P9-CLO-398

Praise for Kathleen O'Neal Gear
and W. Michael Gear

PEOPLE OF THE RIVER

"A story we can't afford to ignore." —*The Washington Post*

"Absorbing . . . Fast-paced and engrossing, [with a] ring of authenticity as well." —*Publishers Weekly*

"There is both delight in the tale of struggles in a time of conflict and peril, and delight in discovery of a civilization now mostly buried beneath tilled farmlands, a prehistory that we have lived atop but have barely known."

—*Scripps-Howard News Service*

PEOPLE OF THE EARTH

"Impressive." —John Jakes

"A novel of suspense as well as a book to give you joy and goosebumps. . . . A great adventure tale, throbbing with life and death. . . . The most convincing reconstruction of prehistory I have yet read."

—Morgan Llywelyn, author of *Lion of Ireland*

Also by Kathleen O'Neal Gear

THIS WIDOWED LAND

"Absorbing . . . Use of period detail breathes life into daily events at the Huron village." —*Publishers Weekly*

"Worthy of note . . . Gear writes with intense historical detail."

—*Booklist*

People
of the
Sea

W. Michael Gear and
Kathleen O'Neal Gear

A TOM DOHERTY ASSOCIATES BOOK
NEW YORK

PEOPLE OF THE SEA

Cover art by Royo

Maps and interior art by Ellisa Mitchell

A Tor Book
Published by Tom Doherty Associates, Inc.
175 Fifth Avenue
New York, N.Y. 10010

Tor® is a registered trademark of Tom Doherty Associates, Inc.

ISBN: 0-812-50745-2
Library of Congress Catalog Card Number: 93-26556

First Edition: November 1993
First mass market printing: September 1994

Printed in the United States of America

0 9 8 7 6 5 4 3 2 1

To Lorena Sanders, and in memory of
    Benjamin Sanders.
For their generous spirits and love of the sea.

We miss you, Ben.

Land of the
People of the Masks

North

the Marsh Peoples

People
of the
Sea

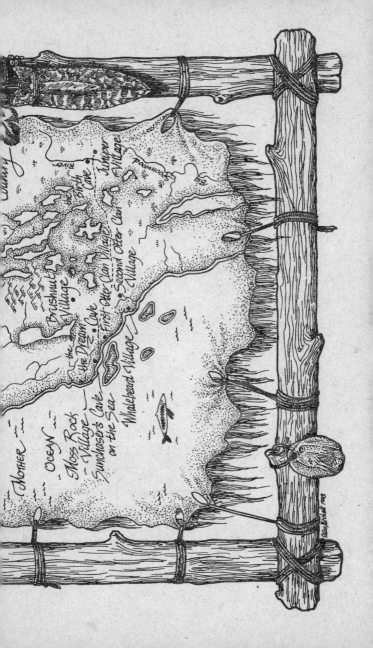

Acknowledgments

We owe debts of gratitude to several people. Dr. Cal Cummings, senior archaeologist for the National Park Service, and Dr. Linda Scott Cummings, director of Paleo Research Laboratories in Golden, Colorado, graciously helped with research. Dr. Dennis Gallegos sparked a book on California in a discussion at the Society for American Archeology meetings in New Orleans. H. Gene Driggers, archaeologist for the U.S. Forest Service, kindly loaned us copies of unpublished reports from projects on which he had worked in California. Sierra Adare spent many hours locating and ordering books and articles—not to mention running front-line defense in difficult times.

Michael Seidman is never far from our thoughts.

Linda Quinton, Ralph Arnote, Yolanda Rodriguez, John DelGaizo, Maria Melilli, Natalie Farsi, Rae Lindsay and Ellisa Mitchell deserve special thanks for their superb work on our behalf.

And Harriet McDougal continues to be the heartbeat of this series. Her talent and caring oversight keep it, *and us*, going.

Last, our readers should be aware that the opinions expressed by the characters in this book are not necessarily those of the authors!

Foreword

During the last Ice Age (the Pleistocene epoch), the Pacific coast, from Vancouver to Southern California, was a very different place than it is today.

The Sierra Nevada mountain range in California underwent extensive glaciation. In the region between Lake Tahoe and Yosemite, an ice cap three thousand feet deep stretched eighty miles long and forty miles wide. The Merced drainage, the San Joaquin River drainage and the Kings and Kaweah basins, as well as Kern Canyon, were sculpted by ice fields and glaciers. A coniferous forest of Douglas fir, cypress, giant redwoods and pines thrived along the coast—where now there is only chaparral.

East of the Sierras, the glacial climate spawned enormous inland lakes. Honey Lake in California and Pyramid Lake in Nevada are tiny remnants of Lake Lahontan, which covered forty-three thousand square miles and was five hundred feet deep. Lake Bonneville, of which the Great Salt Lake is a vestige, was twice the size of Lake Lahontan.

Because so much of the earth's water was tied up in glaciers and lakes, the world's sea levels dropped approximately two hundred and eighty feet. The Pacific shoreline extended ten to thirty miles farther west than at present. Familiar places such as San Francisco Bay did not exist. The Channel Islands, off the coast of Santa Barbara, were one long island, seventy-eight miles long by twenty miles wide, that stretched to within seven miles of the mainland.

The great North American glaciers—the Cordilleran and Laurentide ice sheets, which covered most of Canada and scooped out the Great Lakes—began rapid melting about eighteen thousand years ago. But between ten and twelve thousand years ago, the Sierra Nevada mountains were locked in a glacial advance. Called the Tioga glaciation, it depressed sea surface temperatures, cooled the air and caused increases in precipitation. July probably felt like March. Cooler temperatures decreased the amount of summer evaporation and significantly affected the current desert regions of central and southern California, Arizona and Nevada. Tremendous rains created and sustained over a hundred pluvial lakes that covered the San Joaquin Valley, the Mojave Desert and the Great Basin regions, turning them into marshlands.

Human hunters entered California during this period and found an Ice Age landscape populated by camels, imperial mammoths, dire wolves, horses, giant sloths and saber-toothed cats, among other now extinct animals. The California lion, the largest cat on record, was approximately twenty-five percent larger than the modern African lion. The most terrifying predator of all was the giant short-faced bear, the biggest carnivore to ever inhabit North America; it weighed more than a ton and had long legs designed for great speed and agility.

The question that has plagued scientists for generations is whether the mammoths, mastodons and other "megafauna" were killed off by human hunters or succumbed to the dramatic environmental changes that altered the face of the continent.

We know from paleontological discoveries that before humans arrived, the late-glacial megafauna populations were declining and struggling for survival. The body size and stature of mammoths decreased, probably in response to the capricious weather, which resulted in habitat deterioration. We have a modern analogy to this in several species of caribou in Canada. In order to conserve energy during periods of cold and scarce grazing resources, the basal metabolic rates of these caribou drop by about twenty-five percent and the animals undergo a period of no body growth. But we also know that megafauna populations had survived at least four earlier periods of equally severe environmental stress during the Pleistocene.

So why did they disappear ten to twelve thousand years ago—at exactly the time when human hunters were spreading rapidly throughout the Americas?

The extinctions *could* have been the consequence of the environmental changes at the close of the Pleistocene. We cannot rule out the possibility that for some unknown reason, the megafauna simply could not counter these changes as they had countered similar changes in the past. There may have been climatic stresses that we do not, at present, understand. But the fact remains that they *should* have been able to survive.

We do know for certain that humans hunted these massive animals and killed them with extraordinary skill. We find archaeological sites containing dart points embedded in the bones of mammoths and surrounded by butchering tools. But we also find sites where mammoths appear merely to have died in large numbers—sites where there is no evidence of hunting or butchering.

It is likely that a combination of factors led to the extinctions. The struggling megafauna had undoubtedly been weakened by the dramatic environmental changes and were dying of natural causes; diseases may have attacked them, but their weakened state also made them easy prey for human hunters. Megafauna populations would have sought out and congregated in areas with reduced environmental stress; certainly the coast of California would have been one of these places. The Tioga glaciation of the Sierras would have provided the megafauna with a welcome refuge, a place where the plants they favored and the animals they ate still lived.

Human hunters would have followed. Although various species of megafauna had lived in North America for a million years and had certainly developed skills for combating environmental changes, they had no skills with which to face such a ruthless and relentless predator. While humans were probably not the exclusive cause of the extinctions—

they did not "kill off" all the megafauna—they undoubtedly contributed to their demise and may well have been "the straw that broke the camel's back."

And, as always—witness the Paiute prophet, Wovoka, and the establishment of the Ghost Dance in the 1870s, or the modern environmental movement—when human beings begin to notice the dwindling numbers of animals and inexplicable changes in the world, they become confused and worried. In the times under discussion here, they would probably have prayed for a return to the old days, to the "golden age" of a paradise now lost. We call these "nativistic" movements. In this book, Sunchaser's Mammoth Spirit Dance is such a movement.

The myths and rituals you will find in the following narration are taken from a number of California and Arizona tribes. The Miwok believed there was an opening on the horizon that led souls to the Skyland. The "Dying God" theme is based upon the stories of the Luiseno, who lived in Orange, Riverside and San Diego counties. Sunchaser's maze comes from the Pima and Papago peoples. The Talth Lodge existed among the Yurok tribe of northern California until the 1940s.

Many plants were utilized for their medicinal properties, particularly plants in the willow family such as cottonwood, poplar and aspen, which contain the aspirin-like compound *salicin*—an analgesic and anti-inflammatory. Finally, the Ant Ordeal and the visionary uses of *Datura*, nightshade, morning glory and tobacco—were practiced by tribes throughout California, Nevada and Arizona, but specifically by the Kitanemuk, Luiseno, Tubatulabal, Chumash and Gabrielinos.

People of the Sea takes place at the end of the Tioga glaciation, when the rapidly changing climate generated unstable and unpredictable weather patterns. The great animals that prehistoric peoples had relied upon for food and shelter were swiftly disappearing. The grasses, the trees, even the very ground beneath their feet, were changing.

They must have been deeply frightened. . . .

Prologue

Not much had changed in the last century, Mary Crow Dog decided as she studied the bland conference room in the Bureau of Land Management district office. Just like all the others she'd been in, it had a twelve-foot-long table with twenty chairs arranged neatly around the sides, big windows on the northern wall and a coffeepot that smelled as if it had been sitting on the burner for three days straight. A large map representing southern California hung on the wall. White parts were private land, yellow were BLM-administered public land and green showed the national forests.

A century ago they would have had a map, too, hand-drawn and smudged with dirt and grease. But the faces of the government officials would have looked a great deal like the ones she now saw: smugly superior, thinly masked by a professionally artificial pleasantness. Instead of the noonday sun, fluorescent light illuminated the meeting, and instead of a fire ring, the long, wood-grain veneer table separated them.

As Mary opened her file, still more BLM personnel filtered into the room, coffee cups in hand, note pads or manila folders under arms as they talked softly among themselves—office small talk, to ease the coming tension. Each studiously ignored her.

From the way they acted, their eyes darting uneasily, she had the feeling that the decision had already been made, as it had been in the old days. This meeting, like so many others, was for form only.

Patience, Mary. Endure. Maybe you're wrong.

She reached down, smoothing the brown twill skirt she'd

chosen to wear. A beaded buckle snugged the tooled-leather belt and emphasized her slim waist. She struggled to keep that waist, as small now as it had been when she danced competition in the powwows. Her straight black hair was tightly braided, with two Shoshoni rose berets holding it in place.

Throughout her life, she'd been driven, possessed by her passions of the moment, whether dancing, protesting or, as now, monitoring Native American cultural resources and religious sites. Though only twenty-nine, she had already started to experience emotional exhaustion.

Keep your cool. Professional, all the way. She steeled herself, drawing from Power—from the strength that ran in her blood and the blood of her people. It wasn't something that could be explained to a white guy. Power lived in everything, but its roots lay in the past, in that ability to endure despite conquest and reservation, disease, malnutrition, ignorance, alcohol, drugs and homicide.

Maybe that was why the site they'd recently discovered was so important. Its remains were a link to the past, to a time when the Power carried in Indian DNA had been strong and had pervaded everything in the world. Mary's grandmother was a revered medicine woman, a Healer, but the thread that had passed to Mary was faint. She prayed it would carry her through this government meeting.

She knew most of the BLMers who had come. Wesley Keene, the district manager, had settled across from her and dropped a stack of papers before him like a symbol of state. He wore synthetic stretch pants, a white dress shirt with a bland tie and had a pocket full of pens. She'd come to understand Keene. Like most district managers within the BLM, he'd been promoted because he was a nice guy—"a team player"—not because he was particularly bright or efficient.

The district archaeologist, Jack Riddler, sat at Keene's right and avoided Mary's eyes. She'd been told that eighty-five percent of the people in the BLM were grossly incompetent and that the fifteen percent who really cared actually made the Bureau function—such as it did. If so, Riddler headed the class of the eighty-five percent. Riddler had taken a federal job back in the late 1970s, when *real* archaeologists were still out in the field *doing* archaeology. He had written an M.A. thesis on Minoan ceramics and then hired on with BLM when no one else wanted him. Scuttlebutt had it that one Resource Area even abolished its archaeologist's position in an effort to get rid of him.

One of the realities of life was that once a person received a government job, no amount of ineptitude could get him fired.

Mel Adams, the engineer, and a couple of the others filled in the flanking chairs. Mel Adams carried a quick-draw calculator on his belt and wore a yellow polo shirt, brown duck pants with slit pockets and scuffed brown loafers. He deposited a pile of rolled-up maps, blue-lines and surveyors' plats on the table before him.

The rest of the participants looked the way BLM employees generally did—attired in basic Banana Republic. Why the wildlife biologist, the hydrologist and the landscape architect were attending the meeting would remain to be seen; Keene no doubt saw this as an opportunity to keep them from shooting rubber bands at one another in the main office while the meeting was taking place.

All seemed normal—except for the two men who seated themselves to Keene's left. The look of them stirred Mary's premonition of trouble. Keene's unease was reflected in the way he moved his hands like nervous spiders across the tabletop, continually restraightening the papers before him. His posture indicated complete deference to the white-haired, medium-framed man who lounged in the plastic chair to his left, and to the dandy sitting to that man's left.

Mary studied White Hair, aware that he was vaguely familiar. She had seen him before. And not just around a government office someplace. Something in the newcomer's slouch, in the too-easy smile, bespoke authority. He wore a tweed jacket—unusual for California in midsummer—but his collar was open. He appeared fiftyish, health-spa fit and suitably at ease on this trip to "the field." Capable blue eyes dominated his face. She pegged him immediately: career bureaucrat. This man carried clout within the Bureau; undoubtedly he was one of the shrewder talents who'd risen above the sea of midlevel managerial incompetence.

Washington bigwig!

And to his left sat the Dandy, the nattily dressed lapdog. Mary immediately cataloged the man's prim mannerisms as a classic case of East Coast Urban Wuss. Although he was no more than thirty, his hairline had receded over half of his scalp; the remaining strands had been carefully arranged in an attempt to disguise the bald spot. He wore a three-piece silk suit worth at least a thousand dollars and a snow-white, button-down shirt; a conservative red-and-gray-striped tie pinched his soft white throat.

The Dandy opened an expensive-looking leather briefcase and extracted several sheafs of papers, all of them paper-clipped and clotted with yellow sticky notes that bore clear script. He wore a bulbous silver ring with a yellow stone. The word "Harvard" reflected from the metal.

His fingernails look like they've never even seen real dirt, Mary noted dryly, but he was the danger. She could sense it, like Power whispering to her soul.

The Dandy wouldn't look up, but studied his papers through horn-rimmed glasses before pulling a fancy pen from his inside pocket and jotting more notations on his yellow sticky notes.

". . . think the Raiders will come back this year," Keene's mild voice droned.

That was the district manager's main job, Mary knew: to keep the staff thinking that everything was all right, no matter that Iraq had maybe just bombed the Department of Interior's headquarters in D.C. and none of them had jobs anymore.

"They're bums," the man to Keene's left said. "They'll have to go a ways to whip the Redskins."

Mary's eyes narrowed as she examined the white-haired bigwig. He appeared completely oblivious to his mild words. She used every bit of her control, but asked, "Are the Pale Faces going to make the play-offs, too?"

Careful. Don't antagonize them, or you're going to lose this one. And thinking of Pale Faces, she gave the silk-suited Dandy further scrutiny. He didn't even deign to meet her eyes. He remained engrossed by his papers.

Lawyer? She ground her teeth uneasily, understanding his threat now.

"Do you pay much attention to football, Mary?" Keene asked, aware of her rigid posture in the hard plastic chair. He tried to smile pleasantly.

"That's my busy season, Wes."

"Hunting season, I suppose?" Bigwig asked, his placid government expression carefully in place.

Mary almost snapped a reply, but she was saved when Jess Davis, the contract archaeologist on the project, burst through the door with his usual lack of aplomb. Jess had the kind of absentminded personality that made Mary wonder if a whirlwind hadn't been passing by at the moment of his birth—so that part of its scattered, hither-and-yon soul had merged with Jess's soul. Her only ally for the coming ordeal, he wore blue jeans faded almost white, scuffed Vibram-soled hiking boots that puffed dust with each step and a T-shirt emblazoned with the slogan: "Eat More Buffalo! 50,000 Indians Can't Be Wrong!"

He dropped a pack on the floor as he nodded around the room, that innocent smile on his blond-bearded face. He pulled off his Australian bush hat, ruffled his dusty blond hair, and, already bent over and rummaging in his pack, settled into the seat beside Mary.

"Sorry I'm a little late." His words were muted as he stuck his head halfway into his field pack. "Just got these from the photo center. Thought we might need them."

At that, Jess placed a couple of folders and a thick envelope—the kind photographs come in—on the table.

Keene frowned expectantly.

Mary couldn't suppress a slight smile as tan grains of sand trickled out of the field notebook Jess slapped down next to his other displays. Finally he pulled out a long, square box. It said "Nikon" on the side, but sand, sun and riding over sagebrush in one too many four-wheel-drive vehicles had long since worn most of a marketing director's masterpiece away.

Mary's gaze lingered on the box for a long moment, knowing what it contained. Perhaps their most compelling argument.

When she glanced up, she noticed that the Dandy's concentration had been jolted by Jess's arrival. He studied Jess with the same distasteful fascination he might have leveled at a scorpion crawling across the toe of one of his highly polished, four-hundred-dollar oxfords.

Keene continued smiling nervously, his fingers dancing like ants on his papers as he said, "Well, we're all here. I suppose most of us are old friends, but I'd like to introduce Hal Jacobs on my left, here." He gestured to the white-haired bigwig. "Hal is one of the first-level assistants to the Secretary of the Department of the Interior in Washington. We're fortunate that the Bureau sent him out to check on the project at just this time."

Mary studied Jacobs anew. The man leaned back in his chair, eyes downcast as he smiled. His hair had a thick coating of hair spray to keep it perfectly "puffed." "Just Wes's bad luck that I showed up."

Everyone but Mary and the Dandy laughed.

"And to Hal's left," Wes continued, "we have Peter Preston. Hal needed a solicitor to check some of the papers, and Pres happened to draw the short stick."

They laughed at the right time again, and, this time, Preston joined in.

"Hal, Pres, this is Jess Davis, Principal Investigator for Sayatasha Archaeological Services, the contractor conducting the 'mitigation of cultural resources' for us on the ColPac Water Project."

Jacobs nodded, glancing evenly at Mary.

Keene stumbled slightly, embarrassed that he hadn't introduced Mary first. "Uh, sorry. This is Mary Crow Dog. She's the Native American monitor who works with Jess to make sure that Native concerns are given proper attention and respect. Mary is with the California InterTribal Heritage Coalition."

"So, you're Indian?" Jacobs asked in his pleasant voice, as if it were a delightful new topic of conversation.

Mary just stared at him. He wasn't going to turn patronizing, was he? But then, few of the BLM buddies in Washington had ever even seen an Indian, much less set foot on a reservation. "I'm sorry, I guess I forgot to wear my 'Free Leonard Peltier' button today."

"Your what?" Jacobs asked with a blank look. He glanced at Keene, as though in reprimand that Keene hadn't kept him informed on the Peltier project.

Mary smiled. "Nothing. Inside joke. It's a pleasure to meet you both." Suddenly she remembered where she'd seen Jacobs before. On TV. He was the smart-assed bureaucrat who had advised the Secretary of the Interior to return—at a moment's notice—all Native American skeletal material and burial goods. Some overzealous employees had taken Jacobs' recommendation to heart—prior to the secretary's final decision—boxed every burial they knew of and begun dumping them on the doorsteps of the nearest Indians they could find.

Unfortunately, that had included an aged Navajo Hosteen—a holy man—just outside of Mesa Verde National Park. He'd barely spoken English. The truck had arrived one afternoon as the old man was stepping out of his sweat lodge. Despite his confusion, the DOI people had unloaded forty-seven boxes of human bones in his front yard, smiled, made him sign a voucher with his mark and driven off into the sunset. Only when the old man opened the first of the boxes did he realize what had happened.

By then, it was too late.

His horrified family had found the old man sprawled facedown on the ground, stone dead, his *chindi*—his ghost— mixed wrathfully with forty-seven others. The entire Four-Corners area was in an uproar. Charges of witchcraft were being leveled against the government, the Hopi and other Navajos.

Yes, that was where she'd seen Jacobs. He had been on the evening news, standing in front of the Capitol Building in Washington. One of the major news networks had been interviewing him about the witchcraft accusations resulting from the Navajo Hosteen's death and the return of the skeletons.

"Witchcraft?" Jacobs had asked jovially. "Look, these people want the bones of their ancestors back! We've been inundated by their demands. So we gave them back. That's the problem with this job. Damned if you do, damned if you don't. But witchcraft? Come on! This is the twentieth century. When are these people going to get with it?"

Mary forced her jaws to relax. It didn't look professional to grind molars. She needed to protect this site, needed the information that it might yield about her people.

"Well, let's get down to business, shall we?" Keene glanced around before smiling at Davis. "What have you found, Jess? And what does it mean? It must be pretty serious for you to shut down the dirt contractors. We weren't . . . well, expecting it. We thought the archaeology was all tied up."

Jess was nodding eagerly, that "excited archaeologist" glow brightening in his eyes. "I think we've got a Paleo village site. Possibly intact, but at least in a state of good preservation. I was following the Cat as it cut along the bottom of the slope in section twenty-four. The right-of-way clips the point of one of the hills before dropping off to the Los Angeles basin."

"Right here," Mel Adams, the project engineer, spoke matter-of-factly as he rolled out a U.S.G.S. topographic map and pointed with a pen. A thin red line had been drawn diagonally across one section. "That's all sloughed-off hillside there. What kind of Indian would live on a slope like that?"

Jess rubbed his hands together, oblivious to the fact that everybody was staring at him through slitted eyes. "That's just it. They didn't live on the slope. They lived on the hilltop."

"So, this is trash they threw over the side?" Jack Riddler asked. The BLM archaeologist had watery blue eyes, a grizzled gray beard and hair, and wore a Western-cut red shirt with pearl-button snaps. He leaned forward, bracing his elbows on the table.

Mary stared at him. How could Riddler have failed to read the report she had hand-delivered to him yesterday afternoon? She'd written it especially for this meeting, so he would have all the latest facts.

But then, to most of the archaeological community, Jack Riddler was known as "Jack the Ripper" from his days in the Southwest. His nickname had come from his belief— unfounded in fact—that he could excavate fragile archaeological sites as effectively with a backhoe as an experienced field crew could with shovels, trowels and dental picks.

Jess continued to grin, his eyes focused elsewhere, obviously seeing the archaeological site with his mind's eye. "I think it's the whole village that slid down, Jack. Earthquake, I'd say. I had Roy Fielder out two days ago—you know, the geomorphologist. He agreed that the earthquake had probably happened just after they'd abandoned the village. The whole top of the ridge broke loose and slid down. After the slump, colluvium continued to erode down the slope, slowly covering the site. That's why we've got it. Just an accident of nature."

"Excuse me." Jacobs resettled himself. The air-conditioning had kicked on and whirred to life with a gush of air, but it wasn't affecting his hairstyle in the least. "How do you know all this?"

Jess shrugged. "Geomorphology, like I said. Here, look."

He pulled the photo envelope open, distributed the black-and-white prints to Keene and kept a set for himself. Mary glanced over Jess's shoulder. "Hot off the presses. You can keep that set. Anyway, notice where the Caterpillar is sitting? That's the pipeline right-of-way. We first cut charcoal and FCR at that—"

"FCR?" Jacobs asked, peering at the first photo.

"Fire-cracked rock." Jess glanced up, slightly off balance. "Rocks develop a hackling fracture when they've been heated in fire pits or used for boiling stones."

"Boiling stones?" Jacobs lifted an eyebrow.

"The native peoples heated rocks and dropped them in water to boil stews, soups, teas, what have you."

"Sounds impractical."

Jess blinked owlishly. "Mister Jacobs, if you drop a three-pound rock heated to one thousand degrees into a hide bag filled with ten pounds of water, it's pretty damned efficient. You see, the calories are released immediately and—"

"Jess," Mary interrupted, seeing Jacobs' eyes beginning to glaze, "I think he gets the picture."

"Oh. Okay." Jess sat back.

Keene smiled his plastic smile. "We were a little dismayed to hear that the project had been shut down. Is this site really that important, Jess?"

"Absolutely." Jess pointed to the next photograph. "This is the clincher. See the charcoal level they cut in the trench? We've got FCR and lithic debitage running—"

"Debby who?" Jacobs demanded.

"Debitage," Mary supplied, cutting Jess off before he bored the man to death with a blow-by-blow account of how to turn a chert nodule into a Clovis point. "The chips left over from stone-tool manufacture. Uh, making arrowheads."

"Right. Sure."

"So, you've got a cultural level?" Jack Riddler asked, staring down his long, thin nose. His pearl buttons caught the light as he shifted in his chair. "You've already claimed that it slid down the mountain. You're talking about a lot of disturbance, aren't you? What makes you think any of this is *in situ*?"

"In context," Mary interpreted for Jacobs. He nodded as though he knew that. She went on, "The site's value isn't based only on the artifacts within it, but on the way the artifacts are related to each other. The most valuable archaeological site is one where they are left *exactly* the way they were when the people abandoned the area."

Jess's enthusiasm had cooled as he studied Jack Riddler through sober eyes. The government archaeologist had adopted a "let's get this over with" expression. "Look at this next photo, Jack."

Mary watched as Jess pulled out the picture. There, the man's bones lay partially exposed. The Caterpillar had ripped away the left arm, splintered the ribs and torn away the left innominate, but quick trowel work had uncovered the side of the skull, still intact.

Mary supplied, "Geologically speaking, a human skeleton is a fairly fragile thing. From the preliminary data recovered so far, it looks like we're not dealing with a great deal of turbation—disturbance—of the soil. Again, another freak of preservation."

Jacobs delicately smoothed his white hair and leaned back in his chair. Mary almost laughed aloud. *Just like a Washington politician under fire.* Tense, he extended one hand and made circular motions as he interjected, "Let me get this straight. An Indian village slid down the side of the mountain and you think it's in good enough shape to dig, right?"

"Right!" Jess cried, the gleam back in his eyes.

Jacobs glanced down the table at Mel Adams, who had taken to tapping a pen on the tabletop as he stared at his yellow note pad. "Mel? What's our situation?"

The engineer tipped his head to the side, scratching at his close-shaven scalp. "We've got to pour concrete on Valdez Point by next Friday. We're doing this with a 'just in time' TQM approach—to cut government waste. You know what the directives are on this project. Break a single link in the chain and you've got a logistical disaster on your hands."

Jess hastily dug out the next photograph and laid it on the table. "This is the infant. Neonatal, we think."

Jack Riddler frowned. "Two burials?"

"So far," Mary said quietly. "We could have a whole cemetery there."

"What about the date?" Riddler asked, but his tone didn't convey any real interest. "Jess, you said something about Paleo?"

At Jacobs' glance, Mary stated, "Paleo refers to Paleo-Indian, people whom we know inhabited North America from fifteen thousand to about eight thousand years ago. They were big-game hunters—mammoth, mastodon, California lion—"

"California lion?"

Mary nodded. "Ever hear of the La Brea tar pits? When humans arrived in California, it was a *very* different place. We think that people might have hunted out the large animals such as mammoths, giant sloths, cheetahs."

"Yeah." Keene laughed. "They used to surf on mammoth tusks."

Only the BLM regulars laughed. Mary's eyes narrowed, and Jess just sighed.

Riddler scratched his gray beard and pressed, "How do you know it's Paleo? Did you get a diagnostic? A Paleo point? Faunal association?"

Jess pointed at the picture. "The baby is mostly intact. Look, see the brown thing on its chest?" He carefully opened the camera lens box, gently pulling back the tissue to expose a carved, brown figurine that lay in the padding. Bits of dirt still clung to the side of the piece. "Ivory," he asserted. "*Mammoth* ivory. This was with the infant. Grave goods. What better Paleo association do you want?"

Jack Riddler leaned back, well aware that Jacobs' and Keene's eyes were on him. "Could be intrusive."

Jess sputtered, "Wh—what?" and began to redden. "Are you crazy? Even if it is, the figurine alone is reason enough—"

"Davis! Be real!" Riddler challenged. "So you've got a couple of burials in a site that slid down a mountain? That's why we let the monitoring stipulation ride on the testing and mitigation recommendations. Just in case we missed something like this. Now, let's get the exposed materials recorded and be on our way."

Jess sat stiffly, his back slightly arched, his fingers hanging in midair over the ivory figurine. "Hang on, Jack. I think you've missed something in the translation. We may have a whole village here—a *Paleo* village. And you know that Coastal Paleo is damn near gone! Covered by two hundred feet of Pacific Ocean!"

"Sea level rose over two hundred and eighty feet in the last fifteen thousand years," Mary interpreted for Jacobs when he shot her an inquiring look. "We suspect that many of the most ancient sites in California are submerged . . . gone, for all practical purposes."

"You've got FCR, charcoal, debitage and bones, I admit," Riddler agreed with that "who cares?" smile. Then: "In a site that slid down a mountainside. I don't think that's worth holding up a four-billion-dollar water-diversion project." At that, he crossed his arms and lifted his chin.

Keene and Jacobs seemed relieved. Their smiles had returned.

The veins stood out in Jess's neck. He threw Mary a desperate glance and wet his lips. "Look, Riddler, we've got to *test* the site! You can't just let this one go. Testing will determine whether the strata are intact or not. I've *looked* at the Cat cut. I've got a preliminary profile drawn of the soil levels. They're intact! I swear to God! The data are there for any—"

Riddler waved a hand. "The site fell down a goddamned mountain, Jess!"

Jess sat barely breathing. "The Paleo surface is intact. Damn it, Jack, you can't skid out from under this one. We've *got* to test!"

"We've tested sites like this already, Jess," Riddler replied bluffly. "Three of them. On this same project. We've met our legal obligations."

"Legal!" Jess seemed to run out of breath. He swallowed hard and inhaled, apparently to calm himself, and pointed a finger. "According to 36 CFR 800, this site meets the criteria for nomination to the National Register of Historic Places! You can't blow it off!"

The lawyer was leafing through his papers, the white fingers as neat as the pages they turned. To date, he'd paid little attention to the debate other than to glance curiously at the ivory figurine before returning to his documents.

Jacobs had listened, no expression crossing his face, his mild eyes on Mary. To break the sudden silence, he asked, "What's our bottom line, Mel?"

The engineer continued to doodle with his pen, uncomfortable with Jess's emotion but not getting too upset by it. "If I don't have concrete poured at Valdez Point by Friday, you're going to see a cost overrun that will make the B-Two bomber look like child's play."

A din of objecting voices rose.

"Why?" Mary asked, silencing the debate. "Why not just move farther east on the right-of-way and work there for a while? We can at least salvage some data in the meantime."

Mel gave her a sidelong glance. "I wish I had that kind of flexibility, Miss Crow Dog, but I'm not budgeted for it. Building a pipeline's like building a house. Let's say you have a problem with the electrical wiring. They sent you the wrong gauge of wire, so you can't put it in when you've scheduled it. You can't Sheetrock the walls until all the wires are in, right? You can't finish the trim until the walls are Sheetrocked. You can't lay the carpet until the trim's in. And you can't move in furniture until the carpet's laid.

"My problem is that I've got to move the furniture in—or, more accurately, turn on the water—by December fifteenth. I have a presidential promise hanging in the balance, not to mention two irate senators and a truckload of congressmen landing on my butt. That's my problem. I've got to pour concrete or my pipe can't be placed, and the President's promise is horseshi . . . uh, broken."

Jacobs sighed loudly. "He's right. This is a political sky-rocket. The Administration has billed this as a jobs project for L.A. More water, less social tension, more incentive for business to come into the city. Jobs and bucks, folks. *That's* the bottom line."

Jess was glaring at Jack Riddler, and his callused hands were working—as if he were strangling the BLM archaeologist in his imagination.

Mary steepled her fingers. "As a representative for the Native American community in California, let me clarify that we want this site tested. This is a burial ground. We know that much. I'm forced to agree with Jess. This site is very important. It contains at least two burials and is probably a PaleoIndian campsite—one of the few we have this close to the coast. If we don't dig it, the bulldozers are going to go through and not only destroy what we can learn, but desecrate those graves."

"Miss Crow Dog, we can sympathize," Jacobs told her with his rayon government smile, "but we've got a great deal invested in this project."

Mary nodded her agreement. "Yes, a great deal. But then, it's always been that way, hasn't it? Economic opportunity for the people—so long as they aren't Native people. Mister Jacobs, you've got to understand, I was present when the Bureau rerouted a power line around a white immigrant burial ground. It took a month! I watched a fortune spent to maintain a seventeenth-century historic trail where Spanish priests walked. I do not begrudge this money being spent. But the Valdez Point site is far more important than either of those. This site is almost too rare to believe. Just because PaleoIndian peoples didn't fight in the revolution against George the Third doesn't mean that their legacy isn't part of our national heritage as Americans."

"You don't know that the site is intact," Riddler insisted

smugly. "Look, we've already spent three hundred and fifty thousand dollars on archaeological work for this project."

"And you can't find another three grand so we could at least *test* the site?" Jess barked angrily.

Mary glanced at him. His skin had flushed so red that it made his blond hair look platinum. He'd started raking his fingers in the sand that had fallen out of his field notebook onto the table.

"We don't *have* to test it!" Riddler growled back. "We've met our legal obligations! According to our solicitor's interpretation of the Archeological Resources Protection Act, the intent of Executive Order 11593 and the 1980 amendments to the National Historic Preservation Act, as well as our Programmatic Memorandum of Agreement—"

"The *hell* you have!" Jess had half-started out of his chair. "I can repeat chapter and verse of the preservation laws, too! You can't blow this off, Jack. It's against the law!"

"Pres?" Jacobs looked at the Dandy.

Mary felt what Jess remained oblivious to. Power was shifting in the room.

For the first time the silk-suited Dandy spoke, clearing his throat. He had an appropriately serious expression. "The Bureau of Land Management is within its rights to terminate further work on this archaeological project, Mister Davis." He pushed a paper across the table. Jess picked it up, scowling.

Mary glanced at it, noting the title. Her mouth tightened.

Preston said, "As you can see, that's a copy of the Programmatic Memorandum of Agreement signed by authorized representatives of the Bureau of Land Management, the relevant State Historic Preservation officers and the Advisory Council on Historic Preservation, to the effect that repeated archaeological testing is not necessary on sites considered to share similar values. Since the pipeline crosses several states, Arizona, Utah and Nevada, as well as California, have signed off on the document."

"How can we determine if sites share 'similar values' unless we test them to find out? What idiot would negotiate such a PMOA?" Mary asked.

Riddler answered stiffly, "If there had been problems with my district's formulation of the document, I'm sure that Arizona, Utah or Nevada would have said something about it."

Jess's mouth gaped. He looked almost as though he had gone into shock. Mary grimaced at the way his pupils had dilated. In a choking voice, Jess said, "But we're talking about a *PaleoIndian* village! We've identified nothing similar in the course of this project."

"Come on, Jess," Riddler said with sickening familiarity. "We found Paleo sites in sections six, thirty-four—"

"They weren't *village* sites! There were no burials! They were broken Paleo points surrounded by a few flakes. On deflated ridge tops. With no deposition!"

Riddler, reeking of superiority, had begun grinding his molars. "Jess, we tested sites at the bottom of slopes, too."

"Yeah, late-prehistoric sites dating back five hundred years. You're dumping apples and oranges into the same trash can, Jack. That's *bad* science."

Riddler bristled, as Jess had known he would. "Science isn't the issue, Jess. Compliance with the law is. And that's what our Programmatic Memorandum is designed to see to — efficiently, with no time wasted."

Pres irritably peered over his horn-rimmed glasses and extended another sheet of paper. "This is a copy of the Scope of Work for the final phase of the project, Mister Davis—the phase you are currently conducting. It states, and I quote: 'All ground-disturbing activities will be monitored by a qualified archaeologist. Specifically: the excavation of the pipeline trench, right-of-way, and construction of associated pumping stations. Such monitoring is to identify and record any cultural resources which may have escaped detection during the initial Cultural Resources Inventory for the project. Any such cultural resources located will be recorded prior to impact from pipeline construction. But no further work will be required on sites which are expected to yield redundant information about prehistoric or historic lifeways.' "

Pres added, "I have signatures from the SHPOs and the Advisory Council agreeing to that stipulation."

Jess shook his head in slow agony. "This isn't redundant information! This is a Paleo village site! We can't—"

"You've uncovered no evidence to suggest that it's a village site, Jess," Riddler pointed out. "So you've got a couple of burials. Record the data, return the bodies to whoever requests them and close up this phase of the project." Riddler gave Jess an exaggerated wink, like they both knew what all this was really about. "Don't worry, Jess, you're going to be on the Federal payroll for at least another month. Like we said, this is a *jobs* project. Your field crew—"

Jess shoved his chair back and slammed his fists on the table. "Listen, *Pot Hunter*, my people can find work anywhere, any day! I don't need—"

Mary put a hand on Jess's forearm and softly said, "Let's get back to business, Jess. Sit down. *Sit.*"

Reluctantly, Jess slumped back into his chair, but he continued to glare at Riddler with his teeth clenched.

Preston, appearing indifferent now that he'd passed judgment, looked at the next of his documents, one of the mitigation reports prepared by Jess's firm. A rendering of the Pima tribe's sacred maze, depicting the twists and turns of life, had been used to ornament the title page. As if bored, Pres began working through the route with his expensive pen.

Mary sighed wearily, feeling the inevitability crashing down on her. A century later, and nothing had changed. Nobody cared about protecting her people's heritage. But, boy-oh-boy, if this had been ten feet of the Oregon Trail, the bureaucrats would have been hustling to protect it, rerouting the pipeline, dumping new money into the project. *What did you expect, Jess? You've been in this business long enough to know how it works. The government isn't interested in "the resource." They just go through the motions. Paperwork compliance is the end now, not the means. Only the process matters to them—jumping through the hoops in the right order. That's all.*

Mary turned to Keene and asked, "Have you discussed this specific site with the SHPOs or the Advisory Council, Wes?"

Keene gestured to Riddler. "I don't know. Have we—"

"Such measures are not necessary," Riddler said through an irritated exhalation. "The PMOA acknowledges that this district has the lead on the project and gives us the authority, based upon the PMOA guidelines, to determine when consultation is necessary. I say it isn't. Don't you agree, Wes?"

"Well, I don't know. Maybe we ought to—"

"My recommendation," Riddler interrupted forcefully, "is to get on with this project!"

"Hey, you're the expert," Keene said with a nervous laugh and threw up his hands as if in surrender. "If you don't think we need to consult—"

"There's another thing too, Wes. I didn't want to bring it up because we're not certain yet, but—"

"What?" Keene asked.

Riddler sighed plaintively. "Well, from the map that Miss Crow Dog delivered to us yesterday, it appears that Jess's site may be on private land," he said as he laced his fingers together. "Just this morning I received a letter from the landowner, Mister Black, stating that he waives any need to do further work on archaeological sites on his lands. So you see, no matter how you look at it, no further work is necessary. We've met our obligations under the law."

Pres looked up from his doodling and smiled at Mary. "Would you like a copy of the 'landowner waiver'?"

"Yes, I would."

While Preston shuffled through his papers to find a copy, Mary watched Mel frown in confusion at his map, as if puzzled by the controversy over land status, too.

Preston handed Mary a copy of the landowner's letter. "You're welcome to take this to litigation, of course."

"What for?" Mary asked. "By the time I can talk to a lawyer, let alone find one who knows anything about cultural resources legislation, the site will be gone."

Preston shrugged and used his pen to angrily scribble out the lines in the maze.

Mary flinched as if struck, her heart skipping at the desecration of the sacred symbol. *Get out, Mary! You've lost.*

"I'm sorry it didn't work out this time," Hal Jacobs said. "We're a multiple-use agency. We have to balance the needs of many different interest groups. We can't show a preference for Native American perspectives over those of industry or of the people waiting for that water in the L.A. basin."

A *preference* for—Mary sat stunned. Ninety-nine percent of the archaeologists in the country were Anglos! Preston continued to blot out the Pima maze in a wash of blue ink. *Damn him!* He'd probably been behind Jacobs' decision to send skeletons to that poor old Navajo Hosteen.

Jess reached out, slowly running a finger down the mammoth ivory artifact, as though trying to imagine who had loved that tiny baby so much that they'd placed the figurine on its chest. "If I had any sense, I'd get out of this business." He looked up. "Most of the good archaeologists have, you know. They saw the writing on the wall back in eighty-four, when Operating Order Number One was implemented."

"Please, Jess." Mary glanced at Jacobs, trying to keep the pleading from her eyes. "We *need* data recovery from this site. Wes? Jack? At least let us take you out on the ground and show you the burials up close."

Keene lifted his hands defensively. "I'm sorry, Mary. I really wish I could help. I'm sure you understand the position I'm in. Hal's right. We can't give preference to Native

American concerns here. Given the time crunch and the landowner's waiver, there's nothing more I can do."

The hot California sun burned out of a smog-ridden sky as Mary Crow Dog stepped through the double glass doors and placed her sunglasses on her nose. The skyscrapers downtown wavered eerily in the brown haze. Cars honked as they sped by, but the people hurrying along the street barely noticed. A line of BLM vehicles parked at the curb shielded them from a direct assault by the traffic.

Jess looked as if he could chew cactus when he paused beside Mary, his pack over his shoulder. "Lost again," he muttered dismally.

"Yes, lost again." The heavy sense of depression ate at her gut. "Do you think they ever felt like this? The PaleoIndians? Did they know this futility, the despair and constant failure?"

"Yeah." Jess fished his Copenhagen can out of the back pocket of his faded Levi's. "They were folks, Mary. Just like us. Must have been tough on 'em when the last mammoth died. Some of them probably worked like hell to save their world. Probably had all kinds of nativistic movements afoot to return things to normal. They'd have been desperate trying to understand what was happening. And, God forbid, they must have had spineless wimps like Keene, too. Plus a few conniving bastards like Riddler, Jacobs and Preston." Jess shook his head. "People stink."

Mary stared up at the sky. "First they took our lives, then our land, then our culture and finally our dignity. Now, when some of us are trying desperately to get a piece of ourselves back by saving and studying our own prehistory, they're taking that from us, too."

"Not all of us," Jess reminded her.

"Yeah, Pale Face. You going to write all this up for *American Antiquity*? More archaeology for the benefit of other archaeologists? None of my people read that gibberish. What's the difference? It's all a white man's game. Just like the landowner waiver. How much you think they paid old man Black to get him to sign that letter? Maybe they agreed to that land exchange he's been begging for."

"*If* it's on private land"—Jess spat a brown streak of tobacco juice on the side of a BLM Bronco—"I need your grandmother to come down from Redding."

Mary shot him a sideways glance. "What for?"

"Maybe I've been hanging around you for too long." He glanced up as a taxi swerved around the corner, horn blaring, and shrugged. "I stayed at the site late enough last night to pedestal that infant burial. I wrapped it in a burlap sack and toted it off to the lab. Yeah, yeah, okay—I stole Federal property, or maybe private property. Let 'em come get me. When we finish with the studies, will your grandmother Sing the kid's soul back to wherever it goes?"

Mary's face slackened with wonder. "What made you do that?"

Jess spat more brown insult onto the door handle of another BLM truck. "Just a feeling, Mary. The adult skeleton, well, I guess he could take care of himself—as if he could stop a D-9 Cat. Hell, maybe he can. How do I know? Maybe he'll gum up the injectors or something. The infant, though . . . I don't know. I felt like I could hear it calling to me. Asking for help." He shrugged again. "Just a feeling."

Mary patted him on the back. "Next thing, you'll be like the Navajo, talking about witchcraft. They think you archaeologists are nuts anyway, purposely mucking around with corpse powder. But then, what *chindi* would touch a white guy? Even a Skinwalker won't sink that low."

Jess lifted his blond-bearded face and grinned broadly. "Maybe I ought to go hunt up a good Navajo witch. If I had a stash of corpse powder, I know just the guy I'd sprinkle it on. Jack the Ripper would wish to hell he'd never written that stupid PMOA." He shook his head. "I can't understand the SHPOs agreeing to give the Ripper sole discretion over determining when consultation is necessary on this project. Just doesn't figure. That's why they're there—to watchdog Federal blundering."

Mary let out a breath. "Come on. I'll buy you a beer. Then, I think I'll call the SHPOs and the Advisory Council. Maybe even Jonas Black. Just to check, you know?"

"Yeah, and after that, you can try the Sierra Club, Friends of Brown Dogs and Gray Cats, and the Society for the Prevention of Cruelty to Dead People. It won't make any difference, Mary. Nobody cares what happens to a couple of dead Indians lying out in the desert."

Mary gestured for him to take a right at the intersection of streets. They walked in silence through a seedy section of nightclubs, strip joints and bars. She was leading him to the Broken Arrow Saloon on the next corner. Even at one o'clock in the afternoon, twanging country music blared from the bar's open windows. The scent of food cooking in hot grease hung heavy in the air.

"Cheer up," Mary said and smiled. "If we can just get enough brown dogs on our side, we can violate every BLM tire in L.A."

The Search

Alone she came
To beg for pardon,
Emptying her breath
Into cracks on the desert floor.

She listened for hours
To the Cheshire sage
That evaded her questions.

She stood tall by the cactus
Demanding the afternoon sun
But couldn't get warm.

She called up to Raven,
Tiny onyx set deep in blue,
And his gaze fell beyond her.

She cried for the loss of her art
Tore red welts at her throat
But nothing came.

The skull of the coyote,
Bleached hollow white,
Warned her against
The sound of her sobbing
But she couldn't hear.

Until darkness
Ate into the azure sky
And she sat alone
In its star-spotted belly.

Then she could feel herself
Against the wind,
Hear Raven laugh
And Coyote sing,
Her shadow consumed
In the art of night
But tangible in the dark.

It followed
When she ran away,
Her pockets
Full of Silence.

Kristin Krebs Collier

One

The lodge had grown unbearably hot, stifling. Sunchaser shoved weakly at the mound of hides that covered him. Sweat drenched his naked body, matting his long black hair to his temples and stinging his deep-set eyes. Cold trickles ran down his sides. He was so tall—twelve hands—that his feet rested uncomfortably against the opposite wall. The fire in the center of the dirt floor had been built up high enough that the flames leaped and crackled. Golden reflections danced across the shiny coating of creosote on the hide ceiling. He studied them through fever-brilliant eyes, and the images wavered like a silvery mirage on the desert.

"Good Plume? Aunt?"

He managed to lift his head enough to look around. The lodge consisted of a pine-pole frame covered with hides. It spread in a rectangle, four body lengths long and one wide. Good Plume was gone, but from the dimly lit corners of the lodge, tiny eyes gleamed as field mice froze at the sound of his voice. For long moments he watched the small creatures before they began to scurry about in search of food. One mouse jumped like a grasshopper onto the log that held down the southern wall. Long whiskers shivered in glints of silver as he sniffed his way around the bases of two soapstone bowls, hopped over a curved throwing stick used for hunting rabbits and stopped beside a winnowing basket. He chewed a bit of wheat-grass chaff while he stared unblinking at Sunchaser, his glossy sides pulsing with his rapid breathing.

Then the mouse zipped behind the winnowing basket as Sunchaser sighed and settled into the robes. A nightmare sensation of helplessness possessed him. His mouth had gone as dry as the autumn grasses. Was it the fever, or did he hear voices . . . soft, muted words intermixed with the sputters of the fire?

He let his head fall to the left. Sweat slipped over the skin of his face. Along the northern wall stood a row of thirteen baked-clay figurines. They peered at Sunchaser through sparkling dovesnail-shell eyes. *The Steals Light People.* In their hands they held the timeless ebb and flow of divine Power. Above-Old-Man stood at the far end of the lodge, looking down upon the Steals Light People. Like Mother Ocean, he was not one of the Steals Light People, but was greater than all of them. Because of that, his figurine was twice the height of the others, four hands tall. His entire body had been painted pure white, but he wore a black weasel-fur headdress sprinkled with quartz crystals that had been glued on with pine pitch.

Sunchaser blinked wearily at the figurine. It seemed to be watching him intently. "Above-Old-Man . . ." he murmured reverently. "Your death . . . gave life to the world." Sunchaser smiled.

In the Beginning, Above-Old-Man was all that existed. He was soft and shapeless like the clouds. He knew that to create the world, he would have to use part of himself. It took a great act of courage for him to open his veins and allow the blue blood to flow unheeded, but it poured out and turned into the blue waters of Mother Ocean, from which every other life form emerged. The froth on the Mother's surface gave birth to the Steals Light People: Father Sun, Dawn Child, Winter Boy, the Ice Ghosts, the Thunderbeings, Great White Giant and all the others. Even Sister Earth and Brother Sky were born from the vast blue womb.

First Condor, the biggest bird in the world, sprang to life soon thereafter, created from a ball of Sister Earth's clay. As Above-Old-Man's blood drained away, he called to Condor. When Condor came, Above-Old-Man said, "Please, Condor, I am too weak. Let me give you the Power to breathe Life into the things I have created. You must hurry, before the magic of Creation dies. Otherwise, everything will just be bone and stone and water. It will never feel or think."

Condor had to fly very fast to cover the whole world before the magic was gone.

While Condor did his duty, Above-Old-Man grew weaker and weaker, until he shrank to nothingness and died. The world lived because of Him and Condor, but Above-Old-Man became cold and white and hard. Mother Ocean wept. She begged the other Steals Light People to help her, and they made a net of seaweed and put Above-Old-Man in it. First Condor carried the net high into the sky, where Above-Old-Man was reborn as the moon.

Sunchaser could feel the Power of the Steals Light People; it radiated from them like heat from flames. They made the rains come and winter go. As the children of Above-Old-Man, their prayers gave their Father the strength to rise and cross the belly of Brother Sky every night. If the Steals Light People ever failed to pray, the moon would rise no more.

Pinches of sacred acorn meal lay sprinkled at the feet of the clay figurines, just as it was sprinkled on the living Dancers who represented them at the annual ceremonials. Good Plume had laboriously painted these Steals Light People, crushing the colors from plant roots, flowers, berries and clays, working for long hands of time with a frayed willow-twig brush to get the details right. Then she had dressed them in special, ritually blessed clothing—as befitted gods.

Sunchaser's voice rasped as he asked, "Where is Good Plume, Steals Light People? Do you know?"

They seemed to be whispering; the Thunderbeing's voice was especially loud. Thunderbeings looked like young children, but they had the shining, membranous wings of dragonflies. And talons grew where a human child would have had feet. As they soared through the clouds, their wings caused thunder to rumble across the sky. He couldn't make out the Thunderbeing's words. Or were those sounds only the passing of the mice? Sunchaser blinked to steady the wavering focus of his eyes and fought the drifting sensation that possessed him.

Bright paintings lived over the heads of the figurines. On the long north wall, two zigzags of yellow lightning sliced a path through silver moons and blue stars and lodged in the heart of a crimson sun. The southern wall flamed with orange trees whose branches curled in and around to form the interlocking pathways of a labyrinth. Near the edges of the branches, dark swirls spiraled out, like tongues of black flame. . . . *The Darkness that roasts the soul when it attempts to find the twisting road that leads to the Land of the Dead.*

With all of his strength, Sunchaser rolled to his right side so he could extend a trembling hand and pull the door flap back. His clammy fingers could barely keep their grip on the leather, but he managed to hang the flap on its peg. As he did so, the hides slipped off his chest, exposing it to the cold wind that swept Brushnut Village. He relished the shiver that shook him. The crisp scent of pine flooded his hot nostrils and he inhaled deeply, seeking to fill his soul with the essence of the trees.

Outside the lodge, the green pines gradually darkened into charcoal spears. They stood like dark sentinels against the translucent rays of pale pink light that shot across the sky. Sunchaser could see no clouds, but flakes of snow pirouetted through the trees and landed on the frozen ground.

How long had he been ill? He couldn't even recall when he had retreated to his aunt's lodge to lie down. Where was she? Was the sickness still ravaging the village?

"They need you, you fool," he murmured feebly. "Good Plume is old . . . eighty summers. She can't work all the Healings by herself. It will kill her. Get up. Get up before it's too late and everyone that you care about is dead."

He tried to sit up, but fell back to his hides, panting and trembling from the effort. The interior of the lodge swam around him in a blur of color. He felt sick to his stomach.

Sunchaser had been born here in the mountains at Brushnut Village twenty-five summers ago. He knew and loved each person in the village. How many of them had died since he'd fallen ill? Good Plume's lodge nestled on the western side of the village, down the slope from the others. But he could hear the moans and cries of the sick.

"Blessed Spirits, what's happening? How . . ."

Footsteps crunched on the frozen ground above the lodge, slow, methodic, as if each step required great care.

"Good Plume?" he called again.

"Yes, it's me."

She pushed her walking stick through the doorway before she ducked through herself. Snow frosted the fur of her heavy buffalo coat and glistened in the gray straggles of hair that had come undone from her short braid. Her face had a skeletal angularity; her sagging, wrinkled skin was the color of walnut oil.

Sunchaser closed his eyes for a moment.

Good Plume leaned her walking stick by the door and unhooked the door flap, letting it fall closed again. "Are you trying to kill yourself? Winter Boy is still out and about, looking for souls to eat."

She bent down and covered Sunchaser with hides again, then went to the middle of the lodge, where she removed her coat and laid it by the fire to dry. Her thin arms stuck out from the sleeves of her doeskin dress. She kicked a stump of wood closer to the fire and sat down on it, the beaded hem of her skirt fanning around her feet. Her hands shook as she held them out to the flames. "When I get warm, I'll heat up that raccoon soup we had for breakfast."

Sunchaser wet his chapped lips. "Tell me . . . I have to know. What's happening?"

"It will just worry you. You'll use up your strength—"

"Tell me!"

Good Plume exhaled a heavy breath. "Flint Pond died today. Everyone in the village is going mad trying to figure out who should be the next chief."

"What about Flint Pond's son?"

Good Plume's voice broke when she said, "Little Elk died this morning."

Faint, wavering images of Little Elk's face moved through Sunchaser's thoughts, each like a knife in his heart. They'd laughed and played together as children. "And Little Elk's wife?"

"She's fine. So far. And we had better pray that Above-Old-Man keeps her that way. She's gone all over the village cooking, cleaning, caring for the grieving."

"Standing Moon is a good woman."

Good Plume nodded and lowered her hands to her lap. She rubbed her joints as though the old bones ached miserably. When she scrutinized Sunchaser, firelight flowed into her wrinkles, making her look a thousand summers old. "People miss you," she said gently. "Everyone has been asking about you. Singing day and night, praying for the Evil Spirits to let you go. People need you. They think you're a better Healer than I am."

He smiled feebly. "Then they are all fools."

"You are much loved, Sunchaser. If you up and die on them, they'll never forgive you."

"I'm better, Good Plume. Stronger. Really—"

"Your fever is very high, and the Evil Spirits have held you now for three days. If we can't pray the fever away tonight, I fear for you."

"No, no," he reassured her. "It's not that bad. I just . . . I'm so c-cold, Good Plume." A shudder went through him that made his teeth chatter. He tugged weakly at his hides, pulling them up around his throat. "Aren't there any m-more hides?"

Good Plume rose and went to a pile of folded skins in the rear of the lodge. She carried them back and spread them out over Sunchaser, then tenderly tucked the edges in around him.

Still, he could not stop shivering.

Good Plume's ancient face darkened. "I must pour some hot soup into you. Stay awake for me."

She crossed to the cooking tripod where the hide bag of soup hung and moved it closer to the hearth. Using two sticks, she picked up four of the small rocks that sat on the coals at the fire's edge and dropped them into the bag. Steam exploded upward. A silver wreath encircled her face. While she searched for wooden bowls, Sunchaser said, "I . . . I must get well, Good Plume. The Mammoth Spirit Dance will start at Otter Clan Village in five days."

The Dance was held every moon at one of three villages: Brushnut, Whalebeard or Otter Clan. That way, people from up and down the coast as well as from the mountain villages wouldn't have far to go if they wanted to attend three or four Dances a cycle. The Dances brought great numbers of people together. Many of them walked for days to reach the village where the Dance was being held. And Sunchaser tried very hard to attend each Dance. But sometimes, like this moon, he just couldn't do it. Perhaps Oxbalm, leader of the Otter Clan, would delay the Dance? Waiting for Sunchaser? Occasionally it happened that way. But not often. And Oxbalm couldn't delay the Dance for more than a week, because people would begin leaving. Oxbalm couldn't make them wait just to see if Sunchaser might come.

"Yes," Good Plume said, "that's right. And if you are not there, old Catchstraw will lead the Dance."

"He's led it m-many times before, Aunt. He's not as bad as you think. But I . . . I've missed so many Dances. I should be there. Though Catchstraw tries very hard, he is just not—"

"Do you really believe he tries hard?" Good Plume grunted and walked back to the fire with two bowls and a wooden cup. Scowling, she dipped the cup and filled the bowls. "Have the mammoths grown more numerous with him leading the Dances? Hmm? No. None of them want to come back from the Land of the Dead if they think he'll be the Dreamer to greet them. People wouldn't attend the Dance either if they knew in advance that Catchstraw would be Dancing."

Sunchaser's stomach cramped. Guilt weighted him down like a black wall of earth. "That's my fault. I should be out walking the t-trails, telling people that it's the Dance that is important. They think they need me there, but that is not—"

"Sunchaser," Good Plume said as she set a bowl of soup on the floor beside him, "you try to help too many at once. No matter who asks you to come to their village, you go. You use every shred of your Power for others and save none for yourself." Spirals of steam rose from the bowl.

"I can't tell people that I won't come . . . not when they are frightened or ill. Someone must give them hope."

Good Plume removed one of the deerhides from Sunchaser's chest, folded it and tucked it beneath his head to prop him up. As she tipped the bowl of warm soup to his lips, she said, "It's all right to care about people, Sunchaser, but you must not let your concern disrupt your Dreaming. If you do, in the end even the people you have cared for the most deeply will hate you for it. Dreaming is the only way you can really help them, and they know it."

He took a sip of the warm, delicately flavored soup and sank back against the hide pillow. His teeth had begun to chatter so violently that he barely managed to keep his mouth on the bowl long enough to get another swallow. "Perhaps."

"You doubt me? Don't. I tell you the truth. You must stop giving so much of yourself to people. Pretty soon there won't be enough of you left to Dream."

He started to respond . . . but he heard voices again, faint, riding the wind like lost souls, calling to him. He closed his eyes to listen better.

"Sunchaser? . . . Sunchaser? Hurry! Where are you? Can you hear me? Come and look! There are mammoths coming!"

A brilliant glow suffused the world around him, filled with the desperate cries of a baby. He floated on that tormented sound with the freedom of a curl of smoke on a still day, rising higher and higher, freed from the cage of his sick body.

The Dream lifted his soul and carried it away on wings of gold . . .

He found himself crouching in a condor trap high on a mountain. Rocky cliffs jutted into the sky around him. He huddled down into a ball, but cold seeped from the frozen soil, penetrating his heavily fringed hide shirt and pants. Puffs of clouds were visible through the dense weave of brush. They drifted westward, toward the sea. All day long, snow flurries had intermittently frosted the peak. Above-Old-Man must have been looking out for him. The thin, white coating would help disguise his trap.

The trap was a circle of rocks placed around a pit and covered with brush. Forty hands from the trap lay a dead bighorn, its magnificent horns catching the afternoon sunlight. Sunchaser had killed the sheep at dawn, dragged it down the mountain's rocky slope and slit its belly open so that the internal organs lay in full sight and created a range of smells, from the sweet richness of blood to the stench of torn intestines. Grandmother Condor hunted warily. But only the downy underfeathers of Condor's wings could complete Sunchaser's ritual attire.

He spied two tiny black dots gliding against the background of clouds, and he held his breath. He could just make out the white linings of their enormous wings.

The condors descended slowly, cautiously, circling each other, cocking their red-bald heads as their sharp eyes surveyed the conifer forest for danger. A breeding pair. Sunchaser had located their nest a moon ago. It filled a rocky niche two hundred hands down the slope from his trap.

The huge female let out a glorious cry, tucked her wings and sailed as straight as a well-cast dart to the dead sheep. The male alighted beside her and together they hesitantly approached the exposed guts. The female tore into the liver, while the male pecked at the bloody lungs.

Sunchaser pulled his bone dagger from his belt and readied himself. He waited patiently, twisting the fringe on his pant leg as he repeated a mental chant, a prayer of offering:

I see you, Condor. Hear my prayers.
In clasping one another tight,
Holding one another fast,
May we finish our roads together,
    keeping Beauty before us always.

The condors' eighteen-hand wing span made taking off difficult, and when condors ate, especially in cold weather, they gorged themselves. Flight would be even harder on a full stomach.

The gigantic birds ate in silence, occasionally flapping their black-and-white wings as they tugged at a stubborn gobbet of meat. After two fingers of time, both birds had slowed their consumption, stopping more often now to stare about and strut through the gutted mess they'd created. The male lifted his head and bent his neck back, perhaps to resettle his stomach. They seemed to have eaten their fill. The female ruffled her feathers and plucked at some annoyance beneath her right wing. The male hopped up on top of the sheep and scanned the open meadow. Soon they would fly away.

Sunchaser burst from his hiding place and raced toward the birds. The male let out a cry of shock and flapped hard, trying to lift his heavy body. The female broke in the opposite direction. Sunchaser ran with all his might. Snow squealed beneath his moccasins as he leaped for the female's legs. He managed to latch on to the right one.

The condor squawked in fear, and the frozen puffs of her breath twisted away in the wind. The talons on her left foot ripped at his arms while she attacked the top of his head with her beak. Hot blood streamed down his face and dripped from his chin.

"Please, Grandmother," he Sang as he struck out with his dagger. "Give yourself to me so that mammoths may continue to live in our world." He struck again and again, feeling the sharp point rip through the feathers and puncture the condor's black breast and throat. Warm stickiness coated his hand, and offal leaked from the bird's punctured gut.

The condor shrieked and flogged him with huge, bloody wings. Her mate circled away on the updraft, watching and calling out in terror.

When the female at last toppled onto her back with her wings spread, she stared up with frightened eyes that blinked in the wrinkled redness of her round head. Her large, hooked beak was streaked with gore and bits of tissue. Sunchaser reverently stroked her legs as her neck ceased to writhe. Rasping breaths tore from her lungs.

From tail to head, she stood as tall as many human women, and her wings stretched one third longer than Sunchaser's height. "Thank you, Grandmother. I promise to use your feathers well and to bury your body with many rare seashells and finely crafted dart points."

His people had always revered the great birds, and they buried condors with solemn ritual dignity. Born from the blue blood of Above-Old-Man, condors carried the essence of all Life in their bodies.

Death always gives birth to Life. Even Above-Old-Man was willing to die so that the world might exist.

The female gasped suddenly, and a breath condensed into a white cloud around her open beak. She blinked at Sunchaser, her eyes drowsy with death. Blood spattered her entire body, but the thick coating of red on her white underwings had come also from Sunchaser's torn flesh. A mixing of his blood and hers. He gently traced the forward edge of her right wing with his fingertips. "Forgive me, Grandmother."

He straightened and stood shivering in the glacial air. A dark cloud had blotted the face of Father Sun and left the mountaintop in freezing shadow. The pale dove color of the rock outcrops had turned a deep, dark gray. The male condor still circled above, his head cocked. Alone. Watching his mate's final moments in silence.

Sunchaser's soul ached. His eyes met and held the male's, and they shared their grief. Both understood that death was a fundamental part of their relationship. Condors survived on carrion, much of it either left by human hunters or the humans themselves. Humans had to kill condors to obtain the sacred feathers they used for renewing and sanctifying the world. Human and Condor constantly faced each other asking for life—and knowing that it came only through death.

Sunchaser whispered, "I'll take good care of her, Grandfather. I promise you. She will fly to the Land of the Dead with my people Singing her praises."

Sunchaser gazed down at the female. Her beak rested on the curved edge of her wing. She had stopped breathing.

"Come, First Condor," Sunchaser Sang softly. "Come and guard your child's soul until we Sing her to the Land of the Dead."

He knelt and carefully folded Grandmother Condor's wings. The feathers felt soft and warm. He lashed her wings to her body with a thin yucca cord so she would be easier to carry, then braced himself and lifted the heavy bird into his arms. Her head hung limply, the eyes half open as he started down the mountain.

That night he camped in the lee of a thick stand of fir, sheltered from the worst of the storm. In the flickering firelight, she watched him, her bloody head slightly canted where he had carefully propped it.

Exhausted to the point of collapse, Sunchaser said, "Your body will help the mammoths to live, Grandmother."

As he watched with half-lidded eyes, the condor stirred. A fiery burning traced its way through the wounds she had inflicted on his head and arms. He blinked, sure that he'd seen a shifting of firelight, a trick of the popping embers playing in the breeze. Power moved, loose in the darkness. Desperately, he fought sleep, drifting amidst the sounds of wind, fire and night, hovering in that half-reality of . . .

A breath expanded the condor's lungs, and she lifted her head to stare at Sunchaser. A pale, silver light burned in her eyes. *Now I understand your need for my body, Human. You hunted me with honor. I will take you on a journey. A Spirit*

Journey far away. You shall see why you must pray day and night to keep the mammoths alive."

Grandmother Condor shook off the frail bonds he had wrapped her in and leaped from her resting place. She flapped low over the ground, her wing tips brushing the snow, then gained enough altitude to lift into the sky. She circled and swung back around over the jagged rocks and the swaying trees, her talons outstretched.

Sunchaser screamed, unable to flee. She sank those curved, bloody talons into the shoulders of his hide shirt and bore him upward through gleaming layers of clouds. With every beat of her wings, thunder cracked and rumbled over the mountains.

Bright fear pumped in time with Sunchaser's heart. She needed but to relax her grip and he would fall . . . and fall . . .

"Look down, Sunchaser. What do you see?"

Terror strangled the scream in his throat. Mountains gave way to green, rolling plains where huge piles of carcasses lay rotting in the sun. White bones gleamed, picked clean by predators. Not just mammoths lay there, but four-horned pronghorns, several kinds of horses, ground sloths, dire wolves, giant beavers, shruboxen, saber-toothed cats, short-faced bears, lions . . . so many beautiful lions. They lay touching paws in a field of tall, windblown grass, their golden manes shimmering in the sun.

Horror tightened Sunchaser's chest. "I don't understand, Grandmother. What is this? What am I seeing?"

"This is what the world will be like without mammoths, Sunchaser."

"Filled with the dead and dying? Why?"

Condor tipped her wings, and they soared northward, toward the land of the Great White Giant, where the Ice Ghosts creaked and groaned as they stretched their glacial bodies. Magnificent deserts passed below him. Red ridges snaked across the land, cut and honed by deeply eroded canyons. Enormous stone towers stood like lances, poking their heads up above the ridge tops to look around.

"Because everything is connected to everything else, Sunchaser."

He heard the baby crying again, crying, and crying, and calling his name. . . .

Good Plume awakened when Sunchaser sobbed. She sat up in her robes and rubbed the sleep from her eyes. Wind buffeted the lodge, roaring with the strength of the Thunderbeings. The door hanging had come untied, and it flapped like wings over Sunchaser's head. His hair bore a thick coating of pure white snow. He tossed and turned, writhing as though trying to escape a pursuing monster. His hides had slipped down around his waist, baring his broad chest to the bitter wind.

Good Plume rose and tiptoed over to him. Tears beaded on his lashes. When she put her hand on his brow, relief made her sigh out loud. His fever had broken. But he felt cold, as cold as ice.

"You're going to be all right, Sunchaser," she whispered affectionately as she rearranged the hides to cover him again. "Above-Old-Man must have heard all those prayers your hundreds of followers have been sending up . . . and mine, too."

Before she retied the door flap, she stuck her head outside. Snow fell heavily, sheathing the forest in a thick, wintry blanket. On the wind's chilling breath, cries and groans wavered from the village. Some man coughed and coughed. An infant sobbed.

Good Plume squinted when she caught movement in front of the lodge. A dog sat ten hands away, covered with snow. He wagged his tail when she looked at him. "Who are you?" she whispered. "I know every dog in this village, and you're not one of them."

The dog rose and trotted forward, whimpering softly.

"Are you cold? Well, no creature ought to be out on a night like this."

Good Plume held the flap back, and the dog ran inside. She secured the flap. When she turned, the dog lay curled at Sunchaser's side, his black muzzle propped on his paws. He was a pretty animal, all black except for the tan fur that encircled each of his eyes. The dog lifted his head and peered at Good Plume, and a tingle went up her spine.

"You're not just a dog looking for shelter from the storm, are you? Hmm? No . . . I don't think so. Did somebody send you here? Maybe one of the Steals Light People?"

The dog put his head down again, but the feel of Power that clung to him intensified. A Spirit Helper? Maybe.

Sunchaser had quieted, though lines pinched around his deep-set eyes, and he'd clamped his teeth, setting his square jaw at an angle that made his handsome oval face look longer, his fine cheekbones higher. In the scarlet glow of the dying fire, he looked old beyond his twenty-five summers.

"But Dreaming does that to a person," Good Plume said softly to herself. "Never known a Dreamer to stay young . . . in either body or soul. Spirits won't allow it."

Good Plume massaged her aching hip bones and hitched her way back to her robes. Having lain down again, she stared at the wall paintings—and then her eyes sought the Steals Light People. They were watching her with a concentration that sent a shiver down her backbone.

"I know you were worried, but I told you he was going to get well," she whispered. "It's all those prayers from his followers. Takes that kind of Power to drive out Evil Spirits."

She could hear the figurines speaking softly to each other, their voices like murmurs of wind. The Thunderbeing figurine stared at Good Plume with unnerving intensity. Her wings had started to look ragged. Good Plume would have to see to that.

"Are you trying to speak to me?"

Legend said that it took thousands of cycles for a Thunderbeing's wings to mature. Before that, Thunderbeings lived in the cocoons of clouds and fed upon the rain. Some versions of the story even said that Thunderbeings could become real children if they wanted to. They could send their souls down to earth in the form of a bolt of lightning; when the bolt struck near a woman's womb, the soul could crawl inside the womb and grow into a human.

The Thunderbeing's obsidian bead mouth seemed to move in the wavering firelight.

Good Plume cupped a hand to her ear. The Thunderbeing whispered so low that she could barely hear the words. "Speak up! What woman? What does she have to do with Sunchaser?"

The Thunderbeing fell silent.

Good Plume frowned. "What's the matter? Are you afraid of something?" She shook her head, slightly disgusted. "Well, when you're ready to tell me, I'll be eager to hear. Now go to sleep. All of you. We'll have a lot of work to do tomorrow, Healing, and Singing for the sick and the dying."

She pulled her hides up over her cold ears and closed her eyes. The Steals Light People started talking again, muttering amongst themselves. She fell asleep to the sound of their soft murmurs drifting in and out of the storm's roar.

"The woman's coming . . . almost on her way . . ."

"What if . . ."

"Will she catch his soul?"

"Pray . . ."

Two

Rain fell, misty and cold, from the sodden gray sky. The chilling drops had soaked through Kestrel's antelope-hide dress as she scrambled up the steep slope through the turquoise sage. Heavy steps pounded behind her. She glanced over her shoulder. In the soft, pearlescent gleam of twilight, she could see the two men, coming fast—both of them tall and muscular, with damp black hair that whipped around their expressionless faces. They ascended the slope in quick, measured steps, as though loping on dry ground rather than climbing through clay-slick mud. The warriors of her clan—the Bear-Looks-Back Clan—had legendary abilities as runners. From time beyond memory, they had spent half of every day racing the trails to build their endurance.

Kestrel hugged the bulk of her pregnant belly and desperately ran toward the red caprock ahead. The hoarse hunting cries of saber-toothed cats echoed through the rocky hills as she crawled on hands and knees to clear the gritty lip of stone—hurrying, driven by her pursuers.

In the distance, silver light penetrated the clouds, shot leaden streaks off the wind-painted lakes and coated the gray hills that rumpled the vista. Camp fires gleamed here and there among the villages of mound-shaped lodges. More fires flickered to life as the darkness increased, their twinkles twining through the hills like a necklace of amber beads. Around the villages, hundreds of ponds reflected the orange firelight.

Kestrel could smell the damp reeds and grasses of the marshy lowlands as she staggered along the ridge top. Juniper and pinyon pine speckled the rocky hilltops and slopes in dark green clusters.

"Come on, run!" Tannin, her brother-in-law, shouted as he cleared the caprock behind her. His black eyes, unblinking but wild, were fixed on her like the eyes of a cougar stalking a rabbit. The tension in his thin face had incised deep lines across his forehead and drawn a web around his wide mouth. Soot and grease spotted the chest of his buckskin shirt, and mud matted the fringes on his pant legs. In the dim half-light, the smears looked like clots of dried blood. Tannin sprinted up behind Kestrel and used the stone point on his dart to prod her in the shoulder. "Run!"

"Please!" she shouted. "Please, Tannin—"

"If you don't move faster, I'll kill you here and now!"

Kestrel dashed between two junipers, heedless of the limbs that scratched her face and arms. Locks of long black hair netted her oval face and tangled in her eyelashes. She hadn't the strength to brush them away. Small, frailly built, Kestrel knew that her strength had vanished long ago. Her chest burned as though a fire raged in her lungs. Tannin had kept her running for two days, so long that her feet had swollen hideously.

Cottontail, the young warrior, trotted silently behind Tannin, his sixteen-summers-old body bare to the waist and painted with blue, red and white colors. In the rain, the designs had dissolved into a great purple smear.

"Tannin," Kestrel panted, "please, let me rest. Just for a moment. I can't keep this up."

"Do you think I could show you mercy after the way you've shamed my brother?" Tannin's deep voice wavered in a gust of sage-scented wind that swept the land. "Hurry!" He jabbed her shoulder harder, and the sharp point of his dart bit into her flesh.

Kestrel cried out and turned pleadingly, walking backward. Her moccasins slipped perilously on the mud. "Tannin, listen to me. If you let me go, you know I—"

"Let you go?" He threw back his head and laughed. Rain beaded on his cheeks.

"Tannin, I beg you! Don't make me go back to him." She extended her hands. Tannin had been her friend in the past. When her husband, Lambkill, beat her particularly badly, Tannin always sheltered her in his own lodge. His wife, Calling Crane, tended Kestrel's wounds, speaking gently to her as she washed the bloody fist cuts that covered Kestrel's face and chest.

"He'll kill me, Tannin. You know he will! You've seen—"

Tannin slapped her hard across the jaw. She stumbled backward. He loomed over her, his nostrils flaring with anger. "You deserve to die for what you've done. You *and* your filthy cousin." He grabbed her by the fringed sleeve of her dress and flung her into a shambling trot across the wet sandstone. Juniper trees and brush clung to the patches of soil that had filled the hollows in the stone. She stumbled through them. "I said, *run!*"

Kestrel staggered forward as fast as she could, trying not to trip in the scattered sage that snagged the hem of her dress.

She started down the other side of the ridge toward the village, where seventeen grass lodges were arranged in an irregular semicircle, covering the top of the hill and flowing down over the side; each lodge faced east to receive the early morning blessings of Father Sun. Her own lodge, on the eastern side of the village, sat a little apart, surrounded by a thick grove of junipers that shook berry-heavy limbs in the cold wind.

Her people moved three times a cycle, packing their lodges and belongings and traveling to the shores of the Great Northern Lake in the autumn for the waterfowl migrations, and in the summer making a ten days' walk to the east, to be in the midst of the marshes when the grasses seeded out. This village, Juniper Village, served as both a winter and a spring camp, and her clan spent most of its time here.

Cycles ago, before her marriage, she had chosen the location of this lodge for its privacy. Later, she had regretted the decision. Her husband was a great Trader. He spent half of the cycle of seasons away from home, poling his raft around the huge lakes, traveling all the way to the rainy seacoast far to the north. She didn't know how she'd survived for so long alone, watching the trails, waiting, huddling in her robes at night with only the wind to talk to. Loneliness had nearly driven her mad.

Until Iceplant came . . .

At least Iceplant had escaped. They had split their trails to confuse their trackers, but Kestrel knew that Iceplant was running westward. He was a fast runner, the fastest in the village. He might even now be sitting on the shores of the distant ocean with his mother's people, the Otter Clan.

Thank you, Above-Old-Man. I know I'm unworthy to receive such a gift, but thank you for keeping him safe.

Kestrel placed a hand on their baby and thought she could feel the child's heartbeat, pounding out of rhythm with her own as Iceplant's had done when they'd lain together beneath a mound of furs last autumn. She had known the terrible chance she was taking, but she had taken it willingly, gratefully. Iceplant's warmth had driven the cold from her soul.

All winter she had managed to hide her condition under thick layers of clothing. Not even Lambkill had suspected. She'd spent her time in the menstrual hut with the other women, pretending. But when Spring Girl began to breathe warmth over the frost-laden land, people had glanced suspiciously at Kestrel's heavy clothing. Just after Lambkill had headed north to trade with the Lake People, the rumors had broken loose.

"Ah!" Kestrel cried at the edge of the village when she slipped on a wet rock and twisted her ankle. Her steps faltered.

Tannin shouted, "Do you want to die here in the mud?"

"I—I'm going, Tannin."

Kestrel limped past the first lodge. Made of a frame of willow poles covered with grass thatch, it resembled a shaggy bear hunched over a kill. The scents of fires smoldering, meat cooking and damp furs drifted to her.

People had gathered before a bonfire in the plaza, where flames were leaping twelve hands high. It looked like the entire village—maybe thirty adults and two dozen children—were there. Sparks, winking and sizzling as they rose into the dreary sky, whirled over their heads. When Tannin shrieked a war cry, people turned; men shook war clubs, roaring, while old women wept and tore at their hair. Young women covered their children's eyes to protect them from the wicked sight of Kestrel.

Tribal elders hunched in several lodge doorways, sheltering from the rain, their faces twisted. Kestrel tried not to look at the beautiful geometric designs decorating their shirts. She had dyed the porcupine quills and sewn them onto the garments herself. Each color came from a Spirit Plant that cured different illnesses of the body or soul. Prickly pear cactus fruit produced the rich purple color, juniper berries the tan, rabbit brush the pale gold, sumac bark the beautiful brown.

She stumbled past Old Buffalo Woman, her eyes lingering on the orange-pink color that she'd created from mixing lichen and holly berries. When brewed as a strong tea, the same mixture cured indigestion and eased the tremors of the limb-shaking disease. Even as a child, the *need* to dye and paint had tormented her, as though Above-Old-Man had buried love for the bright pigments deep in her bones. She could not live without her art. And her creations could not live without her, for Kestrel added drops of her own blood to each color. It awakened the sleeping Spirits in the dead plants and gave the designs the ability to come to life. Not every design did. But many of these had. And now, as she went forward, she could hear their voices, soft and pitiful, wondering at her fate, telling her to flee before it was too late. *"Run . . . run . . . !"*

Each elder bowed his or her head as Kestrel went by. Did none of them doubt her guilt? Had she already been judged and sentenced without so much as a chance to defend herself? She'd grown up in their midst, loved them, relied on them for guidance. Would they stand by and quietly watch her murdered?

As Kestrel neared the fire, she saw her grandmother, Willowstem, and then her mother, Owlwoman, standing half-hidden on the outskirts of the crowd. Though neither of them looked Kestrel's way, she could see that tears traced lines down her mother's lowered face.

"Mother?" Kestrel called as Tannin forced her along. "Mother . . . please?"

Owlwoman pressed a hand to her lips to keep them from trembling, but she said nothing.

"Bring her here!" Lambkill commanded. He paced near the flames, his arms crossed over his bony chest. Short gray braids hung to either side of his head, framing his flat nose and heavy jowls. He had passed forty-five summers. The orange light that danced across his lined face accentuated his age and flickered unnaturally in the quartz-crystal necklace that hung over his heart. He'd woven the crystal's chain from strips of mammoth tendon—it was strong enough to pull a buffalo, he claimed. His triumphant black eyes sparkled darkly as Kestrel came forward.

Her heart pounded so hard that she thought it would burst the cage of her ribs. When she was twenty hands from Lambkill, a cruel smile bent his lips. He extended an arm northward. "Look! I've ended it!"

Kestrel turned, then stumbled when she saw Iceplant kneeling by the fire. He rocked back and forth, his handsome face in his hands. A long black braid hung over his right shoulder. She thought she could hear him Singing his Deathsong. The notes lilted like a horrifying lullaby.

No. Oh, no . . .

"Face your husband!" Tannin took Kestrel's arm in a hurtful grip and forced her to look at Lambkill, who had dressed in his finest ceremonial shirt, made of smoked elkhide and tanned to a deep golden color. Red and yellow porcupine quills decorated the breast and sleeves, while rain-soaked feathers drooped mournfully around his ears.

"So, you thought you could escape me," Lambkill whispered savagely as he moved to only a handbreadth from Kestrel. His skin had bronzed so deeply from long days on the trading trails that it resembled desiccated leather. Thick wrinkles hung in folds down his neck and made bulges beneath his eyes.

Kestrel glared at him and braced her shaking knees.

People closed the circle around them, their eyes alert, listening, anxious for the final judgment to be rendered. A few of the young women whispered behind their hands and pointed to Kestrel's belly. She heard someone say, ". . . at least eight moons along."

The words enraged Lambkill. He let out a shrill cry and moved so fast that Kestrel didn't have time to dodge. His blow struck her in the temple and knocked her, staggering, to one side. When she didn't fall, he ruthlessly kicked her legs out from under her. She landed hard on the wet ground.

Iceplant shot to his feet, shouting, *"No!"* Tall and slender, he had soft brown eyes. His medicine pouch hung from a thong around his neck. Covered with Kestrel's own red, black and white designs, it splashed the center of his wolfhide shirt with color. The long fringes on his pants swayed as he tentatively stepped forward. "Lambkill, you . . . you said you wouldn't hurt her. You told me you'd just banish her!"

Horror pierced Kestrel's heart. She stared dumbly at him, like an animal bashed in the head by a hunter's club. Iceplant's eyes tightened when he met Kestrel's gaze, and blood began to surge sickeningly in her ears.

Feebly, she called, "Iceplant?"

"Kestrel, I—I didn't know he'd do this to you. When he caught me, I swear, he told me—"

Lambkill swung around to Iceplant. "Stay out of this, you coward! You're as much to blame as she is."

Iceplant stepped back. Kestrel stared blindly at him, and a dark abyss opened in her soul. *No.* Her lips formed the word soundlessly. *It can't be. He would never betray me . . .*

"Lambkill," Iceplant called in a trembling voice. "Sunchaser says we shouldn't beat our wives. He says that Wolfdreamer watches and listens. We must all—"

"Sunchaser!" Lambkill yelled. His wrinkled cheeks flushed with rage. "That young fool from the seacoast! He's deranged! You haven't started believing *his delusions*, have you?" He glared out at the crowd, taking note of each expression, identifying the believers and the doubters. "What's happened since I've been gone? Have you all been sucked into this madness about your ancestors coming back from the Land of the Dead? I just returned from the great northern lakes. The people there have heard of Sunchaser, but they don't believe in his New Way! How can you? Do you really think that all the mammoths will return if you Sing the idiotic songs Sunchaser teaches? The Mammoth Spirit Dance is nonsense!"

Sunchaser . . . Kestrel exhaled a halting breath. How many nights had she lain awake listening to Iceplant repeat the stories he'd heard from the Traders who routinely stopped at Juniper Village? Sunchaser had barely passed twenty-five summers, yet people spoke his name with hushed awe, as though he were a legend, not a living, breathing man. Stories said he'd died and been carried to the Land of the Dead on the shining wings of the Thunderbeings. There, he'd met and talked to the Ancestor Spirits. They'd taught him a Dance that Sunchaser proclaimed would return the world to its former purity. He said that if people would follow his New Way, the mammoths would return—they'd come tramping back from the Land of the Dead with all of the ancestors who had gone before.

Wolfdreamer himself, the great hero who had led the first clans up from the underworld of Darkness to this world of Light, had promised to return to guide the people. But he would no longer be human. He would return as a dust spiral that bobbed and whirled around the mammoths. Sunchaser carried a square of deerhide with him, on which he had drawn a maze. It showed the Way, he said, to enter the Land of the Dead. He asserted that anyone could go and verify his claims. His new teaching had spread like wildfire in parched prairie grass.

"It's not nonsense," Iceplant said in a shaking voice. He straightened to his full height, eyes aflame. "Sunchaser has been to the Land of the Dead. He's talked with the great leaders of our people. Wolfdreamer told him——"

"Shut up, filth! Do I have to kill you to silence you? Is that what you want?" Lambkill asked. "I could change my mind about your fate!"

Iceplant hesitated. His chin quivered before he clamped his jaw to steady it. "Don't you understand? We have to change, have to return to the old ways of purity and truth."

"You dare to talk to *me* about purity!" Lambkill shrilled.

Kestrel's baby shifted so suddenly that she grunted in pain. All eyes turned toward her expectantly, as though she might speak. She lowered a hand to rub her belly. "Shh," she whispered in a choking voice. "Shh, my baby, don't cry."

"What did you say?" Lambkill demanded. When Kestrel didn't repeat the words, he slammed a fist into her back and sent her toppling into the mud. "Stand up. Stand up! Do you hear me?"

"I hear you, husband."

Kestrel got on her knees, then unsteadily rose to her feet. Mud coated her dress. She felt no indignation, no hatred, only a terror that gnawed at the pit of her stomach. Near the fire, Iceplant had folded his arms tightly across his chest, as if to ease a pain in his heart.

"I am a Trader!" Lambkill yelled to the crowd as he circled Kestrel. Those standing in the wet plaza watched him through frozen eyes, their faces rigid. The elders who had sheltered in the lodge doorways drew their painted hides up over their heads. "You all know that. As you know that I was gone . . . *gone* . . . from the Moon-of-Turning-Leaves through the Moon-of-Flying-Snow."

The raindrops grew larger, splatting on Lambkill's hide shirt and sparkling in his gray braids. His voice had deepened as his movements became more precise. Kestrel's stomach knotted. She had seen him perform a thousand times. He boasted that he calculated each wave of his hand and tilt of his head to affect the crowd in just the way he wanted. His smug voice whispered from her memories: "That's why I'm a great Trader, woman. No one can deny me what I want once they've heard me speak. It's Trader Power." To the outside world, he seemed strong and affable, always in control. Only she knew the real Lambkill, the monster who was born with the darkness.

He had such nightmares. Every night. And they had been getting worse over the past cycle: dreams that woke him from sound sleep and brought him awake gasping. That was usually when he beat her. She never knew why.

Lambkill worked the crowd, walking the circle, placing his clenched fists on the shoulders of the most powerful people while he stared into their eyes. Clan leaders nodded in agreement, and Kestrel's great-aunt wept openly. When Lambkill whirled and strode back, Kestrel took a breath, watching numbly as he pulled a hafted obsidian knife from his belt and lunged at her. Twisting a handful of her waterlogged dress, he slit the soft leather from hide collar to fringed hem and jerked it wide, revealing her huge belly. She staggered to keep standing. Strands of waist-length black hair stuck wetly to her chest, partially covering her milk-heavy breasts; the rest of her seventeen-summers-old body lay bare to the gusting wind. Firelight coated her skin like a sheath of golden pine sap. Kestrel saw her mother close her eyes in shame.

"So, my wife . . . if I was gone all autumn, who fathered this child?" Lambkill thumped her belly with the blade of his knife.

Kestrel forced strength into her voice. "You did, my husband. In the first few days after you returned. I am not as far along as I look. I think I am carrying twins." And sometimes she did think so. Late at night when the world went quiet, she swore she could feel two heartbeats in her womb.

"Liar!" Lambkill shouted, but he appeared to be off balance. He stood stiffly with his hands at his sides, his curled brown fingers tensed like talons while he searched her face. For cycles he had told her of how much he longed for a son. After a few moments, he spun and glowered questioningly at Iceplant. Iceplant shook his head. Speculative murmurs filtered through the village. Kestrel caught parts of the conversations and knew what was being discussed. Lambkill had been married four times and had never fathered a child. Perhaps, finally, his seed had taken root. It would be a great boon to his reputation.

A flicker of hope animated Kestrel. He might claim the child even if he knew it were not his. She concentrated on breathing deeply, evenly. "Your two sisters and your aunt gave birth to twins, Lambkill. Your own mother had twins that died just after birth. Twins run in your bloodline."

Lambkill walked around her; his eyes glowed, lit by an inner rage. Under his breath, he hissed, "Shall I cut the forsaken brat from your womb to see, Kestrel?"

"You would kill your own sons, my husband? Wait until they are born. Then you will know I am telling the truth." *And I will have time to find an escape . . .*

Owlwoman lifted her head to peer at Kestrel with desperate hope in her eyes. The other women in the crowd burst into conversation. Men stood listening intently.

Lambkill's mouth tightened unpleasantly. "The truth?" he hissed. "I already *know* the truth!"

He stalked across the wet ground, twisted a fist in Iceplant's hair and shoved him toward Kestrel. Iceplant did not resist. He came to stand so close that she could count each tiny spiral that encircled the edges of his medicine pouch. She had used alder bark to produce the reddish-brown color. For moons she'd been mixing the powdered bark with Iceplant's food to relieve the stomach pains that so often troubled him. Kestrel was good at taking care of people. She had just started to develop a reputation as a Healer. Easing another's pain helped to ease her own.

In the subdued light, Iceplant's handsome face had a sickly pallor. Kestrel saw hurt in his eyes and fear for her. But more fear for himself.

No, she mouthed the words to him, *please.*

"Tell everyone!" Lambkill ordered. "Go on, Iceplant. Tell them you've been bedding my wife for two cycles. Every time I went away, you sneaked into my lodge and drove your penis into her."

Iceplant's lips parted, but no words came. Finally he murmured, "Yes."

Sobs constricted Kestrel's throat. She bowed her head.

"What?" Lambkill shouted. "Speak up, Iceplant. No one can hear you. Say it again!"

The crowd had hushed, as the buffalo fall silent before the herd stampedes and tramples the plains into dust. No one moved. Only the incessant rain and the sizzling fire gave voice to the world.

Iceplant sucked in a breath. More strongly, he said, "Yes. The child is mine."

Sharp wails erupted from the women in the crowd.

Lambkill slammed a fist into Iceplant's stomach, and when Iceplant bent double, Lambkill kneed him brutally in the groin. Iceplant sank to the ground, gasping.

Lambkill taunted, "Didn't you think I'd ever find out? Do you think I'm stupid? *Fool!* If you hadn't agreed to tell me the truth, you'd already be dead. I should never have consented to let Kestrel stay here, in the village of her birth. By rights, we should have gone to live in my father's village. It was a kindness I did for her—knowing that I would be gone for half of the cycle or more. I let her stay here, near her family, and look what came of my generosity!"

"Don't hurt Kestrel." Iceplant tipped his tortured face to the misty rain. "You promised. You said you wouldn't—"

"It is my right!" Lambkill yelled. He spread his arms and spun around slowly, meeting every eye in the crowd. "It is my *right* as her husband to decide her fate. Isn't that so, Old Porcupine?"

"You promised," Iceplant repeated. "You promised you'd banish both of us."

Iceplant looked up at Kestrel with his whole tormented soul in his eyes, and she suddenly understood what he'd been planning. *He thought it was a way for us to be together . . .* Like a wildflower beneath hot summer winds, Kestrel's soul twisted and shriveled.

Lambkill smiled. "Your confession has decided your fate, Iceplant." He spun to Old Porcupine again. "Isn't that so, elder? I have the right to choose Iceplant's punishment as well as hers!"

Porcupine's ancient face fell into sorrow-laden lines. He adjusted the deerhide over his head, perhaps to better block the chill wind. "It is your right."

"And you, Owlwoman?" Lambkill said to Kestrel's mother. "What do you think? Your daughter is guilty of *incest!* She bedded your own dead husband's nephew! What do you think her fate should be?"

Kestrel gazed for a long moment into her mother's eyes, and a pain began in her chest, like a wrenching scream working its way up from her soul to her lips. It came out a moan as Owlwoman placed a quaking hand on Willowstem's shoulder and turned her back.

A chant rose on the wings of the darkness, rising and falling in mournful tones as Owlwoman Sang Kestrel's Deathsong. Someone else joined in, a man, deep in the crowd. More and more people lifted their voices and tipped their faces to the rain to Sing.

Heya heya a yo ho yo ho yaha.
Hear us, Thunderbeings!
In beauty, it is finished.
In beauty, it is finished.

Our beloved daughter is done.
Heya heya a yo ho yo ho yaha.
With your headdresses of lightning flaming, fly to us!
With your bellies full of rain, come to us!

We beg you to take this beloved daughter away.
Heya heya a yo ho yo ho yaha.
Take her away to the Land of the Dead,
Bear her upon your wings.

Heya heya a yo ho yo ho yaha.
Our beloved daughter is done.
In beauty it is finished.
In beauty it is finished. . . .

Lightning crackled through the clouds, and thunder rolled over the hills. People blinked away the rain, searching for the shining wings of the Thunderbeings, expecting to see them plunge from the heavens.

Kestrel whispered, "No, Grandmother. . . . Mother? Please?"

Lambkill gestured shortly to Tannin and Cottontail. "Get Iceplant out of my way."

Kestrel tugged at her ripped dress, trying to shield herself from the people's eyes and the rain. She watched blindly as Cottontail and Tannin dragged Iceplant back and shoved him down by the hissing fire. Around him, puddles shimmered radiantly in the firelight. Overhead, flashes of lightning slashed the gloomy skies and thunder rolled solemnly from the blackness.

Lambkill lifted both hands and began a speech about his love for clan law, about Kestrel's sacrilege, and of how hard he found it to murder his own wife.

But her eyes stayed on Iceplant, and her ears heard a different voice, three days old, soft, pleading . . .

"Kestrel, please, I beg you. I want to be with you. Come with me to the sea. My mother's people will take us in. The Otter Clan traces its family line through the women—not through the men. You're my father's brother's daughter. You're not my cousin to them!"

"We'd never be safe, Iceplant. Lambkill would search the world to find us and then he would murder all three of us.

He knows every chief and every trail. We'd never escape."

"I'll protect you from him! Kestrel, listen to me. I love you so much. Come with me!"

The abyss in Kestrel's soul yawned wider, threatening to swallow her. Barely audible above the wind and pattering rain, she said, "Forgive me, Iceplant. Forgive me."

Iceplant seemed to hear. He looked up at her through tear-filled eyes, then doubled over as his broad shoulders shook with sobs. The last of Kestrel's soul drained away into the slate-gray echoes of twilight. She felt empty. So empty.

Another paean of thunder shuddered the heavens.

Lambkill strode back to stand nose to nose with her, blocking her view of Iceplant. "The laws of our people say I may do with you as I wish, woman." He smiled and lifted his fist. The force of the blow sent Kestrel reeling backward. Her arms flailed wildly as her moccasins skidded in the mud.

Lambkill danced around her with his knife drawn, bouncing from foot to foot, screaming, "Incest! Incest!"

The obsidian blade glinted as he stabbed her bare shoulder, then slashed across her forehead. Hot blood ran into her eyes, and Kestrel let out a cry of shock. She heard Iceplant moan. Through blurry eyes, she saw him. He was kneeling before the fire, holding his stomach while he vomited.

"I'm going to kill you, wife!" Lambkill yelled and lunged at her, his knife aimed at her heart.

People gasped, rushing forward to witness her death, and a narrow slit opened in the crowd. Kestrel sidestepped and wildly sprinted through the gap and across the plaza, her child-heavy belly bouncing. Cries of outrage laced the misty air.

Lambkill shouted, "Come on!" and an angry mob coalesced from the crowd of her family and friends and followed in pursuit.

When she reached the edge of the plaza and could see the slash of wet trail heading downhill, she heard the swift steps behind her. Frantic, she threw herself headlong down the slope, slipping and sliding, almost falling, but when she braced a hand on a boulder to steady herself, Lambkill caught her by the hair and snapped her head back to glare into her eyes.

"You'll never escape me, woman! *Never*."

"Lambkill, please . . . just let us go. We'll never come back. You'll never have to worry that—"

"Not after what you've done to me!" He wrenched her hair violently, and she kicked and clawed at him, but he used her awkward balance against her. As she swung at him furiously, he slammed his left fist into her face, then grabbed her and spun her around so he could tighten his arm around her throat. He forced her back uphill, into the wet plaza, where her mother still stood, her back turned. But Owlwoman's soft cries pierced the sounds of the storm.

Lambkill pressed his mouth to Kestrel's ear and whispered, "You haven't asked yet what I plan to do with Iceplant."

The touch of his withered lips made her flesh crawl. She stammered, "He helped you to f-find me, didn't he? If he . . . he helped you, you should let him go."

"Oh, yes, he helped me. He told me what time you'd left and which trail you'd taken. He even told me where the two of you had planned to meet. And I *will* let him go . . . just so I can hunt him down!"

"You would break a promise that the entire village heard you make? The elders won't let you do that. The clans will force you—"

"And after I hunt Iceplant down," he continued as though she hadn't spoken, "I'm going to drag him back here and slit him open before your eyes."

"Clan law will forbid it."

He laughed. "Not when I explain to the village that I've changed my mind, that I no longer want your death, but Iceplant's. Oh, his family will be upset. I'll probably have to give them a few buffalo hides, maybe some rare sharks' teeth from the southern ocean. But eventually they'll agree. Everyone knows it's my right to decide your fates. Yes, Kestrel, I'm going to let you live. I want you to suffer for what you've done. The village will disown you. You'll have only me to shield you from their taunts, only me to feed you, only me to keep you company."

Lambkill stroked her bared breast with a callused hand. "But *hear* me. If I ever find you with another man, I will kill you. You can never run away from me. No one can protect you. I will find you vulnerable someday, and I will kill you then. Do you understand me?"

Lambkill tightened his arm over her throat.

Kestrel gasped, "Help . . . someone, help me! Mother . . . *Mother!*" A gray haze formed at the edges of her vision and stealthily began to blot out the world.

"No! In the name of Above-Old-Man," Iceplant screamed. "Lambkill, stop! Stop it!" Through the crowd, Kestrel glimpsed Iceplant running toward her. "Don't hurt her. It was my fault. I forced her. I'm the one to blame! Punish me. *Punish me!*"

"Get back!" Lambkill snarled.

Heedlessly, Iceplant let out a roar and used his fists to beat a way through the crowd, then threw himself at Lambkill, breaking the Trader's hold on Kestrel and toppling him to the ground. They rolled and kicked in the mud as Kestrel staggered away. The crowd surged forward like a pack of hungry wolves closing in on a wounded doe. The people stared at her without pity.

Iceplant, much younger and stronger, slammed a fist into Lambkill's stomach, then straddled him and sank his fingers into his throat.

Lambkill's eyes widened in terror. He struggled vainly against those granite hands, and Tannin and Cottontail pulled their war clubs and waded into the fight. They jerked Iceplant off of Lambkill and started kicking him in the sides and in the face until blood ran down his cheeks. He tried to rise, but they hammered him with their clubs, striking his spine, legs and head and keeping him down. He huddled, covering his head with his arms. Lambkill crawled to his feet and drew his own war club.

"Kestrel!" Iceplant's panicked voice impaled her. "Run! Save our baby! *Run!*" Insanely, Iceplant threw himself sideways, knocking Tannin's feet out from under him. Then he dove for Lambkill's legs, tackling him and wrestling him to the ground again.

As though in a nightmare, Kestrel shoved her way through a group of old women who screamed and clawed at her. Shouts went up as she dashed down the muddy slope. Purple threads of lightning wove an eerie web through the blanket of clouds, partially illuminating her way.

At the base of the hill, she stumbled into a thicket of head-high sage and stood panting. Night had swallowed the land, but she knew the worn paths by heart. Through the blacker patches of juniper that created weaving, serpentine lines across the hills, she could picture the tangle of trails. Which way should she go? Where could she hide? Lambkill would track her. In the mud, it would be easy. How could she—

From out of nowhere, a hoarse scream tore the darkness. It pulsed amid the roars of the Thunderbeings, rising and falling, the wail of a lost soul.

Kestrel's heart almost stopped beating. She spun around.

On top of the hill, Iceplant stood silhouetted against the blazing background of the bonfire. Tannin and Cottontail held his arms apart while Lambkill brutally beat him over the head with a war club. As Kestrel watched, Iceplant's knees buckled. Lambkill took the knife from his belt and thrust it into Iceplant's stomach, then sawed upward, into the chest cavity. A small, wretched cry escaped Iceplant's lips as Tannin and Cottontail let him drop to his knees. The crowd backed away. Dark blood gushed from Iceplant's wound. As though fighting to stay alive, he braced a hand on the ground and dug his fingers into the mud. He coughed. Red foam bubbled at his lips. With great effort, he lifted his head and stared out beyond the village toward her. "Run!" he choked out. "Run, Kestrel . . ."

She thrashed away through the sage, whispering to herself in terror: "Run uphill, *uphill.*" *Wounded animals always run downhill. Lambkill will expect it. He thinks that I'm beaten, that he won't have any trouble finding me. That's why he's not chasing me yet.*

She circled the village and forced her exhausted legs up the slope until she could look down on the bonfire from the red ridge west of the village. When she saw Iceplant, Kestrel started to shake so badly that she could barely keep standing. He lay on his back, peaceful now, rain glistening in his dark hair. Firelight coated his wide, dead eyes with a patina of pure gold, turning them luminous. When the wind gusted, the light flitted through the crowd like a homeless ghost. It fluttered over the face of each person who had witnessed the crime.

Lambkill stood talking to Tannin before the lodge of Old Porcupine. He was smiling, and then he laughed. A harsh, deep laugh that came from his belly. Hatred rose in Kestrel, a hatred so violent, so terrifying in its strength, that it blurred the rest of the world. "I'm going to kill you, my husband," she swore. "Someday I will find *you* vulnerable . . ."

Lightning split the darkness, but the Thunderbeings kept silent as though they, too, feared the dagger of flame that had crept into Kestrel's soul and begun consuming it alive. In the lightning's eerie afterglow, the Mammoth Mountains in the west stood silhouetted like huge beasts shocked abruptly into stillness. One peak looked as though it had its trunk up and was beckoning, saying, *"This is the way. Come this way . . ."*

Kestrel clutched her belly and gazed back at the village. Iceplant's body wavered in the windblown shreds of firelight, sometimes there, sometimes not.

Tenderly, she whispered, "I'm going to the sea, Iceplant . . . as you wanted . . . to your mother's people. I pray they take us in."

Three

White hair fell over Oxbalm's eyes as a gust of night wind swept the beach, bringing the pungent odor of salt and sand to his nostrils. The fringes on his buckskin jacket flapped. He drew his knees closer to his chest and peered at the old woman beside him. Sumac sat like a stone sentinel, her wrinkled face gleaming with spray, and she watched the beach through eyes even more ancient than his own. He gently patted her knee, and she twined her fingers with his.

Snores and the coughs of children echoed from Otter Clan Village in the fir forest behind them. Everyone else slept. Only Oxbalm and Sumac had been up all night. They had sat together watching the Star People sail their canoes through the dark seas in the Land of the Dead, listening to the night birds, watching the fluorescence of the surf . . . remembering.

Through the eyes of their souls, they could penetrate the veil of the present and peer into the past. Only there could Oxbalm still see huge herds of mammoths roaming the coast . . .

He could smell dust. Hear pounding feet. Dust and pounding feet and the voices of mammoths calling. Where the sea breeze parted the haze, trunks lifted, trumpeting in fury. Hunters appeared and disappeared in the dust. Youth pumped in Oxbalm's veins as he ran, his dart nocked in his atlatl, chasing a straggling calf. With his Spirit Song on his lips, he sprinted forward, unafraid of the bulls that watched him, their tusks gleaming in the brilliant sunlight. Other hunters Sang. They all ran to encircle the herd.

Oxbalm shouted "Cast!" and a hail of darts pierced the

warm summer air. They arced up and fell in a shower of glinting chert points. Whoops of joy mixed with the screams of wounded animals. Oxbalm cast again, and again. Painted hunters wove around him, racing through the scattering herd, shouting, killing enough mammoths to feed their people for the entire winter.

Such a good dream. It swelled within Oxbalm like a blossoming flower, reminding him of the days when he had been one of the greatest of his people's hunters, of the days when there had been too many mammoths to count. No one had starved back then. There had been no sicknesses that lasted for moons at a time and ran through the villages like a rampaging dire wolf. For too many winters to count, Oxbalm had watched the number of mammoths dwindle, until now only a few lumbering animals with haunted eyes remained. He hadn't had a mammoth steak in six long cycles, and he yearned for one desperately.

Oxbalm shivered and rubbed his left knee. It ached all the time. "Mother Ocean," he called. He had no teeth left, and his voice always sounded a little slurred. "I felt you tugging at my soul. I got up out of my warm hides and came. Tell me what you need. Send me a sign."

Sumac said nothing, letting him talk to the Mother alone. But she squeezed his fingers more tightly and cast a brief glance over her shoulder toward their lodge in the village. She was worried about their three grandchildren, the two boys and the little girl. Saber-toothed cats had been prowling close to the village in the past cold moon, hoping to catch a child to eat. Mountain Lake, Balsam and Horseweed had been living with them since the death of their mother in the fever two cycles ago. Singing Moss had been Oxbalm and Sumac's last living child, and grief over her had almost killed Sumac.

Oxbalm squeezed Sumac's hand in return and focused his faded eyes on the black expanse of water. He knew the Mother. He'd canoed out into her far reaches, Singing to her, studying her many colors. She resembled a patched old hide, rubbed thin and transparent in places; in other places, darkened almost black from lying close to the bodies of the Earth Spirits on cold, stormy nights. When Oxbalm had been filled with the brashness of youth, he'd canoed out so far that he couldn't see land at all. The Mother played tricks on men so bold. Sunlight rippled off the surface of the water and formed islands that didn't exist, or spun golden whirlwinds from the fog. She spoke to such men, her voice soft and muted. And if it pleased her, she guided them back to land. Often it did not please her. Oxbalm had lost many friends to Mother Ocean.

But a man never forgot the sound of her voice once he had heard it. And the Mother had started speaking to him at sunset yesterday, calling to him, demanding that he come sit beside her.

The fermenting scents of kelp and fish grew stronger as morning neared. Oxbalm filled his lungs and sighed, "I'm tired, Sumac."

"Just a little longer," she responded. "If the Mother hasn't sent you a sign by dawn, we'll go back." She hesitated, then asked, "Do you think it has to do with Sunchaser?"

"I don't know."

Oxbalm put an arm around her shoulders and pulled her close. Long tresses of her gray hair tumbled down the front of his hide jacket. She'd turned fifty-five last cycle, but she wore the bitter winters better than Oxbalm did. Though wrinkles incised her high forehead, her long, straight nose and pointed chin looked as perfect as they had on the day he'd met her. Her full lips had sunken, like his had, as her teeth had fallen out. But he didn't mind. She was still beautiful to him.

Sumac's gray brows drew together. "The Mammoth Spirit Dance starts day after tomorrow and Sunchaser isn't here yet. This will be the fourth Dance he's missed this cycle. Why has he stopped coming? All the surrounding villages will be here. His absence will frighten people. It's as though he's lost faith in the Dance himself. He started it. How could that happen?"

"I don't think he's lost faith, Sumac. He still Sings for the mammoths. Five moons ago he told me he'd been Dreaming every day. You know how hard that is. Keep your faith in him. He's the last great Dreamer left to the sea peoples."

The breeze stung Oxbalm's tired eyes. He rubbed them hard.

Legend spoke of a time when camels and mastodons had covered the hills as thickly as the spring grasses. But now a man considered himself lucky if he saw a few tens of tens in his entire lifetime. The cheetahs had become so rare that Oxbalm could barely remember what they looked like. And the giant short-faced bears had almost vanished— though, Oxbalm had to admit, he wasn't sorry to see them go. Terrifying animals, they ran with the fleetness and speed of Horse, possessed the ferociousness of an enraged lion and stood as tall as a man at the shoulder.

Sunchaser said that all of the big animals, from mastodons to cheetahs, had heard their deaths Sung on the wind and had climbed onto the wings of the Thunderbeings to fly across the sea to the Land of the Dead—to punish humans for overhunting them. The dwindling supply of big meat animals had turned the four-legged hunters bold. Often they sneaked close to the village to grab a child, or a doddering elder. What kind of sign was it when hunter turned on hunter?

Sumac shifted to resettle herself on the sand so as to face him. "But we have other Dreamers. Not as great as Sunchaser, it's true. Catchstraw—"

"Isn't much of a Dreamer . . ." Oxbalm finished ". . . for all that he lounges around his lodge day in and day out claiming to be Dreaming. He never helps around the village. Have you ever seen him hunt? No. Fish? On rare occasions, when he can't pay somebody else to fish for him. Has he ever gone on a war raid? I remember one raid I led when Catchstraw was seventeen summers. All the other young men had readied themselves, but Catchstraw ran and hid in his mother's lodge, shrieking." Oxbalm grunted. "He's not much of a man."

"You've never liked Catchstraw, even when he was a boy."

"It's irritating, Sumac, when a five-summers-old child tries to tell you he knows more than you do."

"Well, he's a Dreamer now. Maybe Mother Ocean never intended him to be a hunter or a warrior."

"If Catchstraw's such a fine Dreamer, why did he start having Dreams only five winters ago?"

"That's when Running Salmon died. You know that. We needed a new Dreamer."

"Running Salmon was smart. Before she went, she told us that Sunchaser would be the next great Dreamer for the people. I guess Catchstraw thought differently. But Running Salmon was right. Only Sunchaser could bring all of the mountain and sea villages together, and keep them together, to work for a single purpose—keeping the mammoths alive in our world. Catchstraw would have driven everybody away with his whining and—"

"You think he's a false Dreamer?"

"I didn't say that. I wonder, that's all. He was always a strange child. Kept to himself a lot. And then, ruining not one but *two* marriages that his mother worked so hard to negotiate. Some of his kin are still struggling to pay back the wedding gifts."

"He was so spoiled that he forgot he had clan obligations."

"Yes. All of his life he's refused to do anything that didn't please him."

"You're being too hard on him, Oxbalm. I think he tries to help people." Sumac blinked contemplatively. "Some of Catchstraw's Dreams have come true."

"And just as many haven't."

"Well, at least Catchstraw is close at hand. Does anyone know where Sunchaser is? He flits around as wildly as the west wind."

Oxbalm used a knobby finger to draw irregular designs in the sand. The grains felt cool and moist. "The last I heard, he was up in the mountains at Brushnut Village. The illness had struck and they begged him to come home and Heal. He couldn't refuse to help his relatives. Before that, he was moving through the other mountain villages, Singing and Dancing for people, performing Healings. I don't know why he hasn't been back to see us. His last trip to the sea was when he came to the Mammoth Spirit Dance held at Whalebeard Village four moons ago. But he has so many villages that he visits, it's no wonder . . ."

Oxbalm could feel the change, the shift of Power. He shivered and cocked his head to listen to the Mother. Her voice had grown low and hoarse.

Sumac asked, "What are you—"

"Shh!" Oxbalm raised a hand, aware of the sudden stillness that even hushed the regular booming of the surf. Power spun eddies in the air, a heaviness growing.

The village dogs started barking, and they both turned. A pack of four dogs raced out toward the beach, peering at something down the shoreline that Oxbalm couldn't see. After a few moments, they began howling and prancing, creating such a commotion that people in the village came crawling out of their lodges, muttering, their hair wild with sleep.

"What is it?" Sumac asked. "What's wrong?"

Oxbalm braced a hand on her shoulder for support while he got to his feet. Dawn Child had touched the horizon with an elusive glow of lavender, and the beach where the dogs stood glistened and sparkled. He took a step forward. For a long time he saw only the surge of the waves and the brightening shape of the big island off the coast. Flocks of sea birds dotted the skies above the dark silhouettes of the island's three major peaks.

"Oxbalm?" Sumac said as she stood.

"Shh. Listen."

A deep-throated groan arose, the sound like the last desperate gasps of drowning men.

Against the dark ocean, something moved.

Oxbalm had to squint his old eyes to see the sinuous trunk

that lifted and weakly splashed the water. The mammoth lay on its side, dying. And there lay another. And another. And . . . The village dogs yipped and howled, bounding back and forth, afraid to get too close, terrified by the huge animals.

"Oh, no. What—"

"Look!" Sumac pointed. "There's another one . . . and another."

Up and down the beach, dark forms appeared, dozens of them. Twenty? No, thirty or more. Their earthy musk carried on the salty wind. They walked out of the trees making soft sounds to one another, their shaggy coats shining, and waded into the sea, the trunk of one holding tight to the tail of another. The little calves squealed as they fought the current to stay beside their mothers. One of the cows lifted her trunk and sprayed water into the air. The droplets spiraled up, capturing the gleam of dawn before they showered down into the ocean. The mammoths walked out as far as they could, then started swimming.

"What are they doing?" Oxbalm blurted in terror and awe.

The domes of the mammoths' heads vanished, and Oxbalm went rigid with fear. Huge bodies began to bob to the surface.

"Oh, no, Blessed Mother Ocean . . ."

Tusks gleamed, some jagged and broken, spearing the sand as the dead animals near shore rocked with the force of the water. Somewhere out in the blackness, a calf bawled. Oxbalm could see it struggling, trying to swim alongside a dead cow, its long auburn hair sparkling in the starlight. It went down, came up, and went down again. Farther out, two old bulls swam with all their might, heading westward, due west. Three younger bulls followed behind them, their trunks up, their massive heads tipped back so far that their tusks thrust straight up at Brother Sky. The lead bull let out a deep, anguished roar when the waves began to drag him under. The other bulls floundered and cried when the lead bull sank. They swam in circles, bellowing, whimpering, then tried to turn back toward the shore, but they'd swum out so far. . . .

Sumac pressed a hand to her throat, clutching it as if in pain. Some of the villagers gathered around them. Silent. Wary. No one had seen a herd so large in cycles. Reverential murmurs eddied through the crowd. The dogs had gone slinking back into the village, their tails between their legs, and now they stood close by their masters, watching with their ears pricked.

"I . . . I don't understand." Oxbalm strained to get the words through his constricted throat. Tears stung his eyes. Why would mammoths, their numbers already so decimated by human hunters, drown themselves? He shook his head. Then awe slackened his face as comprehension dawned. "It's the sign, Sumac! This is why Mother Ocean called me out tonight!"

"Sign of what?"

He started forward, but Sumac's hand closed on his wrist, halting him. Her fingers trembled. "Don't go," she whispered. "I'm frightened."

"So am I. Something's happened. Something terrible. Mammoth Above is trying to warn us." He removed her hand, patted it gently and hobbled across the sand on his rickety legs.

Sumac hurried after him, calling, "Wait! Oxbalm—"

"Find young Horseweed!" he shouted over his shoulder. "Send him to Brushnut Village. Tell him to bring Sunchaser back, at the point of a dart if necessary! Sunchaser is the only one who will know how to make sense of this."

Kestrel clenched her teeth as another contraction left her gasping. The pain seemed to twist her inside out. Her water had broken just before dawn, warm fluid draining down the insides of her thighs, and the contractions had started coming closer together. Breathlessly, she whispered, "A moon early. No, Above-Old-Man, *please*. How can I run with a newborn baby? Lambkill will find us both!"

She braced her hands against the yellow-brown limestone and bit back her cries. She stood in a narrow cleft, rock-filled, clotted with duff and weathered sticks that had been deposited by the rain runoff. The cleft sliced a V into the bluff that overlooked the Big Spoonwood River. Two hundred hands below, muddy water rushed along, whole trees tumbling in the swift current. Across the vast expanse of water, she could make out the caves that pocked the bluff on the opposite side. Did this side have similar caves? Should she chance finding shelter in one of them?

Kestrel wrung some of the water from her long hair, and as she looked down, she saw a white chert flake reflecting beneath the shallow flow of water. She bent to pick it up. As big as the palm of her hand and very sharp, it might come in useful—perhaps to cut reeds with to build a raft—but the rain was falling more heavily, too heavily to think of trying to cross the river today.

Though dozens of crevices cracked the bluff, only this narrow cut had appeared to lead down to the water, and it was becoming steeper as she progressed. On either side of her, weathered walls rose like dark, uplifted wings, reaching so high that they brushed the ominous clouds packing the morning sky.

A series of jagged knobs jutted from the rim of the cleft, reminding her of the ragged wing tips of Crow. Her chest ached with longing. If only she could climb onto Crow's back and sail high above the world. Here, in this crack in the ground leading to the river, she could feel the footfalls of her husband in her heart. Fear took every bit of her strength.

The pain built again. A moan escaped her lips and she gasped, "Stay quiet! Keep moving. You must . . . keep moving."

When the agony eased, Kestrel inched her hands forward over the wet stone, descending the cleft slowly. The shower soaked her to the bone. Ankle-deep trickles of water drenched her moccasins and froze her swollen feet. She'd haphazardly tied the torn front of her dress together, but it provided scant protection from the bitter gusts of wind. Like icicles, they penetrated the soaked antelope hide and stabbed at her breasts and belly.

"And it's going to get much colder," she said, bolstering her courage as she studied the wide, silt-laden river that rushed and foamed where the cleft joined the sandy shore below. Runoff from the heavy rains had caused the water to overflow its banks. Along the shore, a thick layer of dirty froth had accumulated. Reeds, which usually stood at the edge of the water, were visible twenty hands into the current; they poked ragged tips through the surface as if desperate for the sun's warm touch.

"Go on. Hurry, Kestrel. Move . . . move!"

She had to force her exhausted legs to carry her the rest of the way down the narrow defile. Lightning flashed through the clouds, followed by bellows of thunder. Beyond the bluff on the opposite shore, the broken land began its rise toward the Mammoth Mountains, whose deep-blue peaks raked the bellies of the distant clouds. Kestrel gazed at the white mist of snow that shrouded the foothills and wanted to weep. She would be safe there. But she couldn't go. Not yet. Not until the baby came.

She had to find shelter.

That truth terrified her. How long would the baby take to arrive? In the menstrual hut, she'd listened intently when the old women had recounted stories of births that lasted for days and nearly drove the pregnant women mad from pain. She remembered one tale about a woman who gave birth to triplets. The children had been born dead but the woman's screams had gone on for four days.

Days!

And every moment that Kestrel delayed, Lambkill would be closing in. She'd tried to stay on the rocks, where her moccasins would leave no prints, but she'd had almost no sleep in three days and a foggy euphoria had begun to possess her. Sometimes she forgot where she was, why she was running. She kept making mistakes—leaving a heel print here, a snapped twig there. Once, when she'd been hiking uphill, she'd had to grab onto a sagebrush to keep from toppling into the mud. She'd stripped the leaves from the branches . . .

Her trail would be clear to him.

Another contraction bent her double, and she couldn't suppress the sharp cry that tore from her throat. "No! *Oh, no, not now!*"

She squatted on the bank and propped her hands on the ground between her spread knees, letting the pain have its way. When it ended, she couldn't stop trembling.

Kestrel rose and plodded northward along the Big Spoonwood River. She'd been here as a child, and she remembered that the people had built rafts and gathered near a fist-shaped boulder that marked the narrowest stretch of the river. Where was the boulder? She squinted, but she couldn't see it. Around the southern bend in the shoreline? Even at the age of six summers, the raft trip had seemed to take forever.

The river isn't as wide as it looks. Remember? It took no more than two hands of time to cross. But that was in late summer. The water was warm. *No, Kestrel, don't think about that! You . . . you must put the river between yourself and Lambkill.*

Scents of fish and rain-soaked earth filled the air as Kestrel waded into the frigid water. Her teeth started to chatter immediately. She took two steps and staggered when she saw her shattered reflection staring back at her. Her body felt suddenly too tired, too wounded, to continue. Massive bruises covered her face, rising to frame the knife gash that slanted across her forehead. Her left eye had swollen almost shut.

"Someday I'll find him vulnerable," she whispered. "I swear it."

She clamped her jaw and slogged downstream, doubling back to the south, passing the opening to the stone cleft that she had descended earlier. The swirling current would wash away most of her tracks. Perhaps the rain would cover the rest of them. The Thunderbeings had slit open the bellies of the clouds with their wings, and rain now poured down on Sister Earth. If she could get to the rocky terrace that jutted into the river in the distance, she would leave no tracks. She might be able to confuse Lambkill for a short time and stall his progress. As she rounded the curve in the shore, the fist-shaped boulder loomed into view.

Kestrel started to run, splashing through the water, panting. Where the river curved back to the west ahead, the shore vanished. The water had risen so much that it crashed into the bluff and threw foamy lances twenty hands high. Dozens of the tiny round caves that speckled the limestone had been sloshed full of water. Like huge tear-filled eyes, they seemed to watch her as she ran toward the fist-shaped boulder.

When the first squeezing of the next contraction began, Kestrel veered out of the river and headed straight toward one of the caves that gouged the bluff above the waterline. She followed a slender ledge, a deer trail, that ran in front of the caves and eventually led to the crest of the bluff. Along the way, she pulled two handfuls of fresh grass and picked up a small dry stick of chokecherry. The ledge dropped away to a bastion of rocks where water roared as it attacked the stones. Perhaps its fury would cover the sound of her cries. When she reached the entry, she fell to her knees and crawled inside.

Darkness blinded her. With it came the overpowering odor of pack rat dung and the faint sweetness of moss. As her eyes adjusted, she could make out the green-velvet tufts that veined the cracks in the rock. Kestrel blinked. Strange paintings covered the walls, faded, old. Six square-bodied red figures curved upward from the floor, following the arc of the cave so that their eyes peered down at Kestrel from the center of the ceiling. Zigzagging lines of Power issued from their open mouths, shooting toward the floor. Though they bore human bodies, their faces resembled bears, or maybe lions, with their teeth bared. They seemed to be crowding around her, watching, waiting.

"Blessed Star People, what is this place?"

Frightened, Kestrel traced a magical sign in the air to protect her from any Evil Spirits who might be lurking close by. She kept her eyes on the figures as she stooped to arrange the things she had gathered so they'd be close at hand. Softly, she began the Birthsong: *"We crouch before you, Above-Old-Man, tossing in pain, tossing . . ."*

A faint growl rose. It seemed to be coming from the Lion-men. Their red eyes glistened, as though alive and angry that she had invaded their sanctuary.

It's the river, or the thunder. The roar of distant thunder echoing through the cave. That's all it is! But sobs choked her. Had she been in her own village, her mother would have Sung the Birthsong while her grandmother painted wavy lines of black and red from her navel to her breasts. Kestrel kept Singing the Song to bolster her courage: *"We crouch before you, Above-Old-Man. Tossing in pain, tossing. Our blood flows, as yours once did. Bringing Life to the world. Tossing in pain, tossing. Above-Old-Man. Hear us. Lead this child through the dark tunnel. Lead it into the Light born from your blood. We crouch before you, tossing in pain. . . ."*

Kestrel wept. The Birthsong ceremony reenacted the primeval journey of the First People through the World Navel, where they had emerged from the underworld and traveled to the two sacred mountains that marked the boundaries of the Bear-Looks-Back Clan's territory. The world had been perfect then, pristine and beautiful. Had any of those first women felt the fear Kestrel did now? With every moment that the birthing went on, she could sense her husband, coming closer, closer . . .

Lightning flashed blindingly, and Kestrel heard it strike the bluff above her. Chunks of sandstone were blasted from the cliff and flew outward, tumbling as they hurtled toward the river. Dozens of white splashes pocked the roiling gray water.

As the pain intensified, Kestrel wished desperately for her mother. "You're alone. You have to . . . to do this by yourself."

She slipped her torn dress off over her head and threw it down by the sharp chert flake and handfuls of grass. Then she squatted in the opening of the cave and clenched the chokecherry stick between her teeth. The opening spanned barely half of her body length, making it easy for her to brace her back against the dry stone on one side and her hands against the other side. Her legs shook so violently that she feared they might not hold her through the coming ordeal.

It took only moments before sweat ran hotly from Kestrel's naked body. She pushed with all of the strength left to her, moaning at first, then weeping and praying, and when the pain grew unbearable, she screamed. And then, at last, the baby emerged, headfirst.

"It's a girl, Iceplant! I've given you a daughter." She broke into miserable sobs.

With shaking hands, Kestrel lifted the chert flake and sliced one of the fringes from her dress, then knotted it around the girl's umbilical cord and cut it. Kestrel's arms trembled as she lifted her daughter by her feet and shook her until the baby gave her first cry. Then Kestrel's groping fingers located the handfuls of fragrant grass with which to wipe the little girl clean of the smeared blood, tissue and fluid.

The infant's wailing terrified Kestrel. Lambkill had ears like a lynx. Assuming she could cross the river, it would take another ten or twelve days of steady walking to reach Otter Clan Village. Hiding her trail would be hard enough. How could she hope to lose Lambkill while carrying a crying baby? Tenderly, she placed her daughter amidst the soft folds of her antelopehide dress.

Pain twisted inside her again. Sucking in a deep breath, she braced her hands against the wall and pushed. Was it a second child? Or just the afterbirth? She dug her fingernails into the limestone and wept as the agony swelled. "Help . . . help me . . . Above-Old-Man! Help!" She cried out sharply and pushed. And pushed again. Panting for breath, she shifted to spread her legs a little wider. One of her legs buckled, and her knee crashed to the stone floor. Kestrel sobbed brokenly as she struggled to resume the birthing crouch. She braced her hands on the opposite wall again and held her breath and pushed and prayed . . . until the second child emerged. A boy. Tiny. Beautiful.

She knotted a fringe as she had done before and cut his cord, then weakly gripped his arm and jerked on it. He cried. She did not clean him. A short while later, the afterbirth flooded out onto the floor. For another two fingers of time, Kestrel had to sit slumped in the blood, breathing deeply, before she could marshal enough energy to rise. Leaves of fall grass might have had more strength than her quaking legs. She locked her knees, aware of the watery droplets of her blood that fell to splat on the stone in starburst patterns.

All the while, her daughter shrieked urgently and waved tiny fists. The boy mewed softly where he lay on his back in the pool of blood.

Kestrel picked up the boy and cradled his head to her breast. "Shh. Shh, baby," she whispered as he nursed. The feel of that soft mouth against her flesh stabbed her to the soul. She whimpered and patted his back gently. When the infant had finished and lay quietly sleeping in her arms, Kestrel rose, hips aching, and carried him to the entry of the cave.

The wind had picked up. It whipped her drenched hair into a black web that obscured her face. Naked and cold, she stood watching the whitecaps that undulated across the Big Spoonwood River. She tried to close her ears to the wails of her daughter, alone in the cave.

Do it, Kestrel. You must.

The storm had let up slightly. Wavering gray veils of rain swept the vista, but here on the river, only a bare mist fell.

Kestrel could make out the hazy shapes of the mountains that lay a six or seven days' walk from the opposite side of the river—their images only a dim blue band at the base of a rolling sea of gray clouds.

The boy squirmed and shivered. He began to cry again. Kestrel's heart ached. She turned to peer back at the cleft in the bluff from where she'd descended to the river. The trough shone wetly. Nearby, a gull wheeled and dove into the water, then flapped upward with a mussel in its mouth. Spinning around, it hovered over the slick rocks along the shore and dropped the mussel, cracking it open so as to eat it.

No man stood anywhere in view.

But Lambkill was coming, she knew.

Somehow, some way, he would find her—despite the wind and the rain that obscured her trail, and no matter how far or how long she ran. He would find her.

Two crying babies would make it certain.

"The Otter Clan . . . they . . . trace their lineage through the women," she said as she cradled her son in her arms and stepped out onto the ledge in front of the cave.

Her arms trembled so violently that she almost couldn't keep hold of the baby as she walked down the deer trail. Muddy brown water rumbled by below, speckled with juniper needles, twigs and bits of spinning grass.

Kestrel knelt on the sandy shore at the base of the bluff and laid her son down in front of her. Rain beaded on his bloody face. His blue eyes seemed to be searching for her, moving back and forth frantically. He cried and kicked his legs.

"Oh, Spirits, please . . . I . . . I can't do this!"

Sobs shook Kestrel. Desperately, she lifted the baby into her arms again and held him tightly, rocking him back and forth to comfort his fears. "Shh, it's all right. It's all right, my son. Try to understand. I love you . . ." Tears constricted her throat. For several moments, she couldn't speak. *Iceplant, you understand, don't you?* Finally she whispered, "My son, your death may keep your sister alive. And me. Forgive me . . ." She sobbed the words in bitter gasps. "I love you so much."

Kestrel tipped her face up to the cloudy sky and Sang, *"Hear me, Star People. I pray for you to come, to meet this little boy when he gets to the Land of the Dead. Hear me, Star People, I pray for you to come. Please . . . take good care of him."*

She laid the boy on the sand again, then turned and walked weakly up the trail toward the cave. Her son's cries grew shrill, panicked. Kestrel broke into a run that made her exhausted, wounded body scream in pain. "Oh, Spirits, help me! Make him stop crying. I—I won't be able to stand it!"

Gulls squealed.

Kestrel glanced up at them through tear-filled eyes. They swooped over her head angrily.

She ducked back into the cave and sank down atop her antelopehide dress next to her daughter. She could still hear the faint wails of her son. Beside her, the little girl lay as still as a corpse. For a moment, Kestrel didn't breathe. Then her daughter blinked and looked up at the Lion-men who hovered over them. Time seemed to whirl and spin in the wells of those blurry newborn eyes. The growl began again, like animals calling warnings in the night. Deep, barely audible, the sound sent a chill up Kestrel's spine.

"Blessed . . . Mammoth Above . . ."

Her daughter's eyes sought hers, and the girl frowned, as though in answer. The longer Kestrel gazed into those eyes, the brighter they grew, until they were so brilliant and beautiful that it hurt to look at them. Her soul seemed to twist and detach from her body to go flying, up, up—as if it had climbed onto the wings of soaring Thunderbeings.

The baby coughed, and the sound snapped Kestrel from her euphoria.

Trembling, she brought up the edges of her hide dress and tucked them around her daughter's body, then moved the baby to her breast to nurse. "Twisting Cloud Girl . . . that will be your name, my daughter. For your eyes."

"Mother? . . . Mother?"

The Unnamed Boy called forlornly into the black, glittering womb that encased him.

But no one answered.

. . . No one.

Not a breath stirred the dark haze, and loneliness ate at his soul like a starving beast.

"Mother? I want to live! Let me live. I can help you!"

The ebony weave of the womb unraveled into strands that swirled and changed their shades, reweaving into stunning patterns, like the face of Brother Rainbow twisted into multiple, interlacing spirals that spun outward into infinity . . .

Beautiful.

The Boy sucked his thumb as the colorful threads began to sway gently, rocking him back and forth like an invisible hand pushing the side of a cradle board suspended between two trees. He fell into terrible tears.

"Mother? Why can't you hear me? I've been calling and calling to you! I'm not dead, Mother. I'm here. Up here. Alive in the Stars. Let me come down. Let me be with you. Please, Mother. I need to be with you. I won't be any trouble. I promise. I just want to be close to you.

"Mother!" he shouted. "Let me be close to you!"

The rainbow fires turned into a Song . . . faint at first, hard for him to hear, and then the crystalline notes rose like the wails of a thousand mammoths trumpeting in unison. They formed such a magnificent lullaby that it soothed his fears like cool salve on a hot wound.

He sucked his thumb more contentedly—though the music was not like his mother's soft brown nipple. Not at all. The Rainbow fires could never take that memory from him. Not ever . . .

He dreamed about it as he fell asleep, and he whispered

mournfully, "Why can't you hear me, Mother? . . . I need you. I need you to hear me. I want to live."

Four

Oxbalm grunted as he stretched to reach the meat that clung to the interior of the mammoth's rib cage. The entire village had dedicated the morning to skinning the carcass and then to slitting the belly open and hauling out the heavy mass of intestines. The liver had been cut up into slabs and immediately carried away by the children, who giggled and laughed as the red-black blood coated their skin.

The lungs, logged with saltwater, had been hacked away and thrown into the surf for the sea gulls to scream and fight over, and the villagers had moved on to other carcasses. Later, after dark, the crabs would swarm over the lungs as the tide came in. Oxbalm sucked at his lips as he stared at the thick yellow artery that hung limply from the backbone. Someone had already been tired when he'd cut the giant heart out, for the artery had been hacked raggedly.

This old cow had almost no fat around her ribs—she was little more than skin and bones—but Oxbalm's mouth watered just the same. Tough mammoth tasted better than no mammoth at all. The thick quartzite flake had gone slippery from blood, and the joint fever that plagued his hands made holding the flat tool painful. The villagers' bloody feet had tracked in sand, but the footing in the coagulated goo on the ribs below remained precarious.

Pulling on a flap of meat with one hand, Oxbalm used his serrated quartzite to strip the flesh from the heavy bone, trimming ligaments and tendons as he went.

This was the easy work, suitable to an old man, and—he shot a glance from the corner of his eye—to lazy Dreamers who thought themselves superior to the hard work of cutting heavy muscles and using choppers to sever the tendons and ligaments in order to disarticulate the thick legs.

Oxbalm swallowed his disgust and continued to cut the strip of meat loose, sawing along the rib on one side and then the other, exposing a shaft of daylight as he peeled the meat down.

Catchstraw worked silently beside him, his obsidian knife glinting in the light that filtered through the layer of clouds. Tall and skinny, he resembled a big-headed bird. The salty air had turned his gray-streaked black hair into a damp mass. His hooked nose protruded from the middle of his face like a beak. Forty-nine summers old, he looked much older : . . as though the labor of ruining two marriages and alienating half of his relatives had worn on him.

Oxbalm couldn't see very much of Catchstraw's face, but what he could see didn't look to be especially happy. The Dreamer had been mumbling unpleasantly to himself all afternoon. Oxbalm had tried talking to him for the first few hands of time but had given up when Catchstraw started using that authoritative tone of voice that made his words sound as though they came from Above-Old-Man himself.

Since then, Oxbalm had turned his attention to more pleasing things. Children's voices rose and fell against the rhythmic murmur of the surf. The gulls continued to shriek and brawl over the feast. His people laughed contentedly, and the wind had turned warm. Such serenity came along rarely; he wanted to enjoy the day.

Sumac and their little granddaughter, Mountain Lake, sat cross-legged in the bottom of the mammoth, covered with blood. They laughed joyously while they sliced the tenderloin into strips. Mountain Lake had gobbled down so much raw meat that her pretty little face bore a crust that looked like thick red paint. This was the first such feast in her six summers.

Up and down the beach, people Sang as they butchered and skinned. Dogs lay happily in the sun, their bellies bloated. Above them all, insects hovered in clouds of glittering membranous wings.

A ring of guards stood along the perimeter of the butchering ground, their sharp eyes alert for the big cats. Sunlight glinted on polished dart shafts where they rested ready in the hooked atlatls. Beyond the guards, hidden in the screen of forest, saber-toothed cats watched from the shadows, wary of the humans and their deadly darts. When the deep-throated growls carried against the wind, the guards would brandish their darts and the cats would hiss and paw the air threateningly.

"Growl," Oxbalm murmured softly. "One day your voices will be stilled." Even these cats, now so wary, would be dead within the week. Drawn to the carcasses, they would remain to prowl for other prey. Despite precautions, good dogs would begin to disappear, and a child, lost in play, would step too close to the trees, or an old man like Oxbalm wouldn't run fast enough in the twilight.

"What do you mean, 'stilled'?" Catchstraw asked, his eyes narrowing.

"The cats have Power. All silent killers do. But not even that will save them." Oxbalm nodded, remembering a dream he'd once had as a boy. In it, a cat had walked into the camp, crossed the plaza and stood over his bed. Petrified, Oxbalm had stared into those golden eyes, wondering what the silent stalker wished to tell him. If only his ears had been open instead of closed. Or had the great cat judged him—and found him wanting? "Our young men have atlatls and finely crafted darts. I have heard of Blowing Seed, a hunter in the Seal Fat Clan north of here. In his lodge, the walls are covered with skulls of the saber-toothed cat. Over ten tens of them. Filling an entire wall."

"I've heard of him. He claims to have great Power because he has killed so many of the big cats. The fool."

Oxbalm glanced sideways at Catchstraw and cut the strip of meat totally loose from the ribs, grunting as he caught the weight. He staggered to the gaping opening behind the floating ribs and handed the strip to three young boys who fought for the honor of carrying it. "Be careful! Don't drop that in the sand—or everyone will yell at you for getting grit in their teeth." He grinned, exposing his toothless gums. "Everyone but me!"

Oxbalm went back into the mammoth, using a blood-encrusted thumb to rub some of the gore from his big quartzite flake. "Those cats out there in the trees, they're hungry. Their stomachs will overcome their caution, and young Two Toes, or one of the others, will drive a dart through them. Men are smarter hunters than cats."

Catchstraw halfheartedly pressed his thumb against his obsidian blade. "Time to resharpen this," he muttered unpleasantly and then raised smoky eyes to Oxbalm. "Do not underestimate Power, Oxbalm. It is greater than any hunter, no matter how skilled he is in the ways of animals. Someday Power may come hunting you, and no dart of yours will kill it."

Oxbalm's bushy gray brows lifted. "You don't know what you're talking about."

"I know a great deal, old man."

Oxbalm held his tongue and went back to his work, forcing himself to think about the big cats. Yes, now they kept to the shadows, unwilling to show themselves. But Oxbalm knew that when darkness fell, they would fight all night over the butchered carcasses.

Was that the image Catchstraw wanted to conjure with his talk of Power? That of a cat hiding in the shadows by day, prowling ferociously at night? He'd better be careful not to say that aloud to many people. Somebody might suspect him of being a witch and sneak up and bash his brains out. The idea tickled a chuckle from Oxbalm's breast. Catchstraw, a witch! Ha!

Catchstraw gave him a sideways glance. "What's funny?"

"The very idea of it. You don't act like a Dreamer, Catchstraw. Power, Dreaming—they leave tracks on a man the way a deer leaves tracks on a damp forest trail. And I can't see you with saber-toothed Power, or lion Power. No, yours would be badger Power, very loud and vicious-sounding, but if your victim didn't bolt at the noise, you'd stop halfway and run back for your hole." Oxbalm laughed again. "Yes, badger! That's what your Power would be!"

Catchstraw grumbled something.

"What did you say?" Oxbalm asked.

"I said that nobody should be laughing out here!" Catchstraw threw his weight into the slicing off of a strip of rib meat and irreverently tossed it down near Sumac. "This is a very solemn occasion."

"Yes." Oxbalm nodded agreeably. "We are all worried about the meaning of the drownings, but this is also a wonderful time. We'll have new lodges from the hides and more meat than we can eat. Listen to the people. They sound so happy."

"Yes, they do. You ought to be out there telling them to be quiet. They've probably already offended the Spirits of the mammoths. But then, you don't mind offending anything, do you? Not even Power."

Oxbalm sliced through the last bit of ligament holding this strip of meat to the rib and eased the heavy slab down to the floor. He patted the meat gently and silently thanked the cow for feeding his family.

He had never liked Catchstraw, and now even less than before. Mostly, he disliked the cool distance of the Dreamer's manner, but the surly tone didn't help matters. When Oxbalm straightened up, he said, "We did not hunt these mammoths, Catchstraw. They gave themselves to us. I don't know why, but we certainly can't spurn their gift by leaving them to rot on the shore. And accepting their gift makes people happy."

Catchstraw grunted. Then he said, "Don't blame me for what's going to happen. I've been spending every spare moment in the sweat lodge, purifying myself and praying."

"Good. I'm glad. Some of us need more of that than others—"

"What does *that* mean?" Catchstraw's eyes narrowed to slits.

"I wish Sunchaser were here, that's what. He could tell us what this means." The wish was futile, Oxbalm knew. If Horseweed and Balsam had needed to go all the way to Brushnut Village to find Sunchaser, they wouldn't be home for another week at the earliest. Oxbalm had just been hoping they had met Sunchaser on the trail somewhere close by. Clearly, that had not happened.

"Meaning *I* can't?" Catchstraw asked indignantly. "Haven't I been doing a good job leading the Mammoth Spirit Dance?"

"Yes. You have."

"But not good enough? Is that it? That's why you decided to postpone the latest Mammoth Spirit Dance for a week, isn't it? Hoping that Sunchaser would arrive to lead it."

"It's not meant to shame you, Catchstraw. Sunchaser is the founder of the Dance. *He* is the one that Wolfdreamer revealed the Dance to. And now," Oxbalm said diplomatically, "I'd better go check on the fat rendering. I promised Fernleaf I'd be by long ago."

He turned, smoothed his hand over Sumac's gray head and stepped out of the mammoth carcass onto the sand. Sumac gave him a knowing look and sighed softly. She had managed to slice up one of the melon-shaped kidneys.

Little Mountain Lake crawled to her feet and yelled, "Grandfather, can I come? Sometimes Fernleaf gives me a piece of fried fat."

"Sure. Come on. Maybe she'll give us both a piece."

"Will you tell me a story while we eat them?"

"Of course." He smiled.

Mountain Lake awkwardly climbed over the upward curve of the rib cage, jumped down and ran to hug Oxbalm around the leg. Such a pretty child. Her blooded face glowed with childish delight.

"Oxbalm?" Catchstraw called. "Are you really leaving? Before we've finished our discussion?"

"It is finished, Catchstraw."

Oxbalm held Mountain Lake's sticky hand as they started down the beach for the bonfire where Fernleaf and several other women knelt, chopping sun-dried meat and melting fat in soapstone bowls. Waves crashed nearby and water flooded toward them; kelp and small creatures washed onto the shore. A hermit crab scrambled to dig a hole before anything bigger than himself saw him. As they walked, Mountain Lake collected whole horn shells and purple fragments of mussel shells. She kept all of them in her left hand, where their edges poked out between her small fingers.

"Look, Grandfather!" Mountain Lake pointed up at the gulls that circled above the villagers. The birds screamed at them, angry that they couldn't get to the juicy piles of meat, begging for a tidbit anyway. Mountain Lake shrieked and flapped her arms, frightening the birds into higher flight, then laughed. "I told them they'd have to wait until we'd finished our share." Her face radiated happiness. Oxbalm could barely make out her features through the dried blood. He ran his thumb over her cheek and chuckled.

"You look like you were killed by a short-faced bear and dragged around by the cats," he told her.

"Yes," she agreed. "Grandmother and me got a lot of work done. Did you see that big pile of kidney slices we cut up?"

"It was huge. We'll throw them all into the fat and fry them crisp for supper tonight."

Mountain Lake smiled. "I love mammoth."

"This is the first time you've had it, how would you know?"

"We've eaten it for supper three nights in a row. That's enough to know."

She watched her moccasins as she walked, kicking up sand, giggling when the grains showered Oxbalm. He tried to sound stern. "Quit that."

"You like it, Grandfather. You know you do."

She gave him the winning smile that always melted his soul and he sighed, "You're right. Go ahead."

Mountain Lake kicked up a haze of sand and giggled when Oxbalm squeezed his eyes half-closed to fend off the onslaught. Dragging her by the hand, he hiked up to the rocky terrace where the bonfire burned. The delicious aroma of fat hung heavy in the air. On the north side of the fire, two girls used black chert flakes to cut up dried meat and handed full baskets of it to three women who mixed the meat with last autumn's dried berries. The women, in turn, gave the baskets to another woman, who stuffed the mixture into a length of mammoth intestine, tied at one end with yucca twine. Finally, Big Striped Bee held the tube open for her mother, Fernleaf, who poured cupfuls of hot fat over the meat and berries. Big Striped Bee then tied off the open end of the intestine and draped the tube over one of the meat poles. Hundreds of such tubes had already been stuffed.

"The pemmican ropes look like bent logs," Mountain Lake observed as they neared the bonfire. She hesitated for a moment, then twisted her head and frowned over her shoulder. "Uh-oh, Grandfather. Here comes Catchstraw, and he looks mad."

"He always looks mad," Oxbalm said as he turned. Catchstraw strode across the sand purposefully, his gaze riveted on Oxbalm. "Mountain Lake, why don't you go ask Fernleaf for a piece of fried fat? I'll be there shortly."

She craned her neck to look up, then squinted one eye against the sun. "Grandfather, why isn't Catchstraw happy that the mammoths gave themselves to us to eat? Doesn't he like mammoths?"

"I'm not sure that he likes much of anything," Oxbalm answered. "Now go. Run along."

"Yes, Grandfather." Reluctantly, she released his hand and raced away. Female laughter rose as Mountain Lake stopped to greet the women in the pemmican line.

Catchstraw looked determined. Oxbalm had the distinct urge to run in the opposite direction—as if his ancient legs would allow him that luxury. But he folded his arms and stood his ground. The afternoon was wearing on, and mist curled from the deep-blue surface of Mother Ocean. *Coyote is smoking his pipe in the Land of the Dead.*

When Catchstraw was twenty hands away, Oxbalm called, "What is it, Dreamer?"

"We have to finish our discussion, Oxbalm."

"I didn't think there was anything left to say."

Catchstraw propped bloody hands on his hips and expelled a breath. "I'm growing tired of you, elder. *I* have been leading the Mammoth Spirit Dance, Oxbalm. Not Sunchaser. Doesn't that tell you something?"

"What?"

"That I am the new spiritual leader here! I should have some right to talk to you about the matters of the clan."

"Catchstraw," Oxbalm said, "you know as well as I that you'll never be the spiritual leader here until more of your Dreams start coming true. But you do have rights as a member of this clan. Talk. I'm listening."

"No one's Dreams are *always* accurate, Oxbalm. Not even the great Sunchaser's!"

He'd said Sunchaser's name in a mocking, belittling fashion that grated on Oxbalm like sandstone on a raw wound. "When has Sunchaser ever been wrong?"

Catchstraw ignored the question. "Sometimes Evil Spirits tell Dreamers things that aren't true. That's not my fault. It wouldn't happen to me so often if I weren't always Dreaming, trying to see the Way for our people."

"Name one time that Sunchaser's Dreams have been wrong."

Catchstraw wet his lips and brushed damp, gray-streaked hair away from his narrow face. "Oxbalm, I know that you like Sunchaser. I didn't come to fight with you about him. I had a Dream, and I wanted to tell you about it. I know too that you sent for Sunchaser to ask him what the drownings mean, but I *already* know! I was sleeping under that fir tree over there—"

"*What* Dream?"

Dramatically, Catchstraw spread his arms. "It came upon me in a roar like the wings of the greatest Thunderbeings!"

"The *Dream,* Catchstraw. What did you see?"

"Listen for once and you'll find out!" he cried indignantly. "Mammoth Above came to me. She said that her children killed themselves out of anger. Anger at Sunchaser . . . because he refuses to talk to them anymore." Catchstraw lifted his chin smugly. "She said the mammoths need a new Dreamer to talk to."

"I see. And you think you're the one?"

"Who else is there?"

Oxbalm's lips pressed into a thin white line. For cycles, Catchstraw had been struggling to compete with Sunchaser for the spiritual leadership of the sea clans. Oxbalm had never taken him seriously. He suspected that if it ever did come to a contest, it would end like the cat fights—with Catchstraw sprawled across the sands in the morning. But Catchstraw did have a point. Sunchaser's constant absences had diminished his status in the eyes of the people. If Sunchaser didn't take some action soon to repair the damage, Catchstraw might win without any battle at all. There were no other Dreamers for the people to choose from. Good Plume kept to herself, Dreaming only for her family in Brushnut Village. That left Catchstraw and Sunchaser to vie for people's souls.

"What is it you want from me, Catchstraw?"

The Dreamer crossed his arms, his back stiff. "I want you to call a council session so I can tell everyone about my Dream. That's the only way they'll believe me."

Oxbalm shifted his weight to his other foot. *How true.* Without a council session, Catchstraw could recount his Dream all he wanted to, but he'd been wrong so often in the past that few people would pay attention.

"If I am the one to call the council for you, it will appear that I believe your Dream," Oxbalm said. "That's what you want, isn't it?"

"I just need a short session, Oxbalm," Catchstraw said,

sidestepping the question. "I won't take long. And in the end, my Power will win out."

Oxbalm ground his gums in irritation. The request put him in an odd position. Some people actually believed in Catchstraw's Power. Not many, but enough that if Oxbalm denied the request, it would make Catchstraw's followers suspicious and cause a rift in the clan. It might be safer to give Catchstraw the chance to make a fool of himself publicly. It would be even better if he could arrange it so that Sunchaser were present to defend himself at the session. *Yes, indeed.*

"It is my right . . . as a member of this clan," Catchstraw said.

Oxbalm nodded obligingly. "Yes, it is your clan right. Very well. But I can't give you a day yet. There are things I must tend to, people I must consult with, before I can tell you when. And it will certainly have to be after the Mammoth Spirit Dance."

Catchstraw stood as though stunned by the news. "But you *will* call the session?"

"As soon as I can," Oxbalm answered.

"Perhaps I have judged you wrongly, elder." But the voice didn't sound convinced. Catchstraw turned and plodded away across the rocky terrace.

Premonition slipping through him like an eel in a net, Oxbalm studied the man's narrow back as he walked away. Then he sighed and continued toward the knot of women and the crackling bonfire.

Mountain Lake saw him coming and shouted, "Grandfather! I got us two pieces each!" She held up four long strips of fried fat and charged toward him.

Catchstraw sat cross-legged on a thick pile of hides in his lodge. The structure stretched twenty hands long and fifteen hands wide. He'd constructed it by sinking ten whale-rib bones, five on each side, into holes he'd excavated with an oak digging stick. Then he'd lashed the ribs to a central ridgepole of fir with strips of raw wet leather that had shrunk as they dried. After that, he'd cajoled and bargained and bought twelve finely tanned short-faced bear hides to cover the frame with. These he had sewn together with tendons stripped from the bones of elk and deer.

The whole was large enough to house a wealthy man, his wives and family—had Catchstraw ever cared for such trivialities. He'd been married twice, each time as a result of his mother's efforts to arrange a good alignment with another coastal clan. In both instances, the women had left him after several days because he had pointedly ignored them. Each marriage had cost his clan dearly. Wedding gifts, so carefully negotiated, had had to be returned, along with additional wealth to assuage any injured feelings.

While many members of the clan, especially those whose fortunes had suffered, stared at him with resentful eyes, Catchstraw didn't mind. Such actions set him apart, distinct from the rest of his society. Dreamers were always different from ordinary people.

His lodge was arranged exactly to his liking. Brightly painted parfleches filled with exotic stones, carved ivory effigies and sacred plants sat atop the two logs that held down either side of the hide lodge cover. Eight baskets of nuts hung from the ridgepole at evenly spaced intervals. Both the whale-rib frame and the baskets had a single purpose: to prevent rot. The wet air on the coast encouraged decay. Seeds and nuts mildewed quickly in hide sacks, and sapling lodge frames lasted no more than a few cycles before they had to be replaced.

Catchstraw angrily jerked a piece of pine from the woodpile to his left and threw it on the fire in the middle of the floor. Flames leaped and danced. His rage with Oxbalm had yet to fade. "More of my Dreams will have to come true, eh, Oxbalm? Old fool. What do you know? It's not my fault that Dreaming is so hard."

For over a hand of time, Catchstraw had been staring at the irregular piece of deerhide spread across his lap. The supple hide had been tanned to a pale eggshell color, which made the black lines of Sunchaser's maze stand out; they meandered across the surface, weaving drunkenly in and around the center.

Catchstraw had drawn the maze himself, had copied it exactly from Sunchaser's own. In the flickering light, the lines seemed to move, eddying back and forth in the manner of a den of newborn snakes. Catchstraw struggled to concentrate on them, but his attention wandered like the flight of a bee through a field of wildflowers. Everything distracted him: the blue and red designs on the parfleches, the sound of the wind fluttering his door flap, the curls of smoke that drifted toward the smokehole in the roof. Over the long cycles, a thick patina of soot had coated the hide walls and the ribs of the frame, turning them as black and as shining as obsidian. The rich scent of creosote and burning pine surrounded him.

"This maze is meaningless, Sunchaser!" Roughly, he flipped the hide onto the hard-packed dirt floor and rubbed his eyes. "The only thing it's done for my Dreaming is to give me headaches."

For two cycles now, he had been trying to use the maze but had not been able to. Sunchaser claimed that the maze described the twists and turns of the road that led to the Land of the Dead. Catchstraw had never even been able to glimpse the road, let alone worry about its twists and turns.

Besides, his Dreaming had been deepening without the maze. In the past five moons, he'd made monumental strides. Odd that the Dreams began only after Sunchaser started missing Dances and staying away from the sea-coast. Perhaps Sunchaser had been doing something to hinder Catchstraw's progress? Anger seethed in his breast. Regardless, Catchstraw had learned to quiet his talkative soul, to relax his taut body.

But he still felt confused and angry most of the time. He

had never come close to understanding the things the Great Dreamers proclaimed to be true. Sunchaser, for example, said that Father Sun's Light penetrated all things, even the darkest lava tubes that wound through the belly of Sister Earth . . . and that anyone could learn to close his eyes and *see* it. Like the wind, Sunchaser said, the Light moved through every grain of sand on the beach, through every speck of dirt, every rock in the mountains, through humans, and through animals. He said that strands of that Light connected humans to all things so that every thought, every act, affected the whole.

"Pure gibberish. Sunchaser just says those things to drive people crazy." Catchstraw's bushy gray brows drew down over his hooked nose. He remembered one bright day when the Steals Light People had been playing, acting fickle. Spring Girl would breathe warmth, then the Thunderbeings would gather and make it rain while they rumbled their amusement. Showers had come one after another throughout the morning, and by noon, runoff water had inundated the village. He'd kicked one of the miserable dogs that had decided to dig a hole beneath the wall of his lodge and let the water flood in. He'd launched the beast twelve hands high and clapped in delight when the dog yelped and landed rolling and scrambling. Sunchaser had been standing a few hands away, talking with Oxbalm, and had turned and frowned.

"Ah, Catchstraw," he'd said in that curiously deep, soft voice of his, "by that act, you just weakened the stitching in the hides of your lodge. I pity you the next time it rains. If I were you, I'd rub those lodge seams with a thick coating of fat."

"What are you talking about? I didn't touch my lodge."

"No," Sunchaser said, "but the dog's cry did."

The news had spread like wildfire, and, the next time it rained, people gathered around Catchstraw's lodge and pointed and laughed as they watched it leak like a loosely woven net. The village children had run circles around his lodge, screaming and chanting offensive songs, while their despicable dogs barked in glee.

Sunchaser had been gone by that time. But it was small comfort that he hadn't been around to gloat.

Catchstraw had never lived down that day. People still joked about it, and anyone who openly scorned him and his Dreaming mentioned the event to justify their disbelief. He was still convinced that Sunchaser had done something, cut the stitching or slipped a blade into the hide, but he'd been unable to find the proof.

Catchstraw blinked when an idea suddenly occurred to him. For moons, he'd been trying to figure a way of getting back at Sunchaser. "So everything is connected to everything? Maybe you're right, *great* Sunchaser."

Catchstraw leaned forward and brushed dirt from the maze-inscribed hide, then flattened it out on the floor to scrutinize it. Shadows cast by the fire dappled the design. He pulled a stick from his woodpile and thrust the point into the flames to char. When it had a good coating of black, Catchstraw withdrew the stick and lowered the tip to the hide. He chanted the Mammoth Spirit Dance Song as he worked. With the patience of Lion stalking Tapir, he drew new lines, blocking old pathways, creating new twists. An elated chortle escaped his lips.

"Oh, this is amusing."

His actions took on an unreal quality, as if the simple movements of his hand threw him back and forth in time and carried him days, even cycles, from this place and then returned him in an instant.

"I've never felt so much like I'm Dreaming. *Really* Dreaming." His voice sounded far away and unfamiliar. Not his at all. It sent a frightened thrill through him.

He took lines and turned them into spirals, or drew them straight out away from the center of the maze, where they dangled in emptiness.

At times during the long night, he heard the coughs and garbled words of the people sleeping in the lodges nearest him, and the sounds jarred him from his task. He would halt long enough to massage his cramping hand before he bent forward to his work again.

Euphoria possessed him. His body seemed to float on a warm cloud. The lodge grew crystal-clear, the colors brightening until they dazzled, the designs on the baskets and parfleches jumping out at him. When he thought he heard voices in the crackling and hissing of the fire, fear flushed his veins, and he forced himself to stop. He fell back against his hides, panting.

"Blessed Mother Ocean," he whispered hoarsely, "what happened to me? I felt as if—for the first time—I *touched* the Dream world."

He peered nervously around his lodge. "Oh, Spirits, let it happen again. Please!"

The black womb jostled violently around him, and the Unnamed Boy went silent in fear.

Stars shot back and forth across the sky, leaving glowing silver trails in their wakes. He could hear their voices, soft and muted, discussing him and the blue-green world below.

The Boy shivered.

"It's all right," a Man said.

The Boy searched the blackness, trying to see who had spoken to him. But he saw only the flying stars. "No," he answered, "it's not all right. My mother is in very bad trouble. If I could just find a body to live in again, I could help her. . . . And Sunchaser. He needs me, too. Neither of them would have to hurt so much if they had me there to help them!"

The Man's voice swirled around him as though coming from all directions at once, like an echo in a deep canyon. "Suffering . . . yes, pain is always the problem . . . it waxes and wanes like the face of Above-Old-Man beneath the touch of Sister Earth. But the changes are not part of Above-Old-Man. They are only shadows that momentarily dim his brightness. Above-Old-Man's heart doesn't change at all. You must look deeper, Boy, much deeper, before you will be ready to be born again. This is the very reason you have been denied life so many times."

Stars gathered around the Boy, their light hurtfully brilliant, but their warmth built a cocoon around him. Soft voices whispered in his ears, so mixed-up that he couldn't make out anything they were trying to tell him.

The Boy bit his lip and thought about the heart of Above-Old-Man . . . the heart beneath the shadows . . .

"But Sunchaser. What of Sunchaser, Man? Will the shadows catch him?"

In a forlorn voice, the Man replied, "It's difficult to know, Boy. Sometimes humans beg for battles to be taken away from them, not realizing that only in struggling with shadows is the Light made manifest."

Five

Sunchaser walked through Brushnut Village with weary determination, heading for Standing Moon's lodge, nestled between the trunks of two giant firs. Fifteen lodges were spread amongst the trees, arranged around a central plaza where a huge communal bonfire burned. Exhaustion smoldered within his tall body like embers hidden in the ash of an abandoned hearth. His deep-set eyes had sunk so much in the past two weeks that they resembled black holes cut into the tan oval of his face. The buckskin of his long beaded shirt had grown stiff with dirt and sweat. Around him, sobs and fevered moans echoed through the village. The illness had been raging for half a moon, with no sign of letting up.

He hesitated before Standing Moon's door. The last snow

had vanished with the coming of the warm breeze off the ocean, and the wealth of water that had melted into the soil had transformed the surrounding country. Wildflower-scented wind whispered in the thick needles of the firs and ruffled the extravagantly painted hide walls of the lodge. It was like a Song, that breeze, lilting and beautiful as it played over the black, yellow, red and white designs. He granted himself a moment to drown in the beauty of the painted yellow hills covered by red starbursts, where men with atlatls hunted mammoths. He'd been managing scarcely two hands of sleep a night, and he feared his legs might buckle if he didn't sit down soon. *I just need to rest for a moment. Only for a moment.* He set his Healer's pack on the ground and braced a hand on the lodge's ridgepole.

Women moved silently through the bright sunlight. Hunters had come in yesterday, bringing meat, and, in the central plaza, three kneeling girls used flakes struck from a large obsidian core to strip meat from the haunches of a llama. Despite the sorrow in the village, every so often one of the girls would smile and lift a slice of meat, comparing it with her friends' to see whose was the thinnest and longest. Drying-racks stood here and there. Old women monitored them, shooing flies, magpies and small animals from the red meat while it browned in the sunlight.

Good Plume, who never seemed to feel sick, stood a short distance away from Sunchaser. She'd pegged out a fresh pronghorn hide and fleshed it with a hafted chert tool. The chert stone had been flaked along one surface to create a scraping edge. The reddish-brown stone had then been inset into the angle of a branch handle, making a tool that when used with a chopping motion would remove the last bits of tissue and meat by peeling them back from the hide. Tomorrow, when Good Plume finished scraping the hide, she would roll it up with ashes from the fire and soak the whole mixture. The ashes would loosen the hair so that it would slip away under her blade. When she'd shaved away the last of the slipped hair, she would use a rounded river cobble to rub a mixture of brains, white clay and urine into the skin. Again she would roll it tightly and allow it to soak. For several days she would repeat the process. Then, when the tissues had taken the curing, she would pull the hide over a graining post to turn it soft. Finally she would sew it into a fine shirt of the purest cloud-white color. He'd seen her do it a hundred times and had never lost his awe of her skill. No one made more beautiful clothing than Good Plume did.

Sunchaser smiled. Without her, he would have died long ago. His parents' lodge had caught fire in his seventh summer. They had been sleeping closest to the flames and had perished quickly, but Sunchaser's robes had lain along the back wall. He remembered waking up, coughing and choking on the smoke. He had tried to call for help, but couldn't. Frantic voices had yelled outside. Just when he'd thought he would die, too, Good Plume had rushed into the blazing lodge and dragged him out onto the dew-soaked summer grass. She had covered his nose and mouth with her mouth and forced air into his spasming lungs. Days later, she had told him, "My breath is in you now. We have shared souls. You will carry on my work—become a mole." She often spoke like that, in riddles he did not understand. Sometimes she drove him crazy with her curious words. *A mole? What do you mean, I'll become a mole, my aunt?*

But he'd come to understand. Over the cycles when he had lived with her, she had taught him the solitary ways of the Talth Lodge, the secret society of the Steals Light People. Good Plume had shown him how to see without eyes in the darkness. And many other things. She had taught him how to call animals by their secret names, the names they knew themselves by—and to hear them call him by the name they knew him by. Animals thought of humans in very different ways. The elk called Sunchaser "Wildflower Killer," because he collected so many Power plants in the early spring. The ravens called him "That-Howling-Scavenger," because he Sang over dying people. Sunchaser smiled to himself. Yes,

Good Plume had taught him many important secrets about the world.

She seemed to sense his gaze, for she straightened her humped old back and stared at him. No expression crossed her age-seamed face, but her eyes had a glint like that of Weasel with a cornered mouse. Grabbing her walking stick, Good Plume started toward him, each step an effort. Her thin neck stuck out of her doeskin dress, and her long hair, yellowish in the glow of sunlight, hung like old straw over the red and blue quilled chevrons on her collar.

Sunchaser met her halfway. "Good afternoon, my mother's sister," he said. He towered over her like a giant.

Good Plume had to tilt her head far back to look up at him, her sun-blackened face lifting to the light. She had no more room for wrinkles. Her head tottered on her frail old neck. Three white eyes with zigzags of lightning for pupils adorned Good Plume's chin, a sign of her leadership of the Talth. Like real lightning, the yellow slashes seemed to move as she worked her lips over her toothless gums. She remained silent for a time, studying his face. Finally she said, "Go and get some sleep before you fall over dead. You're not fully well yet."

"I'm well enough."

"You'll be of no use to anyone but the coyotes, ravens and maggots as a corpse," Good Plume noted.

"Standing Moon begged me to come and Heal her sister. I must go."

"How long has her sister been ill?"

"For three days."

Good Plume's withered face pulled taut. "Three. That's when most die. Her fever is bad?"

"Very bad. Standing Moon came to me a hand of time ago to say that Wooden Cup had stopped moving last night. She'd been thrashing around, shifting from burning hot to freezing cold, like the others. Until she went still."

"You must hurry, then. But first, tell me quickly about Cedar Branch's three little boys. All night long, you—"

"They died, Good Plume. I . . . I couldn't do anything for them."

Good Plume's old face pinched with grief. She put a gnarled hand in the middle of Sunchaser's chest and weakly shoved him toward Standing Moon's lodge. "Come back to me when you've finished. I'm not done talking to you yet. Something is happening to Power. Something is fooling with it, allowing the Evil Spirits who cause this illness to stalk the land and find homes in people's bodies and souls."

"I'll return as soon as I can."

Good Plume leaned on her walking stick and sighed deeply, as though she planned on waiting patiently right there.

He walked back and picked up his Healer's pack. Clutching it to his chest, he returned to Standing Moon's lodge, bent to the door flap and announced himself: "Standing Moon?"

"Sunchaser? Come. Please."

He lifted the flap and ducked inside. It took his eyes a moment to adjust to the dimness. The powerful odors of sweat, urine and sickness encircled him. He draped the flap up on its hook to open the lodge to the cool breeze. On the low benches that lined the walls, four sick people lay beneath heaps of furs. Moans laced the air. The fire in the middle of the floor had died to gray ashes, but a slight warmth still radiated from it.

"Thank you for coming, Sunchaser," Standing Moon said. She was kneeling on the far side of the lodge. Her hair had been cut short in mourning, accentuating the grief that strained her round face. She held her three-year-old son's hand while he cried. His fever-brilliant eyes darted about in the dimness.

"How is he?" Sunchaser asked.

"He fell ill last night. He won't eat. I went to find the spring tubers he likes so much. I walked very far from the village, Sunchaser, but I couldn't find any. And he won't eat anything else. He shoved away the deer soup I made for him."

Standing Moon kissed her son's forehead, then rose to her feet and wiped sweaty palms on her cathide dress. Long fringes hung from her sleeves; each fringe had a lion's claw knotted at the end. When she moved, the claws clicked together like dry bones rattling in the wind. Bravely, she said, "But it's my sister I'm most worried about."

The eyes of the sick followed Sunchaser as he walked behind Standing Moon to the south side of the lodge. She pulled the hides away from Wooden Cup's face and her mouth trembled. "She's been like this since midnight. I . . . I think her soul has separated from her body. Can you tie it back?"

"If it hasn't traveled too far."

Sunchaser unlaced his Healer's pack and crouched beside the bench. Wooden Cup didn't seem to notice, but stared blankly at the soot-coated ceiling. Sweat-drenched hair framed her slack face. Only twenty summers old, she looked much older. Her skin had gone sallow. Saliva dribbled from the corners of her mouth. Gently, Sunchaser used the edge of a hide to wipe it away. "Could you bring me a bowl of water and a red ember from the fire, Standing Moon? Then build up the fire. Make it hot."

"Yes." She hurried to fill an abalone-shell bowl from a bladder bag and knelt to dig through the ashes until she found an ember. She scooped it out and tucked it into a wrinkle on the top of the shell. Careful not to spill the water, she walked back and handed the bowl to him before placing kindling on the tiny eyes of embers and blowing a crackling flicker alight.

He set the bowl on the bench above Wooden Cup's head. The shell's shiny interior glistened like a rainbow in the murky light. Opening his pack, he removed a white pebble and a green soapstone pipe. The face of Otter peered up at him from the pipe, as if probing his soul. He had carved the image long ago, on his first vision quest.

Very softly, so as not to awaken those sleeping, he began to sing.

Please hear me, Above-Old-Man.
A sacred call I am making.
A sacred call I am making.
My people, behold them in kindness.
The day of Father Sun has been my strength.
The flight of the Thunderbeings shall be my
    road of death.
Please wake the Great White Giant from his
    slumber in the north.
A sacred call I am making.
A sacred call I am making.
Asking for your Breath
    to come into my warm body,
I add my own to yours . . .

Sunchaser continued to repeat the last phrase as he tamped tobacco into his pipe and used a dried leaf to shove the ember into the bowl. He puffed four times to get the smoke going, then lifted the pipe to the west, where the Thunderbeings lived. Their color was black, like the storm clouds they rode. They had the Power to destroy life.

Quietly, he prayed, "Leave this one alone, Thunderbeings. Wooden Cup is not ready to go with you yet. Her family needs her too much." Sunchaser sucked on his pipe and blew a cloud of smoke westward.

Closing his eyes, he turned to the north. For a long while, he faced the land of the snows, where Great White Giant lived. Healing Power came from him. The white pebble had been chipped from Giant's icy foot by a brash young Trader. Sunchaser had bought it at great cost. He'd given four precious moose hides for it and had promised to visit the Trader's village to teach the people the Mammoth Spirit Dance. He'd kept his promise and had made the journey last summer.

Reverently, he took the white pebble and dropped it into the water. Silver rings rippled outward across the abalone-shell bowl. Standing Moon bowed her head when he lifted his pipe again and silently begged White Giant's help in healing Wooden Cup. He blew four breaths of smoke to the north.

Next, he faced east. Dawn Child lived there, wrapped in the red cloak of sunrise. She had the Power to make people see and understand the ways of Above-Old-Man. All the days of men were born of by her. "I beg you to give Wooden Cup a few more days on earth, Dawn Child. She's been a good woman."

He turned to face south, where Summer Girl hid in a blaze of yellow light. Her warmth caused things to grow and flourish. "Summer Girl, cast your light on Wooden Cup's soul so that it can find its way back to her body and flourish again."

Sunchaser lifted his pipe to Brother Sky, then at last lowered it to Sister Earth. He took several more puffs while he waited for his prayers to reach their destination. Like calls shouted from far away, they took time. The sweet fragrance of tobacco encircled him, cleansing and purifying, almost blotting out the reek of sickness. One of the children lying on the bench near the door shouted angrily, as though in fevered dreams. Standing Moon went to kneel beside her and smooth the girl's brow. Her soft voice came to Sunchaser like a mourning dove's, cooing over the crackling snap of the leaping fire.

He took from his pack his sucking bone, a long, hollow tube crafted from the tibia of a condor. The ends had been polished and the smooth sides carefully engraved with the symbols of Power: the spiral, the sunburst, the zigzag of lightning, the shapes of clouds. Chanting, he pulled Wooden Cup's covers aside, lifting her dress so he could place the bone against her navel and suck with all his might to draw the malignancy from within her.

Wooden Cup moaned slightly, and Sunchaser turned to spit a mouthful of saliva into the fire, where it hissed and vanished in the leaping flames. He repeated the process at the hollow of her throat, leaving a red bruise where he had drawn out the sickness. This, too, he spat into the fire. It would be destroyed and carried away in the smoke.

Laying the sucking bone down, Sunchaser puffed on his pipe, gently blowing sacred smoke over the woman and chanting the ancient Healing Songs. Would they work this time? What more could he do?

Rising on tired legs, he rested his pipe near the abalone shell and plucked the white pebble from the water. He Sang as he sprinkled Wooden Cup's face and clothing with the drips that fell from the stone. The water had absorbed the Healing Power contained in the pebble and would transfer it to Wooden Cup's body.

He heard Standing Moon's quiet steps as she came to stand behind him. While he emptied his pipe and tucked the sacred stone back into his Healer's pack, he said, "You must give Wooden Cup a drink from the abalone shell every morning, at midday and at night. It will help her to get well."

"Yes. I will do that."

She pointed to a beautiful leather bag, its sides glittering with dentalium and olivella shells. "Take that, Sunchaser, for your efforts."

He gave her a weary smile. "It's very beautiful, Standing Moon. I appreciate the generosity of your family and clan for offering it to me. For the time being, I have enough things to meet my requirements. Give it to someone who needs it. Give it in my name. The pouch's beauty will Heal someone's grief."

He picked up his pack and started to leave, but Standing Moon gripped his sleeve tightly. "Sunchaser? Will you come back tomorrow? To Sing for my little son? He's so young. I—"

"I'll try, Standing Moon. But there are many others sick in the village. Sicker than your son. . . . You understand, don't you?"

She nodded, but grief glittered in her eyes. "Yes. I . . .

I understand." In a bare whisper, she added, "Thank you, Sunchaser."

She gazed up at him as though she thought he could call the Star People from the sky.

He patted her arm. "I want you to do something for me. Will you, Standing Moon?"

"What is it?"

"You've been washing, cooking and tending the sick for half a moon. You look like you're about to fall down every time you take a step. If I send Good Plume in to watch over your family, will you try to sleep for a few hands of time? This sickness searches for the weak and the tired. We need you to stay strong."

Her chin trembled and tears traced lines down her cheeks. "Yes. Thank you again, Sunchaser."

He stepped over a tumbled pile of hides that had slipped from the bench to the floor, then ducked outside. Sunlight struck his eyes painfully. He paused in the shadow of the lodge to take a deep breath of the fresh air. Good Plume stood where he'd left her, leaning on her walking stick. The vines that curled up the tree trunks and hung like ropes from the branches had begun to sprout leaves. Against that new green background, Good Plume looked brown and withered. She watched him through narrowed eyes.

He crossed the plaza with his pack clutched to his chest. "You wanted to speak to me, Aunt."

Good Plume nodded once, but said nothing.

He waited for a moment, then said, "I told Standing Moon that you would come to watch over her family while she slept. Is that all right?"

"Of course."

"Good." He shifted uncomfortably. "About this sickness, this lingering evil. It's in the very—"

Good Plume banged her walking stick on the ground four times and cocked her head in a birdlike fashion. "Do you know," she said, "that there is a tribe of invisible people? They've been in this world since before Wolfdreamer was born. They move around humans like shadows. Oh, they have bodies like ours, and they use the same tools we do, but they're not human. Where we're always laboring to see the world, they labor not to see it—but to feel it. They become visible only when they die."

"I've never heard that story before. And I don't understand it. What does it mean?"

Good Plume pointed a crooked finger at him. "Once, a long time ago, a human woman married one of the invisible men. He was a good husband. He loved her very much, went hunting every day, and they spent long hours laughing together at night. But this woman, she could not stand the thought that she didn't know what her husband looked like. So one day when he went to sleep, she felt for his chest, took her atlatl and drove a dart into his lungs. She got to see him all right. A handsome young man appeared. She realized too late what she had done and sobbed her heart out. In desperation, she called out to Mother Ocean for help. The Mother killed the woman. Then the Mother took her soul and tied it to the dead man's soul before she brought the woman to life again. So, you see, to this day, human souls are part male and part female. But the other half becomes visible only at death." Good Plume poked her knobby finger into Sunchaser's chest. "How many people have died in this village?"

"Six today. I . . . I don't know how many in the past two weeks."

"All women today, yes?"

"Yes."

Good Plume's wrinkled lips pursed. "I knew it. I've seen strange men wandering around all afternoon. They're lost without their female halves. Soon you must come with me and we'll Sing them to the Land of the Dead. Only you and I can do it. Nobody else has the Power."

Sunchaser nodded, a little lost himself. The older Good Plume became, the more difficult it was to fathom her strange stories. "What would happen, my aunt, if we didn't Sing for them?"

"Why, they'd become witches and go searching for living women to kill so they could be whole again. I have been Dreaming about witches a lot lately. Maybe that's all this illness is—male witches killing women, female witches killing men. Nobody's happy with only half a soul." Good Plume pinned him with a hawkish eye. "You should know that. Where's that square of deerhide you always carry around? The one with the maze on it. Haven't you Dreamed your way through the maze to find out what's causing this sickness?"

Sunchaser folded his arms and hugged himself. A Power like the crushing fingers of Above-Old-Man tightened around his heart. "I wanted to talk with you about that, Aunt. I . . . I'm having some trouble. With the maze. Day after tomorrow, I want to go to the Dream Cave near the coast."

"Trouble? Since when?"

"Just since yesterday. I tried to Dream last night, when I went out into the forest. But I . . . couldn't. I discovered a new . . . turn. A path I've never been on before. I keep getting lost."

"Ah." She shook a finger. "That's a good sign. At least you haven't lost the ability to recognize that you're lost. Because if you did, you *really* would be lost."

He looked at her through the corner of his eye. "But I end up going in circles that lead nowhere, Aunt. I fall into Darkness. I think I need to be alone. So I can rest and think about it."

"So what's the problem with Darkness? What happened to your eyes, Mole?"

He smiled faintly. "Maybe I'm just tired."

"And," she said with a quaver in her old voice, "maybe you've finished with the work of the eyes. Maybe it's time for you to do another kind of work."

"What other work?"

"You've been laboring for cycles to *see* a way out for the mammoths so they can stay here with us. Maybe it's time you gave up your eyes. You must now work on not seeing. Learn to feel your way around."

Wearily, he examined her. "You mean like the tribe of invisible people?"

"Yes."

"And what am I supposed to strive not to see?"

"Your lover's face."

He laughed and dug his fingers into the leather of his pack. "Once I've figured out what that means, I promise to work on it. Then you don't mind if I go and Dream before the sickness ends?"

"Of course I mind, but I can do the Healings that need be done. And I think I understand what's wrong with you," she replied. "I had a Dream. I just didn't know what it meant at the time."

"A Dream?"

"I saw you walking. You were on the hard, black road of difficulties that begins in Dawn Child's belly and arcs across the roof of the world to the home of the Thunderbeings. All humans walk this road while they're alive, of course. But you were very fortunate. You had stumbled onto the crossing that leads to the heart of the maze. Monster Rock Eagle perches in the rocks at that crossing. Very few Dreamers ever see him. He frightened you. You didn't know which direction to take. So you sat right down in the path and cried. It made me ashamed. I thought you were wiser than that."

Sunchaser's brows lowered. "You think the crossing is the new turn in the maze?"

"More likely it's the heart. Only you can figure that out."

"But I want you to help me."

"I can't."

"Why not?"

Good Plume grinned, showing toothless gums. "Because I don't know what it means . . . except that you're in trouble. Don't you think that if I knew, I'd tell you?"

"Not necessarily."

She chuckled. "Come on. We'd better Sing for those half souls right now, before the entire village has been witched and there's nobody left to Sing any of us to the Land of the Dead."

She linked her arm through his and headed him toward the sweat lodge in the forest outside the village.

"You know, Sunchaser," she said as they walked, "I remember when you used to be happy. It wasn't that long ago, either. Remember how you used to let out those bloodcurdling shrieks when Power swelled your chest? Ah, those screams warmed my heart."

"I'll be happy again someday."

"Of course you will, once you've Healed everybody in the world who's sick, saved mammoths, dire wolves, camels and all the other animals who look like they're dying out—and, most important of all, gone back to Dreaming seriously."

Sunchaser shook his head. "Blessed Spirits, I need to sit down. Even if only for fifty heartbeats."

"Well, we're heading in that direction," she said and squeezed his arm affectionately. "Come on."

Six

The sound of cautious feet grating against stone startled Kestrel. She braced her toes on the ledge and lifted herself to peer through the pile of dead branches she had erected to block the game trail here at the edge of the cliff. She stood on a narrow ledge that stuck out like a pouting lip eight hands below the crest of the bluff. Cloud Girl, in her rabbit-fur sack, slept next to her mother's feet.

Kestrel squinted at the trail, seeing nothing, but the sound of approaching footsteps grew stronger as each moment passed. Anxiously, her eyes roved the juniper-dotted uplands. Deep drainages cut meandering swathes down the bluff, creating a series of parallel finger ridges. The bellies of the drainages were so choked with willows and cattails that they resembled green snakes slithering down the bluff toward the river. To the east, a gray haze of rain had devoured the horizon. She could vaguely hear the rumbling voices of the Thunderbeings as they carried the storm northward.

Kestrel sucked in a breath of the pungent juniper-sharp wind and waited.

Her trap had been built in two sections. The first blocked this main game trail that came down from the breaks and followed the canyon rim. The second section lay to the south, where two drainages collided. Her wing walls of brush should force her quarries into that bottleneck. If they didn't balk, if they stayed between the wing walls, they would be funneled to the edge of the sandstone cliff.

Kestrel froze with excitement. Morning sunlight burned along the edges of the bluff and shimmered in the bristly fur of two tapirs—a cow and a yearling calf—trotting toward her on the trail.

Legend claimed that tapirs were the cousins of horses, but they looked much different than horses, with long, wrinkled snouts that curved downward over their lower jaws, and squat, heavy bodies whose legs were much shorter than those of horses. They also had four toes on their front feet and three on their hind feet. Adult tapirs stood maybe six hands tall at the shoulder, but they were powerfully built and dangerous when threatened.

Kestrel studied the cow and her calf. Odd, to see tapirs in broad daylight. They clung to the night like bats and voles. Had something, *or someone,* spooked them from their beds and sent them fleeing? Cautiously, she searched the top of the bluff for any sign of men. The only movement came from high above, where two buzzards soared on the air currents, their wings spread in such freedom that it made Kestrel's soul ache.

All night long, a cold wind had blown down from the north, and this morning, ash-colored fluffs of cloud filled the skies. Could another storm be coming in? So soon?

The cow lifted her head and sniffed the wind when she saw the barricade. Both animals stopped. Kestrel barely breathed. The cow shied, pranced nervously and stopped again. The calf, curious, stepped forward. It cocked its head and twisted one ear, wondering at the new sight on the familiar trail. Gusts of wind ruffled the tapirs' bristly black hair.

Please, Above-Old-Man, let them veer southward to take the trail where I have my trap set.

After a few moments, the calf snorted and trotted off down the southward trail. Kestrel's heart leaped. The cow lifted a front foot, peered intently at Kestrel's hiding place, then hesitantly followed her calf. But she kept looking back, forcing Kestrel to stay hidden until they had moved out of sight over the rounded crest of the bluff.

Kestrel picked up the small pack she'd woven out of strips of juniper bark and yucca fibers and tied it around her waist; it carried the few necessities she'd been able to find along the riverbank. Then she looked at Cloud Girl. Gray tufts of fur framed her beautiful four-day-old face. The pacifier that Kestrel had made from the soft underbelly of a field mouse lay halfway out of Cloud Girl's mouth.

Kestrel had found a flat piece of pine driftwood at the river's edge and turned it into a cradle board. After that, she had killed four cottontails with a throwing stick made from an angled juniper limb. The sweet meat had given her sustenance, and she'd used her chert flake to cut the hides to shape. Then she'd sharpened a chokecherry stick to a fine point on a piece of sandstone and punched out holes in the hides, through which she'd laced rabbit tendons to sew the hides closed; two of the hides covered the cradle board for warmth. Cloud Girl wore the other two hides as a shirt and pants.

Kestrel quickly slung the sack's hide carrying-thong around her neck and scrambled over the lip of stone to follow the tapirs. As she ran, her heavy breasts cushioned Cloud Girl's head.

Magnificent vistas stretched before her. To the east and south, beyond the juniper-sprinkled uplands, chunky red buttes melted into the scudding clouds, while westward, the tortured, muddy swath of the Big Spoonwood River gave way to the slopes of the Mammoth Mountains. Somewhere in the foothills beneath those jagged peaks lay the trail that led across the divide and down to Otter Clan Village.

Iceplant's face flitted through her mind, and Kestrel had to shove the image away to keep her feet moving. Thoughts of him left her trembling. Despite her exhaustion, nightmares had tormented her sleep. She dreamed that she'd met Iceplant at the Pinyon Bark Trails crossing—just as they'd planned—and that he'd played his flute for her while she'd given birth to their children. The sweet, lilting notes had comforted her pain. Afterward, he had smiled and curled his body around hers, keeping her warm through the darkness and the cold. When the golden rays of sunrise had struck their brush shelter the next morning, they'd taken the babies and headed for the sea, laughing, talking about their future . . .

The dream had left her weeping with despair. She couldn't afford to remember such hopes. Someday, she promised herself, she would find a safe hole, cover it with brush and spend time sorting through the wild expectations and the terrors of recent days. She desperately needed to lick her wounds, to cry until her tears dried up. More than that, she needed time to shout at herself in rage. Rage for all the mistakes she'd made. Rage for causing Iceplant's death . . . and the death of Iceplant's son.

Yesterday she'd searched for the baby boy but had found no remains. The hungry animals who roamed the shore must have—

Not now. Don't think about it now.

When Kestrel crested the bluff, darting from scrubby tree to scrubby tree, she could see the tapirs trotting along the next rise. She hastily crouched behind a juniper, peering through the scaly needled branches, and waited until the pair had gone down the other side. The pungent sweetness of the tree lingered in her nostrils, fresh and vigorous. If she spooked the tapirs now, they might break to the right, or worse, to the left, and double back to escape.

"Let's give them a little more time, Cloud Girl," she whispered. "We want them to feel safe when they come to the brush wing walls."

Kestrel had spent an entire day building her trap. She'd twisted sage out of the ground and gathered dead juniper limbs so she could pile them into a long V that progressively narrowed as it neared the face of the cliff—a place where the hard sandstone had been undercut by the wind and weather. The drop was short, barely twenty hands, but it should do the job. She would have to frighten the animals enough to get them running and then force them into a desperate leap over the edge. If she could do that, she would have what she needed for crossing the swollen river.

"Enough," she whispered to Cloud Girl. "Let's go."

She sprinted down the game trail behind the tapirs. Her insides still ached, and every time her foot landed, a sharp pain lanced her abdomen. But she had to keep running; she had to kill at least one of the tapirs. Too much time had passed while she had been trapped by the river's swirling floodwaters. Whenever the wind moaned, she swore that she heard Lambkill's voice saying, *"You can never run away from me. Never . . ."*

Despite the pain, she clutched her daughter against her chest and ran harder, down the dip, up the rise. Gravel bit into her moccasins, and she almost slipped on the wet clay beneath. Before she reached the summit, she slowed and crept up the slope to peer over the crest. The tapirs had unwittingly trotted down the trail between the wing walls. But if she didn't do something fast, they would come to the Place where the trail vanished, veering southward. There, the brush walls funneled them over unmarked stone toward the cliff. Unlike the mountain sheep, who would panic at the obstruction, the tapirs would lower their heads and bull their way through the walls to stay on the trail.

Kestrel picked up her pace and charged over the top of the bluff. When she reached the wing walls, she swerved and sprinted down the trail behind the tapirs. The cow heard her coming and bellowed a warning as it wheeled to face her. The calf danced sideways to see the problem. When it spied Kestrel, it let out a shrill cry and galloped headlong down the brush walls, not stopping until it reached the cliff. Kestrel lifted her arms and hollered as she dashed headlong down the slope. The cow lowered her head and stood pawing the stone with gleaming eyes.

"Run! Run, Mother!" Kestrel shouted. "Hurry! Run!"

The cow stood her ground and began to snort dangerously. A single butt from that thick skull would send Kestrel sprawling to the ground, where she would be trampled.

She kept running.

The cow laid her ears back and took a few threatening steps. Kestrel pulled a juniper branch from the wing walls and slapped the brush as she continued forward, roaring "*Hiyay! Hiyay!*"

Cloud Girl broke into sobs.

The cow sidestepped uncertainly, her coarse hair standing on end; then she took a step backward, and finally she whirled to trot after her calf.

Kestrel ran with all her might, dashing down the narrowing walls behind the cow, shrieking and beating the brush with her branch. The cow reached the cliff, where the calf had stopped to peer over the edge. Frightened, the cow bawled and tried to slow her headlong rush, but her feet skidded on the loose gray dirt. She struck her calf in the haunches, spinning it sideways . . . and toppled over the cliff. The force of the blow sent the calf reeling. It cried out in stark terror, fear bright in its dark eyes as it slid off behind the cow.

Two satisfying thuds came from the stone ledge below.

Kestrel unslung the rabbit-fur sack from around her neck and hung it on one of the branches protruding from the wing wall. Cloud Girl began to scream loudly. On the balls of her feet, Kestrel inched forward to peer down, careful of the slick surface.

The calf had died instantly, its neck broken in the fall. But the cow still lived. She pawed pathetically at the stone ledge with her front feet, trying to force her two broken hind legs to work. When she saw Kestrel, she let out a desperate groan and hoisted herself up on three legs but quickly toppled backward.

"Forgive me, Mother," Kestrel said as she pulled the stout oak branch from the pile of brush where she'd hidden it at dawn. She backtracked to a low place where the descent was less treacherous, moved a juniper stump and eased her way over the cliff. A cascade of sand showered her when she jumped down to the ledge. The coppery scent of blood blended with the musk of tapir to fill the air.

The cow screamed and struggled as Kestrel stepped over the dead calf. Singing the Hunter's Song, Kestrel lifted her club. It took twelve smacking head blows before the cow flopped onto her side and her eyes rolled back. She spasmed, and blood sprayed from her nostrils. With a hoarse gasp, she went limp. Tiny red bubbles foamed around her nostrils and mouth.

Kestrel sank down by that big bloody head and gently patted the black hair, so stiff and warm to the touch. A last breath escaped from the cow's lungs and raised a spurt of dust by her curved snout. "I—I had no choice, Mother. Bless your hide to my use. You will give life to my baby. And to me. We will never stop Singing your praises to Above-Old-Man."

Kestrel crouched and leaned her shoulder against the bluff while she untied the pack from around her waist. Through a narrow cut in the rock below, she could see part of the turbulent river. Pinyon jays cackled and shrilled with their usual good humor as they flocked from tree to tree in search of last year's pinyon nuts, or ripening juniper berries. Because it took juniper berries three cycles to ripen, some of the trees could almost always be counted on to provide food. The cold wind rustled branches and rasped on the worn beds of sandstone. The rabbit brush had begun to turn green. Soon the chimisa would leaf out.

Here in the sun, it was pleasant to clear her mind of any sensation but the warm hide under her callused fingers. If only she could stay like this forever, with the warmth of the sun beating down on her and the satisfaction of fresh meat for her hungry belly.

But a chill like Winter Boy's shadow stole into her heart. She could feel Lambkill's presence, sense him staring at one of her tracks, reaching down to press the rain-spattered soil with a finger to test its age.

There is no rest for you, Kestrel. Not until you find sanctuary—and perhaps not even then.

Cloud Girl had settled down. Her crying had subsided to an almost inaudible whimper. Kestrel climbed back up over the ledge and pulled her daughter's sack from the wing wall where she had left it. Then she edged her way down to the tapirs again.

"Sit here in the sun beside me, my daughter. Smell the rich sweetness of tapir blood. Tonight we will both be full and happy."

Kestrel leaned Cloud Girl's cradle board up against the rocks and opened her pack to pull out the quartzite cobble she had taken from the riverbed, a black-and-white gneiss hammerstone, a flat piece of red sandstone and two yellow blossoms she'd picked from an early-blooming desert primrose.

A flock of cranes passed over the bluff, calling to each other in warbling notes as they sailed toward the river. Against the azure background of sky, they looked like tumbling flakes of snow. Kestrel watched them flap down and alight in the reeds that had been revealed at the edge of the river as the water level receded. She rose. Carefully she plucked the petals from the blossoms and placed them over the cow's and the calf's eyes. It would have been cruel to let them watch each other's dismemberment. Now they would see only a glorious yellow, as if Father Sun himself had descended from the sky to take their souls to the Land of the Dead.

Kestrel gripped her hammerstone and steadied the quartzite cobble so that the blows would drive off the correctly shaped flakes. Under the sharp blows, the stone made hollow cracking sounds as she drove off several large, flat gray flakes of quartzite. When she had a pile of ten flakes, she began the laborious process of skinning the tapirs.

She had to skin the animal "in the round" or it wouldn't be suitable for inflating and floating in the river. That meant that she had to keep any long cuts to a minimum, since every cut would have to be sewn closed again, and each puncture she made with her bone awl would be another opening that water might seep through. The inflated hide had to be perfect, or both she and Cloud Girl would drown.

Kestrel ran her thumb along the cow's front leg to find the notch just below the knee. Then she bent the knee and sawed with her flake until she'd sliced the ligaments. Clear, slick fluid leaked from the joint. Straightening the leg, Kestrel cracked the joint in two and twisted it apart. Gently she laid the lower leg aside with the four toes pointing westward, toward the Land of the Dead. The tapirs would have to climb onto the wings of the Thunderbeings to journey there tonight. Already their Spirits would be eager to go. Kestrel used the longest and narrowest of her flakes to trim around the inside of the knee, separating the hide from the muscle. As she went, she rolled the hide back to the tapir's shoulder and cut off the upper leg. Then she started on the next leg.

When she'd finished all four legs, Kestrel chose a fresh flake with which to slice through the thick neck hide beneath the tapir's skull, at the point where the spine connected to the skull, just back of the ears. It took her a full finger of time to slice through the massive tendons and ligaments to remove the head. Blood, spinal fluid and stiff black hair now stuck to her fingers. She took another long, narrow flake and cut a line from the anus down the back of each leg. She wiped her sweating brow and began the delicate process of skinning around the rear quarters, peeling back the skin until she could pull it over the hips.

"It will go faster now, Mother," she said reverently as she stroked the warm, twitching muscles. In the sun, the meat glistened a rich red, traced by white lines of connective tissue and fat. "I will have to be careful so I don't puncture your thin belly hide, Mother, but the rest is easy."

Kestrel straddled the tapir's midsection and leaned forward. She tugged the skin back with one hand and gripped the flake in the other, skinning quickly, cleanly, although her fingers cramped from the constant battle with the thick, clumsy hide. The limp weight of the animal worked against her, too, making her pant, but finally she had pulled the last bit of hide from the neck and the tapir lay naked before her.

Cloud Girl began to cry halfheartedly. Kestrel smiled wearily at her. "I'm right here, Cloud Girl. You're fine. We're safe . . . for now."

She picked up the sack and draped the thong around her neck, tilting the sack so that her daughter lay on her back. Kestrel untied the front of her dress and drew out her breast. Cloud Girl nursed greedily.

Standing there, holding Cloud Girl and looking at the tapirs, Kestrel's relief was so great that she felt weak. But quick on its heels came the certain knowledge that she had to hurry, *hurry.*

Dropping to her knees beside the forelegs of the tapir, she picked up a fresh flake of quartzite. While Cloud Girl fed, Kestrel stripped out the leg tendons. She laid the gleaming white strings of tissue on the cow's side and then cut out the ulna, the narrow leg bone. It took a finger of time to sharpen the point of the ulna by drawing it back and forth on the piece of sandstone, but after that, the ulna had a good sharp point.

Kestrel turned the cow's hide inside out and dragged it onto her lap. The ulna would also make an effective stiletto if she needed it, but for now she used it to punch a neat line of holes around each of the openings. With the still-wet tendons, she sewed up the anus and the back legs, taking care to double the hide for strength and so that the stitches wouldn't separate. That done, she turned her attention to the neck and one of the forelegs. She closed them and tied strong knots to secure her work. It would hold. She felt sure of it. Last, she cut fat from the animal's back and rubbed thick coatings into the stitches to help seal them. Happiness buoyed her. A sound escaped her lips that was half laugh, half sob. A desperate sound.

Cloud Girl had fallen fast asleep in her rabbit-fur sack. Kestrel tucked her breast back into her dress and sat cross-legged in the lee of the cliff.

Tan stone curved around and over her, like a butterfly's cocoon, shielding her from the bite of the wind that hurled itself at the bluff. But her happiness faded. The muddy river below, although down from its highest level, was still swollen. Two juniper trees flowed in tandem down the middle of the river, whirling and bobbing. Their heavy trunks extended three times the width of Kestrel's shoulders.

How would she and her daughter, clinging to a flimsy tapir hide, ever make it across that water? The debris would surely crush them, or drag them under.

She clutched Cloud Girl tightly and huddled back against the stone. The wind began to prick at her flesh with a wintry intensity. They couldn't even attempt crossing today. Maybe not tomorrow either. Not until the weather turned warmer. No newborn baby could stand the bitter cold of the water.

"It will warm up. Please, Above-Old-Man, let it warm up. It *has* to."

Kestrel closed her eyes for a moment, trying to summon hatred or anger to give herself strength. But exhaustion weighted her. She still had to skin the calf, so she could make a robe to cover Cloud Girl and herself while they slept tonight. She would also have to slice and dry the meat, at least enough of it to last for several days. And she was so tired. Her muscles ached deep down, all the way to the bone. Despair crept through her on icy feet.

Where is Lambkill? Where is he? Why hasn't he already tracked me to the river?

All morning she had expected to see him trotting over the bluff or down along the shoreline. Surely he would have left the village immediately after she ran away. Wouldn't he? Or would he have waited until the storm broke before setting out on her trail? Was he so confident that he could find her?

Yes. Of course he is. Because he will.

An image of his gloating face formed on her closed eyelids; it changed as she watched, shifting to different times in their life together.

One image lingered. From cycles ago. Lambkill still had black in his hair, and wrinkles hadn't cut such deep furrows across his forehead yet. He stood before her, trim and athletic, with muscular arms, and dressed in a beautiful, golden elkhide shirt. *Yes, five cycles ago. I was thirteen summers old.*

It was during the Moon-of-New-Horns at her best friend Waxwing's marriage. Kestrel had been Lambkill's wife for two moons. She had still felt giddy with excitement at being wanted by a man three times her age. A man whose reputation as a great Trader spanned the world. He'd been kind to her, showering her with wondrous gifts the likes of which she'd never imagined.

Kestrel had made a beautiful dress for herself, of soft doeskin bleached pure white, with red and green starbursts of porcupine quills on the chest. Her fringed leggings matched. She had braided her long hair and coiled the braids over her ears, then secured them with mammoth-ivory hairpins. Her mother had told her she looked as radiant as one of the Star People.

She'd helped Waxwing dress, then ducked out of her lodge and walked into the plaza, toward Lambkill. He'd stood near the central cook fire, watching the hindquarter of a shrubox roasting, suspended above the flames. The rich scent had made Kestrel's mouth water.

Lambkill laughed and went on telling the tale of his last

trading journey to the People of the Masks, far to the north. He had accidentally walked between a short-faced bear and her new cub. The sow had chased Lambkill until he'd scrambled into a hole that led underground into a honeycomb of lava tubes. He'd had to stay there for three days, living off of moss and bats, before the sow had left. The young men who stood around listening had rapt expressions. Pride swelled Kestrel's chest.

When she joined Lambkill, he smiled and slipped his arm around her waist to hold her close. His hand on her hip felt so comforting. She remembered gazing up at him as though he were Above-Old-Man himself and hoping that he would never tire of her. More than anything in the world, she wanted to please him.

As more people arrived for the marriage and joined the circle around the cook fire, cousins from distant villages came over to greet Kestrel. She smiled and laughed a great deal as she related the news and told stories about herself and Waxwing, pranks they had pulled when they'd been children.

Waxwing ducked through her lodge door and began the marriage walk down the middle of the village to meet her husband-to-be, Antler Tine. Everyone followed.

The crowd stopped at the foot of the craggy red cliffs west of the village and looked up as Waxwing and Antler Tine climbed to meet Old Porcupine, who draped the white marriage hide over their shoulders. Lambkill had given Waxwing the gorgeous abalone-shell pendants that hung from the edges of the hide and glittered pink in the fading afternoon sunlight. Kestrel smiled and clapped her hands when Waxwing knelt and began Singing the Link Hands Song. Antler Tine echoed each of her verses:

Link hands, link hands, link hands with me now.
Link hands, link hands, link hands with me now.
I have passed you on your roads.

Above-Old-Man's breath brought us together,.
  together this day.
His breath of waters,
His breath of seeds,
His breath of strong spirit,
His breath of Power,
His breath of all good fortune,
  brought us together this day.
Link hands, link hands, link hands with me.
I ask for your breath,
I give you mine.
Together our breaths rise to Above-Old-Man.
He adds his breath to ours.
Link hands, link hands, link hands with me now.

Breath was life. They could offer each other nothing more precious. Joy filled Kestrel.

To get a better look, she stepped sideways several paces— away from Lambkill. People filled in the opening she'd left, and she lost sight of him. She raised herself on her tiptoes to watch Waxwing over the shoulders of two men. One of the men, two or three summers older than she and very handsome, turned to look at her. He smiled. Kestrel, feeling joyous, returned the smile.

"You're Waxwing's best friend, aren't you?" he asked.

She nodded. "Yes, we've been friends since we were four summers old."

"I thought so. I'm Waxwing's cousin, Snow Wind. Didn't you just get married to the Trader, Lambkill?"

"Oh, yes. He's . . ." She tried to see him to point him out, but she couldn't find him and shrugged. "He's over there somewhere."

Snow Wind smiled. "He's a very great man. He used to run the trading trails with my grandfather, Looncry. I've heard stories of Lambkill all my life. You're very lucky to be his wife."

Kestrel laughed at the compliment. "Yes, thank you, I know."

Waxwing stood up, and Kestrel shifted, trying to see better, and tripped over a stone. Snow Wind politely grabbed her hand to steady her.

That's when Lambkill came through the crowd, looking for her, smiling and talking to people on the way. When he saw her holding Snow Wind's hand, he halted abruptly.

Kestrel turned, smiling as she reached out for her husband. But Lambkill stood as still as a carved soapstone statue. His gaze went from her to Snow Wind and back again. His expression had gone from that of a loving husband to that of a dangerous enemy in less than a heartbeat. In dismay, she jerked her hand from Snow Wind's and stood rooted to the ground.

Lambkill came forward, stood between her and Snow Wind and said, "Your grandmother, Willowstem, has been looking for you, Kestrel. Go find her."

"Where—where is she? I haven't—"

"I said for you to *go find her*."

His icy tone made her flinch as if she'd been struck. "Yes. Yes, I will." Kestrel ran through the crowd, shouting her grandmother's name, only to discover that Willowstem had not been looking for her at all. So confused that she didn't know what to do, she started to cry. Tears ran down her cheeks as she shouldered her way back, looking for Lambkill.

By the time she found him, darkness had grown up around the edges of the village. A translucent blue light suffused the sky. Lambkill had been standing with Old Porcupine, but when she got close enough, he roughly grabbed her hand, said "good night," and dragged her back toward their lodge in the juniper grove.

"Lambkill? You're hurting me. Please—"

"You've been my wife for two moons and already you're throwing yourself at other men."

"That's not true! I didn't! Snow Wind—"

Lambkill turned and slapped her so hard that she let out a sharp cry of shock. He leaned down, his nose only a handbreadth from hers, and hissed, "Listen to me, woman. My last wife tried to run away from me. Do you know where she is now?"

"She's d-dead. She died from a fever."

"She's dead all right." He slowly straightened up, a triumphant, gloating expression on his face. "No woman betrays me and gets away with it."

"But, Lambkill, I've done nothing! I love you. I don't—"

"Move!" Lambkill brutally shoved her along the path and into the deep shadows of the juniper grove.

They reached their lodge, and Lambkill pushed her through the hide door curtain so hard that she toppled across their mammoth-hide robes. The long, silken fur cushioned her fall, but it still hurt. She stayed on her stomach, afraid to move. Parfleches lined the walls, filled with dried meat, sunflower seeds, fragments of mammoth tusk and the special exotic trade goods that only Lambkill had the right to possess. The largest parfleche contained the elaborately carved bones of a strange fish that swam in the oceans far, far to the east. Painted hides decorated every wall, depicting hunting scenes.

Kestrel shivered in fear. "Lambkill? Please, I didn't mean to do anything wrong."

Lambkill draped the door curtain carefully over its antler hook, making sure that nothing blocked the cold wind that swept up the slope. The juniper limbs creaked as they swung back and forth. Lambkill ordered, "Roll over."

Kestrel obediently responded to the sharp tone in his voice and rolled to her back.

He fell on her, ripping at her sleeves, pulling them down so that they trapped her arms at her sides. When he fumbled with one hand to unlace his pants, she said, "Lambkill, you don't have to do this. I want you!"

He forced her knees open. Bracing his hands by her hips, he entered her and thrust violently, trying to hurt her.

Weeping, Kestrel cried, "Lambkill! Please!"

"Shut up!"

As his frenzy built, he gripped Kestrel's shoulders so hard

that his fingernails cut into her flesh. Finally he groaned and relaxed. A few moments later, he slid off her and laced his pants again.

In silence, he crawled to the opposite side of the lodge and slumped down on one of the cattail sleeping mats. Within a single finger of time, he started snoring.

Kestrel lay unmoving. Dazed. Hurting inside. She felt as though her soul had separated from her body and floated near the smokehole in the ceiling. . . .

She shook the memory out of her head as she stared at the tapir. The red flesh had begun to crinkle as it dried. *Never again. I'll kill him first.*

She dragged herself to her feet and picked up a fresh flake. A mountain of black clouds bore down on her from the north, blotting out the feeble rays of sunlight as it came. Beneath it, cloud shadows roamed the hills like slate-gray beasts stalking for prey. She thought she could make out the haze of rain.

Wearily, she knelt and slit the thin skin on the calf's belly. She had to bury her arm up to her shoulder to reach the heart. Cutting it loose from its sac took almost more strength than she possessed, but she drew out the organ and tipped it to her mouth. Hot blood coursed down her chin and soaked the front of her dress. She drank greedily, gratefully. Tapir's blood ran like fire through her veins, giving her strength.

The Boy wept with joy! His Mother would live now. And soon, very soon, he would have the chance to be born again so that he could set things right in the world of humans! Only he could do it. No one else had the strength or the determination!

"Yes, good Mother. Drink as much as you can hold. Grow strong! Do you hear me, Mother? I'm calling to you. I have to be born soon. Hear—"

From out of the star-spotted blackness, the Man said, "Come here, Boy. I want to tell you a story."

"I need to watch my Mother! What do you want?"

The Man's voice was as soft and caressing as weasel fur against the face. Tenderly, he said, "There was once a bad Forest Spirit who appeared to a very good Dreamer in the guise of Wolf, and he said to the Dreamer, 'I am your Spirit Helper. Above-Old-Man sent me to you.' But the Dreamer said: 'I don't think so. You must have the wrong woman. I haven't done anything to deserve a Spirit Helper. Perhaps you were meant to appear to my brother Dreamer in the next lodge . . .' Immediately, the wicked Forest Spirit vanished."

Seven

Water pooled, sparkling clear, in the small hollow ringed by moss-covered logs. A mat of needles and rosebush leaves coated the bottom of the catchment. Sunchaser dropped his pack to one side and studied the little creek fed by runoff. Helper, under no such compulsion, stepped forward on hesitant feet, sinking into the moss before lapping eagerly at the water.

The trail crossed the creek here. A man traveling alone was fair game. Bears would be emerging from their winter's stupor, hungry for the lush spring grass and any other food they could find. The roaring of the lions had awakened Sunchaser that very morning, the sound muted by the trees but telling of empty bellies.

Dead branches feathered the gray-brown boles of fir trees and pine, while thick stands of currant and rosebushes clotted the slope to either side of the creek's channel. Overhead, a thick mass of evergreen boughs whispered silently in the midday breeze. The glory of the valley brought peace, and rest.

From the time Sunchaser had left Brushnut Village, his fear had been increasing. When he blanked his mind, he could sense wrongness, a creeping blackness easing over the land like a perverted night fog.

Jumpy . . . I'm still not well. That's all. A bit of leftover fever. He sank down onto the chilly damp soil. His tired legs trembled, and he closed his eyes, happy to rest for a moment.

Everything was going wrong. First his Dreams of the mammoths dying, vanishing from the face of the earth. Then the way through the maze had slipped from his clumsy fingers like a wet fish. In the beginning, he hadn't been worried. Power shifted and fluctuated throughout a man's life. It should have been a simple matter to refocus his efforts and find the way. He'd left Brushnut Village three days ago and had been Dreaming every night, but he hadn't been able to find the path through the maze.

Sunchaser sighed and opened his eyes, aware that Helper had finished lapping up the cool water and come to stand beside him. Absently, he reached out, rubbing the dog's black coat. His hands were immediately coated with coarse black hair.

"Oh, Helper . . ." After his own illness, Helper's hair had started to fall out in clumps.

Sunchaser met Helper's concerned brown gaze. "Everything is going wrong, old friend. The mammoths are dying. Sickness stalks the land."

Helper, his tail slipping back and forth in a loose wag, licked Sunchaser's hand.

"And I can't even find the Power to tie your hair to your body."

Helper whined softly, the sound punctuated by a series of snorts as he pawed the ground with his front feet.

"Do you think so?" Sunchaser asked. "I wish I had your confidence in me."

Helper's high-pitched whine echoed Sunchaser's distress.

"I know." Sunchaser gently ruffled the fur on Helper's side. "We'll go to the Dream Cave, where we'll have the solitude we need to find the Way. You'll help me, won't you?"

Helper bounced on springy legs and tried to grab Sunchaser's hand in his mouth.

"Yes, I knew you would. The cave isn't more than a day's walk from here. We'll build a big fire. Then I'll sweat and pray."

Helper made a *murrumph* that was half exhale and shook his head, an act that haloed his face in floating hair.

Sunchaser leaned forward, bending down to drink—and stopped short. His image stared back at him from the calm water. The interlacing branches of the fir trees overhead made a background for his face, aged now, lined where it hadn't been lined only weeks before. But the greatest shock was something else.

Fear pumped through his muscles as he jerked out a strand of his own hair. The reflection in the pool hadn't lied—his hair was turning snow-white!

Kestrel trotted through the dirty froth that coated the shore of the Big Spoonwood River. Brilliant sunshine warmed her face as she ran, but it did little to ease the terror that stung her soul. Over the past five days, her desperation had been growing, until now she could barely sit still to feed Cloud Girl. Every fiber in her body screamed for her to forget trying to cross the river, to run fast and hard, to get away from here *now!*

But she knew the only way to really lose Lambkill lay in obliterating her trail by crossing the swollen river. Despite the gentle rain that had pattered off and on all night long, the water level had gone down further. Flocks of gulls hunted along the shore, squawking and flapping their wings over the small creatures trapped in the stagnant pools. They screamed at Kestrel when her rapid steps frightened them away from their precious finds.

Looking out over the frothing water frightened her. Whirlpools still sucked needles, grass and small floating bits of bark down into their swirling currents. Farther out in the flow, white water shot up in jets as the relentless pounding of the river drove against the big boulders in midstream. The splintered remains of a giant cottonwood plunged and bucked like a rutting buffalo bull as it lanced the murky flow.

No one can survive that! I'll drown. I'll die out there with my daughter.

Kestrel veered wide around an old mammoth jump site. Dozens of skeletons lay in a huge pile, their rib bones broken and interlaced like long white fingers. She could still see the top of the cliff, even the place where her ancestors had driven the herd over the edge. When the mammoths had realized their error, they must have struggled madly, trying not to fall. Chunks of protruding rock had cracked off as the animals tumbled over the precipice. She'd seen several kill sites in the past two days, but none with as many mammoth skeletons as this one had. As Kestrel trotted by, she aimlessly tried to count them. Thirty or forty animals, she guessed. It must have happened when Winter Boy had been clutching the land to his bosom; that's when the animals came together in enormous herds.

The gaping skulls and impact-split bones haunted her. *This is a place of death—and mine will be but one more.*

Cloud Girl bounced in the rabbit-fur sack on her back, quiet but awake. Kestrel had tied the sack high so that when she turned her head, she could see the baby. Two huge blue eyes stared back at her from the midst of a ring of gray fur. The mousehide pacifier in her tiny mouth moved rhythmically. Usually Cloud Girl went to sleep after she'd been fed, but not this afternoon. Perhaps she could sense the fear that clawed at her mother's heart. Kestrel couldn't keep her eyes from straying to the top of the bluff. She half-expected to see men with atlatls aimed down at them. But only the condors perching on the rugged cliffs met her gaze.

She had waited until early afternoon to test the temperature of the water, and she'd found it barely tolerable. It would still be a freezing trip. They wouldn't reach the opposite shore until just before nightfall, but they could make it. Suddenly she felt sure of it.

Ahead, the inflated tapir hide rested at the base of the fist-shaped boulder. "Are you ready, Cloud Girl?"

Cloud Girl made a soft sound.

Kestrel slowed her pace, examining the familiar layers of rock and earth along the eroded bluff for one final time, then knelt by the tapir hide. Last night she had blown into the unsewn foreleg to inflate it, twisted the leg closed and secured it with a length of wet sinew. Since that time, it had lost some air but not much.

"It's going to be all right, Cloud Girl. Look. The hide held air all night long."

She gazed out across the wide, violent water. Sunlight glittered from the surface, a stunning patchwork of blue and gold. From around her waist, Kestrel removed the pack that held her tools and the calf meat that she'd smoked the night before. Quickly, she pulled out the ulna and a long string of dried tendon. She dipped the tendon in the water until it became slippery.

"The river is so wide this time of season that it will take us three hands of time to cross. Three hands of time. That's all. Then we'll build a fire and get warm again. Don't worry, baby. I'll be right here."

But her heart pounded as she untied the sinew on the foreleg. She put her mouth over the opening and slowly untwisted the leg so that she could blow more air into it, filling it full. Then she twisted the foreleg again and propped her knee on it while she punched holes with the ulna and sewed the opening closed with the tendon.

Blood surged in her ears. She slowly let the twist go. No hissing came from the seam. To make certain it didn't leak, Kestrel plunged the leg under the water and watched for bubbles. Only a few rose to the surface, and she knew that the bristly tapir hair held air pockets.

"It's going to be all right," she repeated tautly, more for herself than for Cloud Girl. But her eyes narrowed as she studied the bluff for a final time, searching the crest and down the trough that led to the river.

At the bottom of the trough, a cormorant hunched on the limb of a dead tree washed ashore in the storm. The master fisher had its black wings outspread, placidly drying them in the sun. A short distance away, two raccoons waddled along the base of the cliffs. A fish flopped in the big leader's mouth. The smaller raccoon kept snatching at it, trying to take it away. When the leader jerked his nose up and broke into a frisky run, Kestrel's mouth tightened.

"The animals see nothing to alarm them, yet I can't even manage a deep breath."

Hastily, she shoved her awl back into her pack, which she tied around Cloud Girl's rabbit-fur sack, high enough that it should stay above the water. Without waiting any longer, Kestrel took the inflated tapir hide and waded out into the river. Goose bumps popped out all over her legs. A single finger of time later, the icy chill began to gnaw at her flesh.

"You can stand it," she assured herself. "By nightfall, you'll be safe. *Safe!*"

She positioned the hide so that the cow's legs stuck out on either side of her hips, to make for better balance. Being careful not to put too much strain on the stitches, Kestrel gripped the hide and pulled herself up until her breasts rested in the middle of the cow's stomach. The hide sank halfway. Kestrel allowed herself to smile. Cloud Girl would be dry, and she herself would be submerged in the bitter water only from the waist down.

As she kicked her legs to propel the hide out into the current, she glanced back at the bluff. She saw no one, but a hollow ache constricted her chest—she felt as though cold, inhuman eyes watched her. Kestrel clamped her teeth to stifle the sudden terror that knotted her belly.

She kicked her feet harder.

Then the current caught them and whirled them out into the midst of the rushing river.

Eight

Spring Girl, exhibiting her usual capriciousness, had slapped the high peaks like a bolt of lightning, splitting winter's dreary clouds and letting in a blinding flood of sunshine. It might snow again tomorrow, but for today, warmth suffused the world. On the distant Mammoth Mountains, glacier fields shimmered whitely against the snow-clotted gray background of the jagged rock that lined the ice-filled hollows and thrust toward the blue vastness of the sky. But here, days from the coast, the enduring wintergreens, fir and spruce, that whiskered the slopes had lost their capes of snow, and the cold, vast, silent body of the mountain had begun to groan and creak as it stretched in the warmth, awakening at last.

Horseweed inhaled deeply as he climbed the muddy path. The rich scents of water, pungent soil and conifer belied the discomfort of soaked moccasins chafing on his water-softened feet. Sunset had taken hold of the land, enlivening the smells of melting snow and newborn grass. They filtered clear to his soul.

His brother, Balsam, followed quietly behind him, watching for animals that might have been weakened by the long moons of darkness and bitter cold. They hadn't eaten since early morning, as the growls of their stomachs kept reminding them. Balsam, only twelve summers old, had yet to fill out in the shoulders, and now his clothing hung from his skinny frame like the hide on a winter-starved buffalo.

Horseweed had two summers on his younger brother, and he stood a full hand taller. He had begun to develop broad, heavily muscled shoulders as a result of his constant training with atlatl and dart. But the boys looked strikingly alike, with round faces, pug noses and owlish eyes. Each carried an atlatl and had a quiver of darts slung over his right shoulder. Small packs rode their backs.

When the trail turned to the right and they could see through the thick boles of the pine and fir, the blue body of Mother Ocean spread in silent glory out in the distance, only a few days' walk from where they stood now. The sparkling water touched and blended with the darkening sky in the west.

Horseweed pushed a pine branch out of his way and began climbing a series of switchbacks. He lost sight of the Mother. The bark of the aspens had been gnawed by the elk's chisel-shaped lower teeth. A man could easily tell where the deepest snow line had been by noting the highest patch of chewed bark and subtracting from that the height of the elk. The drifts here had stood twenty hands high.

Balsam, glancing around at the silent wall of green and shadow, asked uncertainly, "Oxbalm told you to bring Sunchaser back at the point of a dart?"

"Yes. If necessary."

"Don't you think . . . well, that that's a little risky? I mean, Sunchaser is a great Dreamer."

"So?"

"What if Sunchaser doesn't want to come back with us?"

"Then I'll stick my dart in his back and force him to, just as Grandfather said I should."

"If Sunchaser doesn't kill you before you have the chance. Or turn you into a rabbit louse or something."

Horseweed turned to glower, and, when Balsam smiled, he said, "You'd better hope he doesn't. That would mean you'd have to bring Sunchaser back by yourself."

Balsam's smile faded. In silence, they trudged the rest of the way to the top of the switchbacks, where the trail leveled off and meandered due east through a meadow.

An enormous pink granite cliff loomed into the sky along the meadow's northern edge. It blazed in the pastel light, contrasting with the patches of dirty snow lying in the meadow's protected areas. Thousands of cycles of violent wind and storm had weathered the rock until a thick talus slope had formed at the base. High above, boulders perched precariously on the crest. The Dream Cave—about one hundred hands higher than the meadow—made a dark hole in the cliff's lower half. A wide ledge, like a tongue, stuck out from the mouth of the cave, protruding just above the talus. Across the ledge, a deer trail cut a swath through the sprouts of grass, wound down over the talus slope and wedded with another trail in the meadow.

Horseweed's skin tingled just looking at the cave's empty eye socket. They couldn't avoid passing it. The trail to Brushnut Village narrowed to nothingness here where it curved around the base of the cliff. Catchstraw claimed that Evil Spirits secreted themselves in every crevice here, waiting to pounce and eat the first warm body that happened by.

Horseweed slid behind a towering fir tree to study the meadow. Crusted snow clung stubbornly to the ground where the grass met the trees. Only the dainty runs of mice and voles marked the fringes of the meadow. Still, Horseweed searched each tree for the flick of an ear, the swish of a tail. With the stealth of Weasel, he edged up to the next tree and braced himself on the balls of his toes to examine the berry brier that skirted the cliff beneath the cave. A herd of four deer usually grazed there, but no one could hunt them. Catchstraw talked to them in his Spirit Dreams. They gave him advice about the weather and political matters.

Horseweed frowned. There used to be a pile of wood at the base of the cliff. He had gathered it himself during the last Moon-of-Losing-Antlers. What had happened to it? Catchstraw hadn't been to the Dream Cave at all during Winter Boy's reign.

Balsam gasped suddenly. "*Look!* Who is it?" His arm shot out toward the granite cliff.

"Who?" Horseweed spun around. "Where?"

"Up there! In the Dream Cave."

Horseweed squinted against the slanting rays of sunset. An old man balanced on the cave's ledge, his arms spread like Eagle's. White braids framed his square-jawed face. "Can't be Catchstraw. We left him in the village two days ago."

"Then who could it be? Sunchaser?"

"No, don't you remember? We saw him last winter when he came to visit Grandfather. His hair was as black as obsidian. And anyway, he's supposed to be at Brushnut Village."

Balsam suddenly gasped and blurted, "What's *that?* Look at it!"

Horseweed spun again and saw a mottled pink-and-black creature skulking through the brush that ringed the base of the talus slope. Eyes glittered. "Great Mouse, I—I don't know. What kind of animal is pink and black?"

"Maybe it's a . . . a *ghost*." Balsam dropped his young voice to a hoarse whisper. "You know what old Catchstraw says about the Spirits that live here around the Dream Cave. I'll bet that's what it is, a ghost!"

"A pink ghost?"

"Why not? Ghosts can look like whatever they want to."

Horseweed's eyes narrowed as he gripped his atlatl more tightly. Balsam grabbed his brother's arm hard and let out a yip when the "ghost" loped out of the brush and peered curiously at them, one paw lifted.

Horseweed said, "Let go of me. It's a dog! A mostly hairless, ugly dog. That's all!"

Handfuls of fur were missing from its sides and head. Horseweed frowned back at the cave. "We'd better worry about that man. I don't know who he is, but he shouldn't be up there. Nobody's allowed in the cave except a Dreamer. Mother Ocean could turn against us, cause a tidal wave, or . . ." his eyes widened ". . . or kill all the mammoths! Maybe *he's* the cause of the disaster. We'd better—"

A rich, deep voice rose from the cave and echoed down through the meadow. "Who are you, boys? Why are you here?"

Balsam boldly strode by Horseweed and out into the center of the meadow. The new spring grasses rose to his knees. He shouted, "Who are *you?* What are you doing up there? Get out. You're not supposed to be in there!"

The stranger lowered his outspread arms and gazed down at them. Dressed in a fine leather shirt covered with seashells, he looked important, like a visiting chief from the northern clans. "Really? Who says?"

Horseweed wet his lips nervously and edged up beside Balsam. He shouted, "Don't you know that's a Dream Cave? You'd better leave . . . before old Catchstraw finds you and turns you into a liverwort, or a leech!"

"Catchstraw turn someone into a leech? Now there is a frightening fate indeed!" The stranger vented a low, closed-mouth laugh.

Horseweed's eyes narrowed. "What happened to the herd of deer that used to graze here?"

"You mean the two does, the yearling fawn and that three-point buck?"

"That's them. Where are they?"

"A man gets hungry now and then!"

Balsam turned to look in horror at Horseweed. "He slaughtered sacred deer? And *ate* them? He's the bravest man alive."

Horseweed cupped a hand to his mouth and yelled, "Where's the pile of wood that used to be down here? It was a big pile. Took half a moon to collect and stack."

"You didn't think I ate those deer raw, did you?"

"What a stinking *skunk!*" Balsam shrilled. Red splotched his cheeks. "Get down out of there before we come up after you!"

"Come up after me?" The stranger laughed. "Are the two of you planning to drag me bodily from this cave? What if I don't want to go?"

"We'll show you! Get out of that cave or . . . or *we'll kill you!*"

The man laughed so hard that Balsam groaned and stamped his feet in anger.

"Yes! We will!" Horseweed yelled as he shook his darts in defiance.

"Go home, boys. I don't have the freedom to play today. I'm busy."

That made them both pause. Balsam scratched behind his left ear and looked uneasy, while Horseweed fiddled with his atlatl. He nocked and unnocked a dart. He'd fletched the long, polished willow shaft with beautiful, black magpie feathers that shone greenish when the sunlight struck them just right.

"You know," Balsam said, "one of us could distract him while the other ran up that deer trail and skewered him with a dart."

The stranger apparently heard Balsam's comment. He calmly unlaced his new deerhide pants, thumped his male organ as if to get it going and urinated off the lip of the Dream Cave. The stream broke into droplets as it fell, shimmering, into the meadow below. It splashed only a body's length from Horseweed's feet. He glared at the yellow sparkles on the grass.

Indignant, Balsam asked Horseweed, "What do you think that mangy dog will do? Do you think he'll attack the man that tries to climb the deer trail?"

In unison, both boys turned to appraise the animal. The dog had sat down on its haunches, one unfurred ear pricked, eyes steady upon them.

"Might," Horseweed granted. "But I'll dart it in the heart before it gets its jaws around your throat. Don't worry."

"*My* throat?"

The stranger let out a hoarse cry that froze them both in their tracks. He'd opened his arms to the sky again, as though greeting a long-lost loved one descending from the clouds.

Balsam squinted. "What'd he do that for?"

"How would I know?"

The stranger let out another cry, long and breathless, like Wolf on a blood trail. Then he shouted, "Go away, boys! I don't want you here. I don't want *anybody* here. Leave me alone!" Turning on his heel, he disappeared into the cave.

Horseweed swallowed the lump in his throat. "He's one loony old man. He's got to be the reason the mammoths have gone crazy. No telling what he's done to the Dream Cave. I'll bet he's defiled every sacred object in the place."

"Then we'd better get him out of there. Quick."

Movement caught Horseweed's eye, and he barely had time to scream "*Run!*" before the darts started zizzing past his ears. The stranger, back at the mouth of the cave, cast another and another dart. Horseweed raced for the trees, his pack flopping on his back, and dove headfirst into a mound of deadfall. Limbs cracked and showered him with splinters as he jostled to get behind a log from which he could safely peer back at the cave. Two more darts struck, twanging in the deadfall in front of his face.

Balsam crawled up beside him, eyes wide. "How can one man nock darts so quickly and still keep his aim?"

"He's good, all right."

Balsam nervously wet his lips. "Maybe . . . maybe he's not a man, Horseweed. Did you think of that? Maybe *he's* the ghost. Do you remember how Catchstraw said that ghosts wait for warm flesh?"

"Well, I wish he'd come down here and try to take mine. That way, I could dart him up close. But he doesn't seem any too anxious to get near us." Horseweed bent forward to peer through the weave of dead limbs. The stranger had vanished again. "I've got an idea."

"What?"

"See those big boulders on top of the pink cliff? The ones that hang out over the Dream Cave? Come on. We'll sleep on top of them tonight, then tomorrow morning—"

"On top of the rocks?" Balsam objected. "It'll be colder than an elk's hoof in winter up there! Why can't we sleep here in the meadow?"

Horseweed got on all fours and carefully began to crawl out of the deadfall. Twigs crackled with his every movement. "Well, you go right ahead. But in the dark, I won't be able to see well enough to dart that dog before it sinks its teeth into you."

The crimson twilight of the Moon-of-Blossoms had flushed the world with color. Tannin walked across the top of the bluff in a halo of pink light, heading toward the place where Lambkill stood. His older brother had a foot propped on a rock while he gazed out at the swollen, dirty river. The cool evening breeze flapped the fringes on his sleeves and pant legs. Far below, flecks of scarlet twinkled on the surface of the muddy water.

Tannin inhaled deeply, hoping that the strong scents of damp juniper and sage would ease his anxiety. Lambkill had grown progressively worse since Kestrel's escape. Tracking her through the rain had been very difficult. The painstaking process had frustrated Tannin, but Lambkill's rage seemed to feed on it. Every time that Lambkill had found a fringe from her dress hanging on a bush, or picked up a twig she'd broken in her flight, he'd peered at Tannin with glassy eyes, his face running with sweat.

Then this afternoon, when they'd discovered the places where the sage had been twisted out of the ground, Lambkill had gone ominously silent. He'd crisscrossed the area until he found the wing walls. Then he'd stalked down them and peered over the cliff at the tapir skeletons. He'd stood for a long while just staring, refusing to answer any questions that Tannin had asked.

After a full finger of time, Lambkill had started shaking uncontrollably. Frightened, Tannin had tried to help his brother, to get him to sit down, but Lambkill had roared and struck out with his fists, beating Tannin away. Only then did Tannin realize the terrible extent of his brother's fury.

"The quails are cooked," Tannin said.

Lambkill didn't even move. He kept his eyes focused on the churning river.

"Come and eat, Lambkill. We must eat and sleep. Tomorrow we'll get started early."

In a bare whisper, Lambkill said, "Do you see her?"

"Who?" Tannin frowned. He saw nothing but flocks of birds on the shore. A flurry of wings moved on the beach, their feathers reddish in the fading rays of dusk. Farther out in the water, fish jumped, hunting the insects that swarmed over the glistening surface. "Who, Lambkill?"

"My wife. There she is."

"Where?" Tannin searched the riverbank below.

Lambkill lifted an arm and pointed with a crooked finger. "Across the river. She's standing on the other side."

The translucent glow of evening illuminated the distant bluffs, but Tannin could barely make out the major copses of juniper trees on the highlands. He gave Lambkill a sideways glance. "She couldn't have crossed, Lambkill. The water has been too rough. And too cold. She'd never have made it in her condition."

"She's had the baby."

"She's had the— How do you know?"

Lambkill flared his nostrils, scenting the breeze. "I can smell the blood. She gave birth somewhere close by. We must tell people. Every village we come to, we'll sit down with the elders and tell them about Kestrel and her crime." He nodded vehemently. "Yes, and we'll offer great wealth to the man who catches her and brings her to us. You know how fast Traders move. Word will travel as though it were borne on the wings of Eagle. There will be so many eyes watching the trails that she'll never escape."

"Lambkill, I don't think—"

"You don't believe me about the baby? Come on. Come with me. Right now! *Come!*" Lambkill ordered. "I'll show you!" He took off at a dead run along the edge of the precipice. "This way!" he yelled when he found a game trail that led down to the river.

"Wait, Lambkill!" Tannin objected. "Our camp is up here. We can search tomorrow." Their quails would be gone by the time they returned, eaten by the first hungry animal that passed by.

Heedlessly, Lambkill sprinted down the steep path, leaving a thick cloud of dust in his wake. His heavy jowls bounced with the jolt of his stride. "Hurry! Come on!"

Tannin shook his head and slowly followed. The rain-storms had washed stones into the trail, making the footing precarious at best. The dim gleam of evening did not help. As color drained from the land, shapes that had been distinct only moments ago melted into each other. More than once, Tannin's moccasins slipped off an unseen stone and sent him groping for the rocky cliff to keep from toppling over the edge. Lambkill skidded and staggered but managed to reach the bottom without falling.

"Lambkill?" Tannin called. "Wait! Wait for me!"

But below, Lambkill trotted along the sandy shore at the base of the bluff. Tufts of green grass sprouted in the crevices, while pockets of reeds dotted the shore. Lambkill crouched to examine the needles of a scrawny juniper, then hurried on. Suddenly he broke into a run and vanished around the curve of a towering wall.

Tannin trotted warily behind. When he rounded the corner, he saw his brother scrambling up a narrow ledge that led to a cave—a black hole in the limestone that overlooked the river. An eerie shiver stalked up Tannin's spine. There was something about the place, about the roar of the river, which seemed so much louder here . . . This was no place for him . . . no place for ordinary men.

Lambkill shouted "Ha!" and fell to his knees beside a patch of grass. "Come see! I've found her trail!"

A flock of goldfinches that had been perching in a clump of reeds burst into a tumult of chirps and took wing. Tannin watched them soar upward. The way they circled high overhead, they resembled sunflower petals caught in a whirlwind.

"See? What did I tell you?" Lambkill said when Tannin knelt beside him. "See the way these blades are broken? She tore up two, maybe three, handfuls."

Tannin nodded. The blades of grass had clearly been ripped by a hand, not chewed off by grazing animals. Animals would have gnawed the blades evenly. These had jagged edges. He straightened and squinted up at the cave. From this angle, shadows cloaked the interior. Goose bumps like a thousand spiders' feet prickled across his skin. "Do you think she's still there?"

Lambkill snarled, "I already told you! She's on the other side of the river." Gravel screeched beneath his moccasins as he trotted up the incline toward the cave.

Forcing himself to ignore his premonition, Tannin ducked through the entry behind Lambkill—and gave a throttled cry. He stumbled over his feet trying to get out.

"What's the matter with you?" Lambkill snarled irritably.

"Don't you see them? Look!" Tannin pointed to the walls and roof, where strange beings loomed like overarching trees. The red paint had flaked and faded, but their long snouts remained clear. Bolts of lightning zigzagged from their mouths, aiming straight down at Tannin and Lambkill as though to skewer them like bugs. "This is a Power place, Lambkill! We should leave. These creatures—"

"Twins," Lambkill whispered huskily.

"What?"

The silver gleam of evening sheathed Lambkill's hand as he reached down to pick up two umbilical cords. Desiccated, they barely looked human. Lambkill clutched them tightly in his left fist. "She had twins," he repeated and squeezed his eyes closed. "Just like she said she would." For a long time, he didn't move.

Hesitantly, Tannin knelt and touched the pool of dried blood that caked the floor. Ridges of congealed tissue veined the mass. It felt icy cold. He quickly drew back his hand and wiped it on his dirty pant leg. Why had nothing disturbed the blood? Hungry animals should have already lapped up every trace. He glanced up at the ceiling again and a chill settled in his stomach. "Lambkill, let's go. I—"

"No. Not yet. Look."

Lambkill leaned sideways and picked up a strip of antelopehide dress. He carefully plucked a length of long black hair from the leather. "Yes," Lambkill whispered. "Kestrel was here."

Tannin looked around. More strands of hair were glued in the blood, and on the far right-hand side of the cave, a calf tapirhide rested. It had been rolled up and shoved against the wall, as though for the next person who might happen by and need it as a shield against the cold. The pack rats had already gnawed it. A scatter of bristly hair surrounded the hide. Why had the rats eaten the hide but stayed away from Kestrel's blood?

Did they sense the taint . . . the odor of incest about it?

"Twins run in our family, Tannin," Lambkill murmured. His eyes lifted to meet Tannin's, and a curious fire shone in their depths. Fumbling, Lambkill tucked the umbilicals into his shirt pocket, then crawled past Tannin to get outside.

Tannin followed him down onto the sandy shore, past several clots of reeds. Bats darted over their heads as they walked. To block the bite of the night wind, Tannin folded his arms across his chest. He wished for the camp fire that he knew had burned down to red coals on the bluff above. When would Lambkill see fit to return? What could he be thinking? Did he fear that the children were his after all? That Iceplant had lied to him? Tannin shook his head. Iceplant hadn't lied. He'd had no reason to. Why would—

Lambkill stopped suddenly. A cry tore from his throat as he sprinted toward a gnarled juniper tree, his gray hair flying. The tree hugged the base of the bluff.

"What is it?" Tannin called after him. "Where are you going?"

Far to the west, the crescent moon poked through a thin layer of clouds, and its light cast a milky veil over the beach. Tannin saw Lambkill put his foot on the lowest limb of the juniper and climb up into the branches to pull something down. It looked like a small, dead animal.

"Lambkill?" Tannin bit his lip, his legs gone suddenly weak as he stepped cautiously forward. "Lambkill, what did you find?"

Moonlight coated Lambkill's tormented face as he drew a deep breath, then let it go. The wrinkles around his mouth pulled taut. He held the dead animal to his chest and made a wrenching sound. Tears traced lines down his withered cheeks as he carried his bundle out to the water's edge and knelt in the wet sand.

Tannin followed, calling, "Lambkill?"

"*She killed my son!*" he wailed as he rocked back and forth. "My son. My little boy. She *murdered* him!"

Tannin crouched and saw the tiny body that Lambkill held to his breast. His knees buckled. He braced a hand and eased down to the sand. The corpse had shriveled and turned brown. Worse, the birds had been at it. The boy's eyes had been pecked to empty sockets. One foot had been chewed off, leaving a ragged stump. So many raccoons hunted the shore, or maybe a hungry cat had carried the child into the tree.

Gently, Tannin put a hand on Lambkill's shoulder. "It wasn't your son, Lambkill. It was Iceplant's. It's better that the boy's dead. If he had lived—"

Lambkill threw his head back and a horrible shriek tore from his throat. Like a short-faced bear in rage, he dropped the baby on the beach and dove for Tannin, knocking him backward into the river. Icy liquid flooded over Tannin's face and into his lungs. Before he could rise, Lambkill's fingers tightened around his throat, holding him down.

Panicked, Tannin gripped his brother's wrists and tried to break his hold. He bucked and twisted, but Lambkill straddled him and threw all of his weight into the effort, roaring like a madman.

Tannin didn't want to hurt his brother, but when Lambkill bashed a knee into Tannin's stomach, trying to force him to release the breath he held in his lungs, Tannin had no choice. Ruthlessly, he kicked out, twisting onto his side so he could repeatedly slam a knee into Lambkill's groin. When Lambkill gasped and loosened his hold, Tannin shoved him backward into the river.

Panting for breath, Tannin staggered to his feet. He managed to walk three body lengths from the water before he slumped to the sand. His throat burned and his lungs ached. The terror of the moment drained him like the grit-filled water that trickled down his chilled flesh. Stunned, he couldn't speak. His eyes remained riveted on his brother, who was thrashing the water white like a crazy fish in the shallows.

Water cascaded from Lambkill's buckskin clothing as he reeled to his feet in the river. His eyes looked haunted, disoriented, as though he were living a nightmare.

Without giving Tannin a second look, he marched onto the shore and picked up the dead baby. Cradling it to his breast, he slogged upriver through the shallows. His steps sent silver-crested waves undulating outward. He began to sob, a soft, suffocating series of sounds.

"Blessed Above-Old-Man," Tannin prayed as he brought up his knees and braced his elbows on them. Confusion and fear made a sour brew in his belly. The chill of the water and the frigid air barely compared to the cold realization in his soul. "He's my brother. But I—I don't understand what's happening to him. It must be the shock. The pain. I don't know what to do."

"Man? Man, where are you? Where are you! I need you! This is a terrible thing. You know that one of my souls will be tied to that body for four more days! What will happen if that mean man calls up my fleshly soul?"

The Man answered, "Ah, then you will be very fortunate."

"Fortunate! How is that possible? I cannot be born again without both of my souls intact. You know that. This will deny me a real life!"

The Man laughed in an affectionate way. "Just as bees are driven away by smoke, an existence of ease drives fear from the soul and takes from humans their ability to be kind. Pray, Boy, pray very hard that Lambkill tries to summon up your fleshly soul."

"But it will tear me apart! It will kill my greatest hope!"

"Yes," the Man responded softly. A faint sparkle, like a sprinkling of stardust, rained down through the blackness. Like glistening tears, it coated the Boy.

The Man finished: "If that happens, you must give thanks to Above-Old-Man for such a great gift."

Nine

At dawn, Horseweed stepped through the boulders high above the Dream Cave. Legend said that the Ice Ghosts had once waged a terrible battle here, throwing rocks and lightning bolts at one another until they had killed half of their tribe.

The remnant had fled far to the north, where it still lived. As Horseweed looked around at the boulders that ranged in size from the height of three men to head-sized rocks, he believed it. Gravel filled in the spaces between the rocks, washed there by the spring melt and the summer rains. The view was spectacular; the distant peaks of the Mammoth Mountains thrust up in glacial splendor to catch the pink-orange rays of morning light in granite and ice.

To the west, Mother Ocean lay obscured by a low white fog that covered her shining face like snow. Patches of fog also drifted through the dense fir and pine stands that wreathed the meadow below.

Horseweed stepped cautiously to the edge of the cliff, aware of the slick frost that coated the rock, and glanced down toward the Dream Cave. The two-hundred-hand drop made his heart flutter. A man could fall to his death and have plenty of time to regret it before he hit bottom. Puffs of golden clouds clustered around him, wispy and ethereal, almost close enough that it seemed he could reach out and grasp a handful.

The stranger apparently hadn't awakened yet. At least he hadn't come out to the ledge of the cave. Horseweed kept his atlatl clutched in his fist just in case. After yesterday, he wasn't sure the stranger couldn't cast straight up.

Balsam stood on a rock in the distance, next to a scraggly, half-dead fir tree. He had his hands propped on his hips as he surveyed the morning. Great glaciers shimmered between the purple peaks, reflecting the dawn like the finest polished abalone shell. In the morning sunlight, they seemed to burn. Around the fringes of the glaciers, spring's firstborn wildflowers created wreaths of blue and yellow where they had popped up in the wrinkled and humped lines of ice-piled earth and rock.

"It's about time you got here," Balsam called. Wind flapped the two long black braids draping the skinny chest of his buckskin shirt.

"I was out hunting food. You should be glad!"

"We don't have time for food! Put your pack and atlatl down next to mine, over there by that snowberry bush. I've been watching the stranger for a whole hand of time."

"What? Where is he?" Horseweed demanded. Sweat had glued his black bangs to his forehead. He shrugged out of his pack and went to drop it atop Balsam's, then laid his quiver and atlatl down. He'd only managed to dart a fat squirrel, but he'd been looking forward to roasting it. He glanced at his pack forlornly. "I looked down. I didn't see anyone in the cave."

"He thinks he's being clever." Balsam pointed down at the far western side of the Dream Cave. "He's hiding just inside."

Horseweed scrambled up the gritty side of the boulder and squinted. Just back from the mouth of the cave, a tiny fire lit the shadows. A dark shape hunched beside it. It did look like a man sitting there. Horseweed sniffed the wind. The rich flavor of roasting meat caressed his nostrils. "Smells like he's keeping himself well-fed on those sacred deer."

"Smells more like pack rat cooking to me," Balsam said and sniffed the air.

"Ho! Stranger!" Horseweed called. "You! In the cave!"

Balsam leaned over the edge of the cliff and shouted, "It's us! We're planning on getting you out of that cave . . . one way or another. Now, be smart and leave, before you force us to kill you!"

A hoarse cry ripped through the morning stillness, causing the birdsongs to die. Balsam's mouth hung open, but his eyes moved, following the echo of the scream as it bounced around the mountains.

"Blessed Father Sun, there he goes again," Balsam said.

Horseweed ground his teeth as he watched the shadow by the fire. It looked taller now, as though the stranger had stood up. *But it might just be the way the sun is hitting the cave.* Horseweed jumped down from the boulder and began searching the rocks until he found a log about fifteen hands long. "Balsam, come here. Help me with this. We'll get him out of there."

Balsam frowned. "What are we going to do with that? Roll it off on top of him?"

"No. We're going to use it as a lever."

"A lever? What for?"

"To pry the rocks loose. Now, hurry it up. I want you to take the small end." When Balsam had grasped the log, Horseweed continued, "All right, now wedge your end under that medium-sized boulder at the very edge of the cliff."

Balsam shoved the end beneath the rock and turned to squint at Horseweed. His young face had a quizzical expression. "Are you sure this is a good idea? I mean—"

"We're trying to kill him, aren't we?"

"Sure, but—"

"Then stop complaining and start pushing." Horseweed flopped down on the big end of the log and pushed with all his might. The pink tip of his tongue stuck out of the right side of his mouth. The boulder teetered. "Help me, Balsam! We'll show that stranger that he can't just dance in here and take over one of our sacred places."

Balsam scampered up beside Horseweed and threw his weight into the effort, too.

"Push!"

They sweated and grunted until finally the boulder groaned and tumbled over the precipice. Horseweed and Balsam ran to the edge to watch. Balsam jerked when the boulder crashed thunderously on the lip of the cave, bashed its way down the talus slope and rolled out into the center of the meadow. The mangy dog that had been lying at the base of the cliff shot into the trees with its tail between its legs, howling like a lost soul. They heard a crash in the forest, followed by snarling and yipping.

"Well, will you look at that," Horseweed said.

"What?"

"The fire in the cave is still going." Orange flickers glittered through the veil of dust that had risen.

Balsam crowded forward to peer over the edge. "That means he's probably still alive. At least he's stopped that inhuman wailing. It gives me a stomachache. Let's shove some more rocks over."

They hunkered down, wedged the log again and heaved. This time five boulders broke loose and fell at once. Staggering to their feet, they watched them sail downward. The boulders struck the lip of the cave one after another and shook the mountain like the Quaking Earth Spirits that lived under the ground. Dust belched upward in a blinding gray cloud, concealing the cave altogether.

"Where is he?" Balsam asked. "Do you see him? He ought to be coming out after that one."

"I can't see anything."

The glowing face of Father Sun rose higher above the eastern peaks, and an orange gleam possessed the dissipating dust. As it started to clear, Horseweed frowned. Half of the lip of the Dream Cave had broken off and slid down the talus slope. It rested in great chunks at the bottom.

"Fire's out," Balsam noted. "You think he's dead?"

"I don't know, but he's sure deaf by now." Horseweed got down on all fours and crawled to the very edge of the cliff to study the devastation. An avalanche filled in half of the cave's entry. The pounding of the boulders must have loosened the weathered roof and rattled it right off. Anyone inside would have been buried in the dirt and debris, maybe splattered across the walls by flying stone. "Come here, Balsam. Look at this."

Balsam slid forward on his belly, and a slow smile crept over his face. "He's got to be dead after that. Should we go scrape up what's left of him and take him back to Catchstraw?"

Horseweed thought about that. Might be a good thing to do. That way, Catchstraw could Sing the stranger's foul soul into the rocks, where it would stay locked forever. No telling what mayhem such an evil soul could cause if it were left to wander the mountains.

Horseweed nodded. "Let's do it." He rose, dusted himself off and headed for their packs and weapons. Sunlight glittered with blinding intensity from the flecks of mica in the granite boulders. Balsam followed at a trot, grinning.

"We'll be heroes. Did you think of that? People will forever Sing stories about Balsam and Horseweed, the great—"

Before they could reach the snowberry bush where their atlatls lay, a growl erupted and that mangy dog bounded from behind a boulder, its few remaining hairs sticking straight up on its back.

"Look out!" Horseweed yelled. "Run for it!"

They took off like the wind, with the dog chasing them. It snapped at their hands and heels while Horseweed and Balsam leaped deadfall and shoved each other around boulders.

"Head for that dead tree!" Horseweed shouted.

The dead fir thrust black branches into the sky just beyond the slide of boulders. Horseweed managed to shinny up it first. He climbed as high as he could and heard Balsam breathing hard behind him. Horseweed sank down atop a limb. The dog stood on its hind legs with its forepaws braced on the trunk of the tree. It had an odd howl, like a dire wolf with a fresh kill. Balsam had perched on the limb below Horseweed, low enough that if the dog jumped, it might be able to nip off the toes of his moccasins. A swallow went down Balsam's throat, and he let out a choked whisper.

"What did you say?" Horseweed asked. "Have you got an idea?"

"Idea?" Balsam shouted. He craned his neck to look up. "No! I haven't—"

"Well," a cool, deep voice said from down the trail. "If I were you, boys, I'd get down from that tree pretty quick and start digging out the Dream Cave before Catchstraw sees it."

"Who said that?" Horseweed hugged the trunk of the fir and hoisted himself up a little higher to see better. The limb on which he stood creaked and cracked; bits of bark flitted through the sunlight as they plunged to the ground. "Answer me! Who *are* you?"

The man came strolling up the trail, his long white hair blowing about his shoulders. The seashells on his hide shirt glittered as he folded his arms and leaned against one of the boulders. "You're young Horseweed, aren't you? From Otter Clan Village?"

Horseweed shifted on the limb. It took a moment before he could fit those craggy features into his memory. When he did, sickness roiled in his stomach. What had they done . . . almost done? "*S-Sunchaser*, when did . . . did your hair turn *white?*"

"Sunchaser?" Balsam squeaked, casting a quaking glance at the stranger. "You mean . . ." He swallowed so hard that it sounded like a tree frog's croak. "We're going to die . . . be turned into liverworts . . . leeches . . . toads."

"What are you doing up here, bothering me?" Sunchaser asked.

"My grandfather sent us to find you."

"Oxbalm?" Sunchaser straightened. "Why? What's happened?"

"The mammoths are running into the sea! They're dying by the dozens," Balsam piped up. "Grandfather thinks Mammoth Above is trying to warn us about some terrible thing that's going to happen."

Sunchaser's black eyes took on a haunted gleam.

The dog backed down from the tree and silently padded past Sunchaser. When it hit the trail, it broke into a lope and sent up a chilling howl.

"Yes," Sunchaser murmured. "I know I've no choice, Helper." As though very tired, he shoved away from the boulder and turned to follow. His legs moved like an old man's, sluggish and reluctant.

"Helper?" Balsam asked when Sunchaser had disappeared from sight.

"Is that dog his *Spirit Helper?*" He turned to peer incredulously at Horseweed. "He has a *mangy* Spirit Helper?"

"Who cares? Come on, Balsam!" Horseweed yelled. He jumped down from the tree and charged for the snowberry bush where his pack and atlatl lay.

Ten

Kestrel crawled out of the bitterly cold river on her hands and knees, weeping, shivering uncontrollably. No pain she had ever experienced, including childbirth, equaled this. Her body had become the enemy, on the verge of failing her. "J-just a little . . . farther."

She'd picked this place—had started aiming for it—a hand of time ago, because a series of shallow rock shelters scalloped the face of the first river terrace here. Cloud Girl cried in hunger on Kestrel's back, but Kestrel could do nothing about that now. The brutal cold had killed all sensation in her hands and legs. She could not find the thong of the rabbit-fur sack, because she could not feel it.

She forced herself to stand up, and her legs went out from under her as though they were dead meat. Cloud Girl shrieked, and Kestrel hung her head and sobbed wearily.

"Please, Spirits, help me!"

Even if her hands had frozen, she could still run. But her legs . . . her legs! Panic held her riveted for a brief period before she marshaled enough courage to get on her hands and knees again. She had to reach the closest rock shelter. If she didn't, she would die here. The cold would leach into her soul, and her heart would stop.

She crawled, shivering so violently that her teeth clattered like gourd rattles. Body length by body length, she made her way across the rounded cobbles, strips of sand and thick mats of brown grass.

The rock shelter wasn't much, only a place where the river had undercut the sandstone ledge. Eight hands high and ten hands across, it sank about fifteen hands into the terrace. An old pack rat nest filled a wide crack on the southern wall. *Firewood . . . if I can ever make my hands work.*

Kestrel slid as far back as she could to avoid the shrieking wind that raced down the river channel. Just being out of the gale relieved her. She braced her shivering shoulders against the rough rear wall and let her head fall forward. Outside, a transparent, ash-colored sheen spread across the sky. The most brilliant of the Star People already sparkled on the eastern horizon. "Please . . . Above-Old-Man, let the night be warm."

Kestrel had to lift her knees with her hands and position them so that she could hug them to her chest. Tremors shook her so violently that she cried like a little girl. When had she been so helpless and lost?

Long ago, when she'd been nine summers old, she'd seen a woman named Yuccabud fall through the ice of a frozen pond. Before anyone could reach Yuccabud, she'd gone under the water and stayed there for a perilously long time. After her husband had finally pulled her out and started her breathing again, he'd thrown off his clothes—right there in the icy willows—and hugged his wife to his naked body to warm her. She'd been shivering like Kestrel was now. And Yuccabud had lived.

The thought encouraged Kestrel.

She had regained some sensation in her hands—they had begun to ache dully. She used her right arm like a stick, slipping it through the leather thong of Cloud Girl's sack and tugging it around to her chest. By hunching into a ball, she found that she could pull the sack over her head. Her pack, with its supply of tools, fire sticks and dried tapir meat, made a support for Cloud Girl's head, propping her up so that she could see the river beyond the shelter. Her daughter stopped crying to watch the birds swooping and diving over the roiling brown water. Hoarse caws echoed through the evening.

Kestrel rubbed her cheek over the rabbit-fur sack, feeling for dampness. The bottom of the sack was saturated, but most of the upper part felt dry. "Are you all right, baby?"

She put her cheek on top of Cloud Girl's fuzzy head, moved it down the side of her daughter's face. The baby's smooth skin radiated warmth. Blessed warmth. Cloud Girl had started chewing on her fist. Her eyes were bright, despite the tears.

Fearing that her own condition might worsen as night deepened, Kestrel slipped her pack off of the rabbit-fur sack. She used her teeth to work the laces loose, then sifted through the contents for her fire sticks. When she found them soaked, her tears fled as though they'd never been. Cold terror filled her. If she couldn't start a fire—

Kestrel scrambled around Cloud Girl and crawled to the huge pack rat nest. Pack rats scoured the countryside for any kinds of sticks they could carry to their nests, even paddles of spiny cactus. Then they packed them into crevices. This nest filled a floor-to-ceiling crack in the rock, which spanned the width of Kestrel's shoulders. She couldn't tell how deep the nest extended into the rock, but she guessed that it went as far as ten hands. Her numb fingers fumbled aside lesser woods until she found a good hard stick of chokecherry. Above-Old-Man must have heard her prayers, for a beaver had chewed it down to a point. Next, she selected an old, punky slab of pine.

Using her hands like tongs, she picked up her pieces of wood and hurried back to her pack. Shivers racked her again, and she blinked, already having forgotten what she was supposed to be doing. Body-numbing cold did that—it made a person even forget who she was.

She made another trip to the pack rat nest, this time finding a knot of long, dry grass—just the sort she would need for tinder, assuming that she could keep her head long enough to produce an ember.

Cloud Girl had started crying again, loudly and breathlessly.

Kestrel chose a natural depression in the floor near the back wall. Shifting so that her shoulders blocked the wind that trickled into the shelter, she shielded the kindling while she laid out her newly found fire sticks. She put her feet on either end of the cracked pine slab, then placed the point of the chokecherry stick in the middle. She used her chest—wincing at the pain it gave her sternum—to press a dimple into the pine. Not much of a dimple, but enough to steady the beaver-chewed chokecherry in place. She begin spinning the chokecherry stick like a drill between her aching palms. Spinning it as fast as she could.

The motion was awkward. Several times she fumbled. But soon she had bored a tiny hole, and frayed wood shavings had built up like fine dust around it. She continued spinning. The stick dug deeper, and friction began to heat the pine.

She'd reached the threshold of endurance when a thin trace of blue smoke finally rose.

Her fingers had gained some flexibility. She could touch her thumb to her index finger now, but the pain of it went clear to her bones.

You don't have time to hurt, Kestrel. You've got to have fire. She spun the stick faster. When the shavings in the hole began to glow, she quickly dumped them into the frayed grasses she'd retrieved from the pack rat's nest and blew gently. She had to repeat the process four times before the tinder caught. The grass curled blackly, and flickers of flame crackled to life. Kestrel fed them twigs and bit her lip anxiously as the fire hovered at the edge of death. When one of the larger twigs caught, she let out a muted cry of joy. She gathered more wood from the nest and gradually added larger and larger pieces until she had a good blaze going.

She longed to slump right there in front of the fire and sleep. "Not yet."

She completely demolished the pack rat nest and used the sticks, dried juniper branches and small stones to make a wall in front of the fire. It stretched only six hands long and four hands high, but it shielded the blaze and created a tiny refuge for herself and Cloud Girl.

She brought her daughter and her pack into the niche and sank back against the stone wall. The warmth of the flames made her shivering worse, but this pain felt wonderful. Cloud Girl wailed and squealed, waving her tiny fists urgently.

"Oh, baby, just let me sit for a little while."

But Cloud Girl's insistent voice forced Kestrel to untie the front of her drenched dress and lift her daughter to her breast. The baby must have been getting some milk, because she quieted immediately, or perhaps it was just the comfort of the nipple that soothed her.

Kestrel reached into her pack and pulled out a long piece of dried tapir. The meat had gotten wet, but she ate and ate until her stomach cramped. Food would help her body to heat itself.

As night thickened beyond the shelter, the tawny light of the fire seemed a huge blaze. None of the Star People could compete with it. They had vanished. The wall of sticks and branches would diffuse the light, but the glow would be evident from across the river. And Kestrel couldn't afford to care about it. She had to get warm. As she had kicked her feet in the bitter water, she'd dreamed of building a fire so huge that it roasted her bones. If she could just sleep warm for one night—just one night—maybe she would be all right.

She yawned and shivered. When the fire burned down, she pulled sticks from the brush wall and added them to the blaze. Cloud Girl fell asleep with Kestrel's nipple in her mouth.

Kestrel rearranged herself so she could lower the infant to her lap, with the soaked foot of the rabbit-fur sack closest to the flames. It would be dry by morning. Oh, what she would have given for a dry dress. For anything dry to wrap around her shoulders. A musty old buffalo hide would have been magnificent.

She stared at the flickers of flame, and her eyes closed. Racking shivers had ceased to possess her and now came at only sporadic intervals. Her thoughts rambled, their shapes and colors softening like golden autumn trees in the hazy veil of night. Then memories crept up on her, stealing through her soul as subtly as the foul scent of bear on a still, spring morning. . . .

"*Lambkill!*" Kestrel spun around as he burst through the lodge door like a warrior on a raid. He had his war club clutched in a tight fist. His chest rose and fell as though he were suffocating. "What . . . what's wrong?" Terrified, Kestrel backed up against the rear wall.

"Wrong?" he replied in a frighteningly soft voice. He took a step forward, shaking with rage. Sweat poured from his heavy jowls. "Where were you at noon today?"

"At noon?" Kestrel tried to remember. She shook her head. "I—I was at Desert Tortoise's lodge. She asked me to come and paint—"

He leaped forward and brought his war club down on her shoulder. She screamed. The force of the blow sent her toppling to the dirt floor.

"I *hate* Desert Tortoise! You know I do. Why did you go there? I hate her whole family!"

Kestrel threw up her hands to fend off his repeated blows, and Lambkill changed his aim, deliberately smashing at her wrist and fingers until she shrieked in agonized terror. "Lambkill, stop it! Please, stop!"

"You like to paint, eh? I'll make sure you never paint again!"

"*No*, Lambkill! Please!" She hid her hands in her armpits, and he slammed his club into her chest and over the top of her head, trying to force her to defend herself with her hands.

Kestrel fell forward onto the floor, hiding her hands beneath her, and he took out his rage on her spine and legs. She wailed shrilly.

In the village, people yelled, and she could hear their steps running closer. Lambkill shouted, "Stay back! Don't come near! You hear me? She's *my* wife!"

Voices hushed. Steps retreated. But a few people continued to talk in low tones. In rage and fury, Lambkill roared, "Get away from my lodge!" The murmuring went silent, too.

Kestrel scooted back, getting as far from him as she could. Her hands burned. Dizziness made her unsteady, but she knew she had to stay awake. If she didn't, he would crush her fingers, one by one. A pathetic voice in her soul cried, *But maybe he'll love you if you're a cripple. Maybe it would be better* . . . She wept silently. She wanted him to love her. But she *needed* to paint. What had she done to anger him so? She had clan obligations to fulfill. Desert Tortoise was her cousin!

Lambkill whirled and glared at her. "I don't ever want you to go to Desert Tortoise's lodge again. *Never*. If you do—"

"Why, Lambkill?" she sobbed. "She asked me to come. Why can't I?"

Lambkill lunged for her, dragged her to her feet and twisted her arm until she cried out. "Get out of my lodge, woman. Get out and never come back!"

As fast as Antelope, she'd crossed the crowded village, burst into Tannin's lodge and thrown herself into Calling Crane's arms, bawling hysterically, "He *hates* me! He tried to *break* my hands! Why would he do that? Why, Calling Crane? All I did was go to my cousin's lodge to paint her new baby's cradle board! Why would that anger Lambkill . . . why?"

Kestrel jerked awake, panting into the darkness. The mutterings of the river kept her entranced for a moment. Voices? No, no. Water. Just the sound of the river.

The fire had burned down. Cloud Girl still slept in her lap, peaceful, oblivious. The baby's head had fallen sideways, and she had sucked on the fur of her hood. Gray and brown hairs stuck to her little mouth.

Shaking, Kestrel added sticks to the coals. Flames crackled and spat. The rough walls of the shelter gleamed amber. She kept her gaze focused on the darkness beyond. Her fingers crept spiderlike, reaching into her pack for the tapir-bone stiletto. She brought it back and rested it on her knee.

Owls hooted as they ghosted over the shore on silent wings in search of mice or pygmy rabbits that had secreted themselves in patches of willow. The wind had died. Nothing moved except the perpetual rush of the river. Yet the pounding of Kestrel's heart made the shelter seem to quake.

At last, Dawn Child grayed the eastern horizon enough to illuminate the shrubs and rocks. Kestrel fed Cloud Girl, gathered her things . . . and ran.

Eleven

Oxbalm pulled Sumac's wrinkled hand into his lap and held it gently. They huddled together beneath a mammoth-calf hide, watching the beginnings of the Mammoth Spirit Dance. They had waited a week, hoping that Sunchaser would arrive, but when he hadn't, Oxbalm could delay the Dance no longer. People had been filtering in from all over the countryside, from villages that sat several days' walk away.

Thick fog billowed in off the ocean. In the past hand of time, it had started to freeze on the trees, turning them into glittering giants. It was common for this time of cycle. One never knew what Spring Girl would do to trick people into being lazy, thinking that warm weather had come at last.

Icicles hung like pointed claws from the ridgepoles of the lodges that clustered in the trees and spread out across the beach.

The Mammoth Spirit Dance lodge, which they had constructed from eight of the dead mammoths' hides, looked especially magnificent. It was three body lengths wide and seven long and painted with scenes of mammoths on every available space: mammoths grazing placidly in spring-green meadows; mammoth calves lying almost hidden in a field of wild roses; bull mammoths in rut, locking tusks and pushing each other back and forth. On the door flap, the face of a cow mammoth with fiery-red eyes stared at each passerby. Strings of shells scalloped the roof line, and collections of mammoth vertebrae, like bizarre one-eyed heads, draped the ends of the ridgepoles that stuck out from the lodges. They rattled and clacked in time with the wind.

Warmth built in Oxbalm's bony old chest. On holy days, the world always seemed brighter, more beautiful.

"Look at all the people," Sumac said. Her eyes gleamed as she gazed out across the plaza.

"Yes, this is the biggest Dance we've ever had."

Villagers from nearby settlements had been arriving all day, forming a noisy throng in the plaza. They milled around, or sat down when they could find a dry space beneath the towering fir trees. The light of the moon shone weakly through the fog, but it illuminated the joy on people's faces. A mixture of great hope and great fear animated the low voices.

"I pray that Sunchaser gets here before the Dance is over," Oxbalm said. "I overheard one of the women from Robinwing Village say that she and her family had walked for four days straight to be at this Dance. They expected Sunchaser to greet them when they entered the village. Like he used to. Do you remember? When he first started the Dance? Those were great days, indeed."

"Of course I remember," Sumac replied. Her ears and nose glowed red in the bitter cold. Her withered lips had shrunk over her toothless gums, and she spoke as though her cold mouth wouldn't work quite right. "It's those memories that have made me start wondering about Sunchaser."

"What do you mean?"

Sumac's brow furrowed. "Sunchaser used to *feel* it when something was wrong. Remember? He used to show up out of nowhere to offer his help because he'd had a Dream that someone in the village needed him."

"Yes," Oxbalm sighed. "I do remember. Like the time Berryleaf canoed too far out to sea and got lost. Sunchaser came down from the high mountains to tell us that Berryleaf had called to him for help in a Dream."

"Yes, he did. Sunchaser sat right out there on the beach and Dreamed the dolphins and whales in so he could ask them to go find Berryleaf and lead him home. Remember? Berryleaf returned the next afternoon. He came canoeing in amidst a school of cackling dolphins!"

"His wife and children were so happy." Oxbalm laughed, remembering.

Sumac stared unblinking toward Mother Ocean. In the moonlit mist, the Mother's dark face glimmered. "I wonder why Sunchaser didn't Dream about the mammoths running into the sea. Has he lost the ability to Dream? Is that why he no longer comes to the Dances? He's afraid to?"

Oxbalm tucked the hide more securely beneath his chin. "I don't think it's fear of the Dance, or of us. He knows, as we all do, that we must Dance to send prayers to Mammoth Above, asking her forgiveness for our greed, begging her to stop taking her children from the world. These latest drownings must have been guided by Mammoth Above. She's still punishing us for overhunting her children. We must Dance to appease her wrath, before all the mammoths are gone. Sunchaser would be here if he could come. He probably has felt the wrongness. But he's been Healing in the mountain villages. That's all."

Unconsciously, his eyes strayed to the beach, where thirty-four mammoth skeletons lay, keeping silent watch on the proceedings. The whitened bones appeared and disappeared as the mist swirled.

Sumac's fingers dug into his palm suddenly. "Look!"

Sounds of flute music eddied through the fog, the notes clear and pure, like the sweet chirps of chickadees on spring mornings.

A sharp yip.

The crowd hushed and turned.

At the edge of the forest, Humpbacked Woman stood. She stamped forward slowly, one step at a time, the trunk on her mask swaying from side to side, while she grunted in the deep, breathy way of Mammoth. A lane opened for her through the crowd. She dipped her head toward the children in the lane, looking hard at each one for a moment before continuing on. Giggles and a few horrified cries rent the air. One little girl shrieked and scrambled to hide behind her mother's legs as Humpbacked Woman neared.

Oxbalm smiled. Humpbacked Woman wore a fragment of mammoth hide drawn over a hoop on her back and adorned with white circlets of mammoth ivory. His people believed that inside of the hump there were billowing black rain clouds and all manner of seeds—the seeds of the plants that had first grown across this land when Wolfdreamer brought the People up through the World Navel. Humpbacked Woman's Dance sowed restlessness and the yearning for harmony in the human soul, just as rain sowed seeds. She stamped into the center of the plaza, and the clear notes of the flutes gave way to the deep, rhythmic beat of a single pot drum. Finally the music of bird-bone whistles, split-stick clappers and turtle-shell and deer-hoof rattles joined in.

Oxbalm exhaled, and his breath formed a white cloud before him. He watched it twinkle in the firelight until it melted into the body of fog. Soon the other Dancers would rise and begin Singing the mammoths back into the world. Over the next four nights, the entire village would participate, begging Above-Old-Man to guide the people, to help them return the world to its former purity so that the mammoths could come back and live in harmony with humans.

Reverently, Oxbalm whispered, "We begin."

As the beat of the pot drum boomed from the sea cliffs, Humpbacked Woman's voice lifted—clear and powerful— calling the people to join the Dance.

> *In beauty come.*
> *In beauty come.*
> *Come to us trumpeting!*
> *With the zigzag lightning shooting from your trunk,*
> *Come to us trumpeting!*
> *With your leggings of dark cloud.*
> *With your eyes on fire.*
> *With the earth shaking beneath your feet, come to*
> *us trumpeting!*
> *In beauty come.*
> *In beauty come.*
> *Come to us trumpeting.*

At least fifty Dancers, maybe more, ducked out through the doorway of the sacred lodge and stretched their arms to the sky. The seashell-tipped fringes on their long white buckskin shirts clicked as they ghosted across the village in a shuffling gait to form a big circle around the fire. When the circle filled up, Humpbacked Woman trumpeted with all her heart and began a spin that took her out of the circle. In her place, Catchstraw appeared, his gray-streaked black hair and narrow face shining, his white mammothhide shirt pearled over with the tiniest, most colorful seashells.

"Clasp hands!" he called. "Empty your hearts of anger. We're preparing the way for Beauty to return to our world. With Spirit Powers, I make you walk . . . I make you walk, with Spirit Powers!"

The soggy moccasins of the Dancers began to stamp the ground in unison. A dull roar rose on the shimmering wings of fog.

"Who's that?" Sumac asked, jerking her chin toward a man approaching them from the midst of the crowd.

"Isn't that the Trader from Big Horn Village? What was his name? You know, the new Trader who's been working the trading trails for the past two cycles."

"Nighthawk? Is that him? I never liked him."

"You've seen him only three times in your whole life. How can you know that?"

Sumac sighed. "Once would have been enough. Women know people better than men do. That's why we lead the clans, arrange marriages, decide punishments for wrongdoers. People are our responsibility."

Oxbalm scowled at her, then lifted a hand as the youth approached. No more than twenty summers, Nighthawk had already gained a reputation for bringing exotic goods to trade. Medium-sized, he had a lean face with a hooked nose. His black braids stuck out from beneath the furry brim of his beaver hat. He carried a half-chewed piece of mammoth meat in his hand.

"Oxbalm and Sumac!" Nighthawk strode up and clasped each of their hands in turn. "It gladdens my soul to see you both. Sumac, Father Sun has touched your face! You are as beautiful as—"

"As what? Sunburned hide? A dried-up carcass?" She gestured sternly with her hand. "Sit down, boy, and tell us what news you've brought."

Nighthawk chuckled and dropped to the ground beside Oxbalm. His eyes surveyed the Dancers as they bobbed and Sang around the fire. "I've never seen such a huge gathering," he said. "But then, everybody's been scared by the mammoths running into the sea." He shook his head in dismay. "Nobody thought that Sunchaser would miss this Dance. Bad luck, you know. Especially with this being the fourth Dance he's missed." Nighthawk rearranged himself, crossing his legs at the ankles and leaning back. "But it looks to be a very good Dance. Is that Catchstraw out there leading the Dancers?"

Oxbalm sighed glumly. "It is."

"What's wrong? Look at him! Twisting and leaping. I've never seen so much enthusiasm in a Dancer."

Oxbalm narrowed his eyes at Catchstraw. The Dreamer had a knack for drawing attention to himself. Who could avoid noticing his show? He jumped and squirmed like a fish on a hook. If a person's gaze roamed anywhere near the Dance circle, it would have to land on Catchstraw. The realization embarrassed Oxbalm. Sunchaser always conducted the Dance with great dignity and reverence. But Catchstraw? What a fool he was.

"So tell us the news." Sumac shifted around to face Nighthawk. Her short gray braid glistened in the red glare of the fire.

Nighthawk lifted his piece of mammoth meat and sank his teeth into it, pulled off a hunk and chewed contentedly. "It's hard to know where to begin. Everybody's complaining about the scarcity of mammoth ivory. But what can I do? I can't get it. On the other hand, I've been trading much tar from the Bubbling Tar Pits south of here. Everybody's using it underneath the sinew when they tie on their dart points. It lasts much longer than pine pitch. And . . ." he paused to take another bite of his meat, then gestured with the gnawed remains ". . . I'm sure you've heard about the Evil Spirits who have brought diseases to the mountains, but a new illness broke out last week. Terrible, too. People are bleeding from the mouth, raving in delirium. Lots of deaths, I heard."

"Where?" Sumac asked.

Nighthawk waved a hand. "It started at Sleeping Thunder Village, but I think the Spirits have flown all the way to Daughter's Birth Village by now."

Sumac exchanged a horrified look with Oxbalm. The illness was moving very fast to have traveled through six villages in a week. It was frightening. "Were you there, Nighthawk? Did you see what was happening?"

"Not me." Nighthawk shook his head. "I never travel to

sick villages. I knew a Trader once who was killed, yes, *killed*, because people believed he was possessed by the Evil Spirits of the diseases. You know, they thought he was carrying the Spirits from one village to the next. I'm a new Trader. I can't take such chances."

Oxbalm adjusted the calf hide over his shoulders, twining his fingers in the long hair and tugging it up to shield his right ear from the cold bite of the fog. "That must be why Sunchaser isn't here. Have you heard anything about him? Is he still in the mountains?"

"Still at Brushnut, I think."

"He's been there for a long time, then."

"Yes." Nighthawk nodded. His beaked nose caught the gleam of the fire when he peered directly at Oxbalm. Grease smeared his mouth. "The news from Brushnut is very bad. Someone told me that dozens had died."

"Dozens?" Sumac's shrunken old lips quivered. "Are you sure? So many?"

Nighthawk sank his teeth into the last of his meat and chewed it noisily. "That's the story traveling the trading trails."

Oxbalm squeezed Sumac's hand. She had relatives in Brushnut Village. Second cousins, whom she loved. "I'm sure they're all right," he said reassuringly. "When Horseweed and Balsam return, they'll bring news. Don't worry."

"Someone would have sent a runner if . . . if anything bad had happened to my cousins." As though in defense against the worry, Sumac shook her head, "I can't stand to think about it. It hurts too much. What other news is there, Nighthawk?"

"Well, there's always raiding. The Ugly Sloth Clan and the Red Dog Moon Clan are still stealing each other's women and burning each other's villages."

"That's not news. They never stop raiding each other. I think they do it just for fun," Sumac said. "What else is happening?"

Nighthawk lifted his chin and peered sightlessly into the

fog, as though deciding which story to relate. "Here's something interesting. The story comes from the far eastern villages out in the marsh country. It's said that there's a very bad woman coming our way. She committed incest, and her husband is chasing her."

"How do you know she's coming our way?"

"Her husband is the Trader Lambkill—have you ever met him?" When Oxbalm and Sumac shook their heads in unison, Nighthawk shrugged. "He's a very great Trader, but he travels mostly to the north and east of here. Anyway, this Lambkill has been telling his story at every village he passes, hoping someone will send word back to him that his wicked wife has been seen. Her trail leads due west."

"So she may or may not be coming to the coast," Oxbalm said. "Who knows?"

"She may not," Nighthawk agreed. "But if you see her, grab hold of her and don't let go."

"Why? What would we want with a woman who committed incest?" That was the last thing Oxbalm needed in Otter Clan Village. He already had Catchstraw to draw the wrath of every adjacent village; he didn't want another nuisance.

"That husband of hers," Nighthawk said and slapped a greasy hand on his knee while he laughed, "he's as mad as a hornet. He's offering a fortune in trade goods to the person who captures his wife and turns her over to him."

"What's her name?" Sumac asked.

Nighthawk pondered, then shook his head. "I don't recall. She had a bird name. You know, like Falcon, or Eagle or . . . ah, wait. I remember. It was Kestrel. She's from the Bear-Looks-Back Clan."

"Kestrel . . ." Sumac repeated, as though memorizing the name.

"Well," Oxbalm said firmly, "she'll find no one to shield her here. The Otter Clan doesn't put up with such things. Incest is a grave crime."

Nighthawk chuckled. "Yes, she's going to have a hard

time finding a refuge. Of course she'll probably change her name."

"Then how will we know her?"

"She's supposed to be pregnant. But she may have had the baby by now."

"A newborn?" Sumac asked. The wrinkles of her face rearranged themselves into tender lines. "Well, in that case, Oxbalm will offer her shelter for a time. For the baby's sake. It's very cold still, and hard to find food."

"*I'll* offer her shelter?" Oxbalm asked indignantly. "What will the surrounding villages think? I can't . . ."

His voice faded as one of Sumac's gray brows arched. She fixed him with a look that would have sent Grandfather Brown Bear fleeing for his life.

"Sumac, I can't do that. You must understand—"

A low murmur of disapproving voices rose, and Oxbalm looked at the Dance circle. Catchstraw had dropped out and let someone take his place. Several of the oldest people, people who had taken part in Dances that Sunchaser had led, made hissing noises and glowered.

How we miss you, Sunchaser . . . Sunchaser never stopped Dancing. On the last day, the fourth day, the people around him had to support his weight, practically hauling his body every step of the way, but he remained in the circle. And when the Dance ended, he fell down nearly dead, but still Singing. It made people proud.

Nighthawk craned his neck, trying to see what the ruckus was about. "Looks like Catchstraw's age is catching up with him. He's the first one down."

Oxbalm glanced at Sumac. She quirked her mouth. She hadn't taken her eyes from her husband. Flustered, he shouted, "All right, woman! I'll grant this Kestrel a few days of rest. Are you satisfied?"

"You're a good and fair man." Sumac patted Oxbalm's hand fondly. "We can't condemn her until we speak with her. Maybe she didn't commit incest. Maybe her husband is just mad at her and trying to hurt her. Who knows?"

Oxbalm replied, "You always give people too much of a chance. Remember, I warn you about this. If we shelter that woman, the surrounding villages will shriek like a flock of frightened auks."

"Indeed they will." Nighthawk grinned broadly. Around the fire, the Dance circle had split and re-formed into two circles, one inside the other. Another two dozen people had joined in. "But keep in mind what Lambkill has promised—that if you keep this Kestrel long enough for him to arrive, you'll be rich!"

Sumac gave Nighthawk an unflattering look and tugged on Oxbalm's hand. "Come along," she said. "It's time we did our own Dancing to pray the mammoths back into the world."

She pulled Oxbalm to his feet and led him through the wavering fog to the circle around the fire.

Twelve

Through the noisy trill of crickets, horses could be heard whinnying. Tannin could see them in the polished glow of evening, dark shapes charging across the rolling hills at full speed, their tails flying. The rhythmic pounding of their hooves rumbled into the heart of the earth. Like waves, the herd flowed into a valley only to surge over the crest of the next hill.

He smiled and swung the dead grouse in his hand as he made his way up the willow-choked draw toward the hollow in the bank where Lambkill waited. Foxes yipped in the distance, calling to one another now that twilight was descending in a blue haze.

He had never been this far west, and the country—with its strange new trees and plants—fascinated him. He took his time, studying everything in his path. Especially after today, he needed time to walk and appreciate the beauty. They had searched and searched this side of the river, trying to pick up Kestrel's trail. Without luck.

"She may have lost us this time," Tannin said to himself, hoping fervently that she had. After his first wave of anger had passed, he'd lost all desire to see her harmed. As long as she stayed gone, it would be enough for him. And he sincerely believed that Lambkill needed to go home, to speak with his family and to consult a Dreamer.

A dull fear had begun to probe at Tannin's guts, fear that Evil Spirits had entered his brother's body and gobbled up his soul.

He had heard of such things happening. A very long time ago, an ancient Dreamer named Hollowhair had told Tannin that a person could always tell when evil had sneaked into a friend. The friend seemed to change suddenly . . . to grow violent and do things he'd never done before. And if the Evil Spirits stayed for any length of time, the person's soul would simply die and only the body would be left: alive, but not his own.

Lambkill *had* changed. He'd become someone that Tannin did not know. This afternoon when Lambkill had gone into a screaming rage, Tannin had wondered helplessly if he shouldn't just tie Lambkill up and haul him home on a travois.

He loved his brother deeply, the affection going beyond simple blood bonds. Lambkill had been the most remarkable of brothers, a man to be proud of, to emulate. And he'd never forgotten Tannin when he returned from daring trips to the north. That magical pack always contained something special just for Tannin; Lambkill's eyes would gleam with enjoyment as he told Tannin the story of the object and of how it related to an adventure among strange peoples.

The thought of dragging his brother home frightened Tannin. The very act would humiliate Lambkill beyond speaking terms, beyond any repair of their relationship. And Tannin had come to believe that Lambkill, this magical brother he loved so much, would murder him if he so much as raised a hand to interfere with the search for Kestrel.

He shook his head. Bank swallows swooped and fluttered above him as he forded the trickle of water in the bottom of the draw and headed up the slope. He followed the trickle until he reached the place where spring floods had undercut the bank, creating a small shelter. Lambkill had a fire going. It lit the shelter with a warm glow. He could see his brother moving, bent over to avoid the low ceiling. His shadow roved the back wall.

Tannin called, "Lambkill, I'm back," before he climbed the trail and ducked into the shelter.

Lambkill turned and peered at Tannin with unexpected calm. His faded eyes shimmered golden in the firelight. He moved differently, the stiffness of hard days on the trail gone. "I was almost ready to look for you. Did one measly grouse take you so long?"

"She was a clever grouse. Kept ducking behind brush so I couldn't get a good shot at her."

Tannin knelt beside the fire and skewered the bird on a long stick. He glanced at Lambkill. What had happened to bring about this odd serenity? Lambkill acted as if a weight had been lifted from his soul. Had he come to some decision? About Kestrel?

Tannin laid the skewered grouse across the two forked branches that thrust up on either side of the fire pit. The feathers caught and quickly burned off in a cloud of foul-smelling smoke. If he'd been home, Calling Crane would have sealed the grouse in a thick layer of clay and buried it deep in the coals, to cook slowly in its own juices. Here, there wasn't time for such luxuries. But thinking about them made Tannin miss his wife.

She's probably out laughing and talking with the other

women around the central fire in the plaza . . . and thinking about me. Worrying. Fearing for my safety.

Before he'd left, she'd said: "My heart goes with you. Come back to me. And . . . and remember that Kestrel is your sister-in-law. Don't forget the times she came to our lodge begging to be taken in because of what your brother had done to her."

At the time, he had merely nodded and hugged her goodbye. Only now could he hear the undercurrents in her voice—the resentment of Lambkill, the love for Kestrel. As always, she'd said more to him than her words conveyed.

He glanced at Lambkill, who had gone to the rear of the shelter. Shells rattled, and something thudded when Lambkill dropped it. Tannin couldn't see what occupied him.

Tannin stretched out on his side before the fire and sniffed the heavenly scent of roasting grouse. Fat dripped onto the hearthstones, where it sizzled and popped. Down the draw, the moon peeked over the horizon as though hesitant, fearful of what it might see. A corner of silver glimmered through the gnarled branches of a copse of juniper.

Tannin smiled. With the darkness, the wind had cooled and died down to a faint whisper. It fanned their fire gently, turning the coals crimson. Bravely, he said, "Lambkill, I've been thinking. Maybe we should just let Kestrel go. Her trail has vanished and we—"

"We'll find it again."

"Well, maybe, but don't you think—"

"Oh, you can believe me. We will. Because I know where she's going."

"Where?"

"To the seacoast. Iceplant's mother came from there. I don't remember her clan's name, but their village was right on the water. I remember hearing Wind Shadow talk about it twenty cycles ago. She'd been stolen by her husband at a young age, ten summers I think, and in her memories, that village was as glorious as the Land of the Dead."

Lambkill sat down heavily across the fire from him and

opened the pack he propped in his lap. He drew out the dead baby.

Tannin gasped. Lambkill had disemboweled the child! A long slit ran from the baby's throat all the way to its pubis. The internal organs and windpipe had been removed. The flesh had shriveled and blackened like a berry left in the sun too long. A prickle ran up Tannin's spine.

Lambkill stared down at the dead baby. "Did you know that I loved Kestrel, Tannin?"

"D-did you?"

"Oh, yes. Very much. More than I can tell you. I only beat her for her own good. You know, when she did things that I knew were bad for her. You understand."

". . . I understand."

Lambkill lifted his head and smiled. "We'll find Kestrel. I just have to bring my son to life again. That's all. Then he'll be able to *see* her path."

"Bring your son . . . What are you talking about?" A fist seemed to reach inside Tannin's chest to squeeze his heart.

"Far to the north . . ." Lambkill said, and as he turned, the smoky shadows highlighted the purple smudges beneath his wary eyes. His lips parted as if about to reveal some sacred knowledge whose Power could strike dead the man who dared to speak of it. In a hushed voice, he continued, "The People of the Masks, who live with the Ice Ghosts, believe that the souls of dead children stay in the bodies for a long time. And if you're fast and perform the proper rituals, you can tie their souls there."

Tannin watched in horror as Lambkill spread the boy's little ribs back. The stench of decomposition clotted in the overhang. He gagged and turned his head away, struggling to control the nausea at the back of his throat. If he vomited, what would Lambkill say?

Lambkill looked up. "We must prop his body open to smoke for seven nights, until it dries completely." An emotionless smile curled his lips. "The People of the Masks believe that dead babies can learn to speak. Oh, it takes time. Maybe years . . . just like with a living child. But once they learn, they can tell you many strange and wonderful things. The Mask People carry dead babies before them into battle . . . and they say that no dart has ever struck the man with the child."

Tannin couldn't speak. He could only gape as a sense of uncleanliness and corruption leached into his soul. The night air seemed heavy with spiritual pollution. *I'll never be clean again!*

He watched in horrified silence as Lambkill lifted the grouse, slid it off its stick and propped it on one of the hearthstones to cool. Then Lambkill scrutinized the stick and stabbed it through the middle of the dead baby. Blood dripped down onto the dirt.

"See," Lambkill said. "Every night I'll prop my son up, away from the flames of the fire, where he can dry out slowly. Then, in seven days, I'll sew him up and dress him."

"Why?" Tannin asked in a choked whisper.

Lambkill tilted his head, and his eyes glowed eerily in the reflected flames. "So my son can be with me always."

"Oh . . . Man . . . it's happening. Look. Look and see for yourself! I'll never be able to be born again. I'll never be a Dreamer! Or have my chance to save the world! Not as long as Lambkill tries to tie half of my soul to that putrid body. I hate that old fool!"

The Man said, "Boy, do you know why the body exists?"

"No, of course not. You've never let me live long enough to find out anything about the world of men!"

The Man sighed. "If you truly desire to be born again, then wish both of your souls into that putrid body."

Boy gasped, "Why? What for?"

"Because living in that body will teach you everything there is to know about anger. Every day, all day long, you

will be sniffed by dogs that want to eat you, swarmed over by insects that think your leathery body would make a fine home. Flies will crawl all over you, searching for places to lay their eggs."

The Boy blinked. "I can see why such things would make me angry. But . . . why is that good? Is anger good?"

A magnificent blue-violet fire glowed to life around all of the Star People who lived within Boy's sight. The fire encircled each one like a protective vessel of Light. It flickered and blazed. Only Boy didn't have such a beautiful vessel. He frowned.

The Man gently pointed out, "No, Boy. But the worthiness of a Dreamer is revealed by enduring unbearable irritations."

Thirteen

Tall reeds shielded Kestrel as she waded through the cool marsh shallows. The sucking black mud ate at her strength and made her legs cramp, but travel here would leave no trail for Lambkill to follow. Sunset had blushed color into the rocky lowlands rising to the north, and the rounded shapes of boulders glowed with a topaz fire. Southward, two enormous lakes gleamed an unearthly blue, like eyes in a face formed from the rich green marshes.

The air had turned cold with the waning light.

Spotted sandpipers scurried through the water in front of her, hunting insects. When she got too close, they trilled nervously and she slowed her pace to keep them calm. From last year's tawny cattail stems, yellow-headed blackbirds watched with cocked heads. Water snakes slipped between the stems, rustling the newly greening grass. Minnows darted away from her muddy, waterlogged moccasins.

The puffs of clouds on the horizon had begun to blaze orange in the fires of sunset. Soon darkness would cover her movements but until then, she had to be careful not to attract attention to herself.

She had been walking from dawn's first light to well past dusk, walking as fast as she could, feeding Cloud Girl on the move by swiveling the hide thong of the rabbit-fur sack around to her chest. The baby seemed to take the traveling well, but exhaustion weighted Kestrel's body like a granite cape. The knife wounds on her forehead and shoulder had become infected. While the Evil Spirits fed, the constant pain sapped her strength even further.

Her eyes methodically searched the low sandstone outcrops on the fringes of the marsh for a place to make camp. Her hips ached miserably. And, too often, her legs cramped so badly that she had to rub the knots out of them before she could go on. When she thought that she couldn't take another step, she filled her soul with thoughts of Otter Clan Village, nestled in a tall fir forest at the edge of the ocean. She could smell the saltwater, hear the crashing waves. Iceplant had described it to her over and over on the long winter nights when they'd held each other and watched the Star People travel through the Land of the Dead.

Now, those visions kept her sane.

On the opposite bank of the marsh, a small village hid in the shadows cast by a grove of willows. The ten grass lodges, their dome-shaped roofs made from woven cattail, looked new and well-kept. As dusk settled in a blue veil over the land, cook fires glittered to life. The sound of voices carried across the shallow water. A child laughed, and Kestrel glimpsed a boy racing through the village, a spotted dog nipping playfully at his moccasins.

She waded on, fixing her attention on the minnows that shot like silver daggers through the quiet pool. If she'd had the strength, she would have run to get away from those happy sounds. They reminded her of the cook fires—warm and golden—that she'd known as a little girl.

Her mother had taken her by the hand every evening and gone outside to join the other women in preparing supper. The grownups had stood around laughing and gossiping about village events while the children played. Kestrel and Waxwing had usually crouched at the border of the fire's glow, discussing their little-girl dreams of their future husbands, who would be good hunters and give them many sons. They'd wished for rare seashells to decorate their dresses with, and had helped each other memorize the sacred stories so they could tell them to their children.

Kestrel could not recall ever hearing—in all that time—any stories about a man beating his wife or hurting his child. Oh, there had been murders, and one or two rapes, but they had always happened at distant villages.

Kestrel's eyes involuntarily strayed across the water, and she caught sight of a man ducking out of a lodge. He was smiling. He walked toward a woman who stood in the central plaza and softly stroked her hair.

Why couldn't I have been born here, Above-Old-Man? If I'd been born here, I'd have a husband who loved me and Cloud Girl. I'd be kneeling before the fire, frying fish or roasting cattail root and half-listening to the other women whisper about who was going to marry who. Cloud Girl would be sleeping on a silky bed of foxhides in my lodge. I'd smile at my husband when he came to sit cross-legged beside me and finish knapping out his new dart point. We'd talk gently to each other. He'd examine his point, studying the workmanship. Then he'd lay it aside and tenderly squeeze my hand.

Kestrel peered down at her reflection in the water. The dark-blue bruises had faded to purple and yellow. *Tenderness* . . . Did such a thing really exist anywhere, for anyone, now? Did some people's lives just seem beautiful because they kept all of the violence and pain hidden behind the walls of their lodges?

Just as she had, for five long cycles.

"Somewhere, it must exist," she whispered desperately. "Please, Above-Old-Man, let it exist for someone. It can't have all died with Iceplant."

Her right leg cramped again. She groaned softly.

There, that was the place she needed. Warily, cautiously, she slogged toward a rock overhang that darkened the face of a red sandstone knoll barely visible through the screening marsh vegetation. The reeds and mud ended, and moss created a velvet blanket on the rising ground around the knoll, cushioning her steps as she bent low to enter the rock shelter.

Her eyes had deceived her. It was smaller than it had seemed from a distance—barely a body length across and half a length wide. But it would be big enough for a night's rest. Other humans had taken refuge here. Shreds of woven-grass matting were lying about, and someone had knapped out a stone tool here and left brown chert flakes in a pile. A fire pit filled with charcoal marked the middle of the floor. Ash rose when Kestrel slumped down beside it. The jolt brought Cloud Girl awake. She mewed softly.

"It's all right, baby. We're safe," Kestrel soothed. She untied the sack and lifted it over her head, then carefully laid it in her lap. The baby yawned. She had one tiny fist twined in the rabbit fur and the other stuffed in her mouth. She mewed again. "Are you hungry, Cloud Girl? Me, too. We had a long day, didn't we?"

Kestrel stretched. Taking the weight from her shoulders had eased her, but her lower back still hurt. She twisted and sighed. "It won't be long now, Cloud Girl. Another seven or eight days and we should reach the sea. Then we just have to walk by the water's edge until we find Otter Clan Village. They'll let us rest. They'll help us. You'll see. Iceplant told me they would."

She tipped Cloud Girl's sack on its side to retrieve the small pack of tools and dried meat she had tied behind the hood. She couldn't risk building a fire. If the villagers saw the light, they would come to investigate, and no one must know she had passed this way. The last few strips of jerked tapir would have to do for supper.

Kestrel pulled the strips out and chewed them slowly, savoring each bite. She hadn't eaten since before dawn, and the sweet, smoky meat tasted especially wonderful. Her stomach growled. The blue of Cloud Girl's eyes had begun to deepen. By the next moon, they would be a deep, dark brown, like the winter hide of Brother Buffalo. She blinked at Kestrel and began to cry in earnest.

"Oh, I'm sorry, baby. Here."

Kestrel brought up her knees and propped the rabbit-fur sack on them, then loosened her dress and drew out her left breast. Cloud Girl took the nipple and nursed contentedly while Kestrel finished the tapir jerky.

She held the baby to her and sank back against the cool wall. Shadows had devoured the reeds and cattails, melting the individual stems together into a solid indigo wall around the marsh. Westward, only a thin, glowing crescent remained of Father Sun's face. It outlined the distant foothills with gold. To the north, she could just glimpse a slice of the Mammoth Mountains, their jagged peaks turning purple with night.

"That's the way, Cloud Girl. Your father's people are through there. Where the foothills start up toward the peaks, there's a pass. We must go through it, then walk as far west as we can. To the sea. We just have to—"

A tiny whisper of sound made her hush. Her gaze swiftly combed the marsh, lingering on each man-sized shadow. A swarm of gnats glittered in the last rays of twilight, spiraling upward over the water.

Another sound. On the stone above her. A scratching, like moccasins on gravel.

Kestrel's fingers dimpled the hide that encased Cloud Girl. *Lambkill? Oh, Blessed Spirits, how could I have been so careless? I should have kept running until after dark.* Four rapid steps patted across the stone of the overhang. She started to shake violently. *I have to run! Where . . . where can I hide?*

She choked on a cry as a raven walked boldly to the edge of the overhang, caught sight of her and sprang into the sky with a sharp caw.

Kestrel sat back hard, panting, her heart racing. Cloud Girl had not even stopped nursing. She peered up at Kestrel placidly. Her tiny hands kneaded the breast in slow, sleepy motions.

It took several moments before Kestrel could get a deep breath into her lungs.

She stretched out on her side and watched the evening colors vanish in the embrace of night. Nighthawks fluttered over the marsh, their wings whistling when they dove for prey. She clutched Cloud Girl tightly against her and fell into an exhausted sleep.

Gray clouds scudded across the morning sky, sailing eastward. Horseweed glanced at them as he loped down the forest path. Would it rain again? He hoped not. The mud from the last storm had yet to dry. His moccasins were so caked with it that they stuck to his feet like a damp second skin.

"Sunchaser? Wait. *Wait!*" Horseweed called.

Dogwood trees thrust their branches, laden with white flowers, in his way. Petals showered the path as he shoved the limbs aside without losing his pace. Squirrels chittered, chastising him and Balsam for making so much noise. Sunchaser rounded a bend in the trail ahead, and Horseweed lost sight of him. He slowed down. "We're never going to catch him."

"It doesn't look like he wants us to," Balsam noted.

Horseweed twisted his face sourly. They had been tracking the Dreamer for three days. Every time that Horseweed thought they'd caught him, he seemed to vanish into thin air, along with that mangy dog of his.

"He's probably cast a spell on us," Balsam said, "so that we can't see him. I bet he's standing right there in front of us, laughing."

"Dreamers don't cast spells. Only witches do that."

Balsam came up alongside Horseweed and cocked his head. His round face and pug nose were greasy with sweat. "If witches can do it, why can't Dreamers?"

"Well, maybe they can. I don't know. But I've never heard of a Dreamer using spells."

"Doesn't mean they can't. Did you ever think that that's why we didn't see the herd of sacred deer or the woodpile at the Dream Cave?"

Sarcastically, Horseweed said, "Or maybe the deer had wandered into the forest to bed down until dark, and Catchstraw used up all the wood last autumn."

"You think Sunchaser lied about eating the deer?"

"Sunchaser wouldn't eat sacred deer," he admitted sullenly. "He'd be afraid to. Like everybody with sense. He probably said that just to mock us."

The trail broke out into a meadow that sloped off down the side of the mountain. Horseweed stopped to scrutinize the maze of tracks crisscrossing the grass. In the mud he saw elk, wolf, camel and rabbit prints. Nothing that looked human. He shook his head. Maybe Sunchaser had stayed in the trees? A bushy hedge of cypress created an unbroken ring around the edges of the meadow. Horseweed walked next to them, listening to the wind whisper through the dark green foliage. He noted the places where a giant sloth had stripped the branches of new growth and left piles of fresh dung. As he watched, bars of sunlight shot across the meadow. The dewdrops clinging to the blades of grass sparkled. Such a beautiful day. At this pace, they would be home by nightfall. His stomach growled for a good meal, but his soul cringed at the thought of facing his grandfather.

"It's going to be embarrassing if Sunchaser gets home before we do," Horseweed said.

"Why? Who cares?" Balsam's young brow furrowed. "Anyway, there's not much we can do about it. Wonder why he doesn't want to talk to us."

"After what we did to the Dream Cave, I wouldn't want to talk to us either." Horseweed had been feeling increasingly morose as they neared the coast. *How could I have been so stupid?*

Balsam glanced sideways at him. "Oh, that's why you're worried. You think that Sunchaser will tell Catchstraw?"

"Why wouldn't he?"

"I don't know, but I'm not going to tell *anybody*. Least of all, Catchstraw." He grimaced and kept on walking.

They reached the southern side of the meadow, where the trail entered the trees again. A clear slash of brown covered with elk tracks wound down the slope. Horseweed put his hands on his hips and gazed out across the vista. Straight ahead, Mother Ocean spread vast and blue. Her body wedded with Brother Sky's in the distance, marking the hazy border to the Land of the Dead. At the point where Father Sun set, there was an opening. That was where souls entered the Land of the Dead.

To the south, Pygmy Island broke the crystal surface of the water. The big island had been named for the stunted animals that lived there. The mammoths grew to barely the height of a man. Dwarf foxes roamed its shores, and tiny skunks lived in the uplands. The westernmost peak was called Sand Verbena Mountain; the peak in the center was Rush Rose Mountain; and the big eastern peak, Milkwort Mountain.

Legend said that many generations ago, the peaks had been three separate islands. Horseweed could believe it. Just in his short lifetime, he'd witnessed amazing changes. Mother Ocean had been steadily rising. He remembered, as a little boy, his Grandmother Sumac telling him not to play in the sand flats between Milkwort Mountain and Rush Rose peak during high tide, because he might be drowned when the water rushed in. Now those same sand flats were always covered with water, except during really low tides.

The clouds split for a moment and sunlight spilled around Horseweed. Balsam sighed and tipped his face to the warmth.

"Well, come on," Horseweed said. "The sooner we get home, the sooner our humiliation will be over."

They broke into a trot, but when they rounded a bend in the trail, there was Sunchaser, standing with one shoulder against the trunk of a fir tree, his arms folded across his broad chest. The seashells tied to the fringes of his heavy moosehide jacket clicked melodiously in the breeze. Amazing. Moose were so rare. The old people said that the big animals were travelers, just like humans were, and had come to this part of the world only a short time ago. Such a jacket must have cost a fortune. Sunchaser had pulled his white hair away from his oval face and plaited it into a long braid. The style accentuated his deep-set black eyes and made his chin seem more squared.

Horseweed stopped before Sunchaser. "We've been trying to catch you!"

A smile warmed the Dreamer's face. He stepped away from the tree and put an arm around Horseweed's shoulder, as if they were old friends, and headed him down the trail again. They walked side by side, with Balsam following; the younger boy's steps had gone unnaturally quiet.

Horseweed peered at the Dreamer's arm as he walked. "Wh-what did you want, Sunchaser? Did you . . . have something to say to me?"

Sunchaser squinted up at the sunlight glittering in the treetops. "I've been thinking about that earthquake we had in the high mountains."

"Earthquake?" Horseweed asked. "What earthquake?"

"The one that caused the roof of the Dream Cave to collapse. I think it was a sign."

Horseweed gave Sunchaser a curious glance. "A sign of what? Stupidity?"

Sunchaser suppressed a smile. "Not at all. I'm sure that if you and Balsam had not come up and called me out when you did, I would have been in the Dream Cave when that earthquake struck." He heaved a deep sigh. "Yes, no doubt about it. Oxbalm should be very proud of you when he hears of how you saved me."

"That's what you're going to tell him?"

"You did call to me, didn't you?"

Horseweed blurted, "I didn't *mean* to call *you* those things, Sunchaser! I didn't recognize you. You look so much older with your white hair. If I'd known—"

"You called me out, and then the Quaking Earth Spirits poured their wrath on the mountains. Isn't that right?"

Horseweed swallowed hard. "If you say so."

"Good." Sunchaser clapped his shoulder. "It's settled. Now, I need some help from you."

Horseweed squinted skeptically, a sinking sensation in his heart. *Here it comes. What was it Balsam said? A liverwort? A leech?*

Behind him, Balsam yipped excitedly. "We'll be heroes! What did I tell you? They'll probably hold a Dance in our honor. For cycles to come, people will speak our names with pride!"

Sunchaser smiled, but he gazed steadily at Horseweed. "Will you help me?"

The sinking sensation yawned wider. "What do you need?"

"I need to know what Catchstraw has been saying about me. I missed another Mammoth Spirit Dance. Surely he noticed." Sunchaser gazed seriously at Horseweed.

"Catchstraw doesn't like you, Sunchaser."

"I've noticed that. What did he say when I missed the Dance?"

Horseweed shrugged uncertainly. "We left the village the day before the Dance started, but I did hear him tell Grandfather that if you hadn't appeared by the end of the Dance, he was going to . . ." Horseweed paused. How had Catchstraw put it? "I think he said he was going to 'seek advice among the clan elders.' "

Sunchaser's face darkened. He released his hold on Horseweed's shoulder. "He has every right."

"You think he's trying to take your place?" Horseweed snorted derisively. "Catchstraw's no Dreamer! He's a fake. Grandfather's certain of it."

"Yes, but Oxbalm has seen enough Dreamers come and go that he can tell the difference. The other clan leaders . . . well, we'll see. I won't judge them before I've had a chance to talk to them."

"Are you expecting them to condemn you for missing the Dance again? Sunchaser, you were in the mountains Healing. Everybody knows that. How could they condemn you for saving lives?"

"Oh, they may not condemn me." Sunchaser shoved his hands into his jacket pockets. "But most people think that their own needs are far more important than the needs of others. And I suspect that the Otter Clan villagers thought they needed me." He tilted his head apologetically. "They didn't, of course. Mammoth Above hears the Songs, feels the motions of the Dance, whether I'm there or not."

Horseweed frowned. "If they do condemn you, they're fools! Those people at Brushnut Village are our relatives. Cousins. Even aunts and uncles. How could you leave the sick and dying just to lead the Mammoth Spirit Dance for us?" He fiercely slapped a dogwood branch, and a cascade of white petals splashed into the air around them. Sunchaser peered at Horseweed askance.

"Well, it makes me mad," Horseweed said. "I see why you're worried. If you had come to the Dance, somebody would have cursed you for leaving their relatives to die. Since you didn't come, they'll curse you because you didn't lead the Dance for them. You were cursed either way, Sunchaser."

The Dreamer smiled and studied the deer tracks in the mud of the trail for a few moments. "I hadn't realized that you'd grown up, Horseweed. It's good to have a man to talk to."

Horseweed's chest swelled. Though he tried to hide it by turning his head to the side, a broad smile came over his face. *A man!* He was fourteen summers old, true, but had yet to kill his first mammoth or go on his first war raid. Technically, he wasn't a man, although he certainly felt like one. It elated him that the great Dreamer thought he was.

Hesitantly, Horseweed asked, "Sunchaser? What's it like to visit the Land of the Dead? I've always wanted to ask you, but I . . . I've been too afraid before. Grandfather says it's very dark."

"Oh, yes. At first the darkness is so deep and still that you feel your soul will be crushed by it. But then you hear voices. They're familiar, though it takes a while to recognize them. They call out to you, and you cling to the sound of your own name as though it were the only thing saving you from oblivion. You concentrate on it. The darkness changes, becomes a great white light that swallows you and carries you up, up. Then you step out into an alien sky, and you fall toward a new land . . . trees . . . red ridges so jagged and winding they remind you of the skeletons of long-dead monsters . . . a land terrifying in its beauty."

Sunchaser's voice faded, and his eyes took on a faraway gleam, as though seeing that landscape rising before him again.

Wonder tingled in Horseweed's chest. He watched Sunchaser from the corner of his eye but kept quiet, letting the Dreamer remember.

When Sunchaser's steps slowed, Horseweed took the lead down the trail. Balsam eased around Sunchaser very carefully before running to catch up. His face looked plaintive.

"What's wrong?" Horseweed asked softly.

Balsam shook his head. "Dreamers. They're all scary. Sort of half here and half somewhere else."

Horseweed grinned. "That's why we call them Dreamers."

Fourteen

Kestrel bounced Cloud Girl on her knees. Near panic, she couldn't think of anything else to do. The baby had grown irritable after her noon feeding. Then she'd started crying and had yet to stop. Kestrel had made camp early, in an oak grove overlooking a small lake. The newly budded limbs threw a black weave of shadows over her hastily constructed lodge. Made of dead branches propped against each other, then covered with brush, it looked shabby and fragile, but it would keep them dry if it rained tonight. That was all Kestrel cared about. Tomorrow morning they would be running again.

On the lake, a flock of swans floated placidly. Their rich bugling calls filled the valley, providing a beautiful background to Cloud Girl's wails. Everywhere in the grove, birds sang and hopped from branch to branch, birds she had never seen before, with red, blue and bright green feathers.

"Oh, my daughter, please, what's wrong?"

They had made their way through a low, rocky pass at the southern tip of the Mammoth Mountains and entered the foothills on the other side. Northward, snowcapped peaks pierced the blue sky. But Kestrel's eyes drifted to the west, where the land flattened out and gradually sloped downward. Dark patches of mountain mahogany choked the drainages that flowed toward the sea. Between the drainages, a strewn handful of small lakes was burnished a greenish gold by the slanting rays of light.

"Try to eat, baby." Again Kestrel put her breast in the baby's mouth, but again Cloud Girl twisted away to shriek and wave her tiny fists. "Baby, what do you need? What's wrong?"

The cries were driving Kestrel to distraction. Nothing stopped them. Frantic, she put Cloud Girl against her shoulder and got to her feet. Sunlight fell through the trees, warming her face as she walked the trail toward the lake. Cloud Girl seemed to like the motion. Her cries dropped to whimpers. Kestrel patted her bottom, hoping to ease her daughter. Probably Cloud Girl had colic.

"I could cure you easily if we were home, baby. The entire country of the Bear-Looks-Back Clan is filled with bunchberry and nettle, but where would I look for them here? The land and plants are so different."

Kestrel strode through a meadow of blue wildflowers, looking for the winter dung of a buffalo, or maybe, if she were lucky, a shrubox. She found buffalo dung first.

"This won't take long, Cloud Girl. Please, be good. Don't cry."

But as soon as Kestrel laid Cloud Girl on the soft green grass, the baby erupted in shrieks again. At the age of three weeks, Cloud Girl had developed the lungs of a two-moon-old child. Kestrel hurried. She lifted Cloud Girl's shirt, then unlaced and removed her rabbit-fur pants, seeing the soaked crushed bark within. The pants, nothing more than a square piece of hide folded over and stitched up along the sides, with two leg holes in the bottom, had a protective layer of woven bark sewn into the crotch, which was filled with absorbent. The layer rested against Cloud Girl's body, keeping her dry. The women of the Bear-Looks-Back Clan used a variety of absorbents during different times of the year. In the winter, they collected dead moss or dry dung; in the spring, fuzzy cottonwood seeds; and in the fall, cattail down.

Kestrel turned the pants upside down and shook out the old absorbent, letting it fall to the grass. Then she crumbled the buffalo dung and tucked it between the woven bark layer and the hide. It would absorb all the moisture that flowed through the bark layer. She did not re-dress Cloud Girl; instead, she picked up the pants and her screaming daughter and headed straight for the lake. Mixing crushed mint with water, she thoroughly washed the baby. "There, Cloud Girl. Feel better now?" she asked as she slipped the pants over those fat little legs and relaced them.

Cloud Girl fell into a suffocating fit of crying. Kestrel quickly rose and began walking with her again. "Will I have to walk all night to keep you happy, my daughter?" They circled the perimeter of the lake, staying just beyond the thick ring of tules that flourished in the shallows. Redwing blackbirds clung to the stalks and cocked their heads with suspicion as Kestrel marched by.

Swamp smartweed grew in clumps near the tules. Kestrel picked handfuls of the young shoots and ate them ravenously. They tasted bitter, but tender. To keep up her strength, she'd been eating everything she could find, but her milk supply had dwindled, and she'd never been this hungry in her life.

Cloud Girl stopped crying so suddenly that Kestrel came to a dead halt in the grass. "Goodness, my daughter, did the colic vanish so quickly?"

Cloud Girl stared at her from wide eyes.

Kestrel kissed her daughter's forehead in relief. "Let us go and try to sleep. The sky is clear and we'll have a full moon tonight. Maybe we can start walking again at midnight."

The oaks stretched their crooked branches toward her like beckoning arms as she neared her camp. How beautiful the trees were. The afternoon sun shimmered off of their tiny green buds.

So relieved was she that she didn't notice that the birds had stopped singing and that the crickets no longer chirped in the grass. Kestrel got on her knees and crawled into the dark interior of her lodge with Cloud Girl still pressed to her shoulder.

She smelled his male scent before she saw him sitting on her bedding in the rear. A ragged scream tore from her throat as she threw herself backward out on the ground and frantically stumbled to her feet.

He caught her by the arm and whirled her around. Kestrel clutched Cloud Girl tightly. A broad smile split his young face. He couldn't have been more than sixteen summers, but he stood eleven hands tall and had broad, muscular shoulders. A long black braid hung over his left shoulder.

"I heard your baby crying," he said. Then more softly, as though speaking to himself, "A woman and a baby. Yes . . . a woman who looks beaten up . . . and a newborn baby." He scrutinized Cloud Girl. "Oh, this is a great day. I think that maybe Buffalo Bird has just become a rich man."

"What are you talking about?"

He kept a firm hold on her arms, as though afraid she might try to run. "I met a Trader. An ugly old man. He offered many wonderful trade goods to the man who could track down his runaway wife." He chuckled. "You're her, aren't you?"

"Who?"

"Kestrel . . . from the Bear-Looks-Back Clan. Lambkill's woman. You have a funny accent. Like you're from the marsh country."

Her breathing went shallow as hope drained from her soul like water from a torn basket. Her knees wanted to shake, but she wouldn't let them. She could see his indecision. He looked her up and down and peered at her face, as though memorizing the bruises and the festered gash across her forehead. With a violent wrench, Kestrel twisted loose from his grip.

"No. I'm not!" she said. "My name is Lame Antelope and I'm from Otter Clan Village on the sea! Who are *you?*"

He studied her through narrowed eyes. "You're two days from home, Lame Antelope . . . why?"

"That is my business." *Only two days? Blessed Spirits, I'm closer than I thought. So close!*

The youth ground his teeth thoughtfully for a moment. As though testing her, he said, "That Trader, he was as crazy as a foaming-mouth dog. If he'd been my husband, I would have run away, too."

"Crazy?" she asked, unable to help herself. "What do you mean? What did he do?"

Buffalo Bird laughed in disgust. "He carries a dried-out baby around in his pack. Whenever he sees a camp fire, he and his brother—Tannin is his name—walk into the camp carrying that dead boy before them."

Kestrel's heart lurched. She fought to keep her face blank while she tried to figure out how it had happened. Had Lambkill searched the shoreline looking for her trail? And that's when he'd found the baby boy? Her heart pounded nauseatingly. Had he also found the cave where . . . *Yes. He must have.* He knew she'd had twins. "A woman and a newborn baby."

Panic gripped her like the fists of doom. She longed to ask when Buffalo Bird had talked to Lambkill, and where. Instead, she hoisted Cloud Girl up onto her shoulder again and patted her back furiously. A loud burp erupted from Cloud Girl's mouth. Cloud Girl seemed surprised by it; she turned to peer questioningly at Kestrel. "Good girl," Kestrel said. "Can you manage another one?" She patted Cloud Girl even harder, and the baby burped again.

Buffalo Bird watched in irritation. "So you're not this Kestrel, eh? Well, it doesn't matter."

"What do you mean by that?"

"I mean that I have to take you to Lambkill anyway. Just to be sure. I wouldn't want to chance losing my fortune." He gripped her arm tightly. "Come on. My lodge is much bigger than yours, and I killed a deer this morning. You can cook it for me and my brothers for dinner."

"My clan will kill you for this!" she exclaimed. "You can't just kidnap me and my baby for no reason. My family will come looking!"

"Let them. I have many brothers with weapons. Four of them are at my camp right now."

He roughly hauled her up the slope by her sleeve. His moccasins *shished* lightly in the wet grass, a warrior's wary step. "Let go of me!" Kestrel said. "You must at least let me get my pack from my lodge. There are things in it that my little girl needs!"

Irritably, he stopped and let her loose. "All right, but hurry! It will be dark soon."

Dust swept the beach in glittering plumes and sizzled against the hide lodges in Otter Clan Village. Most of the people still slept. Their ears laid back, only the dogs prowled the plaza, slinking through the cold wind that gusted down from the north. With it came a billowing swell of blue-gray clouds and the fragrance of rain. Sunchaser braced his shoulder against the trunk of a fir tree. All around him, the dawn forest rustled with the wind.

He watched two rangy forms saunter from the trees. He had been waiting for them. For four nights straight, they'd arrived at the same time. The lions paid him no attention as they padded silently across the sand, climbed up on the wind-smoothed rocks at the ocean's edge and stood silhouetted against the pale-blue aura of the sky. The male lifted his muzzle, scenting the sea breeze, and the predawn light shimmered in his golden fur. The female stretched out atop the rocks with her huge head resting on her forepaws. They made small, intimate sounds to each other, lovers' sounds, barely audible above the roar of the surf and the screeching of the gulls.

Sunchaser cocked his head to listen. The lions stood no more than a good stone's throw away. But he felt no fear. Lions had been in this world much longer than people had, and their faces reflected a stillness, born of age and wisdom, that humans barely understood. Sometimes when Sunchaser looked into their eyes, he could see and hear things that had long ago hidden themselves from human senses. He'd sat with the lions and heard the mountains Singing at sunset. He'd spoken to the souls of the flakes of snow that fell from brooding winter skies. The lions had taught him that a Presence secreted herself in the dark veil of night, and, if he turned quickly enough, he might glimpse her in the forest shadows. Sunchaser called her *Soot Girl,* because she clung to the darkness the way soot clung to the roof of a lodge.

"It *is* the sign," he whispered softly as he gazed out past the lions to Mother Ocean, whose face had gone ashen with the coming of morning.

In the surging waves, the thirty-four mammoth skeletons lay like huge, white cages. More mammoths than Sunchaser had seen at once in his entire life. They usually traveled in small herds of no more than ten, although six winters ago, he had seen a herd of twenty-seven. Leg bones littered the sand, torn off and scattered by dire wolves and big cats. But the ribs remained intact. Squealing flocks of gulls lit imperiously on them and fluttered through the stomach cavities. The Otter Clan villagers had butchered and smoked enough meat to last the entire cycle. They'd also called in people from nearby villages, begging them to take what they needed. Everyone had gone away with packs full of meat. Most had been smiling.

Oblivious. Like eyeless cave bats.

As Sunchaser looked upon the pathetic remains of those enormous animals, his fear, the fear that had stalked him for moons, metamorphosed into despair. He shook his head, whispering, "Relics of the last·days."

"What does that mean?" Oxbalm asked from somewhere behind him. His moccasins had not whispered against the sand. Sunchaser wondered how a man Oxbalm's age could move with such stealth. "The 'last days'?"

Sunchaser shrugged, unwilling to elaborate, even for this old friend. "Nothing. I'm just tired, Oxbalm."

Oxbalm hobbled forward, touching a fir bough to keep himself steady. Like towering giants, the trees swayed back and forth, pushed by the wind.

"I think it's more than that," Oxbalm said. His llamahide shirt and pants had been smoked to a dark brown, a warm background for his gray braids. As he neared, his elderly face became contemplative. He braced a hand on another fir branch and frowned out at the dead mammoths. His sunken lips pursed. "Were things bad at Brushnut Village?"

"So many died . . . so quickly. I didn't have time to count them."

Oxbalm wet his lips, and his brows drew together. "I could feel your ache. In your silence the past few days. That's why I waited to talk with you. . . . You couldn't help the people in Brushnut?"

"I helped as many as I could. But half of the village is gone. Just . . . gone." Hollow-eyed children reached out to Sunchaser from the mirror of his soul, and anguish coiled around his heart. "Most of them were children. Babies."

"Is that why you missed the Mammoth Spirit Dance? We waited and waited for you."

Sunchaser peered out at the Mother. Spume had collected in thick, foamy drifts at the bases of the rocks where the lions lay. It reminded him of the high mountains. Even with springtime upon them, the granite peaks above the tree line stood wrapped in a glimmering cloak of snow. He wished desperately that he were there. Alone, so he could think.

Oxbalm studied him and muttered, "Mammoths dying . . . villages dying . . . Mother Ocean is always upset. This winter was colder than any I've witnessed in all my fifty-three summers. And our greatest Dreamer is angry with the whole world. . . . Is that what you meant, Sunchaser? When you said that the mammoths are relics of the last days? Did you mean that our way of life is about to die? That we haven't much time left?"

When Sunchaser didn't answer, Oxbalm heaved a sigh and said, "Please talk to me, Sunchaser. I must know what you see. Will you tell me what troubles your soul? I won't accuse. I won't condemn. I need to understand what's happening. You seem to hate everyone, but I can think of nothing we've done to madden you."

"I'm not angry with you, Oxbalm . . . and I don't hate anyone." He turned to brace his back against the tree trunk— so that he could not see the dead mammoths, but instead, faced the southern shoreline and the village of new mammothhide lodges. A few of the lodges had the door flaps pulled back, letting in the cool morning air, and he could see the whalebone frames. They gleamed black with soot. People sat around the fires inside, talking quietly. "Oxbalm, I . . . I've discovered something in the past cycle. Something that frightens me."

"What is that?"

Sunchaser folded his arms to barricade his heart. "I've discovered that there is a Wilderness inside all of us. Oh, we've fought to tame it, to silence its wild voices, but we never will. The Wilderness lives in the bones of our souls. I've been watching the people in the villages I've visited during the past few moons. Whalebeard Village and Brushnut Village are worse than here, but you've seen it, too. People walk the worn paths between the lodges with their eyes downcast and their foreheads furrowed. Back and forth, day after day, moon after moon. Even their children frown as they plod in their elders' footsteps."

"Yes," Oxbalm answered softly. "I've seen it."

Sunchaser met and held Oxbalm's worried gaze. "I've tried asking them why they're unhappy, Oxbalm. What they want out of life. They say they are angry, that Winter Boy was hard on them and that they have to travel great distances to dig the few tubers that are sprouting, or they tell me they need more meat. In rage, they demand, 'Where have all the mammoths and mastodons gone? What happened to the giant sloths that used to skulk everywhere?' Some whisper that the end of the world is near. Haven't I seen it? they ask. I'm a great Dreamer. If they've seen it, surely I must have, too." His voice faded as sickness welled in his stomach. Faintly, he repeated, "Surely I must have, too."

"And what do you tell them, Sunchaser?"

"I tell them to wait. Don't give up, I say. Wait and see what the Spirits have in store for us. But whether they understand it or not, I know the source of their pain."

Oxbalm took a step closer. His eyes narrowed as if in fear. "What *is* the source of it? I've wondered for a long time."

Sunchaser smiled feebly. "It's so clear. Why is it only I who seems to understand? Humans killed all the mastodons and the sloths. We're killing all the mammoths." He shook a fist. "*But we haven't silenced their voices.* The lonesome trumpeting and playful grunts—the voices of all the animals we've killed—seeped into the Wilderness in our souls, where we never stop hearing them. After tens of tens of cycles, the calls of all the dead have grown so loud that they make a deep ache in our souls. It's almost unbearable. And humans refuse to answer the calls. Perhaps we're afraid. Perhaps we don't know how to answer anymore."

Sunchaser stopped, trying to find the right words. His eyes sought the lions. The female licked her paws and purred to the male. At last, Sunchaser said, "Except at night."

"At night?"

"Yes. Last moon, a very old woman, who had seen mastodons as a child, told me that in her dreams she became Mastodon. She said it felt so warm, living inside that hairy hide. She said she could feel the wind ruffling her long hair as she roamed in search of twigs and shrubs. She said that when she lifted her trunk and trumpeted, the whole world trembled.

"And I'll tell you something, Oxbalm. My own Wilderness shook, as if the Quaking Earth Spirits had possessed my soul. I've been thinking about that. Thinking that maybe if everyone trumpeted in their dreams, the mastodons would come back. I've never seen one, yet I miss them. I miss their lumbering tread and the tender way they used to twine their trunks when they mated. I've heard the elders describe it."

The wrinkles in Oxbalm's face rearranged themselves into sympathetic lines. He reached up and touched a lock of Sunchaser's hair. "Is that what has turned your hair white? The dread?"

Gulls fluttered over the skeletal remains of the mammoths, and a cold well opened in the pit of Sunchaser's stomach. He couldn't tell Oxbalm about the maze. Not yet. "Is a world without mastodons . . . or mammoths . . . worth living in, Oxbalm? You tell me. I *must* know."

Oxbalm tipped his face up. As the wall of blue-black clouds moved closer, the first raindrops beaded on his cheeks. "Isn't that why we Dance the Mammoth Spirit Dance? So we can save ourselves and the mammoths? I thought that was what Wolfdreamer told you when you visited the Land of the Dead."

Sunchaser tightened his folded arms, hugging himself. "That's what he told me. Yes."

"But you've decided that the Dance isn't going to work. Is that it?"

"I didn't say that. I meant—"

"That we're going to die. Just like the mammoths on the shore."

"No. No, Oxbalm. I—"

"You've lost faith, Dreamer," Oxbalm said, but his voice held no reproach, only a deep sadness.

Sunchaser wanted to scream, to deny it, but he merely bowed his head.

Oxbalm whispered, "How did that happen? When did it happen, Sunchaser? It doesn't matter, really, but I'd like to know."

"I still have faith," Sunchaser replied, his voice almost too low to be heard.

"Maybe you have hope. Yes, maybe. But hope is not the same as faith. So, tell me, Dreamer, how does a man who has looked Wolfdreamer straight in the face stop believing? Tonight, at the council session, people will ask you that. Catchstraw will ask you. Prepare yourself."

Sunchaser let out a taut breath. "Oh, I'm prepared for many things. I've heard the rumors about Catchstraw's Dream. What frightens me most is that somewhere deep inside me, I fear that Catchstraw may be right. I've been having . . . trouble, Oxbalm. With my Dreaming."

"What do you mean? Trouble? Just because you're having problems Dreaming, it doesn't mean you've been abandoned by Mammoth Above, as Catchstraw alleges."

"No, but—"

Helper barked sharply as he ducked out of the small lodge that Oxbalm had set up for them. The dog had one ear pricked, the unfurred one, and his dark eyes shone like obsidian under water.

Sunchaser frowned. "What is it, Helper?"

The dog trotted by him and loped out across the sand toward the lions. The big male got to its feet and growled, but not at Helper. At something it sensed in the forest. Its breath condensed into a shimmering gray haze. When Helper began to run northward along the beach, toward the mammoths' skeletons, both lions leaped down from the rocks and followed.

"What do they see?" Oxbalm asked.

"I don't know. I see nothing." But Sunchaser's heart began to hammer wildly. "Stay here, Oxbalm. I'll go find out." He had taken three steps when someone in the village screamed, and he whirled.

The first mammoth broke through the trees like a tidal wave, her head swinging, her ears flapping back and forth. The reddish-brown hair on her body hung long and shaggy and shook as she ran. She lifted her trunk and trumpeted in fury, then charged out into the midst of the village, six other mammoths close on her heels.

The lions roared and fled into the forest, seeking the protection of the trees, while the dogs scattered with their tails between their legs, yipping as they ran.

Sunchaser stood stunned as the mammoths thundered by him, shaking the ground with their massive feet, heading into the village. Oxbalm fell back a step, his mouth open in shock.

"Blessed Mother Ocean," Sunchaser whispered to himself. "Why is this happening?" An attack so soon after the drownings? What was Mammoth Above trying to tell humans? She must have been desperate to have—

The village awoke in a shrieking, running horde. Women grabbed their children and raced toward the safety of the densest trees, while men struggled to nock darts in their atlatls. Three of the mammoths trampled lodges while the other three pursued the humans, trumpeting, twisting their thick trunks like writhing serpents.

"Sunchaser, get your weapons!" Oxbalm shouted.

"I . . . I can't kill a mammoth!" Sunchaser blurted. "They're sacred animals to me. I can't do it!"

"You would let them kill us instead?" Oxbalm shouted in rage. "Get out of our village and never come back!" He ran on rickety legs for his own lodge and his weapons.

Sunchaser stood rigid, watching the lead cow bear down on a young child. The girl ran shrieking before the cow, trying to reach her lodge. But the cow reached out with her trunk and lifted the writhing child off the ground. The girl's mother screamed and ran at the cow with a fir branch. The cow dashed the girl into the mother before trampling them both.

"*No!*" Sunchaser yelled. He dodged into his own lodge and came out with his atlatl and quiver of darts slung over his shoulder.

The rage of the herd dazed him. Everywhere, clouds of gray ash rose from the fire pits in pulverized lodges. Two trees had been uprooted and thrown down. How strange this was. Sometimes a bull would go rogue and trample a village—but a whole herd? And why *this* village? Why *now*?

Sunchaser sprinted out into the center of the chaos and sighted on a big cow as she thundered past. His dart took her squarely in the lungs. She swerved, spotted him and let out an earsplitting cry as she charged from not more than forty hands away.

Sunchaser dove to the right. He rolled to his feet as the cow turned, her trunk lashing back and forth with deadly intent. "Mother, why are you doing this?" he shouted. "What have we done to deserve this punishment? Are you angry with us? We didn't cause the drownings!" The cow stopped and stared at him, pain and disbelief in her eyes. ". . . Did we?"

Blood blew from her mouth, showering him with hot drops. He crawled behind a fir tree, pulled another dart from his quiver and nocked it in the hook of his atlatl. "Mother," he said, "please, tell me—"

Before he could finish, Horseweed and Balsam rushed out of the trees and launched darts into the cow's left side.

"No, wait! Stop! She's not—" Sunchaser yelled.

But the cow trumpeted in wild fury and ran at Horseweed and his brother. Sunchaser rose and let fly with his dart, catching her low in the right side. Horseweed struck her with two more darts before her legs went weak, and she stumbled sideways, crashing into Sunchaser's lodge. She regained her balance, stood trembling, then whined softly and fell to her knees. Her huge head rocked on her shoulders as clots of lung blood spewed from her mouth and trunk.

"Balsam! Go help your grandfather. Horseweed, come with me!"

Horseweed followed Sunchaser down toward the southern edge of the village, where two mammoths, one of them the lead cow, had trapped a half dozen people against a rock outcrop. *Don't think. Don't think about it now. Just act!* Shrill human cries mixed hauntingly with the trumpeting of the gigantic beasts. He watched in horror as the lead cow braved a spray of darts to lunge forward and grab a boy around the waist with her trunk.

Sunchaser let out a hoarse scream of "Mother, no!" and ran forward, pitching his dart wildly. Horseweed did the same. The projectiles flopped in the cow's sides as she hurled the boy to the ground and wheeled to face them.

"Sunchaser, look out! To your left!" Horseweed shouted.

An enormous bull broke from the trees, heading straight for him. The dawn seemed to die around Sunchaser. He stood rooted, the lead cow trumpeting her wrath behind him while Horseweed shouted. The bull's tusks gleamed yellow in the early morning light. As the bull reached out with his trunk, Sunchaser instinctively threw himself sideways, out from under the trampling feet.

Somewhere in the distance, a dire wolf howled. The lead cow, swaying on her feet, blood dripping from her sides, lifted her head to listen. All the other mammoths stopped and stood quietly—as though entranced by that call.

Villagers slipped away and ran for the forest.

But Sunchaser fell back at the base of the rock outcrop, breathing hard, studying the animals.

The lead cow let her huge head fall and exhaled a bloody breath. Her whole body shuddered. For the briefest of instants, she looked into Sunchaser's eyes. The hatred there changed to a pain so deep and profound that he could scarcely stand it. His soul felt stricken as a glimmer of understanding flickered through him.

His atlatl thudded softly against the sand, dropped by his numb fingers.

She made a small, pitiful sound, and the two surviving bulls fell in line behind her as she limped away down the shore, toward the place where Helper stood, his pointed muzzle up. The dog howled wrenchingly as they passed by him.

The glowing face of Father Sun slipped over the western peaks of the Mammoth Mountains, and red ripples of light danced across the sea. They gleamed with a translucent fire in the thick coats of the retreating mammoths.

"Sunchaser! Sunchaser, come quickly!"

He spun and saw Oxbalm kneeling, holding a child in his arms. He ran through the scattered belongings, past demolished lodges and dead and dying mammoths, to crouch down beside Oxbalm. The old man buried his face in the blood-soaked hem of his granddaughter's dress. Her beautiful face was still. Long tresses of her black hair brushed the sand by Oxbalm's moccasins.

"Oh, not my granddaughter. Not Mountain Lake. What's happening, Sunchaser?" Oxbalm pleaded. "What are the mammoths trying to tell us? First they kill themselves, then they kill us. What's gone wrong with the world? You walk the path through the maze to the Land of the Dead. You should *know* why this is happening!"

Cries for help rose all through the village, and people moved through the misty morning calling names, searching. Sunchaser's throat ached. He clenched his fists and shook them with weary futility.

"I don't know why!" he shouted, and the village went quiet. As though frozen in time, people stopped to stare at him. "I've lost the way through the maze!"

Voices hissed around him, repeating his words.

". . . lost the way?"

"Sunchaser has lost his way."

"He can't get to the Land of the Dead."

"Oh, Blessed Spirits. What does that mean? Sunchaser isn't a *Dreamer* anymore?"

From across the wrecked village, Catchstraw let out a shrill, triumphant cry and stared dumbstruck at Sunchaser—as though he'd heard news too good to believe.

Helper trotted back, his black eyes wide and unblinking. He took Sunchaser's sleeve in his mouth and whimpered while he tugged him northward.

"No, Helper. I must stay. The council session is tonight. I have to—"

The dog growled and tugged so hard that Sunchaser almost toppled to the sand. "All right. I—I'm coming."

Helper loped out in the lead, keeping sight of the retreating mammoths as they traveled through the forest. Sunchaser followed on weak legs.

The Boy watched through wide, horrified eyes. He cried, "Why are you tormenting them so, Man? What have they done to deserve this? They are good people! They obey your laws. They follow your ceremonials. They give you every ounce of their souls . . . and you do this to them?"

No answer came. But the wealth of stars glittered more brilliantly, as though all the souls in the Land of the Dead were listening. The heavens had quieted.

The Boy cursed and shouted, "Are you good, Man? Or are you wicked?"

When still no response came, the Boy yelled, "I accuse you of wickedness! You are evil! That's why you won't let me live! That's why you want me to commit myself to that putrid dead body! . . . Why do you not defend yourself, Man? I am waiting for your excuse. Speak to me!"

"Boy, boy . . ." the Man replied wearily. "Go down to the earth and find a rock to curse. I want you to curse it soundly."

"But why should I—"

"Just do it."

So the Boy did. He found a big rock, big and ugly and gray, and he spent three days cursing it up one side and down the other. He cursed the rock, and he whipped it with branches until he grew too tired to continue. Then he flew back up to the black sky and took his place amongst the twinkling Star People. "I have done it, Man," he said.

"What did Rock say to you?"

"Nothing."

"Nothing at all? He didn't object to your curses?"

"No. It was a rock. Just a dead rock."

And the Man whispered, "Nothing is dead, Boy. Your arrogance blinds you to the many lives going on around you all the time. That is like most humans. Rock just spent part of his life to teach you a very great lesson."

"What lesson?"

"If you did not understand Rock's silence, Boy, you will never understand anyone's words. . . . Letting you be born would be a curse upon the world."

Fifteen

"It's been only three weeks since Mother Ocean called to Oxbalm and showed him the sign," Catchstraw said from the eastern end of the council fire. They'd set up the meeting away from the devastated village, in a narrow fissure in the sea cliffs, but they could still see the broken fragments of their lives on the beach. Firelight gilded the dead faces of their loved ones, who lay beneath warm hides at the edge of the trees. Before them, a carpet of crushed bones from lodge frames glittered.

Catchstraw pointed at the ravaged skeletons of the mammoths on the beach, then at each of the huge carcasses left from the morning's attack. The stiff breeze that blew in off the ocean whipped his leather sleeve until it snapped. "And I ask you, what do you think the sign meant? Sunchaser *claimed* that he didn't know. What do you think the Mother was trying to tell us?"

Thirty people huddled beneath hides on the ground in front of him. Some peered at him stoically. A few had adoration in their eyes. Most looked skeptical and bored.

I'll show you, you old imbeciles. Not even Sunchaser can stand in the way of my Power! He raised his voice to a shout. "Look around you! Our village is *gone!* Thirteen of our friends and loved ones are *dead.* Illnesses are butchering our sister villages in the mountains. And *when* did it all start?"

Oxbalm sat cross-legged at the west end of the fire, his gray head down. Sumac held an elkhide over his shoulders, hugging him and whispering to him.

Catchstraw could not hear Sumac's words, but he knew from Oxbalm's face that they had nothing to do with Sunchaser. Probably Sumac was trying to comfort Oxbalm about Mountain Lake. *Good. Keep him busy, Sumac. This way, the people can think for themselves for once.*

But the villagers kept eyeing Oxbalm as though expecting him to comment. Preoccupied, Oxbalm drew designs in the sand around his moccasined foot. What a pathetic figure he made.

"I'll tell you when it started!" Catchstraw answered his own question since no one else seemed to want to. "It began when Sunchaser missed the first Mammoth Spirit Dance! Remember? It was right after that that illness ran through Tealwing Village."

The inner circle of elders, they who sat closest to the flames, muttered to one another. Old woman Yucca Thorn waved her sticklike arms, making some point. Dizzy Seal listened to her through half-lidded eyes, his mouth pursed in clear disagreement.

Catchstraw respectfully folded his hands and waited while they discussed the issue. Few of them liked him. He knew that. So he had to be extra careful in the way he treated them. If he weren't, the old fools would never grant him the authority he deserved. They would cast Sunchaser aside and pick some unknown as spiritual leader of the clan—anything to avoid having to rely on Catchstraw.

He patiently studied the beach. Moonlight drenched the sand. Out on the calm water, gulls floated. Every time a wave moved beneath them, their white wings flashed in the silvery glow.

"Are you saying that Sunchaser is the cause of this?" a young man finally asked from the dark edge of the crowd. Catchstraw couldn't see his face, but the voice sounded like young Horseweed's.

"Think about it," Catchstraw urged. "Sunchaser has missed four Dances straight. Four is a sacred number! And he left right after the mammoths destroyed our village. That's when we needed him most! He should have been here to help us pray our loved ones to the Land of the Dead."

"He's never here anymore when we need him," old woman Yucca Thorn yelled. With obvious effort, she rose on crackling knees and let her eyes drift through the gathering. Firelight shone against the carved whalebone beads encircling her collar and reflected from her abalone-shell pendant. "Catchstraw is right. You all heard Sunchaser this morning. He said that he couldn't get through the maze, that he'd lost his way to the Land of the Dead." She made a throwing-away motion with her hand. "That could happen only if Wolfdreamer has given up on him!"

Catchstraw wanted to chortle. He'd heard it himself. Everyone had. Sunchaser had admitted that he could no longer find his way through the maze! This new Dreaming technique had elevated Catchstraw to heights he'd never known, and blinded Sunchaser! He'd been practicing it nearly every night. Of course he couldn't tell that to any of these fools. They'd accuse him of . . . of witching.

It had been cycles since he'd heard about anyone being witched, but he knew the old stories. Witches used Power for wicked things. Generally, witches traveled in human form, but sometimes they transformed themselves, taking the legs of wolves so they could run faster, or the teeth of saber-tooth cats, or the strength of short-faced bears so they could tear their victims to pieces.

One notorious witch from Tides Village, far to the north, was reputed to have undertaken his nightly activities only after removing his eyes and depositing them in a basket in his lodge. He then borrowed the eyes of a lion so he could see better in the darkness. What had his name been? *Yes . . . Cactus Lizard*. The fool. His own dog had found the basket that held his human eyes and gobbled them down, so that he'd been forced to walk the village the next day with his golden lion eyes. People had run screaming. The village elders had ordered that Cactus Lizard be weighted with granite stones, taken far out into the ocean and heaved overboard in punishment.

But what an interesting idea. Catchstraw smiled to himself. What would it be like to prowl the night in the body of a wolf? Dizzy Seal's grating voice jerked him back from his musings.

"Is that it, old woman?" Dizzy Seal demanded from where he sat on the ground. His flat face gleamed like burnished copper. "Or is it that Sunchaser is tired? Eh? All of you! Sunchaser has been traveling from one sick village to the next, Healing people. That's why he hasn't been here to lead the Dances! Would you have him let people die so he could come to Dance with us?"

Shame tightened some of the younger listeners' faces. Murmurs eddied around the fire. Catchstraw saw his chance. In a ringing voice, he said, "I had a Dream!"

Somebody laughed. Who would have dared? Catchstraw peered out beyond the glare of the fire. *Horseweed.*

The boy crouched behind Sumac. Balsam knelt beside him, whispering in his brother's ear.

Catchstraw drew himself up to his full height and shouted, "Mammoth Above came to me! I was sleeping under that fir tree over there, and the Dream came upon me in a roar like the wings of the Thunderbeings!"

"So what did she say, Catchstraw?" Horseweed taunted.

A little girl snickered, then quickly put a hand over her mouth to try to hide her identity. Several adults joined in, chuckling.

"Listen to me!" Catchstraw ordered. "Mammoth Above said that her children killed themselves out of anger. Anger at Sunchaser! Not because he can't get to the Land of the Dead, but because he won't even try. He's given up! He refuses to talk to Mammoth Above."

"Why would he do that?" Horseweed challenged. "Mammoth Above is his Spirit Helper. Without her, he's lost."

"And so are we all, boy. That's the point. Sunchaser admitted today that he's lost! We have to find a new Dreamer to go to the Land of the Dead. And quickly, before it's too late. Before all the mammoths have disappeared from the world!"

"Just who did you have in mind as the new Dreamer, Catchstraw?" Balsam asked in mock seriousness. "You?"

Catchstraw's mouth gaped. "You brat! How dare you?"

"This is silly," Horseweed said and got to his feet. "Sunchaser is the only Dreamer we know who *can* get to the Land of the Dead. Have you ever been there, Catchstraw?"

When Catchstraw hesitated, laughter broke out anew. A few people got up in disgust and left the gathering.

"No, I haven't!" Catchstraw answered swiftly. "And you know why? I copied that maze that Sunchaser has on his square of deerhide. And it leads nowhere! I'm telling you the truth. He claims that *anyone* can follow it to get to the Land of the Dead. Have any of you been able to? Who? Shout out your name."

Silence engulfed the crowd. Even the inner circle of elders appeared to be pondering his argument. Some of the people who had been walking away stopped to listen.

"Bah!" Dizzy Seal shouted. "How many have tried? Oh, yes, we're all content to Dance and Sing for the mammoths' return, but how many of us have actually attempted to find our way through the maze?" He glared around the gathering. "Yes, just as I thought. Sunchaser keeps telling us he needs our help. But as long as we believe that he can get through, we don't think we have to. We can all sit back, knowing that *he's* doing the hard work! Well, I for one am not willing to condemn him until I've tried it myself."

"Go ahead!" Catchstraw yelled. "Try. I'll loan you my copy of the maze." *Just as soon as I can draw one up—and without the changes I made.* "Then come back and tell us, Dizzy Seal. Tell us if you could get through! I promise you'll find that it leads . . ."

His words were consumed by the conversation that flared up when Oxbalm rose. Oxbalm looked small and feeble in the light of the flames, holding his elkhide over his old shoulders. He raised a hand for silence. All eyes focused on him. "This talk of Sunchaser is meaningless," he said. "What we must think about now is our village. The Power is gone from this place. Broken. Scattered to the winds. We must move! Where should we go to rebuild?"

Sumac rose and slipped her arm around Oxbalm's waist. Then they walked away together, toward their robes in the forest. The entire gathering began to disperse, leaving Catchstraw standing almost alone in the windswept plaza.

Only old woman Yucca Thorn came up to him. Her ancient face had pinched into a thousand lines. She gripped his forearm tightly and whispered, "I believe you. Sunchaser is no Dreamer. Not now. Maybe he never has been. I never believed the part about the maze. I will begin talking to people, and listening to them. I don't care what the other sea clans do, but I think it's time that *we* had a new spiritual leader for this village."

Moonlight washed the oak forest as Kestrel hiked northward up the slope toward Buffalo Bird's camp. She panted. Buffalo Bird had kept her moving at a fast walk for over two hands of time. She could see his big hide lodge on the top of the hill, where four young men stood before a fire, their faces glowing orange in the reflected flames, their laughter raucous in the stillness.

Buffalo Bird chuckled behind her. He'd been humming, rapping his atlatl against the dart shafts in his hand to make a rattling sound in time to his Song. "You must be glad to see so many men, eh, Lame Antelope? A woman alone, running from her husband, she needs to be loved."

Kestrel flinched, but she kept on walking. Rape would be nothing new to her. After a time, pain eased. Wounds healed. She only feared what would happen afterward.

"Well, even if you're not glad to see them, they will be glad to see you. We've been out hunting mammoths for over a moon. In all that time, none of us have had the pleasure of seeing a single track . . . let alone the pleasure of a woman. And you're very pretty, despite the bruises and cuts on your face."

Then he slipped his dart shafts into his quiver and reached up to caress her hair. Kestrel twisted away.

He grinned, twirling the atlatl on its sinew finger loops. "Will you fight us? Oh, that would be good. My brothers would like that. Perhaps you could keep us entertained all night long."

Kestrel turned to face him. "Buffalo Bird, speak with me honestly. I don't care what you do with me, but what will you do to my little girl?" Against the deep-blue background of evening, he looked taller, more muscular, than before. "She's only twenty-two days old. She's no threat to you or your brothers. And—and you could sell her. Or give her to someone who wants a baby."

"I don't know," he said. "That Trader only told us he wanted his wife back. And how would we feed that baby if you were gone? The girl would cause many problems."

"What does that mean?"

"It means I don't know."

"Will you kill my baby?" The rabbit-fur sack in Kestrel's arms felt suddenly lighter, as if part of Cloud Girl had already slipped away from her. Her mind raced as she tightened her hold on her daughter.

Buffalo Bird shrugged. "I will have to talk to my brothers about it. But we want to find that Trader as soon as we can. A woman alone can run pretty fast, but carrying a baby? The child is worth nothing to us."

"Nothing?" The air went out of Kestrel's lungs. She looked down at Cloud Girl's beautiful little face, framed in the hood of rabbit fur, and the hard ground beneath her feet melted to quicksand.

At her horrified expression, Buffalo Bird laughed. "The best thing for you, Lame Antelope, is if you really are this Kestrel that the Trader is searching for. Because if you're not and we've already killed your baby . . . well, we can't have you going back to your clan and telling them about us. You could start a war . . . get a lot of good people killed. It would all be your fault."

Kestrel stood rooted to the ground. He'd just told her that he was going to murder both her and Cloud Girl—and had spoken as lightly as if he'd been discussing the killing of field mice. Why didn't she run? Had all of her soul drained out of her in the past few weeks? How could she keep her hands so still, so tight, around Cloud Girl and not lift them to rip out his eyes?

Did Lambkill destroy your will to survive? Why are you just standing here?

Buffalo Bird shoved her shoulder hard, then smacked the atlatl across her rump. "Go on. Walk. I'm hungry. Fresh deer meat is waiting for us in camp."

Kestrel turned. On the hill above, the shadows of his brothers played across the forest like huge shapeless monsters. She began walking. Her eyes scanned both sides of the trail, searching for and finding a thick patch of grass twenty paces ahead, where the trail veered sharply upward through a small outcrop of rocks.

Her steps grew silent, like Bobcat's at dawn. With great care, she shifted the weight of the rabbit-fur sack to her left arm and slowly reached down to unlace the pack tied around her waist. Her fingers barely touched the contents, identifying them without making the slightest sound: flakes, twine, Cloud Girl's mousehide pacifier, the tapir ulna . . . Sickness churned in her belly as her fingers tightened around the ulna. *You can do it. You have to!*

"Besides . . ." Buffalo Bird was very close behind her now, closing the gap between them as they neared the rock outcrop ". . . that Trader's brother, Tannin, told me that Kestrel had committed incest. If you're her, your baby is dead anyway. At least we'll do it fast, so the girl doesn't suffer. I don't know about that Lambkill. He was so crazy, he might torture—"

Kestrel glanced sideways at the thick patch of grass and lifted her foot to the first stone step on the trail. It wobbled dangerously beneath her moccasin. As though falling, Kestrel groaned "Oh, no!" and dropped Cloud Girl into the grass.

"What's happening?" Buffalo Bird demanded. "Just grab onto that next—"

Kestrel pulled the ulna from her pack, braced her feet and spun around. His mouth gaped when he saw the stiletto in her hand. He choked out "No!" as she threw all of her weight into driving the ulna into his chest. She felt the weapon go deep. Blood spattered his buckskin shirt and soaked her hands.

Buffalo Bird let out a cry of shock and grabbed for her as he fell backward. They rolled down the slope entwined like lovers, while dust puffed out around them. In the back of her frantic mind, Kestrel wondered why Cloud Girl hadn't erupted in shrieks. She kept waiting . . . waiting for the brothers to hear the ruckus and come running. They toppled over brush and rocks before they landed hard against a tree trunk. Buffalo Bird caught a handful of Kestrel's long hair and tried to drag her off of him, but she wrapped her legs around his and slammed her fist into the end of the ulna, driving the sharp point deeper. He gasped and half sat up to stare into Kestrel's face. Blood bubbled on his lips.

Slowly, he sank to the grass, then went limp. Kestrel rolled to the side. She put a bloody hand over her mouth and sobbed silently. On the hill, Buffalo Bird's brothers had stopped laughing. Confused voices rose. One of the men left the fire and went to the edge of the hilltop to peer down. Against the golden aura of the blaze, he looked huge.

Kestrel jerked the dart quiver from beneath Buffalo Bird, but the shafts were splintered. One of the finger laces on the atlatl was still wrapped around Buffalo Bird's fingers. Kestrel tore the lace away before she stumbled to her feet and ran for Cloud Girl. When she grabbed for the rabbit-fur sack, Cloud Girl mewed softly, as though asking if Kestrel were all right. "I'm fine, my daughter. Hold on. We have to run, fast!"

She raced around the base of the hill, holding the baby in a death grip in her arms.

She couldn't risk following the trails anymore. She would have to chance the midst of the dark forests. Twigs cracked beneath her moccasins as she jumped a fallen log and dashed for the black heart of the trees. No moonlight penetrated there.

Behind her, someone shouted. Then a roar of angry voices split the night. She could hear men running.

The dream . . . the same dream . . . always the same.

It was a place that no one went to. No one but himself. Because only he still cared about that murdered baby.

The willows and reeds grew thick along the banks of the Goosefoot Marsh. A low terrace of sandstone, no higher than a man's head, encircled the water. Cycles of wind and rain had scoured out dozens of shallow rock shelters, and in the bottom of the shelter at the northern end of the marsh, his baby brother lay beneath a pile of earth and stone. That grave drew him like a starved animal to the scent of blood.

Sunshine warmed Lambkill's face as he braced a hand against the cool stone and followed the narrow path around the marsh. Three hands below, wasps crawled over the shore, flapping their translucent wings while they gathered mud for their nests. Hundreds of the small round structures hung by slender strands of mud from the roofs of the shelters. This place, with its soft sounds, eased his tormented soul. The murmurs of great white pelicans and ducks came from the reeds. Every so often, a line of pelicans beat their wings in unison to drive fish into the shallows, where they could be plucked from the water. Farther out, green-headed mallards flipped their tails up to fish for minnows.

As the trail curved around a dense patch of cattails, Lambkill saw the grave. He stopped and took a deep breath of the fragrant air. Mint veined the cracks in the shallow overhang, and a thicket of ferns fringed the front, creating a sight of extraordinary beauty. A big green bullfrog sat at the edge of the ferns, its throat puffing out in time to its croaking.

"I'm back, little brother. Have you been lonely?"

Lambkill had piled up the stones that marked the grave. Since that day, twenty years before, moss had sheathed them. He approached reverently, Singing a soft Song to the little Spirit that lived beneath the rocks. His people believed that the souls of dead babies would be reborn in the bodies of the next children to grace the family. Lambkill's father, Blue Warrior, had fathered no more sons. Lambkill had the duty to give that tiny dead boy a body to be reborn into.

"Don't worry, little brother. I am to marry. Soon you will be with me again."

Lambkill stroked the mossy rocks and remembered.

His parents had fought. Lambkill had run into the lodge and found his father, bent over his little brother's bed, strangling the baby.

Something had happened to Lambkill on that day. At the sight of the tiny blue boy, something in his soul had broken clean in two, like a dry stick beneath a heavy hoof. He'd screamed and jerked the baby from his father's hands and carried it out into the sunshine, rocking it back and forth in his arms. He . . .

"Lambkill?"

A hand roughly shook his shoulder. He blinked himself awake.

"Lambkill, wake up. You're having a bad dream."

"Yes," he whispered hoarsely and let out a halting breath. He rolled onto his back. The scent of dew-soaked dirt drifted on the wind. Clouds must have filled the night skies, for no light penetrated their brush lodge. He couldn't even make out the shapes of their bedding hides. The horror of the dream lingered like a foul stench in his soul. Groping in the blackness, he found his pack and pulled it against his chest—keeping his son, Little Coyote, safe. "A very bad dream. One I've had many times."

"I didn't know you had such a dream. What is it about?"

"Don't concern yourself with it. I—I'm all right. Go to sleep, Tannin. Thank you . . . for waking me."

Sixteen

High above Sunchaser, clouds painted delicate white brush strokes on the lupine-blue belly of Brother Sky.

Sunchaser carefully worked his way along a creek bed, listening to the water babble as it percolated through a crust of ice. The game trail had veered into a sheer-walled canyon where sunlight rarely penetrated. Wavy lines of snow clung in the shadows. As the day lengthened into late afternoon, a chill breeze blew in off the ocean, rustling through the trees and whistling along the faces of the cliffs. It probed his clothing with such glacial fingers that he couldn't help shivering. He pulled up the collar of his hide shirt and held it closed. Helper had trotted so far into the lead, hands of time ago, that Sunchaser had lost sight of him.

He'd been following Helper for two days. The bulls had fallen behind late yesterday, disappearing into the forest to die. Only the wounded mammoth cow now walked the trail ahead of them. With each step she took, the obsidian points of his darts would be cutting deeper. By now her pain would have grown unbearable.

You're to blame, Sunchaser. You caused her to hurt this

way! When Mammoth Above had come to him on his first vision quest, he'd promised her that he would never again lift his atlatl against one of her children. Would she understand that he'd had no choice? That these children had gone rogue?

He lowered his eyes, studying the pale light that mottled the canyon. On the rocks that poked up in his path, dark red spots gleamed. The cow had lost a lot of blood. How could she keep going?

Ahead, the game trail meandered through a shaded glen and disappeared around a bulge in the canyon wall. Sunchaser plodded forward. As he followed along the curve, he saw a small waterfall cascading down a twenty-hand drop, splashing on rocks in the bottom of the drainage, and heard scavenger birds calling to each other. Ravens and magpies squawked, and buzzards circled overhead. The musty odors of mold and decay accosted him long before he finished rounding the bend.

The first skeleton took him by surprise. Here lay the remains of a mastodon. Though the mastodons had died out long before he'd been born, he knew their bones well.

Good Plume had taken him to a Dying Ground when he'd been a little boy and had taught him the differences between mammoths and mastodons. The massive animal before him was smaller than a mammoth and had a flat skull, not a domed one. The tusks recurved, unlike mammoths' tusks. As he went closer, he noticed that the teeth resembled rounded cones. Good Plume had told him that mastodons needed such teeth because they had lived in wooded areas and browsed on leaves and twigs, unlike mammoths, who needed flat teeth for chewing grasses.

A long dart point lay half buried in the mastodon's third rib. Made of fine red chert, it glittered in the deepening shadows. This animal had been hunted, probably killed, by humans, but its bones showed no signs of having been butchered. So the bull had escaped its hunters and bravely journeyed here to die.

"Bless you, Father. I hope your soul is running free through the forests in the Land of the Dead." Sunchaser stroked the huge skull.

More skeletons met his gaze as he continued into the hidden valley—dozens of them, perhaps even a hundred, some with hairy hides shrunken over their bones, like great gray cocoons. They filled the box canyon.

He heard a soft whine and turned.

Helper lay on the grass with his nose touching the trunk of the dying mammoth cow. He had his ears down and his eyes wide open, peering intently at the mammoth's closed lids. The cow had stumbled and fallen atop her two front legs. She hadn't the strength to rise again. Her back legs twisted hideously in the tall grass. Dart shafts protruded like perverse quills from her blood-soaked hair. But she lived. Puffs of breath condensed into silver clouds near her open mouth. The sight wounded Sunchaser's soul.

"Oh, Mother, forgive me."

His voice echoed in the stillness. The cow shuddered and faintly moaned, frightened by his nearness. Her lids fluttered, as though fighting a great weight, then opened.

Sunchaser knelt at Helper's side and looked into the mammoth's eye. Fear and pain surged in that dark well.

"I haven't come to hurt you, Mother. Not again. I swear it."

Sunchaser reached out and gently touched the gray skin below her eye. The wrinkles felt soft and warm, like sunlit moss on a summer day. For the first time, he noticed the variations in her skin color, from the pale green of her eyelids to the rich reddish-brown spots around her mouth.

Suddenly the cow's body spasmed. Her hind legs twitched uncontrollably and her trunk thumped the grass as though trying to grasp on to something, anything, to keep her here, alive.

When her muscles relaxed again, Sunchaser hurt as though he'd swallowed crushed obsidian. He Sang the cow's soul to the Land of the Dead, praying to Mammoth Above to come and lead her safely on the long journey across the ocean . . . and all the while, he begged forgiveness.

Mammoth blinked lazily at him.

He didn't know how long he held that forlorn gaze, but when the cow's eye became glassy with death, the sky showed stars flickering through a thin layer of clouds.

Sunchaser silently lay down on his side, facing the cow, and placed his cheek on a patch of the long silken hair that hung from her lower jaw. It smelled of grass and sunshine . . . and blood. *Cold, so cold.* He felt colder than he'd ever thought possible for a living man.

Helper trotted over and curled around Sunchaser's back, shielding him from the mist that gathered in the box canyon.

"I—I had no choice, Helper. You know that, don't you? I had to kill this cow. I didn't want to. But that little girl's screams . . . and the boy . . ."

Helper whimpered.

Sunchaser buried his face in the cow's shaggy hair. Grasshoppers sawed their legs in the grass, their songs mixing oddly with the lullaby of the waterfall.

Sunchaser closed his eyes. But he couldn't sleep. He tossed and turned, reliving the battle in the village, seeing again the look in the cow's eyes. His soul drifted. Like an old leaf touched by winter's first gale, he longed to break loose from his body and fly with the cow to the Land of the Dead . . .

Sometime in the night, movement stirred the grass.

Sunchaser scrambled to sit up, panting, and saw the cow staring at him. "You . . . you're alive! I didn't kill you!"

The cow's shape blended with the darkness. But as she lifted her huge head, the glow of the full moon struck her and he could make out her face. A silver sheen coated every wrinkle on her old hide and reflected in the black depths of her eyes. She curled her trunk and tucked it between her forelegs.

"Yes, you did, human. I came to Otter Clan Village to die."

Her voice rumbled in his ears like far-off thunder, soft, deep. "You wanted to die. Why, Mother?"

Mammoth let out a breath that rose in frosty curls around them. *"You have failed us, Sunchaser. There is nothing left for mammoths on this earth."*

"No, not yet. I . . . I've just lost my way temporarily," he said. "I'll figure out the path through the maze. Give me more time!"

"There is no time left, Dreamer. The world is changing too fast for us. As the glaciers melt, the ocean rises, the rain never stops, and the grasses change. The buffalo are growing more numerous, taking from us the few areas of good graze left. We're starving. We're sick. Our weakness makes us easy prey for you humans with your deadly darts and powerful atlatls. It is time for us to go."

"Is that why the mammoth herd ran into the sea?"

"They were trying to reach the Land of the Dead across the water. They had been begging the Thunderbeings to come for them. Finally they decided to try to make the journey alone. How brave they were. It is not an easy thing to admit that your time is finished. Someday, human, your kind will have to face this truth, too."

"Help me, Mother," Sunchaser said. He extended his hands to her pleadingly. "Maybe it's not too late for you. If I can just figure out how to bypass the new turn in the maze, I can go and talk to Wolfdreamer again. He can guide me, tell me how to put the world back in balance so that you will have enough grasses to eat. I've been so busy Healing the sick that I . . . I haven't had time to Dream. But Wolfdreamer promised to bring all your relatives back with him from the Land of the Dead when I've balanced things again. Maybe there is a place where the buffalo aren't so numerous. Maybe—"

"Why can't you just let us die, human? There is nothing wrong with dying."

Sunchaser slowly lowered his hands to his lap. "I can't let you go, Mother. I need you. Humans need you."

"For what?"

"For ourselves. Don't you see? We've hunted and eaten mammoths for so long that we *are* mammoths. Our bodies are made from yours. Like your children's. Your blood runs in our veins. Who will we be when you're gone?"

The cow barely moved.

Sunchaser drew up his knees and propped his forehead on them. "You don't understand."

Winters would be the worst. Now, on bitterly cold mornings when the snow drifted ten hands high around his lodge and he wondered if Summer Girl would ever be brave enough to stir from her long sleep, he had only to see a mammoth to feel warm—as though he knew deep down what it felt like to live inside that thick, woolly hide. But it took seeing a mammoth to remind him that he knew. Maybe his soul would never be warm again. Or maybe he would be warm only in his dreams, like the old woman who had lived with mastodons.

Fiercely, he demanded, "What will happen to our souls, Mother, when our flesh becomes that of sage chickens? Instead of trumpeting in our dreams, we'll have to learn to cluck!"

Despite the darkness, he saw a twinkle of amusement in the eye that peered at him. *"You believe that? That the human soul will change without mammoths?"*

"Yes. I do. Please, I just—I need more time."

The cow went quiet. With her trunk, she pulled out each of the dart shafts that protruded from her hide and dropped them into the pool of blood that had formed by her chest. Then she heaved a great sigh. Her hairy body looked sleek again, unmarked by her sufferings. She lowered her chin to rest it on her front feet and gazed at him steadily. Her eyes burned like torches.

"There is a place by the sea where you must go for your answer, Sunchaser—a rock shelter that hangs out over the

water, suspended atop a narrow ledge of stone. It's very difficult to find. There is only one way to enter it. . . ."

Sacred chanting filtered eerily through the misty coastal forest, punctuated by the wails of the bereaved. Pot drums kept time with the crashing of waves and the squawking of sea gulls. People moved through the devastated village like ghosts, stepping over the ruined lodges, veering wide around the dead mammoth carcasses. They wandered from burial litter to burial litter, placing gifts beside the corpses of their relatives. Everywhere, bodies lay in various stages of preparation. Some were being bathed, others dressed in their finest ceremonial clothing, and still others undergoing the final ritual painting, while prayer feathers were being hung on their litters.

Horseweed bowed his head as Sumac added alternating stripes of red and blue across Mountain Lake's forehead. Balsam crouched beside him, sniffling. Their little sister looked as pale as sea foam in the early morning glow, lying on her litter of pine saplings lashed with rawhide strips. Her once rosy skin had shrunken over her facial bones, making her nose look long and her little mouth protrude like a fish's. Still, she wore her finest wolfhide dress, tanned a warm gold and with green and red porcupine-quill spirals across the breast. Layers of richly painted hides covered her body from the waist down. A wealth of rare and colorful seashells had been piled atop the hides, a testament to the love her family felt for her.

Sumac's soft cries ravaged Horseweed's heart. Tears ran down her old cheeks, pooling in her deepest wrinkles. Her lips had pinched with grief and tightened over her toothless gums, and her white hair straggled damply around her face. For all practical purposes, she had been Mountain Lake's mother, caring for her, teaching her, tending her through one childhood illness after another. Mountain Lake's death must have hurt Sumac more than it did the rest of them put together.

But as Horseweed searched for his grandfather in the crowd, he wondered. Oxbalm sat at the fringe of the commotion, his shoulders braced against a fir trunk, his head back. His gray hair fell around his swollen face as he studied the goings-on through half-closed eyes. His thin body seemed to be visibly wasting away. Oxbalm had barely moved in two days, getting up just long enough to carry out his responsibilities as chief, most of which entailed arguing with Catchstraw over trivial matters.

The false Dreamer had grown arrogant and boastful since the council meeting. He flaunted the fact that Sunchaser had lost his way and whispered that he, Catchstraw, had reached the Land of the Dead and spoken to Wolfdreamer himself. Catchstraw said that he had thrown away Sunchaser's maze and that since then Wolfdreamer had been leading him by the hand.

. . . And he seemed to be gaining a following. Yucca Thorn, Maidenhair and old man Cheetahtail had been staying close to Catchstraw, whispering to him as they eyed the other villagers.

Now the three were among those surrounding Catchstraw, hanging on to his every word, waiting for instructions from the "great" Dreamer. He'd been giving orders as if he were a chief. And he seemed to enjoy his newfound influence. From dawn until dusk, his shrill voice had echoed through the decimated village. He'd kept people scurrying to fulfill his demands.

The very thought irritated Horseweed. People ought to be seeking advice from his grandfather, not from Catchstraw—though right now, Oxbalm wasn't in a condition to give it.

Horseweed watched Sumac paint a wavy yellow line across Mountain Lake's chin. Tears marred the artistry as they fell from his grandmother's cheeks.

"I miss her," Balsam choked out. He grabbed Horseweed's sleeve and buried his face in it to weep. From his shirt pocket, the head of an ivory doll peeked out. The piece had been carved from a section of tusk. Oxbalm had traded for the ivory and given it to Balsam. The doll's hair had been made from a mammoth's tail, and a necklace of tiny dovesnail shell beads draped its neck. Beautiful. Balsam must have carved it for his sister to carry with her to the Land of the Dead.

Horseweed stroked his brother's hair. "It's all right, Balsam. Soon she'll be with Mother and Father. They'll take care of her. You know how badly she missed them after they died."

"Yes, but I wish she didn't have to go."

"So do I."

Horseweed wondered about his own emotions. He felt the way he had two springs ago when he'd gone hunting and almost frozen to death in a freak snowstorm. He remembered how his mind had refused to work. Simple things, like how to start a fire, or how to kill an animal, had vanished from his mind. The effect had been as though his soul had separated from his body and hovered above to observe rather than to participate in life. But when he'd come back to himself, the pain in his body had been overwhelming. He wondered if it would be the same way with his numb soul this time.

Sumac tottered weakly to her feet and squinted at the gutted remains of the camp. Her white llamahide dress bore tiny spots of blood on the sleeves from having bathed Mountain Lake. The carcasses of the dead mammoths lay forgotten, and they'd begun to stink. People had eaten as many fresh mammoth steaks as they could hold before the flies had started to gather in great black swarms. Now no one would touch the meat. It crawled with maggots.

"Horseweed," Sumac said tiredly, "your grandfather is too old for this. Help me lift Mountain Lake's litter. We'll carry it to that big aspen tree straight behind camp. Oxbalm picked the location last night."

"Balsam and I can carry our sister, Grandmother. Why don't you just lead the way and we'll follow you." Horseweed gestured for Balsam to lift the foot of the litter, and Balsam wiped his nose and scrambled to obey.

They walked slowly in Sumac's footsteps, carrying Mountain Lake between them. Balsam couldn't stop crying. Sumac stopped occasionally to comfort a pale-faced woman or to pat the arm of a grieving husband. Partly because of the stops and partly because her ancient legs wobbled so badly, Sumac's path through the village slithered like a snake's.

The tree that Oxbalm had selected was beautiful. It stood on a low rise overlooking Mother Ocean and the forested humps of Pygmy Island. From here, Mountain Lake's soul would be able to watch the whales mating in the summer. She would see people paddle their bull boats out amongst the whales to collect the ambergris that floated on the surface. Sperm whales ate large numbers of squid, and the horny beaks accumulated in the whales' stomachs until the whales regurgitated them. Ambergris held fragrance and color and was mixed with many of the paints the people used in their ceremonials. The hues of the water changed as the eye drifted farther from shore; they were a grayish-green near the beaches and a rich blue out beyond the island.

"Put her in the fork of the tree," Sumac said.

Balsam had to raise the litter above his head and stand on his tiptoes so that Horseweed could lift and wedge it between the heavy branches. Bright-green leaves quaked around him, rustled in the breeze. Gulls wheeled through the sky in huge flocks. Mountain Lake's body would feed them, as well as the ravens, magpies and giant croaking buzzards.

Sumac watched with tears streaming down her face. "Now pull that top hide up over her face."

Horseweed tenderly tugged the hide up and tucked it around his sister's head. "Don't worry, little sister," he whispered. "Mother and Father will come and get you. They'll fly with you and the Thunderbeings to the Land of the Dead."

Balsam let out a sudden cry and held out the doll he had made. "Horseweed? Please. Could you put this under the hide with her?" He shinnied halfway up the aspen trunk to hand the doll to Horseweed. "I don't know if there are toys in the Land of the Dead. She might need this."

Horseweed took the little figure from Balsam's hand and gently placed it in the middle of Mountain Lake's chest. "There. She's sure to see it when she wakes up."

Then Horseweed climbed down. They had to wait for another hand of time while the rest of the villagers secured their dead relatives in the trees before the Death Ceremonial could begin. Oxbalm rose from his position in the fir trees at the fringe of the gathering and hobbled over to stand beside Sumac. Agony lined his face. His bushy gray brows pinched together over his bulbous nose. He'd left his shoulder-length gray hair loose. He gripped Sumac's hand tightly and let his gaze roam the trees. Painted hides gleamed through the weave of branches. The prayer feathers that hung from the litters twirled and fluttered in the wind.

"The burials are beautiful, aren't they? So many colors."

Sumac wiped the tears from her cheeks and nodded. "Yes. Our relatives in the Land of the Dead will be proud."

Oxbalm reached over and patted Horseweed, then Balsam, on the shoulders. "Thank you both for carrying Mountain Lake to her resting place. I should have helped you. I just haven't . . . haven't been myself."

"We loved our sister," Horseweed replied. "We wanted to do it, Grandfather."

Sumac squeezed Oxbalm's hand tenderly. "The weight of the past few weeks would crush any man. You just need more rest, my husband."

"Well, I can't look forward to that for a long time. Tomorrow we will pack our hides and few belongings and leave this place."

"To look for a new village site?"

"Yes. There's no point in staying here any longer . . ." Oxbalm answered ". . . now that the burying is almost done."

Horseweed exchanged a glance with Balsam and they both sighed. They had been born here. Part of their souls lived in these firs, these rocks, this surf. Leaving would be like a little death for them.

People began to gather around the central bonfire, waiting for the ritual to begin. Finally Catchstraw strode out in front of the gathering and lifted his skinny arms high. He wore a fine, heavily fringed elkhide shirt and gaudy pants painted with huge purple and yellow triangles. He lifted his old voice in Song: *"Ya ahe yaa ee ya eye na! Come closer, come closer! See where our sacred Father Sun is walking?"* He pointed to the western sky. *"In the blue robe of day, he is walking. Let us Sing praises! Let us beg him to take our loved ones with him when he travels to the Land of the Dead across the sea. Ya ahe yaa ee ya eye na! Come closer! Come closer!"*

Horseweed put his arm around Balsam's shoulders and hugged him while they Sang their little sister's soul to the Land of the Dead.

Oxbalm stood beside Sumac, his old lips barely moving, his eyes riveted on Mountain Lake's burial. With each flutter of the prayer feathers, his hollow expression deepened, as if his soul journeyed back in time to the days of her playing stick-and-hoop, or listening to his first stories. Against the background of the green sea, his stooped form reminded Horseweed of Grandfather Short-faced Bear walking the tidal pools on his hind legs, searching for black abalone.

Catchstraw clapped and called, "Join hands!" He took the hands of the people closest to him, who in turn joined hands with the people around them.

Horseweed touched Balsam's arm and murmured, "Stand on Grandfather's left. He'll never admit it, but he's going to need help to stay standing. I'll stand on Grandmother's right and help her."

Balsam nodded, impressed by the responsibility given to him. "I understand."

When one big circle had formed around the bonfire, Catchstraw led them in the Death Dance. Horseweed supported his grandmother while he kicked his legs and bobbed up and down in the turning of the circle. Sumac, as he had suspected, seemed on the verge of collapsing. She wept as though she would never run out of tears.

"Grandmother?" Horseweed bent low to whisper. "Let me take you to sit down. Mountain Lake's soul has already risen and is waiting for the Thunderbeings to come. I can feel it."

Sumac nodded, "Yes. So can I. All right," and stumbled out of the circle. Horseweed gently led her to the rock outcrop on the beach and helped her to sit down on one of the wind-smoothed stones. Then he sat beside her. A cool morning breeze flapped his long braids against his buckskin shirt. Catchstraw glowered at them from the circle, as if their leaving might have offended the Spirits. The old fool. No one else seemed disturbed. They all knew that grief drained a person's strength and that the Spirits would understand.

"You're a good grandson, Horseweed," his grandmother said in a shaking voice. She wiped her tears on her sleeve. "Your grandfather is going to need you in the days to come. Badly. I want you to remember that."

"Why, Grandmother? I'm not even a man yet. Why would Grandfather—"

"Because Oxbalm sees things no one else does. He thinks you're a man." She waved a hand weakly. "Anyway, you *might* have killed a mammoth. Nobody knows what happened to that cow Sunchaser followed into the forest. If it died with your dart in it, then you're a man."

The possibility had never occurred to Horseweed. His eyes widened. Sunchaser himself had called him a man. "What do you think Grandfather will need me for?"

"To help him." Sumac lifted her wrinkled chin to the Dance circle. "You can feel it, too, can't you? The people are turning against Sunchaser—even though your grandfather still supports him. Unless Sunchaser does something to turn this tide, Oxbalm will go down with him." She pinned Horseweed with faded old eyes. "All the people Oxbalm has depended upon in the past will start falling away—start turning toward Catchstraw and his idiot babble. *You*, my grandson, will be the only man he can depend upon."

Horseweed patted Sumac's hand nervously. "You know I'll help Grandfather all I can."

"Yes. I do know that. That's why I say it to you. And you'll be doing me a great favor if you keep this conversation to yourself. Your grandfather would not take kindly to my interference in his affairs."

A spider crawled across the sand near Horseweed's left moccasin. It was a big gray spider, with the longest legs he'd ever seen. When he moved his foot, the spider leaped a good two hands away and scurried with lightning quickness into a crevice in the rocks. "He may not take kindly to interference," Horseweed observed, "but he'll accept solid advice. Which is what you've always given. Mother used to talk about it. She said that you were the rock upon which Grandfather steadied himself and gained his strength."

Sumac's lips trembled as she slipped her arm through his and held it tightly. "Blessed Spirits, I miss your mother. She's the only woman I could ever open my soul to. When she died, I lost a part of myself."

"You can talk to me, Grandmother. I would never repeat anything—"

"No, I know you wouldn't." A somber expression creased her face.

Catchstraw fell out of the circle and shook himself like an antelope trying to shed its horns. "Listen!" he shrieked. "Listen, everybody!"

The Dance circle slowed to a stop and people began to mutter fearfully. Balsam cast a glance over his shoulder, looking for Horseweed and Sumac. Horseweed nodded to his brother and gestured to Catchstraw, indicating that Balsam should listen, too. With distaste, Balsam turned back. He disliked Catchstraw as much as Horseweed did.

Under her breath, Sumac said, "I wonder what he's up to now."

Catchstraw grabbed his skull between his hands, pressing hard and groaning. "I see death! Death and destruction! Oh, it's terrible!"

"Some news," Sumac commented blandly.

Dizzy Seal left the broken circle, mumbling irreverently as he went to slouch beneath the trees. Horseweed noted that that made three elders against three: Yucca Thorn, Maidenhair and Cheetahtail on Catchstraw's side, and his grandparents and Dizzy Seal on Sunchaser's side.

Catchstraw raised his voice to a bellow. "Sunchaser is the cause of this! I told you so. Mammoth Above is speaking to me, right now! Don't you hear her voice? It's so loud!" He pressed his fists over his ears and reeled on his feet. People gasped and fell back, staring. "I can't stand it. Oh, make it stop!"

"It's probably your bad gut!" Sumac shouted. "It's babbling so loud, you can't hear yourself. You've always had a weak stomach, Catchstraw."

Old woman Yucca Thorn turned to glare at Sumac, then called, "Go on, Catchstraw. What's Mammoth Above saying?"

"Oh, the pain! She's saying that Sunchaser was never her Dreamer. That he claimed the honor unjustly and now he's being punished for lying. For lying!"

Oxbalm left the circle and limped toward Sumac and Horseweed. Balsam trotted behind him, his eyes wide and fearful.

Horseweed's eyes narrowed. "Do you really think they believe he's Dreaming, Grandmother?"

"Yes, Grandson. They believe. Right now they'd believe anything that might guide them through this terrible time. No matter what—"

"Yes, no matter what it is," Oxbalm finished as he sat down beside Sumac and kissed her cheek. "If a man picked up a chip of mammoth dung from the trail and told these people that he could chart their future by crumbling it and tracing the patterns, why, they would sit right down and wait for the reading."

Horseweed laughed softly.

"Don't laugh," Oxbalm admonished. "I'm not joking. People are frightened. They will cling to any Dreamer who promises them a brighter life."

Balsam hoisted himself up on the rock beside Horseweed. His round face had flushed red from the Dancing. He said, "But look at the people who are listening, Grandfather. They're all stupid! It's old woman Yucca Thorn and her friends. What do they know?"

Oxbalm gently replied, "A great deal, my grandson. A very great deal. Without those people, we have no village at all."

Balsam asked, "Why not?"

"They have the Power to split this village down the middle. If they choose to follow Catchstraw, they will do so, because I cannot follow him. Dreamers, even false Dreamers, are very Powerful. I'll have to take those who will follow me and make a new village somewhere else." Sadness tinged his voice. "I want all of our people to be together. They're my relatives, and precious to me. I don't know who I would be without them. I need them in my life."

Horseweed interjected, "But, Grandfather, why not let them go? It might be better—"

Oxbalm shook his head. "It would not be better. These are important people. *Desperate people.* If a leader fails to heed desperation, my grandson, he's no leader."

Horseweed spread his hands. "But look at them! They're standing out there like frightened fawns. How do they know what's good for them? If Sunchaser were here—"

"Yes, yes, that's true." Oxbalm sighed. "If Sunchaser were here, he would tell people the truth, whether they liked it or not. And they would respect what he said. But he's not here. We don't know where he is."

Horseweed turned to peer solemnly at his grandfather. "You mean that his absence dooms him? That people will believe whatever message they hear the most frequently?"

"He who speaks more often carries greater weight than he who speaks best, Horseweed." Oxbalm massaged his wrinkled chin while he gazed at the villagers. Many had gone to stand beneath the death litters of lost loved ones and weep. "Remember that. It's a very important truth."

"Blessed Mother Ocean," Horseweed breathed. "In that case, I pray Sunchaser comes back to us quickly."

Sumac echoed him. "Yes. Please, Mammoth Above, send Sunchaser back to us soon."

Seventeen

Lambkill slowly circled the dead body, his steps as light as a hunting wolf's. Father Sun had come up bright and hot, making sweat pour from Lambkill's wrinkled face, run down his heavy jowls and splat in the middle of his elkhide shirt.

Tannin stood talking to Buffalo Bird's four brothers a short distance away in the oak grove. Already, ravens had gathered. Twenty or more perched in the trees, their black feathers shining while they cawed back and forth, drawn by the carrion smell. Lambkill admired them. Only the ravens and he would profit from this day.

"Yes," he heard Tannin say to Harrier, the oldest brother. Tannin had his head down, his mouth pursed tightly. They'd gathered around the smoldering camp fire to drink cups of fir-needle tea. "It must have been Kestrel."

Far below, a creek meandered through thick willows in the valley bottom. Copses of oaks and pines dotted the hills beyond it. Lambkill slitted his eyes and studied them for a moment, then returned his gaze to Buffalo Bird. Strands of Kestrel's dark hair wound through the corpse's stiff fingers. The body had been ravaged in the night. A lion had clawed gashes across the chest, partially dislodging the tapir-bone stiletto. Then, when it couldn't move the body, the lion had bitten clean through Buffalo Bird's shoulder. A swath of blood fifteen hands long stained the grass.

By the fire, Harrier said, "The lion came when we were in the forest, trying to track her. We returned and found Buffalo Bird . . . like this."

Harrier's young face twisted in hatred and grief. He had a massive brow, with small eyes and a flat nose. His hide shirt, dyed a deep red, stood out against the background of green oak trees.

Lambkill knelt to touch the blood that had coagulated around the chest wound. Pack rats had gnawed at it for the salt; their tiny, bloody footprints sprinkled the buckskin shirt.

"We will help you find her," Harrier said to Tannin.

"Lambkill will reward you richly. He's a very wealthy man."

"We don't want any reward. Except the chance to see her die." Fiercely, Harrier threw his tea into the smoldering fire and watched it sizzle on the chunks of charcoal. "Buffalo Bird was our youngest brother. He was fun-loving and adventurous, always making people laugh." Harrier's face contorted. "Our village will mourn for days. And our mother . . . Buffalo Bird was her favorite son."

"I understand," Tannin said. "We will welcome your help."

"Yes," Lambkill said, "we will welcome your help." He stood and surveyed the area. "It shouldn't take us long. I can read the night's events very clearly. She attacked Buffalo Bird up near the rock outcrop and then they rolled down the hill and struck that big oak tree, where she killed him.

"And after that," he continued, "she ran away into the forest . . . there." He nodded at the place where Kestrel had entered the trees. He could identify each dead branch she had cracked in her flight. Did she imagine that the depths of the forest would be safer than the trails? Foolish woman. In the tangles of undergrowth and the mounds of deadfall, it would be almost impossible for her to hide her tracks. Especially now. She had a head start of no more than twenty hands of time.

Lambkill laughed. "She can't hide from me. If she climbs over a log, I'll find the place where the bark is scarred. If she follows a game trail, I'll see her moccasin prints beneath hundreds of deer hooves."

Harrier asked Tannin, "Is he really that good a tracker?"

"Yes. He's the best. He—"

Tannin halted when Lambkill knelt by Buffalo Bird's body. With sure fingers, he removed the pack from around his waist and unlaced it.

"Lambkill. No! Please!"

Gently, Lambkill lifted the dead baby from the pack and stood him up on the wound in Buffalo Bird's chest. The tiny body had mummified perfectly. He'd created the boy's clothing by slicing off the beaded sleeve of his extra shirt and cutting holes for the child's stiff arms and neck. Lambkill had found two perfect green stones in a streambed. He'd inserted those into Little Coyote's empty eye sockets and sewn the lids open. He could do nothing about the boy's tiny, shriveled mouth. It had sunk to create a round hole in his face.

"See, Little Coyote," he said huskily. "Your mother did this." He tipped his boy forward so he could stare down at the bloody hole made by the tapir ulna. "She's a murderer. We must find her and make her pay."

When Lambkill saw that Tannin and the other men had stopped talking to stare at him, he rose and carried Little Coyote over to their circle. Two of the brothers stared at the baby with distaste. It triggered Lambkill's rage, but he kept his anger hidden and smiled. *My own brother thinks I'm mad.* Tannin would pay for that look a thousand times over. He should understand. He, of all people! *He was there that day!*

"I promise you, we will avenge Buffalo Bird's death," Lambkill said.

"Yes," Harrier agreed, nodding too quickly. "If we can find your wife."

"You needn't worry about that." Lambkill stepped away from the gathering and lifted Little Coyote over his head, then closed his eyes and, a step at a time, started walking in a circle.

He heard Harrier whisper to Tannin: "How did he do that? To the body, I mean."

Tannin answered, "It's something he learned from the People of the Masks up in the north. They clean out the gut cavities of their dead children, then they smoke the bodies to dry them. They believe that it ties the children's souls to their bodies forever."

"And your brother believes it?"

"Yes, I—I guess so."

"He acts like he thinks the boy is still alive. Does he?"

Tannin responded softly, "He's not well. He's gotten worse since Kestrel escaped."

Rage traced fire through Lambkill's veins. But he maintained his stern control.

"Gotten worse? Was he all right before?"

"He stayed gone a lot, on the trading trail. I can't say when this . . . this began."

They'd never seen! None of them had been that far north. But Lambkill knew. With his own ears, he'd heard those dead babies talk. He'd heard their disembodied voices coming through still mouths, directing, guiding. And *already* he could sense the first stirrings of a voice in Little Coyote. Though the Dreamers among the People of the Masks claimed that it often took years for mummified children to learn to talk, his son was learning far more quickly. Even now, Lambkill could pick up faint murmurings. *"Northwest. She went northwest, Father."*

Lambkill opened his eyes and tenderly tucked Little Coyote back into his pack. Then he lifted his arm and pointed. "There. That's the direction she took."

Harrier exchanged glances with his brothers. Their tension hung in the air.

"But," Tannin objected, "Kestrel's trail heads due west, Lambkill. Harrier tells me that there is a village only two days away—to the west. Maybe we should start there. Those people might have seen her."

"That's *not* where she's headed!" Lambkill shouted. "I told you. Little Coyote says she's going northwest! That's the direction I'm going in. You can head west if you want to."

The four brothers frowned and whispered to one another, while they examined Lambkill like a slab of maggot-ridden meat.

Lambkill angrily walked away. "Go on, Tannin! Take Buffalo Bird's brothers and go. I'll meet you there after I've found my wife."

"No, Lambkill, wait!" Tannin yelled. "I didn't mean that. I'm not going to leave you alone!"

He followed dutifully behind Lambkill as they entered the thick stand of trees. Deep green shadows enveloped them.

Harrier cupped a hand to his mouth and called, "We'll come as soon as we've broken camp . . . and buried our brother."

"He's going to do it, Man. Today, for the first time, I felt the strength in him. He's going to call me back to my body . . . all of me! Not just my fleshly soul. Lambkill wants all of me! Oh, Man, don't let this happen!" Boy wept bitter tears. *"Please, Man. I beg you. Save me."*

A silver glow suffused the black womb, and the Man said, "If you truly want to be saved, you must seek out this tribulation. Because if you run away from it, you will find the same tribulation waiting for you no matter which path you take.

". . . You see that, don't you, Boy? You've thought enough about these things to understand, haven't you?"

The Boy did not answer.

Eighteen

Horseweed walked along the beach at Oxbalm's side, his head down, studying the shells that had washed ashore—anything to avoid hearing the conversations echoing up and down the line behind them. People grumbled. Children cried. A dog barked at something it saw in the dense trees.

Over the past seven days, Horseweed had heard a bellyful of griping and complaints. It wasn't anybody's fault that they'd had to move their village, but people seemed to be blaming his grandfather.

Anger smoldered within him. Only an idiot could doubt Oxbalm's dedication to his people.

He glanced sideways at his grandfather. The old man had braided his gray hair into a short plait that hung over the collar of his buckskin shirt. His lips were pursed tightly, his brow furrowed. It hurt Oxbalm to walk, and the pain showed clearly on his face. Every night around the fire, Sumac threw willow bark into a gut bag and boiled it down to a thick, milky fluid, which she made Oxbalm drink. The potion eased the agony in his knees, but Horseweed could tell that all the walking was taking its toll on his grandfather. Oxbalm's gait grew stiffer every day.

Horseweed tipped his head back and gazed upward. Magnificent mountains of cloud drifted by lazily, their edges glowing a pale gold in the sunlight. Brother Sky's belly had been washed clean and bright. It gleamed like polished turquoise around the clouds. He inhaled a deep breath of the crisp air. He could smell the pines in it, but also the richness of damp earth, saltwater and seaweed.

Everyone was irritable. Oxbalm had barely spoken since they'd Sung Mountain Lake's soul to the Land of the Dead. When he did speak, the words came out sharp, each sentence a command—or, just as likely, an insult.

Mountain Lake's death had wounded Oxbalm deeply. Sometimes, late at night, his grandfather awoke calling Mountain Lake's name, swearing that he'd heard her little steps. "I heard her, I tell you!"

Horseweed closed his eyes briefly and bit back the pain. The first night after the mammoth attack, he had curled up under his robes and buried his face in his sleeve. Feeling lost and sick, he'd longed to cry out his grief. But he couldn't. Balsam had been sleeping next to him, and he'd heard his younger brother crying. He'd pulled Balsam close and held him through the night, patting him whenever his tears started again.

Since that time, eight days ago, a frightening wrongness had possessed the world, and nothing seemed to ease it. It wasn't just Sunchaser's leaving them after the attack, either. Horseweed felt strangely as if the Mother might rise up at any moment and drown them all in anger. Though he couldn't imagine what the anger might be for.

He turned to peer over his shoulder at the long line of people. The women brought up the rear, walking bent over because of the big packs they carried on their backs. Near the group of children, dogs trotted along happily, pulling travois piled high with household belongings. Men walked at the front of the procession with their weapons. Oxbalm and Horseweed had the lead. Everyone had worn his plainest clothing for the journey. Everyone, that is, except Catchstraw. The Dreamer's shirt glittered with beads, quillwork and seashell adornments. He walked along beside old Dizzy Seal, talking incessantly, making extravagant gestures. Dizzy Seal looked bored.

Horseweed turned back around and frowned as he walked. Strange. After having talked to Sunchaser, Horseweed understood his grandfather's disdain for Catchstraw. Catchstraw had no feeling of Power about him. His eyes didn't glow the way Sunchaser's did. He didn't move with Sunchaser's grace. In the days before the mammoths' attack, Horseweed had spent a good deal of time studying Sunchaser, and the man had amazed him. He seemed to think about every step before he took it, every placement of his hand—as though taking care not to inadvertently hurt any of the tiny Spirits that filled the world around him.

"Well, I just don't see why we have to travel so far!" Catchstraw's harsh voice broke Horseweed's reverie. Grudgingly, he turned to see what was going on.

With extreme politeness, Dizzy Seal responded, "I'm sure we'll stop when Oxbalm finds the right place for us. These things take time. We're not like the inland peoples. We've rarely needed to move. Deciding on a new village site requires great care."

"Ha!" Catchstraw scoffed. "How do you think Oxbalm chose the last site? Eh? Do you remember, Dizzy Seal?" Catchstraw opened his arms wide, as if begging Brother Sky for rain. "It was twenty cycles ago, and he'd gotten tired of walking. He reared back, heaved his dart, and we stopped where it landed. Great care! I'm pleased it didn't land in the ocean. We'd all have become relatives of the fishes and sprouted gills by now."

Oxbalm slitted his wise old eyes. Like an enraged bear, he bellowed, "If I hear any more talk like that, you'd better sprout gills, Catchstraw. And with a minnow's speed!"

All the conversations that had been eddying through the procession died at once. The clan elders cupped their hands to their ears to hear better, and the women in the rear ran to catch up. The heavy burdens on their backs bounced and swayed erratically.

"Are you threatening me, Oxbalm?" Catchstraw asked.

"I never threaten, Catchstraw. I make promises that I keep."

Catchstraw's brows drew down over his beaked nose. He stopped dead in his tracks, forcing the people behind him to halt as well. "Well, when *are* we going to stop, Oxbalm? We're all tired. Surely you know that. We've been walking for seven days straight!"

"We stopped for two days when we had that strange snowstorm," Horseweed corrected.

"Yes, strange," Dizzy Seal said and shook his head. "But it's been a strange cycle. So cold and wet. I wonder—"

"How would you know that we stopped for the storm, boy?" Catchstraw sneered at Horseweed. "You were off hunting the entire time we were in that camp."

Horseweed started to reply but closed his mouth when Oxbalm balled his old hands into fists and raised them. The people went stone still. A flock of gulls swooped in from the ocean, scolding the procession with bellicose cries at seeing their territory invaded. They swooped so close to Horseweed's face that he could feel the *whoosh* of wind as they passed. Oxbalm swatted at them angrily. "And my grandson brought in meat, didn't he, *Dreamer*? What have you done for the people?"

"Well . . . I . . . You never ask me what I've Dreamed, Oxbalm. I'll tell you what I've been doing for the people. I've been talking to Mammoth Above! *That's what!*"

A few reverent whispers passed down the line.

Oxbalm rubbed the back of his neck. "Blessed Star People, *again?* Doesn't she have anything better to do with her time?"

Horseweed tried to stifle it, but the snicker escaped his throat and came out a guffaw. Dizzy Seal bowed his head and smiled, but old Yucca Thorn scowled at Horseweed. His grandfather gave him a sharp glance.

Oxbalm said, "And did Mammoth Above tell you where we should make camp, Catchstraw?"

"As a matter of fact, she did." He flung out a skinny arm and pointed toward the high foothills, two days' walk away. "There. She said we should go up into the forest and make camp on a hilltop, so we can be closer to Above-Old-Man."

"Really?" Oxbalm countered. "She wants us closer to Above-Old-Man and farther away from Mother Ocean? Does Mammoth Above realize that we won't find many fish up there? Oh, there are a few in the streams and ponds, but nothing like the wealth of the tidal pools we have here. And clear up there, how can we scramble to the boats and paddle out to hunt sea lions and otters? Do the mussels grow better up there on the rocks?"

Catchstraw raised a fist and bellowed, "She thinks we've become *too* dependent upon Mother Ocean. Mammoth Above wants us to go out and . . ." he shrugged ". . . challenge ourselves more, for her sake."

"I see," Oxbalm responded quietly, a certain glint in his eyes.

Horseweed frowned. He'd seen that glint before and knew that it boded ill for all concerned.

Oxbalm smiled. "And does Mammoth Above realize that water in the foothills gets scarcer with every cycle? Why, down here, on the shore, we barely notice the summer droughts. But up there, it will be much different."

"Mammoth Above knows that very well."

"So, you think she wants to make life harder for us. Why? Is she punishing us, Catchstraw?"

As though proud he'd thought of it, Catchstraw said, "Yes, she is. And do you know why?"

"I have the unfortunate feeling that I do."

Horseweed scowled at Catchstraw. *If only Sunchaser were here to defend himself, you'd never be brave enough to say bad things about him, you false Dreamer.*

"Well, good," Catchstraw responded. His tone had an edge of silken malice. "Because *you're* the one who's always so quick to jump on Sunchaser's side. No matter what he does, *you* always support him. Mammoth Above has abandoned Sunchaser, but he still has Oxbalm to fight his battles for him. Don't you feel a little like a traitor, Oxbalm? Mammoth Above has done so much for us, and you—"

"Tell me something, Catchstraw," Oxbalm interrupted. He propped his hands on his hips. "Is there anything that *isn't* Sunchaser's fault? Hmm? I'd be interested to know. I mean, how about the diseases in the mountains? Are they Sunchaser's fault? How about the peak in the north that just started steaming again? Did Sunchaser do that, too?"

"Oh, stop this, Oxbalm," Yucca Thorn chastised. She limped forward on crackling knees to stand at Catchstraw's side, her ancient face pinched into an ugly expression. "If that's what Mammoth Above wants, why are we standing here?"

"*Is* that what Mammoth Above wants?" Oxbalm asked. "How do we know?"

Catchstraw straightened to his full height. Maidenhair came up behind Yucca Thorn, silently adding her support, waiting. "Because I just told you, that's how. Are you going to defy Mammoth Above's instructions?"

"Never." Oxbalm shook his head. "I am a devout man. If that's where Mammoth Above says we should make our new camp, that's where we will make it."

"Well." Catchstraw flicked his hand. His expression had gone sour and a touch uncertain. His eyes darted around uncomfortably. "Let's get on with it, then."

Oxbalm bowed, a bow so deep that his head almost touched his knees. The act was slowly, perfectly, done . . . and as full of irreverence as urinating on the moccasins of the lead Dancer at a ceremonial.

When he straightened, Oxbalm nodded pleasantly. "I guess you're right, Catchstraw. We'd best get on with it. Grandson?" Oxbalm put a hand on Horseweed's shoulder. Horseweed flinched. The anger and resentment in those old eyes struck him like a fist in the stomach.

"Yes, Grandfather?"

"We will need someone to scout ahead for us. On the beach, we can see, but on the deep forest trails, there are many predators that hide and watch. We wouldn't want a saber-toothed cat or a lion to drop on us from the trees. And right up there where Catchstraw wants us to camp," he indicated the place with his chin, "is where the short-faced bears used to make their dens. I haven't seen any bears in moons, but we don't want any surprises." He slapped Horseweed on the shoulder. "Why don't you pick two more young men to run ahead with you? Then we'll talk about which trail to take."

Horseweed glanced around. A smug grin curved Catchstraw's lips. "Yes, Grandfather," Horseweed said obediently. But as he whirled and trotted back to find Balsam and his cousin Iceclaw, Horseweed shook his head anxiously. The Otter Clan had always been sea people. They knew nothing about how to live in the mountains.

He glowered at Catchstraw as he passed, and the old man chuckled disdainfully. Horseweed clamped his jaw. He vaguely understood Oxbalm's plan—his grandfather wanted people to find out for themselves what a fool Catchstraw was—but Horseweed hated to be sucked into the whirlpool with Catchstraw's followers. He liked the taste of salmon and otter. And he couldn't even imagine life without abalone.

Oxbalm said, "The best trail that leads to that area of the foothills leaves from near Whalebeard Village. We must stop there tonight, tell them where we're going, so no one will worry about—"

"We can't stop!" Catchstraw said. "Mammoth Above wants us in the hills as quickly as our legs will carry us. When we find the trail, we'll just go straight up it. No stopping at Whalebeard Village."

Oxbalm's eyes narrowed, and Horseweed stopped suddenly, his heart pounding. But then Oxbalm smiled and said, "As you wish."

Horseweed shook his head. The world suddenly looked very frightening.

Kestrel stumbled and caught herself by seizing a fir bough. "Blessed Spirits," she whispered. She lowered one hand to rub her eyes. Thick fog blanketed the forest, and shimmering drops of water had formed on the needles of the evergreens. Every time the wind gusted, water cascaded down over her. Cold and weariness had sapped her strength; she had been running for two days and had had no sleep. Sometime last night, maneuvering through the starlit forest, she had lost the game trail she'd been following. Out of instinct, she'd kept heading downhill, knowing that the sea had to be out there somewhere, but now she wondered.

Dark shapes of moss-covered deadfall wavered in the mist. Logs and old branches stood canted at odd angles around her, ten hands high. Duff sank underfoot, soft and forgiving. Mushrooms made thick clumps around the bases of the trees. How would she ever find her way through this forest without leaving signs of her passage?

Kestrel let go of the bough and concentrated on the fallen log directly in front of her. The forest floor had turned treacherous. Wet. Icy in places. She dared not step up onto the log for fear that her moccasins would slip out from under her. She might be able to stand the fall—assuming that Cloud Girl didn't get hurt—but she couldn't risk leaving a scar on the bark. But how could she get around the log? Her mind refused to work. Even the simplest of problems halted her progress for long fingers of time while she tried to reason them out.

Numbly, she ducked beneath a tangle of dead limbs and crawled through. Despite her care, she failed to see the brittle twig that raked across the healing knife gash on her forehead and ripped it open again. Kestrel cried out. Warm blood trickled down the line of her jaw. Angry, she slapped at the twig to snap it off and inhaled a deep breath to calm herself. As she continued forward, the spongy carpet of pine duff squished beneath her hands and knees. Cloud Girl whimpered softly in her rabbit-fur sack on Kestrel's back.

"It's all right, my daughter," Kestrel reassured her, glancing up at the towering redwoods that rose into the sky. She could just make out the shapes of their limbs when the fog shifted. "Today we'll find shelter. Then we'll sleep. I promise."

A new mound of deadfall met her weary gaze. Tiny fir trees had grown up through the weave of dead branches, forming an impenetrable wall.

Kestrel slammed a fist into the duff and choked back the tearful rage that swelled in her throat. She longed to lie down and cry herself to sleep. What harm would it do to rest for a while? Yes . . . In her head, a pitiful voice echoed, "What harm?"

I could dig a hole in this soft duff. It will be dry beneath. I could curl up and be warm. Warm! She brushed damp black hair away from her face. What harm would it do? Pleasant thoughts spun dreamily through her sluggish mind . . .

Violently, she pushed to her feet on trembling legs. Terror had gripped her in cruel fists. "Where's the trail, Above-Old-Man? Help me! Where's the trail?"

A squirrel chirred, and Kestrel heard a loud *crack!* She turned breathlessly. The squirrel climbed down the tree, jumped to the ground and ran to retrieve the pine cone it had dropped. Sinking its teeth into it, the squirrel dragged the cone up onto a fallen log and proceeded to demolish it, eating the seeds as it went.

In spite of herself, Kestrel smiled.

But her smile faded when she saw movement behind the squirrel. A huge eye peered at her through the mist. As she watched, the mammoth's hairy trunk rose and twined through the limbs high overhead to pluck a string of moss from a branch.

How odd to see a mammoth here in the forest. Mammoths lived in the grassy lowlands.

"Hello, Mother," Kestrel whispered.

The mammoth chomped its moss, eyed Kestrel warily, then turned and disappeared—as silent as the fog itself.

Kestrel crawled back through the dead branches and wended around until she found the mammoth's tracks, imprinted in the mud of a game trail.

A wide trail.

How had she missed it? If she'd just walked twenty hands lower on the slope . . .

In the path ahead, the mammoth stood as if waiting. Kestrel shook her head, trying to clear the numbness she felt. Could she be dreaming? The mammoth looked ethereal, hazy. Maybe she had lain down, against her better judgment, and fallen asleep?

When Kestrel moved toward it, the mammoth began walking again, heading down the trail. Streamers of fog spun silver whirlwinds in its wake.

Like a sleepwalker, Kestrel followed.

Catchstraw's thin face shone orange in the light of his small fire. He'd made camp away from the other villagers, in the depths of the forest, where he could be alone. Anyone else would have been thought odd for separating himself like that, but not a Dreamer. Dreamers had special privileges when it came to privacy. The pungent odors of bear dung and crushed grass surrounded him. Trees hunched forward as though watching his every move. He could hear them whispering amongst themselves; they were frightened by his Power.

Catchstraw glowered up at the rustling branches that made a canopy over his head. Through them, patches of stars glittered. "Shut up," he said to the trees. "There's nothing you can do. You're disturbing my concentration."

He went back to the maze. His hand had grown heavy, so numb that he could barely lift it. He chanted softly while he used a chunk of charcoal to draw new lines, crisscrossing the old, obliterating some pathways so that they ended abruptly, as though striking a stone wall. His soul had left his body and floated above, watching, guiding.

"Soon I'll have Dire Wolf's legs," he whispered hoarsely. "I almost managed it last night. Tonight they'll sprout. I can already feel them growing. Then I'll be able to run away, far away. I'll find Sunchaser . . ."

The wind came up suddenly. The branches of the trees clattered together and showered him with small green leaves. The bushes joined the din, sawing back and forth, squealing and shishing.

They created so much racket that Catchstraw finally lurched to his feet and shouted, "You listen to me! There's nothing you can do to stop me. There's nothing anyone can do. I *will* become Dire Wolf!"

A shooting star streaked across the sky, leaving a silver trail. Catchstraw swallowed hard. Witches traveled in the form of shooting stars. Could some long-dead witch be descending from the Land of the Dead to speak with him? He waited, afraid.

"All of my life I've done what others told me to do," he murmured. "I married women that I hated, because my mother ordered me to marry them. Then . . ." he glared at the trees and bushes that watched him. ". . . I . . . I always wanted to be a Dreamer, but clan elders like Oxbalm wouldn't let me. They told me I had no talent for it, that Dreamers were born different, but not different like me, different like Sunchaser! Even after I became a Dreamer, when Running Salmon died, none of the elders sat in council to Sing and talk about their new Dreamer; none came to offer me their prayers or to discuss clan problems. No one has ever asked my advice . . . until I began destroying that maze." It surprised him that a sob lodged in his throat.

The forest went silent, and the wind held its breath.

Catchstraw blinked and slowly gazed around at the still oaks and pines. The Star People gleamed with frosty radiance. "You see now, don't you? That's why you're listening to me. I've found Power! . . . I've never been happy! *Never*. Because I've always been Powerless! And now that I've found Power, no one, human, animal or Spirit, will ever take it from me again.

"I *will* become Dire Wolf, and when I do, people will start doing as I tell them to. No one will dare to shout at me, or . . . or to say that I am useless!"

Another shooting star blazed across the black belly of Brother Sky, and Catchstraw lifted a hand in greeting. "Are you coming to speak with me? Is . . . is that you, old Cactus Lizard? Come. I want to learn the things you knew. Come and talk to me. I'll be waiting."

A gust of wind squalled through the forest again, and the trees clattered and rustled. The bushes hissed at Catchstraw, but he sat down, picked up his chunk of charcoal and lowered it to the distorted maze.

Nineteen

A shimmering blanket of fog covered the coast, obscuring Sunchaser's vision as he walked along the edge of the high sea cliffs, so that he moved by memory rather than by sight. He couldn't see the forest of stunted cypress that sloped upward to his right, but he knew it was there. Just as he knew that two hundred hands below, on his left, the subdued waves of ebb tide caressed the shore. He could hear their faint purl. He held his moosehide jacket closed against the chill mist and followed the curve of the cliff around to the north.

Ahead, he could see the dim outlines of the wind-sculpted pines that grew in the jumbled rock outcrop.

"That's where the yellow ants are, Helper. I found them yesterday," he said to the dog that trotted at his side. "There are a dozen anthills at the base of those rocks."

Helper tipped his muzzle and scented the air, then growled. He loped out in front with his nose to the ground, his back bristling.

Sunchaser flared his nostrils for any scent of camp fire or bear. Of all the creatures that inhabited the coast, the short-faced bear terrified him the most. It was swift, agile and ferocious, and, when walking on all fours, it stood taller than a man. When it raised up on its hind legs, it towered more than twice a man's height. The numbers of short-faced bears had dwindled since he'd been a little boy. He hadn't seen one in nine or ten moons, but just to make certain, he sniffed the air again. Only the sweet, tangy fragrance of cypress mixed with sea met his efforts.

As he walked toward the outcrop, the pines became clearer, growing straight up out of the rocks. Four of them. Their limbs swept back, away from the face of Mother Ocean, like long hair blowing in the wind. Their roots, like clutching fingers, curled down around the boulders and snaked out across them until they could bury themselves in the moist soil. In among the tangle of roots lay the anthills.

Helper stood on the far side, using his front paws to demolish the largest anthill. Dirt flew out behind him. When Sunchaser neared, the dog lifted its dirty muzzle and barked.

"So you found them, did you?"

Helper wagged his tail, the action spraying loose hair.

"Well, let's get busy. We'll have a nice warm fire in the rock shelter."

Sunchaser scratched Helper's now-naked ears and knelt to examine the anthills. No ants roamed the surfaces. The cold must have driven them deep into their tunnels. It had been unnaturally cold, as though Sister North Wind had turned against them and begun to blow air directly from the land of the Ice Ghosts down upon them. He sighed and removed the pack tied around his waist. Placing it on the ground, he unlaced it, then removed an elk scapula and a small, lidded basket, made for him by a woman at Whalebeard Village. He set the basket aside. The heavy scapula felt good in his hands. He began shoveling out the anthill, which Helper had already dug down to ground level.

Helper stretched out on his stomach and watched the process with keen interest. His mange had worsened. A patch of hair three hands wide had fallen from his left side, revealing the black-spotted pink skin beneath.

Sunchaser had dug a hole six hands deep before he saw the first ants: two winged males and a winged female. Sunlight filtered through the fog like a pale reflection of itself, glittering on their yellow bodies.

Sunchaser carefully plucked out the winged ants and set them near the base of the rocks, where they could crawl into the cracks for safety. Only winged ants mated. These would bring new life to the forests. The female would become a queen, if she lived, and the males would die.

Deeper into the hill, he struck a layer of wingless females. These gathered food and tended the eggs. He and the other Talth members monitored ants with exacting patience, charting their life cycles, watching them fight, kill and drag food and touch one another with a gentleness that rivaled that of humans. Some of the workers would live to be five or six cycles old, he knew, while the queens could survive for as long as fifteen cycles.

The ant workers moved slowly in the cold. Sunchaser picked up his basket and shoveled about three dozen of them into it, then clapped the lid on before any could escape. He slipped the basket and scapula into his pack, relaced it and rose.

Helper rose, too, his ears pricked. Worry brimmed in the dog's dark eyes.

"It's all right, Helper. I've done this before. The Ant Ordeal is the first that initiates into the Talth learn. But I understand your concern," he said as he started back the way they had come. Moist sand squished beneath his moccasins. "I haven't needed ants to help me Dream in a long time."

Helper padded by his side, looking up as though for the rest of the story.

Sunchaser shrugged. "I don't know what to tell you. When I was a boy, the Dreams came effortlessly, and with frightening Power. Then, in the past moon . . ."

The dog trotted along in silence.

"What's wrong with me, Helper? Why can't I Dream anymore? I pray that the ants will help."

Sunchaser gazed westward. Over the ocean, the fog bank glittered with a yellowish hue. He couldn't see the border to the Land of the Dead, but he could imagine it, deep blue melting into lighter blue, clouds drifting above. Softly, he prayed, "Please, Wolfdreamer. Help me. I *must* Dream again."

Helper abruptly broke into a run, and, like a dart, shot down the trail toward the rock shelter.

"Helper? *Helper!* What's wrong?"

The dog disappeared into the swirling fog. But Sunchaser heard him whimper and bark. Then he was quiet.

Sunchaser began to trot along the edge of the cliff, straining his ears. Waves crashed below; the tide was coming in, filling the rocky pools of brightly colored anemones, snails and hermit crabs. In the air, sea gulls squawked and squealed, and, high above him, he heard a condor cry.

Then he heard the weeping. He stopped to listen, and fog coiled around him.

"A baby? It sounds like a baby."

Sunchaser's bushy black brows met over his nose as he started forward again. The closer he went, the more it sounded as though the cries came from his hidden rock shelter. His heart pounded, pumping wary blood through his charged limbs.

Cautiously, he studied the edge of the cliff. Entering the rock shelter took a trick of wits, and the fog made the task even harder. Surely no one could have found the shelter without guidance.

Shh. Be still. Perhaps Mammoth Above sent someone to help you. Yes, that must be it. But . . . a baby?

Sunchaser spotted the three boulders piled beside the ancient tree stumps. The trees had been struck by lightning sometime in the distant past. Now only charred, worm-eaten remnants remained. Beginning there, Sunchaser counted the scallops of the cliff's rim. In, out, in, out . . .

He came to a halt when he saw the tracks of the mammoth in the soft sand along the cliff. Swiftly, he turned all the way around, but the fog prevented him from seeing a distance of more than three or four body lengths away.

"Mammoth?" he called softly. "Are you out there? Did you come to speak to me?"

No response came. He stood listening for a while longer, then resumed counting the scallops. Below the cliff, the surf broke onto the rocks, sending white spray high.

At the sixteenth scallop, he found the tiny indentation in the rock. Using it as a fingerhold, he got down on his stomach and slowly, gingerly, lowered himself over the precipice, feeling for the ledge of stone below. For a panicky moment, he hung over empty air. Then, just when he thought he would fall to his doom, his toes struck solid rock. It wasn't really that far down, only eight or nine hands. Helper jumped it with no trouble at all. But Sunchaser wasn't that brave. The edge of the cliff protruded, making it impossible to see the ledge from above unless you leaned far out and looked down. With painstaking care, he planted himself, then released his hold on the indentation and sank back against the stone wall.

The baby's cries had become sharp, almost angry-sounding.

Sunchaser took his time, edging along warily. One hundred and fifty hands below, waves continued to splash and pound the rocks. He glimpsed the shapes of two gulls as they dove through the fog before him.

He rounded the bend and entered the rock shelter—and then he stopped breathing.

Helper looked up as though saying, "Look what I found." He had curled his big body around a woman who lay on her side atop Sunchaser's elkhide robes, fast asleep. The baby lay beside her. The woman had unlaced the front of her antelopehide dress and pulled out her right breast for the baby. But the infant had lost the nipple and was wriggling frantically in an effort to find it again.

Sunchaser exhaled a confused breath and knelt by the child. Gently, he positioned the baby's head so it could nurse. When the child's mouth closed around the nipple, it quieted instantly. Helper lowered his head in apparent satisfaction.

Sunchaser shook his head. "What is this, Mammoth Above? I don't understand."

The woman was beautiful. Sixteen or seventeen summers, he guessed. Maybe ten hands tall. Much too skinny, as slender as a blade of grass, but waist-length hair fell over her chest, shrouding her full breasts like a black silk veil. She had a perfect oval face, with a turned-up nose and full lips.

Sunchaser frowned. The yellow stains of old bruises covered her cheeks, and beneath the web of her hair, a long gash ran the width of her forehead. The wound was raw and swollen.

"That's recent, isn't it?" he whispered to himself. "No more than a moon old."

Her chest rose and fell in the deep rhythm of a dead sleep. To have slept through her baby's cries and his arrival, she must have been exhausted.

His gaze darted over the shelter. Medium-sized, it stretched five body lengths long and four wide. The high ceiling arched over his head. Against the southern wall, his pack and three baskets sat beside three rolled-up elk hides. Next to the hides, he'd leaned the dog travois. He'd brought few belongings with him, but all of them had come in with the aid of Helper hauling the travois. The woman had apparently brought even fewer. Her open pack leaned against the woodpile near the smoldering fire in the center of the floor. He looked in it: a loop of sinew, several pieces of dried rabbit, a mousehide pacifier for the baby. Her only other possession appeared to be a very male-looking atlatl about the length of her forearm, made of sturdy oak, with finger grooves and sinew lacings for a sure grip while launching a dart. The hooked end had been crafted out of polished shell and inset onto the weapon's shaft.

No jacket? No sleeping robes? . . . No extra moccasins?

Sunchaser's curiosity was aroused. He studied her. Brown spots of old blood soiled her dress, and the front of it had clearly been slashed with a knife.

"You've been hurt. By who? A man? Your clan? Whatever your reasons . . . you ran in a hurry. Why?"

Rather than burning off as the day wore on, the fog was thickening. Elusive wisps fluttered into the shelter, licking at the stone like glittering tongues of silver flame. The cold deepened.

Sunchaser shivered. He could smell snow in the air. Snow was not unusual for early spring, especially given the bitterly cold weather they'd had for the past moon, but it could be deadly. He suspected that when night fell, the temperature would plunge.

As quietly as he could, he placed three more logs on the red coals and blew on them. Sparks shot out as the blaze crackled to life.

He warmed his hands, thinking. Finally he rose and gathered up his extra hides. Gently, he draped two of them over the woman and her baby.

The last one, he wrapped around his own shoulders. Then he sat down cross-legged before the fire and untied his pack. He took out the basket and set it down beside the hearth, where it would stay warm.

"Soon," he promised the ants. "Very soon."

Catchstraw writhed on the floor of his lodge, panting, trying to suppress his screams. The pain . . . the pain! He clawed wildly at the dirt floor. He kept his feet braced against the log that held down the northern wall, although his agonized movements made the whole structure shudder. The hide walls vibrated as though caught in a ferocious windstorm. In the middle of the floor, his·fire had died down to glowing coals that watched him with winking red eyes.

"Blessed Spirits!" he cried. "Make this stop! What have I done to deserve this?"

Catchstraw's stomach tied itself in such tight knots that he rolled to his side and pulled his knees against his chest in defense. He'd already vomited until he'd purified himself. What more could the Spirits want? His face contorted. He gasped, and his eyes lit on the freshly plucked trailing stems of morning glory that lay in a neat bundle beside his red-and-green medicine basket. The gray, woolly leaves seemed to mock him.

"That old hag, Running Salmon," he groaned, "said you'd bring visions! Not this . . . this agony!"

Before her death, Running Salmon had described to him in detail all the Spirit Plants that she knew of, especially those that grew near the seacoast. Catchstraw had never expected to see even half of them. Morning glory grew on the dry slopes of the foothills. He'd discovered it by accident two days ago, when they had taken the trail that veered off before Whalebeard Village and begun their ascent into the hills.

"Running Salmon . . . that witch! She probably did this on purpose! You're not a Spirit Plant. You're *poison!*"

He fell into dry heaves that racked his body until he wept.

Running Salmon had said that morning glory had the Power to turn Dreamers into any animal they wanted to be. She'd been dying at the time, her voice a pained whisper:

"The person who uses the plant correctly . . . can become Mammoth, or Condor. He can even roam the skies as a glowing ball of fire. But . . . be careful . . . very careful."

Then her head had fallen sideways, and she had died—before telling Catchstraw how to prepare the plant, or how much of it to ingest! He could have done either wrongly! He'd boiled a handful of the leaves and drunk them as tea, as he would have done with a dozen other Spirit Plants. But maybe only the seeds of morning glory brought on Dreams, and then only when crushed to a paste and rubbed into the temples. How did he know? How would he ever know now?

"Sunchaser probably knows . . . but I'll never ask him. Never! If I die . . ." he gasped ". . . I swear to the Spirits that I'll find Running Salmon in the Land of the Dead. She'll regret doing this to me!"

But as Catchstraw tossed over onto his back, a violent tingle began at his navel and radiated outward in hot lances. He panted in terror and stared wide-eyed at the red hue that sheathed the ceiling. Power grew inside him, like a malignant child swelling his breast to the bursting point.

"Oh, Spirits!" he gasped. "What's happening?"

Voices hissed at him from the dying fire: *"You've chosen your way . . . to witch . . . a witch you will be. What animal have you selected?"*

"Animal? You mean, which do I want to be? I . . ."

The instant the words formed in his thoughts, his body began to burn as though set afire, and a garbled shriek erupted from his mouth. As he watched, his arms stretched and twisted, bending into the shape of Dire Wolf's forelegs. Long yellow claws sprouted from his fingertips. He rolled onto his stomach, frothing at the mouth in terror, gnashing his teeth, growling—and he rose on four legs. He scratched at the dirt, throwing up a haze behind him. He looked down at himself and saw the thick black fur that coated his powerful limbs. It gleamed a dark crimson from the glow of the coals.

Catchstraw managed uneven steps, learning this new body. Sometimes when he looked down he saw skinny human legs, and he had to concentrate hard, very hard, before wolf flesh sheathed them again. Such a wealth of scents! He'd never guessed that the world contained so many smells. His hearing had sharpened, catching even the faint scritchings of insects in the grass outside. He slipped his keen nose past his lodge door flap and wobbled out into the night—and entered a different world, one shaded in dark grays instead of blackness. As he trotted down a game trail in the starlit forest, he growled, then lifted his voice in an eerie howl that echoed through the foothills. A crack of lightning split the cloudless night, lanced across the sky and blasted a nearby hilltop.

The rumble followed him as he jumped a pile of deadfall and loped headlong for the trees.

Twenty

Kestrel moaned softly in her nightmare. She found herself alone again, standing at the bottom of the hill outside of Juniper Village, hearing Iceplant's hoarse shriek pierce the night. Against the blazing background of the bonfire, Lambkill brutally brought his war club down on Iceplant's head. Iceplant's knees buckled . . .

Kestrel tried to scream, but no sound would come from her constricted throat. She flailed about and almost woke up.

Somewhere far away, waves struck a shore, and wind whimpered. Fish was roasting, the scent sweet, delicate . . .

Lambkill took his knife from his belt and thrust it into Iceplant's stomach, then sawed upward. A small, wretched cry escaped Iceplant's lips.

Kestrel tried to run back to him, to save him, but her feet wouldn't move. *"Iceplant!"*

The ground started to quake beneath her. Through the roar of the quake, she heard the snorting and bawling of a short-faced bear. Kestrel staggered back and forth, terror flooding her veins. She had never experienced such anger from the Quaking Earth Spirits. In the country of the Bear-Looks-Back Clan, such quakes rarely occurred, and when they did, they stopped almost instantly. This tremor built until it shook the world. Trees toppled sideways, crashing into each other, and the rumble turned to an earsplitting cacophony. Or was that Bear roaring?

"Iceplant?" she screamed again.

"Run!" Iceplant shouted feebly. "Run . . . Kestrel."

The rage of the Spirits mocked him, jerking the ground from beneath Kestrel's feet and tossing her headlong toward a pile of rocks. She fell, twisting to guard her pregnant belly, and landed hard on her left shoulder. Clawing and gasping, she tried to crawl away from the toppling trees, only to have the earth before her crack with a deafening blast. A shriek tore from her throat. A hissing fissure opened and spat hot steam into the air. In the writhing haze of mist, she tried to scream a name, the most Powerful name she could imagine, but not even she could hear it. The Quaking Earth Spirits trampled it to dust . . .

"It's all right," an unfamiliar voice intruded into the dream. *"You're safe. Everything is all right."*

Kestrel felt herself being tugged away, climbing, climbing . . . Terror and futility swept over her, and silently she wept. Tears trickled down her face. She could sense her body again. It felt like a feather floating on a gentle summer breeze. So tired, but so warm. For the first time in almost a moon, her fingers and toes didn't ache.

And she felt something else. A hand, large and gentle, upon her shoulder, squeezing comfortingly.

"Try to wake up," a man's accented voice said in soothing tones. "You're safe. Your little girl's fine. And food is cooking."

She heard him stand and walk a short distance away. Then

a fire crackled as though more wood had been thrown onto it. Kestrel lay still, feigning sleep, listening while her heart raced. Wind gusted, blowing cold across her face. She realized that a hide covered her. Had he put it there? Clamping her jaw to stifle her fear, she opened her eyes.

Beyond the rock shelter, snow fell. Huge white flakes filled all of the sky that she could see.

The man knelt before the fire, with Cloud Girl in the crook of his left arm. The baby's tiny fists twined in the fringes of his sleeves while she sucked on her mousehide pacifier.

He glanced at Kestrel. Their gazes met and held. His eyes were so dark and deep-set that she seemed to peer into two black, bottomless holes. He had a long straight nose, and the bluntness of his square jaw was softened by the high curve of his cheeks. The deep copper tones of his skin belied his shocking white hair. Not an old man, but a young man . . . and a handsome man.

"Are you feeling better?" he asked. She remembered that curiously deep, gentle voice from her dream. "You had a good long sleep."

Kestrel just stared at him.

He bent forward to turn the three rockfish that roasted above the flames, skewered with a long stick. "Are you hungry?"

She pulled herself to a sitting position and studied the shelter, noting his pack and the baskets along the wall, the big ugly dog that lay in the rear. The animal had lost whole patches of its hair, but it watched her with intelligent brown eyes. Her own pack still rested by the fire.

"Hungry? Yes . . . I am."

"That's an interesting accent you have. Where are you from? Far to the east, I'd imagine."

Kestrel did not answer. She fumbled to retie the front of her dress, and the man averted his eyes, stood and carried Cloud Girl to the mouth of the cave, where he spoke to the baby in a calm voice. Cloud Girl gurgled contentedly.

The background of snow highlighted the shape of his muscular body. He had broad shoulders that narrowed to a slim waist. A long white braid hung to the middle of his back. That fact still startled her. White hair? Why would such a young man have white hair?

"Could I have my daughter?" Kestrel held out her arms. "Please?"

"Oh, of course."

He brought Cloud Girl back and handed her over. "She's a beautiful little girl."

Kestrel took the baby and held her tightly against her chest. "Thank you."

"How old is she?"

"Almost a moon."

"I thought she looked very young. Is it safe to take her on a long journey so soon? I mean, spring weather is so unpredictable."

"She's strong."

The man's gaze touched each of the faint yellow bruises that marked Kestrel's face. He seemed to be thinking about them, wondering. "You both are, I imagine." He smiled, hesitated. "I took your daughter with me when I went fishing. I hope you don't mind. You looked like you could use the extra sleep." Slowly, his smile vanished. "Tell me, how did you find this place?"

Kestrel lowered her eyes to Cloud Girl's face and rearranged the baby's rabbit-fur hood, drawing it up to cover the fuzz of dark hair. She didn't want to tell him the story of the mammoth cow. She wasn't sure that she believed it herself. She had been so tired when she'd seen the cow that she still wondered if she hadn't imagined it. "Thank you for taking care of Cloud Girl while I slept. And for letting us stay here."

He nodded, but his brows lowered. "This rock shelter isn't easy to find, even with instructions. Who told you about it?"

"I heard about it . . . from . . . it was a . . ." She sighed.

What difference did it make if he thought her addled? She would leave soon and she'd never see him again. "A mammoth. A mammoth told me. I don't care if you believe it or not. That's the truth. I know we came into your shelter without your permission. But once I'd climbed down to the ledge, I didn't have the strength to climb back up, and your pile of hides looked so warm." She nervously rocked Cloud Girl in her arms. "I'm sorry. We'll leave as soon as the storm passes."

He peered at her intently. "Tell me more. About the mammoth. Did it actually speak to you?"

"Me?" Kestrel asked in surprise. "Spirits Above, no. I'm no Dreamer. I was lost in the forest when I saw the mammoth. I hadn't slept for two days and I thought I was seeing things. When she saw me, she lifted her trunk, took some moss to eat, then vanished. I found her tracks and saw her again, on the trail ahead of me. She kept looking back to make certain I was following her."

"And you did?"

"Yes. She obviously wanted me to."

"She led you to the handhold in the rocks?"

Kestrel nodded. "And I climbed down, yes."

He ambled out to the mouth of the shelter and propped a hand against the rock. After a moment, he looked over his shoulder at her. "How did you know she wanted you to climb down? You can't see the rock shelter from the top of the cliff. You couldn't have seen my tracks, because I take great pains to walk on the bare rocks up there."

"I just knew." She shrugged. She remembered thinking that the indentation in the stone couldn't be natural, that it appeared man-made, like a handhold, which meant that there had to be something below. "So I climbed down."

He stared unblinking at her, and a certainty seemed to form in those deep, dark eyes. His voice came out low. "You should have. Obviously you were led here. Just as I was. The question is," he said, "why have we been drawn together?"

"What do you mean, drawn together? I'm leaving as soon as I can."

"I wouldn't say that if I were you. You might cause it to snow for weeks."

Great lightning! She hadn't fallen in with a lunatic, had she? "What are you talking about?"

"When Mammoth Above arranges something, she's stubborn about seeing it through. I know."

An odd glint had entered his eyes, like that of a cat hunched quiet and still before a mouse hole. It made Kestrel uneasy. "I don't think—"

"You may not. But believe me, you were brought here for a reason." His face tightened as he scrutinized her more intently. "I wonder how you're supposed to help me."

"You're crazy. I'm not here to help you. I'll be leaving tomorrow, if I can." Kestrel sat up straighter. "You're Spirit-possessed!"

"That would be a nice change," he said, sounding as though he meant it. He shoved away from the rock and let his arm fall to his side. "I didn't mean to frighten you. Sorry. I get anxious when I'm thrust into the midst of a Spirit plan that I don't understand."

He walked to his pack and pulled out a wooden bowl and two cups, then returned and crouched before the fire.

At the edge of the fire pit, a gut bag hung on a tripod made from oak branches tied together at the top. He pulled two sticks from the woodpile and used them to lift a hot rock from the fire and drop it into the bag. Steam exploded when the rock struck the liquid inside. After a moment, he tipped the bag and poured two steaming cups of tea, then set them aside. Next, he slid two fish into the bowl, which he handed to Kestrel. She took it gratefully. The last fish he tossed to the dog, lying in the rear of the shelter. The dog chomped it down in four bites and wagged his nearly naked tail.

"You're not eating?" she asked.

"No."

The man handed her a cup of tea before he sank to the floor, obviously picking a safe distance from her. "It's mint. I picked the leaves this morning, up at the edge of the spring in the cypress forest."

"Thank you." She set the cup by her side.

His gaze scanned her face. "You must let me tend that cut on your forehead. I'm a Healer."

"So am I. I mean—no, not really—but I know something about Spirit Plants."

"Do you?" He gestured toward his dog. "Maybe you can help me Heal his mange. It's getting worse."

"Horse nettle berries fried in grease will cure it."

"Horse nettle? I don't think we have it here on the coast. Or maybe we call it by a different name. In any case, I could get it from a Trader. When does the plant have berries?"

"Not for another four or five moons."

"Did you hear that, Helper?" he called. The dog perked up. "Looks like you'd better get used to the mange. Horse nettle doesn't have berries until near the end of summer."

The dog's ears drooped. He laid his big head on his forepaws.

Gingerly, Kestrel peeled a thick piece of meat from the side of her fish and ate it. It melted in her mouth. "If you don't have horse nettle, nightshade or chickweed will work. You just have to be very careful with nightshade, because it's so poisonous."

The man tilted his head appreciatively and let her eat in silence for a time. When she'd almost finished, he asked, "What's your name?"

Kestrel lowered the bowl to her lap and wiped her greasy hands on her moccasins. Word of Lambkill's reward could have reached this far, moving from Trader to Trader. She couldn't take the chance. "We won't be together for very long, I promise you that. . . . Where did you get that dog?" she asked, trying to lead him to a new subject.

"Helper came to me in a Dream." He reached up and touched his hair. "The same Dream that turned my hair white. When I awoke, I found Helper curled around me, keeping me warm."

"A Dream? You're a Dreamer?"

"Yes. I'm a Dreamer. You're not going to tell me your name, are you?"

"Earlier you said that we'd been drawn together for a reason," she said. "I didn't think that Dreamers—that is, male Dreamers—liked women."

"They don't. That's what makes this all the more interesting."

"Why would Mammoth Above—"

"It's very hard to have a discussion with someone whose name you don't know."

Kestrel picked at her fish uneasily, took another bite of it and chewed it slowly. Outside, snow fell in blinding white sheets. The wind had shifted, coming now from the west. Flakes tumbled in, heavy and wet, creating a glistening fringe at the mouth of the rock shelter. "I can't tell you my name."

He lifted his cup and took a long drink. When he lowered it, he said, "The man who hurt you, is he the one who's chasing you?"

Kestrel's jaw quivered. He noticed, but his face remained blank. Cloud Girl started to twist in her arms. Kestrel tried to take the mousehide pacifier from her daughter's mouth, but her hand shook so violently that she dropped it, grabbed for it, dropped it again and let it lie. Her fingers felt wooden as she fumbled to untie the front of her dress and lift the baby to her breast.

"Is he?" the man pressed.

". . . Yes."

"The snow should cover your trail."

"He'll f-find me anyway."

He sat stone still. Concern lined his face. "Why is he chasing you?"

She shook her head in response. Every muscle in her body had tensed. Cloud Girl began to cry when her milk stopped flowing. "I'm sorry, baby," she whispered. Kestrel closed her eyes and forced herself to breathe deeply and evenly. But nothing helped. Cloud Girl shrieked and waved her fists.

"Here, Cloud Girl. We'll try again in a little while." She tucked the pacifier back into her daughter's mouth. The baby fussed, but quieted.

It took a monumental effort to look up at the man again.

His intent gaze was kind as it moved over her face, logging each detail of it. Then he lifted his teacup and drained it dry. Kestrel noticed that he had gripped the cup so tightly that the tendons stood out on the back of his hand.

"What's your name?" she asked.

He lowered his cup to his knee. "I am called Sunchaser."

Kestrel's breathing went shallow. She was staring at him, but from the corner of her eye she saw the snow spinning, spinning with wild fury, and she felt suddenly dizzy. Her face must have paled, or she must have swayed, because he lunged to grab her arm.

"Are you sick?" he asked.

"Sunchaser?" Her voice sounded pitifully small. "The Sunchaser who started the Mammoth Spirit Dance?"

He held her arm for a moment, then released her. "Yes. That's right."

As though suddenly needing breathing room, he got to his feet and stood before the fire with his broad back to her. He threw another piece of wood on the flames, and a flurry of sparks winked and drifted lazily toward the ceiling.

"Are you really Sunchaser?" she asked. "I mean . . . *really*?"

"I am," he answered, not taking his eyes from the jumping flames.

Kestrel's gaze riveted on his back. His shoulder muscles bulged through his buckskin shirt. Firelight glimmered on his white hair and the portion of his cheek that she could see.

Sunchaser. In her memories, Iceplant spoke that name, his voice hushed with awe, bright with hope. "Lambkill, Sunchaser says we shouldn't beat our wives. He says that Wolfdreamer watches and listens . . ."

Kestrel lifted Cloud Girl to her breast again. This time, her milk flowed. She took a deep breath and held it. With her exhalation, words flooded out: "The man who's chasing me is my h-husband. According to my clan, I committed incest."

Sunchaser bowed his head but didn't turn. "And did you?"

Kestrel patted Cloud Girl to reassure herself. "My lover didn't consider me to be his cousin. He was my father's brother's son. His family traces its lineage through the women. His mother came from somewhere near here. From Otter Clan Village. Do you know where that is? That's where I'm going."

Sunchaser turned to her with a long, contemplative look, as if he'd just perceived a vague pattern in a tangle of cat's-cradle string. "Yes, I know the village. When the storm ends, I'll take you there. Do you know the names of any of your lover's family?"

She shook her head. "No. I . . . not right now. His name was Iceplant."

"Was?"

"Yes, he's . . . dead."

"At your husband's hands?"

"Yes." Tears blurred Kestrel's eyes, but she forced herself to continue holding his gaze. His expression softened, becoming deeply troubled. She noticed for the first time the purple smudges of sleeplessness beneath his eyes, the tiny lines around his mouth.

He dropped his gaze. "Otter Clan Village is two days' walk south of here. I know the Otter Clan people well. We'll find his family."

In a sudden wash, all of her terror and weariness flooded to the surface and a sob rose in her throat. She buried her face against the side of Cloud Girl's rabbit-fur sack and silently wept.

No sounds except the constant roar of the sea and the crackling of the fire invaded the rock shelter for a long while.

Then Sunchaser's buckskin fringes rustled as he moved, and Kestrel heard the soft scraping of his moccasins on the stone floor. Very gently, he put a hand on her hair. She felt the warmth rising from his body, smelled his masculine scent—something more than just wood smoke and sea—and took comfort in those things.

In a choking voice, she said, "My name is K-Kestrel, Sunchaser. Kestrel, of the Bear-Looks-Back Clan. I come from Juniper Village, far away in the marsh country."

Twenty-one

The light of the fire did little to stem the tide of darkness that closed around Tannin. He sat on a rotting log in front of the blaze, his hands laced in his lap. The heated conversation had been going on since sunset, but once again he could hear the forest creaking and moaning in the grasp of the storm winds. Four hands of snow had already deluged the mountains. The pine boughs bent beneath the onslaught, and the underbrush wore such a thick coating that the largest bushes looked like white lions, hunched up and waiting for prey to pass.

Harrier paced on the opposite side of the fire. Despite the freezing cold, his flat nose and massive brow glimmered with sweat.

Lambkill's hostile eyes followed Harrier's every move, though he sat beside Tannin and sipped his fir-needle tea with perfect calm.

Harrier's three brothers, Flint, Trickster and Ravenlight, sat behind Harrier on pieces of deadfall that they'd dragged into camp. None of them could have seen more than nineteen or twenty summers. But they all stood taller than average, twelve hands or more, and had round, heavily browed faces. Snow coated everyone's shoulders and hair, making them look like old men.

"I won't just stay here and do nothing!" Harrier declared sharply, resuming the argument. He'd clamped his jaw in determination. The light of the flames turned his face livid. "We have to keep looking for her!"

"Then go." Lambkill waved a hand dismissively. "We don't need your help to find my wife."

Harrier pointed a daggerlike finger at Lambkill. "Listen, old man, your wife is our brother's murderer. We have to find her soon, so we can go home and tell our clan." He threw up his hands. "I don't understand why you refuse to move from this spot!"

A cold smile curled Lambkill's withered lips. He tipped his face skyward into the falling snow. "You're all boys," he said. "You're not old enough to know anything about tracking. *I* can track a bird through the air! But you—"

Harrier snorted derisively, and Lambkill lurched to his feet, glowering with deadly intent. Harrier's brothers muttered angrily amongst themselves, and Tannin saw that Flint's young fingers had gone tight around the atlatl on his belt.

Tannin put a hand on Lambkill's arm. "Please, Lambkill. *Explain* to them why you want to stay here."

"They're blind. They'll never understand the needs of a great tracker!" He thrust out his chin belligerently. "Why should I even waste my breath?"

"Please," Tannin murmured insistently. "They want to find Kestrel just as badly as you do. If you explain—"

"All right!" Lambkill shouted and jerked his arm from Tannin's grip. Wind tousled the gray locks around his face as he clenched his right fist. "Listen to me, all of you!"

Harrier straightened. "We're listening, old man. What do you have to say?"

Lambkill's lips parted, showing broken yellow teeth. "Tracking a human isn't like tracking a deer, boy. It takes completely different skills. Humans won't always stay on the ground. They'll trick you by climbing trees and working across a forest through the branches, or hopping through piles of deadfall like a squirrel. My wife knows that she's running for her life. She won't leave tracks that *you* can follow. Her trail will be almost invisible. Only *I* know how she thinks and what she's likely to do."

Harrier glared at Lambkill. "And how long must we stay here before we can continue the search?"

"Until the snow melts."

"Melts!" Flint shouted in rage from behind Harrier. "That could take a week or more! She could be all the way to the Cheetah Paw villages in the north by then!"

Lambkill threw down his wooden cup and stood, breathing hard, his hands flexing at his sides. "Don't you think I want to find her quickly, too? She murdered my son!"

"They why can't we—"

"Because!"

The echo reverberated through the forest. The owls that had been placidly hooting the night went forebodingly silent.

Lambkill continued in a low voice. "Only when the snow melts completely will I be able to spot the subtle outlines that her moccasins left behind in the mud. Only then will I be able to find the places where she broke twigs in her flight. The snow must be gone before I'll be able to identify the places where she pulled herself up to climb over piles of deadfall. Finding the crescent marks of her fingernails in tree bark isn't easy, you young fools!"

"Fingernail marks!" Flint laughed so hard that he had to bend forward and hold his stomach. His brothers roared with him. "This old Trader must think we're stupid, my brothers. *No one* can find such things!"

Ravenlight challenged, "Besides, what happened to that dead child of yours? Has he gone blind? I thought you said Little Coyote could *see* your wife's path."

Lambkill's eyes darted wildly across the gathering. "Don't you talk about my son! You're not fit to speak his name!

Little Coyote will kill you all! He has more Power than any of you will ever Dream of. Wait until he learns to speak. Then you'll be sorry you ever scoffed."

"He's going to speak, too?" Flint jeered. "It might be worth sticking close just to witness that. But I think it's more likely that Father Sun will rise in the west."

Harrier lifted a hand, and his brothers fell quiet. He gazed steadily at Lambkill, as if suddenly seeing the precipice upon which the Trader walked between sanity and madness. Briefly, he looked at Tannin. Their gazes met.

Tannin shook his head and lowered his eyes.

Harrier let out a breath. "Lambkill," he said mildly, "I understand now why you want to wait until the snow is gone. Tracking takes patience. But you must see that my brothers and I don't have your patience, or your skill. We will be useless to you out here in the forest."

Lambkill started to say something vicious, but Tannin clamped a hand on his wrist to restrain him. "Please, Lambkill, let Harrier finish."

Lambkill bawled, "Go on!"

Harrier continued in a calm voice. "Tomorrow morning we're heading for the coast. We'll stop at the closest village to see if your wife has shown up there. If she hasn't, we will keep on searching. There aren't many villages that sit right on the water. We should be able to check all of them in a moon. And somewhere, I hope, we'll meet a Trader who can take a message to our mother about Buffalo Bird."

"Then go!" Lambkill shouted. "What do we care? We invited you along only because we felt sorry for you. We will find my wife, and when we do, we'll have no need to find you. You can stay on the coast for the rest of your life for all I care!" Lambkill strode away from the fire, heading toward his robes.

Tannin dropped his head in his hands. He could hear Harrier speaking softly to his brothers, but he couldn't make out any of their words. His heart thudded dully in his chest.

"Tannin?" Harrier said as he walked around the fire. His eyes had a wary look, perhaps calculating what could be said safely.

"What is it, Harrier?"

Harrier tipped his chin in the direction Lambkill had taken. "He's Spirit-possessed. You know that . . . yet you do nothing to help him."

"What *can* I do?" Tannin looked up. "Tell me!"

"Take him home and care for him. Hold a Sing. Perhaps after several moons of good food and rest, this Evil Spirit will leave him, and his soul will tie to his body again."

"Yes, I—I know I should take him home. But he won't even talk to me about it. I've tried."

"If he were my brother," Harrier said, "I would take him home whether he wanted me to or not. If necessary, I would strike him over the head with my war club and carry him every step of the way."

Tannin nodded grimly. "I've thought about doing that."

Harrier bent down to stare him straight in the face. "Don't think. *Do it!*"

Tannin closed his eyes and let his head fall to his hands again. He barely heard Harrier walk away toward his robes, his brothers following.

Tannin's thoughts wandered, pausing here and there. Had it been so long ago that he and Lambkill had been best friends? Yes, thirty cycles. It seemed like yesterday. Tannin had been the runt of the village, small and wiry, not well liked. Lambkill had always defended him. Whenever a boy snickered at Tannin or called him names, Lambkill had bided his time, then caught the boy alone and pummeled him with his fists until the boy had "surrendered" and promised never to tease Tannin again.

He'd been so proud of his older brother. He'd thought Lambkill the greatest hero ever to live.

Tannin folded his hands in his lap and stared hollowly into the flickering flames. The brother he'd loved so much, gone—but where had he gone? Had the long moons alone on the trading trails done this to him? Or had he snapped only when he had discovered Kestrel's betrayal?

For three nights straight, Tannin had been having strange dreams, nightmares, of the times that Kestrel had come to his lodge begging to be taken in, battered and bloody.

As though to torture him, his soul recalled words uttered by Calling Crane: "She's so unhappy, Tannin. Your brother beats her all the time."

"Then why doesn't she leave him? I think she likes the status of being a great Trader's wife."

"Don't be foolish. She's terrified of leaving him. She's afraid he really will kill her then. Now he just threatens. And how many moons a cycle is he gone trading, eh, Tannin? You tell me."

Tannin had shrugged. But now he knew the answer: "Too many moons."

Was that what had driven Kestrel into the disgusting relationship with Iceplant? Lambkill's absences?

He longed to be home lying in Calling Crane's arms. But he couldn't abandon his brother now. Perhaps once they'd found Kestrel, Lambkill's soul would revive.

He prayed it would be so.

He sat on the log far into the night, staring vacantly at the dwindling flames of the fire.

Tannin tossed and turned beneath his hides, mumbling incoherently, calling the names of people who had been dead for cycles. The nightmare images stalked him on cougar-silent feet. He vaguely remembered that he and Lambkill had left Juniper Village in pursuit of Kestrel, but the swimming scenes from his past blotted out everything else. He felt as though time had swept by him and left him frozen somewhere in between moments.

"No . . . Father!" The echoes of his four-summer-old voice swirled around his soul.

Monstrous faces and confused scenes danced in his dream: his mother and father . . . his dead baby brother, who hadn't lived long enough to be named . . . the camp on Goosefoot Marsh, with its thick willows. Tannin fought to shove the visions away, to escape the horrors, but they wouldn't leave him . . .

He and Lambkill huddled outside their family's grass lodge, listening to their parents arguing inside. His stomach ached so badly that he feared he might vomit. They argued every day, but not like this. His mother's hoarse screams pierced the cloudy afternoon like sharp lances. He glanced at Lambkill. His older brother had a stony look on his face, but his eyes blazed with fury. At the age of fourteen, Lambkill was already a man, but he'd yet to marry.

"I didn't do it!" Flamedove, Tannin's mother, sobbed brokenly. "Don't hurt me, Blue Warrior! I am innocent!"

"You're a whore!" his father shouted. A slap sounded. Then another. Tannin's mother shrieked. Something hit the ground hard. His mother's body? "I saw you at Evening Star's lodge. What were you doing there? I watched you go in and you didn't come out for two hands of time!"

"His wife is sick! I was cooking and cleaning."

Tannin's new baby brother began crying, the sound soft and shrill. Tannin slipped an arm through Lambkill's and looked up in terror. Their little brother was only three moons old.

"Lambkill?" Tannin whispered. "Father wouldn't hurt our brother, would he?" Tannin loved his new brother, and he worried about him all the time. He'd watched one brother and one sister die from the fever. Though both had died a cycle ago, Tannin remembered the burials vividly. He could still see the bright ritual clothing that people had worn on that day. Seashells and fine porcupine quillwork had glittered in the brilliant sunlight as the people followed the path to the hilltop. The wailing could be heard for a day's walk.

"I don't know," Lambkill murmured back. His eyes darted around like Eagle's on a hunt.

Tannin bit his lip, but tears leaked down his cheeks. Villagers stood in the central plaza listening, whispering amongst themselves while they cast glances his way. But he knew that no one would interfere. His father was the chief of the village, and a very powerful man. He had alliances throughout the marsh country. Only someone very brave would dare to challenge Blue Warrior's treatment of his wife. It was a husband's right to discipline his family.

The ten grass lodges of their village sat on the mossy flats around Goosefoot Marsh. In the early spring season, the newly patched roofs looked so green that they blended with the reeds and cattails surrounding them. On the calm surface of the closest pond, ducks paddled and squawked, but whenever Lambkill's mother screamed, the birds went silent.

"Blue Warrior, I beg you, stop this! Let me take care of your son. He's hungry and frightened!"

"*Is* he my son?"

"Of course he's your son! How could you say such a thing? I have never—"

Another slap tore the air and was followed by the sounds of suffocating tears. Tannin's father shoved the hide door flap back and dragged his mother out by the hair. She staggered and fell, her knees striking the ground hard, and Blue Warrior kicked her brutally in one kidney. Her face was covered with blood.

"No, Father!" Tannin jumped to his feet. His little chest ached so badly that he could barely breathe. He ran four steps forward. "Don't hurt my mother!"

Blue Warrior stiffened, then turned slowly to glare at Tannin. Tannin's knees turned weak; he started to sob. Lambkill ran to stand beside Tannin and hold his hand.

Flamedove's eyes went wide and terrified. She yelled, "Lambkill, hurry! Take Tannin and run to your grandfather's lodge. Do it! Go on! *Now!*"

Lambkill's lower lip had quivered. He'd squeezed Tannin's hand hard and shouted, "Mother, this is your fault! Why do you always have to anger Father? Why don't you stop doing the things that make him so mad?"

The words had shocked Tannin so much that he'd stopped sobbing to listen. It had never occurred to him that his mother might deserve the beatings she got with such regularity. *What* had she done? Something bad with Evening Star?

"Lambkill," Flamedove ordered fearfully, "go to your grandfather's lodge! Hurry!"

"You lie down for any man!" Lambkill bellowed shrilly and released Tannin's hand. "I've heard stories, Father. Lots of stories about Mother. Everybody says she's a bitch in heat!"

Blue Warrior wrenched Flamedove's hair, and she cried out jaggedly as he slammed her head against the ground. "Do you hear that, Flamedove? The stories have even reached the ears of my sons."

"Lambkill, run," she wept. "Take Tannin and go. Please. Run!"

"No, Lambkill. You and your brother need to witness this. I've known about your mother's ways for cycles. I kept her only because I knew you boys loved her. But now . . ." His eyes glazed with such hatred that Tannin grabbed Lambkill tightly around the waist. Blue Warrior laughed and said, "I must make her pay. That is the way of our people. I want you to see what happens to women who treat men badly."

In a lightning move, Blue Warrior dropped his knee into Flamedove's throat, crushing her windpipe. A horrifying rush of air gushed from her lips. Then the blood came, welling up hotly, pouring down the sides of her face. She struggled, pounding Blue Warrior with her fists while she stared up at him in terror.

. . . Then her eyes moved sideways to Tannin and Lambkill. Her fear for them, and her love, shone brightly for a moment before fading as her arms stilled and her breathing stopped.

Blue Warrior rose and went into the lodge. The baby suddenly stopped crying.

Lambkill wrestled free from Tannin's grip and ran for the lodge, screaming, "No, Father, not our brother! He's not to blame! Please, Father, not the baby!"

Tannin stood rigid with fear as Lambkill ducked into the lodge. And Tannin knew why the baby had stopped crying. Even before he heard Lambkill's hoarse scream of "No! Why did you do it? Why did you . . . why did you . . . why?"

Tannin jerked awake, panting into the darkness, gasped and sat up in the brush lodge they had constructed. His bedding hides fell down around his waist.

Outside, horses brayed and snorted as though they scented a lion or a short-faced bear. They raced with thundering hooves along the game trail two hundred hands downhill from the makeshift camp: six saplings leaning against a rock and covered with brush. Starlight fell through the gaps in silver spears.

Tannin looked over at Lambkill. His brother lay on his back, his pack clutched to his chest. Tannin could sense the malignant eyes of that dead baby staring at him through the hide of the pack. He shuddered and turned his head away.

Lambkill had become a Trader right after the sorrowful day of their mother's murder. And Tannin had known—even then—that his brother had done it to get away from home. Blue Warrior had sent Tannin to go live with his grandfather and had remarried the next moon, taking as wife a silly little fool named Sparrow Hawk.

Both Tannin and Lambkill had hated her, and she had hated them. "Those brats of that whorish Flamedove," she'd called them. "No telling who really fathered them."

Tannin shook his head. How strange that those words still hurt him. Why should they? Sparrow Hawk had died two cycles after she'd married his father, and Blue Warrior had gone on to another young woman. But those terrible words lingered, especially in his dreams.

Lambkill had spent little time at home, and when he did, he had often gone to sit by their dead baby brother's grave.

Not once—not *once*—in all the cycles since had Lambkill spoken their mother's name. And Tannin wondered about that. Lambkill had always been strange with women—as though deep down inside him, he harbored a hatred for all females, an aversion born on that day of their little brother's death. Lambkill clearly preferred the company of men. Yet he had married four times.

Tannin swallowed down his dust-dry throat and stretched out on the ground again. He tugged his hides up over his belly. Yes, Lambkill had been married four times . . . and he'd beaten each of his wives senseless for not giving him a son.

Tannin ran a hand through his sweat-drenched hair, wondering.

"All right, Man," the Boy said in a shaking voice. "I finally understand that only by keeping Death alive in me will I learn about Life—and overcome my cowardice . . .

"So I will be his son. Though I am not. I will sacrifice my ability to be born again and to rest in my mother's arms, so that I can be dead and suffer with this human that I do not even know . . . but it's hard, Man. It's so hard."

Gasps came from the Star People and wavered around him like glowing, gaseous fires.

The Boy's chest shook with sobs.

The Man's voice echoed through the starlit womb of night: "I may have been wrong about your arrogance. . . ."

Twenty-two

Snow.

And more snow.

Kestrel stood in the mouth of the rock shelter and studied the hazy white veil that wavered and flowed across the horizon. Winter Boy had returned with such strength that he amazed her. In the windless morning, the flakes seemed to fall in slow motion, like goose down suspended on the breath of a warm updraft. The Mother, as Sunchaser called the ocean, lay calm and quiet beneath, her voice a bare whisper of waves, as though she still slept. The smooth surface of the water reflected the gray, opalescent sheen of the stormy air.

Kestrel filled her lungs, enjoying the tangy scent of salt mixed with the musk of the shoreline. Damp scents of earth, vegetation and smoke blended, breathing a new life into her soul.

Kestrel's fingers moved absently over the seashells that covered the front of the shirt Sunchaser had given her. He stood so much taller than she that the fringes on his shirt fell to below her knees. She'd cut off two hands' worth of leather from the sleeves so they would fit.

Made of fine mammoth hide with a wealth of beautiful shells that even Lambkill would have envied . . . and Sunchaser simply gave it to me.

Kestrel had risen at the same time as Sunchaser, two hands of time ago. While he had gone searching the forest above for Spirit Plants, she'd located a rill of snowmelt cascading down the rock. She'd bathed in that icy splash and washed her long hair; then she had returned to comb it dry before the low flames of the fire. Clean and shining in the flickering firelight, it hung black and glistening over her shoulders.

In the rear of the shelter, Cloud Girl slept on a soft pile of elk hides. Kestrel had fed her when she'd first awakened, and Cloud Girl had gone right back to sleep. Lately the baby had been sleeping more, crying less, and just sitting propped up in her rabbit-fur sack for long periods, playing with Helper, twining her fists in his tail or clutching at his mange-naked ears. The dog seemed to encourage the attention, staring at the infant with soft brown eyes, periodically thrusting his nose into Cloud Girl's chubby fingers. Even Kestrel missed the dog when he was gone, as now, out hunting with Sunchaser.

She turned her gaze back to the fluttering dance of the falling flakes beyond the entrance. The snow whirled as it settled into the soft mat on the ledge.

"Won't the snow ever stop?" she whispered anxiously to herself. *We won't be safe until we've found Iceplant's family—maybe not even then.*

She looked back toward the fire. Red coals gleamed through the bed of gray ash. From the pile of driftwood that Sunchaser had collected yesterday, she pulled out two pieces and shoved them into the bed of ash. Smoke curled up, and then the dry wood crackled into yellow tongues of flame.

Kestrel folded her arms, entranced by the weaving dance that licked up around the wood. A small basket sat by the fire. Woven of willow bark, it had green and red geometric designs on the lid. She had noticed it last night. Sunchaser had moved the basket when he'd begun preparing dinner and had handled it as though it contained something very precious and fragile.

Curious, Kestrel knelt and removed the lid. A single yellow ant crawled across the sand inside, its antennae wiggling. In the center of the basket, a long quartzite knife lay on a folded piece of deerhide. The knife had a greenish-gray blade, the color of the ocean. She started to replace the lid and saw another ant clinging to its underside. She peered at it speculatively, then resealed the basket.

"Ants?" she asked aloud. "What could he want with ants?"

"Oh, those ants might surprise you. They're very useful. They can teach you everything there is to know."

Kestrel whirled breathlessly. Sunchaser entered the rock shelter with the hind quarter of a deer slung over a shoulder, his fingers laced through the hollow between the leg bone and the thick hock tendon.

For a big man, he moved with the silence and grace of a lion. Snow coated his hair and the shoulders of his moosehide jacket. He headed straight for the fire. Helper trotted at his heels, ears up, tail wagging when he spied Kestrel.

"I found this little doe at the edge of the cypress grove." Sunchaser unrolled a hide and laid the quarter down on it. A thick layer of fat coated the deer's rump. "She stood perfectly still, staring into my eyes, while I darted her."

"She's fat for so early in the spring. Where's the rest of the carcass?"

"I left it hanging in a tree. Hopefully it's high enough to keep most predators from trying to reach it, and it will stay cool up there."

"Yes, especially if this storm continues. Will the snow blow into drifts in the forest here, as it does in the highlands of the marsh country?"

"No, here on the coast, such a thing is rare. This snow is melting almost as fast as it falls, though the water in our boiling bag will probably freeze tonight."

Helper ran across the cave and flopped down beside Cloud Girl with his muzzle on the foot of her rabbit-fur sack. Kestrel tensed, afraid that he might wake her daughter, but Cloud Girl slept on, oblivious.

Sunchaser crouched across the blaze from Kestrel and dug a handful of fresh tree buds from his coat pocket.

"What are those?" Kestrel asked.

"Poplar buds."

"I've never eaten poplar buds. Are they good?"

"Pretty bitter." He gave her an amused smile. "You can eat some if you wish, but I'm going to make a salve for your wounds from the rest of them. They have a power to cure."

"Oh, I see. In my clan, we use aspen buds for the same thing . . . and to bring down fever."

He nodded. "We also use aspen buds, when they're available."

Kestrel watched as Sunchaser pulled his sleeve down over his hand and used it to tip one of the hot rocks that formed the fire ring. He turned it over, revealing the flat surface, then piled the buds atop it. Shortly, they steamed. When he drew his knife from his belt pouch and swiveled around to trim a thick strip of fat from the deer quarter, Kestrel asked, "You're going to melt the fat with the buds?"

"The fat helps on its own, and it also makes a paste to keep the Healing Power of the buds in the wound."

A curious smell arose when he threw the strip of fat atop the steaming buds, pungent, heavy.

"If you'll pull a long stick from the woodpile, I'll cut you a steak," he said. "She was a dry doe. The meat should be wonderfully succulent and sweet. Tender, too, since she wasn't more than two cycles old. Besides, you need to renew your strength. You've had a hard journey."

She lowered her eyes, trying to smile over the worry within. "You—you're not eating. Again? Are you fasting for a reason?"

"Yes," he answered simply and turned away.

Kestrel frowned but did as he'd instructed and placed a long stick at his feet while he sliced into the rich red meat. He skewered a thick steak on the end of the stick and handed it to her. Kestrel used another stick to push the burning wood to one side and expose the glowing coals. She carefully propped her stick away from the flames to keep the wood from burning through. Fat dripped into the fire and sizzled on the coals.

The cooking of meat on an open fire took a certain art. Direct flames charred the outside of the meat, leaving the interior bloody. A thick bed of coals, however, radiated the heat, and if the fire pit was filled with rocks, it held the heat, distributing it evenly.

Kestrel couldn't stop her mouth from watering as the meat browned and the rich aroma filled the air. Helper turned his attention from Cloud Girl, his black nose wiggling as he sniffed and made a grunting sound.

"I haven't had venison in six or seven moons. Since last autumn. It smells so good."

Sunchaser glanced up and smiled. "It's difficult to hunt when you're on the run. I would imagine that you mostly fished and snared rabbits, ground squirrels, pack rats and such."

"That . . . and I harvested the newest spring plants."

The deer fat had melted and combined with the steaming poplar buds. Sunchaser used two sticks like tongs to pull the stone away from the fire so that it could cool and the salve would steep. The mixture had turned a pale green color.

Kestrel removed her steak from the flames and propped it against the woodpile to cool off. Out over the ocean, the haze of snow bore a pale pink tint, letting her know that Father Sun had risen. But the sky still possessed a tarnished-silver look.

"Has Cloud Girl been asleep ever since I left?" Sunchaser asked as he studied the baby.

"Yes. I don't understand it. She's calmed down since we've been here. She used to wake me three or four times a night, wanting to be fed. Last night she woke me only once. Then I fed her again just after you left this morning."

"She probably sleeps more soundly here. The rhythm of the waves is soothing."

"Yes," Kestrel agreed. "It is. I knew it would be."
Just as Iceplant promised.

She'd been so terrified over the past moon that she hadn't had the strength to miss him. But now, after two nights of rest and good meals, she felt the pain in her heart reawakening—

just as nerves shocked by the blow of a club come to life in a stunning flood of agony. Against her will, tears welled in her eyes.

Sunchaser shifted uncomfortably and wiped his hands on his moccasins. Quietly, he asked, "Do you want to talk about it?"

"No. I—I can't. Not yet."

He inclined his head understandingly, and Kestrel turned to pull her steak from its stick. She ate slowly, relishing the wonderful flavor. Her fingers quickly became covered with warm grease. The last time she'd had venison, Iceplant had brought it to her in the middle of the night. Rain had been pattering on the grass thatching of the lodge and slapping into the puddles in the path. He'd been laughing. . . .

She finished her steak in silence.

"Here," Sunchaser offered. "Let me pour you a cup of tea. You can sip it while I tend your wounds." Without waiting for her to answer, he rose and picked up a horn cup, a beautiful thing carved from a desert sheep's horn and engraved with images of animals, men and Spirit patterns. He filled it from the gut bag on the tripod and brought it to her, saying, "You'll have to sit closer to the fire. I'll need the light."

While he went to scoop up a handful of the poplar-bud paste, Kestrel moved to the southern side of the fire, out of the smoke, and sat down cross-legged. From here, she could look northward along the irregular line of the cliffs. Snow frosted every ledge. Naked bushes grew precariously from cracks in the rock, and occasional brave conifers struggled to cling with knotted and twisted roots to the sheer rock. In a few sheltered niches, she could see bald eagles huddled together, their feathers fluffed out for warmth. She wondered if they'd had the courage to go fishing yet on this cold morning.

Sunchaser came over and knelt before her. He'd pulled his long white hair back for hunting and braided it into a single plait. The strands shone wetly. His deep-set black eyes reflected the light of the flames as he examined her face.

Gently, he brushed the hair away from her forehead and frowned at the knife gash. "The wound has been invaded by Evil Spirits. This will hurt."

"I'm expecting it to."

When he began dabbing on the warm salve, Kestrel's belly knotted, told her to pull away, not to let a man touch her. Not ever again. *Iceplant died because he touched me.* But she couldn't move. Weeks had passed since anyone had touched her with such tenderness, and she craved it desperately. Muscles that had stiffened with tension began to let go. Her lungs breathed easier. She wondered about that. Her flesh responded to his gentleness as though it *recognized* that touch. She found herself trembling. Unsteadily, she set the horn cup of tea down at her side.

Sunchaser lowered his hand and said, "I'm sorry, I didn't realize I was hurting you that much."

"No. No, you're not. Can you put some of the salve on the wound in my shoulder, too?"

"Of course."

She unlaced the front of her seashell-trimmed dress and lowered the hide to bare her left shoulder. Her clean brown skin gleamed in the orange light of the fire. Sunchaser's face darkened. Kestrel looked down. Her stomach churned at the sight. It had been hurting, yes, but she'd never taken the time to examine it. A scab had formed over a swollen red lump. Pus oozed around the edges of the crust.

Sunchaser anxiously studied her face. "It may not have hurt when I touched your forehead, but this certainly will. Brace yourself."

Kestrel took a deep breath. Sunchaser had barely touched the wound when a bolt of white-hot pain went through her. To take her mind off of it, she started talking. "What are the yellow ants for? You said they were very useful."

"I'm afraid that you're going to find out tonight. I can't wait any longer. I've fasted for three days. It's time." He looked into her eyes. "You can help me . . . if you want to."

He prodded around the edges of her wound, determining the extent of the infection, and then he pinched the enraged flesh to drain it. Kestrel sucked in a breath as if he'd splashed icy water in her face.

"Sorry," he said. "That's it, I think."

"What do I have to do? To help you."

He began to apply the salve in warm globs. "Just keep an eye on me. Come if I call out to you. I've never performed this ritual alone before. I don't know exactly what might happen to me."

"What does the ritual entail? I mean, what should I expect?"

He smeared the rest of the salve on her wound, and his hand fell to his leg. Conflicting emotions tensed his face. Softly, as if speaking to himself, he said, "I can't really tell you what to expect. I've witnessed others undertake the Ant Ordeal, many times, but each Dreamer reacts differently to the Power. Some weep through the night, some writhe on the ground. Some just stare into the fire. And sometimes, Kestrel, the Dreamer dies."

"The ants have that much Power?" she asked as she laced up her dress.

"Oh, yes. I saw a young girl perish once. It was terrible. After that, the Talth banned young women from participation in the ritual."

"The Talth? What is that?"

Sunchaser rose and stood quietly looking down at her. The seashells attached to the fringes on his sleeves clicked in the breeze. "It's a Power society. A very old one. The elders of the society claim that Wolfdreamer himself was the first shaman of the Talth. I don't know whether that's true or not." He lifted his shoulders and buried his hands in his coat pockets.

"Can't you ask Wolfdreamer? In your visits to the Land of the Dead? Wouldn't he tell you?"

Sunchaser's gaze impaled her with its buried desperation. "I . . ." He looked away. "I need to begin my preparations soon. You won't mind, will you?"

"No," she said as she stood up. "Tell me what to do to help you."

Catchstraw padded quietly through the snowy forest, his pointed ears pricked for danger. The scents that pervaded the world astonished him. He prowled with his long nose to the ground, his tail down so as not to attract attention to himself. A doe and a fawn had trotted down this trail just before him, and a hare had hopped across the path to get to the meadow below. Oh, he could see their tracks of course, imprinted clearly in the snow, but they held no interest for him. The smell, however, made his blood rush. The doe was heavy with fawn, and the yearling buck fawn that accompanied her had been wandering in the shallows of a pond, eating ferns. The buck had sated himself and was drowsy, longing to sleep. He trotted far behind his mother, too confident for his own good.

Catchstraw wrinkled his long nose, exposing his teeth. On occasion they felt like human teeth, rather than a wolf's recurved canines. He shoved the thought from his mind. The buck would be an easy target, either tonight or in another moon, when the doe finally chased him away, forcing him to fend for himself while she searched out a safe niche in the forest and gave birth to her new baby.

Lifting his head, Catchstraw could smell death on the wind. A pine marten had killed a rabbit. He caught the odor of the marten's scent glands and the distinctive richness of cottontail blood. It was not a fresh kill, though. Taking the spoil away from the marten would be unrewarding—the meat would be flavorless. He trotted on, his tongue dangling.

Effortlessly, he leaped a fallen log and veered off on a wide, beaten-down mammoth trail. The powerful muscles rippling beneath his black fur thrilled him. What strength and lusty virility! No human could ever understand this Power. He wondered why he'd never considered taking the path of the witch before. It offered so much more than the Dreamer's path did. As a witch, he could order Power to comply with his demands, rather than having Power use him for its own foolish ends. Dreamers were idiots!

When the trail sloped down a steep hill, he broke into a careless run. What animal could catch him, even if it heard or scented him? Perhaps a short-faced bear, maybe a lion, or a saber-toothed cat—he couldn't be certain, since he didn't know how fast those animals ran. But he knew his own limits well. And in the body of Dire Wolf, he could race the wind and win!

Catchstraw sprinted to the bottom of the hill and sniffed out a new scent . . . it made him halt and look around. A woman's scent. And she carried a baby with her. Through his keen night eyes, he could even spot the places where the woman had halted to strip the soft inner bark of aspens for use as an absorbent in the infant's pants.

That scent set his muscles to trembling. He couldn't be certain whether his response came from wolf or human origins. A baby, tiny and vulnerable . . .

His long, heavily muscled legs pawed the ground, kicking up a haze of moonlit pine duff behind him. Through the overarching branches, he could make out the faint, silverish gleam of Above-Old-Man, though he couldn't see his eye. A cool breeze worked its way up the slope, ruffling his black hair like gentle fingers, chilling his hot blood.

The stiff hairs on the back of his neck bristled. Catchstraw wondered why. His canine body must know something that his human soul could not understand. A low, deep-throated growl erupted from his throat.

He looked over his shoulder and studied his backtrail. He scented the wind. The mountain mahogany, willow and other bushy shrubs obscured the curving trail. . . . But something moved out there. Something clever and quiet.

An uneasy feeling of being pursued disturbed him. The wind blew in from the ocean, carrying his own pungent scent back up the mountain to any animal that cared to lift its nose. He narrowed his eyes, glaring, growling as he searched the forest for any sign of a stalker.

What would a woman be doing up here? No scent of man accompanied her. A woman, alone, with a baby? Strange.

Catchstraw padded softly around a thick clump of ferns. Their long, feathery leaves combed his coat as he passed. He trotted up onto a rocky point and peered through the weave of trees. Mother Ocean spread before him like a vast black hide waving in the wind. Above-Old-Man peeked through a hole in the clouds and shed his tarnished gleam upon her face, silvering the rolling crests of waves, the frosting of snow that had collected on the shore.

Catchstraw put his nose to the packed snow again, following the mingled scents of woman and mammoth as he loped down onto the flat terrace of the sea cliffs.

From somewhere ahead came the deep, low chant of a man's voice, and he could see the orange gleam of a fire reflecting from the water's surface far below.

Catchstraw trotted on, down the fir-clotted slope and along the edge of the cliff.

Twenty-three

Kestrel sat on the pile of furs in the rear of the shelter, rocking Cloud Girl in her arms. Her daughter had eaten, grabbed at Helper's black nose when he pushed it into her palm and now mewed halfheartedly as she drifted back to sleep.

Night had fallen. The orange glow of the fire washed the inside of the rock shelter, throwing Sunchaser's rumpled shadow across the back wall. He knelt at the mouth of the shelter, Singing softly while he created a ground painting around his feet. Crushed seashells trickled slowly from his hand as he moved around the circumference of a circle, painting it white. At the same time, he called for help from the Great Giant in the North. The circle spread a full body's length in diameter and glittered wildly in the firelight.

When Sunchaser had finished, he spread his arms wide and Sang his thanks to Mother Ocean. Then he returned to the center of the circle and filled his hands from the pile of crushed charcoal there. His deep, beautiful voice whispered through the shelter as he rose and began drawing the inner circle. Black and small, it left him barely enough room to sit cross-legged within its confines.

Kestrel watched in fascination. Her own people didn't have this ritual. The Song was unlike anything she'd ever heard before. His movements mimicked a Dance that she felt she should have known but couldn't place. A Powerful ceremony, an ancient ritual. Its beauty and symmetry reached straight to the depths of her soul.

Sunchaser wore only a breechclout. His broad chest was heavily muscled, and a single tattoo—that of a coiled serpent—adorned the space between his breasts. The serpent's tongue flicked out and forked into the spreading branches of a tree that stretched to his collarbones.

When Sunchaser had finished painting the black inner circle, he rested for a moment, Singing very softly, thanking Above-Old-Man for creating a world of such beauty and joy.

Kestrel lowered her eyes. Cloud Girl had fallen asleep. Very carefully, she laid her daughter down on the hides and brought one skin up to cover the baby to her chin. Helper, who lay at the foot of the hides, briefly lifted his head to see what Kestrel was doing, then turned his gaze to Sunchaser again. The dog had a curious gleam in his eyes, almost unblinking, as though quietly observing the last night of the world.

Sunchaser had now filled his hands with crushed red sandstone and had begun to quarter the circles, drawing one wavy line on the north-south axis, then another from the east to the west. Kestrel recognized those symbols: the two giant snakes that held up the earth. Believing it to be their egg, the snakes had been guarding it and waiting for all of eternity to see the earth hatch. Legend foretold of a time when the snakes' hopes would be fulfilled. Father Sun would fall to the ground, and a terrible earthquake would split the world in two. From the broken halves, a fiery serpent would slither out. The serpent would look around, find itself alone and bite its tail in anguish. In the midst of that sacred-serpent circle, a new world would be born, clean and pure, filled with strange new animals and plants.

Sunchaser rose to his feet and bowed his head reverently. His white braid shone as though coated with liquid silver. He looked oddly unreal standing there against the background of falling snow—as if his body belonged more to that glittering haze than to the solid world of soil, water and sky. Slowly, he turned.

"Kestrel, please bring me my basket, the sack of eagle down and a cup of water."

She gathered the things he asked for and carried them to him. He walked to the edge of the outer white circle to take them from her hands. His fingers brushed hers softly during the exchange.

"Thank you." He looked at her with gentle, luminous eyes.

She nodded and backed away, sinking down by the fire, where it was warm. He watched her until she had pulled up her knees and wrapped her arms around them. Then he retreated to the center of the inner circle and lifted his basket of ants. He held the basket up to each of the four directions of the world while he Sang, consecrating the ants and begging the Spirits to help him make his journey to the Land of the Dead.

From deep within Kestrel, awe rose. She had heard a hundred times of his travels down through the maze, where he'd climbed onto the shining wings of the Thunderbeings, who had carried him to Wolfdreamer's Lodge of Light in the Land of the Dead. She could scarcely believe that she was watching the beginnings of that journey.

Sunchaser carefully constructed a bed of eagle down, like a tiny nest, in his left palm and placed five yellow ants in the center. He folded the down around the ants in a protective cocoon and tucked the wad into his mouth. Lifting the cup of water, he took one long swallow to wash it down. He did this seven times. Then he shook himself and flinched. He sank to his knees and bent forward, holding his stomach as though in pain. A shudder went through him.

Kestrel sat perfectly still, not wanting to distract him, but her forehead furrowed with wonder. *Are the ants biting him inside?*

Sunchaser's mouth tensed. He slumped backward to a sitting position and reached into his basket to draw out his long quartzite knife. He gripped it tightly with both hands and squeezed his eyes closed.

He froze in that position, facing east.

Kestrel waited for a full hand of time before he stirred again. The snow was falling more heavily now, forming an unbroken white wall beyond the shelter.

Opening his eyes, Sunchaser looked straight through Kestrel, as though she didn't exist. No expression enlivened his face. His craggy features could have been chiseled from granite. Like an old man with a disease of the joints, he haltingly leaned forward and lowered his knife to the soft surface of the sandstone floor. At the point where the red snake on the east-west axis cut through the black inner circle, he began drawing a wide arc.

At first, she couldn't figure out what he was doing. Then she noticed that he'd carved a circle and had proceeded to fill it with a complex sequence of seemingly unrelated lines. It looked like a labyrinth . . . *or a maze.*

Kestrel straightened to watch more closely. With unblinking intensity, Sunchaser carved twisting line within twisting line, as though following a path of his own making, seeking the way to a center point not yet defined.

He stopped abruptly and redrew a line . . . then drew over it again, etching the turn ever deeper into the stone floor.

The first emotion he'd shown flitted across his face: confusion, or maybe frustration.

Kestrel's eyes went from the maze to Sunchaser's face and back again, not understanding. *What's wrong, Sunchaser?*

Without taking his eyes from the carving in the stone, Sunchaser groped for his basket and pulled out the half-buried square of deerhide. He unfolded it and smoothed away the sand and wrinkles. Kestrel could see another maze drawn on it.

Her breath caught. Was it the maze that Wolfdreamer had given him? The one he carried with him when he went to villages to talk about the Mammoth Spirit Dance? It must be.

Sunchaser seemed to be comparing the mazes. He frowned, shook his head and inhaled a deep breath. When he released it, he bent to the maze on the floor again, carefully retracing the old line. This time he drew it a little longer, so that the line curved up around the interior of the circle, paralleling another line, then angling away from it. At the point of divergence, he stopped and closed his eyes for a moment, as though he didn't know which direction to take.

He made a small sound of dismay.

. . . And tried again, retracing the path through the maze, halting at the same point of divergence.

Once more, he tried.

His hand shook so badly that he drew it back into his lap, put the knife aside and curled his fingers into a fist.

Finally Sunchaser looked up, as though at Kestrel, but she couldn't be certain that he saw her. His eyes had a ghostly look, seeing through her to something far away in another world. Then, like a cat going to sleep, he curled on his side in the middle of the ground painting, his back to her, and Kestrel saw his shoulders shake.

She got on her knees, not sure of what to do. He'd told her not to speak to him unless he called out, but . . .

On coyote-silent feet, she crept forward to the edge of the white circle. When he heard her, he raised his head, and Kestrel saw the tears in his eyes.

She stepped into the circle and knelt beside him. "Sunchaser, what can I do to help you? Do you need something? I could warm you some tea—"

His arms went suddenly around her waist, and before she knew it, he had his head in her lap, his fingers tugging desperately at her sleeves.

"I can't . . . can't get through," he said brokenly. "Trap . . . the turn is a trap."

"A trap?"

"I keep falling . . . going around in circles . . . can't escape! Wing walls funnel me in. Then I fall . . . the blackness swallows me and . . . lost . . . nowhere to turn."

Kestrel's eyes widened. He couldn't mean what he was saying. Sunchaser couldn't lose the way through the maze. What would happen if something so terrible turned out to be true? People everywhere relied on Sunchaser to know the minds of the Spirits. Iceplant had told Kestrel once that Father Sun would fall from the sky if Sunchaser stopped getting up in the morning and offering prayers to him.

She gazed down at that white head writhing in her lap, and her heart went out to him. Being a hero must have placed a great weight on him. His name carried almost as much Power as Wolfdreamer's. Indeed, more people spoke Sunchaser's name with reverence than they did Wolfdreamer's. No, he had not lost his way. That would be unthinkable. Sunchaser had just taken too many ants. He had too much of their poison in his system and it had affected his ability to Dream.

"You just need to try again, Sunchaser," she soothed. "It will work next time."

"No. Not until I understand . . . you see, it's the problem of the wife of the invisible warrior . . . my passion to see . . . I've killed what I love and want most. But how . . . how do I give up my eyes?"

He nuzzled his cheek against her skirt and went deathly still. The large hands that gripped her sleeves turned as rigid as stone. Was this paralysis part of the Ant Ordeal? He hadn't told her this might happen! What could she do? Frightened, Kestrel put a hand on his shoulder and realized in shock that he was crying.

Some people weep through the night . . .

Kestrel knew little about men, still less about the Ant Ordeal, but she had comforted the irrational fears of many an old person. She had smiled away the tears of hurt children. She stroked Sunchaser's white hair. "It's all right, Sunchaser. You'll find the way. I know you will."

"No, I . . . I can't. The Spirits!" he cried hoarsely. "They have forsaken me. I don't understand it."

"Why would they forsake you? You're their Dreamer. Their chosen—"

"Not anymore," he replied. "I'm . . . lost. *Lost.*"

His arms tightened powerfully around her, and he dragged her to the ground with him, stretching out, obliterating much of the painting. He buried his face in the wealth of her hair, his forehead resting warmly against her cheek.

"I don't want to be alone. Stay here with me, Kestrel," he pleaded. "Please, don't leave me."

"I won't leave," she said. "I promise."

For a timeless moment, Kestrel just lay still, feeling his painfully tight grip relax and the wintry chill of the air against her bare legs. Every tiny sound seemed louder: the whisper of the wind, the soft patting of snowflakes on the rim of the cave, the hammering of her heart. She hurt for Sunchaser. She knew about loneliness, about the emptiness that fed on the soul, eating it from the inside out until finally nothing remained but a hollow shell. Yes, the emptiness that drove people to desperate acts. Tears filled her eyes.

Helper trotted across the floor, lay down behind Sunchaser and propped his long black muzzle on Sunchaser's shoulder. The dog peered directly down at Kestrel through warm brown eyes. One of his mangy ears drooped sideways.

You came to Sunchaser in a Dream. Did Wolfdreamer send you? Do you understand what's going on? Can't you help Sunchaser find the way through the maze?

A sparkle entered Helper's eyes. He vented a tired breath.

Kestrel tried to force herself to relax, but she couldn't do it. The feel of Sunchaser's arms around her stirred emotions that she never wanted to experience again.

It's because he's such a great man. You know you don't have to fear him.

She felt safe in his presence, and she hadn't felt safe in such a long, long time. She wished she had the courage to let down her defenses, to allow herself to drown in the comfort he offered. Just to sleep in his arms would have been a precious gift.

No. Not that. She couldn't.

She placed a gentle hand on Sunchaser's shoulder and turned to watch the snow falling beyond the shelter.

From down on the beach, a dire wolf howled. A wrenching, malevolent sound, almost human, as though the animal hunted out of frustrated rage rather than hunger. A shiver went up Kestrel's spine.

She kept her eyes open, wary, listening for familiar-sounding footsteps in the night.

Twenty-four

Sunchaser rolled to his side, sick to his stomach. The elkhide that covered him slipped down to his waist. He felt weak and bewildered, tired to his bones. He shivered. Gusts of cold wind whipped around the shelter. He remembered little of last night, except the terrible pain when the ants were biting him, and a brief period of euphoria before he had attempted the maze.

. . . And he remembered that he'd failed.

His stomach cramped threateningly.

Far below, a calm, deep-blue sea spread beyond the thin veneer of snow that covered the shore. Steam curled from the Mother's surface, the water being so much warmer than the air. The lavender glow of dawn haloed everything, the trees, rocks, waves. Two bald eagles hunted the water, soaring and skimming over the whitecaps with their wings tucked. Three giant croaking buzzards strutted along the shore, scavenging, and leaving loops of tracks in the freshly washed sand.

The storm had broken. Sunlight poured through gaps in the drifting clouds.

Sunchaser lay unmoving, trying to muster the strength to rise. His heart pounded nauseatingly. Behind him, he heard soft sounds: the scrape of a moccasin on stone, the fire crackling as someone threw on more wood. The gut bag's tripod creaked.

He rolled to his opposite side and nausea overwhelmed him. He vomited onto the floor. Kestrel ran across the rock shelter and held his head expertly while the world swam around him in a blur of brown and blue. The balls of eagle-

down came up. He saw a live ant crawl out of the closest
one and scurry across the floor.

"Lie down, Sunchaser," Kestrel ordered as she ran to pick
up two thin pieces of stone and scrape up the mess he'd made.
"There's no need for you to get up."

He obeyed, stretching out on his back. Kestrel tossed the
dirtied stones over the edge and drew the elk hide up to cover
his bare chest, then went back to the fire.

He watched her as she went about making tea: pouring
water into the gut bag, adding mint leaves. She'd left her
waist-length hair loose and it swung around her like a black
curtain as she moved. Another memory from last night . . .
Kestrel in his arms.

He felt suddenly confused, embarrassed. How had that
happened? He'd told her not to get near him unless he
called out. *Which is what I must have done.* Blessed Spirits,
he prayed he hadn't asked anything of her that made her
uneasy. That was the last thing she needed.

"Kestrel?" he said worriedly. "I don't remember much
about last night. The memories from the Ant Ordeal tend
to return slowly. But . . . thank you."

"For what?"

"Well, I'm not certain, but I think that I may have asked
you for things that you . . . I think you helped me more than
I know," he finished lamely.

She walked across the shelter and set a cup of steaming
tea down beside him. His whole body shook when he raised
himself on one elbow to try to sip from it.

"I didn't do anything, Sunchaser. I wish I could have
helped you more."

"More?"

"Yes." She knelt at his side, and the longest strands of
her hair brushed the floor. Sitting there like that, she looked
so young, so innocent—and half afraid. She wet her lips.
"You kept saying that you couldn't find your way through
the maze, and I . . ."

He closed his eyes and weakly sank to the ground. How
could he have done that? He'd made the error in Otter Clan

Village after the mammoths' attack, and now this. How long would it be before everyone had lost faith in him? Before no one Danced the Mammoth Spirit Dance anymore? He could accomplish nothing by himself. It took the combined strength of thousands of believers to effect any change, even a minor one, in the world. He hurt, deep down.

Kestrel's mouth hung open, as though she feared she'd said something terribly wrong. She raised a hand to her lips. "I'm sorry! Did I—"

"No, it's not you," he said. "It's me. Go on. Please. Tell me what I said." The horrifying thought crossed his mind that he might have told her some of his deepest secrets. Not that there were many of them—or that they were particularly interesting to anyone else—but they were *his*. And rightly or wrongly, he preferred to keep them that way.

Kestrel twisted her hands in her lap. "You said that the turn was a trap. That wing walls funneled you to it . . . and then you fell and blackness swallowed you up. Then you said something about having nowhere to turn, about being lost."

He nodded and sighed. "Yes, that's the way it feels. What else did I say?"

"You said that the Spirits had forsaken you." She quickly added, "But of course, that's not true. The Spirits would never forsake you. You're their greatest Dreamer."

"Am I?"

"Of course."

Her eyes were aglow. He felt sicker. Weakly, he propped himself up again and sipped more of his tea. The sweet taste eased his nausea. "Is that all, Kestrel?"

"Yes. At least that's everything important that I can remember." She watched him almost breathlessly, as though expecting him to smooth over the things he'd said during the Ant Ordeal—or to deny them outright.

His mouth quirked as he stared down into the pale green liquid in his cup. "You're very kind to have taken care of me last night. I'm sorry if I . . . made you feel awkward at any time."

Kestrel dropped her eyes to study her hands. A blush

crept into her cheeks. She shook her head. "No. I never felt awkward. And I'm *good* at taking care of people." She said it vehemently, as if she feared he might think her incapable of being good at anything.

Or perhaps she'd just been told that so often by her husband that she'd come to half believe it herself.

"Yes, you are good at taking care of people," Sunchaser said gently. "Too bad your husband didn't realize it."

Kestrel continued staring at her hands. "He did. In . . . in the beginning."

Sunchaser took a long drink of his tea. He had expected her voice to drip hatred and loathing, but it held neither of those emotions. "Did you love him?"

She glanced up suddenly, as though surprised. "Oh, yes. Very much. I would have done anything for him. For a time, I even tried to bury my own being—to deny my nature—so I could be exactly what he wanted. I thought it would make him love me back."

"But it didn't?"

"No."

Sunchaser fumbled with his cup. "If you had become exactly what he wanted, he would have changed his mind and wanted you to be someone else."

Kestrel looked at him with searching eyes. "How do you know?"

"I've seen his kind before. Too often. What you must do now, Kestrel, is to forget about him. You're beginning a new life. You'll have new friends and family—"

"I *can't* forget!" she replied with hushed violence. Her eyes blazed. "He's still out there somewhere, Sunchaser. And he's crazy. He will find me. Even if it takes the rest of his life!"

Sunchaser frowned at the power of her emotions. Could anyone track her through the deluge of rain and snow? It seemed impossible. But she believed it true, and that made the notion matter a great deal.

She stood rigid, embarrassed by her outburst, and lowered her gaze to her hands again.

"Night before last," Sunchaser said quietly, "you tossed and turned in your sleep. You even cried out once. Are you still having nightmares about him?"

"They . . . they've lost s-some of their power," she stammered. "Now when I'm dreaming, I usually know it's sweat on my face, not rain, like the night when . . . And I—I sense that the pressure at my throat is a heavy hide, not a knife." She twined and untwined her fingers. "Most of the time, though, I fear it's the nightmares that are real, that my belief that I'm dreaming is only a blinder against the truth. And I'm afraid, Sunchaser, that someday he'll find me and drag me back to the nightmare, where the rain never ends and he's hitting me."

She crossed to the fire, where she picked up a stick and stabbed ruthlessly at the coals. Sparks popped and crackled. A log broke, and in the resulting flash of light, her skin gleamed with a rosy hue.

As Father Sun climbed slowly over the eastern horizon, each of the rocks on the shore lit up, their crevices filling with golden sunshine. The shells that had washed ashore gleamed with a dazzling intensity against the tan sand. Strings of kelp lay transparently dark green, with pale pods. He could hear the gruff voices of the giant croaking buzzards on the beach below, flapping their wings and jumping up and down, fighting over some tasty tidbit one of them had found.

"Is that what made you turn against him?" Sunchaser asked hesitantly. "The beatings?"

Kestrel's pretty face tensed. "No. No, I thought they were my fault, that he beat me because I was bad. I turned to Iceplant out of loneliness. I just couldn't bear to be by myself anymore. . . . It wasn't the beatings."

Sunchaser stared silently down at the beach. That hurt voice had painted a perfect picture for him. He could see her, young, beautiful, always crouching in her husband's shadow, afraid to breathe lest he think she'd been "bad" and punish her for it. He could imagine Kestrel retreating more and more into her own soul, cutting herself off from family and friends to keep from making a mistake that would anger her husband. And finally the loneliness had grown unbearable. That was when she must have sought comfort elsewhere.

How different from his own life. Solitude had so many compensations. Friends could tell him all they wanted to about the joys of wife and family. He cherished being alone. Only at such times could he really *see* the world around him, and himself. The distress he experienced from being close to people hindered him for weeks afterward. He always said too much, gave too much, cared too much for no good reason at all. Such closeness, even for a little while, drained every ounce of his strength—until he felt that his soul had detached from his body and gone flying to escape.

He put his empty cup down and forced himself to sit up. The cold bit at his bare chest. His belly roiled. "Oh, Blessed Spirits," he groaned, fearing that he might have to vomit again. "I've never understood what the Talth see in ants. I suffered through the same anguish the last time I tried them."

"You mean you couldn't Dream?"

"I mean that all I did was throw up."

"I don't think ants are good for you, Sunchaser."

He laughed and wished he hadn't. She looked so serious. Worse, it made him feel lightheaded again. "I'm sure you're right."

Kestrel smiled then, and he couldn't help smiling back. She didn't realize it, but she looked very beautiful, with her long hair shining about her face and dressed in his Mammoth Spirit Dance shirt, which was much too big for her. Sunchaser suspected that she hadn't smiled in a long time. She did it with such a childlike delight.

"Sunchaser," she said, "I don't know very much about the Ant Ordeal, but among my clan, when we make a ground painting, someone must erase it the next day or it will bring bad luck. May I do that for you?"

He lifted his brows. No one had *ever* done it for him. But the way he felt this morning, he certainly couldn't do it himself. "Yes, if you would like to."

"Where should I begin?"

"With the red serpent lines. You must erase even the places where the colors have been smeared or are gone. Pretend the lines are still there. Because they are . . . in the Spirit World. Work your way outward. The serpent lines, then the black circle, then the white."

"Erase it in reverse of the way I laid it down? Yes, I understand."

She rose and went to the smudged circle. First she spread her arms and Sang prayers to the four directions; then she bowed to Mother Ocean and lifted her face to Brother Sky. Bending over, she began carefully obliterating his painting with her hands. It astonished him. She must have memorized the process last night, because she erased the painting in *exactly* the reverse of the way he had laid it down. And her touch was like that of a mother stroking a sick baby's face.

"You like paintings?" he asked.

"My whole world is painting and dyeing. At least it was. I haven't done either in a long time. I miss the colors. They bring my soul to life."

"I know what you mean. I feel the same way."

Kestrel, reflective, ran her fingers over the carved maze. Awe sparkled in her wide eyes. She drew over each line twice, as though memorizing the twists and turns. In that position, bending at the waist, her knees locked, she looked startlingly like a child playing in the dirt.

She was not a child, he told himself. No one who had been beaten, thrown out by her clan and run for weeks to escape her mad husband could be thought of as anything but a woman. Yet even the way she moved had an innocent appeal. She used her hands to erase the lines, her fingers spread far apart, and appeared totally unconcerned that her long hair dragged in the dirt as she moved around the outer circle. Everything about her affected him with the terrifying sweetness of a Spirit Plant in his veins.

When she had finished, she chanted, thanking the Spirits, then wiped her hands on her moccasins and walked back to him. "Could you eat something?" she asked. "I gathered snails from the rocks at dawn this morning. And I could cut a steak from the deer haunch . . . roast it slowly."

"A steak would certainly kill me. And snails? I'm sure the Spirits would strike me dead if I touched a single one."

"Another cup of tea, then?"

"That, I could face."

She retrieved his horn cup. Deftly, she tilted the bag to refill it.

Sunchaser lowered himself to the ground and pulled the elk hide up over his chest. A chill had begun to eat at him. He shivered. He didn't recall having been this sick or weak after his last Ant Ordeal. But he'd had Good Plume to chant and Sing for him.

Kestrel brought the tea and set it down by his shoulder, then backed away two paces and clasped her hands behind her, an eager, alert expression on her pretty face.

"Is there something else you want to ask me, Kestrel?"

"No. I was just . . . Sunchaser, I know you do not feel well, but the snow has stopped. I was wondering when you might be able to take me to Otter Clan Village. I won't feel safe until I'm there."

As though adding her voice to the discussion, Cloud Girl coughed and began to cry. Kestrel glanced over her shoulder to the pile of hides where her daughter lay, but she made no attempt to go to her. She stood waiting for Sunchaser's response.

"Tomorrow," he promised. *No matter how I feel.* "We'll leave at dawn."

Kestrel's face shone with gratitude. "Thank you."

"Go comfort your daughter, Kestrel. I'm fine. Cloud Girl needs you much more than I do."

He watched Kestrel dart over and pick up Cloud Girl. The baby smiled toothlessly at her, then lifted her gaze to Sunchaser, and her little face slackened gravely. A light flared in those huge eyes, something that drew Sunchaser like a starving beast to food. He felt oddly as though the child were speaking to him, and as though in that silent voice he heard a dread to match his own. It whispered through his soul like a cold wind.

"Kestrel?" he asked softly, so as not to break the fragile strand that connected him to Cloud Girl. "Was it thundering when she was born?"

"Yes. It was one of the worst storms I'd ever seen. Thunder, and a deluge of rain. Lightning struck the bluff over my head while I was in labor with her." Kestrel sat down on the pile of furs and unlaced the front of her shirt, pulling it back so she could feed the infant. Cloud Girl craned her neck to keep staring at Sunchaser. "Why do you ask?"

"In your dreams, Kestrel, have you ever called out to me? Called my name? As though you needed my help?"

Kestrel frowned and shook her head. "No. I don't think so. . . . Why?"

Sunchaser lifted his cup of tea and sipped at it. Cloud Girl moved her head a little more so she could still peer at Sunchaser while clamping her mouth around Kestrel's nipple. Pictures appeared suddenly on the undercoat of Sunchaser's soul, like tongues of fire licking up around long-dead coals: strange images of overpowering darkness and interconnected labyrinths that spiraled out into infinity, flashes of blinding light . . .

"Sunchaser?" Kestrel repeated. Her eyes had been darting back and forth between Sunchaser and Cloud Girl; perhaps she felt their conversation though she could not hear it.

He answered, "I think I finally understand why Mammoth Above brought us together."

Oxbalm tugged his robes up around his throat and frowned at the oak and pine forest that surrounded him. What a strange place. Whereas Mother Ocean lived and breathed, always in motion, always Singing, the mountains' hushed stillness reminded him of death. Frost glittered on the leaves of the trees and on the grass. The night breeze had a bite that ate at his bones.

Piles of furs marked the places where the rest of the villagers slept. Oxbalm had allowed Catchstraw to choose the village site but had immediately regretted it when the old Dreamer had pointed to this tree-covered hilltop. People had been so exhausted that they'd just thrown down their furs and dropped into deep slumber.

But what a site! Half of the trees here had been blasted by lightning, and where was the water? They would have to hike for half a day to get to a river that had any fish. In the summer, when the droughts came upon them, they would either spend all of their time hauling water or they'd dry up and blow away. A ridiculous site. There'd be few animals to hunt up here on this windblown hilltop. What did Catchstraw expect them to eat? Grass and twigs?

Oxbalm heaved a tired sigh. Catchstraw had changed. He couldn't quite put his finger on it, but the man had grown . . . menacing. Almost sinister. Where he used to wheedle annoyingly, now he ordered in a clear, ringing voice. His gestures, which used to be impudent and insecure, had taken on a disturbing confidence. Every wave of his hand now exuded threat.

I'm just angry and worried. That's all it is.

As they'd climbed higher and higher into the foothills, Oxbalm's heart had begun to grieve for Mother Ocean. He felt like a child torn from the womb too early. He missed the heartbeat of the waves. Who would the Mother talk to now, without him there? Would she be lonely?

Not nearly as lonely as you'll be, you old fool. You should have just called Catchstraw a liar to his face and gone on about finding the right village site.

But that would have split the village in two, and he could not bear the thought. False Dreamers didn't last long, though he had to admit that the people drawn to them seemed more loyal than normal, thinking humans were. He prayed that people would come to their senses long before he had to split the village. But even if they didn't, they'd be back. He had seen it before: the strengthening of a Dreamer's following, the greedy way that people flocked to him, and then the sudden toppling of the hero. When people lost faith, they came back wailing and tearing their hair, declaring that they'd been tricked, begging to be taken in by their old clan members.

But what a toll it took. Such family rifts never mended properly.

A little way from him, Horseweed lay sleeping with his head on his arm. Black hair covered half of his young face, but Oxbalm could see one closed eye and his grandson's pug nose. Horseweed had a serious twist to his mouth, as though dreaming of frightening things.

Oh, how you've changed, my grandson. Horseweed had grown up in the blink of an eye. Oxbalm had first noticed the change when Horseweed returned with Sunchaser. But his grandson's maturity had been steadily growing since then. What had the Dreamer said to cause Horseweed to begin looking at life so deeply . . . to turn Horseweed from a boy to a man? No one else recognized his grandson's new status, because Horseweed had yet to seek a vision or kill a mammoth. But Oxbalm did. Almost unconsciously he'd begun delegating more authority to Horseweed, asking things of him that he would never have asked a moon ago, depending on Horseweed as on a seasoned adviser.

Curious, the effect Sunchaser had on people.

He prayed Sunchaser hadn't taken his words to heart when he'd told him to get out of the village and not to come back. The thought of never seeing Sunchaser again wrenched Oxbalm's soul. He believed in Sunchaser and Sunchaser's Dreams.

"I wish you were here with us right now, Sunchaser," he whispered mournfully.

Something scampered through the branches over Oxbalm's head, rousing the sleeping birds into a cacophony of whirring wings and squawks. Against the stars, a small dark shadow was jumping from limb to limb. Then abruptly the little animal shrieked and fell, thumping the ground a short distance from Oxbalm. He sat up. The squirrel writhed and flopped on the ground, squealing as if in pain. Oxbalm and Sumac's fire had burned down to glowing red coals. It didn't cast enough light that he could see the animal very well.

"What is it?" Sumac asked. She clutched her sleeping hide against her chest and propped herself up on a spindly arm. Soft locks of gray hair draped around her face.

"It's a squirrel. Something's wrong with it."

Sumac focused on the animal, and her eyes widened. In a hoarse whisper, she said, "There's something . . . on it."

"What do you mean, 'on' it?"

"I mean attached to the squirrel. Look. Aren't those wings?" She pointed.

Oxbalm squinted until his nose wrinkled up. But he still could not make it out. "I don't see any wings."

"Well, get up and find out for certain. If it threatens a squirrel, it might threaten our children."

"Blessed Mother Ocean!" he whispered irritably. "It's probably an owl with dinner, and you want me to go attack it!"

"Hush and go see!"

Oxbalm threw off his hide and forced his aching knees to hold him up, but he'd taken only four steps when a prickle climbed his spine and he stopped. The squirrel lay five hands from him, on its stomach, with its legs sprawled every which way, its paws twitching.

A bat lay atop the squirrel's back. It had snugged its wings around the squirrel's sides, keeping the little animal still. Three hands long, the bat looked huge. Only the squirrel's white throat and head showed beneath those midnight colored wings. The squirrel had begun making a soft, pitiful sound. The bat held the squirrel's shoulder between its sharp teeth while it watched Oxbalm through black, shining eyes.

Oxbalm had not seen such a bat since his youth. These bats lived in the foothills. He'd seen them often while hunting or going on war raids, but it had been so many cycles, maybe twenty or more, since he'd done either that he had practically forgotten that the bats existed. The squirrel chirred weakly and tried to fight again, but the bat just sank its teeth deeper and spread its wings to brace itself until the squirrel's strength failed.

Oxbalm crouched down and the bat went still. It kept its wings spread, as though trying to blend with the darkness. But its eyes, those black, glistening eyes, looked at Oxbalm frantically. The longer Oxbalm peered into them, the more the differences between them slipped away. *As one predator to another,* the bat's eyes seemed to plead, *don't take my squirrel away from me. I hunted long and hard to catch it. You understand. I need to eat. Let me have my squirrel.*

"Don't worry, little fellow," Oxbalm murmured. "You made a good hunt. You earned your dinner."

Very slowly, so as not to scare the bat, Oxbalm rose and took three long steps backward. The bat tucked its wings around the squirrel again and began to make sucking sounds, feeding on the rich red fluid from the squirrel's shoulder wound.

"What is it, Oxbalm?" Sumac asked.

He turned and saw her sitting up in their robes, an alarmed expression on her face. The faint gleam of the coals had dyed her skin reddish.

"Oh, it's just a bloodsucking bat. Nothing to worry about. I've never heard of one attacking humans."

Sumac frowned. "A bloodsucking bat? You mean—"

"Yes. It's feeding on the squirrel."

Sumac shuddered visibly.

As Oxbalm started back toward his robes, he saw movement from the corner of his eye. He craned his neck to look down the western slope they'd climbed earlier in the day. Four men walked out of the mottled forest shadows. Their dark faces gleamed in the starlight. He could hear their voices, low, speaking quietly to one another.

Oxbalm cupped a hand to his mouth. "Hello!" he called. "Who are you?"

A ringing voice called back, "I'm Harrier, from the Blackwater Draw Clan. My brothers are traveling with me. Are you the Otter Clan?"

Oxbalm frowned. "Yes. How do you know that?"

"We followed your tracks from your former village site. We've been trying to find you for days."

Sumac exchanged a questioning look with Oxbalm and shouted, "What for?"

The yelling had brought the entire village awake. As people roused, mutters of alarm laced the cold night air. Oxbalm saw Horseweed grab his atlatl and quiver of darts, peer down the trail, then throw off his robes and get to his feet. Other men rose and walked forward with weapons in hand, while women shushed their children. A few dogs ran down the trail to sniff and bark at the strangers.

Horseweed came to stand beside Oxbalm. "Who are they, Grandfather? Do you know them?"

Oxbalm shook his head. "No, I don't think so."

The four men crested the hill. They were tall youths, burly, with atlatls in their hands and quivers slung over their broad shoulders. The leader, probably Harrier, had a massive brow and a flat nose. He walked straight to Oxbalm and took his hand in a firm grip. In the pale gleam of the coals, Oxbalm saw the beautifully dyed red-leather shirt he wore beneath his buckskin jacket.

"You are Oxbalm, aren't you?"

"Yes," Oxbalm replied cautiously. "Do I know you?"

Harrier let his hand drop to his side and gave Horseweed a quick, evaluative glance. Horseweed's eyes narrowed. Harrier said, "I met you when I was a boy, Oxbalm, but it's been fifteen cycles. I wouldn't expect you to remember. Please, talk with us. We're looking for a woman."

"What woman?"

"Her name is Kestrel." Harrier's brothers crowded around, their young faces hard. "She murdered our brother."

From out in the darkness, Catchstraw's grating voice cried, "What is it? What's happening? Somebody should have awakened me!"

Oxbalm glanced over to see Catchstraw pulling on his moccasins, anger on his face. As he jerked on his deerhide coat, he shouted, "Yucca Thorn! Dizzy Seal! Where are you? Why did no one inform me that visitors had arrived?"

Harrier's eyes narrowed speculatively, and Oxbalm placed a friendly hand on his shoulder. "Kestrel . . . yes. I have heard that name before. Come, sit down. I'll build up my fire and we'll talk."

The Star People called across the blackness, worrying, terrified that Mother Ocean and Above-Old-Man had lost control of the situation on the world below. "Why aren't you already down there, Boy?" one old woman shouted. "Get moving! I thought you wanted to be a great Dreamer so you could help her!"

The Boy closed his eyes in shame. "I haven't been called yet. The Man says it will happen soon, though. Very soon."

The Star People's voices hushed to disagreeable whispers, but he caught fragments of their conversations:

". . . he's afraid. He'll never be able to help anybody."

"Boy is a coward."

"Too young . . ."

". . . can't expect him to know anything important . . . don't understand why Man chose him. Boy, a Dreamer? Ridiculous!"

The Boy huddled in upon himself and peered at his own inner light that shimmered a pure white. "I can do it. I can so."

"Can you, Boy?" The Man called softly from the deep dark belly of the blackness, and his words fell around the Boy like handfuls of stardust. "Being a Dreamer is very hard. Harder than you could ever imagine."

The Boy breathed out a shuddering breath. "I can do it, Man. I—I just wish I knew exactly what I'm supposed to accomplish in that dead body. What should I do, Man? How should I deal with this wicked human?"

"Tell him what he wants to know."

Boy frowned. "You can't mean that. More than anything, he wants to know where my mother is. You're not asking me to betray my mother? Man," the Boy asked in horror, "are you?"

All of the low conversations that eddied through the blackness died suddenly. Stars twinkled and burst, while others shrank into nothingness, and beyond them all, spirals of whole dead villages turned in their inexorable rotations.

"Man? Man, please answer me. I must know the answer to that question. I can't betray my mother!"

"Is that what frightens you most?"

"Yes, of course it is! She is my hope . . . my only hope."

"Then you have answered your own question, Boy. Haven't I told you that every Dreamer must face his greatest fear before he can Dream the world back into balance?"

Twenty-five

Catchstraw wandered aimlessly around the edges of camp, his hands shoved into the pockets of his heavy elkhide coat. He'd pulled his furlined hood up to keep his ears warm. Mist filled the meadow below and coiled around the trunks of trees. A bitter chill had settled over the foothills last night, though not a single cloud marred the translucent blue of the early morning sky. Crickets chirped monotonously in the grass, and a haze of gnats glittered in the calm air. The fragrance of dew-soaked earth saturated the hills. Unless a storm moved in later, it should be a perfect day for cutting down trees and digging postholes to set them into. Not that Catchstraw particularly cared. He was a Dreamer and above such work.

He studied the people near their crackling fires, cooking food, getting ready to begin a day of hard labor building lodges and unpacking belongings. Most of the children still slept, but two boys—Cloverleaf and Little Puppytail—had a dice game going between the lodges, using walnuts painted black on one side and white on the other. Puppytail kept squealing shrilly when Cloverleaf rolled pairs of whites. Each yell set the dogs to barking excitedly and running to peer down the trails.

The brothers who'd arrived around midnight sat in a knot by their own small fire on the far western side of the hilltop. Harrier, the oldest, kept glancing speculatively at Catchstraw, as though he wanted to come over and speak to him but hadn't yet gained the courage to, probably because Harrier had witnessed the people's reverence and caution around Catchstraw last night.

"Well, you should be timid about approaching me, boy," Catchstraw whispered to himself. "I have more Power than you could ever understand."

The fact had begun to seep in. He had actually started *seeing* differently. Even now, he appraised people through the eyes of a predator, a hunter looking to kill. He could recognize people by their distinctive scents. Pregnant women bore a peculiarly musky odor. They were easy to identify, even those who did not yet know about their pregnancy themselves. Once he'd learned to tell the sex of the unborn child just by the mother's smell, he would gain a following the likes of which Sunchaser would envy. People would view him with awe. And he *would* learn how. Already he could distinguish a certain earthiness clinging to some women, but not to others. He thought it indicated that they would give birth to sons, but he couldn't be sure yet. He'd have to wait to verify his suspicions.

Catchstraw chuckled to himself and folded his arms smugly. Strange. All his life, he'd felt like the prey, tormented by his relatives because he was *different*, because he hated clan law and clan obligations.

Since he'd learned to witch, a new strength had flooded his veins. His muscles had begun to develop at an astounding rate, and his night vision had sharpened to the clarity of a cat's. He expected in a few moons to be as feared and renowned as old Cactus Lizard—though of course he'd never boast of his witchery to *anyone*. He wanted people to believe that his Power came from Dreaming. Dreamers stayed alive a great deal longer than witches did.

Harrier stood up by his fire and stretched his stiff back muscles. He said a few quiet words to his brothers and walked away from them, heading bravely toward Catchstraw.

Catchstraw observed his approach with narrowed eyes and lifted his hooked nose to sniff the air. The boy smelled like a predator, too. That made Catchstraw wary.

"Good day to you, Dreamer." Harrier bowed respectfully.

"What do you want, boy?"

Harrier blinked at Catchstraw's harsh tone. "If I'm disturbing you, please tell me and I will return later."

Catchstraw waved a hand irritably. "No, go on. I'd just as soon get it over with. What do you want?"

Harrier shifted his weight to his other foot and gazed at Catchstraw curiously. "One of the old women told me last night that you are a Dreamer. I was hoping I might be able to talk with you about some of your visions."

"*Which* visions?"

Harrier spread his arms and smiled nervously. "As you know, my brothers and I are looking for this Kestrel. Have you seen anything of her? Or of her crazy husband, Lambkill? Their locations, perhaps?"

Catchstraw shoved his hands in his pockets again and ground his teeth for a moment. "The only Dreams I've had lately are about terrible things happening to Otter Clan Village. You're not the cause of those things, are you?"

"Me?" Harrier yipped in surprise. He took a step backward. "No . . . I mean . . . how could I be?"

"Doesn't matter. Just see that you're not. Understand, boy?"

A swallow went down Harrier's throat, and the fear on his face pleased Catchstraw enormously. Harrier nodded obediently. "My brothers and I did not come here to cause you trouble, Dreamer. We want to capture our brother's murderer and go home. That's—"

"Good. The sooner, the better."

Harrier stood with his mouth slightly open. As sunlight brightened the forest, the birds broke into song and the bright blue jays, goldfinches and vermilion flycatchers flitted through the tops of the oaks. Catchstraw heard Oxbalm's soft voice as he spoke to Sumac. They were rising late today, but they'd been up very late last night. From the edge of his vision, Catchstraw saw them rolling up their bedding hides.

Harrier turned to follow Catchstraw's gaze and said, "I can see that you're busy, Dreamer. May I return to talk to you again after breakfast? Perhaps on full stomachs we'll both be—"

"You may," Catchstraw granted, "but don't disturb me if I'm out in the forest gathering Spirit Plants. That's a sacred time for me."

"I understand." Harrier smiled halfheartedly and bowed once more. "I hope to see you again later. Thank you." He turned and practically ran back to his fire. Questions burst out from his brothers. Harrier shushed them and whispered his responses while he eyed Catchstraw gravely.

Catchstraw sighed and lifted his hooked nose again to survey the array of meats being cooked for breakfast. Maybe he would join old woman Yucca Thorn's family. They'd propped a porcupine over their fire and it smelled fat and succulent. Yes, Yucca Thorn would be glad to share her meal.

Twenty-six

Moist sand squished between Kestrel's toes as she walked barefoot across the beach. A stiff wind tousled her long hair about her shoulders. She saw Sunchaser, back in camp, holding Cloud Girl while he tended the fire. They had left their rock shelter yesterday, and Sunchaser said they would reach Otter Clan Village tomorrow afternoon. The sudden freedom affected her like a tonic. She extended her arms and spun around with her head thrown back. The fringes on her dress danced. *Blessed Mother Ocean, perhaps I should have been praying to you all along. Thank you . . . for making me feel this way.*

When she lowered her arms, she hugged herself tightly and basked in the joy that swelled her heart. They'd passed four people today, from a place called Whalebeard Village, and each had seemed friendly and happy. So unlike her own stodgy clan, with their dour faces.

"I'm going to be happy here. I just know it."

She started walking again, checking each shady place beyond the reach of the salty water for chickweed. The plant grew in thick clumps in the shadows of rocks. It had scraggly branches that ended in tiny white blossoms. Whenever she spotted one, she plucked the entire plant and tucked it into the hide bag tied around her waist.

The afternoon sunlight flushed her cheeks with warmth. Kestrel took her time, picking up an occasional shell, rubbing it clean and studying its texture and colors, smelling it to absorb the scents of fish and kelp. She fought her own best judgment and deliberately shoved all thoughts of Lambkill from her mind. She just wanted to pretend for a short while, to let her soul believe that she was thirteen again and had never married.

Mother Ocean rocked turbulently in the high wind. Dark gray swells rolled in, one after another, roaring as they curled and crashed, shattering on the beach. The water rushed in white and boiling, almost up to the place where they'd made camp. Then the waves exhausted themselves, melting back into the body of the Mother once more as they undercut their advancing brothers in ripples of streaked brown sand.

Kestrel skipped and broke into a run. As fast as the wind, she leaped over anything that lay in her headlong path, and she sped down the shore with her hair flying.

Sunchaser smiled as he watched from the lodge he had crafted from saltgrass, tied shock upon shock, and propped around a water-worn oak limb screwed into the sand. She ran down the beach with childlike abandon, stopping occasionally to spin around with her face tipped to Father Sun, her arms outstretched. Her bright laughter wafted on the wind.

They had made their camp by a rocky outcrop surrounded by a mixed grove of pine and flowering dogwood trees, where a tiny moss-covered spring bubbled up. Windblown pink petals scattered across the sand and heaped against the bases of the boulders.

Twice the height of a man, the eight rocks of the outcrop formed an irregular semicircle that opened to the sea. The rocks had been smoothed and shaped by thousands of cycles of wind and rain until they seemed to have faces. Eerie faces. Pits of eyes and mounds of bumpy noses protruded over wide cracks of mouths. Sunchaser sensed Power here. Faint, old, but here nonetheless. He had the uncomfortable feeling that he was being watched.

Quietly, he eased the sleeping Cloud Girl into the crook of his left arm and used his right hand to pour a sack of fresh clams into the cooking bag that hung from the tripod at the edge of the fire. They had dug the clams and collected firewood a hand of time ago, just after they'd set up camp. He had purposely camped early tonight. It might take them another day to reach Otter Clan Village, but at least Kestrel would be rested when she arrived. A moon of exhaustion had sapped her strength. She hadn't complained, but by noon he could tell that she was already getting tired. She'd fallen silent in an effort to hide her hard breathing. Did she think him so unapproachable that she couldn't tell him when she needed to rest? He would have to fix that.

With his elk scapula, he scooped a hot stone from the flames and dropped it into the bag. Steam exploded. He added more hot stones until the water boiled, then sank back to the sand and gently lowered Cloud Girl to his lap. Her mousehide pacifier had glued itself to the corner of her open mouth. The sound of the baby's breathing soothed a weary part of his soul. He carefully pulled up the rabbit-fur hood and arranged it around Cloud Girl's face to shield her from the chill.

Helper lay on the opposite side of the fire, sleeping. He'd tucked his pointed nose into the bits of remaining fur on his tail for warmth. The orange light of the flames reflected in his patchy coat. Behind Helper, Sunchaser had thrown out two piles of sleeping robes. The camp faced north, so that he could watch their backtrail.

He honestly did not believe that her husband could have tracked her through the storms they'd had.

But just in case, he kept a lookout.

When he glanced up again, Kestrel was heading back toward camp. She walked slowly, as though deep in thought. Wind whipped a web of black hair across her pretty face. She made no attempt to brush it away. She folded her arms and tucked her hands into her long sleeves. The seashells on the shirt he'd given her glittered in the late-afternoon light.

The wind was blowing with a violence he hadn't seen since last autumn. Pine branches clattered, and the flames of Sunchaser's fire pranced back and forth wildly. Their colors alternated between orange and blue, tinged with a lavender so rich and beautiful that it reminded him of the inside of a mussel shell. He poked at the fire with a long piece of driftwood, waiting for Kestrel.

She walked into the half moon of standing stones and knelt beside Sunchaser to stroke Helper's neck. Helper lifted his head inquiringly and thumped his tail on the ground.

"Tonight," Kestrel informed the dog in a soft voice, "you're going to feel better. Just wait. No mange can stand up to a good chickweed poultice."

Sunchaser smiled. "Should I pull out a wooden bowl for you?"

"Two would be better. That way, I can cup one on top of the other."

He glanced down at Cloud Girl, taking care not to awaken her as he drew the bowls from his pack and handed them to Kestrel. Unlacing the small bag around her waist, Kestrel tugged out five handfuls of scraggly chickweed plants and piled them into one bowl, then turned the other bowl upside down and placed it on top of the first. They didn't fit together very well, but the top bowl would help to contain the steam.

"It won't take long," she said. She used a stick to drag several glowing coals to the edge of the fire pit. Then she covered the coals with a thick layer of sand and set the bowls atop it to heat slowly. "When the plants have cooked down enough, we'll plaster them on Helper's mangy spots."

Helper apparently understood. He wagged his tail again and licked Kestrel's forearm. She laughed and scratched his ears. "It's all right, Helper," she said. "You would do the same for me. I know you would."

The dog crawled forward on his belly to lay his head in her lap.

"The clams are ready," Sunchaser said.

"Good. I'm starved."

A serenity had entered her eyes. Sunchaser held her gaze for a long while, probing those dark brown depths in search of the soul beneath. It wasn't hard to find. She opened herself to him unabashedly—as though perfectly willing to let him see her many vulnerabilities. *Because she trusts me with them.*

He smiled. "I'm starving, too. I thought you'd never get tired of feeling the sand squishing between your toes." He reached for his pack. "We'll have to use our cups since our bowls are filled with chickweed."

"Here," she said. "Give Cloud Girl to me and I'll put her down on my . . . your hides . . . the hides that you've kindly loaned us." She held out her arms.

"They're your hides," Sunchaser said as he stood. "I have plenty without them. Every time I perform a Healing, the sick person's family showers me with hides and other gifts. It's actually become a nuisance. I don't know what to do with them all. I usually can't refuse the gifts or I'd insult the givers, so I leave them with my aunt in Brushnut Village. Her lodge is stuffed full." He handed Cloud Girl into Kestrel's waiting arms. "I hate to let go of her," he said honestly. "I've held a lot of babies before, but none have affected me the way Cloud Girl does."

Kestrel pulled back one of the hides that formed her bed and placed Cloud Girl in the midst. When she drew the fur up around her daughter's tiny face, she said, "All babies touch the heart. I think—"

"No, it's more than that." Sunchaser crouched before his pack to pull out two cups. He set them on the sand and hesitated. "Cloud Girl is special. Do you understand what I mean?"

Kestrel nodded. "Yes, I think so. If you mean the—I don't even know what to call it—the strange look in her eyes."

"Yes. That's what I mean."

Sunchaser dipped his elk scapula into the boiling bag and ladled out two cups of steaming clams. He gave one to Kestrel. "Be careful. They're very hot."

She took the cup and set it aside to cool while she patted the top of Helper's head affectionately. He let out a groan of what sounded like sheer delight. "Sunchaser, you know more about these things than I do. What do you think that 'look' is?"

He stretched out in front of the fire, braced himself on an elbow and picked up his cup of clams. "I don't know exactly. She's connected to Power. But I'm not sure how."

"Connected to Power?"

"Yes. A lot of children are. It's only as they grow older that they lose their natural ability to touch and hear things beyond this world."

Kestrel frowned thoughtfully. "When I first really looked into her eyes, I felt as if my soul had been severed from my body." She pried open one of the clams in her cup and tore out the succulent meat.

Sunchaser dug into his own cup. The clams tasted sweet and juicy. "I hesitate to say it," he said, "but I think that Cloud Girl's going to be a Dreamer when she grows up. I—"

"Oh, I'd like that. Very much," Kestrel said. "It will give her the chance to help people. There are so many people who feel lost and confused. They need to know there's someone who cares about them, no matter what they've done. I hope you're right."

Sunchaser's hand halted midway to his mouth. Is that how Kestrel saw him? As someone who cared "no matter what"? He lowered the clam back to his cup solemnly. How little the average person understood about Dreaming. He did care, very much, but he would have preferred not to. Tending to the needs of others left him feeling bereft, and too exhausted to Dream. And, as Good Plume had noted, Dreaming was what *really* helped people.

He prayed that Cloud Girl would learn to balance the needs of others and the needs of Power better than he had. He'd known Dreamers who had so exhausted themselves in serving others that they'd lost their way to the Land of the Dead. They'd always ended up hating themselves . . .

Sunchaser sat for so long staring into the fire, remembering those haunted Dreamers, thinking about his own problems with the maze, that he missed the brilliant shades of sunset that kindled the heavens. When he awoke from his contemplation, darkness had swallowed the day and only a faint gray haze limned the western horizon. The wind had died down to a whisper of breeze. He looked at his bowl. His clams had gone stone cold.

Kestrel was quietly applying the chickweed poultice to Helper's mangy spots. Helper had his chin propped on her knee. She took special care to rub the chickweed gently into his ears. The dog peered up at her with a mixture of relief and adoration. When she noticed Sunchaser's gaze, she smiled faintly and said, "Are you back?"

"Yes. Sorry. I didn't mean to do that." He rattled the cold clams in his cup. In the firelight, the faces on the boulders looked even more alive. Shadows filled in the hollows of cheeks, nostrils and throats. Eight old men. That's what they reminded him of. Had they heard his thoughts? Felt his worries?

"Do you often drift off that way?" Kestrel finished coating Helper's mangy spots and rubbed her hands in the sand to clean them. Helper rose, walked around in circles until he found the right place, then flopped down and went to sleep again.

"To tell you the truth, I don't know. I may, but I rarely have anybody around to tell me about it."

"Isn't it hard? Being alone all the time? I'd die from loneliness." Kestrel wrapped her arms around her knees and propped her chin atop them. Her long black hair draped her shoulders.

"Oh, I'm far more lonely when I'm with people than when I'm by myself."

"I don't understand."

Sunchaser held her gaze but concentrated on the burbling of the spring in the dogwoods. Its soft, silken sound soothed him. "Loneliness, at least for me, happens only when I don't like myself very much. I generally like myself when I'm alone. It's only when I'm with others that I don't."

"Why don't you like yourself when you're with people?"

"Oh, I suppose it's because the reflection of myself that I see in their eyes terrifies me." He hesitated and shoved the cold clams around in his cup with one finger. "I see myself as they see me—and I know I can never live up to their expectations. I know I can never be the man they think I am."

Kestrel tilted her head questioningly. "And so you're lonely then?"

"Yes." Sunchaser smiled. "Lonely for the me that I like. I haven't seen that man much in the past cycle."

"Then being with others hurts you?"

He nodded. "Nearly every conversation, every moment I spend with someone else, is like a collision. I feel injured when I walk away."

"I've never thought of loneliness that way. I'm happier when I can hear someone talking or moving about close by." She hesitated awkwardly, as though words had failed her, and Sunchaser filled in the gap in the conversation.

"Dreamers are more fragile than normal people. Easily bruised."

"You? Easily bruised?" She pulled her head back in teasing disbelief. "The great Sunchaser?"

His smile waned. He studied the dogwood petals that tumbled across the sand in the breeze. They flipped back and forth like fluttering butterfly wings. "Too easily, I'm afraid."

Kestrel lightly rubbed her chin across the fine hide that covered her knees. In the fire's glow, her black hair glinted golden, as though woven with strands of summer sunlight. Sunchaser picked up his long piece of driftwood and tapped it on the stones in the hearth ring. She affected him oddly. Despite what he'd just said, the past five days had not been a collision. They'd been filled with easy talk and laughter.

"But I didn't mean that being near you makes me lonely, Kestrel. I've enjoyed the time we've spent together."

A silent communication passed between them, warm and powerful, like a strengthening current.

"So have I, Sunchaser."

Her eyes held him riveted. Suddenly he felt as though he stood on a high ridge in the middle of a lightning storm. His whole body prickled. When he began to feel it in all the wrong places, he hastily dropped his gaze and grimaced at the fire.

Helper groaned.

Sunchaser assumed it to be a comment on his behavior, but when he looked over, he found the dog sound asleep, his feet twitching while he dreamed.

"He's probably hunting rabbits," Sunchaser mused.

Kestrel smiled. Then she put a hand to her mouth, covering a yawn.

"Do you want to sleep, Kestrel?" He started to rise, but she reached out and put a hand on his arm. The chill of her slender fingers penetrated his shirt.

"I was wishing that we might talk more. If that's all right?"

He sank back to the ground. "What about?"

"Oh, I . . . I don't know."

"Not more about Dreamers, I hope. I think I've bared my soul enough for one night."

She laughed at his wry tone. "No. Let's—" She leaned back and took a deep breath, as though preparing herself for a painful discussion. "I was hoping you would tell me something about the Otter Clan."

Sunchaser's brows went up. "Oh, Kestrel, forgive me. It should have occurred to me long before now that you'd be wondering about them." *Wondering, hoping, desperate to know what sort of people her new relatives would be.* "I think you will like them very much. And I know they'll like you."

"It doesn't matter about me. I just . . . they *must* like Cloud Girl. If anything happens to me, I want to know that there's someone among them who will take care of her and love her."

"There will be," he said kindly. He cracked open another

clam and tugged out the cold meat. Before putting it in his mouth, he added, "And as for anything happening to you—"

"Let's not—I don't want to talk about my h-husband. Please, tell me more about the Otter Clan. How big is their village?" She peered at him through eyes as wide and intent as an owl's.

"About thirty people, maybe a few more. I'm not certain of how many children have been born this past winter. Their leader's name is Oxbalm. He's a dignified, feisty man of fifty-three summers. A good leader. He—"

"And the village sits in a fir forest, doesn't it? At the very edge of the sea?"

Sunchaser nodded. "It does. Yes."

"And they make their houses by setting up whale or mammoth bones and covering the bones with hides . . . isn't that right?"

He smiled. "Iceplant must have told you those things."

"Yes." She laced her fingers over her shins. "Sunchaser, have you ever heard of a woman named Wind Shadow?"

He thought about it, then shook his head. "No. Why?"

"She was Iceplant's mother. I remembered her name last night. I just thought maybe . . ." Kestrel lifted a shoulder gracefully.

"No. Sorry. I haven't heard of her. Was she born here on the coast?"

"I can't say for certain. Iceplant told me that she was 'from' the Otter Clan, that they were her people. I know she told him many stories about the village and the sea. I've always assumed that she was born here, but I'm not sure."

Stars had begun to pop out across the indigo slate of night. Against that background, her flame-dyed face seemed unearthly, almost too beautiful to be real. Sunchaser couldn't take his eyes from her. "So Iceplant wasn't born here?"

"No. He was born among my people in the marsh country. His mother married my uncle. She died when Iceplant was very young."

"And you don't know the names of any of Wind Shadow's family? Didn't Iceplant ever speak of them? Surely Wind Shadow would have told him about his grandparents, aunts and uncles, cousins?"

"No."

"Wind Shadow never spoke to him about them? Or, if she did, Iceplant never told you?"

"He never told me."

The despair in her voice when she talked about Iceplant made his stomach ache. He shifted to peer at the clamshells charring in the fire. The flames had dwindled. He threw on another piece of driftwood and poked the fire with his long stick to get it going again. "Tell me about Iceplant. What did he look like? Maybe I can . . ."

His voice faded when he saw Kestrel's jaw tremble. She bowed her head, but she did not cry.

"He . . . He was tall. Almost as tall as you are. And he had a very round face with a straight nose and a pointed chin." She drew the lines with her hand.

"I didn't mean to hurt you. I'm sorry. I should have known it wouldn't help much. Nearly everyone in the Otter Clan fits that description."

"I want you to ask me questions, to ask anything that might help. I-I've been having nightmares that I'll finally get to Otter Clan Village and there will be no one there who's ever heard of Iceplant. And then . . ."

He could fill in the rest for himself: and then she would be truly alone and without hope. He'd been worrying about the same thing. For ten cycles he'd been visiting the Otter Clan, and he had never heard of anyone there marrying into the Bear-Looks-Back Clan. The "whys" and "why nots" had begun to weigh on him. But it was such a large clan, with people spread out all over, including some who lived in his own home village of Brushnut. In the cycles since Wind Shadow left, her relatives could have moved a dozen times.

"I've been trying to prepare my-myself." Kestrel crumpled the hide of her dress in her fists. "But it's very hard to do."

Sunchaser nodded. The sea had calmed. The crests of the waves resembled undulating silver serpents as they rolled toward the shore. "Kestrel, please, don't take this the wrong way, but is it possible that Iceplant was wrong about being related to the Otter Clan? That he—"

"No." She shook her head vehemently. "I know what you're thinking. He wouldn't have lied to me. Not ever. He asked me to marry him and come with him to the sea. We tried to escape. To-to do it. But Lambkill captured Iceplant and forced him to reveal which trail I'd taken and—"

Sunchaser looked up. "Iceplant told Lambkill which trail you'd taken?"

"Yes. Iceplant . . . he thought it was a way for us to be together. Lambkill had promised that if Iceplant admitted to being my lover and told him which trail I'd taken, he wouldn't kill us. Lambkill promised to banish us both."

"And Iceplant believed him?"

Kestrel wet her lips. "Yes."

Sunchaser quietly laid his stick down. Surely Iceplant had known of Lambkill's madness. Kestrel would have told him. Therefore Iceplant had knowingly risked Kestrel's life and that of their unborn baby. So all three of them could be together, she said. Strange, the way the human soul worked at desperate moments, making up reasons to justify things the person would never ordinarily say, or do.

"What are you thinking?" Kestrel asked softly.

"Hmm? Oh, nothing really. We humans think we're so clever and strong, but when we are asked for real loyalty or sacrifice, most of us fail."

"You mean . . . Iceplant?"

"Not just Iceplant. Everyone." He picked up his stick again and began peeling the bark from it. Bits and pieces fell around his moccasins. "I think we're all selfish at heart, though there are glorious moments"—he shook a finger emphatically—"when people rise above their inborn preoccupation with themselves. But not often."

Kestrel bit her lip and studied the toes of her moccasins that showed beneath her dress. "He didn't betray me, Sunchaser. Really. I worried about it for a long time. But he would never have done that."

"No, of course not, Kestrel. I only meant—"

"He tried to save me!" She reached out pleadingly. Words poured from her as though she feared that if she didn't say them now, she would never be able to again. "That's how I escaped. At the very end, Iceplant wrestled Lambkill to the ground and told me to run. And I—I did. It was right after that that Lambkill m-murdered—"

She put a hand to her trembling mouth. "He loved me. He did, Sunchaser."

"Of course he did." *She saw her lover killed before her eyes. Blessed Spirits.* "I never doubted that, Kestrel."

She struggled to stand. He rose and offered her a hand. She took it, and he helped her to her feet. He could see her legs shaking beneath her dress. Powerful emotions flitted across her face: anguish, sick confusion, emptiness . . . so much emptiness.

Sunchaser tightened his grip on her hand, and they stood for a long while just staring at each other. Tears slowly filled her eyes.

"Oh, Kestrel, don't cry."

He released her hand and wrapped his arms around her shoulders, pulling her close. The top of her head barely reached the middle of his chest. He patted her back gently. "It's all right. It's over. You're going to be fine. You're safe now."

"I can't let myself believe that, even though I feel safe with you." She slipped her arms around his waist and nuzzled her cheek against his shirt. "Thank you . . . for helping me. My husband will probably kill you for it."

His brows lifted. "I'll do my best to jump sideways when he aims."

"Don't joke," she said as she lifted her chin to look at him severely. "Really, Sunchaser, Lambkill will never stop hunting for me. You've placed yourself in grave danger."

He stared down into her eyes, and blood started to pulse deafeningly in his ears. The feel of her body pressed so warmly against him stirred terrifying sensations.

"Yes," he said and smiled with grim amusement at the irony in his voice. "I can see that I have." It took a deliberate act of will to pull away from her.

Kestrel's extended arms hovered uncertainly for a moment while she frantically searched his face. "I didn't mean—"

"I know you didn't. My fault." He shrugged nonchalantly, embarrassed by how rapidly he was breathing.

"Are you all right? I know about Dreamers and women. I haven't hurt your ability to Dream, have I? I would never—"

"No." He gave her a lopsided grin. "No, you're not responsible for that. Any problems I'm having are strictly my own fault."

For a time, she didn't move. Then, hesitantly, she said, "I . . . I think I'll sleep now."

He jerked a nod. "Sleep well."

She turned away toward her robes. "Good night, Sunchaser."

He watched her crawl in beside Cloud Girl. She curled herself around her baby and pulled the hides up to her chin, but her eyes remained open, peering out into the darkness.

Sunchaser shoved his hands into his coat pockets. Before he realized it, they'd clenched into fists. He felt foolish and vulnerable standing there, but he couldn't convince himself to sleep. He knew he would just lie there and stare blindly at the stars.

"I think I'll gather some more wood," he said.

Kestrel tugged her hide higher, covering half of her face. "Thank you."

Waves whispered gently, rhythmically, against the shore as he walked. The wind cooled his hot face, calming him enough that his shoulder muscles finally relaxed. His gaze brushed the sable belly of Brother Sky. The Star People glittered like a million snowflakes frozen midway in their fall to earth. Charcoal plumes of cloud drifted above the western horizon.

"It's all right," he murmured to himself. "Tomorrow I'll deliver Kestrel and Cloud Girl safely to Otter Clan Village. Then I'll return to the rock shelter and start Dreaming seriously."

When he stooped to pick up his first piece of driftwood, a mammoth trumpeted. The call echoed through the foothills, deep-throated and anguished.

Sunchaser stared wide-eyed at the forested slopes. Another mammoth joined the first, blasting the night.

Their cries blended into agonized wails.

It took him a while to find his voice. When he did, he murmured, "Don't be afraid. I'm not lost yet."

Twenty-seven

The spring leaves of the oaks trembled in the cool breeze that swirled through the forest. Wildflowers covered the open spaces, painting the slopes with blazes of red, blue and white. Oxbalm inhaled their sweet fragrances as he dragged a cut pine sapling along the game trail toward the new village site.

Though he had trimmed the branches, the sapling stretched thirty hands long and kept catching on the bushes and rocks that lined the trail. The effort of constantly tugging it loose had tired him and slowed his pace to a snail's crawl. What could people expect? At his age, he was lucky just to be able to tug on a log, let alone move it! He minded only that his dallying would be holding up the lodge construction.

The day had begun warm and sunny, but now towering gray thunderheads pushed across Brother Sky's belly, and Oxbalm could smell rain on the wind. He forced his miserable legs to go faster. The last thing he wanted was to sleep out in the open during a downpour. He feared that his bad knees would freeze up and never unthaw again.

On the hilltop, people were building new lodges while they roasted haunches of venison over open fires. Excitement pervaded the air. The din was punctuated by the uneven staccato of adzes rapping into hard wood as men used the hafted tools to chip away at stubborn branches while they fitted the logs. These would be placed into holes excavated with digging sticks, and the whole thing would be lashed together where the ridgepole was run across. After that, braces would be placed as needed and the entire structure covered with hides.

Several of the children had a game of hoop-and-pole going. The hoop, made from a willow stem and bound with sinew at the joint, spanned barely half a hand in diameter. The children had laid the ring flat on the ground and set up a throwing line forty hands away. They took turns throwing a pole, as long as they were tall, at the ring. If the pole lodged in the center of the ring, it counted as five points; if it touched the ring, as two points. They played to fifteen points. Shrill laughter rang through the hills.

Oxbalm panted as he began climbing up the slope. His moccasins skidded on the loose gravel. For every two steps forward, he seemed to slide one backward. He groaned and clutched the sapling tighter. At times like this, he missed little Mountain Lake the most. Had she been alive, she would have been jumping around him, laughing, asking him a thousand questions, and he would have completely forgotten the pain in his old body.

Oh, how I miss you, my little girl.

When he made it to the top of the hill, Horseweed and Balsam saw him coming and hurried to help him. The long fringes on their sleeves flapped against their sides as they ran. A broad grin split Balsam's young face, but Horseweed had a serious expression. Had it been only a moon ago that they'd seemed the same age?

"Here, Grandfather," Horseweed said as he took the sapling from Oxbalm's hands. "Why do you do this? Balsam and I can carry the poles. Let us know the next time you're going out into the forest. Why don't you go sit down by the fire? Grandmother made a delicious soup. It's hanging in the bag on the tripod."

Balsam trotted around to pick up the other end of the sapling, and Oxbalm smiled and put a hand on Horseweed's shoulder. "I do it because I still can, Grandson. But food sounds good. Have you eaten yet?"

"Yes," Balsam piped up. "We ate as soon as Grandmother would let us."

"I'll bet you did. Well, I hope there's enough left for me."

"There is," Balsam assured him as he snugged the sapling under his arm. "When the soup bag started getting close to the bottom, Grandmother beat us away with an oak branch."

Oxbalm chuckled. Sumac always made certain he got the biggest portion of every meal. When their children had been young, that had proven to be a feat of no little accomplishment. Love for her warmed his chest. When everyone else in the world had abandoned him for being a silly old fool, she would still be there—probably giving him an evil look. "How are the lodges coming along?"

"The frames are almost done," Horseweed said.

Oxbalm hung onto Horseweed's arm as they plodded through the camp. The people had decided to make two big lodges rather than several small ones, because they had brought only a few hides with them, and because it would be far colder here in the foothills than down closer to the sea. Four families would be assigned to each house so they could share one another's warmth.

People crowded around the lodge sites, babbling back and forth as they inspected the postholes dug into the rocky soil.

People did things that way, with a great deal of pointing, head shaking and gestures—unlike Coyote, who simply buckled down, dug like mad with a violent spray of dirt shooting out between his legs and growled only when he had to chew off a stubborn root.

For each lodge, twenty saplings had been set into holes in the ground, ten on either side, and spaced about ten hands apart and thirty hands wide. While the women pressed dirt around the bases of the saplings to secure them, four men set the ridgepole by bending and tying the ends of the saplings to it.

Oxbalm glanced upward. The clouds had melted together to form a bluish-gray blanket that blotted out Brother Sky. He prayed they would finish their lodges before the brunt of the storm struck. Then they would see whose shortcuts had been critical. Lodges never fell down in nice weather, only when the wind was howling like a wounded saber-toothed cat and the rain was blasting the earth like Above-Old-Man's very wrath.

Horseweed and Balsam left him, hauling the sapling to the second lodge site, right beside the first, and Oxbalm hobbled unsteadily over to the fire, where Sumac knelt stirring the soup. Straggles of gray hair had come undone from her short braid and fell around her face in wisps. She pushed them back, revealing a streak of soot that slanted across her high forehead.

When Oxbalm dropped down atop an old stump, every joint in his back and hips popped like green fir in a hot fire. He groaned at the rebellion of ancient muscles and frail bones. *Ah, but in your youth, Oxbalm, you could have carried ten such poles up the hill! Yes, in my youth . . .*

Sumac had filled a wooden bowl. As she handed it to him, she said, "You old lunatic, I thought maybe you'd fallen down dead out there. I was getting worried."

"If I'd been dead, you wouldn't have had anything to worry about."

"I would have worried anyway. It's become a bad habit."

Oxbalm patted her cheek gently, then lifted the bowl and sipped the soup. The delicate flavor of venison fawn mixed with phlox blossoms and onion coated his tongue. "This is delicious. Where did you get the onions?"

"Down in that wet meadow at the foot of the hill." She pointed to a broad, flat expanse filled with white and pale rose-colored flowers. "They're growing everywhere. Along with spring beauty, beavertail grass and some cow parsnip."

The warmth of the flames made him shiver. He finished drinking his soup and raked out the last bits of meat and vegetable, discarding a spall from one of the cooking stones. Grit always collected in the bottom of the cooking sack.

Finished, he set his bowl down and extended knobby brown hands to the fire. He rubbed them briskly together. A cacophony of shrieks and claps erupted from the children. Oxbalm squinted and saw that someone had cast a pole straight into the center of the ring. He clapped his hands approvingly, too. "Who did that?"

"It was Coyote Paw!" Little Waterbell yelled.

"Good girl, Coyote Paw!" he shouted. "Keep that up and you'll be a great hunter someday!"

The little girl tucked her chin shyly and smiled at the praise, then darted forward to pull her pole out of the ground and take her place at the rear of the line of children. Excited cheers and yips went up at the next throw, though it didn't come anywhere close to the ring. Oxbalm laughed.

"It looks like you have company coming, my husband."

"Hmm? Who?"

Sumac tipped her withered chin toward the second lodge site. Harrier had laid down the stone ax and hammerstone he'd been using to thin the bases of the saplings and was walking across the camp toward Oxbalm. Such a tall young man. Almost Sunchaser's height. He'd left his black hair loose and it swayed with his gait, partly obscuring his massive brow.

Oxbalm lifted a hand in greeting. "Good day, Harrier."

"Good day, Oxbalm," Harrier said as he settled himself cross-legged before the fire. His red shirt reflected the flickering flames like a calm pond. He narrowed his small eyes and said, "I hope you don't mind, Oxbalm. Last night you were so tired that I didn't want to burden you any longer, but I would appreciate it if you would speak with me some more."

"Of course. What else do you need to know?"

Harrier brushed his hair behind his ears. When he held his hands out to the warmth of the fire, the shell beads sewn around his cuffs in a scalloped design glittered. "My brothers and I talked last night. We would like your permission to stay here for another half a moon."

"To wait for this Kestrel?"

"Yes. She may not have arrived yet, but we are certain she will. A group of hunters from Whalebeard Village came by while you were cutting saplings. They said they hadn't seen her. Nor did they know of anyone who had. That narrows the number of villages we have to search."

"Why are you so sure she'll come here? She could have headed for the high mountains. There are many more villages up there than down on the coast. And maybe she got eaten by a saber-toothed cat. Who knows?"

Harrier laced his fingers around one knee. "It's possible. But if she's alive, she may well end up here searching for her family. Her husband, the Trader Lambkill—"

"The crazy one?"

Harrier nodded. "Yes, he's as bad as a rabid skunk, but I'm sure he told the truth when he said that his wife's dead lover had relatives on the coast. Lambkill believed that Kestrel would seek refuge with those people. The Otter Clan."

"She may find Otter Clan members long before she reaches this village."

"Maybe."

Oxbalm propped his damp moccasins on the warm hearthstones. "These Whalebeard Village hunters, were they just passing by on the way to their hunting grounds, or did they come here for a reason?"

"They came looking for Sunchaser. They said that illness had just struck their village and they needed a Healer. Catchstraw told them that no one here had seen Sunchaser in a long time. The Whalebeard hunters spent another hand of time talking, then they left."

"I see." *More illness? Blessed Mother Ocean, protect us from this disease. We have so many little children in our village.*

Sumac knelt beside Oxbalm and studied Harrier through brooding eyes. "And what will you do, Harrier," she asked, "if we decide to grant this Kestrel refuge? She is traveling with a newborn baby. We will listen to her side of the story before we decide, and if she had good reason for running away from her husband and for murdering your brother—"

"*Good reason!*" Harrier blurted as he lurched to his feet. Anger strained his face. "Buffalo Bird would have done nothing to deserve such a death!"

Sumac tilted her head unsympathetically. "You are his brother. Of course you think that. But a desperate woman with a little baby might see danger where you would not. Maybe she thought she was protecting her child."

Harrier made a deep-throated sound of disbelief, and Oxbalm put his arm around Sumac's bony old shoulders, lending her his support, though he wondered what he would do when faced with Kestrel's stories. Could he offer her shelter? Ever? Even if she were innocent of all the charges against her, so many rumors had run the trails that half of the neighboring villages would care nothing about her side of the story. They would simply want her dead. Sheltering her would be very risky.

"It will be all right, though, don't you think, my wife, if Harrier and his brothers stay with us for half a moon?"

Sumac frowned thoughtfully. "Yes, if you think it best."

Harrier bowed his head, the flush in his cheeks subsiding. "Thank you. We are grateful."

Sumac rose and went to help the circle of women who had begun sewing the hides together with which to cover the completed lodge frames. The Thunderbeings soared through the clouds, shaking the world with their rumbling flights. In the distance, a transparent gray veil wavered over the hills, moving toward them quickly. The women were obviously rushing to get the lodges finished.

"But, Harrier," Oxbalm added gravely, "if Kestrel has not shown up here in that amount of time, we will ask you to leave. You understand? We want no more trouble over this matter."

"I understand," Harrier said. "We will leave with no complaints." Uneasily, he shifted his weight from foot to foot, then continued. "Your wife . . . she does not believe the stories about Kestrel?"

"She may believe them. But for her, that's not the point. She's stubborn. Even if a man were killed before her eyes, she would force me to give the murderer time to tell his side of the story." He shook his head. "She's always been that way. I've never understood it. But I *respect* her for it. No one can say that justice is rendered hastily in this village."

Harrier nodded, but a ruthless glint lit his eyes. "Our clan will demand the chance to render justice, too."

"Yes, I imagine so."

"Then if you find Kestrel innocent, you will hand her over to us so that we may take her home to face our people?"

"No." Oxbalm shook his head. "I didn't say that. I don't know what we would do in that case. We would have to consider."

Harrier cocked a brow. "If you denied us the right to judge the murderer of a member of our clan, you could start a war. Do you realize that, Oxbalm?"

"It is a risk I'm willing to take."

Harrier's eyes slitted. "Then I think it would be better for all of us if I try to catch this Kestrel before she makes it to your village. That will save you from having to make such a decision. Let it be known that my brothers and I will be establishing two lodges of our own—one on each of the trails leading here."

In a clipped voice, Oxbalm responded, "If that is what you wish to do, do it. But you should know that if the relatives of this woman's lover discover that you have murdered her without just cause and they come to me demanding retaliation, I will be forced to send out my warriors to hunt you down and bring you back here. Do we understand each other?"

Harrier answered, "It seems that this strange woman from the marsh country may cause a war no matter how hard we all try to avoid it. But I understand you, Oxbalm."

"Good."

Harrier lifted a hand airily. "I was talking to your Dreamer, Catchstraw. He has great Power. So much so that he scared me!" Harrier laughed nervously. "He told me that he's been having Dreams about terrible things happening to this village. I hope this war is not what he meant."

Oxbalm's moccasins had begun to feel unpleasantly hot. He moved his feet from the hearthstones to the dirt and said, "So do I. What else did Catchstraw tell you?"

"Very little. After hearing our stories about Lambkill's wife, he said he would see that she was punished for her crimes." Harrier inhaled a breath and let it out slowly while he stared Oxbalm in the eyes. "He said that most of the village elders will support whatever punishment he thinks is appropriate. Is that true? Does Catchstraw have that sort of influence?"

"He has followers, yes."

Harrier nodded. "Thank you for agreeing to let us stay for half a moon."

"Don't make me regret it."

Harrier inclined his head and went to call his brothers together. Several questions were yelled back and forth. Then the brothers dropped their tools and the four of them trotted down the trail to begin cutting trees for their own lodges.

Oxbalm's moccasins, cooler now, were still damp. He vented a disgruntled sigh when the first drops of rain struck his face like icy needles. He folded his arms and shivered lightly. "I hate bickering with other clans."

His eyes drifted over the village. The first quilt of sewn hides was being pulled over the closest lodge frame. The children raced to get under it before the lances of the Thunderbeings pierced the clouds and the heavens opened up.

Oxbalm rose and headed toward the lodge to see what he could do to help.

When the Star People sailed to midway in their evening journey, Lambkill rose silently from his robes, picked up his pack and walked out along a damp earthen path that led through the marshes. Crickets sawed their legs around him, while bats flitted through the starlit heavens. Their flights inscribed a lilting song across the indigo slate of night. Cattails and reeds grew as high as Lambkill's head here. Their rich green scent carried on the cool breeze. The path slithered in serpentine patterns, winding around one shallow pond of water and between two others. A few cypress trees with their aromatic foliage threw windblown shadows over the rippling pools.

He knelt on a moss-covered slab of granite, facing east, toward the land of Dawn Child, the Life Giver. The Seven Old Women had just risen. Their faces glittered in the moonless darkness, watching him with interest.

Lambkill smiled, gaps dark among his broken teeth. "Yes, you watch, Old Women. Tonight you will see a sight that will strike fear into even your cold white hearts."

Reverently, he unlaced his pack and drew out his son. He carefully unwrapped Little Coyote's otterskin sheath and turned him over on his back. Starlight gilded the boy's face, which had darkened and shriveled like an old dwarf's. Dwarfs had great Power. Above-Old-Man had given them a special ability to speak with him. Everywhere, in all of the clans across the country where Lambkill traded, dwarfs held seats of honor, and nowhere more so than in the lands of the People of the Masks.

"You're even more beautiful than I'd imagined, my son. I feel your soul tugging at mine. I've heard you whispering to me in my head for over a moon. Now I must give you the ability to speak aloud."

A draft from the marshes moved cool air across his face as he gently placed his son on the dew-soaked moss. He could have used help with this ceremony, but not from his traitorous brother. Tannin had become the enemy, though Lambkill couldn't let his brother know that. He needed Tannin too much right now. That was why Lambkill waited until late each night and left their camp to talk to his son alone. What Tannin didn't witness, he couldn't object to.

"If I were in the far north, my son, I'd have a dozen men helping me. They understand your Power. But here, you frighten people. Especially my weak-spirited brother."

He stood and peered back through the weave of reeds to their camp. The fire had long since died, but a faint crimson effulgence danced in the cracks between the stones that formed the hearth, making them look like pulsing blood vessels. Tannin lay still in his robes, his face shining in the starlight. The sound of snores drifted on the wind.

Quietly, Lambkill knelt again. "My brother wouldn't understand this," he whispered to his son. "So we must be very careful. When you can speak loud enough for Tannin to hear, we won't have to sneak around like this."

Lambkill lifted his arms to Dawn Child and Sang a soft, poignant prayer, begging her assistance in bringing his son to full and robust life. His voice sailed across the ponds and echoed gently through the tall reeds, silencing the crickets like the roar of the Thunderbeings.

Lambkill bent over and placed his mouth against his son's shrunken lips. He breathed life into that tiny dead baby, as a man would craft a finely made dart point. Between breaths, he called for Dawn Child's help. Little Coyote tasted like dust and smoke. For five hands of time, Lambkill breathed and Sang, until Dawn Child's pale blue glow swelled over the eastern hills. The Star People retreated in reverence.

Lambkill blinked.

His son's shadow was running lightly across the calm surface of the eastern pond—as though a figment spawned by the darkness. The dancing gleam of Dawn Child clung like a glowing aura around Little Coyote's shadow. Elated, Lambkill braced himself. But he kept on breathing life into his son's dry, smoke-flavored mouth.

Little Coyote's shadow stepped off of the water and came trotting down the path toward him. Tiny and dark. So dark that his shadow blotted the reeds and the reflected gleam of the water. Blacker than black. The shadow crept inside Little Coyote's body, and a voice, high and childlike, murmured:

"Hello, Father . . . I am here. What do you want of me?"

Lambkill fell back to the moss panting, his eyes wide. He braced a hand on the cool green carpet to steady himself. His son's face glowed as though from an inner fire.

He stood Little Coyote up. "Oh, my son, my son! I finally gave you a body. I've been trying to for cycles. You must believe me."

"I waited a very long time for this dead body."

"Yes, I—I know. It's the best I can do right now. I tried for a long time to give you a living body. The women in my clan whispered that my wives couldn't give birth because I'd been cursed by the Spirits . . . but I *knew* better. Why do you think I married a baby like your mother? She was fresh and unspoiled. I selected her the day she first entered the menstrual hut." He chuckled softly to himself. "Yes, I *knew* that someday my seed would take hold in that virgin ground."

"What do you want of me?"

The boy's voice shook as though he were frightened. Lambkill wet his lips and leaned forward, putting his face only a handbreadth from his son's. Those tiny green stones of eyes silvered, as though frozen beneath a crust of water.

"The truth, my son. That's all. Your mother is out there, running from me. Where is she? I must find her and make her pay for what she did to you . . . to us."

Little Coyote's mouth moved ever so slightly, like a trick of starlight. The boy's voice sounded sad. *"There is a witch who knows. You must meet him. When you do, all of your questions will be answered. And she will be a breath from your hands . . ."*

"Boy? . . . Boy?"

Silence pervaded the glittering darkness of the Land of the Dead.

"Boy, can you hear me?"

The Man parted the Darkness with his hands, and his gaze lanced through the layers of cloud and rain to the Boy far below. Boy's soul glowed a rich blue that suffused his ugly dead body.

"Boy, your fear is like an icicle piercing my heart. . . . I can help you, if you will let me."

Very faintly, the Boy's voice drifted upward. "Did you not tell me, Man, that I should learn to be like a dead child to all those who love me? That to die to one's friends is to cease to judge them in anything? . . . I am now dead to you, Man."

But the Boy's tears struck the earth like lightning and sent a rumbling quake through the Land of the Dead.

Man said, "If you are truly dead to me, Boy, then you should not fear talking with me. Perhaps you should consider why you fear me. Have you judged me, Boy? Is that why you will not speak? Boy? Boy . . . ?"

Twenty-eight

"But where could they have gone?"

"I don't know," Sunchaser replied as he wandered through the bleak remains of Otter Clan Village. Helper awkwardly followed his master, hauling a travois with their bedding hides and other belongings piled atop it.

Whalebone lodge frames littered the ground in haphazard disarray, some of them crushed to sparkling white splinters. Sunchaser knelt and picked up tools, fragments of clothing, a beautiful seashell hairpin. He touched each tenderly before putting it down again. His deep-set eyes had a haunted look. "Oxbalm must have known that the Power here had vanished."

"Vanished?"

"Yes, or been driven out, depending upon the way you look at it." He squatted next to an old fire pit and proceeded to sift through the debris testing it for warmth.

Kestrel stared again at the dozens of ravaged mammoth skeletons that littered the beach. When they had come upon the first dead mammoth, Sunchaser had broken into a run, heading toward the abandoned village. Kestrel had passed by the skeletons in silence, but now they drew her full attention. She folded her arms and dug nervous fingers into her flesh.

The scent of death pervaded everything like a foul wind. *Oh, Kestrel, do the Spirits hate you so much that they would do this to keep you from finding a sanctuary?*

"You mean that the mammoths who attacked the village drove the Power away?"

"Yes," he answered.

"For what purpose?"

"They knew it would force the Otter Clan to leave."

Kestrel kept her face blank, trying not to alarm Sunchaser any more than he already was, but her knees had gone weak. The empty village lay in ghostly silence. Scaffold burials nestled in the limbs of the fir trees. Many of them stretched no more than six hands long. Little children. Babies. Brightly painted hides covered the bodies, but here and there the wind had torn the hides away and revealed a tiny bloating face. Flies swarmed in glittering clouds around the scaffolds.

"Why would Mammoth Above have wanted to force the Otter Clan to leave this place?"

Afternoon sunlight gleamed in Sunchaser's loose white hair as he rose. He spoke softly, as if to remind himself. "To force the crossing upon me . . . Yes, Good Plume, now I see. What a fool I am. I expected a different kind of threat, one that winged over the ground of the human heart. So, from here on out, I must learn to feel my way. *But why now?* Where is Monster Rock Eagle?"

"What—what does that mean?"

He shook his head lightly, and Kestrel knew that he wouldn't explain.

Unable to bear it, she turned away and walked toward the shore. Cloud Girl twined a hand in Kestrel's hair. The baby had been quiet since they arrived, riding content in her rabbit-fur sack and looking around. Kestrel reached over her shoulder to pat that tiny hand. "It's all right, baby. Everything's going to be all right. Your father's people can't be far."

For ten moons, this place had been a sparkling apparition in her dreams. She wondered what Iceplant would say if he stood beside her now, witnessing the desolation. Would he rage at Above-Old-Man? Or would he just walk away quietly, as she was doing, eaten by a despair that sundered the soul?

Kestrel heard the sound of Sunchaser's graceful steps as he came to her. A scarcely concealed fear strained his handsome face. He'd clenched his right hand into a fist. "I'm sorry, Kestrel."

"It's not your fault."

"Isn't it?"

She frowned up at him. His eyes scanned the surface of the ocean, touching on each floating bird or piece of driftwood as though searching for an answer to this disaster.

More softly, he repeated, "Isn't it, Kestrel? I'm not nearly as certain as you are."

"How could it be your fault?"

Sunchaser sighed wearily. The pale glow of the waning day glittered from the seashells on the fringes of his moosehide coat. He glanced at her, and the misery in his face deepened.

"I feel very lonely today, Kestrel."

Turning without another word, he trudged down the beach, the quiver slung over his left shoulder swaying with his movements.

She saw him kick at a rock, and she lagged behind, letting him be alone with himself.

As the bright afternoon wore on, Catchstraw trotted along the crest of the sea cliffs. Gravel crunched beneath his paws. The wind had turned warm, bringing him the scents of many animals: rabbits, mice, birds, deer, even mammoths, making his empty stomach growl ravenously. Gusts caressed his black fur like gentle human fingers. He wove in and around the cypress trees that crowded the cliffs, marveling at their gnarled branches and twisted shapes.

Father Sun's rays coated the evergreen needles like pale yellow honey. The first spring butterflies had appeared as if by magic in the past two days, swarming over the meadows in a fluttering wealth of orange, yellow and white wings. He'd eaten a few of them, but they didn't even dent his hunger, and their wings coated his tongue with a foul, chalky taste. They seemed to like the wintercress and mustard flowers best. Whole stocks of the plants were encrusted with butterflies.

Catchstraw leaped over an old stump and trotted down a deer trail that dove off the edge of the cliff, followed a narrow ledge and wound down toward the beach. Mother Ocean's constant roar filled the air. The water bore a blinding patina of light, as did Pygmy Island. The pines on the three main island peaks had turned a fiery gold in the sun.

In the distance, he could see the old village site. A twinge of homesickness assaulted him. He had spent his entire life next to the soothing sounds of the Mother, the lapping of the waves, the shrieking of the bald eagles and the roaring of the lions. He missed them, even though life here had been devilish for him. He'd been disdained, after all, by nearly everybody. It seemed strange to him now that he'd put up with it for so long. If he'd only known the Power of witching sooner! He could have taken revenge on everyone who had ever dared to slight him, and no one would have been the wiser. With Dire Wolf's legs, he could cover enormous distances in only a few hands of time. He could attack, kill and be gone like a figment of moonglow. At least, he thought so. He'd been eating so many Powerful Spirit Plants that he was no longer certain about the passing of time.

Catchstraw wrinkled his snout. *They'll all pay. In this body, the fatigue of age can't touch me. If it takes me the rest of my life to find each person who ever so much as looked at me crossways—*

He stopped suddenly and pricked his ears. Two people strode down the beach ahead of him. A tall man and a tiny woman. *It couldn't be!* He lifted his nose and scented the sea breeze.

A tingle crept through his veins. He took a wary step backward. *Sunchaser . . . and the woman with the baby!* Yes, he could identify each of their scents. Fear made his belly knot. His tongue lolled as he started to pant. Why was he so frightened of Sunchaser? In the form of a human . . .

yes, it was understandable. But as Dire Wolf? What could Sunchaser do to him?

That's the problem. You don't know. What can *Dreamers do to witches?* He'd never heard of a Dreamer even challenging a witch . . . perhaps a Dreamer wouldn't dare to?

Curiosity curbed his fear. What a glorious experience it would be to fight Sunchaser as Dire Wolf! Why, Catchstraw could rip his throat out effortlessly. How wonderful, to watch Sunchaser bleed to death!

When he'd first run the coast in the body of Dire Wolf, he'd found Sunchaser's rock shelter, seen the light of his fire reflected on the dark ocean. And he'd smelled the woman there, too. But he hadn't thought about the implications. Why would Sunchaser be with a woman? He was supposed to be Dreaming for Mammoth Above. At least that's what he told people. Perhaps lust had eaten his Dreamer's soul?

Catchstraw loped into the coastal trees and wound his way through the forest, following unseen behind Sunchaser and the woman.

The woman walked about twenty paces behind Sunchaser. She had slipped a dart through a loop on her pack and wore an atlatl tied to her belt. Did she have only one dart? Strange. She had clamped her lower lip between her teeth and reached over her shoulder to hold her baby's plump hand—as though deeply worried about something and needing comfort.

Fool. Didn't she realize that a hungry animal his size could leap on her from behind, jerk the baby from the pack on her back, run into the forest and gobble down the child before anyone knew what had happened?

At the thought, his stomach squealed and growled with eagerness. Human blood. In the depths of his wolf soul, he remembered that taste, rich and coppery, a little like mammoth mixed with fish. A stinging wash of desire, almost sexual, rushed through him.

He broke into a run and dashed through the forest.

But when he spooked a grouse hidden in the underbrush and it burst into flight, he whirled and leaped instinctively. He snatched the bird out of the air with expert grace and closed his jaws around its neck. The grouse squawked in terror and flapped wildly, struggling to escape. Ecstasy possessed him! He peered down at the terrified bird's face and knew that the creature saw its death reflected in his eyes. The grouse went silent, trembling.

Catchstraw bit down, crushing the grouse's windpipe, then brutally shook the bird to break its slender neck. Blood flowed into his mouth with the sweetness of phlox-blossom nectar. It inflamed his blood!

He ripped the feathers from the bird's thin belly and tore open the gut, which he ate ravenously, swallowing the kidneys and liver whole, then chewing the intestines down a rope at a time. Dark blood soaked his muzzle and dripped into his chest fur. From the corner of his vision, he saw Sunchaser pass among the weave of tree trunks. The Dreamer's head was down, his brows pulled together over his straight nose. His white hair glimmered with an unearthly light.

A frenzy overtook Catchstraw. He tore the grouse to shreds in a growling, snarling rage . . . imagining it to be his enemy.

It won't be long, Sunchaser. Soon you and I will face each other with all of our Powers rushing in our veins . . . and I will kill you.

Twenty-nine

Tannin trotted steadily beside Lambkill, absorbing every detail of the sea; it was so blue, so *vast!*

All of the Traders' tales were true. The fir trees grew so tall that they speared the clouds. Huge eaglelike birds roamed the sandy beaches. Their black wings spanned a distance greater than a man's height, and they charged each other with massive ugly beaks. Lambkill called them giant croaking buzzards.

Tannin smiled. He and Lambkill had been running since dawn, talking sporadically and laughing, basking in the splendor of the sunlight. Since they had lost Kestrel's trail, Lambkill had become his old self again, joking, smiling, telling stories. Tannin could not believe the change. They'd followed Kestrel deep into the forest, to a dense section of black timber where the deadfall stood ten hands high. Lambkill had found the place where she'd crawled under a pile of dead branches. A single strand of her hair had clung to a twig. Then, suddenly, her trail had vanished. They'd searched for two days to find it again, but it seemed as if she had been lifted straight up from the ground by a whirlwind. Lambkill had laughed— actually rolled in the pine duff and laughed!

And from that moment on, he had been the brother that Tannin knew and loved. He hadn't brought Little Coyote out of his pack even once, a fact that brought no little relief to Tannin's worried soul.

Perhaps tonight he would try to talk sense to Lambkill, try to convince him to quit this insane hunt.

As they followed the rounded arc of the shore southward, a small village came into view. Seven hide lodges nestled at the edge of a pine grove, facing west. How different from his own people, who turned their lodges eastward to receive Father Sun's early morning blessing. The outside of these lodges bore elaborate paintings, using every color of the rainbow. Orange and yellow sunbursts decorated the lower parts of the lodges, while the upper halves sported blue and purple geometric designs. People lounged about outside. The sweetness of roasting fish pervaded the air. Two large rafts floated out in the water. Bull boats, made from hides wrapped around a sapling frame, bobbed beside them. Tannin could make out the women who stood atop the rafts and knelt in the boats, spears in their hands, fishing.

"Ah," Lambkill said. "Perhaps these people will be able to give us some information."

"I hope so."

"I don't see Harrier or his idiot brothers anywhere, do you?"

"No, but . . . they're not idiots, Lambkill. They're just young. Young and impetuous."

Lambkill grinned, as though he'd read Tannin's thoughts like tracks in fresh snow. "Don't worry, Tannin. I'll be pleasant, at least until we find out what they've discovered. If anything."

Tannin breathed a sigh of relief. Lambkill squinted, then began to run, his heavy jowls and short braids bouncing.

Four old women sat weaving baskets on the northern edge of the village. They had their knees drawn up, their feet spread wide and their shoulders bent to the task. A bowl of water nestled at each woman's knee. They dipped their fingers frequently and moistened the basketry materials to keep them supple while they worked them. An array of tools lay scattered about: shell knives for cutting twine and splitting wood; bone awls sanded to fine points for puncturing holes, or pressing home the weft; cups of sticky pine rosin to cement the frame.

Tannin recognized the loose weave as belonging to a family of baskets called "nut" baskets, though people used them for many other seed crops as well. The weft consisted of very strong twine made from the inner bark of nettle plants. The warp extended from a rigid top hoop, made of split willow, to the bottom, where the weaving twine knotted. The basket gained its sturdiness from two bowed rods that crossed at right angles at the bottom and were lashed with sinew and cemented to the top hoop. Lambkill traded extensively for them. The wide spacing in the weave allowed nuts and other large seeds to breathe, so they wouldn't mildew.

When the village dogs spotted the two oncoming men, a series of barks and sharp yips went up as a pack raced toward them, ears pricked, tails wagging. People stood and pointed, calling to one another.

"Let me do the talking," Lambkill said.

"Yes, big brother."

They trotted past the old women, through a passel of squirming, shouting children and into the plaza. Young women had gathered around a big cook fire where five boiling bags hung from tripods. Silver wreaths of steam whirled around the women. Over the flames, racks of fish sizzled. From every direction, men walked toward the newcomers and surrounded them. One man, a medium-sized youth with a lean face, pushed through all the others and trotted forward with his arms spread wide. He wore a furry-brimmed beaver hat pulled down over his ears.

"Lambkill?" he called.

Lambkill cocked his head suspiciously. "Who are you?"

The man lowered his arms. His smile faded. "It's Nighthawk! I'm the Big Horn Village Trader."

"Oh, of course! Forgive me, Nighthawk. We met at the Pure Water Renewal, didn't we?"

Nighthawk nodded, and the smile came back to his face. "What are you doing here? Trying to steal my trading partners?"

"Bah! I have enough trouble keeping up with my own partners, I don't need yours." He strode forward to embrace Nighthawk. They patted each other's back heartily. The surrounding villagers smiled.

"Well, come over here and meet Chief Staghorn. This is Moss Rock Village. These people are my third cousins. They will treat you well. Staghorn, come and meet my good friend, Lambkill," he called to an old man who stood beside the village's central and largest lodge. "Come! Lambkill is the great Trader from the marsh country."

The elder hobbled forward. He wore a heavily painted shirt made from the hide of an old dire wolf. He'd turned the fur inside out to warm his body, and gray fur spiked up around his throat. He nodded politely to Lambkill, and Lambkill gave him a deep, respectful bow.

"I am honored, Staghorn. Your reputation as a great and wise chief spans the country."

The hostile look in Staghorn's eyes abated only a little. His mouth puckered as though he wanted to spit. "I have heard of you, too, Lambkill. You're the man who's searching for his wife, aren't you?"

"Yes," Lambkill said softly, "I am, great Staghorn. As a matter of fact, we were hoping you might be able to help us."

"Why are we standing?" Nighthawk asked. "Come, sit down by my fire. I have a bag of fir-needle tea already made."

He led the way. Staghorn and Lambkill walked side by side, while Tannin brought up the rear. Lambkill's voice sounded almost reverent as he spoke to Staghorn. Tannin marveled at that. Could this be the same man who only a week ago had been tearing himself apart with rage?

Thank Above-Old-Man that Lambkill had returned to normal.

The villagers scrutinized them as they passed. People's smiles had vanished with the rough tone in Staghorn's voice; now women whispered behind their hands, and children clung to their mothers' skirts, peering up through fearful eyes. The skin between Tannin's shoulder blades crawled as if an atlatl were centered on his back.

Blessed Marsh Hare Above, what stories have these people heard about us? He glanced around uncomfortably. The sooner they left Moss Rock Village, the happier he would be.

Tannin took his place at Lambkill's side, dropping to the sand in front of the low fire, his back to the lodge, but his eyes roved the village vigilantly. Nighthawk sat to Tannin's right and Staghorn to Nighthawk's right. But Staghorn left a noticeable gap between himself and Lambkill, as if he thought he might be tainted if he sat any closer. Tannin glanced sideways at Lambkill. His brother smiled pleasantly, seemingly ignorant of Staghorn's slight.

"Here, have some tea!" Nighthawk offered with too much eagerness. He dipped four abalone-shell cups full and handed them around the circle. "So, Lambkill, tell us how your search is going. You haven't found this wayward wife of yours yet?"

Lambkill waved a hand carelessly. "It's only a matter of time. We know she's headed for the coast. She—"

"How do you know that?" Staghorn demanded. His ancient eyes narrowed to slits.

Completely taken aback, Tannin leaned forward to make a hot reply, but Lambkill put a hand on his shoulder and gently pushed him back. In a soft voice, Lambkill responded, "Forgive me, elder. I meant to say that we 'believe' she is headed for the coast. That's where her lover's family came from. We think she mistakenly believes that his mother's clan will shelter her from us."

Tannin peered at Nighthawk. The young Trader had clamped his jaw so tightly that it looked malformed. His gaze kept darting from one person to the next, as if waiting to see which way the wind would blow before he revealed his own thoughts. Tannin decided that there were a lot of people he'd rather be stranded in the desert with than Nighthawk.

Lambkill spread his arms wide in a gesture of surrender. "I don't understand, Staghorn. Why are you being so unfriendly? What have I done to you?"

Staghorn brought up one knee and propped a reedlike arm atop it. "Tell me about your wife, Lambkill. What has she done to you?"

Lambkill bowed his head and hesitated for a moment. His voice came out pained. "She committed incest, elder. With her cousin. While I was gone trading, she bedded him in my own lodge."

Staghorn lifted his chin haughtily. "And if I say I don't believe you?"

"I speak the truth, elder. Why wouldn't you believe me?"

"Lambkill." Nighthawk bent forward and licked his lips. "We have had news."

"*What* news? You have seen her?"

"Well, perhaps. We're not sure. Our people did not ask for her name, but yesterday . . ." He paused to glance at

Staghorn, and the old man nodded. Nighthawk continued. "Yesterday four people from this village returned home talking about having seen a woman and a tiny baby. A newborn."

Lambkill shrugged nonchalantly. "So? How many women with newborn babies are there on the coast? Eh? It could have been anyone."

"I don't think so," Nighthawk said and sat back. He tugged at a ragged fringe on his pant leg. "It wasn't the woman who mattered as much as who she was traveling with."

Lambkill sat completely still, and Tannin almost burst before Lambkill asked, "Who was she with?"

Nighthawk went silent, yielding to Staghorn. The old man fixed Lambkill with a glassy stare. He said in a prayerful way: "Sunchaser."

Lambkill's nostrils flared. "And you think it was my wife?"

"No one had ever seen her before," Staghorn said. "My people know everyone within a ten-day walk of here."

Lambkill nodded. "Did they give you a description of her?"

"Yes," Nighthawk answered. "They said she was very beautiful, although very slender, a small woman. She had waist-length black hair, an oval face, big eyes and full lips. A healing scar crosses her forehead. Like so. She carried her baby in a rabbit-fur sack on her back."

Tannin felt Lambkill go rigid, but his brother showed no signs of tension. Lambkill tilted his head obligingly. "This woman does sound like Kestrel. Why was she with Sunchaser?"

"No one knows. That's the problem. He's a Dreamer. He's not supposed to spend time with women!" Nighthawk shouted the last and quickly looked around, as though he'd surprised himself. "It has me very upset," he said. "Who could even think of trying to capture her when she's with a man like Sunchaser? Only a fool would challenge him."

Lambkill's eyes gleamed. "Which way were they going?"

"They—"

Staghorn broke in, "Our people couldn't say."

Lambkill eyed Staghorn unpleasantly. "It doesn't matter. We will look up and down the coast until we've found her."

"Then you have a long way to go and had best be on your way." Staghorn rose on rickety legs. "You are not welcome in our village, Trader Lambkill. I ask that you and your brother respect our wishes and leave as soon as possible." Staghorn hobbled back to his lodge and ducked beneath the door flap.

People throughout the village murmured and returned to their duties, ignoring Lambkill and Tannin as though they didn't exist. Women gathered silently around the cook fires, children raced out to chase the dogs, and men returned to their places in front of the lodges, where they smoked pipes or threw out dice crafted from the wrist-joint bones of deer. Conversations and laughter slowly rose again, but at least one person in every group kept watch on Lambkill and Tannin.

"This is hardly the welcome I expected, Nighthawk," Lambkill said sourly.

"It's not my fault!" the Trader whispered insistently. "These people are only third cousins! What do they know?" He dipped another cupful of fir tea from the bag hanging on the tripod. "May I offer you more tea?"

"Let's go, Lambkill," Tannin urged. "We'll learn nothing else here."

Lambkill put a hand on Tannin's knee, keeping him still. "Don't be so hasty, my brother. Nighthawk is a Trader. He understands these things."

"Of course," Nighthawk agreed as he sloshed tea into Lambkill's shell cup. He aimed next at Tannin's cup, but Tannin turned it aside. Nighthawk dumped the tea back into the bag. "People are all the same, no matter where you go. They have stupid loyalties. Like this passion for Sunchaser. I mean, do you know how many Mammoth Spirit

Dances he's missed this cycle? Four. A sacred number. It's a sign from the Spirits. Everyone says that Wolfdreamer has abandoned him and is looking for a new Dreamer to lead the sea clans."

"Really? Tell me more," Lambkill said with an amiable smile as he sipped his tea. "Sunchaser is missing Dances, and now he's been seen traveling with a woman? This is interesting. But how could Sunchaser possibly have met Kestrel? I'm puzzled."

"Lambkill," Nighthawk said. A swallow went down his throat. He rocked forward, closer to the fire, to stare Lambkill in the face. He dropped his voice to a bare whisper. "All I can tell you is that people here think that Sunchaser is her protector. That he's taken her under his wing. If that is so—"

"Yes. I understand." Lambkill chuckled contemptuously. "No one will think of trying to claim my reward. They fear Sunchaser's Power too much."

"Exactly." Nighthawk leaned back in relief. He almost knocked off his beaver hat when he reached up to wipe sweat from his forehead. "I'm glad you see the problem. I was afraid—"

"Oh, of course. I understand. Though I must admit, I hadn't expected to be received so belligerently by the People of the Sea. My wife committed *incest!* No one condones that. I don't care where they're from."

"True. But . . ." Nighthawk heaved a sigh. "No matter what crime your wife committed, in the eyes of my people, her violations have been washed away by her association with Sunchaser. Just to be with him is to undergo a ritual cleansing. You see that, don't you?"

Lambkill roughly swished his tea around in his cup. Tannin noticed that he'd clutched the cup so tightly that his fingernails had gone white. "The blessed Sunchaser. Yes. Kestrel's lover was an admirer of Sunchaser's, too." A broad, genial smile graced Lambkill's face. He laughed softly. "I killed him for it."

Nighthawk's gaze faltered. He frowned at the sand as though he'd found something very interesting amidst the grains. "Lambkill, I can't shelter you here. Not after what Staghorn said. The people . . . well, they would never forgive me."

Lambkill got to his feet and threw his teacup down on the sand. "Oh, yes, I understand, Nighthawk. You make your living by trading with these people. Of course you can't afford to be *soiled* by association with me!"

Lambkill's voice had risen to a hoarse bellow. All the eyes in the village focused on them. Grim mutterings eddied back and forth. Staghorn pulled his door flap aside and peered out. He gestured to two of his warriors. The men quietly went to their lodges and came out with atlatls in their hands and quivers of darts slung over their shoulders.

Tannin got to his feet cautiously and grabbed Lambkill by the wrist. "Let's go, Lambkill. These people are useless to us. We don't need them. We'll find Kestrel by ourselves."

Lambkill shook off Tannin's hand and turned to glower venomously at Staghorn. In response, one of Staghorn's warriors pulled a dart from his quiver and silently nocked it in his atlatl.

"Lambkill!"

Lambkill's gaze shifted to Tannin. Cold. Emotionless. It was like being stared at through the eyes of a snake. Then Lambkill casually faced Nighthawk again. "Tell me one last thing, Trader."

"What?" Nighthawk asked nervously. "What is it?"

"Have you seen four brothers from the Blackwater Draw Clan? The oldest is named Harrier."

"No, Lambkill. I promise. They have not been here."

"You're sure?"

"I swear it! I have no reason to lie to you. I don't even know who these brothers are or what they have to do with you."

"I'll tell you what they have to do with me." As though greatly pleased by being able to relay the news, Lambkill explained, "My wife killed their youngest brother, Buffalo Bird. She drove a tapir-bone stiletto into his heart. Beware, Nighthawk. She is not as frail and innocent as she seems. If you so much as mention my name in her presence, she'll kill you without a second thought. Evil Spirits have possessed her soul."

Nighthawk rose to his feet and wiped his clammy hands on his pants. His beaver hat sat canted at an odd angle on his head. "That may have been true a moon ago, Lambkill. But by now, Sunchaser will have driven any bad Spirits out. No one among my people will believe she's still evil. Evil cannot exist in the shadow of Sunchaser's Power."

Lambkill's cheek muscles twitched. "You have helped us, Nighthawk. I thank you, as one Trader to another." He extended his hand and gripped Nighthawk's firmly.

Nighthawk glanced around anxiously and leaned forward. In one last effort to keep his valuable trading connections alive, he whispered, "There is one other thing that might help you, Lambkill."

"What is that?"

"The villagers who saw Sunchaser and the woman yesterday? They said that Sunchaser asked them where Otter Clan Village had gone."

"Gone? Do you mean this village has moved recently?"

"Yes," Nighthawk said and straightened up cautiously. "We don't know where it went. But apparently that was where Sunchaser was headed."

"Where did Otter Clan Village use to be?"

Nighthawk gave lengthy directions, but Tannin only half listened. He kept his eyes on the camp, watching each and every movement. Dislike now lined faces that formerly had shown only suspicion.

". . . can't overlook it. The skeletons of thirty-four mammoths are lying on the shore. If you keep going farther south, another three days' run along the beach, you will come to Whalebeard Village. Then—"

Lambkill interrupted, "I am obliged to you, Nighthawk.

I would appreciate it if you would answer a final question: Have you heard of any witches in this area, on the coast?"

Nighthawk's face froze. He shook his head once. "No. Not in cycles."

Lambkill whirled and tramped away through the center of the village, glaring at anyone who had the courage to meet his eyes.

Tannin followed, wary, his hand on the atlatl that hung from his belt thong.

Thirty

"Witches?" Tannin asked. "Why did you ask about witches? What would we do if we met one?"

Lambkill tossed a piece of pine onto the fire. Sparks spurted into the air to whirl and wink as they floated upward. Lambkill had been pacing restlessly. They'd made camp in a grassy meadow on the high cliffs above the beach. A few dogwood trees stood to the north, their blossoms shining brilliantly in the moonglow. Two hundred hands below, Mother Ocean rocked and roared, dashing the shore angrily.

"*Do*, my brother?" Lambkill answered. "Why, we would ask the witch to curse Kestrel. Maybe to curse her feet so she couldn't walk, or to curse her eyesight so she couldn't see her way. Witches have many valuable uses. I'm surprised that you would even ask."

Tannin shifted, stretching out on his side by the fire. "But they're so dangerous to work with. They can't be trusted."

A small school of finback whales moved through the

waters between the shore and Pygmy Island, their fins gleaming against the dark waves. They'd seen a school in the daylight yesterday, and Tannin had thought them magnificent. But tonight, in the moonlight, they seemed unearthly, like disappearing phantoms.

"I've always hated Sunchaser," Lambkill continued. Dirty strands of gray hair matted his cheeks.

"I didn't know you'd ever met him."

"I haven't, but it doesn't matter. I know he's driving his penis into Kestrel."

Tannin grimaced at the lukewarm tea in his wooden cup. "Lambkill, that's not possible. Dreamers don't do that. At least not Dreamers of Sunchaser's status."

Lambkill's lips pressed into a white line. The bags beneath his eyes had turned a dark blue. "You're gullible, brother. I've seen dozens of Dreamers. None of them are as holy as they claim. Each has a fatal flaw."

"And you think Sunchaser's is women?"

"Yes, he's the type. He's very young. And the greatest Dreamers are usually fools at heart."

Tannin shook his head impatiently. "What difference does it make? Our task is to find Kestrel and take her home."

"Who will turn her over to us if she's with Sunchaser, brother?"

Tannin had been wondering the same thing, but he'd come up with no solution. He set his empty teacup on the grass beside him. "Only someone very brave."

"Such people are becoming as rare as mammoth ivory."

"Then what should we do?"

Lambkill tossed the remainder of his tea into the fire and propped his hands on his hips to stare up at the Star People. In the strong silver gleam of the moonglow, they looked like faded reflections of themselves. "We must find the new Otter Clan Village, my brother, before she does. That will give us time to talk to the village chief and explain our unpleasant chore. Then"—he laughed maliciously—"we'll surprise Kestrel when she arrives."

"What if the Otter Clan has already heard that she's been seen with Sunchaser? We'll face the same hostility that we found today in Staghorn."

Lambkill filled his lungs with the sea-scented wind. "Then we'll have to catch her *before* she arrives."

"And just how will we do that?"

Lambkill looked up blandly, but he'd set his jaw. "My son has started to speak, Tannin. I didn't tell you because I knew you wouldn't believe me. But he has. He speaks as well as you or I. He's been talking every night . . . and even during the day, he often whispers to me. Little Coyote will tell us about Kestrel when the time comes. We'll catch her all right."

"Horseweed! *Horseweed, wake up!*"

Horseweed roused from a deep, dreamless slumber and rolled to his back. Balsam knelt beside him, his young face wild with fear. In the starlight that streamed through the smokehole in the roof, Balsam looked as white as snow. A thick dusting of something like pollen coated his pug nose and the shoulders of his buckskin coat. His two black braids had come half unraveled.

"What is it? What's wrong?" Horseweed braced himself on one elbow.

Balsam glanced around the dark lodge, making certain that everyone else still slept. Seven adults and eight children crowded the rectangular structure, their piles of hides unmoving around the three fire hearths. People had hung their belongings, baskets, atlatls and quivers on the walls. Starlight glinted from the stone points of darts. Several men snored.

Balsam bent down and hissed, "Hurry! You must come with me. He's in the meadow. I . . . I don't know what he's doing!"

"Who?" Horseweed whispered as he sat up and pulled on

his moccasins. He groped in the darkness to find his coat, shrugged it on, rose and followed Balsam across the hilltop and out into the forest.

Balsam waited until they were well away from the lodges before he spoke again. "It's Catchstraw," he said. "He's up to something."

"He's always up to something. What do you mean?"

Balsam shook his head for silence and trotted down the slope to the trail that veered around the base of the hill and headed straight westward, toward Mother Ocean. They ran by an ancient oak. Lightning had riven the trunk at some time in the distant past, killing the tree, but its gnarled branches still reached upward, pleading mutely to Brother Sky for rain. An owl perched on the top branch. Its eyes glinted as it turned its head to watch them pass.

Night came earlier here in the mountains than it did on the coast. Unlike the Mother, whose face sparkled and glimmered all night long, even in the depths of storms, the oak forests held a nearly tangible gloom. Blackness filled the spaces between the trees and undulated in choppy swells of hills for as far as the eye could see.

Horseweed's uneasiness had been growing for days, as if this alien darkness spawned unseen horrors.

Balsam's steps grew more cautious as they neared a broad meadow. The bright hues of the wildflowers had been washed silver by the light of the Star People, but the blossoms' sweet scent filled the cold air. Balsam dodged behind a tree, and Horseweed crouched down on his hands and knees. Tall grass tickled his throat, and he knew now how Balsam had been covered with purple-nightshade pollen. The delicate little blossoms had sprouted everywhere. Out at the far edge of the meadow, near a copse of pines, movement stirred the shadows. A thin, high voice drifted on the wind.

Horseweed crawled over beside Balsam, rose to his feet again and stuck his head out on the other side of the thick trunk. He squinted and could tell that Catchstraw knelt on a broad, flat piece of sandstone. For decades, women had been using the outcrop as a place to pulverize seeds and nuts, and small round grinding holes covered the stone. Only this morning Sumac had gone there to grind a basket of dried pine nuts, which she'd mixed with water and fresh onions and fried for breakfast. What could Catchstraw be doing out there? He seemed to be drawing something on the rock with a piece of charcoal.

Horseweed whispered, "What's he doing? Can you tell?"

Balsam looked up with wide eyes, and Horseweed saw that his brother was shaking with panic. "I . . . I think he's *witching*, Horseweed! I swear that's what he's doing. Come on. We can get closer. Let me show you."

Balsam got down and crawled through the tall grass with the calculated stealth of a hunter. Horseweed followed at his heels, but he kept glancing over at Catchstraw.

The ugly Dreamer had stood up, skinny and old against the background of starlit forest, but the gray in his hair glimmered with the brilliance of mica dust. He spread his arms and began Dancing. He spun and stamped his feet . . . like a Condor Dancer at the annual winter ceremonial. But then he sidestepped and spun in the opposite direction. . . . And his Song. It had no words. Or rather, the words were broken, confused, said in a curious accent, though recognizable. He was calling down the Power of the giant bird, calling it into himself. Horseweed's heart pounded. The sound filled him with an inexplicable terror.

They crawled behind a chaos of deadfall, and Balsam whispered, "Have you ever seen that Dance before?"

"No."

"He's been doing it, off and on, for the past hand of time. He draws on the rocks for a little while, then he rises and Dances. Did you hear the Song?" Balsam shuddered. "It's as if he's taken the sacred verses from the Condor Dance and deliberately corrupted them. That's against the *laws* of our people!"

"He's never cared anything about clan law."

Balsam wet his lips anxiously. "He's a bad man, Horseweed. Look at the rock by his feet. Can you see the black lines?"

Horseweed eased his head over the deadfall and looked. "Yes."

Catchstraw lowered his arms, laughed softly and began erasing his drawing with the toe of his moccasin. He took his time, going over each line with the care of a loving artist. A condor shrieked somewhere close by, and Catchstraw froze, an awed expression on his face. He leaped off the rock and ran, disappearing down the slope of the hill.

Horseweed watched in horror as a huge condor flew up from the other side, its massive wings blotting the stars as it soared away.

Balsam gripped Horseweed's arm and sank his fingernails into the warm flesh. "Let's get out of here!"

Horseweed patted Balsam's hand. "I have to see the drawing first."

"There's probably nothing left of it. Horseweed . . . do you think . . . I mean, he was doing the Condor Dance!"

"Stay here, Balsam. I'll be right back. Then we'll return to the village."

Horseweed rose slowly, scanning the meadow and forest as he did so, looking for danger. The condor had winged out of sight. Cautiously, he stepped around the deadfall and into the dew-soaked meadow. The scent of wildflowers mixed with the sweet tang of onion here. By the time he reached the flat stone, his pant legs stuck to his skin wetly. He braced a foot and climbed on top of the stone, then crouched, surveying the meadow again. The condor swooped up over the treetops in the distance. Its shadow skimmed the path that led up the hill to the village.

Nothing else moved.

Fearing that the giant bird might be able to see him, Horseweed stayed down. He duck-walked to the drawing and stretched out on his belly to examine it more closely. Field mice skittered around him, feeding upon the meal left in the grinding holes.

Balsam scurried up onto the rock, panting. "Catchstraw—I mean that condor—is coming back! Hurry!"

Horseweed's brows drew together. "Look at this." With his finger, he followed the lines. Catchstraw had not finished erasing them. The charcoal had smeared, but the winding paths remained visible. "What do you think this is?"

Balsam wiped his mouth with the back of his hand. In a tense whisper, he answered, "It looks like a maze, doesn't it? I mean, that's what I thought when I first saw him drawing it. That it looked like a maze."

"Why would he—"

"Don't you remember?" Balsam asked urgently. "The day of the mammoths' attack. Sunchaser said that he couldn't get through the maze anymore."

"You mean . . . you think this is Sunchaser's maze?"

"What other maze is there?"

"Well, none that I know of, but—"

Balsam's eyes scanned the dark skies. "He's *witching*, Horseweed! He's witching Sunchaser!"

Horseweed cocked his head warily. "Careful. That's a serious charge. It could get Catchstraw killed."

Balsam got down on his stomach beside Horseweed and breathed, "We have to tell Grandfather. He'll know what to do."

The unmistakable sound of condor wings slicing the air came from somewhere close by. Horseweed and Balsam went rigid. A huge, dark shape floated above the trees.

Balsam panted, "Do you think he sees us?"

"Not yet," Horseweed whispered. "*Don't run.* Follow me."

With the silence of Water Snake, Horseweed slid off the stone slab and dropped to his knees to crawl across the meadow. Though Balsam tried to scramble past him several times, he managed to keep his brother calm until they reached the base of the village hill. Then Balsam leaped to his feet and sped up the trail like a jackrabbit.

Horseweed stood and turned to look back. The condor had landed on top of the stone and bent to examine the charcoal maze. The bird was huge. Horseweed swallowed hard. Condor moved across the granite, cocking his head, listening.

Then Condor lunged and struck like lightning. He came up with a mouse in his glinting beak, lifted his head and choked the creature down whole.

I've never heard of a condor hunting. They just don't! They're scavengers. A terrible chill gripped Horseweed's heart. Terror ran icy fingers through his guts. *I have to tell Grandfather about this, too.*

Slowly, Horseweed backed up until he'd rounded the base of the hill. Then he raced up the trail with all his might, legs pumping.

As he sped toward the hilltop, Condor saw him and lifted into the air with a high-pitched squeal.

Thirty-one

Sunchaser sat in the starlit darkness at the edge of the water, both knees drawn up, his elbows braced on them. He'd been here for three hands of time. He had eaten nothing since they'd left the old Otter Clan Village, for fear that his aching stomach would heave any food right back up. Dread writhed like a living creature inside him, twisting and turning.

A hundred hands away, Kestrel knelt before a fire that had burned down to wavering red coals. She'd laid out their hides and fixed dinner and tea, all in utter silence, leaving him be. She snugged an elk hide over her shoulders and unlaced the front of her dress. She lifted Cloud Girl to her breast and patted the baby absently as she nursed. Kestrel's pretty face was tense and pale.

What game are we playing, Mammoth Above? Sunchaser picked up a large pebble and flung it into the black body of the ocean. *You can do with me as you wish, but Kestrel doesn't deserve this. All she wants is a home.*

They'd camped on a narrow spit of sand, out in the open. Mother Ocean surrounded them on three sides, undulating restlessly. A few pale lavender blossoms of seaside daisy thrust up from the sand. But nothing else grew out here. Wind Girl stalked the beach vigilantly, hungry for prey; she clawed at Sunchaser's clothing with icy fingers, trying to shake sense into him, to warn him.

But Sunchaser needed no warning. He understood the signs clearly.

Mammoth Above had brought Kestrel to him.

Mammoth Above had driven the Otter Clan away so that he would be forced to stay with Kestrel.

. . . Because Mammoth Above *knew* what was happening to him.

The strength of his feelings shocked him. He had known Kestrel for such a short time. Yet it seemed that she'd filled his dreams forever. He ran a hand through his hair and shook his head.

Helper whimpered.

Sunchaser turned to look at him. The dog lay behind him, his head on his paws, watching the world through huge brown eyes. A fuzz of black hair had begun to grow in his mangy spots. "Why didn't you stop this, Helper? Isn't that why you're here? To keep me on the path? To remind me of my duty to the Spirit Powers?"

Helper's eyelids drooped, half opened, drooped again and closed. The dog groaned and flopped over on his side.

Sunchaser scratched his ears. "Spirit Helper, can't you even stay awake when I'm talking to you?"

When Cloud Girl had finished nursing, Kestrel tucked her between two soft elk hides and spoke to her softly for a time. Sunchaser could hear the baby mew in return and saw Kestrel bend over to kiss her daughter's forehead.

Kestrel stood glancing between Cloud Girl and Sunchaser, clearly trying to decide whether or not to disturb him. Then she resolutely walked out across the cool sand.

With his heart in his throat, Sunchaser watched her approach. She took her time, her arms folded over her chest to block the wind. When she stood in front of him, she hesitated before kneeling to face him.

He looked at her in a kindly way. "What is it, Kestrel?"

"Could I talk with you?"

"Of course."

She bit her lip. "Sunchaser, I'm frightened. I—I fear that you may hate me because I—"

"No. I don't hate you."

She ignored him, rushing on. "But you don't hate me nearly as much as I hate myself. I know I'm a burden to you. I'm keeping you from Dreaming. I really don't understand why we've been thrown together—"

"But we have been."

"Yes. And that's the problem . . . isn't it?"

"It is," he answered gently.

"I'm so sorry." Misery twisted her face. She rose and gazed down at him with wounded eyes. "I'm leaving tomorrow, Sunchaser. I can find Otter Clan Village by myself. That way, you won't have to worry about . . . a-about anything. I want you to go back to Dreaming. I have the feeling that that's the only thing that's really important. And I've been keeping you from it. I know that. I regret it very much. Please, don't hate me for . . . distracting you."

"Kestrel, I told you, I don't—"

As quick as Pine Marten with Coyote in pursuit, she turned and ran. He had to pitch himself on his stomach and make a mad grab to seize the fringes of her hem and halt her flight. She stopped, but made a soft, dismayed sound.

He tugged lightly. "Kestrel?"

When she didn't turn to look at him, he pulled harder, making her stumble backward.

"Sunchaser, please! Let me go."

"No. I can see that you're right. We need to talk. Sit down here beside me. . . . Please?"

She walked back and stiffly fell to her knees. A grudging action. She refused to meet his eyes, keeping her gaze fixed instead on the sand. Starlight edged the high curve of her cheeks with silver and glimmered in the windblown wisps of her long hair.

"Sort of a half-sit, eh?" he said.

"I'm here."

"Yes. You are." He let go of her dress and gave her leg a comforting pat. "Thank you."

Drawing up both knees, he wrapped his arms around them. "I'd like to be honest with you. Would it be all right if I am?"

"I would appreciate it very much."

He filled his lungs with air and let it out slowly, girding himself against his own foolishness. What could he say that wouldn't hurt her? And how should he say it? Kestrel appeared to have stopped breathing.

"This is difficult for me," he began. "I'm—"

"I know you're upset, Sunchaser. And I know I'm the reason. All day long, I've been wishing I were dead so I wouldn't be causing you this pain."

A stinging sensation lanced his soul. *No, Kestrel. Never say that*. Looking at her young guilt-ravaged face, he felt very, very old, and a little wistful for days long ago, before he became a Dreamer. A tender ache swelled his heart. "Kestrel, I think you know that I have come to love you. But—"

"I'm sorry, Sunchaser. I never meant—"

"But that isn't what's worrying me," he interrupted. He had the feeling that she might be about to embarrass herself on his account, and he couldn't bear the thought. "I could overcome my feelings for you. At least," he smiled wryly, "I think I could. Let's just say that Dreamers have had thousands of cycles in which to devise ways. What worries me is that apparently I'm *supposed* to feel this way about you." He waited for bewildered questions, or a surprised silence.

She lifted her eyes and stared at him with unnerving calm. "Why?"

"I'm not sure."

"I thought such things were bad for Dreamers."

"Usually they are. Some Dreamers can manage responsibilities to both family and Power, but they're very rare."

Kestrel shifted to sit on her left hip. She curled her knees around, then braced a hand on the sand. The concern in her voice was touching. "Sunchaser, why would Mammoth Above throw an obstacle in your path when you're trying so hard to save her children?"

"Are you an obstacle, Kestrel?"

"What else could I be? I mean, I thought—"

"I've been trying to answer that question all day. Mammoth Above has gone to great lengths to assure that you and I will be together for several more days. She's my Spirit Helper. I trust her. But I don't understand this. The only reason I can see for Mammoth Above to chance it is that you or your daughter can help me to solve the problem I'm having with my Dreaming." He lightly brushed his fingers over the sand that covered the toe of his right moccasin. "Forcing us together is very dangerous for Mammoth Above. She could lose me. She knows that. And I don't think she wants to."

The moon had risen above the dark peaks of the Mammoth Mountains. Kestrel frowned at the rings of translucent color that haloed the pale orb. Nearby clouds shimmered with a frosty iridescence. "You have been so kind to us, Sunchaser. I would do anything to help you. But I . . . I don't know how I can help you Dream. And Cloud Girl is just a baby. What could she do?"

"Please try to think, Kestrel. Perhaps I'm wrong about Cloud Girl. Maybe there's something you know, or do, that ties you to Power. It could be as simple as weaving nets or—"

She leaned toward him and put an urgent hand on his wrist. "I paint! The only times I feel Power moving through me, Sunchaser, are when I'm painting or dyeing. It must be that!"

His eyes rested on the thin fingers so cool and comforting on his wrist. Tomorrow he would try Dreaming again. He must, or his soul would shrivel to dust and blow away in the next gust of wind. Mammoth Above needed him to Dream, and he needed to Dream for her. He could sense her presence all around him, watching, supporting, trying to help him, though desperation clouded her hopes.

He wiped his sweating palm on his pant leg before he reached over to grip Kestrel's hand. "Will you paint for me, Kestrel? I think I need you to very much."

"It would give me great pleasure, but . . ." She squeezed his hand gently, and her brow furrowed. "Sunchaser, please tell me what you're thinking about Cloud Girl. A few days ago, you said you thought you knew why we'd been drawn together. I didn't ask you to explain at the time . . . I was too frightened to. What did you mean?"

He moved his fingers over the smooth, tanned skin of her hand. "Do your people in the marsh country know of the Steals Light People?"

"No. Who are they?"

"Special messengers of Above-Old-Man. They live on the roof of the world, the highest mountain peaks. The Power of Above-Old-Man enters our world through the hands of the Steals Light People. We—that is, my clan, the Steals Light Clan—keep small figurines of each of the Steals Light People in our home lodges to serve as portals for the real people's Power. That way, the Steals Light People can speak to us, direct us, help us when we are sick or in trouble. But sometimes," he said, stroking the top of her hand tenderly, "sometimes the People ride lightning bolts down from the roof of the world and walk among humans without anyone's knowledge. They can even choose to enter a woman's womb and be born again."

Kestrel's full lips parted as if to speak. Then she closed them, pondering. "You think she . . . that my little girl . . ."

"I don't know," he answered the unfinished question. "But she might be."

"What would that mean?"

"It would mean that I've been given a very great gift." He smiled sardonically. "And one that I haven't the slightest idea of how to appreciate."

Oxbalm studied the charcoal lines through narrowed eyes. They wove in and around, crossed over each other, back-tracked. Some of them even shot outward from the body of the maze and tied themselves in intricate knots. Horror throbbed in his breast. All morning long, the Thunderbeings had been restless, angry. They crowded the skies, rumbling and throwing bolts of lightning about within the clouds. The scent of snow rode the breeze. Oxbalm had never liked Catchstraw, but he'd never thought the man capable of this. Especially not when they needed Sunchaser so badly.

Oxbalm started to rise, and Horseweed and Balsam took his arms, supporting him as he struggled to his feet. He patted their backs absently and studied the top of the hill where the village sat. He had asked Catchstraw to help Sumac design the lodge paintings—to keep him busy while Oxbalm investigated Horseweed's whispered accusations. Not that he had doubted his grandson. He hadn't. But such things required delicacy, corroboration and great courage.

A few red starbursts and two wavy blue lines decorated the exterior of the lodges . . . but little else had been done. Had Sumac been designing the paintings herself, the lodges would have been finished by now, and beautifully.

Oxbalm let out a shuddering breath. "We must say nothing about this. Not to anyone. Not yet. Do you both understand?"

Balsam nodded and bit his lip.

Horseweed shivered, rubbing his arms with nervous hands. "Yes, Grandfather. But how long can we wait before we take action? We can't let this go on."

Oxbalm gazed up into that boyish face with the dark eyes and saw a man looking back, a deeply worried man. "No. We can't. But remember, he has followers. And they all know that I don't like him. We must wait for an opening before we accuse him. Witchcraft is very dangerous, frightening. A rash action, or one too soon, could bring terrible disaster down on us."

"How long, Grandfather? How long can Sunchaser wait?"

Oxbalm shook his head. "Only Mammoth Above knows the answer to that question. We must pray that Sunchaser has been able to fend off this monstrous attack."

Horseweed shifted uncomfortably. "And if he hasn't?"

Oxbalm's mouth tightened. "Then we must end it quickly."

"What if . . ." Horseweed and Balsam exchanged a frightened look, and Horseweed's gaze scoured the trees and sky. "Grandfather, what if Catchstraw has learned how to change himself into Condor? Or other animals? What will that mean once we bring charges of witchcraft against him?"

Oxbalm's chest felt as if a granite boulder sat atop it, making it almost impossible for him to breathe. He slipped his arms around both of his grandsons and hugged them. "Then we are in worse trouble than we think. Much worse."

The sun had slipped through the opening on the horizon and entered the Land of the Dead, but whispers of its brilliance flitted across the surface of the ocean and reddened the specks of clouds that dusted the deep blue. Tannin stood with his atlatl gripped in both hands, watching Lambkill pillage the abandoned Otter Clan Village. His brother growled

maliciously as he crushed a beautiful seashell hairpin beneath
his foot, then reached down, picked up a clamshell atlatl
hook and tucked it into his shirt pocket. Rage smoldered in
Lambkill's faded eyes. He kicked at the scattered remnants of
a whalebone lodge frame and muttered darkly to himself.

Tannin exhaled hard.

Cold gusts of wind rustled the firs growing thickly along
the shore. Slate-gray waves curled into white breakers to
thunder on the sand, and gulls wheeled around them, cawing,
flapping, cocking their heads in curiosity. Two dozen of the
birds sat atop one of the giant mammoth carcasses that lay in
the midst of the devastated village. Flaps of moldering hide
clung to the skeleton, but the meat had been cleaned out
long ago by predators. Tannin wondered how much those
magnificent ivory tusks would bring if traded to the right
people. Lambkill would know, but Tannin dared not ask
him. Not now. Tannin feared that anything he said would
trigger Lambkill's insane temper.

Lambkill tramped across the sand and jerked a long pole
from a pile of deadfall. He tested its strength and then thrust
the pole up into one of the tree burials.

Blessed Mammoth Above . . .

Lambkill levered the burial out of the tree, letting the
rotting corpse tumble limply onto the sand, spilling maggots
and grave goods helter-skelter.

Tannin stared with disbelief, his breath caught in his throat,
fear prickling along his veins. "Lambkill, no . . . *no!*"

Heedless, his brother dislodged another burial, and a little
girl's corpse thudded headfirst onto the ground.

Tannin gaped in horror as Lambkill kicked the brightly
decorated burial wrapping apart, unconcerned with the putrid
reek of death and corruption. The child's head lolled amidst
a disarray of long black hair that came loose in patches.

"Here!" Lambkill cried, picking up a carved ivory doll.
"This is worth a fortune inland."

Tannin fell to his knees, his sleeve draped over his nose
to block the stench.

The little girl's body lay hunched and stiff, half desiccated. The empty eye sockets, long picked clean by ravens and gulls, stared accusingly up at Tannin; the flesh around her mouth had dried into a death's moan.

Trembling, Tannin crawled away on rubbery knees, sobs choking him.

Lambkill stopped suddenly and knelt down to brush at the sand. His loose, shoulder-length gray hair hung in dirty strands around his wrinkled face.

"Look here, my brother!" Lambkill said and grinned. *"See these prints? We have her!"*

Thirty-two

Father Sun—a fiery orange ball in a smooth blue sky—gleamed through the canopy of trees over Kestrel's head. Where the sun pierced the thick branches above, damp logs on the ground steamed. Ghostly wisps of fog filled the forest. Kestrel's moccasins cut a meandering swath through the dew-soaked grass as she skirted the meadow and headed down the slope toward the beach. She still needed to gather lichen for the rich yellow that would be the focal point of her design. She hurried, afraid that Sunchaser would be waiting for her. He'd told her that he wanted to sweat and chant until noon. After that, they would begin.

She would paint, and he would Dream.

Anxiety gnawed within Kestrel's belly the way Porcupine chewed on winter-shed antlers. She had been feeling strange all day, jumping every time a squirrel chittered. She wanted so much to help Sunchaser. But could she? The possibility of failure terrified her.

You don't even know for certain what the problem with his Dreaming is. She sighed uneasily. What was it? The turn in the maze? That was what he had said during the Ant Ordeal.

All night long, she had been designing her painting with that in mind. But if she'd guessed wrong, her painting might make things worse for him.

Be sure, Kestrel . . . you must *be sure.* Colors held Power. They came from the very soul of Sister Earth. "Some of my paintings come to life," she whispered.

With Cloud Girl's sack bouncing against her back, Kestrel stepped over a rotting log and knelt in a lush bed of ferns before a granite boulder wedged between two towering fir trees. The grayish-green leaves of lichen covered the rock. "When my paintings come to life, the Spirits in them grow minds of their own. No one can predict what such Spirits will do."

Kestrel unlaced the pack around her waist and drew out a chert scraper the size of her palm. The lichen adhered to the stone like boiled pine sap, forcing Kestrel to gouge, cut and scrape for a full finger of time before she had enough of the leathery plant to fill half of her pack. Lacing up the pack, she stepped out of the ferns and trotted toward the game trail that led downhill.

When she emerged from the trees, the salty sea breeze hit her, rich with the scents of smoke and boiling paints. They'd moved their camp from the spit of sand to the edge of the trees so that Sunchaser could set up his sweat lodge in a sheltered location. They'd constructed it at dawn, making a round frame from pine saplings, then covering the small frame with the hides they used for bedding.

The lodge nestled in the middle of a small grove of aspens whose new green leaves quaked and rustled in the wind. In front of the lodge, a bed of hot coals lay covered with rocks.

Kestrel could see that Sunchaser had removed several of the rocks. Using sticks as tongs, he would have picked them off and carried them inside, placing them in the pit dug into the floor of the sweat lodge. Water sprinkled over the hot stones would produce the steam.

Legend claimed that Wolfdreamer had built the first sweat lodge, and that it cleansed the soul as well as the body.

To the right of the sweat lodge, a large flat rock lay tilted slightly toward the sea. At its base, Helper lay on his side in the thick grass, watching Kestrel with his pointed ears cocked.

She went directly to the fire, where her paints were boiling. She'd collected large clamshells, heated them and mixed her ingredients with the fat from the rabbit she'd snared and eaten for breakfast.

Sunchaser hadn't eaten or drunk anything since yesterday. He'd been worried about it all morning. "Dreaming well requires the denial of the body," he'd told her. "I should have been fasting for the past three days. Even attempting to Dream today is dangerous, but I'm desperate. So many strange things are happening . . . I must try to reach the Land of the Dead. Perhaps the Spirits will forgive me this once."

Kestrel unslung Cloud Girl's sack and gently propped her daughter up against Sunchaser's pack beside their rolled-up hides, the only two left after making the sweat lodge. Cloud Girl smiled happily.

"I have to tend my paints, baby. Be good for me."

Cloud Girl chewed her fist as Kestrel knelt before the fire. The flames had burned down to a few weak flickers. Kestrel used a dead branch ripped from the bottom of a fir tree to snake out and turn over the shell she'd shoved into the ashes before going to find the lichen.

From her pack she pulled the folded bark container that held the remaining rabbit fat and a handful of the lichen. With her fingers, she scraped the fat from the bark onto the hot shell. The fat melted instantly, sliding down to pool in the hollow of the shell.

Kestrel rubbed the lichen between her palms, crushing it over the hot grease. When the bits of plant landed, they began oozing a beautiful orange-yellow color. Kestrel stirred the mixture with a stick and went to pull her other paints away from the flames to cool.

She positioned the shells in a neat row. Then she unwrapped an obsidian flake from its protective leaves and slit the tip of her index finger. Blood welled. She Sang softly and squeezed drops of her blood into each color.

Willow bark produced the rich red paint; a mixture of walnut leaves and bark, the deep black; sagebrush, the pale ivory. When the lichen had finished steeping, she would have the four sacred colors she needed in order to create her designs.

Sounds came from the sweat lodge in the aspen grove. Helper rose and stretched, wagging his tail. Sunchaser ducked through the door flap and stood naked against the background of spring leaves. A sheen of sweat coated his sun-bronzed skin. Beads of water glistened like a net of pearls over his white hair and braid.

For a brief instant, Kestrel allowed her gaze to linger on the curving muscles covering his tall body. The blue-and-green serpent tattoo on his chest gleamed. When he turned to look at her, his deep-set eyes appeared blacker than she had ever seen them before, like caves in moonglow.

"Are you ready, Kestrel?" he asked softly.

"Yes. Where do you want to sit?"

"Here, in the aspen grove."

While he went about tying on his breechclout and climbing up on the low rock, Kestrel carried Cloud Girl and her paints over. It took her four trips—the sacred number. By the time she'd finished, Sunchaser sat cross-legged on the rock, eyes closed, back straight. The clear notes of his low chant caressed the air like hushed flute music. Helper had curled up before the sweat lodge, ten hands away. His knowing gaze rested on Sunchaser.

Kestrel hung Cloud Girl's rabbit-fur sack on the closest tree and took a deep breath before she turned back to gaze at Sunchaser. Spears of sunlight penetrated the quaking leaves and dappled his hair and face with a wavering golden patch-work.

Kestrel understood why so many people spoke his name in their prayers. His handsome face had a soothing peaceful-ness, as though the sweat bath had washed him clear down to his soul. Power radiated from him like water from a spring. The hair at the nape of her neck prickled. Despite her awe, fear stirred within—not fear of him, but for him. What would he do if he couldn't Dream again today?

How many people have ever seen you cry, Sunchaser? Or heard you earnestly talk about loneliness? Please, Mammoth Above, let him find his way through the maze.

Quietly, Kestrel climbed up beside Sunchaser and arranged her paint shells near her right hand. Sunchaser smelled pleas-antly of mint. He must have thrown a few sprigs into his water bowl before he poured it on the hot rocks. She folded the hem of her dress to cushion her knees from the gritty bite of the granite and waited.

The thin white trunks of the aspens clustered around them, seeming to lean inward as though eager and anxious about the happenings below. Kestrel took a deep breath to prepare herself. The pungent odor of wet hides drifted from the sweat lodge.

In the distance, the spit of sand where they had camped last night pointed out into the water like a narrow finger. A flock of black-and-white auks floated near the tip, diving for squid and small fish. Mother Ocean rocked calmly around them. The squawks pulsed in an odd rhythm with the sound of the surf.

Sunchaser stopped chanting and bowed his head. Kestrel saw his shoulder muscles contract. "Kestrel?"

"I'm here, Sunchaser."

"Have you ever seen someone Dream before?"

"No. Except in the Ant Ordeal."

He paused. "This will be different. Don't be afraid. I may not awaken for days, because I'm trying so hard to find my way. Do you understand?"

"Yes."

He extended a hand around behind him, and Kestrel took it between her hands and squeezed hard. She said, "Dream well, Sunchaser. I'll do my best for you."

"I know you will."

His deep, steady voice eased her fears. Kestrel released his hand and he closed his fingers slowly, as though to hold the feel of her with him for a time longer. Finally he pulled his hand back to his lap and began his low chant again.

The shadows of the quaking aspen leaves flitted around the grove like dark butterflies.

Kestrel dipped the first two fingers of her right hand into the black paint, warm and oily.

All right, Kestrel. Picture the design in your mind. It's a tree, but the branches circle around like segments of the maze that Sunchaser carved into the floor of the rock shelter. Yes . . . yes, that's it.

She put her left hand on Sunchaser's shoulder and began painting with her right hand. At her gentle touch, a brief shudder went through him. Across his lower back, Kestrel carefully painted the trunk and the three branches sprouting from it. The two outside branches curved up like stubby buffalo horns, but the center branch slithered like a snake, swaying sinuously, first up, then down, veering off at a tangent, then to the left, then to the right.

Kestrel sat back to examine her work, and her hide skirt spread around her in a fringed halo. She cleaned the black paint from her fingers by rubbing them on the rock. Sunchaser's Singing had grown quieter. She could no longer make out the words, they'd blended into a harmonic whole.

The rest of the painting would be far more difficult to do. The segments of branches had to connect and disconnect at just the right places. And she would have to create an ending, praying that her artistry didn't somehow confuse Sunchaser's soul.

As she dipped her fingers into the red paint, a bird fluttered down to sit on a branch over Helper's head. A red-breasted nuthatch. Such a beautiful bird. Blue-gray above, it had a rust-colored breast and a bold black eye stripe. In a flurry of nasal *nyak-nyaks*, two more swooped low and landed in the same aspen. Kestrel smiled. The first nuthatch hopped down the side of the tree, unconcerned, and began pecking, looking for insects that had secreted themselves beneath the bark.

Kestrel lifted her fingers again and noticed that the flock of auks that had been floating near the sand spit had waddled to the edge of the aspen grove and were craning their necks to watch. Forty or more of them. Soft chirps of curiosity eddied through their ranks.

Helper studied the birds suspiciously, one eye half open.

Cloud Girl grinned. Her shrill piping didn't seem to alarm the birds.

When Kestrel touched Sunchaser to draw the next segment of the maze, a tingle invaded her fingers. His body radiated warmth. She jerked her hand back reflexively.

Where are you, Sunchaser? Already on the path? Is that what the animals sense? She swallowed hard, glanced at the auks and nuthatches and lowered her fingers again to draw the sinewy red lines. Then the white. . . .

Kestrel concentrated so hard on creating the correct interplay of red and white lines that she didn't even notice the changing slant of the daylight. Father Sun methodically journeyed across the belly of Brother Sky until his body wedded with Mother Ocean's. At the joining point, a swath of light flooded outward, turning the surface of the water to molten gold.

Kestrel lowered her hand to the cool granite to watch the glory. The high, wispy clouds blazed like fire-engulfed spiderwebs.

A faint grunt sounded behind her and Kestrel tensed. She spun around and her eyes widened.

How long had they been there? The mammoth calf lay on its side in the lush grass, his trunk securely twined around his mother's.

How could they have come so close without her having

heard them? The calf's tail flicked up and down playfully.

The cow met Kestrel's gaze with equanimity, but dark emotion stirred the brown depths of her eyes. Like a chill breeze on a warm day, Kestrel sensed the mammoth's fear.

She whispered, "He's trying, Mother. Really he is. He's walking the maze right now, trying to get to the Land of the Dead so he can help you."

The cow tilted her huge head as though listening. She took a step forward, stopping no more than six hands from Kestrel, looming over her. A person never really understood how big a mammoth was until she looked up at one.

The cow's musky scent filled the air, and the sun's dying light burned redly in the long hair that clothed her twenty-eight-hand-tall body. Mud caked the blunt feet that rested so easily on the ground. Kestrel was so close that she could see flakes of skin peeling on the front of the cow's long trunk.

Kestrel nerved herself to ask: "How's Sunchaser doing, Mother? Is he all right?"

The cow gracefully knelt on her front knees, then lowered the rest of her body to the ground beside her calf. Her left front foot pressed against the rock upon which Kestrel and Sunchaser sat. Grass stained the curve of her short tusks. How silently mammoths moved.

"Can you help Sunchaser, Mother? He needs all the help he can get."

The cow flapped her ears lazily, but that burning brightness remained alight in her wizened eyes.

On the opposite side of the rock, the auks had bedded down with their necks stretched across each other's backs. The nuthatches sat on their branches, their feathers fluffed out. The breeze stilled, and the aspen leaves ceased their soft rattling.

All were waiting . . . The whole world was waiting.

Kestrel uneasily turned back to her paints. The lichen had steeped to a flaming gold tinged with the barest hint of green. She brought the shell closer and set it by her knee, then closed her eyes again and saw her design. This part had to be perfect. She could risk no mistakes.

Yellow. For you, Sunchaser.

Yellow would outline the twisting route that led to the heart of the maze. When completed, the path would resemble serpentine flashes of lightning. Yes, that was it. To help light the way for Sunchaser.

Kestrel opened her eyes and lowered her fingers to the paint. But as she began to chart the circuitous route around the edges of the maze, she caught movement from the corner of her eye.

The mammoth cow's dark gray trunk eased up over the edge of the rock and tenderly coiled around Sunchaser's bare foot, holding it in a lover's grasp. The cow vented a small, satisfied sigh.

Kestrel looked down and smiled. The cow had tilted her massive head sideways, mashing down the tall grass so that she could see Sunchaser's face. Her short tusks gleamed. The calf had shifted, falling asleep near the cow's hind legs, sprigs of fern sticking out of his mouth.

Sunchaser didn't seem to feel the cow's touch, but he had ceased chanting. His breathing had become so shallow that Kestrel could barely discern the rise and fall of his broad chest. Anxiety tickled her stomach. How long would he be Dreaming? All night? For days?

There were so many things she wanted to tell him . . .

So many things she feared.

But they would have to wait, at least until after he had talked to Wolfdreamer and knew better where his path led.

He had avoided the opportunity to let her speak her feelings.

And she knew that he'd done it deliberately—sparing them both—because he feared, as she did, that the next time he saw Wolfdreamer, the Spirit might tell him to start using some of those gruesome techniques that Dreamers had spent thousands of cycles devising.

Kestrel lifted her fingers to finish the route that led to

the heart of the maze. But when she touched Sunchaser, her hand froze.

The auks squawked suddenly, and the mammoth cow lifted her head. Helper growled and stood with the hair on his back bristling. Kestrel gaped, startled, then she felt it, too: a fluttering like velvet wings at the edges of her soul. A tremor shook her as Power flowed into her from all directions, creeping from the trees and animals, from the rock she sat upon, from the very air itself. She had never felt it so strongly before. Like a frostbitten foot thrust into warm water, the sensation grew more painful as moments passed; it seeped upward and inward from her fingers and toes until it enshrouded her whole body in a tingling cocoon.

"Blessed Spirits . . ."

With difficulty, Kestrel concentrated on finishing her painting. Her hand shook as she threaded the yellow strand through the red segments, around the black and between the white lines. It required painstaking attention not to cross over, not to smudge any of the maze's colors.

When at last she'd reached the center of the tree—the heart of the maze—Kestrel's arm ached so badly that she could barely hold it up.

Darkness had settled like a hazy charcoal veil upon the land. Mother Ocean washed the beach quietly, as though aware that Sunchaser Dreamed, and was careful not to disturb him.

Kestrel lowered her arm and let out a breath.

Helper crept closer, to within four hands of the mammoth cow, and stared knowingly at Kestrel. Then his gaze shifted to the painting on Sunchaser's broad back.

"What do you think, Helper?"

The dog wagged its tail.

Kestrel shivered in the chill breeze that rustled through the aspens. She would have to build a fire soon. But for a short while, she wanted to sit and stare at her artistry. The sense of rightness ran like spring breezes through her blood. It felt so good to be painting again, as though a severed limb had been miraculously reattached to her body.

The bright colors formed a glorious picture, the strands winding in and out and around each other.

... Already she could feel the first stirrings of life in the painting.

Catchstraw didn't breathe.

He sat stone still, watching, listening. The distorted maze at his feet had been forgotten.

The swooping creatures observed him with unblinking eyes as they soared through the trees. Moonlight reflected blindingly from the translucent membranes of their dragonfly wings. They had come upon him suddenly, invading his forest sanctuary like quills shot from a terrified porcupine.

Since he no longer had a private lodge, he had been forced to move his secret activities out into the open. He couldn't risk lighting a fire, so he'd been working the maze in darkness ... and the Thunderbeings seemed drawn to his activities like thirsty beasts to water.

Perhaps because he'd done so well tonight! Twisting the path like a knot of screwbean vines, stretching some runners out into linking, interwoven spirals.

The Thunderbeings dove at him. Were they ... angry? Trying to frighten him away? They streaked through the forest like silver darts, coming close enough to rip off his head with their talons!

"You're so beautiful," he whispered hoarsely.

The human faces glared down at him. They looked like children of no more than five summers. Some of them had the fat faces of infants barely out of the womb. And their wings! The smallest stretched a single body's length, but the largest spanned five or six body lengths. How could they maneuver so gracefully through the dense forest? But Thunderbeings had magical souls.

How had he summoned them?

The more Catchstraw became entranced by their motions, the more his mouth gaped. "It must be the nightshade."

He had found the purple flower at the edge of the meadow, in the dry, rocky places beneath the oaks. Though he'd never seen the plant before, he had recognized it immediately from Running Salmon's description: "It has a bright-yellow center and frail, violet petals, transparent, almost too purple to believe."

How wise he'd been to demand that Oxbalm take the village into the foothills! He'd found half a dozen new Spirit Plants, and he wanted to try every one of them. When Catchstraw had first seen the purple nightshade, he'd dug it up roots and all. Then he'd begun experimenting. First the blossoms. Then the leaves. Tonight he'd ground the roots and mixed a small amount with his tea.

The plant's deadly Spirit must have allowed him to call to the Thunderbeings. *What Power!* It intoxicated him.

He'd intended to change himself into a short-faced bear tonight and go hunting. But he'd lost his body somewhere in the first moments of glory. Now he seemed to be floating off of the forest floor, suspended between the worlds of earth and sky.

I feel like a tiny Thunderbeing cocooned in clouds, feeding off of the rain. Maybe . . . is that why you came? You want me to become one of you? The thought had never occurred to him . . . but why not?

He floated higher and higher, until he looked over the tops of the trees. Against the Star People, the flights of the Thunderbeings wove a flaming web of light. It resembled a net, caging . . . *caging?*

The Dream tattered like sun-warmed mist, and Catchstraw let out a scream as he fell.

He awoke with his face buried in the tall grass of the forest floor, panting. Terrified, he flopped onto his back to look up. The Thunderbeings had vanished.

A huge amber halo encircled the crescent of Above-Old-Man that hung over the eastern horizon.

"What happened? Why did I fall? I wanted to fly! Come back! All of you!"

The dark forest whispered malevolently around him, and he could sense presences growing in the shadows. Like poisonous vines sending up shoots after a summer shower, they grew, and grew . . .

"I want to be one of you! I'm tired of becoming animals!" Catchstraw shouted. "Give me wings!"

Silver eyes coalesced from the glitters of moonlight scattered in the forest.

"Oh, there you are. I thought you'd gone. You hate me, don't you? Well, I don't care. You hear me? I'll grow wings whether you like it or not." He pouted. "I *must* have dragonfly wings!"

The eyes blinked, off and on, off and on, like a million tiny stars falling through the trees.

Catchstraw scrambled to his feet. "I *will* be a Thunderbeing!" he bellowed in rage. "I can do *anything!*"

"Father? Father, do you hear me?" the Boy asked from the dried mouth of his smoked body. *"Father, wake up."*

Lambkill roused and blinked at the gloom of the brush lodge. The lean-to walls had gaps so wide that moonlight flooded the interior, shadowing the packs and haloing the bedding hides with a burning line of liquid silver. "What? Who called me?" He propped himself up on his elbows and scowled. His jowls looked like white sacks in the darkness.

"I did, Father," the Boy replied through a weary exhalation. *"I have something to tell you."*

"What is it, my son?"

It hurt the Boy to do as this human asked. What greater punishment could have been inflicted upon him? He wondered why the Man had commanded him to tell Lambkill what he wanted to know.

"*Mother is on the seacoast, near Pygmy Island. She is alive and well. And that witch I told you about? He is growing too arrogant for his own good. He's tired of running and flying in the bodies of animals. Now he wants to join the ranks of the Thunderbeings.*"

Lambkill sat up suddenly. "Does your mother know I'm following her?"

"*She suspects. That's all. She can't believe that you would ever let her go.*"

"And where is this witch I am to seek out?"

"*In the foothills. Don't worry. Soon another Trader will tell you how to get there. He'll tell you that—and much more.*" Things that I cannot bear to, no matter what the Man might say.

The Boy's soul coiled into a tight spiral and lay restlessly in that dead body, watching the man he hated more than any other drift back to sleep.

"*Man? Man, can you hear me?*"

"*Yes, Boy. I hear you.*" The voice whispered on the eddies of night wind that penetrated the brush lodge.

"*I can't stand this, Man! I feel filthy. I—I hate myself as much as I hate Lambkill! Why are you making me do this? What am I supposed to learn from betraying my mother?*"

The Man's voice took on a wavering, windblown timbre. "*Oh, a very great deal, Boy. Only when a soul learns to do violence to its own will, for the greater sake of Power, can it hope to save the world.*"

The Man paused, and Boy thought he heard a moan of despair on the wind. "*Boy, do you know that after I died and went to the Land of the Dead, I spent a full millennium in despair, mourning the fact that Power had forced me to kill my own brother?*"

"*You . . . you had to kill your brother?*"

"Yes."

Boy thought about that. How could Power make its chosen Dreamers do such terrible things? What purpose could Power have in generating such misery? Man wouldn't ask him to kill his own mother, would he? Fear quivered in Boy's soul. He couldn't force himself to ask that question, so he asked instead, "What made you stop grieving, Man?"

"I discovered that my soul was like a hide bag, and that my thoughts, regrets and fears were like slices of meat filling the bag. If you leave such a bag for a long time, the contents will rot. So I turned the bag upside down and emptied it into the blackness of the Land of the Dead."

"And that helped?"

"Yes. You see, I hadn't fully learned the teachings of my friend, Heron, during my life. Teachings about the One, and Nothingness, and Emptiness. So I was forced to grapple with them after I died. Just as you are grappling now, Boy."

"But what did you learn?"

"I learned that only when I had become Empty, could I stop hurting."

"I'd like to make this putrid body empty, Man. To free my soul! Nothing would make me happier. But I don't know how to get out now that I'm here. Set me free, Man. Please. I can't stand this anymore!"

"If you want to be free, Boy, you must learn to empty your soul. To make yourself as empty as Above-Old-Man's bloodless heart."

Thirty-three

Kestrel lay curled behind Sunchaser on the rock, drifting in and out of tortured dreams where she found herself running madly for the Pinyon Bark Trails crossing—with Tannin's moccasins pounding behind her.

The temperature had dropped dramatically after sunset, and the night had a bitter bite. She'd tied a hide around Sunchaser's bare shoulders and rolled herself and Cloud Girl in another.

Her daughter slept soundly at Kestrel's back, with her head pillowed on Helper's black tail. The dog had climbed up on the rock, shivering and wagging its tail pathetically. Kestrel had turned the elk hide sideways so she could cover Helper as well as herself and her daughter. It meant that she had only her dress between the chill granite and her skin. Cold seeped up to nip at her, but not unbearably.

She had been afraid to demolish Sunchaser's sweat lodge, fearing they might need it later tonight. Moonlit clouds sped across the sky like ghosts racing for cover. Behind them, a dark haze had gobbled up the glimmers of Mother Ocean.

"That's not rain, is it?" Kestrel murmured anxiously.

The mammoth cow that lay at the base of the rock lifted her head. Her eyes glinted in the gloom. She made a soft sound and flapped one ear. An icy grass-scented breeze fanned Kestrel. The little calf had moved farther out beyond the aspen grove, planting himself in a thick bed of ferns. The darkness outlined his auburn-haired body.

"I'm sorry I woke you, Mother," Kestrel whispered. "You can go back to sleep. Sunchaser's still Dreaming."

The cow used the tip of her trunk to reach the thick fringe of grass around the front of the rock, where she ripped up a handful, then put it in her mouth and chewed, the grinding sound loud in the night.

With her toes, Kestrel pulled the bottom of the elk hide up and folded it under so that she could tuck her cold feet into the niche.

As she closed her eyes, dreams flitted across her soul . . . images flaring and dying in a single instant.

Kestrel heard Sunchaser calling her. His deep voice rang with such urgency that she thought he'd awakened, but when she sat up to stare at him, she found him still Dreaming, his body silhouetted against the backdrop of green leaves and white tree trunks. His expressionless face, with its deep-set eyes, hadn't changed. White hair still bordered his high cheekbones. His braid hung over his left shoulder.

Kestrel closed her eyes again, and his voice grew louder . . .

"Kestrel? Kestrel? Can you hear me?"

"Yes, I hear you . . ."

He kept calling, and she followed his voice and found herself trotting along a narrow dirt path through a magnificent wind-sculpted land. An infinity of canyons cut this desert to ribbons, leaving red ridges and needles of orange sandstone to slice the brilliant blue of Brother Sky. No birds soared on the thermals or perched on the rocks. No wind blew. An unnatural silence and heat gripped this place. Sweat ran down her chest, trickling between her breasts. Her long hair danced in the gusts of searing wind. The seashells on her dress clicked melodiously as her feet thudded on the dry soil.

In the distance, jumbles of rounded rocks dotted the desert, like balls rolled into place and frozen by the gods. Cactus bloomed at the base of the outcrops, creating fringes of yellow. The closer she came to the rocks, the louder Sunchaser's voice became. She could feel it pounding against the suffocating air.

"Sunchaser?" she called. "Where are you? I can't see you!"

"Kestrel . . . Kestrel . . . I'm here. Over here."

She crested a low rise and plunged down the other side into a tangle of trails. She slid to a stop. Dust spirals coiled into existence, twining toward the sky, then guttering out and weakly splashing Kestrel with grains of sand. Sunchaser's voice seemed to come from everywhere and nowhere at once. She scanned the landscape, her gaze following the bone-dry drainages and sweeping up the red spires.

"Sunchaser?"

Which direction should she take? She scrutinized the knot of pathways. They resembled a twined heap of unraveled yucca cord, strand dropped upon strand, looping off in every direction.

"Kestrel . . . Kestrel . . . !"

The sound of his voice made her frantic. "Where are you, Sunchaser? I'm at a trail crossing. I don't know which way to go!"

"I'm here. Here!"

Kestrel ran back along the way she'd come, trying to find his tracks. Only her own moccasin prints showed on the sandy soil.

A new voice called to her. *"Kestrel?"* It had a harmonic sound, like several people speaking at once. *"Kestrel, you'll never find Sunchaser if you stay on the trails. They're being witched. You have to fly above them. Tell Sunchaser. He has to fly."*

She spun around, scanning the rocks. "Who are you?"

"Run, Kestrel. Fly over the trails. Fly . . . you must fly."

"I don't know how to fly! I'm not a Dreamer!"

"Try. Try to fly. Go on, Kestrel. You can do it. Just spread your arms . . ."

She turned, raced forward and leaped over the chaos with her arms outstretched. When she sailed through the air, suspended above the tangle, she could clearly tell the direction from which Sunchaser's voice came. Joy filled her. She hit the dirt running, heading for an orange needle of sandstone that gleamed like fire on the eastern horizon, and never let her gaze waver.

"Sunchaser, I'm coming!"

A hundred trails crossed her path, but she refused to look at them. Her route cut through the twists and turns like an arrow, slicing the knot in two.

And through some magic she did not understand, she seemed to be looking down on the desert from high above. As if following the route of a cat's-cradle string woven between a child's fingers, she could make out the simple single strand that formed the basis of the chaos. It led to the heart of the maze, where the knot tied the two ends together.

The knot resembled a deep canyon filled with dark shadows. . . . *Like the hole through which Wolfdreamer led humans into this World of Light.*

She sprinted forward at a headlong pace, her shining black hair streaming out behind. Her slender body felt young again, as though she'd never undergone the travails of childbirth or abuse. A feeling of utter freedom possessed her. Her beaded moccasins barely seemed to touch the burning desert sands. The horrifying burdens that weighted her soul vanished. She no longer cared whether Lambkill would find her or not. Her husband didn't exist here. She felt as though she had stepped out of her own life and into someone else's.

And this someone was happy.

Buttes rose on either side of her, their blunt noses sniffing the belly of Brother Sky. Wind blew streamers of red sand from the crests and whipped them into spirals that curled upward into the sky.

"Kestrel, can you hear me? Where are you? Are you still coming?"

"I'm here, Sunchaser! I'm following the sound of your voice. Keep calling my name!"

"Kestrel . . . Kestrel . . . Kestrel . . ."

He sounded so forlorn, so lost.

She picked up her feet and ran like the wind, down a steep drainage filled with sage and up the opposite bank.

A broad plain fanned out before her, bordered on either side by scrubby bands of pinyon pine. A euphoric sense of purpose tingled along her limbs. For the first time in cycles, she knew why she was alive. She lived here now to help Sunchaser unravel the maze. He needed her.

I've escaped, Lambkill. You'll never find me. Never.

After all the weary burdens she'd borne in the past five cycles, this wasteland affected her like a heady brew of fermented juniper berries. She didn't want to go home. Not ever.

But Cloud Girl . . . oh, my baby . . . my baby.

Kestrel passed the central knot, her eyes focused solely on the orange spire, and trotted between two enormous ridges that rose like jagged rows of teeth on either side of her. They narrowed as they approached a deep, dark chasm.

She whispered, "Like the wing walls of a trap."

The sheer sandstone walls funneled over a cliff. The ethereal orange spire sat across the gap, floating on a bed of fluffy clouds. Kestrel slid to a halt so fast that she stumbled backward and fell to the ground, breathing hard. Between the precipice and the spire lay nothing. Nothing but Darkness. "Sunchaser? Sunchaser, where are you?"

"Call me, Kestrel! Please, keep calling me!"

"Sunchaser? I'm here. Up here, on the cliff. Sunchaser, Sunchaser, Sunchaser . . ."

Kestrel awoke with a start.

Clouds had rolled in and eaten the Star People. Tiny flakes of snow were drifting out of the black. The aspen limbs bore a white coating half a hand thick, as did the hide that covered Kestrel and Cloud Girl. Helper sat beside Sunchaser, his ears pricked, his tail thumping the rock happily.

Kestrel didn't understand until she heard Sunchaser gasp and saw him fall sideways, crumpling like a water bladder punctured with a quill. Helper lurched out of the way with a sharp bark and dove off the rock to slide through the snow on his chin.

"Sunchaser!" Kestrel yelled and scrambled to slip her left arm beneath his head so he wouldn't bash his skull on the granite. His shoulder struck hard; weakly he flopped over onto his back, crushing her left side. His white hair glimmered with snow crystals. He seemed to be breathing, but she wasn't certain of it.

Kestrel wriggled from beneath him and sat up. "Sunchaser? Sunchaser!"

He made feeble swimming motions. "K-Kestrel?"

"Sunchaser, it's snowing. We have to get into the sweat lodge before we freeze to death!"

She slid off the rock, pulled the elk hide up over Cloud Girl's face to shield her from the snow and ran around to the front to help Sunchaser. The mammoth rose, her eyes wide.

"He's all right, Mother," Kestrel assured her. "He's come back to us."

But the cow watched intently as Kestrel helped Sunchaser sit up.

As though mustering his strength, Sunchaser took several deep breaths, then sluggishly swung his legs over the rock's edge and fell into Kestrel's arms. She staggered but managed to hold him up.

The mammoth groaned as though in pain.

"Kestrel . . . wait," he whispered. "Give me just a bit more time."

Sunchaser turned and held the cow's forlorn gaze for several moments before he reached out with a trembling hand. The cow lifted her trunk and touched Sunchaser's fingers lovingly. She curled the tip of her trunk around his wrist, holding it tight.

"Sunchaser," Kestrel said, "you're as cold as ice. I have to get you inside the sweat lodge. We must hurry."

"Just a little longer."

He bent his hand so that he could cup it around the cow's trunk, then raised his other hand to gently stroke her. Kestrel had to brace her feet and wrap her arms securely around Sunchaser's chest to keep him standing. His legs trembled so badly that she feared she couldn't manage it for long. And all the while, Cloud Girl peered at her over a thin horizon of elk hair, as if holding her breath.

Finally Sunchaser let go of the cow's trunk, and his knees went weak.

"Sunchaser! I can't hold you up by myself!"

They both fell to the ground and rolled in the snow. Kestrel came up spitting flakes from her mouth, while Helper bounded around them barking.

"Sunchaser?" She bent over him. "Are you all right?"

Slowly, he lifted himself on his elbows. "I can reach the lodge by myself. Gather the hides, and—"

"Yes. Go on! I'll hurry."

Kestrel climbed back up onto the rock, threw one hide over her shoulders and wrapped Cloud Girl in the other. The baby peered at her gravely, her eyes slitted, mouth pinched. Kestrel carefully eased her way over the slick rock to the ground.

By the time she ducked into the cramped sweat lodge, Sunchaser lay on his side in the rear, breathing as if he had just run a difficult race. She took the hide from around Cloud Girl and put it over him. Then she set Cloud Girl down at Sunchaser's feet.

"I have to gather wood. I'll be right back."

She ducked outside and worked quickly, cracking dead branches from live trees, piling them in the crook of her left arm until she could carry no more. She turned back to the lodge again. Inside, she dropped her wood to the right of the door flap.

Darkness pressed down around her while she felt for the stone hearth and arranged the dry twigs and larger sticks into a pyramid.

"Oh, my pack . . . my fire sticks."

She went out into the snow again. There was now a sheath of white on the rock; she patted it until she found her pack.

She dragged the pack back to the lodge and dug through it for her fire sticks.

Before she even attempted to generate a spark, she felt the roof for the place where the hides overlapped and shoved one slightly to the side, making a smokehole. A few snowflakes sneaked through.

Cold, so cold. Her hands might have been made of wood, and just as clumsy. *Not as bad as after the river crossing,* she reminded herself, and fought a bout of shivering. By feel, she placed her sticks and began to spin the hard wood between her palms. The thought kept going through her head that if Power really wanted to help people, it would find a way of generating fire at a snap of the fingers.

When she finally had a good blaze going, Helper poked his black nose around the door flap and whined.

"Come in, Helper. There's room for you."

The dog ducked beneath the hanging, spied Cloud Girl and went to flop down at the foot of her rabbit-fur sack. He kept his gaze riveted on Kestrel, his dark eyes wide and worried.

"Sunchaser's all right, Helper. Really, he . . ."

But when she turned, she found Sunchaser shivering uncontrollably. He'd rolled to his back and crossed his muscular arms over his chest; his handsome face was twisted with agony. His long legs stuck out beneath the hide from the knees down.

"Sunchaser?"

". . . F-freezing," he murmured through chattering teeth.

Kestrel piled more wood on the fire, then rearranged the elk hide. But it didn't seem to ease his tremors. He continued to shake violently.

"You were out in the cold for so long," Kestrel said. "It will probably take two or three hands of time for you to get really warm. After I'd floated across the Big Spoonwood River, I thought I'd never be warm again."

Sunchaser's breathing came in short gasps, and his stiff fingers clutched desperately at the hide that covered him. His black eyes fluttered open and closed, as though he were half-conscious, and fading fast. When she could see his pupils, she saw that they looked dull and glazed.

Panic struck within her like sparks off of chert. "I'm getting under that hide with you, Sunchaser. Do you hear me? I've got to warm you up fast . . . and I know of only one way."

Kestrel slipped her dress over her head and spread it out over Helper. The dog licked her hand and she patted him. Naked, frightened, she crawled beneath the hide and covered Sunchaser with her body. Cold bumps prickled his skin. At the feel of her flesh against his, he wrapped his arms around her back and hugged her so tight that she could barely breathe. His shivering shook them both.

"Thank you, K-Kestrel," he whispered. "For coming to find me. I was . . . lost. I couldn't have found my way out of that Darkness without you. I'd gotten turned around and so confused that I . . . that's when I started calling to you. I . . . I prayed that you'd be able to f-follow my voice and that together we could backtrack on your trail to find this world again."

Kestrel rested her forehead against his cold cheek and stroked his hair gently. "I thought it was a dream."

A smile curled his lips. "It was. A real Dream. You were on the t-trail that leads to the Land of the Dead."

Kestrel patted his shoulder and sighed. "I never expected that I'd see it until . . ." *Until Lambkill finds me.* "Sleep now, Sunchaser. You're home. You're safe."

"Safe . . ." he whispered. "S-safe."

A hand of time passed before his shivering subsided and his muscles relaxed. With every breath he took, his arms slid down a little more until they rested at his sides.

Kestrel stared at the flames. The tiny lodge had warmed quickly, but she would have to awaken often during the night to add more wood to the fire. If she didn't, they would all be frozen by morning.

Sunchaser's head lolled to the side, and he fell into a deep sleep. His handsome face looked peaceful. Kestrel tightened her hold on him, trying to memorize the sensation of his body against hers, the way his white hair tangled with her black, the warmth of his skin. Deep inside her, a terrible ache grew.

"I'm glad you're back, Sunchaser," she whispered forlornly.

A gust of wind penetrated the door flap, and the flames crackled and spat. One of the branches popped in two, and a lurid flare of crimson light illuminated the sweat lodge.

She closed her eyes and tried to sleep.

Sunchaser awoke in the middle of the night when Kestrel rose to throw wood on the fire. He lay still, watching the red glow on the back of his closed eyelids, feeling her careful movements . . . and her return to him. Her full breasts pressed warmly into his chest. Her thighs rested against his.

He tried to stop the hot flush that ran like fire through his veins, but he couldn't. His physical responses surprised him. First, his heart thundered, then he broke out in a sweat. And finally, against his will, his body began to respond to her closeness. He opened his eyes and found her peering at him worriedly. Her long hair fell around him in a silken curtain.

"Kestrel? I . . ." His voice faded when he saw the tears that welled in her eyes. She looked frightened.

"Are you sure you want this to happen, Sunchaser?"

"I'm not sure of anything anymore, Kestrel."

"But it will endanger your Dreaming, won't it?"

Perhaps it was because he felt so tired and helpless, or because he loved her. A pain tore at his chest, like sharp talons ripping at his soul. The loneliness swelled until it blotted out every other emotion. He needed her more desperately than he had ever needed anything in his life. She had braved the Land of the Dead to come to him when he'd called her. She had warmed him with her body when he'd been freezing. Mammoth Above had guided her to him. His gaze caressed the bluish glints of her hair, the smooth lines of her face, the silken bare skin of her shoulder against his.

"Yes. It probably will, but . . ." He slipped a hand beneath the wealth of her hair. He pulled her face down so he could kiss her gently.

She blinked back her tears. "I love you, Sunchaser, but I don't want to hurt you. The last man who loved me is dead and I—"

"That wasn't your fault." He brushed away the glossy hair that stuck wetly to her cheeks. "No more than this is."

But in the depths of Kestrel's soul, memory of a hoarse voice whispered: *"If I ever find you with another man, I will kill you. You can never run away from me. No one can protect you. I will find you vulnerable someday, and I will kill you."*

Sunchaser put an arm around her shoulders and rolled her over onto her back. He stared down at her.

Kestrel shivered as he tenderly smoothed a hand down her bare side. In his eyes she saw desire . . . and the reflection of her own certainty that this should never happen.

Tannin's steps pounded a steady rhythm against the dragging sand. Lambkill had taken the lead and now he ran three body lengths ahead, his gray braid lashing the back of his soiled buckskin shirt like a whip, driving him ever onward.

Rolling green hills rose to the east, where Dawn Child's golden glow had just touched the tops of the tallest fir trees. To the west, the ocean barely moved. Waves purled softly as they caressed the shore. Coyotes yipped and howled, serenading the new day.

Tannin concentrated on his feet.

Lambkill had been pushing him hard. They had eaten little yesterday, and slept less. They had run through the snow until they'd hit a rocky section of shoreline, where they'd kept tripping and stumbling. Lambkill had reluctantly agreed to stop. Still, Tannin had had barely two hands of rest last night.

Then Lambkill had awakened him long before sunrise. They'd rolled their bedding hides in silence and trotted through the luminous gray world of predawn. Snow had coated the beach, but stars had gleamed over their heads.

Tannin's stomach growled. The hunger took a toll on his strength. He trotted faster, catching up with his brother, but Lambkill didn't even glance over at him; he kept his eyes squinted at the curving shoreline, like a wolf on a fresh blood trail.

"Lambkill?" Tannin said as they ran through the dappled shadows of a copse of trees. The scents of melting snow and dogwood flowers rose strongly. "Let's stop and eat. I'm sure the tidal pools are brimming with snails. Maybe a few abalones."

"You're weak, my brother. You used to be able to run for days on an empty stomach."

"I'm not as young as I used to be, Lambkill."

Lambkill pointed ahead. "We'll stop at the village just over that rise. Someone will offer us food. And we will learn where we are."

"What village?" Tannin shielded his eyes and searched the distance.

"It's there. Believe me. See the tops of those scrubby aspen trees? Near there."

Lambkill picked up the pace, forcing Tannin to run with all his might. He hated running in sand. It ate at his muscles like the poison of the shiny black spiders that lived under rocks. Yes, that was it, poison from dark places.

He couldn't help but stare at his brother's back when that thought twined into his soul.

When they veered around the base of the rise, splashing through the shallows of the sea, the village came into view. Tannin glanced at Lambkill, amazed.

"How did you know it would be here?"

"Simple, brother. Nighthawk said that Whalebeard Village sat exactly three days south of the old Otter Clan Village. I assumed that Nighthawk meant 'at a Trader's pace.' That's why I've been pushing you. I knew that if we ran hard, we could reach it in half that time."

Tannin looked at the village. Fifteen hide lodges sat in a semicircle at the base of a low hill, facing the sea. Three women stood near cook fires, and a few children played at the edge of the water, but only four men lounged on the sand in the plaza. It looked as if they played a shell game, for the man in the center had three clamshells laid out in a line. No laughter carried, nor any strains of conversation or the happy shrieks of children.

Tannin glanced at Lambkill. "This is a somber village, brother. You think they'll know something about Kestrel?"

"We shall see."

When the men in the plaza saw them pounding through the surf, they rose and spoke to one another. One man, short and wearing a frayed, soot-stained bearhide coat, ran toward them, waving his arms.

"What's he saying?" Tannin asked nervously. Terror lined the man's face.

"I don't know."

Then the words reached them: "Go back! Don't come any closer! We have sickness in this village!"

Lambkill grabbed Tannin's sleeve and brought them both to a dead halt at the edge of the waves. Gulls squealed and dove over their heads. The short man walked to within forty hands of them and slowed, his hands held up to stop them. He had an elderly face and white braids.

Lambkill called, "Thank you for warning us! We are looking for a woman."

"What woman?"

"Her name is Kestrel. She's my wife. Young, very pretty. She's traveling with a newborn baby."

The man straightened. "Yes. We have heard of you. You're the marsh-country Trader, aren't you?"

Calmly, Lambkill responded, "I am. Have you seen my wife?"

"No."

"Have you seen any men from the Blackwater Draw Clan? We are supposed to meet them somewhere near here."

The man propped his hands on his hips. "You mean Harrier and his brothers?"

"Yes! That's them. Are they here?"

"No. They came through many days ago, looking for the Otter Clan."

Lambkill's hands clenched into tight fists at his sides, and Tannin's blood started to boom in his ears. "We are also looking for the Otter Clan," Lambkill said. "Where is their new village? Do you know?"

The man hesitated, then he answered, "In the foothills. Two days' walk to the east. Some of our hunters went through their village only days ago. Turn around and go back to the other side of the rise; you will see a trail that winds up through the hills. Their new village is on that trail. You won't be able to miss it."

"Thank you!" Lambkill called and started to back away.

"Wait! Wait, please," the man yelled. He ran ten hands closer. "Please. Have you seen Sunchaser? Or heard of where he is? We need him desperately! We've sent word up and down the trails, but no one has seen him. Have you heard anything?"

"No." Lambkill's face twisted in disgust. "We've heard nothing."

Lambkill trotted by Tannin, but Tannin still stood, unable to leave, holding the man's tortured gaze. The elder wet his lips, and a difficult swallow went down his throat. He lifted a hand in a genial way.

"If you happen to meet Sunchaser," the man called, "please tell him that we need him."

Tannin nodded and backed up two paces. *Sunchaser. Always Sunchaser. Everyone thinks they need him.*

He turned and ran.

Thirty-four

Sunchaser folded the hides that had covered the sweat lodge frame and carefully packed them on Helper's travois. The bent poles of the frame stood naked now, gleaming reddish in the morning sunlight. The aspen leaves rustled softly in the breezes that breathed out of the foothills. Father Sun had just barely chased away the fires of Dawn Child, and purple shadows pooled in every undulation on the beach. Lines of curling breakers rolled endlessly toward the north. Seabirds soared as they called to each other and filled the sky with dark, gliding shapes.

Kestrel laughed as she stepped out of the ocean waves and started back with a hide sack full of mussels.

Sunchaser had been surreptitiously studying her for over half a hand of time while she waded the shallows, collecting breakfast. The size and colors of the mussels seemed to amaze her . . . as they did everyone not native to the coast.

The mussels were almost two hands long and had beautiful violet shells, covered by brown skin. A series of flattened ridges textured the skin. On the inside, the mussels gleamed grayish-white and had two small teeth. They attached themselves to rocks along the tide lines with hairy bundles of fibrous fingers.

Long before Sunchaser had awakened, Kestrel had bathed and then combed her wet hair behind her ears. The style accentuated the perfection of her face and the fullness of her lips. She looked so much like a child but for the scar on her forehead. Tiny and slender, her size and actions belied the strength within. A child? He remembered very well that she had been a woman last night. He tingled just thinking about it.

She swung her sack happily as she walked, Helper trotting at her heels. The seashells on her dress sparkled magnificently. Cloud Girl sat in her rabbit-fur sack across the fire from Sunchaser, half asleep, sucking noisily on her new pack rat–hide pacifier.

Kestrel smiled at Sunchaser. She knelt before the fire and dumped the mussels into the boiling bag on the tripod. Her quick eyes surveyed the campsite and she noted, "It looks like you have everything packed."

She seemed so casual, so calm. But then, she'd had far more experience with mornings after lovemaking than he'd had. He felt awkward and uncertain, his thoughts absorbed by last night's sweetness. He returned her smile. "Almost. After breakfast, we'll need to gather our tools and fill our packs. Then we'll be ready to go."

"But *where* will we go, that's the question."

"Down the beach. Whalebeard Village isn't far. We'll stop there. Perhaps Oxbalm left word of his whereabouts."

Kestrel used two sticks to lift a large hot stone from the edge of the fire. Gingerly, she dropped it into the boiling bag. A violent explosion of steam made her fall backward to the sand, her brown eyes wide. The fracturing of rock sounded as loud and sharp as cracks of thunder. "That rock was much hotter than I thought! I hope it doesn't split the bag!"

"Won't matter. The mussels will be cooked long before the water drains out," he noted evenly.

"They certainly will." Her eyes sparkled as she laughed.

The sound of that childlike amusement warmed something old and cold in his soul. He looked at Kestrel, his whole heart in his eyes. She sat with her hands braced behind her, her hair tumbling wild and tangled over her shoulders. The posture accentuated her enlarged breasts, breasts that had pressed against him in the urgency of their lovemaking.

"You look very beautiful this morning," he said.

She sprang up from the sand and ran to kiss him soundly, then returned to stirring the boiling bag before he could even move. She added two more hot stones to the bag, small ones this time, and gazed at him adoringly.

He smiled and shook his head.

Blessed Spirits, how alien all of this was to him. Oh, he'd loved once. Ten cycles ago. Her name had been Mistletoe, though it surprised him that he could remember. They'd had a passionate relationship for two moons. He'd given Mistletoe every shred of his heart, but she'd demanded his soul. That, he could give to no one. Only Power had claims on his soul. He recalled painfully how he'd sat down with Mistletoe, taken her hands in his and apologized for making promises that he couldn't keep. She'd nearly beaten him to death in rage before she'd run screaming back to her mother's lodge. Good Plume had aptly remarked, "Driving you to Dreaming is probably the only good thing that girl will ever do in her life. Show some gratitude. Forget what a fool she is."

He must have done it. He couldn't even recall clearly what Mistletoe had looked like.

Steam spun a lacy pattern around Kestrel's face. If he lived to be as old as Mother Ocean, he would never forget Kestrel's childlike beauty. "You know," Sunchaser said, "you can't collect those big mussels in the summertime."

"No? Why not?"

"They eat small creatures that make poisons. It doesn't seem to bother the mussels, but the poisons can make a human very sick."

Kestrel's dark, graceful brows drew together. She seemed to consider everything he said with great seriousness. "They don't eat those same creatures in other seasons?"

"I imagine they would if they could, but those tiny animals flourish only in warm weather."

"I must collect the big mussels only in the cool moons," she said, as though to memorize it. "Good. Thank you for telling me. In the marsh country, we don't have such mussels." The smile returned to her face. "I'm sure they're done. Are you ready to eat?"

Kestrel set out their bowls and scooped five mussels into his bowl and three into her own. Rather than handing the bowl straight across to him, she rose and carried it, knelt before him and placed it ceremoniously at his feet, her eyes downcast as though waiting for his approval.

Sunchaser frowned. He put a hand beneath her chin and lifted her face to look into her bright eyes. "I don't know the ways of your people, Kestrel, but you don't have to do this for me. If you were from my clan, I would make no move without your consent. I would go to live in your mother's village. You would own all of my belongings—our lodge, our children, everything except my Healer's bag. I'm allowed sacred things. But only those. My people trace their lineage through the women. Men rule—*after* having their decisions approved by the female elders of the clan."

Eagerly, she said, "Iceplant told me about that. That's why he said I wasn't his cousin."

That fact seemed important to her . . . as though it absolved her from crimes she couldn't bear to face. He sighed silently. He didn't know very many things, at least not in the sphere of human emotions, but he thoroughly understood the anguish of self-accusation. "That's right. Among my people, you and Iceplant would not have been cousins."

Kestrel lowered her eyes to the mussels in his bowl. The boiling water had shrunk the brown skins and revealed the beautiful violet shells beneath. She sat still for a moment. Then she reached out and lifted Sunchaser's right hand, unfolded his fingers and tenderly pressed his palm to her cheek. Her skin felt cool and soft. "You are so kind to me."

"I wasn't being kind, Kestrel. I was being honest."

She kissed his palm and released it. Her young face slackened into grave lines. "Sunchaser, there wasn't time last night, but . . . soon we must talk about the Land of the Dead. When you're ready."

The tone of her voice sent a chill through him. "I'm ready now. What did you want to talk about?"

Kestrel leaned sideways to retrieve her bowl of mussels, then shifted to sit beside him, the wooden bowl in her lap. She used both hands to pry open the first mussel and tug it from the shell. It was steaming hot. "When I came to find you, I heard voices, Sunchaser. I don't know who they were or where they came from, but it's important that I tell you what they said."

"They were the Spirits in your painting, Kestrel. I heard them, too. They helped me to avoid the first trap along the trail."

She looked up, startled. "Is that who they were?"

"That's who they were. Did the Spirits of the painting tell you something they didn't tell me?"

"Well, I . . . I don't know." She bit into her mussel and chewed it slowly. "They said, 'Kestrel, you'll never find Sunchaser if you stay on the trails. They're being witched. You have to fly above them. Tell Sunchaser.' I didn't really understand, but when I leaped over the tangle of trails, I could tell the direction from which you called. I sighted on an orange spire on the horizon. That's how I found you."

Sunchaser felt as though she had just kicked him in the stomach. "*Being witched?* How? I mean, by whom? Who is the witch?"

Kestrel shook her head. "The Spirits didn't tell me. Perhaps they didn't know. But—"

"They always know. They just won't say . . . for their own reasons." He waved a hand apologetically. "I'm sorry. Go on. What else did they say?"

"Nothing. Just that you'd better learn how to fly over the trails."

His face slackened. "I've done that before. Once on the backs of the Thunderbeings. Another time with the help of Grandmother Condor." He clenched a fist. "But they took me only because they thought I was dead."

Kestrel stopped in mid-chew. "Dead?"

His eyes squinted at the memory. "The first time, I'd been Dreaming for so long that Good Plume had pronounced me dead. She couldn't find my heartbeat, so she prepared my body for burial and called to the Thunderbeings to come for my soul. And they did. That's how I reached Wolfdreamer's Lodge of Light."

"And that's when he gave you the maze?"

Sunchaser nodded. "Yes. So I could find him again— without the Thunderbeings' help."

"Then why would the Spirits tell you that you had to fly?"

"They must mean that I can't counter the witching, that the maze is useless now." He sat back, stunned. "Ordinarily, witches are easy to identify, and all you have to do is threaten them to make them stop. I've never even had to battle one." A chill, colder than ice floating in a winter river, settled on his heart—the same heart that had been so happy just a moment before. "Perhaps the time has come."

Kestrel's eyes seemed to darken, to expand in her small face. "This must be a Powerful witch, Sunchaser. I could see the tangle of trails. They coiled and knotted, and some even spun off and led nowhere."

"But I can't think of anyone who would want to . . ." His soul sped back to the day of the mammoths' attack on Otter Clan Village—and a shrill, triumphant cry. "*Catchstraw?* No. No, it couldn't be. He's not that Powerful . . . or that malicious. Is he?"

"Who?"

"He's a Dreamer. At least he claims to be. From the Otter Clan."

"Sunchaser," Kestrel's voice had gone serious, "do not let my words anger you, but you don't seem to realize the extent to which humans can enfold evil into their souls. You love everyone, and everything. Suspicion isn't part of your nature. I've learned, firsthand, about hatred, and about how deep the human soul can sink. Think. Could Catchstraw be a witch?"

"He's the only person who might want to stop me from entering the Land of the Dead. He has always resented me."

Sunchaser balled a fist against the emotions that cramped his belly. His mouth had become a hard line. How could the day that had begun so wonderfully have descended so quickly to these dark depths? A rage possessed him that he had not felt in cycles. How stupid he had been! It had never even occurred to him that his problems might have sprung from witching. For cycles, he had defended Catchstraw! As he would have defended any Dreamer. He knew how many demands Power made. He would never condemn someone unless he had substantial evidence.

Blind! I've believed in the good sides of people. And doing so has left me in darkness as black as if I'd burned my eyes out.

Kestrel continued. "Maybe it isn't this Catchstraw, Sunchaser. Maybe it's someone else. Even if Catchstraw resents you, why would he want to stop you from entering the Land of the Dead when he knows that the survival of mammoths depends upon you? And Dreamers do know such things, don't they?"

"Maybe he thinks he can do it himself." Sunchaser shoved his bowl of mussels aside, no longer hungry. He braced his elbows on his knees and dropped his head into his hands. "I'd gladly yield to him if I thought he could. I don't know why Power works the way it does—choosing one Dreamer instead of ten or tens of tens."

"Perhaps Power has limitations, too."

He lifted his head. Kestrel's wide, innocent eyes concealed a perceptive soul. "How strange that you understand that. Most people think that Power can do anything it wants to. It can't, of course. The Spirits groom Dreamers very carefully, preparing them for the final desperate moments of a certain age. But not even they can force the world to be what they want it to be, what they know it needs to be."

"My grandmother told me once that Power has to start very early if it wants to affect a person's life. It must begin with a child—"

"Yes, with the child, and work persistently on shaping the adult for its own purposes. Dreamers are tools—nothing more, nothing less." Did he really believe that? That Power cared nothing about the Dreamer? No, he didn't . . . not really. He knew that Above-Old-Man and Mother Ocean worried about him constantly. And he could sense Wolfdreamer and Mammoth Above working for him all the time, helping him, encouraging him.

"Resentment is a festering thing. It eats at the soul, turns it black and ugly. Just as it's done with Lambkill." Kestrel slowly finished her last mussel and watched the morning brighten over Mother Ocean.

She looked sad, thoughtful. Giant croaking buzzards flapped sluggishly above the water, hunting the shallows for marine creatures washed up by the high tide last night. Their black wings flashed with the echoes of dawn's lavender gleam. Far out in the distance, a whale blew, and a pillar of water fountained up. Sunchaser's eyes narrowed at the calm beauty. The scents of the sea, the drying kelp, fish and dew-soaked ferns pervaded the air.

"Sunchaser, why do you think Power always demands so much of its chosen Dreamers?"

"Because," he answered through a taut exhalation, "salvation can be bought only with the price of the soul. But we should thank Above-Old-Man, Kestrel, that it can be bought at all."

For an instant, her eyes glowed. He noted the way she clenched her hands in her lap. Sunchaser forced himself to pry open one of the mussels in his bowl and choke it down. They had a long walk ahead of them, and he'd developed the urge to run all the way. He managed to eat two more mussels and fed the last two to Helper.

"Sunchaser, tell me about Catchstraw. What's he like?"

"He's an old fool." How could he have said that? The words had slipped from his tongue before he'd suspected their presence. He didn't even know for certain that Catchstraw was the witch. *I'm starting to sound like a sullen boy.*

"A fool? Yet the Otter Clan believes he's a real Dreamer?"

"Some of them do. Maybe all of them. I don't know."

Silence fell. Kestrel bit her lip nervously and fit the mussel shells in her bowl back together, arranging them with care. They clattered when they fell apart.

Sunchaser gestured helplessly. "Catchstraw led the Mammoth Spirit Dances while I was in the mountains, Healing. I heard that he was always the first one to fall out of the Dance circle." *What's the matter with you? What difference does any of this make?* "His dedication to Mammoth Above lasts only as long as his comfort."

"So he's not much of a Dreamer."

"No. Not much of one." *Mother Ocean, make me stop this! I'm making a fool of myself.* "Kestrel," he said in a strained voice, "I think we should be going."

He rose, feeling sick to his stomach. As he passed her, he put a hand on her shoulder, tenderly, and went to stuff more things into his pack.

Kestrel shifted to look at him. "If it turns out that this Catchstraw is the witch, can you stop him?"

Sunchaser picked up a tiny colored basket, the one he had placed the ants in. "Yes, if the time comes." Anger seared his veins again. He closed his eyes, trying to kill its Power. "Dreamers know very well how to fight fire with fire. We just hate to have to do it. It takes a great deal of Power. Power better spent trying to mend an out-of-balance world." Brutally, he jammed the basket into his pack.

Oxbalm hobbled through the trees behind Horseweed. His knees ached with a fiery intensity. The cold in these mountains ate at his bones like a starving coyote. He shoved a smoke-tree branch laden with dark blue blossoms out of his way and stepped over a fallen log.

"Here it is, Grandfather," Horseweed whispered as he knelt by a slab of weathered granite.

Oxbalm did not even have to bend over. He stood breathing hard, logging the details of the perverted maze. Catchstraw had taken special pains to make his artistry perfect. He'd used crushed charcoal and red sandstone. Black lines curled and wove about, enmeshing red spirals until they strangled for lack of Spiritual direction. On the periphery of the maze, condor feathers lay scattered on the ground. It was as if one of the great birds had been captured here and killed. But no blood marred the stone. "He's not even bothering to erase his mazes anymore."

"No," Horseweed replied. His nostrils flared with repugnance. He'd left his long black hair loose. It fluttered in the chill breeze. He stood and shoved his hands into the pockets of his buckskin coat. "He's grown arrogant, Grandfather. And careless."

Oxbalm nodded. "We must not wait any longer. Sunchaser is in grave danger. At least one of the elders of the clan must be made aware of this now, before it's too late. Find Dizzy Seal. And your grandmother. Bring them here. I want them to see this obscene maze—and the condor feathers—with their own eyes. We will need their support to end this madness. But . . ." He lifted a warning hand. Horseweed held his gaze. "Let no one else know what you're doing."

Horseweed murmured, "Yes, Grandfather," and hurried away through the forest.

Oxbalm peered down at the tangled lines. No human could make sense of them. And what of the condor feathers? How had they gotten here? A shudder went up his spine. Fragments of stories he'd heard long, long ago drifted through his thoughts . . .

"It's old Cactus Lizard! I'm telling you the truth. He turns himself into a short-faced bear at night. He's the one causing this. . . . No, it's not Cactus Lizard. Wounded Bull is the witch. Listen to me! I found a thick pile of lion fur in his lodge. He's shed his human skin and grown the hide of a lion! He roams the shore at dusk, hunting for humans to eat. That's where all the children have disappeared to. It's not the saber-toothed cats coming into the village at night! . . . Don't you see?"

Oxbalm hobbled over to sit down on a nearby rock. Songbirds filled the trees, but none sang. They sat motionless, peering down at him with gleaming eyes.

Oxbalm squinted warily at the sky, then muttered to himself. "Is that what Catchstraw has done? Turned himself into a witch? It would be just like him. He couldn't Dream, so he took the coward's way out. Started using Power for his own ends, instead of letting Power use him to accomplish good things in the world."

Oxbalm shook his head violently, as if the action would cast off the horrible possibilities. "The old fool. If he's hurt Sunchaser, everyone for a ten-day walk will come running just to drive a dart through him."

Yes, it could happen just that way. Old age could be such a curse. Eventually one had seen so much, so often, that everything seemed clear, the facts etched as precisely as quartz crystals. "But I'll be the first to pierce your heart, Catchstraw. I promise you that."

Thirty-five

Sunchaser and Kestrel walked side by side down the beach. Angry surf battered the shore, pounding waves that drove white, foaming sheets racing up the dark sand. Beyond the breakers, the sea chopped up and down, gray and brooding like the sky. Clouds had begun moving in at dawn, and by noon, they had swallowed the blue of Sky Boy's belly. A chill rode the wind, one cool enough to echo the cold within his soul.

Sunchaser pulled up the collar of his moosehide coat. Ahead of them, an eroded hill sloped down to the shore. Twisted firs grew thickly on the crest and dotted the rocky flanks. On the other side of the hill, the branches of a few scraggly aspens thrust up, their pale green leaves trembling in the wind.

"Will they follow us all the way to Otter Clan Village?" Kestrel asked, looking over her shoulder. Her black hair swept around and netted her face.

Sunchaser frowned at the mammoth cow and her calf plodding silently at the fringe of the water. The mammoths had emerged from the trees just after he and Kestrel had left their old camp and had fallen into line behind them. The calf held on to his mother's tail with his trunk. "I don't know. I guess we'll find out."

"I'd like that," Kestrel said and smiled.

"Would you?"

"Oh, yes. I never feel whole unless there are animals close by."

"It is said by the wise ones that it's only through the eyes of animals that we see ourselves correctly . . . as we really are. Because animals see a person's soul, unlike humans, who often see only the body."

Kestrel snugged Cloud Girl closer to her breast, turning slightly to shield the infant from a sudden gust that carried spray off the water. Her eyes narrowed, as if lost in thought.

Sunchaser pointed. "Whalebeard Village is just around the base of that hill, Kestrel."

Helper trotted at Sunchaser's right side, hauling the travois effortlessly, though his tongue hung out. His hair had grown back in a thin black wealth. The fur made his nose seem longer, his ears more pointed. He looked strikingly like a wolf, but pale tan fur encircled his eyes and was the only light color on his entire body. His tail had become a dark bush.

Kestrel lifted a hand to hold her fluttering hair out of her eyes while she scrutinized the hill. Cloud Girl awoke and blinked at the world from her sack. "Whalebeard Village?" Kestrel asked.

"Yes. I haven't been here in two cycles, but the leader used to be a man named Woodtick."

"So his wife will be the clan matron. Is that right? And she and her sisters will be the owners of the village?"

"You're learning very quickly. Yes, that's the way it works here on the coast. And when those women die, their daughters will take over the administration of the lodges and the clam-collecting beds. They will also inherit the possessions of the dead women."

Kestrel shook her head in amazement. "It's so different from the ways of my people. Men own and rule everything in my clan. A woman has nothing of her own. I don't know if I'll ever get used to the laws of the sea people."

Sunchaser smiled, and when she smiled back at him, his throat tightened. He reached out and clasped her hand, twining his fingers with hers. Her touch reassured something deep down in his soul. "Yes, you will. It won't take long. I'll bet that you understand almost everything within three or four moons. This way is easier, you see. And it makes sense. People don't fight over which family gets what if a man and woman decide they don't like each other anymore. No one fights over the shellfish beds, or the root grounds."

"What will be hard for me, Sunchaser? Are there some things that are very complicated?"

"A few. For example, kinship and how it affects social relationships are difficult. I've lived for over twenty-five summers and still don't fully understand the way kinship works. But as a man, I'm not supposed to. Kinship and property, those things are the province of women. Political alliances are established based upon the economic advantages to be gained. In other words, you won't just marry Cloud Girl to any man who comes along and takes a fancy to her. He'll be someone who will advance the interests of the Otter Clan."

She swung his hand happily. "But what if she chooses someone who won't advance the clan's interests?"

Sunchaser laughed. "She won't. Cloud Girl is your daughter and therefore she will know where her duties lie."

Kestrel tipped her face to the cool breeze and let it wash her tanned skin. Sunchaser's gaze caressed every line, every tiny imperfection. A faint scar created a white ridge near her right ear. Another zigzagged down the side of her throat. Both of them were barely visible. And she had the healed scar that slashed her forehead. He knew how she'd gotten that one. But he wondered about the others. Childhood accidents? Or the legacies of Lambkill's rage? The thought of someone hurting her made his blood rise hotly. He prayed he never had the misfortune to meet Lambkill. He couldn't guarantee that he would behave in the dignified manner required of a Dreamer. Last night, he'd dreamed that he'd torn Lambkill to pieces with his bare hands. And he'd felt good about it, which worried him a little.

They rounded the base of the hill, and Whalebeard Village came into view. On the leeward side of the hill, more than a dozen lodges clustered in a crescent, facing the roaring waves of Mother Ocean. A flock of gulls swooped and dove above the lodges, squealing and cawing.

Sunchaser frowned. No one was outside. On such a pleasant day, children should be playing in the sand, men gambling in front of the lodges and women weaving fishing nets from yucca cordage. The fire hearth in the central plaza had burned down to nothing. Only the heaviest of the dead coals had survived the wind. They'd rolled into a pile against the eastern edge of the hearth.

"Kestrel," Sunchaser said apprehensively when they neared the first lodge, "wait for me here. Something's wrong. I don't know what, but I'd feel better if you didn't come with me."

Kestrel studied him with worried eyes. Yes, she, too, sensed danger in the ominous quiet. "I'll wait over there by the aspen trees, Sunchaser."

"I'll be back when I know what's happened."

His moccasins dug into the soft sand as he walked forward calling, "Woodtick? Shining Hunter Woman? *Anybody? Where is everyone?*"

A little old man, as frail as a stalk of winter thistle, ducked through a lodge door. He squinted, then made a deep-throated sound of surprised joy before running forward. He'd tied his short gray hair into a braid that hung down his back. His doeskin shirt and pants bore sweat stains and splatters of blood.

"Sunchaser? Oh, Blessed Spirits. We've been praying for you to come!" He grabbed Sunchaser around the waist and hugged him frantically. "We've been so desperate, Sunchaser. More than twenty people have died. Even . . ." tears brimmed in the faded old eyes ". . . even my beloved Shining Hunter."

Sunchaser held the old man tightly and let him weep. "I didn't know you had illness here, Woodtick, or I would have come long before now."

The old man pushed away and stared up through his misery. "But you're here now. Bless the Spirits. I can't tell you how glad I am to see you."

"Tell me about the sickness."

Sunchaser linked his arm through Woodtick's to support the frail elder, and together they walked toward the cold hearth in the plaza. A stack of wood sat by the stone circle. It looked untouched. As they walked past the lodges, Sunchaser heard soft cries and groans. Odors of urine and vomit drifted out to him.

Woodtick held Sunchaser's arm tightly. "This must be the same sickness that attacked the mountain villages, Sunchaser. High fever. People have been bleeding from the mouth. The little children . . ." His voice broke. "The children, they just seem to shrink and disappear before our eyes. We have only twelve people left in the entire village!"

Sunchaser paled. Whalebeard Village had numbered thirty-five the last time he had been here. "Let me get my Healer's pack. Then take me through the lodges so I can identify the sickest people. I know how this illness works. If there's anyone who has been sick for three days—"

"Several people." Woodtick squeezed his arm even more desperately. "But Little Sage and her son, Four Darts, are two of the worst. They live in the last lodge." He lifted a trembling arm and pointed.

Sunchaser nodded. "Wait for me there. I'll be right back."

He released Woodtick's arm and ran, the deep sand eating at his muscles, to where Kestrel stood in the aspen grove. She had already begun unloading Helper's travois, stacking hides, separating Sunchaser's things from hers. Sunchaser grabbed his Healer's pack from the ground. "Kestrel, please, don't come into the village. Stay here. There's sickness. I've seen it before, and it's deadly. I don't want to take any chances with you or Cloud Girl. I'll be back soon . . . no, maybe not until tomorrow. But—"

"Don't waste time telling me about it, Sunchaser. Go to them." Worry lined her pretty face. "I'll set up the lodge, build a fire and wait for you. Help as many people as you can."

He hugged her to him, hard, then backed away and trotted across the sand to the southernmost lodge. Woodtick stood before it. A large structure, it spread four body lengths long and three wide. The exterior looked poorly tended. The red and blue geometric designs had faded badly.

"Hurry," Woodtick pleaded. "Please, hurry!"

The chief held the door flap open, and Sunchaser ducked through into darkness. The odors of excrement and sweating bodies nearly suffocated him. The fire in the center of the floor had burned down to white ashes. As his eyes adjusted, he made out the loops of cordage attached by thongs to the back wall, and the brightly colored nut baskets hung from the ridgepole. The sweet fragrance of buckeye meal drifted from the closest basket. On the log that held down the long northern wall lay a few shell spoons and bowls, some bark platters inlaid with haliotis shell, a wooden stirrer and several soapstone pipes worked into the shapes of sea mammals.

There were three people in the lodge: two women and a little boy. The only one well enough to greet him was an old woman wearing a dress covered with magnificent quillwork; blue, yellow and white wavy lines decorated her chest and the hem of her dress—but the garment was filthy. Gray hair hung in damp straggles around her flabby face. She rose slowly and tottered forward.

"Sunchaser," she whispered reverently. Her fingers twined in the fringes on his sleeves, holding on to him as though she feared he might vanish at any moment. "I am Falcontail. This is my daughter, Little Sage." She held out her hand to the young woman shivering beneath the mound of hides on the far side of the lodge. A little boy lay at her feet. In the gloom, Sunchaser could make out only their pale faces. "And this is my grandson, Four Darts."

The boy looked worse than his mother. His eyes rolled aimlessly and his skin had a mottled flush. He moved his lips in soundless words.

"How old is Four Darts?" Sunchaser asked as he went to kneel by the boy's side. He pulled back the heavy hides and put a cool hand on Four Darts's bare chest. The flesh was very hot.

Falcontail's withered face tensed. "Three summers. He's . . . he's the only grandchild I have left." She stifled her cries by covering her mouth with a translucent elderly hand.

"He's going to be all right, Falcontail," Sunchaser promised. "I'm sure of it. I've seen many of these cases before. Power can heal him."

The old woman dropped her face in her hands and wept openly.

Sunchaser unlaced his pack and removed his abalone shell, his otter pipe and the white stone cut from the foot of Great White Giant. He arranged them in a row at the boy's side. Then he drew out a small sack filled with a mixture of dried willow bark and poplar buds.

"Falcontail? I'll need your help."

She hurried to his side, her eyes wide and still shining with tears. Red flushed the high arch of her cheekbones. "Anything, Sunchaser. What do you need me to do?"

He held up the sack. "Could you boil some water and throw the contents of this sack in? When the water has boiled down to a milky fluid, we'll start giving it to Four Darts and Little Sage. It will bring down their fevers."

Falcontail took the sack and hobbled quickly across the lodge to collect a soapstone bowl. She set it beside the fire hearth while she used a stick to dig around in the white ash, looking for a hot ember. She scraped all the cold coals to the side and mounded the ones that glowed in the center of the hearth, then added kindling. Fire crackled, and the little flames threw a wavering orange halo over the interior of the lodge. Falcontail added more wood to the flames. Sunchaser's eyes took in the faded paintings on the walls: Above-Old-Man with his single eye open wide and shining silver, followed by different shades of red crescents, until Above-Old-Man's eye closed completely and a black circle stood silhouetted against a charcoal-gray background.

Such beautiful, painstaking work. He wished that Kestrel could see it. He could imagine her face, soft and smiling. Her expression always became tender when she looked upon careful artistry.

"Sunchaser?" Woodtick called from the door, where he stood anxiously. He wore a pinched expression. "Is there something I can do to help you?"

"Yes, please go and ask Kestrel, the woman I'm traveling with, to gather more willow bark and poplar buds for me. She'll know the kinds I need. But, Woodtick, I'm worried about her and her baby. Could you make sure that she doesn't come near the lodges? The baby is so tiny, and Kestrel—"

At the concerned tone in Sunchaser's voice, Woodtick smiled. "Yes, I understand. I'll make sure. I'll go right now." He started to duck beneath the door flap, but stopped and wet his lips before he slowly straightened up. "Did you . . . did you say her name was *Kestrel*?"

Sunchaser had so absorbed himself in preparing Four Darts for the Healing ceremony, throwing off the boy's hides, brushing his hair back, that he didn't notice the chief's horrified tone. "Yes. She's setting up our camp in the aspen grove to the east of the village. Hurry, Woodtick. Everyone who is feverish will need this willow-and-poplar tea. It would be best if we could hang a large boiling bag over the plaza fire pit. That way, anyone who needs it can get to it quickly."

Woodtick swallowed hard. He jerked a nod. His voice came out soft, hesitant. "Yes. I'll . . . I'll tell . . . Kestrel." He ducked beneath the lodge door flap and his moccasins patted softly against the sand as he broke into a painful trot.

As Kestrel knelt in the cool shadows of the aspens, filling her gut bag from the spring that bubbled up clear and cold through a crevice in the rock, she saw Woodtick coming. Young aspens, willows and an array of ferns and mint clustered thickly around her. She had yet to slip Cloud Girl's sack from her back, and her daughter piped shrilly at the sight of the old man running across the sand. Back at the camp, Helper barked and wagged his tail. But he stayed there, on guard, as Kestrel had told him to.

"Shh," Kestrel said to Cloud Girl. Reaching around and gripping her daughter's tiny hand, she stood up. Cloud Girl hushed, and Kestrel tightened the strings on the water bag, then draped it over her right forearm.

The chief trudged wearily toward her, panting, his elderly face running with sweat, and she could see the bloodstains on his doeskin shirt.

"Kestrel?" he called. "Sunchaser . . ." he breathed hard ". . . he needs you to gather fever plants for him!"

Her brows drew together. She trotted forward. "Which fever plants?"

"No, stop!" Woodtick ordered, throwing out a hand. "Don't get close to me. Please. I may carry the Evil Spirits of the sickness." He bent forward and propped his hands on his knees to take several deep breaths. His gray braid fell forward, partly obscuring his wrinkled face.

"*Which* fever plants, Woodtick?"

He straightened up. "Poplar buds and willow bark. If you can gather them and leave them near the plaza fire pit—" he flung out his skinny old arm to point "—I'll get them and put them in the boiling bag."

"Yes. All right," she replied. "I'll hurry!"

Woodtick's frightened face slackened when Kestrel immediately hung her water bag on an aspen branch and fell to her knees before a thick tangle of willow. She drew her chert scraper from the pack around her waist and began sawing the red stems in two.

Woodtick's faint smile contained more gratitude than Kestrel had ever received in her life. She hastily gathered the willow stems and ran around the spring to a cluster of young aspen saplings. She trimmed off several of the newest buds. She didn't know why, but aspen, willow and poplar seemed to have the same ability to bring down fever.

Woodtick cupped a hand to his mouth and shouted, "I'll wait for you by the fire pit!"

"I'll be there soon!"

He nodded and trotted unsteadily back toward the village. His aged legs wobbled with fatigue, and perhaps with the stress of tending ill relatives.

Kestrel turned back to the saplings. "Oh, Cloud Girl, I wonder how much Sunchaser needs. From the number of lodges, there must be thirty or forty people who live here. But not all of them will be sick—and I don't know how long the illness has been going on." She frowned. "I'll assume that he needs at least enough for twenty people tonight. Then I'll gather more tomorrow morning."

When she'd trimmed off enough aspen buds, she stuffed them into her pack and returned to their camp in the tall grove. White trunks created a dense fortress around her. Over her head, the triangular leaves trembled and rustled. She sat cross-legged by the pile of hides and pulled out her chert scraper to strip the willow stems. She peeled off the red outer bark and isolated the white strips of fibrous inner bark.

Cloud Girl cooed and blew bubbles over Kestrel's shoulder. She twisted to look at her daughter, and Cloud Girl smiled broadly.

"How lucky you are to be a baby," Kestrel told her. "You don't understand how sad being here is. These people are desperate. Did you see the way Woodtick grabbed Sunchaser? He looked as though he'd just seen his Spirit Helper in the flesh. But everyone feels that way about Sunchaser. He's the only man in the world who gives every ounce of his soul to everyone who needs him. I don't think he can say 'no.' Not when he knows people need him."

Kestrel's brows drew together as she emptied her pack on the sand and filled it with the strips of willow bark and the aspen buds.

Helper sat on the other side of the pile of hides, watching her. His warm brown eyes glowed.

"I'll be back in a little while, Helper. Stay and guard."

She rose and trotted across the deep sand, sinking up to her ankles. Shimmering grains flooded over the tops of her moccasins and ate their way down inside to grate against the pads of her toes. If she'd been running on hard dirt or stone, it would have hurt. But in the sand, the grains only irritated her sweaty feet.

When she ran past the first lodge, she could hear cries and coughs . . . and Sunchaser's deep voice. He was chanting the Healing Song. The lilting notes floated above the sounds of suffering like bright jewels suspended on a warm breeze.

Kestrel knelt before the plaza fire pit and emptied her pack onto one of the flat stones that formed the fire ring. She rose to her feet.

"Woodtick?" she called.

The old chief ducked through the flap of the southernmost lodge, and Sunchaser's voice grew louder for a moment. Kestrel caught a glimpse of him, kneeling, his white hair glinting in firelight, before the flap fell closed and Woodtick hobbled forward.

"Let me know when Sunchaser needs more."

The old man nodded. "Thank you, Kestrel, I will." He lifted a hand appreciatively.

Kestrel turned and trudged back toward their camp in the aspens. Now to make a shelter. Helper wagged his tail and bounded around as she approached. She bent down and scratched his ears.

Helper trotted at her heels as she walked through the dappled shadows of the trees. Back at their camp, she crouched to untie the pack of hides, secured with a thick length of yucca twine, then took the length of twine and tied it to two trees. One by one, she threw hides over the twine to make a tent. Not as secure as a lodge, it would do for temporary housing. She prayed no storm winds ravaged the beach tonight.

Kestrel went to the spring and loaded her arms with stones, while Helper bounded around, jumping over deadfall and barking gleefully. When she headed back toward camp, he grabbed a rock in his mouth and sprinted after her. She placed the rocks around the base of the hides to hold them down.

"Well," she said with a sigh, "we should start a fire and make some tea."

Kestrel lay asleep, fully clothed, on top of a soft pile of hides when Sunchaser's voice woke her. "I don't know, Woodtick. I wish I did. Then I could change it."

Kestrel rolled onto her back. Darkness cloaked the world. Her fire had burned down to a bed of brilliant scarlet coals.

She had threaded short lengths of leather through the roof twine, to which she'd attached Sunchaser's precious baskets of Dreamer's herbs, her pack and Cloud Girl's rabbit-fur sack, to keep them from being chewed by hungry rodents. They gleamed with a reddish hue.

"I don't understand why Mother Ocean is doing this to us," Woodtick lamented. "Our clan has been faithful. Why would she curse us with this calamity?"

"It's hard to understand the ways of the Spirits, Woodtick."

Kestrel nuzzled her cheek into the soft elk hide. Cloud Girl lay beside her, her tiny face gleaming in the carnelian light cast by the coals. Kestrel ached for Woodtick. What if she lost Cloud Girl, as Woodtick had lost members of his family to this illness? The grief would devour Kestrel's soul. Gently, she folded a corner of the hide over her daughter's pale little body. Cloud Girl whimpered sleepily but didn't awaken. She had grown thick black hair. It hung over her ears like strands of midnight-colored silk.

"But, Sunchaser," Woodtick said in a choking voice, "if you can't Heal my people, who can? What hope is there?"

Sunchaser's moccasins scuffed the sand uneasily. A weak gust of wind buffeted the tent's walls, making them puff in and out, as though taking a deep breath and letting it go.

"I'll try again tomorrow, Woodtick. Get some rest. You need it very badly. There's nothing more you can do tonight."

"Yes, Sunchaser," Woodtick said faintly. Then he added, "You asked earlier where Oxbalm had taken the Otter Clan. We were so busy, I didn't have a chance to answer. They're in the foothills. If you take the trail that splits off on the northern side of the hill, you'll find them."

"Thank you, old friend. We'll go in a few days—after your village is well again."

"Sunchaser . . ." Woodtick hesitated. "About the woman you're with . . . this Kestrel. Who is she?"

Kestrel dug her fingers into the sandy soil beneath her. The sounds of the evening filled the pause; waves crashed and wind rustled through the aspen leaves. Cloud Girl's soft breathing seemed thunderous.

"Don't worry about Kestrel, Woodtick. Some Dreamers can get along just fine with women in their lives. I'm one of those. Please, don't worry. Go to sleep. You must get some rest."

Softly, Woodtick responded, "And you, too, Sunchaser. Let's . . . I want to talk with you more tomorrow. About Kestrel."

"Yes. We'll do that. Good night."

Kestrel heard the sound of steps retreating. The tent flap opened and moonlight flooded inside as Sunchaser ducked through. The rhythmic chorus of Mother Ocean intensified, then hushed when the flap dropped.

Sunchaser looked at her through weary eyes. Sweat glued wisps of white hair to his temples.

"Hello, Sunchaser. How are things in the village?"

He shook his head. "Worse than I want to admit." The lines around his black eyes deepened as he lowered his head and sighed.

"Well, there's nothing more you can do tonight. You need to sleep, Sunchaser." She lifted Cloud Girl's sleeping body and moved her to the other side of the tent, behind her, then scooted over to make room for Sunchaser.

He threw more wood on the coals and removed his garments, piling them by the fire pit. Kestrel knew he'd done that so his clothing would be warm in case he needed to put it on again in the middle of the night.

Sunchaser stretched his tall body out beside her where she lay on the hides. He leaned his head sideways to rest his chin against her hair.

When he didn't speak, she asked, "Sunchaser, how many did you Heal today?"

"None."

Kestrel looked at him. He stared unblinking at the ceiling, white-lipped and silent. He began unbraiding his hair.

"You just arrived," she soothed. "Tomorrow—"

":What's wrong with me, Kestrel?" he whispered. His face tensed painfully. "I used to be able to Heal people. Why can't I do it now?"

Kestrel wrapped her arms around him, holding him. "You're exhausted. Wait. Tomorrow you'll be able to Heal, once you've had a good night's rest."

He ran a hand tenderly down her throat, but his voice sounded flat, as dry as dust. "Kestrel, I . . . everyone I touched today . . . they died."

When Kestrel glanced sharply at him, he withdrew his hand and clenched it into a fist over his heart. He turned his face away to stare blindly at the pile of firewood she'd gathered and stacked by the entry. The low flickers of the fire gave his taut face a curiously ethereal quality.

Her heart sank as she remembered where she had seen that look of hopelessness and desperation before: in the eyes of a dying man. Outside, a cool gust of wind rustled through the aspens and carried the sounds of misery from the village. A baby cried and cried . . .

Wrenching grief filtered through her. In an attempt to soothe herself and him, Kestrel braced herself on one elbow and kissed Sunchaser with all the urgency she could summon.

He looked at her in uncanny understanding—almost as though he had been there that day, had been standing beside her when she'd gazed into Iceplant's living eyes for the last time.

Sunchaser returned her kiss, his lips moving softly at first, as if to comfort her, but it quickly became more than that. He kissed her so passionately that all other concerns vanished from her thoughts. Accustomed to his usual leisurely gentleness, she froze when he roughly pulled her dress over her head and tossed it over by the door flap. He rolled her onto her back and caressed her body hungrily.

"Oh, Kestrel, I love you so much," he murmured.

He made furious love to her.

While her body responded to his frantic need, her soul echoed: "I used to be able to Heal . . . why can't I do it now? . . . What's wrong with me? . . . Kestrel, I love you . . . love you so much."

Helper nosed the door flap aside and entered the tent. He met and held Kestrel's gaze, then went to flop down on Sunchaser's shirt by the fire. He watched her through wide, glistening eyes. In them, she saw deep sadness.

Thirty-six

Sunchaser woke before dawn the next morning. He blinked wearily in the graying darkness. The futility hadn't fled in the night. Today he would have to try that much harder, give that much more of himself—and he couldn't be sure that he had enough left to do what he had to.

He turned his head, seeking Kestrel, and found her gone. He shoved away the hide that covered him and blinked again at the dimness. "Kestrel?"

She had probably gone out to scour the tidal pools for breakfast. He rolled onto his side, aware of the soreness in his groin, the ache in his testicles. The discomfort brought warm memories of the pulsing release he'd experienced.

But if he ached, how did she feel? Shame flushed his cheeks. She was such a tiny woman. Had he hurt her?

He reached up and pulled the tent flap back to look outside. Mother Ocean moved with a tarnished silver glow. Already, gulls hunted the water, diving and squealing, their wings flashing in the lingering glory of the Star People. He scanned the beach. The black silhouettes of the mammoth cow and her calf lay bedded down at the base of the hill, as though to keep watch on the trail. The cow's huge head was up, staring at his tent.

Sunchaser let the flap fall closed and rolled onto his back again. Where could Kestrel be? She might have gone around the hill to search the pools of the inlet. Yes, that would make sense. A wealth of clams, crabs and mussels lived there.

Helper peered at him across the dead fire. The dog blended with the darkness; only the pale fur around his eyes showed.

"Good morning, Helper. Where's Kestrel?"

The dog propped his chin on his paws.

"Did I hurt her last night, Helper? Where is she? I—I didn't mean to. I just felt so desperate."

Sunchaser sat up and tugged his clothes out from beneath Helper, slipped his shirt over his head and pulled on his pants. His nerves had begun to tingle as if they'd been flayed. Using a stick from the pile of firewood, he rolled together a few red coals and steepled several dry twigs over the top of them. Flames danced to life. In the tawny gleam, he noticed that Kestrel had taken Cloud Girl with her. She often took her daughter, so she could talk to her while she combed the shore. But her pack and a single deerhide were also missing from their place in the back corner.

Sunchaser hesitated, a thoughtful gaze on the spot where Cloud Girl had been. *No, she wouldn't . . .*

He hurriedly tied on his moccasins and lunged to his feet, shoved the door flap aside and trotted across the sand toward the mammoth cow and her calf. They watched him quietly, unmoving.

"Kestrel?" he called. "*Kestrel!*"

He headed north toward the shallow inlet. The eastern foothills rose like dark swells of water. Above them, the faint bluish gleam of Dawn Child lit the heavens, dimming the twinkle of the Star People. The trail that led to the new Otter Clan Village shone clearly, a pale streak through the black trees. She wouldn't have gone on without him, would she? It was too dangerous.

"Kestrel!"

He ran beside the ebbing water until he panted, but no human form showed in the false dawn. The retreating surf flooded the shore and contracted into the whispering waves. He turned back and sprinted southward. His moccasins left pockmarks in the damp sand.

She'd tensed when he'd taken her last night. In his desperation, he hadn't cared that she'd gone rigid. Only later had she responded to his movements.

You're no better than Lambkill! The thought burned within him. Lambkill had probably treated her that way—frantic about his own needs, unconcerned with hers.

As he neared Whalebeard Village, he saw a man standing alone by the central fire pit. Low flames leaped and crackled in the cold breeze.

A faint voice called, "Sunchaser?"

"Woodtick?" He trotted toward the fire pit.

The chief's white hair hung loose, blowing in the wind. He wore a tattered camelhide coat, grimy and darkened with soot. Only his pale face gleamed in the light of the flames.

"She's gone, Sunchaser."

His steps faltered. "Gone? When?"

"I couldn't sleep. I saw her walking down by the shore, maybe seven or eight hands of time ago."

"She left in the middle of the night? Where did she go? Which direction?"

Woodtick folded his arms and let out a tense breath. "Northward. That's all I know." He paused. "Sunchaser, I must tell you something. I don't know if she's the same Kestrel, but—"

"What do you mean, 'the same Kestrel'?"

Woodtick canted his head sympathetically. "For one thing, days ago two men stopped here. I waved them away, but not before they asked me about a woman named Kestrel. The gray-haired man, a Trader called Lambkill, said she was his wife and that she was traveling with a newborn baby. He asked if we'd seen her. When I answered 'no,' he asked for directions to the new Otter Clan Village. I gave them to him."

"What . . ." Sunchaser swallowed his terror. "What else?"

Woodtick gestured aimlessly. "Four hunters from the Blackwater Draw Clan came through. They said that Trader Lambkill might be following them and that we should beware because he was crazy. They said he carried a dead baby in the pack on his back and claimed that it spoke to him. . . . They said they also were hunting this Kestrel because she had killed their brother, driven a tapir-bone stiletto through his heart. Then when you arrived and I heard the name of your companion, I couldn't believe she could be the same woman. Especially not when I saw how much you cared for her. But now . . . is she the same?"

"Yes," he answered, "though I don't know whether the things you were told are true." Kestrel had killed a man?

Woodtick examined Sunchaser's face, his rigid stance. "Don't leave us, Sunchaser. We need you. I know you must be worried about Kestrel, but we're desperate. Our needs are so great. You see that, don't you? She is one woman. *Ten* of my relatives are sick."

Misery, like tiny splinters of obsidian, shot through Sunchaser's veins. He couldn't speak, couldn't think, without agony. A voice in his soul whispered, *You're a Dreamer. Your duty is here.*

Over by the hill, the mammoth cow rose to her feet. Wan blue light flashed from her short tusks and reflected with a fiery sheen in her eyes. The calf stood and shook himself, sending a gleaming wave through his long auburn hair.

Woodtick turned in the direction of Sunchaser's gaze, then extended his hands. "Kestrel has been running for a long time, Sunchaser. She'll be all right. She knows how to hide from her husband. But we—"

A garbled cry strangled in Sunchaser's throat. He ran stumbling through the sand toward his camp.

The fragile scents of spring grasses and damp rocks surrounded Kestrel as she climbed the winding trail through
the foothills. Last night's strong moonlight had lit her path
like a torch. She had made good time. Westward, Mother
Ocean's face shone a deep indigo, frosted with glimmers of
silver. To the east, the land grew more rugged. The coastal
forest changed as she ascended, going from sparse firs to
dense, intermixed oaks and pines. Outcrops of granite spiked
up jaggedly on several hills. Patches of grassy meadows
softened the effect. In the dim predawn glow, the palest
wildflowers resembled strewn handfuls of silver dust.

You should never have let him touch you.

*Don't. Not . . . not now. Later, when you've rested and can
stand thinking about it.*

Cloud Girl stirred in her sack on Kestrel's back, and a
tiny hand twined comfortingly in her mother's hair. Kestrel
reached up and patted those little fingers. "I'm all right,
baby."

A merciful dullness had possessed her. It numbed not only
her heart, but the tired ache in her body. She needed to sleep,
but she feared the nightmares that she knew would come. If
she could just keep pushing herself, perhaps she could make
it to Otter Clan Village by nightfall, even though Woodtick
had said "two days." Somewhere at the end of this trail, she
had to believe, was safety, a place where she could sit with
other people, watch children play—and try to heal the raw
wounds in her soul.

If she could just hurt for a while without fearing that
her weakness would endanger Cloud Girl, she might be all
right. She hadn't realized when she'd started loving Iceplant
that the price she would pay for that brief warmth and joy
would be everlasting fear. How precious those moments had
been . . . and how desperately she needed to let them go.

And to let other things go as well.

The trail grew steeper, and Kestrel hurried her pace, forcing her weary legs up the slope as fast as she could. As dawn approached, the dark silhouettes of the hills and trees gave way to a watery lavender light. The trail became clear and wide, cutting a path through rich meadows. She concentrated on the Otter Clan, trying to find some hope to cling to. She thought about the things Sun . . . the things she knew about the clan.

You can't even say his name, Kestrel?

A lump rose in her throat. She'd felt safe with him—safe for the first time in her life—and only now did she realize what it had cost him. By allowing himself to be her refuge, he had failed in his promises to Mammoth Above. The memory of his anguished face last night haunted her. He had looked shamed, bewildered. Why hadn't she left him that day after the snow stopped? She had known very well that he wanted to be alone to Dream. He could just as easily have given her directions to Otter Clan Village as taken her there himself. It would have been abandoned anyway, but Sunchaser would have been spared this pain.

"Oh, Sunchaser . . ."

Kestrel started to shake, but not with tears. It was the dry shakes of naked emotion.

Would he hate her now? Now that she had made him love her, killed his ability to Dream and run away from him without a word? Blessed Above-Old-Man, she had hurt him in a thousand ways!

In the depths of his passion last night, when his white hair had hung like a glistening fire-dyed veil around her face, she had seen utter terror in his eyes, the terror of a man who suddenly realizes that he has become enmeshed in his own evasions and can't find the will to end them. It had shocked her enough to wring her from her euphoria.

I had to go, Sunchaser. You see that, don't you?

He could return to Dreaming now, and she could get on with raising her daughter. Sunchaser had given her so much.

Gratitude filled her for the time he had shared with her. Not so long ago, she'd desperately feared that tenderness had vanished from the world. In his presence, at least, that fear had died.

Kestrel lowered her gaze to the trail and the dew that glittered like diamonds on the pine needles scattering the path.

"Thank you, Sunchaser," she whispered. "Thank you so much."

Thirty-seven

Birds sang in the trees, greeting the first Star People who gleamed on the eastern horizon. Oxbalm tightened the lacings on the front of his shirt, fending off the coming night chill. He sat on a deerhide between Sumac and Dizzy Seal.

Horseweed and Balsam hunched on the opposite side of the fire, staring unblinking at the flickers of flame that licked up around the oak log. They both had their atlatls and quivers close at hand, as though they sensed danger afoot this evening.

Oxbalm worked his jaw back and forth, feeling the threat in the air. It had reached such strength that the hair on his arms stood straight up. He hadn't felt evil this potent since the days when old Cactus Lizard had roamed the darkness in the bodies of Lion and Bear. Oxbalm's stomach knotted into a hard ball. Even the flames in the fire pit seemed wary.

Most of his people had already retreated into the lodges to cook their dinners and tell their children stories. The few villagers who remained outside had huddled around fires and were talking in low tones . . . as though they, too, felt the unseen horror growing.

A witch was loose. Even those who didn't know it were catching the scent of evil in the air. Like a winter mist, it seeped through everything, chilling the souls of men, women and children alike.

A tripod with a bag of phlox-blossom tea stood to the left of the fire, beside Dizzy Seal. The old man kept tapping his fingers on the warm bag in a nervous gesture. His shrunken face was grave beneath the beaverskin hat that covered his gray hair. To Oxbalm's right, on the other side of Sumac, a pile of chopped oak logs was stacked, enough to last for three or four days. None of them had said anything in half a hand of time. They'd been watching the blaze of sunset ignite the translucent vestiges of clouds that limned the sky . . . and surreptitiously studying Catchstraw.

He had built himself a sweat lodge down the slope right next to the trail. The small hide-covered structure nestled in the shadow of the hill, where it turned dark long before the west-facing slopes did. The lodge sat like an ominously hunched black beast.

Dizzy Seal's mouth pursed. "Most Dreamers would build their sweat lodge out away from people, not on a busy trail."

"He wants to be seen," Sumac said. Sweat beaded on her nose. She'd unbraided her gray hair and let it hang loose down the front of her heavily fringed doeskin dress. She wet her lips and lowered her voice to a whisper, afraid that Catchstraw might hear. "This newfound Power of his has made him arrogant and boastful. I've never known a conceited Dreamer."

"Catchstraw is no Dreamer," Oxbalm reminded her. "He does everything the opposite of the way a Dreamer would. As if he's deliberately mocking the sacred ways of compassion and charity."

"The old fool." Dizzy Seal's deeply incised brow creased into a hundred folds. His beaver hat slipped down to cover half of them. "He's walking on a thin crust of ice."

Horseweed hissed, "Shh," when Catchstraw looked up at the hilltop.

They all fell silent. Oxbalm calmly dipped his wooden cup into the phlox tea and sipped the warm, flowery liquid.

Catchstraw's hooked nose lifted, and he scented the wind, then bent over the glowing hearth before his sweat lodge, his stick poking at the rocks heating atop the red coals. He'd stripped down to his breechclout. A beautiful tortoise-shell comb pinned his gray-streaked black hair on top of his head.

To Oxbalm's eyes, he looked skinnier, paler, almost as though the very breath of life was being sucked from him. Evil did that. That's how it survived; it nursed itself on the strength of the body and the soul. And if a man let it, it would drink him dry, leaving nothing but a hollow shell of flesh. The soul would rot out of the body, all black and twisted, like a slice of liver left in the hot sun for days.

Once, a very long time ago, Oxbalm's parents had taken him to the village of the famed witch Pineburl. They'd gone to meet a Trader who brought rare shells from far to the east, pink things, huge, with spikes on them. As his mother had been arguing price with the Trader, the old woman had walked out of the forest. She looked like a half-dead white weasel, unbelievably thin, and with glinting amber eyes that bored holes in anyone who dared to meet her gaze.

At the age of five summers, Oxbalm had dared. He'd stared openly, not knowing any better. Her face had been as gaunt as a corpse's. Pineburl had smiled at him with broken teeth, and his soul had shriveled. As though every unnameable terror that lurked in the shadows beyond the village had suddenly risen and come crowding around him, he'd gone cold inside. In those eyes, he'd seen nothing but angry wickedness. Oxbalm's mother had told him later that evil had eaten away all the softness in Pineburl's soul.

Catchstraw had started to look like that. His eyes darted constantly now, like a rabid wolf's. He sought out and lambasted anything that didn't please him. He shrieked at the children for playing games they had always played. Yesterday he'd darted a little dog that had come too close to his new sweat lodge.

Oxbalm had listened to the seven-summers-old owner's tears all night. Half of the village ran when they saw Catchstraw coming . . . the other half gazed at him worshipfully. His followers sensed the Power that swelled in him. But they couldn't even guess at its malignant source.

So far, only Dizzy Seal, Sumac, Oxbalm and his two grandsons had witnessed the perverted mazes scattered in the forest. Oxbalm had been too frightened to tell anyone else. When it came to such lethal matters, he could trust few people.

Catchstraw ducked into his sweat lodge, carrying three hot rocks on a litter composed of two sticks. He stepped outside again and took in three more rocks. After four trips, steam puffed up around the lodge's door flap. It glittered in the dusk, rising in thin, serpentine wisps until it vanished in the breeze that rustled the tops of the tallest pines.

Oxbalm hunched forward in relief, ran a hand through his damp hair and gazed around the circle. Everyone stared at him through questioning eyes. "Not yet," he said. "We must wait until we have proof that he's harmed someone. Without that, his obscene mazes are not enough."

"But, Grandfather," Horseweed murmured solemnly, "do you remember what Sunchaser said that day after the mammoths' attack? He said he could no longer find his way through the maze. Isn't that proof enough?"

Oxbalm shook his head. "Not unless Sunchaser stood here before us and told us that he couldn't get through because he'd been witched."

Dizzy Seal leaned forward and ran his tongue over the gaps in his teeth. Against the background of green oaks and pines, he looked as brown and brittle as an autumn leaf. He laced his fingers in front of him. "If someone is found guilty of witching, the sentence is death. I've never heard of any other punishment. Have you?"

Oxbalm shook his head, and Sumac said, "No."

Balsam whispered, "Good riddance."

"The problem," Oxbalm reminded, "is that someone has to kill the witch. I saw Pineburl when I was a boy. Everyone knew she was a witch, but no one could find the courage to kill her. Witches are Powerful. You have to sneak up on them and kill them on the first blow. Because if you fail, they'll get you. Witch you. You'll die horribly."

Balsam sat up suddenly and lifted his hand to shield his eyes against the last polished rays of opal sunlight that haloed the western horizon. His pug nose wrinkled. "Grandfather, Harrier is coming up the trail, and he has two strangers with him."

Oxbalm swiveled to look over his shoulder. The newcomers were a full hand shorter than Harrier and wore a slightly different cut of hunting shirt, the kind that Oxbalm normally associated with the Marsh Peoples to the east.

The shorter and older of the strangers looked to be in his mid-forties and had gray braids and heavy jowls. His flat nose seemed to sit right on top of his thin upper lip. Thick folds of skin hung loosely on his throat. He wore a grimy buckskin shirt and pants and carried a bulky pack over his shoulder. Despite the pack's weight, he walked naturally, as if born to the burden. A Trader?

The second stranger was taller than the first, and maybe ten summers younger than his companion. He'd knotted his hair into a black bun at the base of his skull. A thin band of red beads encircled his collar, but the rest of his elkhide clothing was plain. No fringes, no quillwork. Unease, even reluctance, marked the younger man's walk and posture.

The older man's eyes scanned the village with the care of a hunting saber-toothed cat. Not the sort of manner a Trader generally brought to a new village. No, this was something different—and too many things were already different as it was.

Trouble! the voice in Oxbalm's head said.

Oxbalm stood. Harrier lifted a hand to him as they came up the trail, and Oxbalm nodded courteously in response, despite feeling no joy at the sight of Harrier. The youth had been coldly polite for days, coming into camp every morning to ask what news Oxbalm had received. A hot tightness tickled the back of Oxbalm's throat, as though his body fought to tell him something that he didn't want to hear.

Sumac whispered, "It's *them*, Oxbalm."

"Who?"

"That crazy Trader and his brother. The men hunting the woman with the newborn baby."

Dizzy Seal got to his feet, while Horseweed moved his atlatl to his side with such stealth that the movement appeared to have been accomplished through sleight of hand. Balsam had rocked to his knees, tensed as if to spring.

Oxbalm glanced down at Sumac. "What makes you think it's them?"

She sat with her back painfully straight, her chin thrust out as though preparing to do battle with Above-Old-Man himself. "Look at the smile on Harrier's face. He's as anxious as Mouse cornered by Marten. Notice how his hand grips the atlatl tied to his belt? It's them, all right. Harrier's probably wondering what to do with them, since the Trader's wife hasn't shown up here yet."

Oxbalm's eyes narrowed as the three men walked briskly toward him. The villagers who sat around the other fires burst out in conversation. A few reached for their atlatls and drew them warily into their laps. It eased Oxbalm's soul to know that a half dozen darts would be aimed at the Trader if he got too crazy.

Night had begun to fall quickly now, draping the forest in a veil of luminescent charcoal.

"Sumac," Oxbalm said quietly, "I would feel better if you were safe in our lodge. Why don't you—"

"I'm staying."

"Why do you always insist on arguing with me when I'm trying to protect you!"

"Because usually," she replied matter-of-factly, "that's when you need me most."

"I do not need you! I have three men here—"

"That," Sumac said and gazed at him with equanimity, "is exactly why you need me. This whole matter is over a woman. There should be somebody here who understands what she must have gone through. Or do you, as a man, know everything that moves a woman?"

Dizzy Seal bowed his head to hide his smile, and Horse-weed chuckled softly. Oxbalm glowered at both of them, then turned to face Harrier as the youth strode up with his hand extended.

"Good evening, Oxbalm," Harrier said, taking the old man's hand in a reluctant grip. "You remember my telling you about the men who were looking for—"

"Yes," Oxbalm said and faced the short man with the gray braids. "You must be the Trader, Lambkill."

The man bowed deeply and nodded. "I am. And this is my brother, Tannin. We're from the Bear-Looks-Back Clan out in the marsh country."

Oxbalm inclined his head respectfully, but said nothing.

Lambkill continued. "It would seem that we owe you a debt of gratitude. Harrier has told us that you've helped him, allowing him and his brothers to stay and watch the trails for my wife, Kestrel."

Oxbalm gestured to the fire. "Please, sit down and help yourselves to the tea."

Oxbalm lowered his old body to sit beside Sumac again, while the men found places and removed their packs from their backs.

Sumac's eyes tightened when she saw how reverently Lambkill placed his pack in his lap and arranged it just so before unlacing two ties and removing a wooden cup.

Tannin crouched warily beside Lambkill, his arms braced on his knees as he took out his cup. Powerful leg muscles bulged beneath his pants. Harrier filled Lambkill's and Tannin's cups with tea, then pulled a piece of oak from the woodpile, tipped it on end and used it as a stool.

Silence stretched until Oxbalm said bluntly, "I'm sorry

to say, Trader Lambkill, that your wife has not visited our village yet."

"She will," Lambkill replied. "She is on her way. It's just a matter of time."

Oxbalm tilted his head doubtfully. "Well, perhaps, but—"

"No perhaps about it," Lambkill interrupted. He met Oxbalm's gaze balefully. "We were at Whalebeard Village two days ago. They told us they'd seen her."

Sumac slipped her arm through Oxbalm's and shifted to rest on her hip, peering across at Lambkill. In a chill voice, she said, "That is no proof that she intended to come here."

"No," Lambkill agreed, "but the man she was with asked for directions to your new village site. That strongly suggests that they intended to come here."

Sumac saw Tannin's sharp glance at his brother and tightened her hold on Oxbalm's arm. Apparently she sensed, as Oxbalm did, an undercurrent in that statement. Something left unsaid—purposely. "Is it true," Sumac asked, "that your wife has a newborn baby with her?"

Lambkill nodded. "She gave birth after she ran away from Juniper Village. She had twins. We found the place—"

"A woman, pregnant with twins, ran, and escaped?" Sumac asked, awed. "She must have been very desperate."

"With good reason." Lambkill's wrinkled face pulled into new lines as he frowned down at the pack in his lap. He stroked the hide gently. In the darkening sky behind him, bats soared and dove, hunting the insects that floated over the meadow. "She had been condemned to death for committing incest with her cousin."

Tannin sipped his tea casually, but he gripped his cup in both hands as though his tension had built to unbearable levels. He kept glancing fearfully at Lambkill.

Harrier tipped his log stool forward and braced his elbows on his knees, then extended his hands to warm them over the flames. "Oxbalm, Lambkill and Tannin ask your permission to stay here—"

"Only for as long as you and your brothers are here,

Harrier. And you have three days left. More time than that, I cannot grant. Already you've upset my village. Every man here has started sleeping with his atlatl, worried that this event might cause a war between our clans. The women are keeping their children close to the village. It's unhealthy having you and your—"

"But, Oxbalm, listen. Lambkill knows that Kestrel is coming here. Maybe not in the next few days, but soon, and we'll catch her when she does. If you will just—"

"I have said no. Must I repeat it?"

Harrier straightened and his eyes narrowed. "Where is Catchstraw?" he asked softly. "If you will not give your permission, we would like to ask his."

Dizzy Seal made a low sound of disgust and threw the dregs of his tea into the fire. As the flames sizzled, one of the burning logs broke and a flash of lurid light chased back the darkness for a few moments.

Sumac surreptitiously patted Oxbalm's elbow. The gesture made him suppress the bitter words that had rushed to his lips. That and the fact that he saw Horseweed silently pull a dart from his quiver, then nock the dart in his atlatl with unobtrusive skill. Oxbalm waved dismissively at Harrier.

"Catchstraw is in the sweat lodge down the hill . . . Dreaming." The word stuck in his throat like a clot of tar. "He said he didn't want to be disturbed. But perhaps he just meant disturbed by his fellow villagers, rather than by you and your friends. Would you like to chance angering him?"

Harrier and Lambkill exchanged looks. "No," Harrier replied. "We will see him tomorrow morning."

"If he's finished Dreaming by then," Lambkill said. "Some Dreamers stay in the Spirit World for days at a time."

"Not Catchstraw," Oxbalm commented blandly. "He'll be available tomorrow."

Harrier stood up, and Lambkill and Tannin gathered their belongings and rose beside him. When Harrier didn't offer any conciliatory words, Lambkill said respectfully, "You've been honest and forthright with us, Oxbalm. We thank you. We will cause you no trouble, I assure you."

"I hope you are right, Trader. As I have told Harrier—"

Horseweed gasped suddenly and bolted to his feet. All the color drained from his face as he peered down at the meadow. Oxbalm spun around . . . and his heart rose into his throat. A dire wolf, black and huge, loped through the wildflowers, heading for a copse of pine on the southern end of the meadow.

Harrier gasped. "Where did it come from? They're so rare now. Maybe we should mount a hunting party to kill it."

"No," Lambkill murmured, and his faded eyes glimmered with something like recognition. That look sent a tingle up Oxbalm's spine. "No," Lambkill repeated. "Leave it be. So long as it doesn't bother us, why should we bother it?"

Lambkill walked away across the hilltop, and Harrier and Tannin followed. But Lambkill kept glancing back and forth between Catchstraw's sweat lodge and the place where the wolf had disappeared into the trees.

. . . As though he knew.

Oxbalm fought to still his labored breathing. *How could a Trader from the marsh country know a secret that even I am not certain of?*

His gaze drifted over the dark branches of the oaks that filigreed the indigo vault of the sky. The wide eyes of owls flashed as they turned their heads to watch the retreating men.

"Tomorrow, Grandson," he said to Horseweed, "I want you to organize a scouting party. Pick four men, two to run the western trail and two for the eastern trail. Maybe we can warn this Kestrel and her friend before they walk into Harrier's trap. If she is a relative, she deserves at least that much from us."

"Yes, Grandfather, I will," Horseweed whispered and looked up through haunted eyes. "But the wolf. Do you think—"

"It could have just been a wolf. That's all," Dizzy Seal

responded. But he didn't sound as though he believed it himself.

Oxbalm grimaced. "There's one way to find out. Sumac, please, for my sake, stay here with Balsam. Balsam, take care of Grandmother while Dizzy Seal, Horseweed and I go down the hill."

Terror welled in Horseweed's eyes. He swallowed hard. "Where are we going, Grandfather?"

"To talk to Catchstraw. If he's there."

"Oxbalm," Sumac murmured as she rose, "don't do this. What if the wolf sees you and comes back?"

"Then I will take it as a great favor, wife, if you would scream to call out all of our warriors."

Balsam said, "Don't worry, Grandfather, I'm a very fast runner. I'll have our warriors out of the lodges and with atlatls in their hands before Grandmother can yell twice."

Oxbalm nodded proudly. "Yes, you are a fast runner. The fastest in the village. Keep watch on us, Grandson."

"I will." Balsam picked up his atlatl and went to stand by Sumac.

Oxbalm turned to Dizzy Seal and Horseweed. "Come. Let's get this done."

Horseweed had gripped his atlatl in his right hand, while a long dart lay balanced in the fingers of his left. As if anxious to fly, the dart twirled as he rolled it in his fingers.

They took the trail that led off the eastern side of the hill and wound down around the base through a blaze of pink snowberry flowers. The shrubs sent trailing tendrils across the path. Oxbalm took his time, avoiding them so he wouldn't trip. He doubted that his bad knees could take such a jolt. They would probably snap in two just to spite him.

And wouldn't Catchstraw like that!

As they curved around the base of the hill, the sweat lodge came back into view. Catchstraw had built it large enough to hold ten men, though he'd invited no one to participate in the purification ceremonies with him. A shimmering haze of steam haloed the structure.

Oxbalm sucked in a deep breath, fortifying himself, as he stepped around the woodpile and stopped before the door flap. Dizzy Seal and Horseweed flanked him. Horseweed held his atlatl in a death grip, the dart nocked and ready. Dizzy Seal's elderly eyes roved about frantically. In the orange firelight, he looked like a dying man.

"Catchstraw?" Oxbalm called. "I'm sorry to bother you, but I would like to speak to you. It's urgent."

No answer.

"The two men who are looking for the woman named Kestrel have arrived. . . . Did you hear me?"

Oxbalm hobbled closer and put his ear close to the door flap. Hot rocks sizzled inside, but nothing else could be heard. No movements, no breathing. "Catchstraw? Are you in there? It's Oxbalm."

Gingerly, Oxbalm pulled the door flap aside and peered into utter darkness. He couldn't see a thing. "Horseweed? Please throw more wood on the fire out there."

Horseweed did so, and as the flames leaped higher, the interior of the lodge glowed faintly. Steam shimmered like sunlit fog. Oxbalm hooked the flap on its peg and stepped inside.

A dozen colored baskets sat in a neat line along the back wall, and Catchstraw's bedding of hides lay piled on the south side of the central fire pit. A mound of hot rocks currently filled the pit, but a fire had been in it earlier. White ashes ringed the rocks. On a log that ran the length of the north wall, abalone-shell bowls stood heaped high with acorns, walnuts and strips of jerked venison.

Oxbalm shook his head. Catchstraw was such an old fool. Didn't he realize that in the damp environment of a sweat lodge, nuts and meats were sure to mold? And leaving them close to the ground was an open invitation to every rodent within two days' walk. His bedding, too, would mildew and harden.

Oxbalm frowned. But . . . of course Catchstraw knew these things. Why would he make such obvious errors?

Unless he's not thinking right. Not thinking like a human because he's filled with Spirit Plants.

Oxbalm fingered his chin as he studied the baskets, damp hides and hot rocks. Dizzy Seal's breathing sounded half-strangled as he peered into the dark lodge. Sumac had told Oxbalm days ago that Catchstraw spent half of every morning out prowling the meadows, collecting plants he would let no one see.

"No wonder Catchstraw built this so big," Oxbalm said. "He's moved all of his belongings down. This isn't just a sweat lodge. He's going to live here."

Dizzy Seal bravely ducked in behind Oxbalm and in a hoarse voice, said, "Careful. See the maze on the floor?" He pointed.

Oxbalm stopped dead in his tracks and looked down. The red, black and white lines wove an intricate labyrinth to the rear of the fire pit. Carefully, he hobbled forward and hunched down. As he extended his hand to touch the painting, he saw the sparse scatter of wolf hair that sprinkled the maze. His hand began to shake so badly that Dizzy Seal ran around the opposite side of the pit and hissed, "What's wrong?"

"Do you see them?" Oxbalm indicated several of the closest hairs.

Dizzy Seal stumbled backward. "He . . . *it was him!*"

Oxbalm rose and wiped his clammy hands on his pants. "Maybe."

Horseweed ducked through the entry, his eyes wide. "What did you find?"

"Come and look at this, Grandson. Quickly. Then we must get out of here."

Horseweed knelt before the scatter of wolf hair, picked one up, then threw it down as though it had burned him. He lurched unsteadily to his feet, breathing hard. "I think we should go hunt him down and dart him to death right now."

"Yes, I—I agree," Dizzy Seal said.

Oxbalm's eyes widened. "This is no proof. There are those who will defend him. They'll say that Catchstraw just went out into the forest to gather plants again, and that when we saw the dire wolf and found Catchstraw gone from his lodge, we jumped to conclusions. Old woman Yucca Thorn will accuse us of hating Catchstraw and trying to malign his character. The village will split. Half of our relatives will go away and never want to see us again. No . . ." he sighed. "Not yet. We must wait a little longer."

Lambkill rose from his seat by Harrier's fire. The youth had made camp along the western trail that led to the sea. Lambkill's haphazard grass lodge was a good distance from the fire, well away from the smoke, in the soft meadow grass. At least he would sleep well there. To his left, on top of the hill, he could make out the dark forms of people moving through Otter Clan Village and the faint gleam of Above-Old-Man silvering the sky. Hushed strains of conversation carried.

Lambkill stretched his stiff muscles. "That was a long walk. I don't think my body will ever be the same again."

Harrier smiled grimly. He sat across the fire playing with a woven yucca cord, looping it, tying it, then nervously untying it. "It has been a hard half a moon. I'm anxious to get home."

"So am I," Tannin said. He sat on a dead log with his head down, a cup of tea clutched between both hands. He'd grown too sullen to bear. Just looking at Tannin's grimace made Lambkill want to strike him.

Idiot brother. Don't you think I want this over, too? Do you think I enjoy being shunned and slighted by every village we come to?

Lambkill lifted his pack from the log and slung it over his shoulder, smiling genially. "I'll be back shortly. I just need some time to pray to Above-Old-Man."

"I understand," Harrier said softly, but he eyed the pack as though he suspected Lambkill's true reason for going into the forest.

Tannin glanced at the pack, and his mouth pursed disdainfully. "Hurry back, Lambkill. I want to talk to you . . . about Kestrel."

Rage fired Lambkill's body, but he merely nodded. "As you wish. I'll return soon."

He tramped out into the forest, ducking low beneath several thick oak branches. Deadfall and brush clogged these foothills. It made walking difficult. A mass of deer trails crisscrossed here, going off in all directions. Lambkill picked one that led due north. He followed the winding path until it led him into a dense thicket of berry vines. Tiny white flowers covered the brier. Sweetness filled the cool night air.

Lambkill examined the surroundings, the trunks of trees, the fallen logs. When he found a small patch of wildflowers, he stopped and sat down. Above-Old-Man had risen, and moonlight fell through the canopy of branches here, lighting the ground.

"We must talk, my son," he whispered.

He sat down and gently laid his pack in the midst of the fragrant wildflowers before him. As he unlaced it, he Sang a soft Song of praise to Above-Old-Man and Mother Ocean. He lifted the flap on the pack and peeled it back. Little Coyote lay still within, resting on a bed of sage leaves.

"Come, son. Stand in the moonlight. Feel the wind on your face. It feels good."

He reverently removed his son and propped him up against the pack. Little Coyote stared at him through his stony green eyes. "You're so tiny, son. So beautiful. . . . Are you awake? Can you hear me?"

"*I hear you, Father.*"

Lambkill heaved a sigh of relief. "I was afraid for a moment . . . but of course you're still here. I need you, my son. These Otter Clan people are plotting against me. I can feel it. They want to protect your mother."

Little Coyote's withered brown mouth moved faintly. *"They won't be able to, Father. You're more clever than they are."*

Lambkill tenderly stroked his son's shriveled bald head. "Yes, but it will be hard for me to take her away from them, son. I must catch your mother before she reaches them. Where is she now? Can you see her?"

Little Coyote's stone eyes glittered. *"Yes, Father. She's coming up this very trail. She'll be here in less than a hand of time."*

Blood surged in Lambkill's ears, giving him a throbbing headache. He rubbed his temples. "I'll try, son. I'll try to catch her, but—"

"Don't worry, Father. She's not traveling with Sunchaser now. She's alone and frightened. Well, not quite alone. She has my sister with her. But they'll be easy prey for you."

Like a lust in his body, rage filled Lambkill. "Thank you, my son. I knew you wouldn't let me down. Thank you. I'll catch her. And when I do, you and I will spend hands of time watching her die."

"Tannin is going to try to talk you out of killing her, Father. Do you know that?"

Lambkill ground his teeth. "Yes, I know. His time is coming, my son. He'll pay for his disbelief, for his weakness! Just wait, Little Coyote. I will avenge every wrong that has ever been done you . . . and me."

Lambkill frowned. Little Coyote had stopped talking and the glitter had vanished from his eyes. The green stones had gone dull, opaque. "Son? What's wrong?" Lambkill asked. "Are you all right?"

From that withered mouth, a faint whisper came. *"I'm tired, Father. Very tired . . ."*

"Yes, I'm certain you are. We've had a long, hard journey to get here, haven't we? Why don't you sleep, Little Coyote. Sleep until I catch your mother."

Carefully, Lambkill lifted his son, kissed him on the forehead and put him back into the pack. "Yes, sleep well, son. It will be a long walk home after we're finished here, too."

"Boy? Boy, I hear you crying. I want to tell you something. Listen, will you?"

". . . I don't want to hear anything you have to say. I hate you!"

"Listen anyway, please. There was once a very young Dreamer, a Dreamer in the making, named Roseroot. Everyone loved her. And she loved everyone. She was very happy in her village. But one day her village was attacked and burned to white ashes by enemy warriors.

"She ran away, out into the desert, where she found a cave to live in. The only water she had to drink fell from the sky and pooled in a tiny basin in the stone outside of her cave. The only food she could find to fill her empty stomach was a wispy grass that grew in the rocky crevices.

"Hatred ate away at her soul, hatred for the warriors who had hurt her by killing her people. Hatred for Power for not warning her so she could save them. She made herself miserable with this hate.

"Many cycles later, a very old man came hobbling by her cave and dipped his hand in her water basin to get a drink. Roseroot ran outside to scream at him.

" 'Get away from my water! You have no right to drink from my pool!'

"The old man looked up and squinted his eyes and gasped. 'Why, aren't you Roseroot, who used to live at Red Canyon Village?'

" 'Yes,' she replied. 'Who are you?'

" 'I'm your Spirit Helper!' the old man replied. 'Don't you recognize me?'

"Roseroot frowned, looked him over carefully and said, 'No. I do not. And my Spirit Helper was no Helper at all.

He didn't warn me before the attack on my village came. And he fled afterward and left me alone!' She began to weep bitterly.

" 'Hmm,' her Spirit Helper said and heaved a deep sigh. 'Then I guess you'll never understand the ways of Power.'

" 'What do you mean?' Roseroot demanded.

"The old man spread his arms wide. 'Well, look around you, young Dreamer. What do you see?'

" 'Nothing. I see nothing! This is a terrible place of barren sand and bare rock. I hate it!'

" 'Exactly,' said the old man. 'Power went to very great efforts to drive you out here so you could learn about hatred without being distracted by love, but apparently you've spurned the gift . . .'

"And the old man vanished, as though he'd never been there at all."

The Man stopped talking.

Boy blinked thoughtfully at the dark leather that surrounded him. Lambkill's jarring steps made the pack sway. The scent of sage encircled the Boy. "I haven't spurned your gift, Man. I'm trying to keep Death before my eyes at all times. But it's so hard. Sometimes I fail."

"And then you hurt, don't you, Boy? You hurt and you hate."

". . . Yes."

"You must try harder. Clutch Death to your heart with all your might. Try, Boy. You must try harder."

Thirty-eight

Sunchaser hiked the trail with his atlatl in one hand, a selection of darts in the other. Pines jutted up above the rest of the forest, their pointed tops darkly silhouetted against the slate-blue opalescence of the evening sky, their branches swaying gently in the cool wind. A hand of time ago, Helper had started growling, the sound low, from deep in his throat. The dog's eyes searched the forest vigilantly. He trotted at Sunchaser's side with the lanky stride of a prowling wolf.

"I know, Helper. I feel it, too."

Some dark Power pressed down on them, smothering. So close and suffocating that it should have been visible, like a dirty mist in the air.

The skin prickled on Sunchaser's neck, and tickles ran across his skin like invisible ants. Danger . . . there . . . ahead of them, in the trees. But he didn't know how far ahead.

Sunchaser slowed and cocked his head. From long practice, he cleared himself of worries and fear, blanking himself to the sensations of Power, seeking the source of . . . what?

Violent anger. Feral rage.

It burned like a fire in Sunchaser's soul. And hate. Festering hate. White hot. So much hatred for everything alive.

The searing sensation increased with the darkness, as though the beast fed upon and gained its Power from the deepening shadows. Once when Sunchaser had accidentally cornered a short-faced bear in a box canyon, he'd felt this same intensity of blind fury. Could it be a bear? He lifted his nose to scent the wind. Short-faced bears had a rank odor from the carrion they routinely fed upon.

Test the wind as he might, he smelled only the damp exhalations of grass and pine.

The urge built: *Flee! Run from the creature's path!*

But Kestrel would be walking this same trail, not so far ahead. Perhaps on a collision course with that enraged animal. Sunchaser had pushed himself mercilessly, trying to catch up with her before darkness fell. His exhausted legs ached, but his panicked soul kept saying, *Hurry. You must hurry. You have to find her before Lambkill does!*

Oxbalm wouldn't simply turn Kestrel over to Lambkill; of that, Sunchaser felt certain. Sumac would demand a council session to consider the charges . . . assuming that Kestrel made it to the village before her husband captured her. And if she didn't, how would Sunchaser find her? Where would Lambkill take her? Back to Juniper Village?

Or would he kill her here, in the depths of the forest, where no one would know?

"Come on, Helper. Let's run again. We can do it."

Sunchaser shook back the sweaty strands of white hair that had glued themselves to his forehead and sprinted up the hill, pushing his muscles until they trembled in protest.

Helper—a black shape gliding through the darkness—ranged out in front of him. Helper had stopped growling, had gone quiet the way a wild dog does when he has prey in sight. Sunchaser's nerves crackled like fur rubbed by an angry hand. Only tame dogs yelped and panted their eagerness, foolishly warning the prey.

Helper vanished silently over the next grassy swell.

Beyond the shadowy outlines of the foothills, a lustrous arc of silver lit the sky. Above-Old-Man would be up soon, and his mighty presence would chase away half of the Star People. Sunchaser prayed that the trail cut across meadows and not through the tree-choked forest. In the open, moonlight would illuminate any enemy who dared to attack and give him a target for his dart. Most of the animals that roamed the night would cling to the densest brush and trees, waiting for unsuspecting prey. If the trail veered into the forest, could he afford to stay in the meadows? He might lose his way . . . and precious time.

All day long he'd been frantic for Kestrel. He knew why she had gone. She'd tried before to tell him that she thought herself responsible for his inability to find his way through the maze. His failures at Healing yesterday must have tormented her.

And I made it worse—forcing my needs upon her. It's not your fault, Kestrel. Those things are my fault. You're not to blame!

Blessed Spirits, how he missed her. He'd never understood before what Good Plume had meant when she'd said, "Nobody's happy with only half a soul," but he did now. Kestrel's departure had left him feeling fragmented, only half alive.

The undulations in the trail made his moccasins slip and slide, but he kept up a steady trot, his gaze ever sweeping the shadows.

He dipped down the side of one hill and ran up another. When he reached the crest and looked into the narrow valley below, he saw a strewn handful of dove-colored ponds. The weak, inverted images of the trees stood perfectly preserved on those still, reflective surfaces.

Sunchaser didn't see Helper. But he heard the soft rustle of fur catching on brush. He turned to look over his shoulder.

"It's just darkness," he whispered to himself. But he shivered, *feeling* something out there, as if danger coalesced from the threads of shadows.

"Helper?" he called. "Is that you, boy?"

Something stirred in the inky shadows at the edge of the trees east of the trail. Did the failing light play tricks? Or did eyes gleam there?

"Helper?"

Without warning, the huge animal burst from the darkness. On powerful legs, it shot up the hill toward him, its tongue lolling. Fear rushed through Sunchaser's veins. He fell backward a step and pulled a dart from the quiver

on his back. He nocked it in his atlatl and braced himself
to cast.

Dire wolf! What a huge animal!

For its size, the wolf moved with unnatural silence and
grace, as though it ghosted over the path rather than ran
upon it. Shaggy black fur rippled with its pace. A ridge of
hair stood straight up on its spine, as high as the middle of
Sunchaser's chest. When the animal was close enough, he
would dart it in the heart and run.

Dire wolves are so hard to kill!

He'd heard of wolves that had been darted twelve times
and before they'd succumbed to their wounds, had still managed to tear out the throats of their hunters.

The wind shifted and brought Sunchaser a strange, cloying
odor, oddly human, tainted with smoke and the aroma of
roasting meat.

The dire wolf crested the hill. Those brown eyes bored
into Sunchaser like red-hot pokers, and he perceived something . . . familiar . . . in that hate-filled gaze. The wolf let out
a triumphant howl and charged.

Sunchaser braced his feet, his left arm forward, and
launched his dart with all of his strength. The dire wolf
leaped aside like a Spirit Dancer, whirling, then staggering
and yipping.

The dart had lodged in the front shoulder, where it flopped
with each tortured leap the animal made.

Sunchaser stumbled—his senses blurred by panic—and
ran for the trees.

The thumping feet of the wolf sounded terrifyingly close
behind him. Its smoky, human reek clogged Sunchaser's
nose. He pounded into the forest and ran for the closest
pine, slipped his atlatl through his belt, then jumped to grab
the lowest limb and swung himself up so he could hook
his knees ver another branch. But before he could climb
higher, the glint of fangs flashed in the corner of his vision
and the muscles in his chest and right upper arm screamed
in pain as claws ripped through his flesh. The force of the

impact jerked him from the tree and slammed him to the ground.

He hit the pine duff hard, rolling up on his knees. The wolf stood no more than ten paces away, glaring hate.

Why doesn't it charge? Sunchaser panted for breath, collecting himself.

A glimmer of something akin to fear lit the animal's dark eyes.

Sunchaser slowly slid his hand toward the darts on his back. Running would be futile. Before he could even get to his feet, the beast would leap and knock him flat again. Blood spread warmly across his torn shirt and ran in rivulets down his arm. The wolf's fangs had merely glanced across his chest but had cut deep through his arm, almost to the bone, slicing an artery. He couldn't possibly cast another dart, at least not with his right hand. And he couldn't do it accurately with his left, nor with the strength he would need in order to penetrate the animal's vital organs. He would have to wield his dart like a spear—and with his left hand.

Trembling, Sunchaser lifted the dart before him, pausing only long enough to breathe Spirit into the beautifully flaked stone point. The rippled surface of the blood-red chert gave off a faint sheen, deadly, ready for this final conflict. Bound with sinew to a chokecherry foreshaft, the long, fluted point had been crafted by his now dead friend, Little Elk. The edge was sharp enough to shave hair.

The wolf growled, a low sound from deep in its throat, then stalked forward, as silent as mist. Saliva dripped from its muzzle, coating its chest with a silver froth. It had broken the dart shaft during the chase, but a short length of the smoothed willow still protruded from its front shoulder. Sticky blood clotted around it. The wound would not kill, not even in time, unless Evil Spirits entered and festered in the raw flesh—but it would slow the wolf for weeks.

As the wolf came closer, it probed the forest floor with its nose, licking hungrily at the spots of Sunchaser's blood on the duff, the way a Dreamer would drink from the nectar of sacred plants to gain their Power.

Sunchaser set the long dart in the atlatl's hook and crouched, mouth dry, ready to thrust. The animal sensed his fear, sensed that final desperation. It jerked up its head and sprang forward with a sharp bark.

But as if it understood the threat, the huge wolf twisted sideways, sidestepping the dart point at the last instant.

Sunchaser made it halfway to his feet before that massive body struck him and knocked him backward, sending him sliding through the pine duff. The dart shaft snapped hollowly, leaving only the foreshaft, and its keen point to use like a knife.

Wolf's jaws closed around his left leg, and Sunchaser twisted away, lashing out with his blade, cutting a gash in Wolf's black side. A frenzy of madness possessed Wolf. With jaws locked on Sunchaser's arm, the animal shook him the way Coyote shakes Rabbit to kill it—and the dart point was flung into the darkness.

Wolf lunged for Sunchaser's throat, and Sunchaser kicked out and twisted wildly while Wolf's canines ripped at his blocking arms. Sunchaser screamed in rage and pain. He squirmed backward, trying to reach the dart point.

Wolf hesitated, looked up, suddenly distracted . . . and Sunchaser dove for his dart point. With all of his might, he plunged the blade deep into Wolf's right hind quarter, ripping, sawing, seeking to hamstring the beast. Wolf yipped and attacked again, but a hurtling black body slammed into the animal before it could sink its teeth into Sunchaser's side.

Sunchaser rolled free, scrambling to recover. What . . . *Helper!*

Dog and Wolf rolled across the forest floor in a snarling, biting fury of black that ripped patches of brown duff from the ground.

Sunchaser staggered forward, seeking to drive his dart point into the dire wolf but finding no opportunity in the milling legs, snapping teeth and thrashing tails.

In an instant, the dire wolf tore free and raced away into the trees, Helper slashing at his rear.

"Helper! *No!*" Sunchaser screamed before dropping to his knees, spent and panting. "Don't . . . don't chase him! Let him go."

Silence. Not even Owl's plaintive voice carried on the night.

But Dire Wolf might return to finish the kill.

Sunchaser's entire body throbbed as he slid backward, leaving a broad trail of blood. He managed to drag himself into a dense pile of deadfall, deep into the smell of moldering wood and new grass. He collapsed on his left side, trying to catch his breath. Here, at least, his back and sides were protected from attack.

A soft whining.

Sunchaser weakly lifted his head. "Helper? *Helper?*"

A black blot in the darkness, Helper crawled in, sniffing at the blood, licking Sunchaser's hand, then his face, the tongue warm and reassuring.

"You all right?" Sunchaser asked, hearing the tail thumping hollowly against the tangle of dead branches that sheltered them.

Weary, so very weary. Sunchaser couldn't reach down to pat his friend. "Good boy, Helper. Good boy. Are you all right? Did Wolf hurt you?"

Helper pawed at him, as if trying to get him to move.

"Guess you're . . ." Sunchaser shifted his mangled leg and gasped. "You're in much better condition . . . than I am."

With every beat of his heart, blood drenched his ripped shirt and pants, and a numb sensation filtered through him. He felt strangely detached from his body—as though his Spirit floated high above him. Was he losing so much blood?

"Helper?" Nausea overwhelmed him. He choked the sourness back. "Helper, go find Oxbalm. He's up the trail. Go find . . . Oxbalm . . ."

Helper went silent, then madly scrambled out of the deadfall.

Sunchaser didn't hear him run away. His ears seemed to be stuffed with cattail down. He could feel himself slipping away ... grayness ... fading. Pain flayed him as his shocked nerves awoke in a flood of agony. So light-headed. Drifting. Something nagged at the back of his mind, something about the wolf ... what ... the wolf ... those burning brown eyes, that fetid human scent. Its mad frenzy. Why had it ...

Sunchaser rolled to his back and peered unseeing at the dimness.

Dire wolves have yellow eyes.

"Oh, Spirits, no."

His thoughts wavered, moving like whirlwinds of dust created by the feet of racing children. His body spun, pulsing, as though on the fourth night of the Mammoth Spirit Dance. He could scarcely feel his flesh, was aware only of the cadence of the sacred motions, the movements of the Dance, becoming Life, lifting him off the ground, taking him flying to the stars ...

Then a hand, bright and golden, appeared before Sunchaser's eyes—like a figment spawned by death, or by extreme thirst. He blinked at it, disbelieving. A beautiful voice issued from the blackness. *"Come with me, Sunchaser. Take my hand. I need to show you the twists and turns of the Starweb."*

Sunchaser opened his eyes, but he perceived only hurtful brilliance. His voice came out in a hushed croak. "The Starweb? What is that?"

"Your heart, Dreamer. Yours—and everything else's. Come. Take my hand. Before it's too late."

"But where are we going? Who are you?"

"You're hurt, Sunchaser. You don't recall, but we've met before. Cycles ago, in a different world. I'm Wolfdreamer. I led the First People up from the dark underworlds to this World of Light. But the Light is going to die, Sunchaser. Mammoths and lions will go first, then bristle snails and saltmarsh harvest mice, a few tiny pupfish and finally eagles

*and bears. Everything else will follow. Too soon . . . unless
you help me."*

Sunchaser's heart thundered. Deep in his soul, he knew
what the final moments of Light would be like. He could hear
and see those eternal instants as though they'd been burned
into his soul with a fiery brand: a deluge of misty rainbow
fires, swallowed by stunning Darkness . . . music like none
he'd ever heard before, the notes lilting powerfully as the
sparks of eternal brilliance cried out and perished beneath
the onslaught of oblivion . . . then utter Blackness, complete,
devastating. Infinite.

With all of his dwindling strength, Sunchaser reached
into that blinding golden radiance and felt warm fingers
clasp his.

"I'm ready, Wolfdreamer. Take me."

Lambkill stretched out on his side in the soft grass before
Harrier's fire. Around them, oaks lifted gnarled branches
toward the sky like supplicating hands. Beyond them, the
fires of the Otter Clan blinked and winked where they dotted
the top of the ridge. Why had the Otter Clan come here?
Half of the trees had lightning scars on them. The violent
fall winds had also left their marks on the trees, and more
winds would ravage the village when the seasons changed.
Oxbalm must be a fool.

No matter. Oxbalm's leadership wasn't a concern of
Lambkill's. By the time the Otter Clan realized how badly
they had chosen, Lambkill would be long gone . . . and Kestrel
but a memory.

For the first time in moons, he felt calm and free of care.

Tannin, however, sat cross-legged beside him with a
worried expression on his face, and his shoulders hunched
beneath his buckskin shirt. He stared into the green liquid in
his wooden cup as though at something repulsive.

Across the fire from them, Harrier and his younger brother, Ravenlight, sat on rocks they had dragged in from the forest. They'd shoved the end of a pine log into the fire, and it burned bright and fragrant. The orange glow shadowed their faces, making their massive brows and flat noses stand out while it created hollows of their eyes. They both wore red-painted shirts. Ravenlight's collar had a zigzagging line of blue and white porcupine quills.

Lambkill swirled his tea. "Where are your other brothers, Harrier? Did they run home when they discovered how arduous this trip would be?"

"No." Harrier's jaw tightened. "We split up to watch both of the trails that lead into Otter Clan Village. We assumed she would come up from the west, but of course none of us could know for certain. Trickster and Flint have a camp on the eastern trail."

Lambkill said mildly, "She's coming up from the coast. Cocky and confident, too."

"Why would you say that?"

Lambkill felt Tannin shift beside him. He turned and caught his brother's warning glance. Tannin's long braid hung straight down his back. He'd rested his teacup on his knee and held it with one hand. *What an idiot.* Did he think Lambkill would be fool enough to mention that Kestrel had been seen with Sunchaser? Never. And anyway Sunchaser had left her by now. Tannin was unbearable.

Lambkill smiled at Tannin, then gestured negligently to Harrier. "Because she'll think she's almost safe. Why shouldn't she be confident?"

He casually sipped his tea. He could *smell* Kestrel's approach. Her scent carried on the breeze with as much pungency as that of the pines. Yes, she would be here soon. Very soon. And he would be waiting. He grinned smugly to himself.

Harrier lifted his tea and took a long swallow, then wiped his mouth on the back of his sleeve. "Let me tell you some things about this clan. Oxbalm's wife, Sumac, has always taken sides with Kestrel whenever we've discussed her. Be prepared for that."

Lambkill nodded, half-amused. "Women stick together. That's to be expected. It won't change things."

"How can you be so sure? What if Sumac makes a fuss when we try to take Kestrel out of the village? Oxbalm said that Sumac would demand a council session to hear the charges against your wife."

"So we sit through an Otter Clan council, then we go. We've hunted this long, another day won't make much difference."

"And what if they find her innocent of the incest and murder charges?"

"How could they? We are all witnesses to her guilt."

"It will still be our word against hers. The Otter Clan traces its descent through the women. They might not believe six men. They *could* vote to set her free. Or worse. Since she claims to be related to them, they could admit her into the clan. In that case, we would have to fight them to get her back."

Lambkill chuckled disdainfully. "It will never go that far. Believe me."

Ravenlight leaned sideways to whisper something to Harrier, and the warrior's face darkened. He nodded. "Yes, Ravenlight is right. Perhaps we should talk to Catchstraw before we take the chance of a council session."

Lambkill heard Little Coyote whisper from his pack: *"Yes, Father. Catchstraw is the one I told you about. Go to him. He's seen Mother. Talk to him about Mother before Sumac has her chance to stop you."*

Lambkill realized that his face went blank when he listened to Little Coyote, but the looks that Harrier and Ravenlight were giving him made him smile grimly. They peered at him as though he'd just called a ghost from the air. Could they hear his son's voice? he wondered. No, if they had, they would have shown astonishment, not suspicion.

Lambkill stared at the fire, assuming a relaxed posture. "Yes, we must talk to this Catchstraw. The four of us should go to see him at dawn tomorrow."

Harrier laced his fingers before him and nodded. "I think that's wise. Ravenlight won't be there, though. Tonight it's his turn to run the western trail, searching for your wife. If he's back by dawn, he'll want to sleep. But I'll go with you."

Thirty-nine

On her stomach, Kestrel moved with the stealth of Bobcat through the moldering deadfall, her ears straining to pierce the sounds of wind through the oak leaves and the croaking of frogs in the meadow. Powerful scents of spring flowers and deer dung stung her nostrils.

You just imagined it. She'd been telling herself that for half a hand of time, but the voice had imprinted itself on her soul like a poisonous taste on her tongue.

It's because you're so close. That's why you think you hear his voice. It's not real, Kestrel. It can't be real . . . please, Mother Ocean, don't let it be real!

Cloud Girl slept in her sack, and Kestrel prayed she would stay asleep. Darkness, the rustle of the wind and the sound of male voices from the camp beyond the trees should cover any sounds that she herself made. The voices were unfamiliar, but for a moment, for just a brief moment, Kestrel could have sworn she'd heard Lambkill's gruff laugh.

Warily, she dragged herself up to a tangle of brush and parted the branches. On top of the hill stood two large hide lodges. People moved through the flickering auras of plaza fires. She heard children laughing and dogs growling playfully. A woman was speaking in a low, melodic voice.

Otter Clan Village? As if being crushed beneath the weight of Mammoth's foot, her chest ached. She longed to rise and run all the way up the trail. But she pulled her gaze away.

Closer, a dart's cast to the south, a small camp fire lit the shadows. Three men sat around the blaze, one lounging on his side, his back to her. Gray hair hung down his back . . .

Kestrel began to shake with such violence that she had to concentrate on letting the branches close slowly, so they didn't flail against each other like dry sticks rattling in the wind.

Mother Ocean, oh, Mother . . .

She clenched her hands into tight fists to still their tremor.

If the village on top of the hill belonged to the Otter Clan and they had allowed Lambkill to camp beside them, then they had already judged her guilty of the crimes her husband accused her of.

Dry sobs racked her. Kestrel curled on her side and dug her fingers into the forest duff. How soft the ground felt, and how soothing to lie here with her cheek pillowed against it. The fragrance of damp earth filtered up around her in a sweet, invisible haze.

With the stealth of an assassin, the horrifying truth sank in.

. . . There was no haven.

There never had been.

The path that should have led her to the safety of Iceplant's family had led to nothing. Nothing at all. She had merely imagined the sanctuary . . . in the same way she had imagined suckling babies before she'd had any, or the way she could look out across the meadow down the hill and imagine it covered with deep snow that wouldn't be there for seven more moons.

She had built the haven from the wisps of her soul, and her soul was the only place where it had ever really existed. How could she so desperately want to weep for the loss of something that had never been?

Kestrel's breath trembled in her lungs. A queasy emptiness seeped through her. She'd known the truth for weeks. But she'd denied it, even when it had been thrown in her face. For two days she'd been rehearing Woodtick's voice when he'd said, "Sunchaser? About the woman you're with . . . this Kestrel. Who is she?" He'd heard her name before. She had known that just from the way he'd said it. And, like a fool, she'd shoved the warning out of her thoughts.

"Oh, Cloud Girl, I'm sorry. Mother's so sorry."

Her mind raced, considering options, seeking a future already denied her. Coming to the Otter Clan had been a mistake. Lambkill had been bound to realize someday that she would seek it out.

Why didn't I go straight north once we'd crossed the Big Spoonwood River? If I'd walked in the shallows, he'd never have been able to track us, and by now, we'd be in the country of the Ice Ghosts.

But then she would not have met Sunchaser.

And even if Lambkill murdered her tonight, she would never regret that. But Cloud Girl . . . what of Cloud Girl?

Her eyes were drawn to the hilltop again. One old woman had hobbled out to the edge of the crest and stood with her arms crossed, peering westward into the darkness. Firelight created an amber halo around her. She had a worried, an almost frightened, expression on her withered face. Was she the clan matron? Kestrel wondered. A great-aunt, or great-grandmother, of Iceplant's?

Blessed Above-Old-Man, how I wish I could go and ask. But I can't. Even if the Otter Clan adopted Cloud Girl and me, Lambkill would find a way of killing us. He would hide in the depths of the forest and wait for cycles, if necessary, to find them, together or alone.

Memories flitted past, of Iceplant, Owlwoman and Juniper Village.

Kestrel's stomach heaved. She vomited silently, her body writhing again and again until she had nothing left to bring up. At last she lay unable to move, tortured by dry heaves. But with the cleansing came a new emotion, one that chased away her terror: hatred. Pure. Fiery. It filled her the way a drowning man's lungs filled with water: hatred for Lambkill, for what he had done to her, and to Iceplant. For what he would do to Cloud Girl if he had the chance.

A frightening clarity stole through Kestrel's veins. It felt like a Spirit Plant's presence. Whispers breathed from the bottom of her soul, directing, guiding. With utter calm, she raised her arms and slipped the baby's sack off her back, then hung it on a snag of deadfall.

Her daughter didn't stir. She slept with her head tilted sideways, resting on her soft rabbit-fur hood. Her lips had parted, making her seem more innocent and vulnerable than ever.

Kestrel's eyes blurred with tears. No matter what happened to her, someone from the Otter Clan would find Cloud Girl and adopt her. *Yes. Yes, of course they will. Children are so precious. Who could resist that beautiful face?*

She ran gentle fingers down the front of Cloud Girl's sack, stopping over her daughter's heart. She smiled and wept. *I love you, baby.*

Kestrel pulled herself forward on her elbows, maneuvering around rocks and clumps of brush until she had a clear line of sight. She peered around a pine trunk. That was Tannin, sitting cross-legged beside Lambkill. He looked as though he'd eaten something rotten. His mouth had puckered in distaste. Kestrel recalled Calling Crane's tenderness and love; Tannin's wife had never treated her with anything but kindness. She missed Calling Crane.

Please, Mother Ocean. I don't want to have to kill Tannin. Calling Crane would hate me for it.

Kestrel wished she could hear the words of the hushed conversation. Who was the youth in the red shirt? A warrior from the Otter Clan? Why would he be sitting with Lambkill and Tannin? *Waiting with them for me to arrive?*

Kestrel's jaw clenched. She nocked a dart in the shell

hook of her atlatl and squirmed forward on her belly like Snake.

She could see Lambkill's face now, old, so old. His jowls looked more pronounced than before, and the thick wrinkles beneath his chin hung in loose, overlapping folds. But his smile hadn't changed. Gloating. Confident.

I'm going to kill you, my husband. Tonight!

Kestrel scrutinized his narrow back, imagining the placement of her dart. Sitting there like that in the light of the fire, he wouldn't even know what had hit him. The dart would slice through the muscles of his back and penetrate his lungs. He would drown in his own blood.

. . . And Tannin would catch her and kill her.

But it didn't matter. Cloud Girl would be safe.

Kestrel started to creep forward toward the cluster of mountain mahogany that created a blind no more than thirty hands from Lambkill's camp . . . but a sound behind her made her freeze. Something was running full tilt through the brush.

She stared wide-eyed at the darkness.

Then she saw the dog emerge from the shadows, its pink tongue dangling. *Helper!* As he came closer, she saw the wet stickiness that clotted his black coat and then smelled the coppery odor of blood. Kestrel shoved up on her elbows.

She stroked his dark fur, and the dog leaned into her hand as though desperately needing the comfort she offered. Then, after licking Kestrel's hand quickly, he bounded away, back down the trail. Kestrel's soul went cold.

Helper trotted back and stuck his pointed nose in her face, whirled lightly and ran down the trail again. When she didn't rise, he let out a sharp, agonized bark.

Cloud Girl woke and shrieked in response. Terror flooded Kestrel's veins. Lambkill shouted, "What was that?" and turned to look in her direction. Kestrel scrambled to her feet and started to run back to her daughter . . . and then saw the old woman from the village running down the trail with all of her elderly strength. Kestrel's steps faltered.

You'll be better off here, Cloud Girl. If Lambkill has no idea that you're my daughter, you'll be safe.

Voices muttered in the village on the hilltop. Several more women and two men ran after the old woman. Moccasins scritched on the gravel as people slipped in the darkness. Lambkill and the men at his camp rose and stared at the forest shadows where Cloud Girl's sack hung on the dead snag.

Kestrel still stood transfixed. Helper loped back and clamped his jaws around her hand, tugging at her cruelly, his canines digging into her flesh. She forced herself to back away. It was the hardest thing she'd ever done in her life. Cloud Girl burst into pathetic, shrill cries. Kestrel thought she could see her daughter's tiny hands reaching out to her.

Sobs choked her as she followed Helper into the black depths of the forest.

Sumac stood anxiously on the crest of the hill, her arms folded, peering westward. In the distance, wind pulled the clouds into thin strands of pale gray. She had been irritable all night, feeling strangely as though silent voices called to her from the trees and the earth, trying to warn her. When she'd first walked out, she'd half expected to see the woman named Kestrel coming up the trail. But she saw only Harrier and the two Bear-Looks-Back men sitting around their fire at the base of the hill. They'd erected a brush lodge twenty hands down the trail from their fire. It looked like a small shaggy bear.

Then she heard the baby's wails rising out of the depths of the trees, and her eyes jerked wide open. The older man—Lambkill—lurched to his feet when he heard the child's cries. The look on his withered face sent a chill up Sumac's spine.

"Oxbalm?" she shouted. She didn't turn, knowing that he sat beside the fire, sipping phlox-blossom tea.

Without waiting for his answer, she ran down the starlit slope, her old knees crackling. In her rush, she dislodged rocks and dirt. Three large stones bounced and tumbled ahead of her, followed by a flood of dark earth.

"What is it? *Sumac?*" Oxbalm responded.

"There's a baby in the forest!"

She heard a dozen people start down the hill behind her. Speculative murmurs broke out. By the time she reached the bottom of the hill, Lambkill had disappeared into the trees. Sumac rushed headlong after him, her old heart pounding so hard that she could feel it in her throat. The baby's cries had intensified, become breathless now, as though the infant were scared half to death.

"Blessed Mother Ocean," she whispered, "if he hurts that baby . . ."

She found Lambkill holding up a fur sack with a child in it. He held the sack at arm's length, as though frightened of the baby.

Without a word, Sumac rushed forward and jerked it from his hands, then cradled the child to her breast. The baby tipped a tear-streaked face up and frantically twined her fists in the fringes on Sumac's dress. Sumac didn't know why she assumed the child to be a girl, but she did. A thick wealth of black hair covered her tiny head. Softly, Sumac stroked her cheek and said, "Shh, it's all right, baby. I'm here."

A haunted expression twisted Lambkill's face. He glanced from Sumac to the child and back. "Whose baby is that?"

"Mine now." Sumac turned away, trying to catch her breath, and headed for the trail. She could see Oxbalm and several other villagers standing there next to Harrier. Tannin, Lambkill's younger brother, stood a short distance away, beyond the glow of the fire, his face dark and inscrutable.

"What do you mean it's yours? Who gave birth to it?" Lambkill demanded as he thrashed through the brush behind her.

Sumac hobbled out across the grass and thrust the baby

into Oxbalm's arms. He looked at his wife in puzzlement, but held the baby close. Then he peered over Sumac's shoulder at Lambkill. When the child fussed, Oxbalm rocked her gently—as he had rocked tens of tens of babies over the long cycles.

Sumac whispered, "I'll explain later. The baby is ours now."

Lambkill strode into the amber glow and clenched his fists at his sides. His face had turned an ugly shade of red, as if he suspected he were being played for a fool. "Who does that baby belong to?"

Oxbalm glanced at Sumac's face, and his faded eyes lit with understanding. He shifted the child into his right arm and reached out to take Sumac's hand. His warm touch comforted her. He replied, "This child belongs to the Otter Clan."

"Are you telling me that someone from your village left her baby in the forest . . . alone! *At night?*"

Calmly, Oxbalm replied, "What I'm telling you is that this is none of your concern, Trader Lambkill."

Voices rose like a flock of frightened birds and fluttered through the firelit darkness. Men and women whispered behind their hands and stared at the baby.

Oxbalm ignored them. He hobbled up the trail toward the hilltop, dragging Sumac with him. Very quietly, Sumac said, "I think it's *her* baby. All night long, I've been feeling odd. I think she was here, saw her husband and decided to leave her child and run away."

Oxbalm's thick gray brows drew together over his bulbous nose. A faint sliver of Above-Old-Man's face crept over the eastern horizon and sprinkled the sky with diamond fires. The light flowed into Oxbalm's wrinkles, making him appear uncounted winters old. As he huffed and puffed up the steep slope, he threw Sumac an affectionate, if reproachful, look. "Then this Kestrel must have known that her lover's relatives are fools for children."

"Perhaps."

Gladness swelled her chest. She timed her steps carefully, walking in stride with Oxbalm. It made both of them steadier. Maybe this little girl would fill the hole in their souls left by Mountain Lake's death. Sumac reached over and drew the rabbit-fur hood up over the girl's head to protect her from the night's chill. The baby watched her through wide, unblinking eyes—*strange eyes, so deep and bright they seem filled with the knowledge of eternity.*

Oxbalm crested the hill and headed across the grass for the central fire. "Who will you ask to feed this infant, my wife?"

Sumac said, "Against the Clouds has a son about the age of this little girl. She has enough milk for two. She's always complaining about how much milk she has. She's been leaking all over her finest leathers. She'll be glad to have another child to feed."

Oxbalm stopped beside his cup near the fire and handed the child to Sumac. "You're too kindhearted for your own good. Did you know that? If this is Kestrel's daughter, we'd better keep quiet about it."

She clutched the baby firmly. In the firelight, she could see Oxbalm's eyes soften. Sumac smiled at him and patted the baby's back. "Afraid you'll have to go to war with the surrounding villages to protect her?"

"Yes, I am."

"Well, then that's the way of things. This little one needs a home. You know, you can't have too many children around. It would be worth a war to give her a family."

"Yes," he sighed and put a tender hand on Sumac's shoulder. "It might be."

Wolfdreamer stood on top of a red ridge overlooking a canyon filled with crumbling stone villages. Around him, a dry, rough-hewn landscape spread. Deeply eroded plains stretched

as far as he could see, dotted with sandstone buttes that poked their square heads against the azure sky. Dusty drainages sliced meandering canyons through the vastness, marked by the serpentine lines of scrubby trees and brush.

The tang of sage drifted on the hot wind. Wolfdreamer inhaled deeply, letting it bathe his face in memories of a time when the scattered ruins below had housed thousands, and voices shouting "Hututu! Hututu!" had sundered the heavens to call the Rain God from the sky.

Dressed in a wealth of colored feathers and copper bells, Wolfdreamer had walked with men here. The People had sprinkled his path with blue cornmeal and Sung his praises while shaking their deerbone rattles. In return, he had showered them with the richest of life's gifts . . . rain.

Now only field mice, snakes, scorpions and coyotes roamed the crumbling ruins in this empty canyon.

Wolfdreamer braced a hand against the boulder beside him and studied Sunchaser.

The Dreamer knelt in the middle of the disintegrating plaza below. His white hair stirred in the wind that swept the faces of the sheer canyon walls. Sunchaser's eyes focused on the huge, five-storied building that curved around him like the cold arm of a dead lover. His face had gone slack with wonder, as though he could see beyond the desolation to the great civilization that had once thrived here.

"Do you see the ghosts, Sunchaser? Can you hear their voices?"

Wolfdreamer could. He saw the men leaning against the clay-washed faces of the buildings, knapping out arrow points, and the women sitting in the plaza, talking as they rolled out clay and coiled it into beautiful pots. He could hear the gobbling of the tamed turkeys that strutted the grounds and the laughter of the children who had once raced so freely through the cool shadows of this monumental village.

Nevertheless, he had chosen this time—when they had been dead for over two centuries—to teach his lesson.

Wolfdreamer had arrived before Dawn Child awoke. But he'd left Sunchaser alone. The Dreamer had wandered the ruins like a little boy, running, calling out, exploring the thousands of rooms within walking distance . . . and finally he had returned here to fall on his knees and stare in awe at the crumbling magnificence. He'd Sung for a while, beautiful lilting Songs, calling forth the shreds of Power that lurked in the fallen stones, gathering them around him like a transparent fortress wall.

Then the Dreamer had gone quiet . . .

Wolfdreamer walked the trail that led over the crest of the ridge and wound down into the canyon. The shell bells on his moccasins clicked melodiously, while the long fringes on his mammothhide shirt and pants patted out a muted rhythm. He'd braided his long black hair into a single plait that hung down to the middle of his back.

The path between the silted-in villages had been lined with crushed potsherds. The fine black-and-white designs on them blazed beneath his feet. Murmurs of ghosts haunted these ruins. Their words rose and fell with the intensity of wind, drifting homelessly around the looming masonry walls as if searching for surviving relatives, sisters or cousins who could save them. But they'd already obliterated every possible refuge.

The ghosts would never leave this place.

As he rounded the corner of the building, he started to Sing. The notes echoed through the shadows.

Sunchaser didn't even turn at the sound of Wolfdreamer's soft voice. He just gazed at the ruins. The magnificent paintings—depicting the Gods—that had once covered the white-plastered walls had flaked and crumbled into chunky piles. Only the thirty-hand-tall figures of the Yamuhakto, the Great Warriors of the East and West, continued to grace the front of the building. They carried lightning bolts in their hands, aimed down at the plaza. But the rich reds, blues and yellows that had detailed their terrifying masks had paled to insignificance.

When Wolfdreamer stood beside Sunchaser, he saw that the Dreamer clutched a stone knife in both hands, one of the rare turquoise knives used by the great priests in their ceremonials. Sunchaser had gripped the stone so tightly, for so long, that he'd snapped it in two.

Wolfdreamer sat down and leaned back on his elbows. Sunchaser's hair and craggy face bore a thin coating of red dust. The dirt had mixed with tears and puddled in the lines at the corners of Sunchaser's black eyes. He looked very tired, and hurt.

Wolfdreamer tipped up his face. As Father Sun sailed westward on his afternoon journey, shadows stalked across the plaza, cool on Wolfdreamer's bronze skin.

"This is a majestic place," Sunchaser said. His voice sounded hoarse, as though his throat was raw from so much praying.

"It was. I remember a hundred glorious summer-solstice celebrations. When Father Sun peeked above the eastern horizon, shafts of light pierced the sacred ceremonial chambers here, and the clan elders burst out in Songs that shook the foundations of the world. They Sang the Gods into existence. They Danced the world back into harmony." Wolfdreamer paused and gestured to the Great Warriors. "In the last days, the People painted everything they could, trying to prevent Power from abandoning the canyon."

Sunchaser's face betrayed shock. "But the Power . . . it's almost dead. I've been trying all day—"

"Yes, over the centuries a few traces have returned, but not many."

"You mean there was a time when all the Power had disappeared?"

Wolfdreamer nodded. "With every tree they cut, every field they tilled, every war cry they uttered, they bled away the strength of their civilization, until the last trace of Power fled in the searing summer wind."

"But how could that happen? Why would Power abandon them?"

Wolfdreamer squinted at the sunlight playing along the jagged edge of the high cliff. Flecks of light glimmered in the rock carvings that covered the flat sandstone walls. The Spirals called to him, their voices faint but impassioned, "Save us! Don't let us die. It wasn't our fault! We tried!"

He lowered his gaze and brushed his fingers over the gritty sandstone. "Because by then, it was too late."

Sunchaser held the halves of the turquoise knife more tightly. "Their Dreamers weren't strong enough to bring the Power back?"

"Their greatest Dreamer—named Born of Water—had failed long before, and not all of the Dreamers alive could save them then. Though they tried.

"The Old Ones who built this sprawling civilization called all of their Dreamers together, the great as well as the small, and isolated them in that subterranean ceremonial chamber over there—" he pointed *"—on the north side of the plaza. They Sang and fasted for almost a moon, sucking every bit of Power from the rocky cliffs, the animals, the clouds that drifted by."*

"And still they failed?"

"There was so little Power left, Sunchaser, that the amount they could collect did them little good.

"This place, while one of the most spectacular, is not the only one. There are others, scattered across time and land. I could have taken you to Cahokia, or Etowah, the Medicine Wheel, Tippecanoe, or Wounded Knee. All of them are places where people Sang and Danced and prayed . . . and died."

Sunchaser stared at Wolfdreamer with astonishment in his eyes. "Why did you bring me here, Wolfdreamer? What am I supposed to learn from these palace builders?"

"I wanted you to see the great heights your people will reach ten thousand cycles from now." Wolfdreamer smiled gently. *"And to tell you that over that vast span of time, tens of tens of Dreamers will fail . . . yet your people will still build this magnificent civilization."*

"At what . . . what cost?"

"*Many things will change. Beautiful animals will die, along with different kinds of trees and butterflies. Some of the sweetest flowers in the world will pass out of existence.*"

Sunchaser gripped his stone knife so hard that his fist shook. "I have not failed yet, Wolfdreamer! Mammoths still exist in my world!"

"*Yes . . . for now. I haven't given up on you, Sunchaser. I just wanted you to know that I realize how hard it is. I, too, loved once. She was beautiful and kind. I made a different choice than you have. But that doesn't mean you'll fail because of your love. A few rare Dreamers actually need love to keep them Dreaming well. But sometimes even the best, the most faithful, Dreamers fail. Some fail because they choose worldly responsibilities, others because they're just not strong enough. And some fail because they're being witched and don't even know it. But failure is not the end. Power will just select someone else and pray that its new Dreamer can accomplish the impossible task set before him or her. . . . And there's something more you should know, Sunchaser.*"

"What is that?"

Wolfdreamer let out a breath and smiled forlornly, watching the whiffs of dust that curled up along the ruined walls when the breeze gusted just right. The reddish-tan streamers sailed upward and vanished against the blue sky like the long-dead souls of hunting serpents. Wolfdreamer's brows drew together. "Just this, Dreamer. Failure is not wasted effort. Mammoths may vanish from the world . . ." *Sunchaser started to protest, but Wolfdreamer lifted a hand for silence* ". . . but that doesn't mean your efforts are smoke in the wind, Sunchaser. Every moment that humans spend cherishing and worrying about the Life around them is another spark added to the ocean of Light; it drives back the Darkness for just that much longer.*"

Sunchaser frowned, bewildered. "Wolfdreamer, please help me. I feel lost. I don't know what's right anymore. I can't get through the maze. People are losing faith in me. What am I doing so badly?"

The agony in those words reminded Wolfdreamer of a thousand such pleas he'd heard—and each of them had pierced his soul like a needle of ice. He smiled and put his hand over Sunchaser's fist that held the halves of the turquoise knife. "I came to help you. You don't realize it, but all the suffering, all the confusion and exhaustion you've gone through, were necessary. A beginning. Even the witching had a place. The wrong paths you think you've taken weren't wrong at all. You've just been concentrating so hard on the twists and turns that you missed the reason why you were traveling."

"But isn't that why you gave me the maze? So I could study it? Because it represented the sacred geography of the Land of the Dead? I thought that if I understood the twists and turns, I'd be able to find my way to you at any time I needed to."

Wolfdreamer sat up and laced his fingers over his drawn-up knees. "No. That wasn't the reason. I gave you the maze in the hopes that you would stare so hard at the lines that you'd finally see the spaces between them."

Sunchaser blinked. The dust on his lashes glittered as he straightened. "I don't understand."

Wolfdreamer sighed. "Answer this for me. What would the maze be without its background? Without the hide or the stone or the bark you draw it upon?"

"What would it be?" Sunchaser cocked his head and seemed to be thinking hard. "I . . . I don't know. It wouldn't be anything, would it?"

Wolfdreamer lowered a finger to the dusty plaza. He patiently drew each of the maze lines, but overlapping, until they obliterated the spaces between the lines. "What is this, Sunchaser?"

Sunchaser leaned forward. He glanced sideways at Wolfdreamer, then back at the lines. "It looks like all the strands of the maze have pulled tight into a knot."

"Does it?"

"Well, yes. I mean, that's what it looks like to me. What do you think it looks like?"

The question made Wolfdreamer laugh. "I think it looks like an eagle. Monster Rock Eagle, actually."

Sunchaser's face slackened as a glimmer of understanding lit his eyes. "Monster Rock Eagle, who sits at the crossing that leads to the heart of the maze?"

"The very same. Few Dreamers ever see him. And he's very hard to kill, but you must kill him. Or you'll never find your way through the maze."

Wolfdreamer waited while Sunchaser digested that bit of information and related it to Good Plume's Dream. Sunchaser's face went from intrigue to fear in less than ten heartbeats. He looked up at Wolfdreamer with his whole soul in his eyes.

"You mean that the heart of the maze is a tangle? A knot? I know it has always been the twists and turns that have frightened me, but I thought the Land of the Dead was the heart of the maze."

"Monster Rock Eagle keeps watch over something far more precious. He guards the Center."

"The center of what?"

"Life. And Death. To unravel the knot and find the Center, you must live Monster Rock Eagle's death, at the same time that he is dying your life. Don't you see? When you've both died, there will no longer be any Dreamer to seek him, nor will there be any Eagle to block the path. The point where the two of you meet in death is the Center."

"But what's there . . . at the Center, I mean?"

"Emptiness. Just Emptiness. I can make the explanation no simpler than that, Sunchaser."

Wolfdreamer got to his feet and stretched his back muscles. Scents of greasewood and prickly pear blossoms blew in with a whirlwind of dust. The whirlwind bobbed and careened across the plaza, then struck the sage and dissipated into a reddish haze that evaporated as it floated upward.

Sunchaser stood beside Wolfdreamer and folded his arms over his chest as though to keep all the confusion locked inside.

Wolfdreamer gave him a pained smile. "You make things too hard, Dreamer. Whatever convinced you that the lines of the maze were the path? The lines are only markers on the way. They'll just lead you in circles. You have to walk the empty spaces between the lines to get anywhere."

"How can I walk the spaces between the strands of a knot, Wolfdreamer?"

Wolfdreamer threw back his head and laughed harder than he had laughed in cycles. It felt good to laugh. And to be here in the warm sunshine, bathed in the sacred fragrances of the desert. Oh, how he cherished them. "Everything is connected to everything else, Sunchaser. Remember?"

"That sounds like a knot if ever I heard one."

Wolfdreamer turned and gazed at Sunchaser, praying, hoping that the Dreamer had at last understood, hoping he now saw that the strands of the Starweb that connected all living things and the slithering, disconnected lines of the maze were the same . . . but the Dreamer only met his gaze with a pained frown.

Wolfdreamer sighed. "It's time for you to go home, Sunchaser. Go home and think about it. Don't forget what we discussed here. First you must challenge the witch who's trying to kill you, and then you'll be free to continue Dreaming, working for Mammoth Above. But go home now, Sunchaser . . ."

Forty

Horseweed drifted through the trees like Owl's shadow, stepping toe first, checking the ground before he lowered his heel. He couldn't even hear his own movements, so he knew that she couldn't either. Nevertheless, if she turned at just the right moment, she might catch sight of him.

He slowed down, stopping briefly behind a tree trunk so that he blended with the night. The young woman and the dog followed a deer trail that wound from meadow to meadow through the timber. Two fingers of time ago, he'd seen her face reflecting in the moonlight and had started following her. She didn't have a baby with her, but she carried an atlatl and a long dart in her right hand.

Kestrel! He felt almost certain that she was Trader Lambkill's wife. She fit the description perfectly: tiny, with long black hair and a turned-up nose. Her beauty stunned him, as did her dress. He'd seen that shirt many times before. Sunchaser wore it when he led the Mammoth Spirit Dances. Had she stolen it? Maybe she'd killed Sunchaser—the way she'd killed Harrier's brother?—and taken the shirt. Anger and fear warmed his veins.

The woman he saw now seemed incapable of the strength necessary to drive a tapir-bone stiletto into a grown man's chest with her bare hands. But looks could be deceiving. Horseweed took a dart from the quiver on his back and nocked his atlatl. His steps took on the caution of Cougar stalking a wounded bear.

Bending low, he crept by a lichen-covered boulder. On the other side, he cautiously peered around the gritty curve of the stone. The woman had stopped and crouched down to touch something on the ground. She lifted her fingers and stared at them. A soft, choking sound came from her. The dog bounded back and forth in front of her. It didn't bark, but it seemed frantic.

The woman stood. "Where is he, Helper? Take me to him. Hurry!"

She ran forward as the dog led the way through the dense underbrush and into the lurking shadows of the towering pines.

When they'd almost vanished behind a huge tumbled pile of dead wood, Horseweed rose. His pulse roared in his ears.

Helper? Sunchaser's dog was named Helper. He recalled Balsam's ironic question that day high in the mountains: "Is that dog his Spirit Helper? He has a *mangy* Spirit Helper?" This dog didn't have mange. Could it be the same animal?

So, what was going on? The tone of her voice was worried, like a mother for a child . . . or a wife for a husband. Prickles of unease traced patterns down Horseweed's back. Witching, hunted women, the mammoths' suicides—and he was right in the middle of it all.

Horseweed ran lightly down the trail the woman had taken, then ducked from one tree to the next as he followed her. Where had she gone? He squinted into the darkness.

A dog whined, giving him a target in the blackness. Horseweed crept closer, then stopped when he saw her feet sticking out from beneath a head-high stack of deadfall. She'd left her atlatl and dart on the ground outside. Her moccasins had dark, wet splotches on the bottoms. In the moonlight, the splotches looked like . . . blood? He gripped his weapons more tightly.

"Oh, Sunchaser! No . . . no!" the woman cried. "Helper, go around me. You have to get out so I'll have enough room to drag him. *Move!*"

A scuffling sounded from under the arch of deadfall and

the dog emerged. It got up and shook the pine duff from its thick coat. Dust glittered and spun little whirlwinds in the silver light penetrating the branches.

When Helper saw Horseweed, he let out a growl, and the hair on his back stuck straight up. Horseweed knelt and extended a hand. "Come here, boy. It's all right. I'm a friend. Remember me?"

That's when he saw the broken dart shaft. It lay at his feet in a puddle of old blood. What had the dart struck? An animal? Or a human predator?

Helper stepped toward Horseweed to sniff his hand. He wagged his tail and whimpered. Just then the woman's head appeared at the end of the logs. Long hair trailed around her. Her eyes had dilated enormously. As she crawled out, Horseweed could see the tears that streaked her cheeks.

"Who are you?" she demanded. She'd hooked her atlatl on her belt. Her hands were empty. "Never mind. Come over here! I don't care who you are, I need help. *Now!*"

Horseweed put his dart back into his quiver and tied his own atlatl to his belt thong, then walked over cautiously and knelt beside her. He could smell the pungent scent of blood. "Who's in there? Is it Sunchaser?"

She searched his face anxiously and nodded. "Yes. Do you know him? You told Helper you were a friend. That's the only reason I didn't dart you when I first came out."

"I know Sunchaser. He comes to our village often."

"Then help me. Please! He's injured and unconscious. That space is big enough for only one person and I . . .." she made a panicked gesture ". . . I don't think I can manage to drag him out!"

"Let me try."

She rose and stepped aside. Horseweed glanced at her as he tentatively placed his atlatl and nocked dart on the ground beside her weapons. She didn't seem to notice. Her eyes were riveted on the pile of deadfall. He got down on his stomach and crawled into the dark womb formed by the fallen trees and tangled branches. Thin lances of moonlight pricked the darkness. The scents of moss and pack rat dung mixed eerily with the pungency of blood.

Sunchaser was lying on his left side, one arm stretched out. His clothing had been torn to shreds, baring his chest. Horseweed gasped and scrambled forward. Claw marks covered Sunchaser's arms and legs. Horseweed touched one of the dark pools that glistened on the ground. It felt sticky and cold.

Blessed Spirits . . .

"Sunchaser?" Horseweed called as he slid closer. He couldn't see Sunchaser's face very clearly, but the Dreamer's deep-set eyes looked sunken and blood spattered his square chin and white hair.

A staccato of fear began to beat in Horseweed's chest. Sunchaser wasn't dead, was he? No . . . no, the wounds didn't look that severe. Still . . . Horseweed reached out and placed his fingers against Sunchaser's throat. Relief spread through him when he felt the steady rhythm of a heartbeat. He let his hand sink to the ground. "Sunchaser?"

"Hurry!" the woman said from where she knelt in the entryway. "Get him out of there so I can have a good look at his wounds."

"Bringing him out safely isn't going to be that easy," Horseweed called back. "I think he was attacked by a bear, or maybe by one of the big cats. I found a broken dart shaft outside. The animal must have gotten away. I'm going to need your help so we don't break the wounds open again when we move him. He can't afford to lose more blood."

Horseweed backed out. The moonglow seemed brilliant compared to the darkness of the deadfall. An old forest giant, its trunk as thick as three men, had fallen here, toppling the lesser trees around it. For a moment, he studied the dead wood, then braced himself, heaving with all his might. One of the logs lifted, but try as he might, Horseweed could not pull it loose from the mass that pinned it.

He puffed a sigh, sat back against the end of a log and looked at the woman. "If you can go in first and get above

Sunchaser's head—there's enough room for you, I think—
then fold his arms over his chest and keep them there, I
can pull on his feet. I'm afraid his tattered sleeves might
get caught on a snag and do more damage than—"

"I understand. Get out of my way, so I can get inside."

Horseweed leaned sideways, and she pushed past him.
He could hear her soft voice as she spoke to Sunchaser,
the words filled with tears. "I'm here, Sunchaser. You're
going to be all right. Don't worry. I'm here."

Horseweed rolled to his belly and peered into that blackness.
He could see the woman. She had gently lifted Sunchaser's
white head so she could ease around him into the niche at the
opposite end of the hole. Two splintered branches had been
driven into the ground by their fall, creating a V-shaped space
barely large enough to admit her. She stroked Sunchaser's
cheek gently before she carefully arranged his arms over
his chest.

Horseweed's brows lowered. Even an idiot could have told
from the tone of her voice and the way she touched Sunchaser
that they were lovers . . . no matter how unlikely it seemed
that Sunchaser would have taken a lover.

"I'm ready," she called to Horseweed. "As you pull, I'll
hold his arms."

"Let me get a good grip on his feet." He reached in and
clamped his fingers around Sunchaser's ankles, holding them
just beneath the torn flesh of the calves. The blood made his
hands slippery. "I'm going to start pulling."

"Go ahead."

Horseweed tugged, and Sunchaser came slowly. The woman held the wounded Dreamer's arms to his chest with one
hand while she used the other to cushion his head.

When at last Horseweed had managed to pull Sunchaser
out into the moonlight, the woman fell by Sunchaser's side
to check his wounds. She made soft sounds of pain as she
touched each injury on Sunchaser's tall body.

Horseweed asked, "You're Lambkill's wife, aren't you?"

She didn't even look up. She held out a hand. "Give me

your knife, a sharp flake, anything. I need to cut his sleeve to bind his arm wound. That seems to be the worst one."

Horseweed reached into his pouch, located his chert-bladed knife and gave it to her. She sawed off a square of Sunchaser's sleeve, revealing the swells of muscles beneath—and the deep slashes. Gore and old pine needles had clotted together to form thick mounds on his upper arm. She cut the ends of the square, then wrapped the piece around Sunchaser's arm and tied the split ends.

"We can't risk washing any of his injuries here," she said shakily. "We have to get him to your village, where he can be properly cared for. I'll need to make a poultice, to find the right plants to Heal him. Pray that Evil Spirits don't smell the blood and come to feast before we have a chance to clean and bind his wounds."

Horseweed nodded. Helper sat a few hands away, his black ears up. Through the branches behind him, a few of the brightest Star People sparkled on the slate-blue undercoat of moonlight. Horseweed rose and said, "Cut a handful of fringes from his jacket. We'll need them to tie a travois together. I'll start looking for dead saplings for the poles."

She stroked Sunchaser's bloody hair, clearly reluctant to move away from him. "I saw a small grove of pine saplings up the trail. From the looks of it, the big trees starved them of light." She hesitated, biting her lip, then said: "Wait. I'll come with you. It will be quicker that way."

Horseweed stood quietly, waiting for her, watching her rise to her feet and clench her hands into fists. She had to be around his age, maybe a little older, fifteen or sixteen summers. What was it about her that touched him so deeply? He didn't have enough experience with women to understand the effect she had on him. The way she moved, her gestures . . . all gave the appearance of a little girl dressed up as a woman.

And yet something about her went straight to his heart with the sharpness of an obsidian dart point. He swallowed hard. It would be just like him to stumble into love with Sunchaser's woman. Sunchaser would probably turn him into pond scum in retribution.

Hastily, he stepped out. "Which way did you say those poles were?"

She led the way, and Horseweed followed her to the grove where the unlucky saplings had tried to grow under the spreading bulk of a sequoia. The gray skeletons of six small trees had reached nearly fifteen hands in height before they'd starved in the shadows. They would do. The woman pushed the first tree over until the base cracked with a loud pop. Horseweed toppled another as Kestrel snapped off the thin dry branches.

They worked in silence until they'd knocked down and stripped four of the trees. Then Horseweed said, "That will be enough. We'll use the two longest poles for the sides. Then we'll snap the two smaller trees into segments and lash them to the side poles to make six inner rungs."

She nodded and wet her full lips. "Good. Let's hurry. Give me the small ends. You take the big."

As he gathered the saplings, Horseweed said, "Your husband is waiting for you on the trail ahead. Do you know that?"

"Yes. I—I know."

"You don't have to go into camp with me if you don't want to. I can take Sunchaser by myself. In fact, if I were you, I'd find a place in the forest to hide. My grandfather is the chief of Otter Clan Village. He gave your husband and the Blackwater Draw men until the day after tomorrow to wait for you. Then they must leave. It will be safer for you to come in after they're gone."

She took a deep breath. "Please, I don't want to think about that yet." More softly, she added, "When we get closer to the village . . . I'll decide."

Horseweed turned his attention to the task at hand, retracing the path toward the pile of deadfall. The resignation in her voice struck him hard. Glancing back, he noted the set of her shoulders, the way she walked with bowed head.

Horseweed turned away. Helper had lain down by Sunchaser's side and propped his muzzle on Sunchaser's shoulder.

As they lowered the poles, Horseweed said, "The decision is yours, of course, but you should know that my grandmother is on your side. She—"

"Your grandmother?" the woman asked. "Who is she? What does she know of me?"

"Her name is Sumac. She is the matron of our clan. I don't know how much she knows about you. Only what your husband and the Blackwater Draw men have told her."

"Then . . . you're Oxbalm's grandson?"

"Yes," he answered proudly. "How do you know of my grandfather?"

"Sunchaser told me about him. He has great respect for Oxbalm. What's your name?"

"Horseweed."

"So, Horseweed," she said through a long exhalation, "what have my husband and these other men told the Otter Clan about me?"

Horseweed shrugged as he picked up one of the smaller poles, studying its shape in the darkness. "Your husband has accused you of incest, and he said that you claim to be related to our clan. Harrier says you killed his younger brother, Buffalo Bird. Both said you had a baby with you."

The woman's jaw quivered before she clamped it still. "So you know my name."

"They said it was Kestrel."

She stared at the scattered triangles of silver light that lit the forest floor. "Yes. That's right."

Horseweed placed the pole just so, its end on one of the fallen logs, and jumped on the middle of it, cracking it in two. "I'll need those strips of leather," he said, "to lash on the rungs."

She tenderly ran her fingers over the long fringes that made up the hem of Sunchaser's bloody shirt, then deftly cut off several of them. She did it reverently, as if each were a ceremonial object, specially blessed by the Spirits. And perhaps they had been at that. Horseweed couldn't count the number of sacred Songs he'd heard Sunchaser Sing to Mammoth Above while he'd worn that shirt. He stood awkwardly, feeling guilty that she had to savage that shirt for a travois.

She handed his knife back. "I'll tie on the three lower rungs if you'll tie the top ones."

"All right."

He took six of the strips of hide from her and laid the side poles out, forming a steep angle. Then he placed the rungs and lashed them securely, making certain that the top rung was wide enough for his hips. Kestrel triple-wrapped the ends of the bottom rungs before she knotted the hide strips.

"Don't you want to know why my grandmother is on your side?" Horseweed asked as he rose and dragged the finished travois over beside Sunchaser's tall body.

Kestrel walked around Horseweed and very gently rolled Sunchaser onto his side. "Push the travois beneath him," she instructed.

When Horseweed had the litter positioned, she rolled Sunchaser to his back again, suspended over five of the rungs. His arms flopped lifelessly. She carefully bent his long legs so they wouldn't drag on the ground. Rising, she unlaced the small pack from around her waist and placed it beneath Sunchaser's head as a pillow.

"He looks so pale," she murmured.

"He'll live. I'm sure of it. We just have to get him to my grandmother. Sumac will take good care of him."

"Is she a Healer?"

"No, but she knows how to take care of people. She's very good at it. She raised me and my brother and sister after our parents died."

Kestrel blinked somberly. "She sounds like a good woman. A woman who loves children. . . . Come on, then. Let's get moving."

Horseweed picked up his weapons, put his dart in his

quiver and tied his atlatl to his belt thong. Then he handed the woman her own weapons. She took them, saying, "Thank you. After the things you must have heard about me from Lambkill, I'm surprised that you would give me back my weapons."

Horseweed lifted the narrow end of the travois and ducked under it so that the top rung pressed against his waist and the poles rested over his hips. The ends of the poles provided handholds. "It is because I've met your husband that I gave them back, Kestrel. He's . . . well, you may need them."

He walked forward slowly, testing the travois' strength. The litter seemed stable. He pulled it out onto the trail, feeling the heavy drag.

He squinted at the moonlit path—all of it uphill. He'd make it to the village, all right. Somehow, some way, he'd summon the strength and endurance, but it wouldn't be fun.

Kestrel walked beside Sunchaser, her weapons in one hand and the other hand knotted in what remained of his left sleeve, making certain that his limp body didn't slide off the travois when they hit irregularities in the trail. Helper trotted in front, scouting the path with his nose in the air.

When Horseweed reached the top of the first rise, he stopped to take a breath while he looked out over the vista.

"Oh!" Kestrel cried, stepping to the side and returning with her pack, which had fallen from beneath Sunchaser's head.

Horseweed glanced around. "This must be where he was attacked. Here, in the middle of the rise. But that doesn't make sense. Predators generally hunt from the shadows, from ambush. Not from the open."

As Kestrel retied her pack to the side of the travois, Helper trotted down the trail ahead of them, his bushy tail up. Horseweed threw himself back into his labor, the eerie wrongness clinging to his soul like morning dew to a spiderweb.

The hills bore a shining powder of moonlight that resembled snow during the Moon-When-Wind-Sings, breathtakingly beautiful. Every blade of grass in the meadows shimmered.

Slender feathers of clouds floated across the bleached belly of Brother Sky. Horseweed breathed deeply of the damp redolence of the night and steadily pulled the travois.

Somewhere out there, a wounded animal hid. It would be angry and in pain, eager to even the score. He glanced down at his atlatl on his belt, making certain it would be close at hand if needed. It would be hard to draw a dart from his quiver, however, while hauling the litter.

He leaned into the rung over his waist and tugged the travois down the slope and across a field of wildflowers. Too many things were happening—as if all the world were coming undone. And, yes, he *was* right in the middle of it.

"Did you commit incest?" Horseweed asked bluntly.

"I don't know," she answered. "According to my people, I did. But my lover's mother came from your clan, the Otter Clan. He said you traced your kinship through the women, so he didn't consider me to be his cousin."

Horseweed frowned. "How does your clan trace its kinship?"

"Through the men."

He shook his head. "I've heard of such a thing, but I can't even imagine how it would work. When you marry, do you go to live in your husband's lodge, in his mother's village?"

"In his *father's* village. But often Traders' wives continue to live in their own villages—it's a kindness. Life in their husbands' villages would be very difficult. Traders are gone for half the cycle or more, and the woman would be lost in a group of strangers. But usually women go to their husbands' villages. Among my people, everything belongs to men. The lodge, the children. Even a woman's body."

Horseweed cocked his head when he heard the scurrying of field mice across the trail ahead. He saw their tiny forms darting over the bare dirt. He scanned the next rise, searching for any sign of danger. "Your lover was related to your father, then?" He grunted as he tugged the travois around a deep hole in the trail.

"Yes. Iceplant was my father's brother's son."

"He wouldn't have been your cousin as far as my clan is concerned. I've never heard his name before, though. What was his mother's name?"

"Wind Shadow."

Horseweed chewed his lower lip thoughtfully. For her sake, he prayed to Above-Old-Man that someone had heard that name before. "Don't worry. She must have left a long time ago. Maybe some of the clan elders will remember her."

"I hope so, Horseweed."

Kinship through the father instead of the mother? How could people think so differently? He'd been brought up on the coast and had never traveled more than two weeks in any direction. Everyone he knew was related through his mother's family. If his people did things the way Kestrel's did, none of his relatives would be his relatives. The thought was unsettling. It must have been terrible for Iceplant's mother. How could her parents have forced her to marry into such a strange life? Which of his relatives had done that to Wind Shadow?

Horseweed struggled against the weight of the travois for over half a hand of time, then stopped, catching his breath. His legs ached. The muscles in his back felt strained and hot.

"Are you all right?" Kestrel asked.

"Fine." He smiled at her, trying to disregard his quivering limbs. Why did Sunchaser have to be so heavy? He threw himself into the struggle again, forcing himself forward. The last thing he would let this pretty Kestrel think was that Horseweed was a weakling!

The moon had slid halfway across the sky, and sweat ran down Horseweed's sides in trickling rivulets. His legs shook as the poles ate into the skin on his hips. His breath came in gasps, but he ground his teeth and stumbled forward.

"Could I help?" Kestrel asked. "Maybe if I—"

"No. Fine. I'm fine."

Horseweed glared at the steep hill before him and called up yet another fistful of energy from his empty reserves. When he reached the next level spot, he paused, taking another breather.

"My village is over that next rise." He turned to look at Kestrel. Despite the cold breeze, perspiration had beaded on her smooth brow. It had matted tiny curls to her temples. "Are you going in with me?"

Kestrel's eyes narrowed as she gazed at the hill. "I guess I . . . Horseweed, I'm not leaving Sunchaser. Not again."

"What about your husband?"

"I don't know. I—I just don't know. But go on. I'll follow you in."

Horseweed watched her smooth her fingers over her atlatl and nocked dart, and he started to climb the rise. She had a right to protect herself, but he fervently hoped that she wasn't contemplating murder. The Otter Clan's punishment for such a crime came with breathless swiftness.

"Kestrel," he warned, "don't attack him first, no matter how frightened you are. My people . . . they wouldn't understand."

"Thank you, Horseweed. I don't know the ways of your people, and I need your help." She unnocked her dart, then tied her atlatl to her belt and gazed at her long dart, as if wondering what to do with it.

"You can put it in my quiver if you want. I'll stay close by you. You'll be able to reach it, I think, if you need it."

"Thank you." Kestrel walked forward and slipped her dart into his quiver.

He dropped his eyes back to the trail. The travois poles raked over a section of upthrust rocks, creating a high-pitched screech. "You're a brave woman. Stay behind me. If trouble starts, I'll reach for my own atlatl. No one will question my actions to protect you."

They passed Harrier's empty camp. The fire had burned down to flickering red coals. The scent of smoke mixed with the fragrance of the dew-soaked meadow where Harrier's lodge stood. From the corner of his eye, Horseweed saw that Kestrel's legs had started to shake so badly that she could barely walk.

His own legs were shaky, too, though for different reasons. *Come on, Horseweed, just a little farther! Sunchaser called you a man . . . prove it!* He leaned into the travois, every muscle in his body rebelling.

Kestrel bit her lip. On top of the hill, Horseweed's kin had built up the central fire. About two dozen people stood in view, talking. A wavering golden aura arced over the camp, blotting out the stars. Shouts rang out. Her expression betrayed the fact that she was living a nightmare—one she had suffered through a thousand times.

But she stiffened her muscles and kept on walking. That courage steeled Horseweed's flagging endurance. He nodded to himself. This night would be a test for both of them. Hers of the strength of her soul, his of the strength of his body. He licked dry lips, placing one step ahead of the last as he dragged the travois up the western trail toward the village.

Lambkill's voice rose above the others, yelling in rage, "Whose baby is that? Bring the mother forward! I want to see her!"

Kestrel had to clamp her teeth to halt the cry in her throat. He sounded exactly as he had on the night of Iceplant's murder when he'd stood red-faced before her, thumping her pregnant belly with his knife.

Blessed Mother Ocean, I'll do anything you want! Just protect my baby.

Kestrel released Sunchaser's sleeve so she could clutch the hook of her atlatl. She would heed Horseweed's words and would not pull it unless she had to. But it comforted her just to feel the smooth wood beneath her fingers.

Horseweed halted before the crest of the hill, breathing hard. He glanced at her over his shoulder, firelight gleaming on his sweaty face. "Ready?"

Kestrel could see the leaping flames now, and Lambkill.

He stood next to Tannin beside the fire. He had his chin thrust out, and his jowls were mottled with crimson. On his back, he wore a small pack. *Is that where he keeps the dead baby? That beautiful dead baby boy . . .*

Something in the way Lambkill waved his arms caused a black bubble to begin swelling in Kestrel's breast, swelling until she feared she might be sick.

"Yes. I'm ready."

Forty-one

Dust sparkled faintly in the gleam of firelight, stirred up by the feet of the people who milled nervously in the plaza, their braids frizzy as though they'd been driven from their sleeping robes with no warning. Kestrel watched, her soul panicked, as she and Horseweed crested the hill. She glanced at the youth.

His stumbling pace had slowed while he examined the scene. The elders sat in a ring around the fire, their hides pulled over their shoulders. The rest of the village crowded around behind them, murmuring, shouldering one another aside to see better.

"If that's my daughter," Lambkill shouted, "you have no *right* to keep her from me!"

Kestrel leaned to the side to see Lambkill. He stood between Tannin and the man with the red shirt, his fists clenched, his body stiff. His violent glare was directed across the fire at an elderly man and woman. The quartz crystal that hung from the braided mammoth hide around Lambkill's neck glinted wildly. He yelled, "Give me that baby!"

The old woman Kestrel had seen earlier—the one who

had looked down at her from the hilltop—stood up from her crouch beside a young woman feeding a baby . . . *Cloud Girl!*

Kestrel couldn't take her eyes from her baby. Cloud Girl nursed quietly. She seemed well. Contented. Kestrel wanted to weep. Her breasts began to ache and her milk flowed, warm against the hide of her dress.

As she stood there staring at Cloud Girl, she heard the labored breathing of the crowd, the shuffling of many feet and the constant hooting of owls hunting the forests for mice and rabbits. *Iceplant? Can you see your daughter? She's here with your family. Just like you wanted her to be.* A hard knot grew in Kestrel's chest, as though all of her fear and desperation had frozen around her heart.

The old woman cleared her throat to gain attention and said, "We don't know whose baby this is. It may belong to your wife, Lambkill, but it may not. And anyway, I thought you said your wife's children came from incest. Are you telling us now that you claim her children as your own?"

"If that baby is hers, it *belongs* to me!" He stabbed a dirty thumb into his chest.

The old man across the fire from Lambkill shifted and narrowed his eyes, and the villagers hushed one another in anticipation of his words. He said, "Not according to our clan laws. Not even if you are the father, Lambkill—and you've yet to say you are. The Otter Clan considers all children the property of their mothers."

Lambkill hissed, "Are you *begging* me to kill you? Don't you know what will happen if you don't turn my family over to me? It will be war! The Bear-Looks-Back Clan and the Blackwater Draw Clan will band together to wipe the Otter Clan from the face of the earth!" He shook his fists in rage. "Do you *hear* me, Oxbalm?"

"Yes, I do," the old man responded, a fierce glint in his eye. "And so do my warriors. I wouldn't say that again if I were you."

The name made Kestrel's heart pound. She mouthed it like

a ceremonial prayer, *Oxbalm. Chief of the Otter Clan.* Was the woman to his left Sumac, then?

Horseweed had stiffened as he listened.

Lambkill didn't move a muscle, but his gaze swept the faces in the crowd as though he'd forgotten that so many watched. All around him, men and women fidgeted with atlatls and bone stilettos. Half of them looked angry enough to dart Lambkill if Oxbalm so much as pointed at him. Children hunched in a line outside the nearest long lodge, clutching their dogs by the scruffs of their necks. The animals had their ears up, and low growls rumbled in their throats. They didn't like Lambkill either.

The argument had grown so intense that no one even noticed Horseweed and Kestrel until Horseweed accidentally dragged the travois over a rock that hid in a thick patch of grass. Kestrel let out a small cry when the travois bounced and Sunchaser almost slid off.

The argument around the fire died. Lambkill spun and shouted, "Who's there? What's happening?"

People whirled to stare. A boy near the old woman lunged to his feet and shouted, "Horseweed!"

"Horseweed," Kestrel echoed from where she leaned over Sunchaser, "let's . . . let's put the travois down. We're close enough, aren't we?"

Her stomach curdled. In the subdued light of the fire, she really saw Sunchaser for the first time, and all of Horseweed's comforting words about how the Dreamer would not die flew away like petals in the wind. Blood-soaked hair framed his gray face. He lay canted slightly to the left, with his right cheek resting on the travois frame. His lips and the flesh around his eyes had turned a pale blue. His nostrils moved with swift, shallow breaths, like a man fighting to breathe at all. "Oh, Spirits . . . Horseweed, put the travois down!"

Horseweed immediately levered the travois off the rock and laid it flat. When he came around to stand beside Kestrel, he had his atlatl gripped in his hand, and fear shone in his eyes. "Is he all right?"

"I don't know." Kestrel dropped to her knees, steadying herself before she collapsed. She lifted Sunchaser's limp hand from where it had fallen to the ground and put it back on the travois.

"He's going to be all right, Kestrel," Horseweed soothed. "Really. I've seen wounds like this before. He'll live. And my grandparents won't let anyone hurt you." But he glanced over his shoulder at the people around the fire, pulled a dart from the quiver on his back and nocked it in the hook of his atlatl. "Don't worry. You're safe here."

"I won't be safe until my husband is dead, Horseweed. He hates me. He'll never let me go. And Sunchaser . . . may Mammoth Above help him." She looked down again at Sunchaser's sunken face, and the thought of a world without him was more than she could bear. Exhaustion and despair had emptied her of tears. All she could do was to gaze at him with anguish in her eyes.

"Horseweed!" The old woman ran across the plaza, her gray braid swinging back and forth with her uneven stride. She'd sucked her lips in over her toothless gums. Behind her, a line of people followed, including Oxbalm. Scents of the dust and smoke that clung to their hide clothing strengthened as they neared.

Kestrel tenderly smoothed her fingers over Sunchaser's face, mouthing, *I love you. Live, Sunchaser. Not just for me, but for everyone who needs you.*

She closed her eyes for a moment, mustering her courage. The dew had soaked her moccasins; they chafed at her toes as she rose to her feet. Standing side by side, she and Horseweed blocked the view of the travois.

Horseweed's chest expanded with a deep breath. He whispered, "Easy, Kestrel. Don't move too fast or say too much. Use your head."

Lambkill let out a hoarse roar when he saw Kestrel, and her knees went weak. He took two running steps forward, but Tannin grabbed his arm and jerked him back. They shouted at each other and began a shoving match, which the man in the red shirt tried unsuccessfully to break up.

Lambkill finally calmed down and shook off Tannin's hand. He stood breathing hard, hatred on his ugly face. Tannin spoke to him in a gruff voice—probably advising him not to act rashly.

Kestrel watched them for a moment, knowing that since she stood on the edges of the fire's glow, they probably wouldn't be able to make out her features. Lambkill looked older, his wrinkles deeper, his flat nose broader. His heavy jowls hung more loosely. The gray hair that brushed his shoulders fell in a stringy mass—as though he hadn't bathed in a moon. Soot and dirt covered his elk-hide pants and shirt. Tannin, tall and burly, hadn't changed at all, except for the look in his eyes. Kestrel didn't see hatred there, and she'd expected to. If anything, she saw pity.

And it struck at her heart. Had his anger finally died, even after all she had done to his brother?

The red-shirted youth muttered something to Lambkill, and when Lambkill nodded, he stalked across the plaza like a bull elk in rut. Dark circles of sweat stained the leather of his shirt beneath the arms and around his collar. When he was twenty paces from Horseweed, Helper bounded from the crowd and blocked his path, barking and snarling viciously. People faded back, creating a semicircle around Harrier, watching and pointing.

"Get this dog out of my way! Whose dog is this?"

"That's Sunchaser's dog, Harrier!" Horseweed yelled. "Leave him alone!"

"Despicable brat! I've never heard of Sunchaser having a dog. Get it out of my way before I slit its throat!" He pulled his knife from his belt sheath.

Horseweed grinned broadly, making a gesture that subtly changed his position, freeing the arm that held the atlatl and nocked dart. "Go ahead. The dog is Sunchaser's Spirit Helper. You'll probably lose your sight, or go deaf, before you can even get close to Helper!"

Harrier ranted, "If this is Sunchaser's dog, where is Sunchaser?"

Neither Horseweed nor Kestrel responded, and Harrier brandished his atlatl at Helper, trying to make the animal get out of his path. Helper barked and bared his teeth.

"Good boy, Helper," Horseweed whispered, for Kestrel's ears alone. Then he added, "That old woman running in front of the others, that's my grandmother—the woman I told you about. Her name is Sumac."

Kestrel let out a shuddering breath and prepared herself.

Sumac ran forward and grabbed Horseweed to hug him. "You found her! You're a good tracker, Grandson." When she released Horseweed, she stepped hesitantly toward Kestrel.

Kestrel reached out, took her withered hand and held it tightly. "My name is Kestrel. I'm hoping very much that I'm related to you, Sumac."

To Kestrel's surprise, Sumac squeezed her hand. "So am I. I found your little girl. She's going to be all right. I promise you that."

Tears welled in Kestrel's eyes. Softly she said, "I knew you'd take care of her. Bless you. But, please, Sumac. I don't want Lambkill to know she's my daughter. He'll never leave her alone. He'll find a way to kill her."

"Then he'll never know," Sumac whispered and started to turn to Horseweed, but when she saw Sunchaser lying on the travois behind Kestrel, she gasped and screamed, "Oxbalm! Oh, Mother Ocean, no. Hurry. It's Sunchaser! He's hurt!"

A roar went up from the crowd. Everyone in the village rushed forward in a dark wave . . . except Lambkill and Tannin. They remained standing by the fire. Tannin had placed a restraining hand on Lambkill's forearm again, while he spoke in a low voice. Kestrel wished she could hear what Tannin was saying. His forehead had furrowed deeply, while Lambkill's jaw clenched.

Sumac pushed between Horseweed and Kestrel and crouched by Sunchaser's side. A groan escaped her lips when she pulled back his tattered shirt and saw the bloody slashes across his chest. "Blessed Spirits, what happened, Horseweed? Was it a bear?"

Oxbalm ran past Horseweed and straight to Sunchaser. His sharp intake of breath silenced the rest of the crowd. "Quickly," he ordered. "We must get him over to the fire so we can tend his wounds. Hurry!"

Horseweed slipped his dart back into his quiver and settled his atlatl through his belt. He lifted the travois again. "Kestrel," he asked, "do you want to walk at my side?"

"Yes," she answered gratefully and saw that he gazed at her with resolute courage. "Thank you."

She walked forward, and Horseweed tugged the travois toward the fire. Harrier glared hatefully at Kestrel as she passed. Her knees shook, but she kept her head high and clutched the hook of her atlatl in a death grip.

People crowded around them, murmuring as they gazed wide-eyed at Sunchaser. Someone in the crowd began to cry. Oxbalm caught up with Horseweed and asked, "How long has Sunchaser been like this, Grandson?"

"I don't know. I saw Kestrel in the forest and followed her. She was running after Helper. The dog led us both to Sunchaser. From the way his blood had clotted, I'd guess he'd been attacked one, maybe two hands of time earlier."

"Do you think it was a bear?"

"It could have been a lion, or a saber-toothed cat, or even . . ." Horseweed faltered. His mouth hung open. Why hadn't it occurred to him earlier? The thought terrified him so much that he could barely speak the words: "Or a . . . a wolf, Grandfather. Maybe a dire wolf."

Oxbalm looked up at him and nodded. His bushy gray brows lowered. "That's what I feared."

Sumac, who had overheard their quiet exchange, whispered, "He wouldn't dare attack Sunchaser . . . would he? Where would he find the courage?"

Kestrel asked, "Do you mean Catchstraw? Sunchaser said—"

"Shh!" Sumac jerked Kestrel's arm hard to silence her and glanced over her shoulder at another old woman who walked not far behind. "Yucca Thorn is one of Catchstraw's admirers."

The skinny old hag had her head cocked, listening with the intensity of Coyote hunting for the sound of Mouse moving beneath the snow. Kestrel wondered what she would do if she'd caught the gist of their conversation. Would she warn Catchstraw about their suspicions? Give him time to defend himself? Or time to kill all of them before they could publicly accuse him of being a witch? Blood surged hotly through Kestrel's veins. Who would want to see Sunchaser hurt? She'd strangle the evil one with her own hands.

Oxbalm leaned forward slightly. "Later tonight, Kestrel, I want to talk with you about this. Once we've taken care of Sunchaser."

Kestrel nodded. "I'll tell you what I know." In a faint whisper, she added, "And what Sunchaser suspected."

Sumac studied Kestrel thoughtfully. For a moment, she said nothing. Then she asked, "What are you doing with Sunchaser? I've never known him to take up with a woman before."

"He . . . he was bringing me to you. We went to your old village site and tracked you down the beach to Whalebeard Village. There they told us where you'd made your new camp. But the rest . . . I'm afraid it's a long story."

"I want to hear every word of it," Oxbalm said. "Later."

Kestrel wondered why she hadn't told them that she and Sunchaser were lovers. Sunchaser wouldn't care. What did she fear?

Lambkill's response if he knew . . . He'd want to kill Sunchaser. Just as he had killed Iceplant. Hatred gave her the strength to walk bravely past Lambkill, following Horseweed as he hauled the travois to the opposite side of the fire and eased it down.

The warmth of the flames touched her face and made her shiver. The woman holding Cloud Girl to her breast sat only ten hands away, but Kestrel couldn't look at the baby, couldn't give herself away to Lambkill. If she so much as dared to gaze at her daughter, such love and longing would color her face that he would know for certain whose child Cloud Girl was. Hers . . . and Iceplant's.

Sumac took a young boy's hand and commanded, "Go fetch my bag of Spirit Plants, Balsam. And bring one of the water bags."

"Yes, Grandmother." He raced away and ducked into the closest lodge.

Horseweed stood by Kestrel, took his atlatl from his belt again and calmly nocked a dart in the hook. He gave her an encouraging glance while people gathered around them, fighting to get a good glimpse of Sunchaser in the light. Once they'd assured themselves that he was alive, they stared at Kestrel with curiosity. She met each gaze with a bland expression.

Balsam raced out of the lodge carrying Sumac's beaded Spirit Plants bag and a water bag. He shouldered through the crowd and placed them at his grandmother's side. "Here, Grandmother."

"Thank you, Balsam." Sumac squinted at an old man who hovered over Sunchaser like a mother hen. "Dizzy Seal, bring a boiling bag and a tripod. We need to warm some water so we can wash his wounds."

"Yes, Sumac." The old man trotted away.

Sumac continued, "Oxbalm, where's that hide you had over your shoulders earlier? Get it. Sunchaser is icy cold."

Kestrel knelt by Sunchaser's side and put a hand on his brow. Blessed Spirits, he did feel cold. Her stomach cramped. She could feel eyes upon her, evaluating the way she touched Sunchaser, speculating about it. She fought to keep her emotions hidden.

"Horseweed?" Kestrel asked as she looked up. "Could I have your knife, please?" He removed the finely knapped chert blade from his belt and handed it to her, antler handle first.

"Thank you." She turned to Sumac, who knelt beside her. "I'm going to cut off Sunchaser's shirt, so we can get a better look at his chest."

Sumac nodded.

Kestrel steadied her hands by clenching them tightly into fists, then reached out, peeled the blood-clotted hide back and cut it away from Sunchaser's arms. Firelight fluttered over the wounds ripped by huge teeth, and a chorus of gasps and moans went up. So many people spoke at once that Kestrel caught only fragments of conversation:

"Oh, no! Look at the gashes!"

". . . only a bear . . ."

"Could have been a cat . . . dropped on him from a tree."

Kestrel worked silently, aware that Lambkill watched her with hatred in his eyes. She couldn't think about him. Not yet. Not until she'd satisfied herself that Sunchaser had truly escaped death.

While Kestrel finished sawing through the sleeves and gently peeling them back, revealing the bloody, bruised flesh beneath, Sumac took the boiling bag and tripod from Dizzy Seal and dropped two hot stones into the water. It sizzled and spat, sending up a puff of steam. Next, she removed a small sack from her bag of Spirit Plants and unlaced it.

"What is that?" Kestrel asked.

"Crushed greasewood mixed with sea salt. Evil Spirits hate it because it tastes so bad. It keep wounds clean. Will you help me wash them down?"

"Yes."

Sumac removed two dry, shriveled sponges from her bag and threw both of them into the warm brew, where they swelled as they sucked up the water. Then she handed one of the dripping-wet sponges to Kestrel, who held it over Sunchaser's chest and squeezed it out, making sure that the liquid pooled around the clotted blood. Sumac moved the tripod in between them, and Kestrel dipped her sponge again to soak Sunchaser's right arm, which was very badly clawed and chewed. Sumac squeezed her sponge out over Sunchaser's bitten legs.

"Blessed Above-Old-Man," Sumac whispered, "I'd bet he has lost enough blood to fill a small pond."

Horseweed said, "When we found him, the pine duff around him was sodden with it."

Sumac shook her old head and sighed. "It's no wonder he's unconscious. He's lucky, he is. Keeps him from feeling the pain. Well, he just needs proper care. He'll be all right. Kestrel, I'll wash his legs if you'll finish up his chest and arms."

Kestrel nodded, dipped her sponge again and gently started cleaning Sunchaser's left arm. Less severely wounded than the right, it took her almost no time to wash the bites there. Red blood flowed anew from the gashes. She wrung out her sponge and soaked it in the greasewood brew, preparing to start on Sunchaser's lacerated chest.

Through the corner of her eye, she saw Harrier push forward to stand on the opposite side of the fire. He fixed Kestrel with a look of loathing, his head tipped down and his massive brow shadowing his eyes. "Are you Kestrel?" he demanded. "Lambkill's wife?"

Softly, she answered, "I was," as she painstakingly washed each claw gash on Sunchaser's broad, muscular chest.

Harrier bellowed, "Did you kill my brother?"

Kestrel stared at him uncomprehending. "Your brother?"

"Buffalo Bird! He was killed on the Oakcreek Trail—high in the hills. His murderer drove a tapir-bone stiletto through his heart. Did you do it?"

"Yes, I killed him." Kestrel's voice had a curiously far-off timbre, like that of a child awakened from a dream and not wholly in this world.

The people broke out in furious conversation. Their firelit faces showed shock and bewilderment. Even Horseweed swiveled to peer at her.

Harrier roared, "Oxbalm! She admitted the murder! I now put in a claim on this woman. I ask that you grant me the right to take her back to my village so she may be judged by the Blackwater Draw council!"

The possibility didn't affect Kestrel at all. As long as Cloud Girl and Sunchaser were safe, what happened to her made little difference. She wet her sponge again and leaned over Sunchaser to clean his right arm further. This time the thick crust of blood and pine needles melted beneath her warm sponge, revealing a deep slit. The wound had swollen and turned violet around the edges, but it didn't start bleeding again, much to her relief.

"Just a moment," Oxbalm replied. He moved to stand directly behind Sumac. To Kestrel, he said, "Why did you kill Buffalo Bird?"

Kestrel responded, "He told me that Lambkill had offered a reward for me. He started dragging me toward his camp. In the process, he told me that I would provide pleasure for him and his brothers—and that if I wasn't Kestrel, he and his brothers would kill me after they had raped me. That way, the Otter Clan would never know that one of their relations—a lone woman—had been raped and murdered. My death would stop a war, Buffalo Bird said. I was defending myself."

Sumac threw Kestrel a knowing glance, and Kestrel bowed her head and clenched her jaw. Sumac seemed to understand that Lambkill had offered a reward for Kestrel, but nothing for her daughter. Did Sumac guess that Buffalo Bird had seen Cloud Girl as a worthless nuisance? It didn't matter. Kestrel could not mention Cloud Girl. Not even in her own defense, not without endangering her daughter.

Lambkill let out a low, disbelieving laugh that turned Kestrel's blood to ice. Against her will, she started to shake again. The seashells on the front of her dress quivered, reflecting the firelight with a stunning radiance. To soothe herself, Kestrel dipped her sponge and began washing Sunchaser's handsome face. Just looking at him eased her terror. Could his Spirit see her? She thought it might. She sensed his presence around her like a protective shield. But Kestrel shivered anyway, unable to stop.

Lambkill laughed louder, pleased by her fear. Boldly, he shoved Tannin out of his way and walked around the fire. Kestrel counted each of his calculated steps, *five, six, seven, eight, nine* . . .

Horseweed shifted to stand in front of her, his atlatl in his hand, ready. Lambkill looked at the youth as he might regard a slab of maggot-ridden meat. "Get out of my way, boy! You've no right to keep me from my wife!"

"I'll move," Horseweed answered calmly, "when *she* asks me to."

Kestrel swallowed the lump in her throat. Horseweed didn't know her, yet he bravely stood between her and Death. Iceplant had been right about the Otter Clan. They were honorable people.

Lambkill's steely gaze shifted to Kestrel. He seemed riveted by the way she touched Sunchaser, by the lightness of her fingers, as though he understood the intimacy it conveyed. Madness entered his eyes. It filled him like a flood of foul water pouring into clear. His withered mouth puckered threateningly.

Kestrel scarcely glanced at him. She finished cleaning Sunchaser's wounds and dropped her sponge into the boiling bag. Folding her shaking hands in her lap, she clenched them tightly, keeping them away from her atlatl, and dared to look her husband full in the face. Lambkill's eyes blazed with malice.

"No one can protect you, Kestrel! Do you hear me?" he shouted. In a whining whisper, he continued, "I gave you everything, and you turned against me! You grew as cold as ice!"

"You beat the warmth out of me, Lambkill."

"The beatings were for your own good. I had to teach you how to behave like a proper wife!"

Kestrel felt so numb that she stopped shaking. She focused on Sunchaser, remembering his gentleness. Sick, dead, tens of tens of tens of cycles from now in the Land of the Dead, the memories of his warm body against hers would comfort her. She placed her fingertips on his wrist, letting the steady rhythm of his heart brace her.

Lambkill shouted, "You're a bitch in heat! Everybody knows you'll spread yourself to the first man to walk past! First you commit incest with your cousin, then you seduce a *Dreamer!* For the sake of Above-Old-Man! Is no one beyond your witchery?"

At the word, Horseweed tensed as if he'd been slapped. A glint sharpened in Oxbalm's eyes, and Dizzy Seal stepped back uneasily.

Sumac threw her sponge into the boiling bag, gave Lambkill a scornful look and reached over to put a cold hand on Kestrel's arm. "Now, tell us the truth, Kestrel. Did you commit incest?"

Kestrel peered into those keen old eyes, a *woman's* eyes, filled with more knowledge about clan matters than Kestrel would ever have, and she knew she would be treated fairly. "I don't know, Sumac. According to the Bear-Looks-Back Clan, yes, I did." Gasps of outrage went up, and several of the men cursed Kestrel openly. She took a deep breath and waited for the clamor to subside. "But my lover claimed to be from your clan, since his mother was. Because he was my father's brother's son, he didn't call me his cousin."

The hand on Kestrel's arm tightened until it hurt. Sumac nodded. "What was his mother's name?"

"Wind Shadow."

A cry of shock rose from across the fire, and Kestrel turned with her heart in her throat. She couldn't make out the woman's face until she shouldered her way into the light. It was the old hag who had been following Kestrel earlier, the one named Yucca Thorn. The woman's mouth trembled. "Wind Shadow was my granddaughter! She was stolen from my daughter when barely ten summers old! We never knew what happened to her . . ." Yucca Thorn swallowed down her wrinkled throat. "Is she still alive? Where is she?"

"No," Kestrel said. "I'm sorry. She died when Iceplant, her son, was very young. She was killed in a raid. But she never forgot you. She told Iceplant stories about all of you—" her voice constricted "—every night until her death. My clan expected Iceplant to claim kinship through his father. But he never did. He always considered himself related to you. He . . . he wanted to bring me here, to live with you, so our children could be born and raised in the ways of the Otter Clan."

"Then you weren't his cousin!" Yucca Thorn declared flatly and fixed Lambkill with a glare of disgust. "Your wife didn't commit incest!" She turned back to Kestrel. "Where's the baby you're supposed to have with you? Is she the child we found tonight? That baby would be my great-great-grandchild!"

Kestrel lowered her eyes and gazed at Sunchaser's bruised face. "My baby died. The journey was so difficult, so long . . . finding food was very hard. She died right after she was born."

Old Yucca Thorn seemed to deflate. Her bony shoulders sagged forward and the wrinkled lids over her faded brown eyes blinked. "Blessed Spirits . . . I was hoping . . . at least you're safe." Yucca Thorn lifted her ancient face to peer sternly at Kestrel. "If you're willing, young woman, I'll adopt you into this clan, as part of my family. My great-grandson loved you. That's enough proof of your character for me. I'd like the chance to know you myself."

Lambkill's eyes darted through the murmuring crowd. People studied Kestrel intently. They noticed that everything seemed to enrage Lambkill. First her touching of Sunchaser, then the argument about tracing kinship. Lambkill set his jaw, and his eyes traveled over her, surveying every spot of dirt on her dress, every scar on her face, with loathing.

"You're a filthy woman! Filthy!" To the villagers, he shouted, "She's done terrible things! Other things! You can't imagine. My people condemned her to death for her monstrous crimes! She *murdered* my son! My little boy. He was so tiny . . . just born." Lambkill slipped the pack from his back and held it out to the crowd. "This baby—"

From across the fire, Tannin shouted, "Lambkill!"

Lambkill halted for a moment, as though considering the warning, and Kestrel drew a breath to speak to him, but a sound distracted her—a weird, lingering scream that rent the night. It sent shivers down her spine, chilling the blood in her veins. It was the cry of a wounded animal—or of a man nearby, coming up the eastern trail.

"What's happening?" Sumac asked as she rose to her knees and squinted past the glare of the fire. "Who is that?"

"Blessed Spirits," Horseweed rasped. "It's . . . it's Catchstraw, Grandmother." He clutched his atlatl more securely. "He's staggering. It looks like he's been hurt, too."

Forty-two

Kestrel's soul froze. *Catchstraw*. The witch! Her eyes narrowed as she craned her neck to see him.

Helper uttered a moaning growl, his head down and the fur standing straight on his back. He loped forward and the crowd dispersed abruptly; people ran like a school of fish when a pelican splashes into the water over their heads. With snarling barks, Helper charged toward the tall, thin man with gray-streaked black hair who staggered across the hilltop.

"Oxbalm!" Catchstraw yelled hoarsely. "Oxbalm, this is *your* fault!" He wove on his feet as though possessed by a Powerful Spirit Plant. As Helper closed, Catchstraw jabbed the dart point toward him. Helper veered off, circling and barking.

Oxbalm straightened and squinted at Catchstraw, who glared back. Catchstraw wore only a breechclout and carried the dart in his hand like a firebrand. The translucent chalcedony point glimmered in the flickering light. Horrifying wounds covered his skinny body, and blood trickled down his pale skin in bright, crooked patterns. He held his free hand pressed against a wound in his shoulder, hindering the rush of blood, but the long gash down his left side flowed unheeded. Kestrel noticed the gore that crusted over the wound on his right thigh, just beneath the flap of his buckskin breechclout. That was what made him limp so.

"Get out of my way!" Catchstraw shouted and slashed at people with his long dart. He appeared demented with hatred. "I despise all of you! Do you hear me? Every single one of you!" Children shrieked and fell to the ground, crawling out of his reach.

The mob faded back, creating a path for him. He dragged himself forward, sliding his bad leg. His hooked nose flared repulsively, as if tormented by a gruesome stench. "Sunchaser?" he screamed. "Where's Sunchaser? What have you done with him, Oxbalm?"

Yucca Thorn spun. "Over here! He's lying by the fire, Catchstraw!"

Catchstraw came forward like an avenging Spirit Helper, his eyes glowing as he limped into the glare of the fire. "Oxbalm!" he railed shrilly. "Look at me. Look! Sunchaser attacked me while I was out gathering plants by the light of the moon. He caught me off guard, darted me in the shoulder and tried to slit my throat with his knife! He's no Dreamer! He's a murderer!"

Kestrel's hand slipped down to her atlatl. She wouldn't do anything so bold as rising to pull her dart from Horseweed's pack, but she could use the atlatl as a club if she had to. This man looked as if insane enough to attack Oxbalm, Sunchaser or anyone else who got in his way.

Catchstraw's malignant gaze fell upon Kestrel with such Power that she flinched.

Catchstraw shrieked, "Sunchaser's evil. He's been consorting with wicked women! Satiating his lust in their flesh!" He gestured at Kestrel, then looked at Oxbalm. "And you have been defending Sunchaser! Calling him 'great' and 'good.' You old fool! He's betrayed us all!"

"You're a liar!" Kestrel shouted.

Behind her, she heard Lambkill laugh coldly. The sound struck her like a slap in the face.

Horseweed glanced at Lambkill, then at Kestrel in panic. "Shh. Don't say anything," he whispered urgently. "You don't need to make enemies so soon." He lifted his atlatl and spread his feet, ready to drive the long point into any enemy. He wet his lips anxiously as he glowered at Catchstraw. "You're the one who's betrayed us! You *witch!* I call you a witch, Catchstraw! I accuse you of witching Sunchaser and attacking him in the form of Dire Wolf!"

"*You* accuse *me!*" Catchstraw bent forward in suffocating laughter. "*Me?* A witch? What proof—"

"Look at Sunchaser's wounds!" Horseweed interrupted. "They were clearly made by an animal. Look at the claw and bite marks. If you fought with him and made those wounds . . ."

Kestrel's heart thundered when people surged forward like a tidal wave, closing in around the fire, peering at Catchstraw in amazed terror, then glancing disbelievingly at Horseweed and Sunchaser. Horseweed stood his ground, though he looked as if his nerves thrummed.

"I call Catchstraw a witch, too!" Sumac said.

"So do I," Dizzy Seal chimed in from where he stood to Horseweed's left, looking very small and frightened.

When Oxbalm lifted his hands for silence, the people quieted down to nervous murmurs. The gathering seemed to split before Kestrel's eyes, half of it aligning behind Catchstraw and half drifting in Oxbalm's direction. Catchstraw lifted his chin smugly. A gust of wind swept the hilltop, carrying the pungent scent of fear-hot bodies to Kestrel. She noticed the beads of perspiration that dotted people's foreheads. Many of the men had nocked their atlatls and stood poised to cast at the slightest provocation.

Kestrel glanced at the woman who held Cloud Girl; she

looked more scared than anyone, her eyes wide, her mouth ajar. Desperately, Kestrel wished she had Cloud Girl in her own arms . . . but no matter what happened here, her daughter was safer without her. She struggled to keep her anguish at bay, hoping that Cloud Girl didn't feel it. But the baby started crying and waving her fists, shrieking as if terrified. Cloud Girl reached out to Kestrel, in a "Take me! Take me!" gesture.

Kestrel shook her head weakly as tears stung her eyes. Cloud Girl shrieked louder.

Oxbalm raised his old voice. "It's true! Catchstraw is a witch! For weeks, Sumac, Dizzy Seal, Horseweed, Balsam and I have been seeking out and finding the evidence of his witchery! He—"

"What evidence?" Yucca Thorn demanded. She strode up to stand at Catchstraw's right. Her withered face had a pinched look. "Name one thing Catchstraw has done that suggests he's a witch!"

"Out in the forest," Oxbalm called, "he's been leaving perverted mazes. Sunchaser's mazes, ruined by Catchstraw's hand! He's been drawing over the lines, confusing them, erasing some and destroying others."

Sunchaser stirred feebly, and Kestrel smoothed his hot brow, brushing wet hair away from his face.

"That's no evidence," Yucca Thorn defended. "If you're accusing Catchstraw of witching, you'd better have more proof than that! You know Catchstraw never believed in the maze. He said it led nowhere. Maybe he was trying to fix it, to correct Sunchaser's errors so the maze would be useful— the way Wolfdreamer intended it to be."

At the repetition of his name, Sunchaser awoke. He looked as if it took every ounce of strength he possessed to open his eyes. When he saw Kestrel, his mouth tensed and he struggled to rise. "No, Sunchaser. It's all right," she said. "You're in Otter Clan Village. You're safe."

He whispered, "Kestrel . . . Kestrel, run. Run . . . your husband . . ."

"Yes, I know. It's all right," she said with false confidence, praying Lambkill couldn't hear Sunchaser's soft voice. "Save your strength. You're going to need it to get well."

Yucca Thorn yelled, "If Sunchaser thinks he's been witched by someone, let him name his assailant!"

"W-what?" Sunchaser asked. Feebly, he squinted across the fire, probably seeing nothing but the glare that swelled so high that it drove the moonlight back.

Kestrel said, "They want you to name the witch—the person who attacked you in the forest."

Clearly, Sunchaser murmured, "Catchstraw . . . he's been witching the maze. He's learned to become Dire Wolf . . . attacked me . . . on trail . . ."

"Liar!" Catchstraw let out a roar of rage and lunged forward, using his fists to beat a way through the crowd around the fire. Screams rang out as people hit the dirt crawling. Catchstraw lifted his dart and dove at Sunchaser.

"No!" Horseweed screamed.

Kestrel leaped forward and grabbed Catchstraw's arm, dragging him sideways to the ground. He slammed a fist into her face. In fury, Kestrel clawed Catchstraw's wounded shoulder; he shrieked madly and bashed her in the head with his elbow. The force of the blow sent her reeling backward, and she landed on her side on the cold ground.

"Look out!" Horseweed shouted. "Get out of the way! He's going after Sunchaser again!"

A fight ensued around the fire. Horseweed let fly with his dart, and Kestrel saw it lance clear through Catchstraw's right arm as he fell atop Sunchaser in a writhing, kicking fit.

Oxbalm cried, "No, Grandson! No! Stop! Get back, everyone!"

Shrieks and hoarse shouts pierced the air as people broke away and ran in confusion. Horseweed leaped on Catchstraw and tore him from Sunchaser, forcing him to break his grip. They rolled, slamming fists, gasping and groaning . . .

Kestrel started to scream, but a callused hand clamped over her mouth. Powerful arms jerked her roughly to her feet and shoved her through the crowd and around to the rear of the closest lodge. Kestrel jerked her atlatl from her belt, but he batted it away effortlessly. Horror gripped her like the fists of doom. She groaned and twisted like Snake. The scent of smoked lodge hides wafted in the moonlight-silvered darkness.

They stumbled through belongings that had been piled behind the lodge: grinding slabs, axes, things too big to be carried away by animals. But the noise around the central fire had grown so deafening that it covered the sounds of their movements.

Lambkill whispered, "Didn't I tell you I would kill you, my wife, if I ever found you with another man?" He slammed a fist into her stomach so hard that her feet went out from under her. Kestrel shouted, "Help!" But Lambkill covered her mouth again, hauled her upright and dragged her down the slope.

"Lambkill? *Lambkill!*" Tannin called from someplace behind them.

Through blurry eyes, Kestrel saw Tannin sprinting down the hill, his jaw clenched, his eyes wide. Lambkill shifted, hooking his left arm around Kestrel's throat so he could use his right hand to draw his knife. The blade glinted with a pewter gleam.

"Stay back, Tannin!" Lambkill ordered, pulling Kestrel with him as he backed up. "Get away. I don't *need* any more of your advice!"

Tannin halted a body's length away, breathing hard, and unslung his quiver of darts and his atlatl and laid them on the ground. "I mean you no harm, my brother." He stood and spread his hands. The tiny shell beads that lined the seams in his shoulders sparkled; they had been sewn with such care by Calling Crane's hands. "Listen to me, Lambkill. Just . . . just let her go. There's no point in hurting her. What good will it do now? Let's go home. I miss my wife, Lambkill. And I want to take you home. You need rest. It's over. Let's get out of here!" Tannin took a step, and his foot snapped a twig in the grass.

Lambkill jerked Kestrel backward so hard that she choked. She tried to scream, but her voice came out in a rasping whisper: "Tannin! . . . *P-please!*"

Lambkill laughed and brandished his knife, but he kept glancing at the commotion on the hilltop. Kestrel's fear for herself paled when she heard Catchstraw screaming: "Sunchaser is the witch! Look at the bite and claw marks on *my* body! He's the one who's learned to become Dire Wolf. He devised that accursed maze in the first place. Gather stones! We must stone him to death now, before he has a chance to regain his strength!"

From the corner of her vision, she saw people running around the fire, their shadows huge, amorphous, on the trees in the background. Were Catchstraw's followers gathering stones? She strained to hear more, but Lambkill's voice blotted out everything else.

"My *brother*," Lambkill snarled. "You've been a coward this entire journey, always whining, complaining, wanting to go home. Now that we're at the end, you can't stand to go through with it. Well, I don't need you! I never have! Go on. I can kill my wife by myself. Get away from here. Go!"

Tannin licked his lips and took another step closer, raising his hands, showing that they were empty, harmless. Sweat created a sheen on his neck in the moonlight. He never looked Kestrel in the eyes, but wisely kept his gaze locked with Lambkill's. "You know this is wrong, Lambkill. We've already killed her lover and caused the death of her little girl by pushing her so hard—"

"You can't believe that! Do you think that baby found in the forest tonight was left by the Thunderbeings?"

". . . Let her go. She'll never come back to Juniper Village. That's punishment enough. She'll never see her mother or grandmother again. Never see any of the friends she's had since childhood. Even if the Otter Clan adopts her, she'll still be alone among strangers. What else—"

"Are you *blind* as well as a coward?" Lambkill answered. With the slow expertise of a killer, he waved his knife before Kestrel's eyes and gradually lowered it to her belly, where he pressed the tip hard against her. She moaned in fear. "You saw the filthy way she touched Sunchaser. If we let her go, she'll still have him."

Tannin shrugged. When the fire on the hilltop flared in the breeze, the reflected light danced across his sweating face. "If Sunchaser lives. He didn't look so good to me. But so what? Why should we care?" Tannin laughed as though greatly amused. "You know the stories about women unfortunate enough to be snared into marriage with a Dreamer. They're miserable!"

Still laughing softly, Tannin spread his arms wide in a negligent gesture and shook his head. "Come on, Lambkill. Let's go. Kestrel isn't important enough to cause this rift between us. You're my brother and I . . ." He leaped forward with the swiftness of Weasel snatching Vole and grabbed Lambkill's knife hand.

"Ah!" Lambkill blurted and shoved Kestrel to the dirt.

Tannin kicked Lambkill's feet out from under him and fell on his brother, and Kestrel crawled away, trying to find a rock or a branch to use as a club. Tannin and Lambkill struggled against each other, rolling over and over, fighting for the knife. Dirt caked their pants and shoulders, and the pack on Lambkill's back. The mica flakes in the pack glittered darkly in the moonglow.

"You . . . traitor!" Lambkill raged from where he lay beneath Tannin. "You've always hated me!"

Tannin slammed a fist into Lambkill's face and chest, then used Lambkill's weight against him by lifting him off the ground by his short arms and slamming his head down until Lambkill grunted.

Through gritted teeth, Tannin responded, "That's . . . not true . . . Lambkill. I love you. I have always loved you. That's why I came on this . . . journey with you."

Scrambling to her feet, Kestrel snatched up a palm-sized stone and held it over her head as she stepped forward across the damp grass, waiting for an opening to use it on Lambkill.

When he saw her, he went wild. He shrieked and twisted, throwing Tannin first one way, then the other, until he could bring up his knee and bash Tannin in the groin repeatedly. When Tannin gasped and bent double, Lambkill shoved him over on his back, seized the knife and straddled him.

Kestrel lunged forward with her upraised stone, but before she could strike him, Lambkill slashed out with his knife and cut a deep wound in her right thigh. She stumbled sideways and fell, throwing her stone with all her might. It struck Lambkill in the back, and he roared in rage.

"Lambkill, don't do this!" Tannin pleaded, fighting to keep his grip on his brother's knife hand. Lambkill's skin seemed to slip from his grasp like a wet eel.

"I've wanted to kill you for over a moon, brother," Lambkill said as he wrestled with Tannin, trying to wrench his hand free.

"Lambkill, you don't know what you're saying. You're not . . . well. That dead baby has made you—"

"Don't speak about my son!" Lambkill bellowed. "Never talk about him! You wanted him dead. I made him live!" He tore his hand free from Tannin's grip and with one quick movement, slashed Tannin's throat.

Kestrel screamed when blood gushed. Tannin made a hideous choking noise and flailed desperately at Lambkill, but Lambkill only caught his arms and pinned them over Tannin's head, staring his brother in the eyes as the blood drained from his body. Each panicked pumping of Tannin's lungs blew a crimson spray over Lambkill's face and chest. Red bubbles frothed at Tannin's lips as his mouth worked in soundless pleas. He kicked and squirmed against Lambkill's hold.

Kestrel wove drunkenly as she limped away up the hill. Only a croak would come from her bruised throat: "Help! Horseweed! Horseweed, I'm down here! Sumac! Yucca Thorn!"

"I'm coming!" Lambkill yelled at her. "I'm right behind you. Hear my footsteps?"

And she did hear them—they were closing fast. Kestrel fell into sobs when she reached an especially steep part of the trail and her moccasins slipped on the dew-slick grass. Blood ran hotly down her leg from the knife wound. She clawed at the grass, hauling herself up, scrambling five more steps.

"Listen, woman." His voice had dropped to a horrifying whisper. "I'm coming. I'm almost on top of you! Soon you'll be dead!"

Kestrel stumbled and fell to her knees, screaming. She slid ten hands back down the grassy slope on her stomach. When she rolled to her back and scrambled to rise, she found Lambkill leaning over her, a savage glitter in his eyes. The faint reflection of the village bonfire coated his jowls as they shook with laughter.

"Oh, yes, my loving wife. It's time we left here. You and I. Together." He extended a hand to her in such a genial way that it terrified her.

Kestrel shrieked "No!" and twisted sideways to dive head-first down the slope.

She tumbled like a loose boulder, slamming into old stumps, sliding and rolling uncontrollably. She threw up one arm to protect her face, and the act changed her balance enough that she went careening sideways into the trunk of a towering pine. Her wounded leg struck the tree so hard that when she scrambled to her feet to run, she could only stagger forward with agonizing slowness.

A hand twined in her long hair and jerked her backward to the ground, where she sobbed and kicked aimlessly.

Lambkill bent over her, his mouth twisted into a grin. His quartz-crystal necklace swung back and forth above her face, reflecting the silver light in prismatic patterns. Affably, he murmured, "Come, wife. I have someone I want you to meet."

He gripped her arm hard and dragged her to her feet. By sheer brute force, Lambkill hustled her out across the meadow and into the blackness of the forest . . .

* * *

Horseweed used his atlatl like a club, battering the side of Catchstraw's head, horrified at the animal strength in the man. Fetid breath, reeking of rot and death, puffed from the witch's mouth, adding to Horseweed's panic. With all of the might in his young body, he smashed his head full into Catchstraw's face, the impact blasting sparks of yellow light across his vision.

Catchstraw's grip weakened, and Horseweed butted him again, and again, aware that something was shaking Catchstraw from behind.

The witch threw his head back, and a scream ripped from his throat that sounded half wolf yip, half human cry. Then Catchstraw spun away, bucking and twisting, pulling free.

Horseweed shoved to his feet, watching Catchstraw run blindly through the crowd, wailing like a wounded dog, while Helper continued to slash at his legs.

Horseweed wiped the back of his bleeding mouth with his hand and reached down for his atlatl. But all of the darts in his crushed quiver had been broken.

"No," Oxbalm said, gripping Horseweed's hand. His faded old eyes showed horror and pain. "No, Grandson. That's enough. We'll . . . we'll deal with him later. Stay here. I need you to take care of Sunchaser and guard Kestrel. We—"

"*Kestrel!*" Horseweed cried. He scanned the crowd. "Where's Kestrel? Where did she go? Grandmother—"

"I've problems of my own! I didn't see!" Sumac cried. She was bent over Sunchaser with the heels of her hands pressed against his bleeding right arm, as though she could force the blood back into his body. But red flowed over and around her old fingers in thick streams. The fight had opened the deep gash.

"Sumac," Sunchaser said as he thrashed feebly, struggling to rise, "let me go. Let . . . let me go!"

He managed to shove Sumac's hands away and to roll to his hands and knees, but he sprawled face-first onto the ground.

"Sunchaser, stop this!" Sumac yelled. "Horseweed, help me get him into the lodge. He's going to kill himself!"

Horseweed ran to help as Sunchaser's fingers dug into the dirt and he clawed his way forward, getting up on shaking hands and knees again. His white hair draped in a damp, glittering veil around his face. "Help me . . . up!" he ordered.

Horseweed knelt and lifted Sunchaser to his feet. He had to wrap his arms securely around the Dreamer's bloody chest to keep him standing. "Sunchaser, you're badly hurt. You can't—"

"Horseweed . . . listen," Sunchaser whispered. "Go. *Find her!* He'll . . . he'll kill her. Hurry! She doesn't have long. He can't afford to . . . trifle with her. I'll help you as much as I can . . . from here. Hurry!"

"From here? I don't . . ."

Sunchaser's broad chest shuddered as he inhaled; then he slumped in Horseweed's arms. Horseweed let him sink slowly to the ground again.

"Go!" Sumac said frantically as she knelt by Sunchaser. "Do as he said. Find Kestrel!"

Oxbalm gripped Horseweed's hand hard. His elderly face was as wary as a young hunter's. "But be careful, Grandson. Lambkill is crazy. There's no telling what he'll do to you if he catches you."

"He won't catch me," Horseweed answered confidently, but he recalled the insane glow in the old Trader's eyes.

He took one last look at Sunchaser's bloody face, then ran with all of his strength, weaving through the crowd, shouting, "Did anyone see where Lambkill took Kestrel? Who saw them? Somebody must have—"

Balsam waved his hands from across the gathering and yelled, "I didn't see them, Horseweed, but I saw Tannin. He ran down the eastern trail!"

Horseweed lifted a hand in thanks and sprinted away into the grass-scented darkness. Moonlight slanted through the branches and fell across the hillside in bars and streaks of smoky white. Every rock and bush shone like polished shell.

He hadn't run even a few tens of paces before he saw the sprawled figure at the base of the slope. He slowed and approached cautiously, his gaze searching the shadows for hidden figures. With a hoarse gasp, the man's tall body spasmed, his lungs drawing air frantically.

Horseweed approached warily and knelt to get a closer look. "Tannin?"

The man's throat gaped. Blood had puddled around his head. How had he lived so long?

For one brief instant, Tannin's panicked eyes met Horseweed's stricken stare. Then he moved his right arm up and curled shaking fingers to point to the south. A garbled cry came from his ruined throat, like a plea for help . . . and he died. Breath escaped his gaping lips in a final whisper.

Horseweed remained staring at his still face, serene now. "Blessed Mother Ocean, if Lambkill would murder his own brother . . ."

Horror possessed him. He hadn't felt this terrified since he'd been a boy and awakened in the night to find his mother lying dead beside him. He'd run screaming for his grandparents that night. But tonight he had only his own wits to keep him safe. His hearing seemed to sharpen, like Deer listening for the almost soundless padding of Lion's paws in the darkness.

He rose on nerveless legs and looked out across the dappled grayness of the foothills, fearing that Kestrel might already be dead. He couldn't track Lambkill in the darkness. No one could. He would have to trust Tannin's last gesture. *They went south . . .*

Horseweed's eyes followed Tannin's pointing finger to a small thicket of newly leafed-out berry vines across the meadow. Quickly, he pulled the darts from Tannin's quiver and shoved them into his own. Then he trotted forward on a warrior's light feet, whispering the Mammoth Spirit Song as he ran.

Sunchaser lay beside the fire, wavering in and out of consciousness, listening to the yells and shouts, weaker and more helpless than he'd ever been in his life. His body had begun to shake uncontrollably, as though in fevered chills. But he knew that it was more from lingering fear than from loss of blood. When he'd looked into Catchstraw's crazed eyes and seen the eyes of the dire wolf staring back, he'd cried out in horror. And Lambkill . . . He'd been standing there, behind Kestrel, looking just as she'd described him, old and gray and maddened with hate.

Kestrel needed him! And he could barely gather the strength to breathe.

"Hurry!" That was Sumac. "Dizzy Seal, find me some cord so I can tie off his wounds! If we don't stop this blood from pouring out of him—"

"Here, take my belt."

Sunchaser felt someone lift his right arm. When the cord was jerked tight, he groaned.

"Oxbalm," Sumac cried, "give me your belt, too!"

Sunchaser blacked out briefly, then heard the roar of the wind as it rushed through the forest like a flock of enraged Thunderbeings. Tree branches cracked against each other and moaned, as though frightened by the force of the sudden storm. It took all of his will to raise his eyelids enough to gaze upward. The golden glare of the flames blinded him to the sky. Had clouds moved in? Or was this the trick of a desperate witch?

"Which way did Catchstraw go?" Oxbalm yelled. "Who saw him?"

"I did!" Dizzy Seal responded. "He ran down the western trail and veered off into the trees near Harrier's camp."

Sunchaser struggled to force himself to think. *Think!* How could he best help Kestrel and Horseweed, and battle Catchstraw at the same time? Would Catchstraw change himself into Dire Wolf again? Yes . . . yes, undoubtedly. If he could find the time and the courage. In the body of Dire Wolf, he would be able to run all the way to the seacoast, even injured as severely as he was. If he could find a place where he could rest and lick his wounds, he would be a far more dangerous enemy when he returned to face Sunchaser the next time.

"Wolfdreamer?" he murmured weakly. "Help me. Help me find the strength. You know what I must do . . . and it takes so much strength. I have to call the animals. To . . . to call their Power into myself—"

"What?" Sumac asked. Her breath felt warm on his cheek as she leaned close to his mouth. "What did you say, Sunchaser?"

He could smell the fragrance of yucca soap in her hair and hear the fear in her voice. But he couldn't respond.

He focused his soul and called, *Wolfdreamer, Wolfdreamer, will you help me? I beg you . . . help me . . . help me to draw Catchstraw into the Dream.*

He felt his soul rising out of his wounded body. Up and up . . . The violence of the storm flowed into him with the potency of Brother Hurricane's wrath. A Song burst from his lips. In it, he called the animals by their secret names, the names they knew themselves by, and he heard the stirring in the foothills as each lifted its head to listen. Sunchaser solemnly pleaded for their aid.

Power flushed his soul as he sailed over the camp and flew away on the shoulders of the gale.

Forty-three

The towering black trees seemed to breathe around Lambkill.
They swayed back and forth in unison, rustling and whimpering, watching him through the eyes of silver spots of
moonlight. He could sense their malignant Spirits reaching
out for him, hoping to snag his soul and rip it from his
body. Their touch slipped like wet tentacles over his skin.
Where had this windstorm come from? He'd seen no clouds
gathering!

"What do you want?" he demanded. "Stay back. Stay back
or I'll kill her right now! *Stay back!*"

The tentacles retreated into the darkness, but he could
hear the hoarse whispers of the Forest Spirits echoing around
him.

He kept his left hand clamped over Kestrel's mouth and
shoved her down the dim game trail ahead of him, causing
her to trip and stumble, letting the dead branches rip at her
flesh. The knife wound in her leg must have pained her badly,
for she had begun leaning into him, forcing him to carry her
weight. How strange to feel her young slender body in his
arms again.

He moved his right hand down and ran it over the seashells
on her dress, then groped for her full breasts until she let out
a muffled cry. Rabid desire flushed his system. His penis
hardened with the need of her.

She felt it and whimpered pathetically. If he let her speak
now, she would beg him to stop, not to hurt her, to let
her go. Knowing that stoked the triumph rushing within
his soul.

"So, my wife," he whispered in her ear. "You thought you could escape me, didn't you? *Didn't you!*" He twined his right hand in her thick black hair and wrenched her neck agonizingly.

She nodded weakly. Lambkill felt tears running warmly over the fingers of his left hand.

"Silly fool," he hissed. "I told you. I told you I would find you. Didn't you believe me? You know what a great tracker I am. No one is better than me. I found every heel print you left, every tiny fragment of your dress. I even found the place where you gave birth to my children."

Kestrel twisted to peer into his eyes. Sweat coated her face, turning it luminous. Her long black hair fluttered in the cool wind that swept the forest trails. Oh, how he used to love to wrap himself in that glossy wealth and couple violently with her.

"Yes, wife, I know now that the twins were mine, not Iceplant's. My son told me. The first moment that I brought him to life, he called me 'Father.' "

Horror shone in Kestrel's eyes, and Lambkill laughed in disgust.

"You don't believe me, do you? Well, Tannin didn't either. I tried to show him, but he closed his eyes and ears to me. That's why I had to kill him. He thought I was crazy. I'll bet you do, too."

He tipped his head back and laughed into the gale. "Just wait. Wait and I'll show you our son. I've taken good care of him—unlike you did. You tried to *murder* him. He would have stayed dead if not for me and my knowledge of such things."

A shudder went through her body, and it thrilled him.

If only he could slit her open now and leave her for the wolves and coyotes. He had been planning her death for days. As he forced her down the brush-choked game trail, he talked to her.

"Do you remember what I told you I was going to do to Iceplant? Hmm? I said I was going to let him go so I

could hunt him down and slit him open before your eyes."
A chuckle shook his bony chest. "I didn't have the chance
with him—he forced my hand, forced me to kill him before I
could play with him. But now I have you. Oh, my wife," he
said softly, intimately, as she stumbled over a fallen tree. He
continued shoving and prodding her down the winding trail.

The faint roars of lions sounded in the distance, calling
back and forth to each other across the hills. The birds
perched sleeping in the trees awoke and chirped, as though
startled by the sound.

"Let me tell you what I'm going to do with you, Kestrel.
I'll tell you so you can think about it while we're running.
First I'm going to stretch you out on your back between two
trees and tie your hands to one tree and your feet to the other.
Then I'm going to use my knife to carefully slice open the
smooth skin of your belly. I want to sever the tissue sac that
holds your internal organs. Yes, think of that. Imagine what
the pain will be like.

"Finally . . . when I get ready . . . I'll reach inside you and
pull out your stomach, liver and intestines. But unharmed,
Kestrel. I want them to keep functioning. And they will, you
know. For a long, long time. I'll leave your insides on the
forest floor to dry in the cold and wind. It will take hands
of time for you to die. Maybe even days."

He laughed, racked by the glorious justice of it. "Or maybe
it won't be days, hmm? You'll probably be eaten alive before
any of those fools from the village come looking for you and
put you out of your misery."

A muted wail resonated in her throat, and he clamped his
hand harder over her mouth while he searched the dark
shadows of the forest. Spatters of moonglow shifted as the
wind blew through the trees.

But Lambkill had the eerie feeling that something else
moved out there, something huge, with eyes as black as midnight. His heart had begun to pound like a hunted animal's.

"Shh!" he hushed Kestrel when she moaned, and he realized that he'd crushed her lips so hard against her teeth

that the inside of her mouth was cut. Blood soaked his hand.

Lambkill cocked his head. "What was that? Did you hear it?"

Kestrel didn't make a sound, as though she, too, were listening breathlessly for movement in the forest.

"What's that *sound*? I . . . I can feel the vibration of feet striking the pine duff. Don't you feel it?"

Lambkill squinted to catch sight of the beast. But the creature slipped through the dense trees with the deadly stealth of a giant cat. He saw nothing except the wavering branches of brush and trees.

Fear began to sour in his belly.

Hurry! Hurry! To defuse his panic, he jerked Kestrel to a halt in the middle of the game trail and put his cheek against hers, the way he used to in the old days when she'd loved him. The scent of her sweat filled his nostrils.

"Yes, think of it, my wife." He wet his lips anxiously. "The ravens will smell your blood and descend in huge black flocks to perch on your soft limbs and caw hungrily while they peck out your eyes. The foxes, wolves and bears will come next. The animals will be frightened by your screams at first, but gradually they'll grow accustomed to the sharp sounds. Within a hand or two of time, they'll lunge forward to rip at your disemboweled organs."

He lightly kissed her temple. "Close your eyes. Imagine it, Kestrel. Use your wonderful imagination, the one you use to paint with. How will it *feel* when the foxes pull your insides out of your body?"

Kestrel twisted violently and wrenched her head free from his grip to scream. *"No!"*

She kicked him and made three running steps before he tackled her and knocked her to the ground. The scent of the molding logs encircled him. Her wiggling body, so firm and shapely, fed that growing sexual desire. He could feel her muscular buttocks pressed against his groin. He moved his hard penis against it and laughed.

Kestrel managed to cry, *"Help! Someone help me!"* and tried to scream again.

He cut the scream short by pulling his bloody knife from his belt and pressing it to her throat. "Shall I mix your blood with Tannin's, wife? So soon? I wanted to have time to talk to you. To tell you things that any other human would give his very life to know . . . to *see* with his own eyes!"

Kestrel had flinched at the touch of the knife. Through his tight grip, he could feel her heart hammering in terror—the way a bird's did when, as a child, he used to pluck the feathers from its wings before he left it to flop on the ground.

Now he would pluck another bird . . . this one a Kestrel!

"Yes, good. That's better. Sit up and lean back against that dead log behind you."

Kestrel did as he ordered and brushed away the thick web of hair that had fallen over her face. Her breathing came in rapid, shallow gasps. She looked thin and tiny there, her oval face blued by the diffused shawl of light that draped the forest.

Lambkill smiled at her.

"Oh, I'm so disappointed," he said as he leaned back and wiped a hand across his mouth. "I've been dreaming of how glorious it would be to build a tree perch and watch your death from high above. But it's out of the question now. With the first gray rays of dawn, the Otter Clan villagers will be able to track us. There's probably some fool already thrashing about searching for you."

He glanced around the night, his head cocked as he listened to the rustlings in the trees. *Was the creature out there human? A searcher?* "I can't risk waiting around to see justice done. No, I'll be denied that pleasure. But it will be enough to know that you, my wife, are dead and that I still have my son. Yes, my son. Little Coyote will keep me company forever. Oh? Do you doubt that?"

Kestrel sat rigid, watching him through wide, unblinking eyes. Several of the seashells on the front of her dress had been ripped loose, and they dangled from their hide thongs. Rare shells. They would bring a fortune back in the marsh country.

Lambkill reached out and yanked off two of the exquisite, ruffled jingle shells. They came from the lands of the Ice Ghosts far to the north. She cried out shrilly at the violation and looked as though she wanted to snatch them back from his hands. Her mouth trembled as tears filled her eyes. Lambkill cocked his head. What would she find so precious about these shells? She knew nothing of their worth in trade.

"Don't move, wife. Don't even breathe." He lifted his knife. The flaked facets of the blade glittered. "Remember, the longer you can convince me to let you live, the more chance you have of being rescued." He chuckled. "Yes, hope for that. It's very unlikely. No can track at night. But be quiet. Live longer. Hope, Kestrel. Hope all you want."

In a shaky voice, she murmured, "L-Lambkill, tell me about my son . . . our son. What did you do to bring him to life?"

He studied her through half-lidded eyes. Was she just making talk to delay him from performing his final duty? Or did she really care about Little Coyote? The haunting sensation of being watched by invisible eyes intensified. Lambkill squinted at the smoke-colored trunks of trees, the stacks of deadfall, the clots of brush.

Owls hooted close by. Their calls drifted on the wind, mixed with the rustling of pines and oaks. Vague premonitions of danger taunted his soul. What creature could cloak itself so well with darkness that even his trained Trader's eyes couldn't spot it? Something black, blacker than tar from the coastal pits, and as silent in its approach as Death.

The vibrations of the forest floor had stopped, but his discomfort didn't ease.

Cautiously, he slipped his pack from his shoulders and unlaced the ties. "Now you will see, my wife. Yes, finally you will know the great Power of the husband you spurned."

He lifted Little Coyote out and cradled him in his arms. The baby boy's tiny body had become browner and more shriveled than ever. It smelled of smoke and sacred sage, which Lambkill had stuffed into his pack to make a soft bed for the boy.

Kestrel whispered, "Blessed Spirits . . ."

Lambkill sat down cross-legged across from Kestrel and stood Little Coyote up on his knee, facing his mother. The boy's mouth had pulled taut to form a puckered black hole. The green stones that Lambkill had placed in the empty eye sockets glittered.

"Do you remember your mother, Little Coyote?" Lambkill tilted his head to listen for the boy's voice. "It's all right, son," he encouraged. "You don't have to fear her anymore."

Futile tears poured from Kestrel's eyes. She remembered the warmth of the baby boy's naked flesh against hers, the pain of giving him birth, the terror of that rainy day not so long ago when lightning had flashed all around her.

How shocking to see the gentle way that Lambkill held the dead infant. Despite the paralyzing fear that pumped bright in her veins, she could still wonder. She had never seen him display that much tenderness in their entire life together.

"How . . . how did you do that?" Kestrel asked hoarsely. Her throat ached. Cautiously, she lifted a hand to rub it.

Lambkill grinned at her, his broken yellow teeth reflecting dully. Shadows played across his wrinkled face, while moonlight flashed in his eyes. "I disemboweled him. Then I smoked him over an open fire for seven nights in a row. After that," he said, leaning forward to whisper, "I called up his Spirit and tied it to his body."

"Why? Why . . . would you do that?" How horrible, unthinkable, to tie a soul to a dried, rotted husk like that. She didn't believe it, but what if he really had done it? The poor little boy . . . "How, Lambkill? How could you do it to him? How could you condemn his young soul to living in a dead body?"

Lambkill frowned as though she must be mad to ask. "Because *I* love my son. That's why. I wanted him to be with me forever!"

He cradled the dead baby in his arms again and rocked him gently, as though trying to get the boy to go to sleep. The baby's puckered brown body moved in and out of the shadows. Kestrel's soul writhed at the sight. All around them, storm winds whipped the trees, making their boughs groan and creak.

Lambkill would kill her—just as he had killed Iceplant. She wanted to hate him, but he looked so pitiful. An expression of desperation creased his face . . . as if he *needed* to believe that the baby still lived.

Kestrel extended a hand and in a kind voice, she said, "Lambkill, let me help you bury Little Coyote. We'll do it together. We'll bathe him and dress him in a new foxhide shirt. Then we'll Sing his soul to the Star People. He'll be happier there, where he will have a body of Light—"

"I'll *never* bury him!" Lambkill shouted. Brusquely, he slipped the dead boy back into his pack and laced up the ties. "Never! You hear me? *Never!*"

Without looking at Kestrel, he said, "At least here, he has me to love him. You wouldn't understand that. You've never really loved anyone. You . . . you bitch! *Bitch in heat!*"

Kestrel closed her hand on air, dazed. He'd hunted every trail for a two-moon walk to find her, and she wondered now if he hadn't done it just to show her that he finally had someone who truly cared about him, someone who would never make him angry or hurt him.

With a weary voice, she said, "I loved you, Lambkill."

He rose and walked a short distance away to lay the pack atop a dead log. He patted the pack softly while he shook his head. "No, you never did. You just pretended."

"I didn't pretend. No one could pretend the kind of feelings I had for you."

He rubbed his eyes. When he turned, his quartz-crystal necklace sparkled. His head was bowed. Stringy gray hair framed his face. "Do you hear it?" he asked and lifted his eyes to her in panic. "You hear it now, don't you? That sound like massive feet hitting the forest floor somewhere close by?"

Kestrel listened. She did hear something, a rumble, like far-off thunder. "I . . . I think it's just the storm in the distance, Lambkill. That's all. You know how the sound of thunder carries across the hills."

He returned and sat cross-legged before her, his shoulders hunched forward. He looked beaten, and frightened. He kept glancing out into the forest as though to penetrate the shadows. Kestrel's eyes narrowed. She'd been afraid of him for most of her adult life. But now, seeing his fear, she could scarcely believe him the same man who had tormented her for five cycles. Had he changed since she'd left? Perhaps grown a human heart? The way he'd treated that dead baby made her wonder. And hope! Maybe she could talk him out of killing her . . .

"Lambkill," she said carefully, "I'm sorry I hurt you so much."

"You did, Kestrel, you tore my soul in two."

"I know. I—I didn't mean to. I was just so lonely. You were always gone, and then when you came home, you beat me so badly. That's . . . that's why I turned to Iceplant."

"What?" he said, as though he hadn't heard. He had occupied himself with rubbing his fingers in the pine duff.

Quietly, she repeated, "That's why I turned to Iceplant. You were never home. I was lonely. And you beat me for things I didn't do. Can you understand?"

Slowly, Lambkill lifted his face and peered at her. No emotion crossed his face. None at all. He just stared blankly.

Kestrel mustered her courage and reached out to touch his knee, hoping to show him that even after all he'd done to her, she could forgive him. Her fingers trembled when she placed them on his pants. He flinched slightly. "Lambkill, please. I . . ."

He leaped forward with stunning swiftness, grabbed her by the shoulders and threw her down onto the ground, where he crawled on top of her. He'd pulled out his knife again and held it to her throat. She could feel the sharp obsidian blade pressing into her flesh, his hard penis against her abdomen. She squirmed, trying to move away. He used the antler handle of his knife to bash her in the temple. It was a warrior's trick, to stun the enemy.

"Lie still! Be quiet!" He shifted, cocking his head to listen.

The vision in Kestrel's right eye blurred, and sickness welled into her throat. The forest seemed to dim suddenly, as though a thick curtain of black clouds had been drawn across the face of Above-Old-Man. *Oh, Blessed Spirits. I must stay awake. He'll kill me for sure if I don't!*

She fought to get deep breaths into her lungs, though the weight of his body on her chest made it difficult. She dared to look up at him. His mouth opened as if to speak, but he said nothing. He bent down almost nose to nose with her and stared unblinking into her eyes. Then he kissed her.

Mad. He's completely mad. Behind him, she saw the brightest Star People glittering through the cloak of moonlight. Tree limbs danced above, clattering against each other violently.

When Lambkill pulled his head up, a smile curled his lips. "Are you ready to die, my wife?"

Kestrel felt the knife lower to her throat again, and a trickle of blood flowed as the sharp obsidian pricked her skin. "Lambkill, wait. I . . . I want to talk to you more about Little Coyote. Y-you said earlier that you'd brought him to life. Does that mean . . ." She gasped for a breath. Lambkill was staring at her intently. His whole body had gone rigid. The knife hadn't moved. "Does that mean that you've actually been able to hear him speak? Has he . . . talked to you?"

Lambkill's wrinkles fell into reverent lines. "Oh, yes. He speaks to me almost every night, guiding me, helping me to find you. I didn't just chance upon Otter Clan Village, wife. Our son led me here."

Kestrel wet her lips. "What else has he told you? Does he—"

Out in the forest, a snuffling sounded, then a snort. Lambkill shoved away and lurched to his feet to stare down their backtrail. Kestrel rose behind him on trembling legs. A low growl echoed through the trees. It had been cycles since she'd heard that sound, but her body remembered it better than her soul did, and a wave of new fear blinded her.

On the trail, a huge black shape blotted out the moonlight. It had its blunt muzzle to the ground, sniffing out their tracks. Taller in the front than in the rear, the short-faced bear had a chest as broad as Kestrel's height. It looked up and went *whoof* in surprise. Its eyes glinted in the darkness, and it bared long white teeth. The growl that issued from its massive jaws this time warned them to run . . .

But Lambkill had his back turned to her!

If she didn't take the chance now, she would never have another. She leaped on Lambkill like a cat pouncing on prey, grabbed the back of his mammothhide necklace and twined the braided hide in her fist to take up the slack. Lambkill lost precious moments, tottering from foot to foot, reaching for her as she spun around and yanked him off his feet and onto her back.

He tried to scream, but the strangling cord allowed only a panicked *ach!* that choked to nothingness as he flailed. Frantic hands beat the air around her as she used her hips against him, turning as she pulled, keeping him off balance.

Gargling sounds rasped in his throat. He gripped her skirt and tugged furiously, trying to make her stumble, while he battled to flip over.

Kestrel tightened her grip on the thick braid, praying it would hold, and staggered forward up the trail. She struggled to stay on her feet. Her wounded leg wanted to buckle.

Behind her, she heard the short-faced bear growling, closing. The ground shook as the huge animal bounded forward.

Don't look! If you don't kill Lambkill, you'll be dead before Bear can get his jaws around you!

Lambkill released her skirt suddenly and kicked out with all his strength. The force sent Kestrel toppling forward. Her knees struck the ground hard before she flopped on her stomach, but she kept his necklace thong pulled tight over her shoulder.

Twist it! Tighter! Her forearms ached, her hands were going numb.

The viciousness of Bear stunned her. He bawled and snorted. She heard the sound of hide clothing ripping while Bear tore at the struggling Lambkill, who kept making strangling sounds that she knew would be screams if he could breathe. He lashed out with his hands and feet.

A deafening *crack!* erupted when the enraged beast batted a dead log and ripped it up from the damp forest floor. Splinters of wood showered Kestrel as Bear flung the log down. It struck with a thunderous crash, and Lambkill's wild flailing grew to desperation, forcing Kestrel to twist madly to keep her grip on the necklace. She heard a horrifying sound, and at first she didn't recognize it as her own agonized screaming. Lambkill's hands tore at her hair and clawed her face.

Then Lambkill frantically braced a knee on the ground and rolled off of Kestrel, turning his back to Bear.

Kestrel jerked the necklace with all her might, hauling Lambkill to the ground again as she fell on her back. Bear reared, standing up on two legs, watching them with unearthly concentration.

For an eternal instant, Kestrel stared into Lambkill's face. The image burned into her soul: his bugged-out eyes, wide in panic; the tongue protruding from his open mouth; the muscles in his face working spasmodically.

She refused to let go as he dragged her across the forest floor, trying to break her hold. He slammed a fist feebly into her face. Kestrel sobbed in misery. His face had turned crimson. The heaving of his lungs, sucking at the choked throat, racked his entire body.

He mouthed, "I . . . curse you . . . wife!"

Behind Lambkill, Bear took a step forward and used one huge paw to rip at Lambkill's legs. The force of the slap sent Lambkill tumbling sideways into the deadfall, hauling Kestrel with him. Lambkill struck her once more on the side of the head, trying to get out of Bear's reach as well as hers, but gradually his body went limp.

Too terrified to let go, Kestrel kept pulling on the necklace. She scrambled onto her knees and threw all of her weight into keeping the cord tight where it puckered the skin of Lambkill's neck.

Her body quaked so violently that she thought for a moment the Quaking Earth Spirits had risen from their underworld graves and decided to thrash the whole world in rage. Her sobs sounded like breathless screams.

A strange light shone in Bear's eyes. He made a soft sound and eased forward to sniff at the bloody knife gash in her leg, then tilted his head in an almost tender gesture, as if silently asking if she was all right. Kestrel could only weep uncontrollably. Bear blinked and held her gaze for a long moment. Then, slowly, he backed away and trotted into the trees with his square muzzle up, scenting the wind as though hunting.

"Kestrel?" a familiar-sounding voice called.

Hoarsely, she answered, "Horseweed! I'm over here!"

She saw him loping down the trail, his head moving cautiously as he scanned the shadows. He had a nocked atlatl lifted in his right hand. The stone tip of his dart glittered in the flashes of silver light. He broke into a run when he saw her. "Kestrel!"

Horseweed knelt beside her, and his young eyes tightened as he appraised Lambkill. Gently, he reached out and put a hand over Kestrel's aching fists, still knotted in the necklace thong.

"You can let go now, Kestrel. He's dead. Let go, Kestrel. Easy now. Please."

"No, no! He might . . . still be alive. I . . . I can't let go. Not yet. Just a little longer. I have to . . . hold on a little longer. For Cloud Girl's sake. Sh-she'll never be safe if he lives!"

Horseweed nodded sympathetically and lowered his eyes to examine the wounds in Lambkill's legs where Bear had clawed deep gashes. Blood still ran in dark streams, soaking the pine duff.

Softly, Horseweed said, "Bear did a good job. Almost as though he knew. He sliced through the big arteries. Your husband would have bled to death even if you hadn't strangled him, Kestrel."

He turned back and gazed at her in a kindly way. His hand lay warmly on her skin as he patted her aching fingers. "Please. Let go now, Kestrel. He's dead. I promise you. He's gone. He'll never hurt you or your baby again. Let go. . . . Let go now, Kestrel. You've done it. It's over."

Blinded by the silver rush of tears, she couldn't. Her cramped hands would not let go.

Forty-four

Kestrel trudged wearily up the eastern slope that led to Otter Clan Village. All of her strength went into the monotony of placing one foot ahead of the other. Tired, so thoroughly exhausted. Would she ever feel rested again? She glanced at Horseweed, who walked beside her, a grim look on his smooth face.

Despite the numbness of her battered body and soul, she wondered what he must think of her now. She was his relative . . . and a murderer.

She could hear a man talking beside the fire on the crest of the hill. Someone was still up. But then, on a night like this, how many could sleep? Charges of murder, witchcraft and violence had flown like fall leaves in an early winter gale.

She glanced up. A diffuse membrane of clouds had slipped across the sky. Most of the Star People had vanished, but the clouds had spawned a majestic multicolored halo around Above-Old-Man's face. The wind had calmed to a gentle breeze. On its breath, it bore the smell of rain and the haunting howls of wolves. Dew had formed a thick gloss on the spring grass, making the footing precarious.

Horseweed kept glancing sideways at the pack she carried cradled in her arms. The dead baby was so light, as though perhaps not lying on the bed of sage inside at all. But she could *feel* the boy there. Since she'd picked up the pack, a strange glow of warmth and contentment had been radiating through the soft leather. It grew stronger with each moment that passed. She'd never planned on being reunited with this tiny child that she'd given birth to. But gladness swelled her heart.

My poor son, you've gone through so much since that terrible day. Forgive me. Had I known, I'd never have left you there by the river, where Lambkill could find you.

Kestrel clutched the dead baby closer when she passed the place where Tannin had been killed. Tannin's body was gone, but sadness still pervaded the area, clinging to the black-crimson stain of his blood as if his Spirit lingered, trying to figure out what had happened. How could he have been murdered by his own brother?

"Poor Tannin."

Horseweed nodded. "My grandfather will have taken him into camp so the women can prepare him for burial tomorrow."

"I'm grateful. . . . but I'll prepare him. He was my brother-in-law. He was very good to me, Horseweed, even at the last." An ache thumped in her heart, remembering how he'd fought to stop Lambkill from hurting her.

"Then . . . then I'll send word to his wife, Calling Crane." Her voice constricted, and she swallowed the lump in her throat. What would Calling Crane do? Would she hate Kestrel for having caused Tannin's death? *Not now, Kestrel. Accept the burden of that pain when you can take it.* "She'll be worried until she knows her husband's fate for certain."

"I understand."

Kestrel took a deep breath when they crested the hill and walked across the plaza toward the fire. Oxbalm, Sumac, Dizzy Seal . . . and Harrier sat around the blaze, sipping tea from their wooden cups. Harrier had his back to her. His red shirt glimmered orange in the light of the flames. Several others stood close by, but Kestrel didn't recognize them. Oxbalm was speaking in a low voice.

She frantically looked for Sunchaser. The travois she and Horseweed had made stood on end against the far lodge.

Sunchaser lay nowhere in sight, not within range of the dancing flames. A thread of terror stitched her chest as her mind accosted her with questions too frightening to be borne.

No, no, Kestrel. They must have taken him inside. That's all.

But the image of his sallow, blood-spattered face formed with crystal clarity on the wings of her soul. And where was Cloud Girl? The woman who had been feeding her earlier had vanished. Kestrel's feet suddenly felt as heavy as granite.

As though Horseweed could read her thoughts on her taut face, he said, "I'm sure Sunchaser's all right, Kestrel. My grandmother would have finished cleaning and binding his wounds. Then she would have had him carried inside and covered with a pile of hides to keep him warm. You'll see. Sunchaser will be in the far lodge, the one closest to the fire. It's my grandmother's. She would have wanted him near so she could keep an eye on him throughout the night. It's just her way."

Kestrel reached out and gently squeezed his forearm. His muscles bunched beneath her touch. "Thank you, Horseweed.

You've helped me more tonight than I can tell you. You were very brave to come into the forest after me, especially when you knew about Lambkill's madness. I'll never be able to repay your kindness."

He bowed his head as though embarrassed by her praise. "I wasn't being brave, Kestrel. You're my . . . my cousin, or something. And Sunchaser asked me to find you. I had to." He glanced over and smiled wryly. "Not that you needed my help."

Kestrel tilted her head. "If you hadn't found me, Horseweed, I'd still be sitting in the forest."

She blinked solemnly. Horseweed had been forced to pry each of her fingers open while he told her over and over that Lambkill was truly dead.

When she'd finally gotten to her feet, she'd had to run a short distance away before she could persuade herself to look back at Lambkill. Part of her still believed that he might rise up and come after her again. His body might be dead, but he continued to live in her soul. Cycles would pass before she would be able to sleep through a whole night without waking in terror because she imagined his voice, or his stealthy footsteps, or just because she *sensed* him standing over her.

When Sumac saw them coming, she rose and pulled the hide more securely over her bent, elderly shoulders. Worry made her face resemble a dried berry. Her gray hair gleamed in the amber glow of the fire. Oxbalm followed her gaze and stood as well.

Horseweed whispered to Kestrel, "Don't worry about Harrier. Let me handle him and his brothers. It would be best if you didn't say a word to them. They've already made up their minds about you. Nothing you can say will change that."

"Thank you, Horseweed. Again."

He nodded gravely. "Find Sunchaser. Stay close to him. Even unconscious, his holiness protects you far better than any of my darts can."

"I'll find him. All night long, I've felt him near me. Almost as if he'd opened the arms of his soul and embraced me to keep me safe."

Harrier turned and saw Kestrel. He lifted his voice in anger, yelling, "Look! She's alive! She's mine now, Oxbalm. Give her to me!"

Sumac raised a fist and slashed the air with it. "Hold your tongue, boy," she ordered. "This is no longer your affair, since we've decided to adopt her into our clan. Unless you *really* do want a war?" She shot a hard glance at Harrier. "But then, your brother wouldn't have threatened to murder her in order to keep her quiet after you raped her if you *really* wanted a war. Would he?"

"You're taking *her* word!" Harrier's expression was calculating.

Sumac hobbled around the fire and met them halfway across the plaza. She hugged Horseweed and gave him one of those proud nods that caused red to flush his young cheeks. "I knew you'd find her, Grandson," she murmured softly. "Now, please, go to stand beside your grandfather. He might need your support."

"Yes, Grandmother." Horseweed trotted toward the fire, where Oxbalm stood.

Sumac and Kestrel stared into each other's eyes, probing the depths of each other's soul. In the background, Kestrel heard Harrier cursing Oxbalm, and the old man calmly answering, "My wife has spoken. You heard her, didn't you, Harrier?"

Harrier waved his arms angrily and began a tirade.

"It won't be easy," Sumac said, covering Harrier's words. "Harrier and his brothers have put in a claim on you. They want to take you back to their village to be punished for Buffalo Bird's murder. But you're welcome here, Kestrel. We'll do our best to keep you safe . . . if you decide to stay."

Kestrel smiled wanly. "Iceplant was right. He told me you were good people. But . . . I need to talk with Sunchaser about it. To find out his plans. Where is he?"

Sumac peered intently at the pack in Kestrel's arms, then led her to the entry of the far lodge.

They both ducked beneath the door flap, and Kestrel saw Sunchaser lying, just as Horseweed had said, beneath a pile of hides. Helper lay beside him with his black muzzle on his paws. He wagged his tail when he saw Kestrel. A small fire burned a few hands away, throwing a golden veil over the Dreamer's handsome face. Sumac had combed and braided Sunchaser's white hair. The long plait rested over his bandaged shoulder. His eyelids trembled, as if in the throes of a powerful Dream.

Quietly, Kestrel went to kneel beside him. She put her dead son down on the edge of the hides and leaned over to look at Sunchaser's pale face. Helper rose and trotted around to sniff the pack with the dead baby inside, then flopped down beside Kestrel, his black ears pricked. She patted his side. Sunchaser lay deathly still. To reassure herself, she pushed the hides away to see the rise and fall of his broad chest. Relief flooded her. She didn't want to awaken him, but she had to touch him. Gently, she smoothed her fingers over Sunchaser's sweating forehead.

He stirred. In a barely audible voice, he asked, ". . . All right?"

"Yes," she answered. "Lambkill is dead, and I'm safe. Horseweed found me. He brought me back."

". . . Love you," he whispered.

Sunchaser's head rolled to the side instantly, and his body went limp. Kestrel put her hand on his chest, feeling his lungs working. She frowned with concern as she pulled the hides back up to shield him from the cold.

Her old eyes shining, Sumac knelt beside her. "I think he was trying to stay awake until you returned . . . to make sure you were unharmed."

Kestrel tenderly squeezed Sunchaser's hand, and all of her strength vanished at once. She sat back on the hard-packed floor and braced her elbows on her drawn-up knees. The flickering of the fire threw strange shadows on the wall to her left, like animals fighting a battle to the death.

"I'm so tired, Sumac."

The old woman nodded. "You must get some sleep. But before I find hides for you, could we talk for a while?"

"Yes. What do you wish to know?"

Sumac shifted to sit cross-legged beside Kestrel. Her brow furrowed deeply. "Your little girl."

"Is . . . is Cloud Girl all right?" Kestrel felt the ground quaking beneath her again. "Did something happen?"

"No, no, she's fine. But I'm worried. I've been watching Harrier and his brothers. They have a mean streak. I'm afraid that if they can't get back at you . . . well, children are so vulnerable."

Kestrel steepled her fingers over her mouth and nodded. "I think, Sumac, that the best thing for all of us—including your village—is for me to take my girl and just go away. Last night, I realized for the first time that coming here was wrong. I wish I'd—"

Sumac gripped her wrist hard. "No, it wasn't wrong. Now you know you have family. Your children will always have a place to come to, people who love them. Everyone needs to know such things. Especially children. Don't be sorry you came here. I'm not."

Tears blurred Kestrel's vision. She patted Sumac's hand. "We'll come back often, I promise. I want Iceplant's daughter to grow up knowing you."

"Good." Sumac released Kestrel's hand, and her gaze shifted to rest on the small pack that lay beside Sunchaser. "That's the dead baby, isn't it? Lambkill never showed him to us, but I heard people say that's what he carried in that pack."

"Yes. That's the dead baby."

Sumac searched Kestrel's face, noting every line. "Do you want me to take it away? I could take it outside and put it beneath the hide beside Tannin. He's under that big oak tree to the north of the village. Oxbalm posted a guard, to keep the predators away."

Kestrel ran a hand through her black hair and shook her head. "No. I . . . I want to keep my dead son close to me tonight. So he knows I haven't abandoned him again. I can't explain it, Sumac, but I think he needs me."

Sumac lowered her eyes. "Yes, I know what you must be feeling. After my granddaughter died, I sat up with her all night, making sure she was warm. Let me get you those hides. Is there anything else you will need?"

"No. Thank you. Not tonight. But . . . tomorrow I must prepare both Tannin and my son so that they'll be ready for the journey to the Land of the Dead. Will you help me Sing their souls to the Star People?"

"The whole village will help. But, Kestrel, haven't you already Sung your son's soul—"

"A long time ago. But I'm afraid, Sumac. Lambkill claimed that he'd called the baby's soul back and tied it to this body. I—I have to make absolutely certain that my son isn't trapped here. He deserves the chance to be born again."

Kestrel reached out and placed a hand on Lambkill's pack. She swore she could feel a tiny hand desperately reaching back to her, struggling to touch her. She lifted the pack again and cradled her son against her breasts. The desperation ebbed away.

"Sumac? I know I gave my little girl to you, but—"

"Let me get her and give her back." Sumac grinned toothlessly as she rose. "Cloud Girl will be happy to see you. She's been whimpering all night."

"You are a kind woman. Sumac? I'm not sure, but I've been hearing a voice, trying to tell me . . . perhaps you will know." Kestrel reached into the pack and removed a carved ivory doll—a small figure that brought a gasp to Sumac's lips.

"Where did you get it?"

"From Lambkill's pack. Do you know the doll?"

Sumac's jaw trembled and tears welled in her faded old eyes. "It . . . it belongs to my granddaughter, Mountain Lake.

My grandson placed the doll on her burial litter after the mammoths killed her. Where did Lambkill . . . how could he . . . how could anyone take it from a dead child?"

"We will return it to Mountain Lake. In the Land of the Dead." Kestrel smiled sadly. "My son will take it to her. I know he will. He'll explain to them all about Lambkill." She tenderly reached into the pack and touched the hand of the mummified boy. "Won't you, my son?"

Sumac watched her through sober eyes. "Let me go get Cloud Girl for you. Tomorrow we will Sing and try to make many things right again. And as soon as Sunchaser can move, the Otter clan will leave here, Kestrel. Leave everything behind and return to Mother Ocean's side . . . where we belong." She shook her head. "This village has been tainted by witchcraft. It will bring nothing but heartache and sadness to anyone who sets foot in it."

As if in answer, a faint tremor shook the earth—a warning, perhaps, of things to come. The ridgepole shuddered and creaked, while the hide walls trembled. The conversations outside the lodge halted abruptly as a soft rumble rose. Kestrel held her breath until it stopped.

Sumac's eyes widened. Softly she said, "I hear you, Quaking Earth Spirits. Just let us leave this place and you can slide it right into the valley and bury it!"

Sumac ducked beneath the door flap, and Kestrel sat quietly, staring at Sunchaser and holding her son.

Down the length of the lodge, people slept beneath mounds of hides, their faces reflecting the burnished gleam of the low flames in the fire pit. Baskets hung from the pine poles that made up the lodge frame, and nets filled with beautiful, glittering shells lined the base of the walls. Carved wooden dolls stuck out between the fingers of sleeping children. As Kestrel looked around, she saw all the things that created a *home*.

But she would be leaving this place very soon.

Homeless again.

And she didn't know where she would go.

Kestrel placed her fingers on Sunchaser's white braid, trying not to awaken him this time. "Where will we go, Sunchaser? Where will you be happy?"

Forty-five

Catchstraw loped painfully down the trail. His huge paws patted the ground silently, despite the awkward gait caused by his wounds.

Ahead, he could see Mother Ocean glimmering beneath the pastel touch of Dawn Child. The waves rolled and winked purple, as if strewn with crushed mussel shell. The pointed tips of the fir trees lining the shore had just caught the first rays of morning. Birds chirped. The sounds of an awakening Whalebeard Village eddied around him; dogs barked to the squeals of children and the reprimanding shouts of women.

Catchstraw slowed. He'd stopped bleeding, but his powerful muscles screamed in agony, as if hot coals filled the dart and knife injuries. He'd been trotting all night long and had neither seen nor scented anyone pursuing him. But the wind had come up with such a fury that it might have blown away the distinctive smells of humans. To make sure that no one was behind, he kept turning to glance over his shoulder. The shapes of a brightening forest met his searching gaze, but nothing else.

Catchstraw trotted out onto the sandy shore and headed north. He couldn't let the villagers see him. The slightest glimpse of a dire wolf would rouse the entire community, and every able-bodied warrior would grab his atlatl to hunt him down.

Catchstraw leaped a wind-smoothed rock and ran into the trees, where he found a game trail. Lavender light scattered his path in irregular patches. Despite his exhaustion, he had begun to feel better, stronger. Part of it could be attributed to his continuing euphoria from the Spirit Plants. The sight of Sunchaser lying on that travois, bleeding and half-dead, had sent Catchstraw's soul soaring.

Satisfaction filled him, bubbling within like a fermented berry drink. He would find a place to hide—perhaps even the obscure rock shelter where he had first scented Sunchaser and Kestrel—and he would Heal himself. The blood of Dire Wolf carried more Power than human blood did. In this muscular body, Catchstraw's wounds would mend faster.

Then he would return to Otter Clan Village and take up his place as the rightful chief. He would be required to kill Oxbalm, but that would be a small task. The old man was as brittle as a dry stick. Once Catchstraw had become chief, he would intimidate the nearby villages into joining him, and together they would wage war on the Desert People, cutting off the trade routes and intercepting any rare goods that came through. The wealth and Power gained from that triumph would establish his prestige. As the generations passed, his name would be Sung, echoing clear to the Land of the Dead, where the ghosts would hear . . . and hear . . .

Catchstraw! Catchstraw! Catchstraw! Catchstraw! The legends of men and Gods would never forget! And perhaps, with his Power as a witch, he could live forever!

Catchstraw halted and pricked his ears. Was that Singing? Where could it be coming from? And such a deep, beautiful voice! He couldn't understand any of the words—it was as though they were spoken in a foreign tongue—but the notes seemed to breathe from everywhere, from the surf, the wind, the chirping of the birds. The hair on his back stood straight up in a black ridge. A low growl involuntarily rumbled in his throat.

He lifted his long nose and sniffed, cataloging the rich scents of salt, fish and fir needles that saturated the air. Beneath the heavier fragrances, he identified the odors of fox and mammoth. His nostrils flared wider when he caught the faint musk of a big animal, a predator. The scent of blood drifted with the musk. It was from an old kill, so dry that he could barely detect it.

The Singing grew louder.

Fear raced through Catchstraw's veins in a stinging wash. He held his breath to listen. He could sense his stalker's approach, though he heard nothing but that magnificent Singing! Any earthly creature would have been snapping the twigs that lay in clumps along the trail, or frightening the small squirrels and chipmunks that chattered in the trees and brush. This predator moved through the woods like an ethereal wisp of mist. Nothing seemed startled by its passage. Nuthatches hopped up and down the fir trunks, hunting insects, while a cottontail sat placidly eating grass.

Irrationally, Catchstraw leaped forward and raced up the trail. He spooked a flock of ravens feeding on an ancient deer carcass, but he barely slowed. He vaulted over a fallen log and bounded off the trail through a tangle of underbrush. Thorns raked at his thick fur, while willow limbs slapped him in the face. He kept on running.

As he broke out into a crowded copse of newly leafed-out aspens, he noticed that the ravens soared through the trees at his sides, cawing to each other, following him. He saw the evil glints in their black eyes. Two of the birds had soared high into the sky. They were tiny black dots against the brilliant gold of the birthing day. The birds flapped and screeched as they circled his location.

What were they doing? Spying on him?

Catchstraw barked and snapped threateningly at the ravens when they sailed close enough, but they merely tipped their midnight wings and veered away, only to return.

Finding a game trail that skirted the very edge of the sea cliffs where the indigo shadows still lived, he stopped again to listen. His panting breath fogged in the cold morning air. Frozen puffs hung before his eyes. The ravens swooped down on the rocks to watch him. They *thocked* knowingly to each other.

Catchstraw sniffed for scent again and bent an ear backward. The traitorous wind had shifted, sweeping his own distinct wolf odor down his backtrail.

To his amazement, the ravens lifted their heads, ruffled their wings and one by one, piped out a single note. But when woven together, their calls created a rhapsody so enchanting, so glorious, that it held Catchstraw entranced. Only when he realized that their notes repeated the melody of the faint Song that continued to ride the wind did panic grip him.

He jerked his head around when he glimpsed a huge amorphous shadow moving silently along the face of the cliff, as if camouflaging itself in the lingering echoes of night. He stared hard. *Imagination! There's nothing there! It's just the changing light through the tree limbs . . .*

But he let out a shrill yip when the creature rose on its hind legs and swaggered toward him like a man, growling hideously. Its sheer size struck terror into his heart, but when the subdued dawn-gleam reflected stunningly from Bear's extended claws, Catchstraw froze, his heart thundering. A moment later, Catchstraw shot up the trail, his legs pumping in panic and his tongue dangling from the side of his muzzle. The flat path wove through the forest until it blended with another trail and led him up a narrow ledge to the crest of the cliff—a dead end.

Mother Ocean spread below in a vast chaos of shifting motion. Sunlight had gilded her face with an amber hue. Far out, a school of dolphins bucked the waves, their fins glittering as if set afire by Father Sun's presence.

Secreting himself behind an enormous redwood, Catchstraw cautiously slid his muzzle around the curve of the fragrant bark to study his backtrail.

Seven sea gulls joined the flock of ravens and winged up the slope to squawk and squeal as they circled him.

Catchstraw barked and leaped around madly, cursing his feathered accusers for their betrayal. But his frenzy died in a stillborn howl when he spotted his pursuer loping along.

Great Lightning, the bear was huge! Three times his own size. A prickle crept through him that left his wounded muscles shuddering.

He darted through the redwoods like the hunted animal he was, and, with every step he took, the Singing grew louder. The gulls and ravens swooped low to fly beside him, echoing the crystalline notes. He felt as if he'd been captured in a net of tinkling shell bells. The weave tightened around him until he panted for breath.

He took another trail, this one looping eastward, its narrow sides bordered by thick brush. Here the trail doubled back and led him into a series of switchbacks that climbed the steep side of a hill—only to culminate in another dead end, this one bounded on three sides by sheer rock walls.

The Singing grew to a deafening roar.

Catchstraw whirled on his back legs, despite the pain in his wounded haunch. Desperately, he raced back the way he had come, searching, ducking to the right as a gap appeared and charging frantically forward on the new trail.

Was this trail the one that would save him? It, too, doubled back, taking turns, leading him around in a curious circle.

Catchstraw fought to still his soul by Singing a Song of his own . . . but the melody only fused with the birds' Song. He went silent when he began choking on that grand music.

What's happening to me? Blessed Spirits, has my witching lost its potency? How could that be? Who could compete with me? No one has my Power!

He sprinted across a wildflower-filled meadow and angled down a dew-slick trail lined with overarching dogwoods. Most of the blossoms had fallen away, but a few bruised petals clung stubbornly to the tips of the highest branches. Catchstraw's paws were soaking and cold in less than a heartbeat. This time he knew he'd found the right trail. This one would lead him beyond the reach of that hideous short-faced bear! A faint roaring grew louder, covering the lilting melody of the Song. Victory lay just around this last bend in the . . .

Catchstraw stepped out onto a spit of sand that lanced into the middle of a pool of water. The soft roaring came from the waterfall that tumbled down the black rock in white, churning cascades. The water danced and dashed, changing its roar into the rhythmic cadence of the Song.

Catchstraw's heart ached as he pounded blindly back the way he'd come, searching for the meadow, seeking to find his way through the twists and turns of the trail. It couldn't be this far! He stopped, his thoughts gone thick with panic.

He bolted through a hole in the vegetation and found himself on yet another trail. Now he ran with horrified desperation. He had to get out. Escape! Find Mother Ocean again, and regain his bearings!

As he ran over the swell of a hill, he saw a mammoth cow and calf ahead. They stood blocking the trail. When the cow saw him, she lifted her trunk and released a trumpet blast that shook the ground. The vibration tingled through his quivering legs. The cow then lowered her trunk, poised her short tusks and charged him.

Catchstraw stumbled sideways before he caught his balance and darted into the thickest of the underbrush. The mammoth and her calf pursued, thrashing through the shrubbery after him, trumpeting and whining in fury.

He evaded them somehow, floundered out and scrambled up a deer trail like a clubbed fawn, despair firing his veins. Exhaustion sapped his wolfish muscles, but he staggered onward, hope blunted to the point that he stopped numbly as this trail, too, ended abruptly in a cleft in the rocks. Red sandstone walls towered above him, cloaked in blood-colored shadows.

Every trail he took turned into a dead end! The sunlight gave no clue as to direction. The Song carried through the very air, magical, Powerful. He turned, backtracking, aware that Mammoth hunted him somewhere back along this trail.

He took yet another turn, another trail. Leading where? To another dead end? Or to the center—where short-faced Bear, in all of his huge fury, awaited him? What *were* all these paths? He'd lived along this shore for his entire life and he'd never seen this . . .

. . . *this . . . maze!*

His weak legs failed him. He sat down hard in the middle of the trail and stared wide-eyed at the sky as the truth sank in.

A growl echoed. He turned in terror, rising again and spreading his legs to prop himself up.

Bear lumbered up the trail like a swaying mountain of muscle. Blood stained his square muzzle and streaked his massive chest. When Bear saw Catchstraw, he rose on his hind legs and roared. Gleaming strands of saliva dripped from those teeth that could crush a mammoth bone into splinters.

Catchstraw howled in indignation and attacked, springing for Bear's vulnerable throat.

Bear brought his huge paw around and effortlessly smacked Catchstraw to the side with a loud pop. The blow stunned Catchstraw, and he rolled head over tail into a pile of rocks, limp, breathing hard.

Agony, like nothing he had ever experienced, burned through his body. He scrambled to rise, to escape, but Bear bounded forward and closed his jaws around Catchstraw's wounded foreleg. Insanely, Bear shook him. Just as, not so long ago, he himself had shaken Sunchaser . . .

Catchstraw shrieked when he heard his bones snap and felt splinters drive through his muscles. Blood welled hotly in his mouth. Had fragments of broken ribs pierced his lungs?

Abruptly, Bear spit Catchstraw out and paused to peer down at him.

Catchstraw blinked through the thickening gray haze, swallowed the flood of metallic-tasting blood that clogged his throat and whispered, "Oh, no . . . Sunchaser! I—I didn't think Dreamers could change into animals. I thought only witches . . ."

The mammoth trumpeted, and a whole herd of mammoths responded from scattered positions in the foothills. Bear's eyes widened, and he lifted his bloody muzzle to listen.

Catchstraw sagged against the rocks; his skull smacked dully on the ground. Through the dense layer of pine duff and earth, he heard Bear's rhythmic steps pound away at a headlong run.

Catchstraw's eyes felt heavy, so heavy that he couldn't keep them open.

He didn't know how long he lay there listening to the wind rustling through the grass, but finally rumbling rain clouds pushed across the sky and the Thunderbeings plunged down from their black bellies. With their wings glittering, the Thunderbeings swooped through the trees. Rain patted his blood-caked black fur. The scent of wet earth and pine rose powerfully. Flies were hovering over him, already laying eggs in his torn hide.

The maggots would come, along with the other scavengers. For the maggots, a dead dire wolf was a triumph of wealth. Maggots, wiggling maggots. They would Sing his praise . . . and Sing it . . . and Sing . . .

Darkness closed in around Catchstraw. He fought it, his ruined legs pawing the air trying to run, though he knew the effort was useless. The gulls and ravens called back and forth, reporting on his every movement, and he could smell the mammoths as they quietly came to stand over him. The cow smelled like ferns and grass. The calf still bore the sweetness of milk on its breath.

Through the tears in his eyes, Catchstraw saw their blurred images.

"*Foolish human,*" the mammoth cow said as she extended her trunk to pull up a handful of grass that grew tall beside the rocks. She tucked it into her mouth and chewed slowly.

"*Did you think you could use Power for your own purposes and never have to pay the price? Either you let Power work through you to accomplish its goals or you die.*

You're lucky you lived this long. Power always wins . . . in the end."

"Boy?"

The word sent starlit ripples through the Land of the Dead. All of the Star People blinked and flared, listening. Blackness flooded out around them like waves washing across an endless shore.

The Man cocked his head. From far below came the faint pattering sound of rain against oak leaves and dry soil, the rich smell of blooming mountain harebell. Then a little boy's voice responded.

". . . Yes, Man?"

"I want to discuss something with you."

The Boy asked, "What is it?"

"Tomorrow your mother will Sing you back to the stars again. Does that make you happy?"

The Man could sense the Boy thinking, wondering.

Finally the Boy answered, "I don't know, Man."

"But I thought you hated being there in that dead body."

"At first I did. But I used to fear so many things when I lived among the stars. Things I no longer fear. I have learned something, Man."

"Tell me about it."

Boy let out a serene breath. "I have learned that a soul that truly clothes itself in Death is never afraid of anything. And seeing the world through the eyes of Death is a vision of heartrending beauty."

The Man closed his eternal eyes and smiled to himself. The words were like a balm on his wounded soul.

He replied, "Come, Boy. Come back to the Land of the Dead. You have more to learn . . . but I think it's time you were born as a living, breathing Dreamer. Perhaps you can help your mother . . . and the world after all."

Harrier, the last of his brothers to remain loyal to the task, lay stretched out on his belly, atlatl and darts clutched in one hand, watching as Kestrel led the way on to the beach. Sunchaser limped beside her, a light pack on his shoulder, and Helper followed, hauling a travois filled with hides.

Harrier slid along the rise, making sure that the grass broke his form should either of his targets look up.

Sunchaser!

Harrier shook his head. Too much had happened for him to understand all of it, but one single fact clutched at his soul. Kestrel carried his younger brother's atlatl. Even from here, he could see it swinging at her hip.

He'd skulked along the trail taken by the pair, awaiting the opportunity to drive a dart into Kestrel's body—but it had never come. The two stuck to each other like glue boiled from an elk's hoof.

Therefore, to kill Kestrel, Harrier had first to kill Sunchaser, for if he didn't, the Dreamer would seek revenge—and Harrier, having trouble nerving himself to kill a Dreamer, quivered in fear at the thought of a Dreamer trying to kill him!

They passed below, so close that he could hear their voices. *Steady now, steady!*

"Will there be fir trees there, Sunchaser?" Kestrel asked and smiled serenely at the Dreamer.

Sunchaser shrugged and laughed. "I don't know. I've never been that far north before. I've heard that there are firs and gigantic redwoods, twice the size of the ones we have here. Why, Kestrel? Have you grown to love the firs so much?"

She nodded. "Yes. They're very beautiful. And I love their scent when the rains soak them."

"Then I hope there are firs. And many of them." Sunchaser took Kestrel's hand and held it tightly. She smiled again. Strands of her long hair danced in the sea breeze.

Harrier slowly rose to his knees, settling a dart into the hook of his atlatl, easing his arm back.

He would have to cast just so, driving the dart into Sunchaser's back, hopefully sending the point of the missile through the man's spinal column. Then, as Sunchaser fell and Kestrel bent down in panic, Harrier would drive a second dart through her. The baby in the pack on her back would die from the cold tonight.

His arm had extended to full reach now and was balanced, the obsidian point at the end of his dart glinting in the sunlight.

Harrier choked the cry in his throat as a sharp pressure in his back was followed by a pain.

"Don't move," the calm voice ordered. "Just open your hand and let your weapons fall."

Through clenched teeth, Harrier said, "Who—"

"Do it!"

Harrier's atlatl and darts clattered against the rocks hidden in the grass. The noise was drowned by the crash of the surf, and Sunchaser and Kestrel walked away oblivious, smiling at each other.

Harrier turned, staring over his shoulder, squinting into the sun to find Horseweed standing above him, pressing a dart into the small of his back. "Are you going to kill me, boy?"

Horseweed made a face, slowly shaking his head. "I have to admit, you do tempt me, Harrier. The Otter Clan, as in your own clan, considers a youth to be a man when he's killed a mammoth or a man. I may have killed a mammoth. I could certainly kill you. But earning that distinction isn't worth a war, Harrier."

"Then you will be a youth all of your life! Are you a coward?" And as soon as he'd said it, Harrier regretted his words. No coward had ever battered a witch like Horseweed had done. The boy was brave.

"You may believe that, if you wish," Horseweed told him evenly.

"What do you want of me?"

"Your word that you will leave the coast, follow your brothers back to your people and never bother Sunchaser, Kestrel or the Otter Clan again."

Harrier cocked his head. "And you will take my word?"

Horseweed nodded. "I will. Despite your actions, I think you are an honorable man."

Harrier looked back at the beach, where a man, a woman, a baby and a dog followed the curving line of surf and sand northward. Sunchaser's white hair gleamed with an unnatural brilliance. Waves crashed and rolled up over their moccasins. They didn't seem to mind. "Buffalo Bird was a fool to tell Kestrel the things he did. He was so young. Too eager to gain wealth and status. I understand why she killed him. But . . . I loved my brother." Harrier squinted at Sunchaser and Kestrel. Their joyous laugher echoed through the air. Helper barked and bounded happily around them, the travois jerking up and down.

"Perhaps . . ." Harrier sighed. "Perhaps Buffalo Bird's foolishness shouldn't continue to guide my life." His brows pulled together. He wanted to go home. When his brothers had refused to join him in a battle against Sunchaser, he'd felt alone and frightened. The feeling had only grown worse in the past few days. "Yes, Horseweed, you have my word." And with that, he sank down on the grass and exhaled a deep breath. "I will leave them, and you, alone."

At that, Horseweed nodded and lowered his weapons. But he didn't look at Harrier. His eyes had riveted on the people on the beach. A smile touched his young face. "Live long, Harrier. I can already tell that you will be a great and wise leader someday."

Selected Bibliography

Adam, David P., and John D. Sims. "Late Pleistocene and Holocene Remains of *Hysterocarpus traski* (Tule Perch) from Clear Lake, California, and Inferred Holocene Temperature Fluctuations." *Quaternary Research: An Interdisciplinary Journal* 8, no. 2 (September 1977). New York: Academic Press.

Applegate, Richard B. "The Black, the Red, and the White: Duality and Unity in the Luiseno Cosmos." *The Journal of California and Great Basin Anthropology* 1, no. 1 (Summer 1979): 71–88.

Blackburn, Thomas. "A Query Regarding the Possible Hallucinogenic Effects of Ant Ingestion in South-Central California." *The Journal of California Anthropology* 3, no. 2: 78–81.

Elsasser, A. B. "Notes on Yana Ethnobotany." *Journal of California and Great Basin Anthropology* 3, no. 1 (1981): 69–77.

Fagan, Brian. *Ancient North America.* New York: Thames and Hudson, 1991.

Foster, Steven, and James Duke. *Medicinal Plants.* Boston: Houghton Mifflin, 1990.

Gifford, Edward, et al. *Californian Indian Nights.* Glendale, Calif.: Arthur H. Clark Co., 1930.

Guthrie, R. Dale. *Frozen Fauna of the Mammoth Steppe.* Chicago: University of Chicago Press, 1990.

Harris, Arthur H. *Late Pleistocene Vertebrate Paleoecology of the West.* Austin, Texas: University of Texas Press, 1985.

Haynes, Gary. *Mammoths, Mastodons, and Elephants. Biology, Behavior, and the Fossil Record.* Cambridge University Press, 1991.

Heizer, Robert F., ed. *The Handbook of North American Indians: California,* vol. 8. Washington, D.C.: Smithsonian Institution, 1978.

Henshaw, Henry W. *Perforated Stones from California.* Bureau of American Ethnology, Bulletin 2. Smithsonian Institution, Washington, D.C., 1887.

Heye, George G. "Certain Aboriginal Artifacts from San Miguel Island, California." 7, no. 4 (1921). Heye Foundation.

Hudson, Travis. "A Charmstone from the Sea of Point Conception, California." *Journal of California and Great Basin Anthropology* 1, no. 2 (1979): 363–366.

———. "A Rare Account of Gabrielino Shamanism from the Notes of John P. Harrington." *Journal of California and Great Basin Anthropology* 1, no. 2 (1979): 356–362.

———. "The Integration of Myth and Ritual in South-Central California: The 'Northern Complex.'" *The Journal of California Anthropology* 5, no. 2 (1978): 225–247.

———. "To Sea or Not to Sea: Further Notes on the 'Oceangoing' Dugouts of North Coastal California." *Journal of California and Great Basin Anthropology* 1, no. 2 (1981): 269–281.

Johnson, Donald Lee. "The Late Quaternary Climate of Coastal California: Evidence for an Ice Age Refugium," and "The California Ice-age Refugium and the Rancholabrean Extinction Problem." *Quaternary Research* 8 (1977): 149–179.

Keesing, Roger M. *Kin Groups and Social Structure.* Chicago: Holt, Rinehart and Winston, 1975.

Lyman, R. Lee. *Prehistory of the Oregon Coast.* New York: Academic Press, 1991.

Moratto, Michael J. *California Archaeology.* New York: Academic Press, 1984.

Moratto, Michael, Thomas King, and Wallace B. Woolfenden.

"Archaeology and California's Climate." *The Journal of California Anthropology* 5, no. 2 (1978): 147–161.

Oetteking, Bruno. "Morphological and Metrical Variations in Skulls from San Miguel Island, California." *Indian Notes and Monographs* 7, no. 2 (1920). Publications of the Museum of the American Indian. Heye Foundation.

Orr, Phil C. *Prehistory of Santa Rosa Island.* Santa Barbara, Calif.: Museum of Natural History, 1968.

Parkman, Edward Breck. "Soapstone for the Cosmos: Archaeological Discoveries in the Cuyamaca Mountains." *Journal of California and Great Basin Anthropology* 5, nos. 1 and 2 (1983): 140–155.

Pielou, E. C. *After the Ice Age. The Return of Life to Glaciated North America.* Chicago: University of Chicago Press, 1991.

Simmons, Marc. *Witchcraft in the Southwest.* Lincoln, Neb.: University of Nebraska Press, 1974.

Suzuki, David, and Peter Knudtson. *Wisdom of the Elders. Honoring Sacred Native Visions of Nature.* New York: Bantam Books, 1992.

Thomas, David Hurst. "A Diegueno Shaman's Wand: An Object Lesson Illustrating the 'Heirloom Hypothesis.'" *The Journal of California Anthropology* 3, no. 1: 128–132.

Thompson, Lucy. *To the American Indian: Reminiscences of a Yurok Woman.* Berkeley: Heyday Books, 1991.

Waters, Frank. *Masked Gods: Navaho and Pueblo Ceremonialism.* New York: Ballantine Books, 1973.